WITH A QUIET HEART

ALSO BY EVA LE GALLIENNE

At 33

WITH A
QUIET HEART

an autobiography by
EVA LE GALLIENNE

New York
THE VIKING PRESS
1953

Library of Congress catalog card number: 53-5201

Printed in the U.S.A. by the Vail-Ballou Press, Inc.

To Mimsey

ILLUSTRATIONS

(*Following page viii*)

FOREWORD

Twenty years ago I wrote a little book called *At 33*, and I was tempted to call this one *Plus 20*. But I am not the same person that I was at thirty-three—and for that I am not sorry—so this is not a continuation of that story.

A thirty-three I was concerned mainly with action; at "plus twenty" I find myself more interested in experience. At thirty-three one is very opinionated, supremely confident of one's knowledge and understanding of almost any problem; at "plus twenty" one is—or it seems to me that one should be—aware that one is, after all, not *quite* the center of the universe.

There is, of course, something immensely engaging about that supreme egotism of youth, and *At 33* appealed tremendously to young people. I doubt if they will like the me of today as well as they liked the me of twenty years ago. They may find me less ambitious, less flamboyant, less triumphant. Or they may be able—for youth has surprising insight—to see that these former characteristics have been merely tempered and disciplined by time, have been reassessed but have not vanished.

At "plus twenty" one is quieter, stronger, less turbulent, but, perhaps because of that, more ardent.

I confess that I have not lost an ardent sense of life; in that I have not changed. Life seems to me mysterious and wonderful; it always has and always will. And this mystery and wonder exist quite apart from events. They are like those "harps in the air" of which Hilda speaks in *The Master Builder;* they are a part of that intangible music heard by those whose awareness of life is acute and joyous. This music, it seems to me, grows ever better with the years, ever richer, ever clearer.

I'm afraid my book may be thought old-fashioned; it is so thoroughly innocent of anything sensational. But to me sensational things are strangely lacking in excitement; there is something fictitious about them that gives out a hollow sound.

I have tried, as honestly as I know how, to tell this story, beginning with the violent cataclysm that cut my life in two. I have set down a few thoughts and beliefs and discoveries about my work and things in general, in the hope that they may be of use, of amusement, of interest—or perhaps even of help—to those people who care to accompany me.

So, if you are with me, let's turn to the story.

As Mrs. Alving in *Ghosts*—"with whom someday I hope to become
better acquainted"

With Mother in Copenhagen, 1938. "I suppose it's natural to be proud of one's parents, and I am very proud of mine"

In the station wagon at Weston. "I always planned to have a little place in the country that was my very own"

My father, Richard Le Gallienne—"a mercurial being . . . a patient worker, an understanding friend"

As Julie in *Liliom*. "It is the inner performance of the actress that makes the role so telling"

As Marguerite Gautier, "the fragile Lady of the Camellias"

With Ethel Barrymore in *L'Aiglon*. "The death of *L'Aiglon* is my favorite"

With Joseph Schildkraut in *The Cherry Orchard*. "Pepi loved playing Gaev and was most engaging in the part"

As Ella Rentheim in *John Gabriel Borkman*—"hailed by many as the finest of all the American Repertory Theatre's presentations"

Two of Nannie's kids—some of the "numerous animals that peopled my little domain"—with Marion Evensen

Graphic House

With Dame May Whitty in *Thérèse*. "Thomas Job had fashioned a
grim melodrama out of Zola's powerful book"

As Hedda Gabler. "Ibsen's deep knowledge and acute observation of the female heart and mind are little short of miraculous"

Bambi Linn at the recording of *Alice in Wonderland*. "Bambi's little
face seemed to me exactly right"

As Mirandolina in *The Mistress of the Inn*, "the first Goldoni play ever
to be presented professionally in English on the New York stage"

Vandamm

As Marie Antoinette in *Madame Capet*. "Here was a play I should
really like to work in"

At the loom. "I took up weaving and proudly produced linen hand-towels, rough, nobbly bathtowels, table runners . . ."

Vandamm

As the Comtesse de la Bruyère in *What Every Woman Knows,* "Barrie's delightful comedy"

The Civic Repertory Theatre. "Passers-by stopped in amazement to read . . . names the like of which had not been seen on Fourteenth Street for many a year"

Alexander Alland

Taken during the demolition of "the old Fourteenth Street Theatre of happy memories"

Vandamm

As Catherine of Aragon in *Henry VIII*. "We were all of us proud to be a part of this wonderful production"

Alfredo Valente

With Joseph Schildkraut. "I am always happy to play with Pepi"

WITH A QUIET HEART

CHAPTER ONE

THERE is something nightmarish about working in your garden on a heavenly afternoon in June, feeling peaceful and serene, and five minutes later looking down in bewildered horror at your hands hanging in shreds, like gloves turned inside out. Too much shock to feel pain as yet. That was to come.

All day I had been working hard in the garden. I was wearing a heavy flannel shirt with long sleeves, and workman's overalls. They probably saved my life.

Since the day was warm, my little French maid, Marinette, had decided to give the dogs a bath—cairn terriers, of course; I have always been a cairn fan. She called out to me from the house that she couldn't get the hot-water heater to light. In those days the house was in quite a primitive state, and the stove and water heater used bottled gas that came in cylindrical containers. This gas, called propane, was very practical but highly inflammable and completely devoid of any odor. It was much used at that time in summer cottages and on yachts, for the cylinders were quite small and easy to install and replace.

I had another half-hour's work to do on the rose-bed, but I said I would go in as soon as I'd finished and help Marinette get the heater started.

The hot-water heater stood in the far corner of the cellar. A steep flight of steps led down from the kitchen. Sidonie, the cook, was standing by the icebox in the kitchen, next to an open window.

As I ran down the steps I struck a match on the side wall.

3

There was a deafening explosion, and the whole cellar became a mass of liquid fire. The force of the explosion was so great that Sidonie was nearly thrown out through the kitchen window.

Evidently the gas valve had been left open, and for the past half-hour the gas had been pouring into the cellar; but, since it had no odor, we were none of us aware of it.

Three things saved my life: the heavy clothes I wore, the fact that I lit the match while still some way from the heater, and the fact that, temperamentally, I am not a screamer. Had I opened my mouth and drawn a breath to scream, my lungs would have been fatally injured.

I remember a series of vivid impressions, disconnected, sharply etched, like a landscape seen intermittently by flashes of lightning.

My first instinct must have been to save my eyes, for I put my hands before my face—which is the reason, I suppose, for their having been so severely burned.

I remember rushing back up the steps. I remember my hair being on fire. I went to the kitchen sink and put my head under the faucet. I must have gone a little mad, for I went outside and rolled over and over on the grass to extinguish the flames.

I remember the shrill cries of the two Frenchwomen. They came from a little village in the foothills of the Pyrénées and, when excited, they broke into their native patois, an incomprehensible mixture of French and Spanish. They sounded like agitated birds.

They helped me tear off my clothes, and one of them threw a sheet around me, while the other ran out to catch the gardener, who was on the point of leaving.

It was then that I saw my hands, hanging in long bloody strips.

They put me in the station wagon, and Tony—a tiny little Italian of incredible strength—drove over the bumpy dirt roads at seventy miles an hour to the hospital. I remember his heavy breathing and, with almost every breath, his cry, half prayer, half curse: "Jesu! Jesu Maria!"

He somehow got the old Ford up the steep hill to the hospital. They half carried me into the lobby, and then I blacked out.

Nature is kind. She does not allow us fully to recapture the experience of agony. I thought I should never forget the weeks that followed. Yet now I find that, though my mind remembers the torments I went through, my body refuses.

Before actually experiencing suffering, we think we can readily imagine what it is like. But this is untrue. In the same way, though we may in retrospect try to describe it, we find ourselves incapable of doing so.

I suppose one of the very few good things that emerge from wars is the constantly improved method of dealing with various forms of physical pain and mutilation. Had I been burned yesterday as I was twenty years ago, it would have been a comparatively simple business. The treatment of such cases today makes the treatment used twenty years ago seem archaic. But in 1931 the ultimate recovery from such an accident depended largely on the physical and mental stamina of the patient. Organically I had inherited a remarkably tough constitution, a physical resilience of quite unusual power. Mentally I must have been quite tough too, for the possibility of my being permanently defeated by this sudden catastrophe never even occurred to me.

I regained consciousness for a few moments in the emergency ward. I remember a pattern of voices; I could see nothing, but the voices seemed to flutter round me in hushed agitation, and I kept hearing my name repeated over and over again in tones of shocked surprise and consternation. I felt an excruciating agony in my hands; I suppose they were giving them some preliminary treatment. The pain was so great that I felt as though my hands had been separated from the rest of my body; they were remote from me in a strange way, as though they had assumed an entity of their own, and my mind was watching them suffer from a distance; yet all my nerves and senses seemed concentrated in them alone. I was often to experience this strange sensation in the weeks and months to come, so that I came to think of my hands as something apart: poor, lacerated creatures whose agony I was somehow forced to share.

I mercifully blacked out again and remembered nothing until the following day.

I suppose it was morning when I regained consciousness, but I could see nothing. I came to the awful conclusion that I must have lost my sight. I found it almost impossible to make myself understood, for my mouth was swollen and shapeless so that I couldn't move my lips.

Someone was in the room, and to my great joy and relief I recognized the voice of my dear friend Mary Benson—"Mimsey," as I've always called her. She has had a house in Weston, Connecticut, for many years; in fact, it was she and her husband, Stuart Benson, who "discovered" the valley. While staying with her, in 1926, I found my little piece of land and have made it my home ever since. Her house is only two miles from mine, and Sidonie must have sent for her after the accident.

There is always a sense of comfort where Mimsey is. Somehow one has the feeling that everything will be all right. She has a genius for smoothing out difficulties and making hard things seem comparatively easy.

One never has to explain anything to Mimsey—she always knows. She sensed at once what was in my mind, for I heard her say, "It's all right, darling; you're not blind. It's just that your face is so swollen that your eyes can't open." Had anyone else said this to me, I should have thought they were trying to comfort me with lies. But since it was Mimsey's voice that spoke the words, I knew they must be true.

She then told me she had sent a reassuring cable to my mother, who was in London. And thirdly she said that Mrs.

Bok had called her up and sent word to me not to worry about the financial end of things—that my one thought must be to recover. Mrs. Edward Bok (now Mrs. Efrem Zimbalist) had been a good angel to me for many years; she had great faith in the Civic Repertory Theatre and was one of its chief supporters. The wonderful work she has done for music through her Curtis Institute in Philadelphia is world-famous. She has helped innumerable artists, young and old, and the aura of grateful thoughts that surrounds her should make her life a happy one.

And so, in three sentences, Mimsey relieved me of the mental anguish that had overwhelmed me when my mind began functioning again. I have often tried to express to Mrs. Bok the great contribution this peace of mind on the money question made to my recovery. But no words could ever adequately describe my gratitude.

I afterward learned that my poor mother was told the news by a "kind" neighbor, before receiving Mimsey's cable. This good woman had come to Mother's apartment bearing a newspaper which carried the alarming headline: "Famous Actress Burned in Explosion; May Live." Fortunately the cable arrived a few minutes afterward, presenting the facts in a more hopeful manner.

Actually, I was on the danger list for over a week.

One of the next services Mimsey did me was to rid me of a particularly brash and brusque nurse—a very young and pretty one, I was afterward told—who, because I was blind and almost dumb, imagined I must be deaf as well, and shouted things at me in anything but a soothing manner. She was transferred the next day to another case more suited to her particular brand of ministration—a young and wealthy man who had broken his ankle. I have always hoped he managed to leave the hospital a bachelor. Nothing can be more dangerous to an eligible young man than the predatory nurse!

At seven o'clock that first evening my night nurse came on the case. In those days nurses worked on twelve-hour shifts.

This woman was an angel who went about the world as Nurse Green—or "Greenie," as she is invariably called.

I liked her voice at once; it had bread and salt in it. She said to me, "I'm afraid when your eyes open and you can see me, you'll get a shock. I'm very fat and very ugly. Not like that pretty young thing who just left you."

But, oh! the comfort of those hands of hers. The sureness with which she tucked in the covers round my shoulders. The easy way she picked me up in her arms while the sheet was smoothed out under me. I was completely helpless, and she handled me as if I were a baby.

If ever there was a great nurse, Greenie is one. And how rare they are! No one could have helped me get through those dreadful nights that followed as she did. For two weeks I was allowed no dope of any kind. It was considered dangerous. It was explained to me that the more pain I could stand, the better my chances of recovery would be. So, of course, one just had to bear it—and it was tough. There were times when I didn't think it possible to endure such torment.

Greenie had been through World War I, at the front. She is a Canadian and went overseas with the Canadian forces. She lost her husband and her brother in that war—and came out of it with the Victoria Cross, one of the highest military decorations and rarely bestowed on a woman. She was a master psychologist, for during those sleepless nights she would tell me of all the agonies she had seen the men endure, of the unimaginable suffering they bore so unflinchingly. This had the effect—just as she intended—of making me ashamed of showing weakness; in thinking of all those many thousands had gone through, I toughened my will and stood the pain with a courage that was a reflection of theirs. As I dwelt on their immense suffering, my own seemed trivial by comparison.

The days were very different from the nights.

My day nurse, successor to the brash young lady who had mercifully been removed, was also enormously fat—for Greenie had not lied in her description of herself, except that one would never describe her as ugly. Her face radiated such goodness, such character and strength, combined with a grave tenderness, that one might have been tempted to call it beautiful. But fat she was. In fact I had drawn the two fattest nurses in the hospital—both considerably over two hundred pounds. But Greenie was hard and trim and firm, whereas my day nurse looked like a large and very wobbly blancmange—a revolting form of dessert much in vogue during my childhood.

She was a good-hearted, sloppy Irish soul, and certainly well meaning, but she was not a great credit to her profession. Her idea of being a good nurse was to please the doctor—and to hell with the patient! This is an all-too-frequent attitude I've found in nursing tenets. The sheets were tucked in so neatly and so ruthlessly, so that not a wrinkle should offend the medical eye, that one felt encased in a strait jacket. And since for the first weeks I was completely helpless, I had no means of destroying my blancmange's immaculate work.

Every other day the bandages were removed, and my hands were put to soak in saline solution. This was a painful business and was supposed to last for a half-hour at most, when the doctor would arrive and take over. But my blancmange was so afraid of keeping the great man waiting that she often allowed me to soak in misery for well over an hour.

The business that followed the soaking was grim indeed. I shall never forget the first time I was able to see as well as feel it.

The bandages on my hands made them look like two huge boxing gloves. When they were taken off I saw two masses of tumefied flesh, utterly shapeless, and with no trace of fingers or bone-structure of any kind. It was a shocking sight, and it was hard to believe that I should ever have hands again, though the doctor assured me that I would.

I had been very fortunate that first night, for the doctor in charge of the emergency ward happened to be Dr. William Tracy, Jr., a very brilliant and sympathetic young surgeon, who was much liked and admired and whom everyone called "Dr. Bill" with very real affection. Every other day he had the horrid business of treating these lumps of burned meat, picking away the dead flesh and gradually, and with great skill and patient care, whittling down to the healthy cells that would build me my hands again. The pain he had to cause me—for he could use no anesthetic—hurt him, I believe, almost as much as it did me. I watched great beads of sweat form on his forehead and pour down his face as he worked.

I felt so sorry for him that I made herculean efforts not to cry out, and to wince as little as possible. I asked them to put a hard pillow at my feet, and I used to brace myself and kick against it; it helped me to endure the torment. Dr. Bill kept telling me that the more I could stand the better the final result would be, and that thought helped me too.

Mimsey had sent for the famous specialist Dr. John J. Moorhead the morning after the accident. The first time he came I couldn't see him, but I was aware of a very forceful personality and a dry witty voice, rather like an actor's voice, which had the unmistakable ring of greatness and authority. He visited me again about ten days later, and this time I was able to see him and talk to him.

He reminded me of George Arliss in one of his famous characterizations—a very small man, wiry and nervous, tremendously alive, with something rather birdlike in his bright piercing eyes and prominent bony nose, a grand sense of humor, and an unerring understanding of the nature of his patient. I had complete faith in him, and we trusted each other from the first. At this stage of the proceedings he was there only in an advisory capacity; in his opinion, it was not possible to use surgery on my hands for another year or more. I was to come to know him very much better later. He seemed to have great faith in Dr. Bill, who had trained under him at Post-Graduate Hospital in New York City. He approved of the treatments and left me, for the time being, in Dr. Bill's care.

In hospitals time loses its meaning. The days and weeks seem interminable, and yet one is surprised at how quickly they actually pass. Hospitals are little worlds in themselves, and the tiniest occurrences assume the importance of events. Hospitals are filled with comedy as well as pain. Greenie and I, in our night sessions, had many a laugh at the foibles and eccentricities of some of the characters that drifted in and out of our small domain.

There was the matron—an extremely efficient woman, I understand—who used to open the door a crack, peep at me, and exclaim in cooing tones, "Eyes like Lake Tahoe!" and disappear again. It was she who named the two bundles at the ends of my arms, which were placed carefully outside the covers on either side of me, the "little kittens"! She used to say, "Now *which* little kitten is going to get well *first?*" Lake Tahoe turned to blue ice at that!

Once she asked me, "Why do you suppose God snatched you from your roses and brought you up the hill to us? *That's* to teach us *courage!*" More blue ice! But the occasion that almost caused Greenie to mutiny was the evening when this good lady, as she went off duty, "popped in" to see us and presented Greenie with a copy of something called *The Cheerful Cherub*, which she advised her to read aloud to me. As soon as the door closed on her cooing, Greenie threw the offending cherub on top of the wardrobe.

All this, of course, was intended to cheer me up and comfort me; but alas, I'm afraid the dear lady was no psychologist and had sadly overrated her patient!

At the end of two weeks Greenie was allowed to give me some morphine. Every night at nine o'clock she gave me an injection. All day long I lived for that moment; such a release from pain can amount to ecstasy. It was as though my hands were unscrewed from my arms and went off somewhere, taking their hell with them, and I was left in peace. For five or six hours I could sleep. From then on my recovery grew more rapid, and the doctors were very pleased with my progress.

Except for nurses and doctors, no one but Mimsey had been allowed to see me. She had always been famous for her poker face, and never by word or look had she indicated that there was anything odd about my appearance. I hadn't given it much thought myself; I had other things to cope with. But one morning, about three weeks after the accident, Mimsey brought a friend with her. The friend evidently was not prepared for what she saw, and before she had time to control her expression I knew that I must be a horrid sight. She only stayed for a moment in the doorway and waved to me. As soon as she had gone I asked Mimsey to give me a mirror. I wanted to know the worst.

I couldn't help laughing at what I saw. I looked like a very ugly Chinese Buddha. My hair was charred jet-black and stood up on my head like short stubble, with a longer tuft standing up in the middle. My face was bright red and quite swollen, with eyes like very small "Lake Tahoes." There were dark brown scabs all round my mouth, and the end of my nose was encased in something that looked like the discarded shell of a beetle. It was lamentable and somehow very funny. Mimsey and I laughed till we cried.

I shan't go into all the details of the weeks that followed. Some things stand out in sharp relief. The boxing gloves were gradually reduced in size, and the nurses started to take me around the hospital in a wheel chair, to see the sights. I was able to sit out on the sunporch, a glass-enclosed room in which some rather badly tended plants—old-fashioned begonias, mother-in-law's tongues, and philodendron—struggled for life as though they too were invalids. I longed to comfort them but was still completely helpless as far as any use of my hands was concerned. Everything had to be done for me. I had to be fed and washed and dressed; my nose had to be blown for me, my teeth brushed, and the stubble on my head combed. I found all this very trying. I have never been the sort of person who enjoys being waited on hand and foot; I've always done things for myself. I was fired with ambition to scratch my own ear again, blow my own nose, and do up my own buttons!

One afternoon, as I sat out on the sunporch, I had the great joy of a visit from Katharine Cornell. It was so like her to think of coming to see me. She brought me a box of fresh figs, which she had heard I was fond of, and sat talking to me for an hour or so. I was deeply touched by her kindness. It is that rare quality of genuine warmth, of simple human understanding, that comes across the footlights and fills her audiences with such love and respect.

Altogether the goodness of people amazed and overwhelmed me. I was filled with gratitude and humility. I realized how much I had taken for granted, how selfish and arrogant I had always been.

At last the day came when I could leave the hospital. Greenie came with me, as I was still unable to take care of myself. The bandages were removed from my hands. The left hand, slightly less damaged than the right, had healed, and I could use it to some extent. The back of the other one was still open, and it was amazing to watch the little islands of new flesh forming and gradually coming together, so that they finally closed in a semicircular scar. Several times a day Greenie had to expose my hands to the sun, and I was given various exercises, such as clutching and unclutching a ball, and trying to flex my clumsy new fingers on the edge of a table.

I was too nervous to go back to my own house—the scene of the crime. A friend lent me a car and chauffeur, and Greenie and I went on a little motor trip up through New England. We visited Mrs. Bok for a few days in Camden, Maine, and then drove to the Cape, to Provincetown, and I saw my dear friend Susan Glaspell at her house in Truro.

It was rather difficult for me to appear at public places, for I still looked most peculiar, and my accident had received so much publicity that people everywhere were very curious about me. I remember one time in particular, when Greenie and I were having lunch at an inn in Provincetown, and large parties of ladies kept passing and repassing our table, staring at me, and especially trying to get a good look at my hands, which were anything but prepossessing. These are the less attractive forms of public adulation.

Mimsey let me stay at her house in Weston, since I did not yet feel strong enough to return to my own. She had gone to Europe, but Greenie and I were well looked after by her Angèle, a wonderful Frenchwoman, aunt to my own little Marinette.

One day I was actually able to put on my own clothes, and I remember so well dear Greenie's face. She was torn between satisfaction at my progress and sadness that her "child" was growing up and would no longer be dependent on her. To a nurse with her clear, uncompromising sense of dedication, the recovery of each patient becomes a kind of personal loss, though mingled of course with a great sense of pride. The suffering we had lived through together had brought us very close and had created a bond that the years can never break. Though we meet but seldom, I think of her always with deep affection and gratitude.

CHAPTER TWO

A MONTH before my accident I had rung down the curtain on the fifth season of the Civic Repertory Theatre.

Had it not been for what in recent years I have come to look upon as a miraculous dispensation of Providence, the year that followed would have been even more difficult to face than in fact it turned out to be. I should have been confronted with the necessity of rapidly improvising a way of continuing the work of the Civic, though I myself would have been unable to take an active part in it, since my injuries, both physical and spiritual, precluded for some time any personal participation in a theatrical program. But I was mercifully spared any such problem. Against the counsel of all my friends and advisers, in the face of stunned bewilderment on the part of the Civic's many admirers, I had decided—or thought I had decided—to close down for a season. The strain of the first five years, with their unremitting effort, had exhausted me; I felt empty and in need of renewing the innermost sources of my creative energy. The destiny of the Civic for the season of 1931–32 had therefore been established in every detail. The executive staff, whittled down to a bare minimum, was to use the time to enlarge our membership, to procure additional patrons, to spread propaganda for our reopening in the fall of 1932. The acting staff had been reduced to a dozen of the major players, who had agreed to hold themselves ready for the resumption of activities, at a minimum weekly salary—a sort of retaining fee—while busying themselves in other fields during this suspension. It was to be a salutary fallow period for us all, during which we would have the opportunity of catching our breath, of reflecting on the achievement of the past years, while girding ourselves for the infinitely better work to come.

So it turned out that what appeared to be a purely arbitrary decision on my part was, in fact, the dictate of some guardian spirit.

Anyone strolling along Fourteenth Street between Sixth and Seventh Avenues in the year of 1953 will search in vain for any trace of a theatre there. But in 1866 a fashionable new playhouse, at the time hailed as the apotheosis of elegance, was opened on the uptown side of the street near the corner of Sixth Avenue—the French Theatre.

Through the years this playhouse suffered many vagaries of fortune. It knew triumphs and disasters—as all theatres do— but by the year 1926 it seemed irrevocably relegated to decay.

It stood, crumbling and shabby, flanked on one side by the hideous travesty of a medieval fortress known as the Fourteenth Street Armory, and on the other by disreputable-looking buildings housing an anomalous collection of small private factories and stores, whose filthy windows rattled mournfully at the passage of the Sixth Avenue elevated trains.

The paint had peeled off the once-beautiful portico of the old theatre; the plaster fell in dangerous showers from its dilapidated cornices; and a few tattered posters announced occasional performances of tenth-rate burlesque shows, and "foreign-language" presentations, mostly Italian.

But during the summer months of 1926 the building underwent a sudden change. The motheaten façade was encased in scaffolding on which painters worked feverishly. Windows were mended; sagging doors were reset on brand-new hinges; the filth of years was laboriously carted away in veritable mounds.

At last, over the marquee, electricians mounted one by one

the large letters which proudly spelled the name CIVIC REPER-
TORY THEATRE, and, spanning the street, a blue and white banner erected by the Fourteenth Street Association fluttered,
bearing on one side the words GOOD LUCK CIVIC REPERTORY and
on the other WELCOME LE GALLIENNE.

On each pillar of the colonnade supporting the venera-
ble portico neat frames appeared, bearing the titles of such
plays as *Saturday Night* by Benavente, *The Three Sisters* by
Chekhov, *The Mistress of the Inn* by Goldoni, *Twelfth Night*
by Shakespeare, *The Cradle Song* by Martínez Sierra, *The
Master Builder* and *John Gabriel Borkman* by Ibsen, and *Inheritors* by Susan Glaspell. Passers-by stopped in amazement
to read these names, the like of which had not been seen on
Fourteenth Street for many a year.

On the evening of October 26, 1926, an unprecedented procession of cars and taxis drove up to the long-neglected doors,
and a crowd of curious, somewhat skeptical first-nighters, bewildered at finding themselves so far from the familiar Broadway
scene, surged into the brightly lighted lobby.

From the subway, elevated, and Hudson Tube exits streamed
another crowd, making its way in eager expectation to the rush
seats in the gallery.

Backstage high excitement reigned, for this night was the
culmination of many months, indeed years, of thought and
careful planning. It was the beginning of our attempt to realize
a dream, a dream that we had been assured was impossible of
realization, impractical, fantastic, and foredoomed to immediate failure. We had taken up the challenge and now prepared to embark on our first battle.

What was this Civic Repertory Theatre, which, through the
unique quality of its achievement, has already become a legend?
What were its aims? What was its purpose?

The Civic was founded in an attempt to provide the people
of New York with a popular-priced classical repertory theatre

similar to those that have existed as a matter of course for many years in every large city of Europe—not only in such great capitals as Paris, Berlin, Vienna, and Moscow, but in such comparatively small towns as Brussels, Amsterdam, Prague, Budapest, Stockholm, Oslo, and Copenhagen.

The first sixteen years of my life were spent in countries where such "libraries of living plays" were considered mandatory. These theatres were as important to the mental and spiritual well-being of the people as bread was to sustain their bodies. Their presence in no way precluded, or impinged upon, the lighter and more sensational forms of entertainment, which it is also the function of the stage to provide; but in European cities the theatre was not limited, as it is in our country, to the best-seller of the moment.

It was this limitation of an art which I had been brought up to consider on a par with poetry, music, and painting—and which can be, in its finer aspects, a synthesis of all of these—that shocked and startled me, as it does so many newcomers to our shores, on my first arrival in New York in 1915. There was plenty of cake in the showcases of Broadway, but the bread was missing.

I determined then and there that, once I had won my spurs and proved my worth, I would devote my energies and talents to filling this need in the American theatre scene, and this determination never left me.

In 1925 I felt ready to attempt the realization of my purpose. A series of consecutive successes, starting with Arthur Richman's *Not So Long Ago*, followed by *Liliom* and *The Swan*, had placed me in the front rank of the young actresses of that time, and enabled me to gain access to men and women of wealth and influence, some of whom, happily, saw the value of my scheme.

I started modestly with some special matinees of *The Master Builder* in the fall of 1925, and when these proved a success I added *John Gabriel Borkman* to my incipient repertoire. At first these plays were offered at the regular Broadway prices, but since popular prices were the crux of my whole plan, I cautiously presented the two plays on alternate mornings at a top price of $1.50. Even at the unlikely hour of ten-thirty a.m. the houses were packed, and hundreds of eager people had to be turned away.

After the Christmas holidays I took the two plays on a spring tour of the Eastern cities, charging as low a scale as the booking office would permit. The results were immensely encouraging, and during these months I worked out, down to the smallest detail, the schedule for a proposed season of repertory to open in the fall.

One morning, in Cincinnati, I called the company together and outlined my plan to them. I explained that the work would be hard and the salaries only moderate, but in spite of this they one and all decided to join me in my adventure.

The plan once clearly formulated and set down on paper, I flung myself wholeheartedly into the job of translating theory into practice. I was predatory and ruthless. No rich person was safe in my presence. My crusading zeal was such that few people had the strength to escape my attacks on their bank accounts. If I met with resistance I was quick to point out that since I, possessed of no fortune but my talents and industry, was willing to donate nine-tenths of my earning capacity to this work, it would seem niggardly of them, secure in their steady incomes, to begrudge me a tiny fraction of their wealth. This argument amused some and impressed others and usually clinched the matter; I seldom went away empty-handed. I never failed to make it clear that these sums were gifts, neither loans nor investments; there could be no hope of repayment or profit. The Civic was designed as a subsidized theatre; only in this way, it seemed to me, could popular prices be combined with the necessary high standard of production, and the policy remain stable and safe from compromise.

There were three reasons why I chose the old theatre on Fourteenth Street. To my indignant surprise, the uptown theatre managers refused to permit regular performances at the popular prices I had decided on—thirty-five cents to $1.50 top. They were afraid of lowering the prestige of their houses. I therefore had to find a place outside of their jurisdiction.

With few exceptions the stages uptown were too small to accommodate the repertory scheme, with its constant changes of scenery.

I felt, too, that since our theatre in no way intended to compete with the regular run of Broadway attractions it might be best to remove ourselves completely from that particular arena. So it came about that the Fourteenth Street Theatre was rescued from oblivion.

On that Monday night of October 26, when we opened our doors with Benavente's *Noche del Sabado*—translated somewhat erroneously by John G. Underhill as *Saturday Night*—we had three other plays in readiness: Chekhov's *The Three Sisters* and the two Ibsen plays already produced the previous season.

The notices on Tuesday morning tried to be kind—the critics seemed to feel a respect for the venture, mingled with surprise and amusement at its sheer audacity—but they were far from being good. We were able to brush them off lightly, however, for we had many other strings to our bow and, thanks to my Robin Hood tactics with various wealthy patrons, we were assured of a full season, no matter how meager the box-office receipts might prove to be. On Tuesday, our second night, we opened *The Three Sisters*, the first professional performance in this country of a Chekhov play in English, and over this Mr. Woollcott flung his famous hat in the air, and there was general jubilation among his colleagues. By the end of our second week *The Master Builder* and *John Gabriel Borkman* had joined the repertory, and these four plays rotated on the Civic program while rehearsals were in full swing for Goldoni's *Mistress of the Inn*, which opened the Monday of our fifth week. This was the first Goldoni play ever to be presented professionally in English on the New York stage. Five weeks later Shakespeare's *Twelfth Night* took its place beside the other productions. In early February *The Cradle Song* was added to the list and proved a veritable smash hit, and finally Susan Glaspell's *Inheritors* was produced, giving us an active repertory of eight plays. I remember that the last week of our first season we gave ourselves the luxury of playing a different play at each performance. I had not announced "repertory" for nothing!

We closed the end of May, and I retired to the country to plan our second year of work, making occasional sorties to the yachts and palaces of Long Island to strengthen our finances, for, as I had expected, the deficit that first year was very high.

I was amazed at the praise and honors that began to shower upon me, and decidedly embarrassed by all the eulogies about my "great sacrifice" and "unselfish devotion" to the theatre. I felt lucky to be doing what I wanted; I could see nothing unselfish about that! Honorary degrees were conferred on me, gold medals, and, best of all, the *Pictorial Review* Award for "the most outstanding accomplishment by an American woman"—a prize valuable from several angles, since it carried with it the handsome sum of five thousand dollars, with which I was able to refurbish the carpets and chairs in the orchestra and put cushions on the bare benches of the gallery rush seats.

Each year we added four or five productions to our growing library, and by the end of the fifth season we had some thirty plays actively rotating in repertory. Besides the staples that should form the backbone of such a repertory—plays by such giants as Shakespeare, Molière, Goldoni, Chekhov, and Ibsen —we had introduced Giraudoux to the New York theatre-goers —a fact often forgotten—through his *Siegfried,* and several other modern playwrights such as Jean-Jacques Bernard, Claude Anet, Wied, and Mohr. We had won a Pulitzer Prize with Glaspell's *Alison's House.* We had inaugurated a free school, known as the Apprentice Group, whose graduates included such well-known actors as Burgess Meredith, John Garfield, J. Edward Bromberg, Richard Waring, Arnold Moss, Howard da Silva, and many others. Our acting company had been strength-

ened by the presence of such artists as Alla Nazimova, Jacob
Ben Ami, Paul Leyssac, and Josephine Hutchinson, and the
Civic Repertory, from being a mad quixotic experiment, had
assumed an air of permanence.

Many of our productions—notably *The Cradle Song*, *The
Cherry Orchard*, *Peter Pan*, *Camille*, and *Romeo and Juliet*—
had been smash hits in the full Broadway sense of the words,
and I had much difficulty in resisting tempting offers to cash
in on these successes by moving them uptown and presenting
them at the regular commercial scale. It seemed to me that
such a step would be not only shortsighted but a betrayal
of the basic purpose for which the Civic had been created.
Since our aim was to establish a permanent repertory theatre,
I felt it would be decidedly foolish to throw away our trump
cards. The full houses that these plays drew each time they
were performed enabled us to keep alive our other productions, which, though all of them worth while, had a more
limited box-office appeal. I wanted to keep faith with the
public that had shown faith in me, and by strictly adhering
to its firmly stated policy the Civic won the loyalty of its many
followers and the respect of critics and newspapermen in general. I was proud of the reputation we had acquired of always
living up uncompromisingly to the plans that we announced,
and when we rang down that fifth year on a performance of
Camille the extraordinary demonstration that followed the
final curtain was proof enough of the public's genuine appreciation for the consistent integrity of the management.

All those who were present on that memorable evening will,
I'm sure, remember it as vividly as I do. It is only in the living
theatre that such a communion between audience and players
can exist. From all over the house people shouted to us, "Come
back! Be sure to come back! Don't go away!" Those in the gallery and the back of the orchestra fought their way down the
aisles to get a closer view of us. The entire Civic personnel—
office staff, stagehands, and actors—stood on the stage with
tears in their eyes as the curtain rose and fell to the seemingly

endless applause; and when I came out to take a final call alone I suddenly found myself ankle-deep in flowers, thrown singly and in small bouquets from every part of the auditorium.

It was one a.m. by the time the crowd dispersed. People found their way backstage through the pass-door, and I stood on the threshold of my dressing room, shaking hands with these unknown friends as they filed slowly past. As I started upstairs to my apartment on the top floor of the building, exhausted by the emotions of the evening, the porter told me that there was still an immense crowd at the stage door, which refused to go away without a final glimpse of me, so I hurriedly threw a cloak over my Camille nightgown and went out into the street to wave farewell. Again came the shouts—"Come back! Be sure to come back!" I was tempted then and there to abandon our year of respite and continue the work without interruption; yet I felt this much-needed break would bring us back armed with fresh ideas, a clearer perspective, and renewed energy to serve. Little did I realize what this "much-needed break" held in store for me.

A few weeks later, when I found myself painfully struggling through my unexpected ordeal, the memory of this demonstration of friendship on the part of the public was a potent factor in my fight for recovery. I felt that, like the legendary salamander, I must somehow emerge from the fire unscathed and keep the promise to "come back" to which I had pledged myself that evening.

CHAPTER THREE

GREENIE stayed with me until I recovered sufficiently to be more or less independent, but work was of course out of the question, and I grew very restless. I decided to go to Europe and spend some months in travel.

Alice De La Mar lent me her delightful Paris apartment in the rue Gît-le-Cœur, so full of pleasant memories for her innumerable friends. I made this my headquarters. My hands were both healed by then, and I wore very large soft gloves to protect them and hide them from my own and other people's eyes. They were ungainly and stiff and horribly painful, but, although quite useless for any delicate work, they served well enough, and I was delighted to find I could drive a car without any trouble.

As always, the impact of Europe was soothing to me. Although for many years, and most happily, I have been an American citizen, still my roots are in Europe, and whenever I go back I can't help feeling profoundly moved. There is something about the smallness and shabbiness of things, the well-worn look, the patina that time has cast over everything—giving to quite ordinary little villages a nimbus of beauty—that is enormously touching. The smells, the taste of the food, the light on ancient walls and buildings, the faces of the people, their clothes, and the way they wear them—somehow they seem to live less self-consciously than we do over here. They seem to touch life more nearly; there is no effort to be smart, or "in the groove," or to seem successful when one is not. Tired old men and women are not ashamed of looking tired and old. Plump young peasant women glory in their plumpness, with no "Hollywood figures" to mar their healthy enjoyment of being alive. A poet glories in being a poet, and a laborer in being a laborer. Values seem simpler—richer, perhaps. These countries have gone through so many centuries of prosperity and famine, of wars and peace, of freedom and oppression; they bear the marks of so many scars, and the insignia of so many glories, that they can afford to move in a slower rhythm. When one has been physically and spiritually shattered, old people are better medicine than the very young. And so, when I landed at Le Havre and felt old Europe take me in her arms once more, I wept—but I was happy.

After leaving the bulk of my luggage in Paris, I made a flying visit to England to see Mother and my dear sister Hesper and prove to them that I was still very much among the living and looked forward to complete recovery. I then returned to Paris and the rue Gît-le-Cœur for a couple of weeks before leaving with some friends on a trip to Spain. I had never been there before, and, while I found it interesting and saw many wonderful things, the country and the people did not greatly appeal to me. Perhaps I was handicapped by not knowing the language; it is hard to get a true impression of any country under such conditions. When I saw my one and only bull-fight, however, I was grateful for my ignorance. Had I spoken Spanish as I do French, for instance, I'm sure nothing would have prevented me from rising up and proclaiming to the crowd my horror at the whole proceeding. I should probably have been removed to a jail or a lunatic asylum, from which the American consul would have had to extricate me!

At first it all seemed splendid enough. The blare of the trumpets, the brilliant costumes—those of the *espada* and *banderilleros* elaborately embroidered in gold and silver—the *picadores* mounted on richly caparisoned horses, the throng of gaily dressed spectators, the great sand-covered oval shimmering in the hot sunlight, created a sense of vivid excitement.

But then the gate was opened and the bull entered the arena. He seemed very quiet, almost tame; he looked somehow small and rather patient. Then the "sport" began. First the *picadores* went to work with their pikes; then the *banderilleros* planted their darts, garishly decorated with colored paper streamers, in the bull's neck; and each time they drew a little spurt of blood the audience yelled with delight. In front of me were sitting two old people with a tiny child, their grandson. The little boy screamed with joy as the blood flowed, and the old people encouraged him with laughing approval, clapping their hands.

At first the bull shook off the attacks almost languidly, as one might brush off a mosquito. But little by little, as the superb *banderilleros* kept up the incessant barrage, it grew angry and started to try to retaliate. This, of course, was the moment they were all working for—to turn that patient beast into a raging fury, bellowing with pain and charging wildly at its tormentors. At last the great man of the day, the *espada*, mercifully saw fit to give the *coup de grâce*. With an elegant and expert gesture he buried his sword in the dying animal's neck, close to the head, cheered to the echo by the delirious crowd. The bull stopped quite still for a moment and then very slowly crumpled up and collapsed on the bloody sand. Chains were fastened to it, and it was dragged out of the arena in triumph.

Though I was reminded that five more bulls were to be killed that afternoon, and that this was only a beginning, I had had quite enough. I staggered out as fast as my shaky legs would carry me and was quietly sick under the arcades near the entrance, to the great amusement of a crowd of Spaniards, who laughed scornfully at another foreign woman who was too soft to enjoy such glorious, full-blooded sport. But I suffered their contempt in silence.

I know that to many people my feelings may seem squeamish and ridiculous, but it is not lack of courage that makes me dread seeing an animal tortured. I can't help thinking that man was given his much-vaunted superiority of intellect for better reasons than gratuitously to torment helpless creatures. It is true that there is a great element of risk, once the bull is roused to fighting pitch; but deliberately, and by crafty, vicious means, to rouse it to that pitch is something in which I can take no delight. The *espada* and his assistants may be brave men, but they act from free choice, and that seems to me to make all the difference.

Fortunately Spain has many other glories besides the *corrida*; one of the greatest of these is certainly the Prado. Never shall I forget my first sight of the Velázquez paintings in the Oval Gallery there. I had often heard artists speak of Velázquez as the greatest of all painters. Having hitherto seen only reproductions of his finest works, I was rather puzzled by this insistence; but, coming face to face with these pictures, I began to understand. They seem to walk right out of the walls to meet you, alive and glowing and infinitely wonderful. It is worth going to Spain just to see them. Their vitality is so powerful that, as you stand looking at them, your own life seems to disappear and become absorbed in theirs. The infinite precision and perfection of detail never interfere with the magnificence of breadth and scope, and the over-all effect is overwhelming.

There is so much for actors and stage directors to learn from looking at such paintings. The amazing rhythm of the grouping is in itself a valuable lesson. There is nothing that seems studied or arty about it. I have often watched the patterns that crowds of people naturally fall into and wondered why stage crowds nearly always look so wrong. I think it is because the real crowds are unaware of being observed, are wholly absorbed in what they are interested in, with no thought of pleasing anyone's eye or engaging their attention. And because they are thus unselfconscious they inevitably respond to the rhythm of nature, which is always faultless.

In the theatre, as in most other arts, we should of course observe and learn from nature; but sometimes we are lazy or unaware, and walk about the world with unseeing eyes. Often a great work of art has the power to open doors for us and show us things in nature that we might not be acute enough or wise enough, or simple enough, to discover for ourselves.

For a young actor—especially our young actors, who have so little scope for using their bodies—to study the way in which people in great paintings stand or sit, or walk or turn their heads, or use their hands or wear their clothes, the balance and line of each part of the body expressing so accurately, so unerringly, the slightest thought and emotion, is worth many months at a dramatic school.

And there's no need to go to Spain either! Or anywhere else, for that matter. Our museums are full of pictures immensely valuable to the aspiring actor, and most libraries have collections of art books that are well worth careful study. Studying for the stage is not just a question of mastering certain basic technical problems—though it is necessary to know such things, the "traffic of the stage" demands it; nor should it be limited to a self-conscious absorption in one's own personality. The art of the theatre is, or should be, all-embracing, and the knowledge and perception of an actor should be widely catholic in range. I remember Granville Barker's saying to me when I was a child of twelve, "Learn anything and everything. Sooner or later you will have use for it in your work."

From Spain we went over to Mallorca, the wonders of which I had heard many people rave about. George Copeland in particular had often spoken of it to me with tears of nostalgia in his eyes, and I had thought of spending a few weeks in this enchanted island of his. But somehow the enchantment failed to work on me. Perhaps it was the wrong season of the year; perhaps I was too nervous and high-strung to appreciate its somewhat parched and arid beauty. In any case, the combination of sirocco, swarms of flies, uneatable food, and total lack of water was too much for me, and I fled back to the mainland and to France as rapidly as I could.

We drove through Provence—Carcassonne (so badly and thoroughly restored that it seemed like a movie-set); golden, lovely Arles, of Van Gogh memories; incredible Les Baux (so

little known, but one of the rarest places in the world); Nîmes;
Avignon, blessed home of that most heavenly wine, Château-
Neuf-du-Pape—then up through Auvergne, its chestnut trees
dripping wet-gold in the November rains; and at last back to
Paris and the rue Gît-le-Cœur, where I settled down for the
next few months.

CHAPTER FOUR

I<small>T</small>'s strange; on the morning of June 21, 1951, I read in the *New York Times* of the death of François Fratellini. I was just about to try to write of him and his two brothers, Paul and Albert, for they were an important part of the pattern of my life during this winter in Paris.

I had been troubled at how to put into words some faint reflection of the Fratellinis' inimitable artistry, and was finding it tough going.

Under the name of "The Fratellinis" they were famous all over Europe as great clowns, and had delighted audiences for many years—one might almost say for generations, for they came of a long line of clowns, going back to the days of the Italian *commedia dell' arte.*

François was always the leader of the team, the most articulate—vocally, at any rate—and since I believe there is much truth in the old saying that the dead help the living, perhaps he will help me now. I read that he died at seventy-two, so at the time I saw so much of him and his famous brothers he must have been fifty-two. Actually, however, twenty-two, thirty-two, fifty-two, or seventy-two makes no difference, for such artists have no age. They are born old, and yet they never lose their youth. Chaplin is as young now as he ever was. The great clown must combine the wisdom and sadness of the ages with the effervescent, wide-eyed innocence and simplicity of childhood. If he is merely funny he is not a great clown; there is much more to it than that.

By far the greatest theatrical experience I had during this Paris visit was my discovery of the Fratellinis. They were appearing at the Cirque d'Hiver, one of the permanent circuses of Paris. The other is the Cirque Médrano. These circuses are quite unlike our three-ring super-colossal Ringling Brothers variety. They are housed in permanent structures built especially for the purpose and used for nothing else.

These auditoriums resemble to some extent our theatres-in-the-round, except that they are much larger. There is, of course, only one ring—no self-respecting circus artist would appear by choice in a three-ring circus, and that is probably why the Fratellinis never came to the United States. The ring is covered with the traditional sawdust, and in one section of the circle is a large opening, where the principal exits and entrances of the various acts take place. Above this opening the brass band is lodged, so that the audience actually surrounds only about four-fifths of the ring—a plan, incidentally, which would make our theatres-in-the-round far more practical.

The Fratellinis appeared all winter long at the Cirque d'Hiver. Their repertory of acts—or *lazzis*, as they would call them—seemed inexhaustible, and each Friday they changed their entire program.

Each brother played a very definite role in the proceedings. François followed the classical clown tradition in make-up, costume, and manner. He was a small man, with a closely knit, rather stocky body, which yet had the agility and control of a dancer's, or, more nearly, an acrobat's—the kind of effortless, perfectly coordinated, concentrated control that one sees in most animals. His face, in the traditional clown white, with scarlet circles on his cheeks and *bouche en cœur*, the lashes painted round his eyes with bold strokes of black, giving them a look of starlike, wide-awake guilelessness, was so sensitive and mobile that it expressed his slightest thought or change of mood with a minimum of movement. He never mugged.

His body, dressed in a classical one-piece satin garment of some vivid color, embroidered with flowers and suns and moons and stars in glittering spangles, was equally expressive. He never made an unnecessary gesture; his economy and accuracy of line were a source of perpetual wonder.

His brother Paul, the eldest, who died some years before François, was much softer and rounder. He had no fixed costume but appeared under various disguises, often as a fat lady. I have one memory of him as a fantastic duchess, dressed in a green hunting costume, riding sidesaddle on an incredible "horse" manned by some minor clowns, and wearing a Queen Mary toque crowned with a nesting bird. At one point in the action the bird was shot at and flew off, leaving her nest, complete with eggs, on the duchess's head. Paul seemed less impressive than the other two; he was principally a "feeder," a straight man—or woman, as the case might be—but any comedian will tell you of the vital importance of this role.

Then there was Albert—there still is Albert, for he is still alive, and one feels sorry for him for that; he must feel so lost and lonely. These three were so bound up together, such an integrated whole in their art, that to think of one without the others seems impossible.

Albert was the silent one, and perhaps the greatest artist of the three. How can one describe the profound melancholy, the side-splitting funniness, the touching, grotesque hideousness of Albert's creation? He wore a black suit, green with age, several sizes too large for him; his pants trailed on the ground in a double train as he walked; his shoes were at least two feet long and turned up at the immense toes. He wore a bulbous red nose, capable of lighting up in moments of emotion, and a wig with a fringe of black hair encircling a bald pate. This black hair occasionally stood on end, and, at times of great stress, revolved on his head.

He seldom changed this costume, though I remember him in one act, dressed as a milkmaid with a very short, full skirt disclosing legs encased in hairy pink fleshings, and wearing balloons for bosoms, which of course burst with a mournful whistling sound, at strategic moments in the action. In this guise he "milked" a "cow"—animated, like the horse, by minor stooges—and from her concertina-udders gave a soulful rendering of "*Parlez-moi d'amour.*"

All the Fratellinis were fine musicians, dancers, and acrobats—even magicians. These accomplishments were a necessary part of their work, and enabled them in a thousand different ways to project and impart to others that humanity, that sense of the grotesque and ludicrous—sometimes broad almost to vulgarity, sometimes subtle and shrewd, but always based on universal and timeless truths—that marvelous observation of the foibles and absurdities of mankind, that made them such great artists.

I have been privileged to watch many artists in my life: Bernhardt, Duse, Réjane, Lucien Guitry, Isadora Duncan, Mrs. Fiske, Charles Chaplin, Ethel Barrymore, Mei Lan Fang—all great people who, in one way and another, have enriched my understanding, widened my horizons, and sharpened my perceptions, and to whom I shall be forever grateful. And on this list certainly belongs the name of Fratellini.

From the night I discovered them the Cirque d'Hiver became my favorite haunt. The whole atmosphere of the place enthralled me. During the long intermission you were allowed to go through that magical opening in the back of the ring and mingle with the performers. There were great stables back there for the beautiful trained horses that were always an important part of the show; there were cages for any other animals that appeared from time to time as guest performers. Opposite the stables there was a large café-bar where you could sit at little marble-topped tables and order drinks and refreshments served by the clowns who were engaged as part of the permanent circus staff; the tips were a welcome increase to their meager wages.

Many of these minor clowns were English, mostly Cockneys. I struck up a friendship with one of them, called George. We had long talks about circus life.

One evening I asked if it would be possible to attend a rehearsal. I longed to see these people at work, without the bright lights and glitter and trappings of a regular performance. George had no idea that I had any connection with the theatre; I told him nothing about myself. He just put me down as circus-mad, and he was right!

He told me their working hours, which appeared to be practically continuous, and proudly suggested that I ask for George, and he would see that I was admitted.

The very next morning I turned up around ten o'clock. Of course I didn't recognize George without his paint and putty nose and carroty wig; he looked like a rather seedy little assistant groom on an English estate. He welcomed me with open arms and, in atrocious French, informed a gentleman in charge of the rehearsal that I was a cousin of his just over from England. I followed him through the promenade that encircled the ring. The entire building seemed filled with activity of every sort. I saw tumblers, acrobats, dancers, weight-lifters, all busily practicing their various acts, all hard at work.

One balancing act, made up of a large family—mother and father, daughter and son-in-law, son and daughter-in-law, and an assortment of their children of all ages and sizes—was training the littlest one of all, who looked about three, to stand on his head on grandpa's head. He seemed to be doing pretty well, but if ever he showed the slightest hesitation he was hurled briskly through the air from one member of the family to another, round and round in a circle, until he seemed quite grateful to be allowed to come to rest once more, on grandpa's head! George tore me away with difficulty from this fascinating spectacle and led me into the empty amphitheatre; there he sat me down in a seat close to the ring and went off about his business.

They were working on a special Christmas attraction. It was to be an English foxhunt. The ring was full of horses, and there was a large pack of beagle-hounds, held in leash by two Yorkshiremen who shouted curses at them in a strong North-Country accent. Altogether, the mixture of tongues was unbelievable.

The master of the horse was Russian, the clowns all either English or Italian; only the ringmaster was French. He wore dirty riding breeches and an old shirt. He seemed in a foul temper, which was expressed in a continuous stream of foul language, shouted in a high nasal roar and punctuated by the cracking of his whip, which curled about the legs of animals and people alike with a kind of relish, as though it had a life of its own.

I laughed as I remembered the suave, courtly gentleman, with the gleaming smile, waxed mustachios, and dark ogling eyes, whose sartorial splendor dazzled the customers of an evening.

His wrath seemed to be mainly directed against a half-dozen young women who, as members of the hunt, were supposed to mount their horses rapidly and in unison, then, after circling the ring once, jump a very low fence and make a dashing exit. Two of the young women seemed just to have made their first acquaintance with a horse, and they didn't like what they saw, and the horses didn't like them either, so of course they just couldn't get together. And the more the ringmaster swore and cracked his whip, the more nervous both the young women and the horses became, and the less progress was made.

The ringmaster finally flung down his whip and tore his hair, and the young women ran shrieking from the ring.

With a great effort the ringmaster pulled himself together and glared round the amphitheatre. There were a few stray people sitting about, besides myself, and he appealed to us in agonized tones. "*Y-a-t-il quelqu'un ici qui puisse monter en piste? J'ai besoin de deux jeunes femmes qui sachent monter en piste! Le temps presse! Il me faut deux jeunes femmes . . .*"

I suddenly found myself standing in the center of the ring at his side. How I got there I shall never know.

"*Vous, mademoiselle?*" he shouted at me. "*Bon! Essayons! Donnes lui tes culottes!*" This last was addressed to a young groom standing by.

I was ushered backstage, pushed behind a curtain, and in a moment a pair of riding pants was hurled in at me.

"Well, I've gone so far, I might as well go through with it," I thought to myself as I struggled into the unsavory pants. I was fortunately wearing a suit and, though the pants were much too big for me, I managed to keep my shirt in them by fastening my belt very tight. I had on low-heeled walking shoes, and the legs of the breeches were so long they looked almost like jodhpurs and concealed my silk stockings. I must have been a queer sight as I emerged into the lighted ring. I was scared stiff, but, having got myself into it, I was grimly determined to land the job.

"*Allons, allons! Dépêchons, mademoiselle!*" came the voice.

As I approached the horse I caught a glimpse of George's face out of the corner of my eye. It was a study. "So that's wot she was after!" I could hear him think. "Wanted a bloody job —that's wot!"

Then suddenly I thought of my hands. I had on gloves, of course—at that time I was scarcely ever without them—but I had no idea how well I'd handle the reins. However, there was no time to think of that now.

I took up my position. The music started. At the sound of the whistle we were to mount. I stroked the horse's muzzle and whispered a prayer to him. He danced a bit and then was quiet. I felt as though I were in a dream. I heard a voice shout, "*Alerte!*" Then came the whistle. I remember nothing until I found myself dismounting with the others, out by the stables.

It was over, and I had landed the job!

The ringmaster came up to me, quite amiable now. "A *la bonne heure, mademoiselle!*" he said. "*Très bien.*" I was called to rehearsal for nine o'clock the next morning. My pay was to be twenty-five francs a show. I had joined the circus!

That first day I hadn't seen my beloved Fratellinis. They were in their dressing room, working on some props for a new act. But in the days that followed I had the joy of watching them work and of getting to know them.

Although I was one of the humblest members of their entourage, and an outsider at that, they were as kind to me as they were to everyone else, no matter how insignificant. I came to know that incredible dressing room, which was like Merlin's cave—a very long, low, dirty, unbelievably untidy room, badly lit and devoid of the simplest comfort. A make-up shelf was built along one wall; above it hung a series of old mirrors, with here and there a bare electric bulb of the usual French wattage, which bears economy strictly in mind.

The opposite wall held a long rack on which hung a medley of fantastic garments; and from nails stuck into the wall all over the place, seemingly at random, hung masks, false noses, funny hats—which would have delighted the heart of our own dear Bobby Clark—trick wigs, whiskers, balloons, and a bewildering collection of props and accessories of every kind and description.

There were no windows, and the atmosphere was thick with cigar and cigarette smoke; thick, too, with an amazing blend of smells—spirit-gum, greasepaint, coffee, burnt cork, sour wine, garlic, and the sweat of many a great performance. Never, before or since, have I seen a room remotely like it.

And it was always crowded; the door was never shut. These wonderful little men made everybody welcome. Not a corner of the long make-up shelf was ever vacant; young boys who aspired to follow in the Fratellinis' footsteps were encouraged to try different make-ups and effects and were given salutary criticism and pointers. Old clowns, who for years had toiled in obscurity, always on the fringe of the laughter and applause, were given praise and comfort, a cigarette, a glass of wine. In spite of its gloom, its dirt, its stifling atmosphere, the place seemed radiant; it was a place of magic.

At rehearsal the Fratellinis wore turtle-neck sweaters—very old, with faded stripes—and trousers so worn and ancient that they had acquired definite personalities of their own. Without

their comic make-ups the brothers' faces were inclined to be
serious, almost grave, and, in the case of Albert, handsome and
quite definitely sad. They never actually played any of their
own acts at rehearsal, merely outlined them, occasionally going into a huddle in the middle of the ring to decide on a
specific point of timing or movement. But when the work
involved any of the minor supporting clowns, they were tireless in giving them precise instructions, in helping them to make
the most of their small parts, in showing them just how best
to get the coveted laugh. These lessons were priceless; I shall
never forget them.

Later on, while rehearsing for the White Queen in *Alice in
Wonderland*, I realized how much I had learned during those
days, and if I played the part at all well, my success was entirely due to my masters, the Fratellinis.

But I soon found that circus life is not all comradeship and
sweetness and light. From the first day, the regulars were highly
suspicious of me. I had given a false name, and no one knew
anything about me. They assumed I must be French, for I had
no accent—that in itself might have seemed odd in that
polyglot world—but they sensed I was a foreigner and, more
than that, an "outsider." They had a dim feeling that I was not
unfamiliar with the entertainment field, and yet I was definitely not one of them—not of the circus.

Several of them asked me what circuses I had performed in.
I tried to indicate vague connections with establishments in
Scandinavia, Germany, and Russia, and I spoke a smattering
of all of these languages, which gave these fantasies some semblance of truth, but I knew no one was convinced.

Some of the things that I saw going on around me I found
very hard to take, particularly the treatment of the animals.
It may have been ignorance on my part, but there seemed to
me to be a great amount of unnecessary cruelty. One morning
I had words with one of the Yorkshiremen in charge of the
beagles. One of the dogs kept barking, and the man struck it
repeatedly across the muzzle with a heavy whip-handle until

the poor beast howled with pain as the blood streamed from its battered nose. I did try to hold my tongue and mind my own business, as I was told to do in no uncertain terms, but it was hard.

I noticed that small, mean tricks were being played on me. I always set my stirrup at the proper height myself before my horse was led into the ring; but on several occasions, when I came to mount it under the eagle eye of the ringmaster, I would find that some anonymous hand had shortened it so that my foot couldn't possibly reach it. Had I had the normal use of my hands, I might have been able to vault into the saddle, but as it was I had to rush round the horse and mount from the wrong side. This, of course, delayed me slightly, as well as spoiling the neatness of the ensemble, and I was duly called down by the maestro, no doubt to someone's great satisfaction.

But it was not this petty persecution that made me give my notice, though I've no doubt some of my colleagues rejoiced and imagined they had won their victory.

I resigned for personal reasons. I awoke from my dream one day and faced the fact that my mother would be arriving from London at any moment, to spend Christmas with me. I dared not face her outrage when she discovered that her darling daughter was indulging a mad whim by working as an obscure super in a circus!

I had not written to her about it. I knew her prejudices too well, and saw no reason gratuitously to offend them; that was my main reason for working under another name. But it would be impossible to conceal the awful truth from her once she was on the spot. Besides, special matinees were to be given daily all through the holidays, and they would have allowed me scarcely any time to be with Mother and entertain her as I wished.

When I mention Mother's prejudices I don't want to give the idea that she was in any way stuffy or lacking in fun and understanding—quite the contrary! But she belonged very much to her period—she was born in 1864—and there were certain things that ladies just didn't do. The circus episode was the second of two particularly unorthodox episodes in my somewhat unorthodox career, and I never told Mother about either of them.

The first happened when I was a small child of about ten and we were still living in Paris. An old lady and her daughter, the proud possessors of a beautiful gray donkey and several goat-teams harnessed to various little carriages, used to ply their trade of selling rides to the innumerable children that played about the *bassin* in the Luxembourg Gardens. I discovered that on Sundays and holidays they were short of help and were willing to pay the handsome sum of ten centimes an afternoon to anyone willing to lead the donkey-cart on its appointed rounds. Not only did I find this a job after my own heart, but the money was a useful addition to my weekly allowance of fifty centimes, the pocket money that Mother provided me with. When she inadvertently discovered this undignified oc-cupation Mother was very angry. She felt that "Richard Le Gallienne's daughter" should be otherwise engaged! As a pun-ishment, my fifty centimes of pocket money was docked for six months. This was a grave error on her part, for it gave rise to a far more ingenious way of making money. (I must have been born with an incorrigible desire to be independent!)

I suddenly switched my field of activity to the Bois de Boulogne. I persuaded our English maid—a young woman of what now seemed to me in retrospect rather dubious morals, who had replaced my beloved Nanny—to accompany me there on a Sunday, rather than to the Luxembourg Gardens; and since the Bois de Boulogne was a much more satisfactory place for her meetings with the various young men she "went" with, providing as it did pleasantly secluded nooks, conveniently masked from the public gaze with trees and shrubbery, she gladly consented.

As soon as I had made sure that she was happily engaged with her current "fiancé," I slipped away, knowing that for a couple of hours she would be oblivious of my whereabouts, so engrossed would she be by the delicious pastime of what was known in those days as "spooning."

I then stationed myself at one of the crowded *carrefours* in the Bois, where two of the main paths reserved for pedestrians crossed. I removed my large straw hat and placed it on the ground at my feet and proceeded with my performance. This consisted of a fairly large and varied repertoire of songs in several languages: Danish and German folk songs, French songs, English music-hall numbers that I had picked up here and there, incongruously mixed with nursery songs taught me by my darling Nanny. My French numbers were an equally strange mixture of songs I had learned legitimately and some others that I was not supposed to know, and whose meaning of course was largely obscure to me.

After a few minutes a sizable crowd would gather round me —people who looked in astonishment and amusement at this respectably dressed, well-fed child, apparently all alone, who, with seemingly imperturbable aplomb, entertained them with this motley program. Every now and then, at the psychological moment when I felt some members of the audience were about to give way to new arrivals, I passed round the hat. I would collect as much as five francs on a good day—it seemed to me a small fortune. And it was fun too; the sense of risk added a fillip to the whole business, since there was always the chance that a friend or acquaintance of Mother's might happen to catch me. But this never occurred.

So, those many years later, I decided that since I had successfully spared her the knowledge of the first escapade, I would also keep her in blissful ignorance of the second. I handed in my resignation at the circus and prepared myself to perform my filial duties and give Mother a happy holiday.

CHAPTER FIVE

MY MOTHER loved the theatre, and I had saved up most of my theatre-going until her arrival. I had been several times to the Comédie Française and the Odéon, for I knew she wouldn't care much for that kind of play-going. She loved what she called "glamour" in the theatre—the latest successes, the spectacular hits. She was quite a bandwagon girl, was my mother, and there was something very young and engaging in her attitude. She had a marvelous capacity for having a good time, and that made her fun to do things with. I think that's why she had so many young friends; she never lost her eager interest in new things, new achievements, new personalities. She was a born journalist, and up to a couple of years before her death, at seventy-nine, she was still writing articles for *Politiken*, the famous Scandinavian paper for which she had been correspondent for over forty years.

We saw Jouvet and his company in Giraudoux's *La Guerre de Troies n'aura pas lieu* and in *Dr. Knock*, the Molièresque satire by Jules Romains. As usual at Jouvet's theatre, both productions were impeccably staged and acted, with the unity of form and rhythm that constant playing together in repertory under a fine director gives to such companies.

We saw the Pitoëffs in Ibsen's *A Doll's House* and Shaw's *Saint Joan*. To me their productions were always a bit arty, and, from a scenic point of view, decidedly sloppy. They always did great plays, however, and many people thought Ludmilla Pitoëff a superlatively great actress, but her marked mannerisms of speech and *plastique* always tended to spoil my complete enjoyment of her work.

I was interested in Mother's criticism of her Nora. Mother had seen almost all the great Noras since Fru Dybvad, the great Danish actress who created the role. In her opinion, Alla Nazimova was the finest Nora she had ever seen. She thought that Nazimova succeeded as few actresses ever do in playing both ends of the character: the frivolous, spoiled, and bullied child-wife of the first half of the play, and the suddenly awakened creature, faced all at once with an awareness of her "duty to herself," the grave young woman who finds the courage to slam that famous door and start life over again alone, in an effort to grow up and make of herself a "human being." Mother felt that Ludmilla Pitoëff played the first part of the character almost too thoroughly, so that one found it difficult to conceive of the possibility of such a complete reaction; one was inclined to doubt the seriousness of the change, to suspect that this was still the same child-wife dressed up in grown-up's clothes. I think there was much truth in this opinion.

In *Saint Joan*, one of Madame Pitoëff's most successful roles, she was extremely engaging, though, I should think, very far from Shaw's idea of the part, and equally far from what one imagines the real Jeanne d'Arc to have been. Perhaps it was her very tininess of person that always made her seem like a slightly neurotic, precocious child. It was hard to believe that she could ever have been robust enough to go through Joan's rough, hard experiences; and her spiritual quality seemed to me to belong more to a saint of the type of Thérèse, *la Petite Fleur de Lisieux*, than to the honest, unselfconscious girl who answered the devious questions of her judges with the homespun practical logic of the French peasant.

We saw an enchanting performance of Sacha Guitry's comedy *Mozart*, with music by Reynaldo Hahn, in which Yvonne Printemps played the title role, looking adorable in her eighteenth-century satin breeches, like a *porcelaine de Saxe*, and playing with delicious wit and humor.

One afternoon we were invited to attend a dress rehearsal at the Odéon of *La Dame aux camélias,* in which Ida Rubinstein of Russian Ballet fame was playing the famous lady. She herself had financed the entire production, which was designed by the great Russian painter Benois.

Years before, Mother had taken me to see the Ballets Russes, and I remembered Madame Rubinstein vividly in *Le Martyre de St. Sébastien* and *Schéhérazade.* She was a marvelous mime. Later, however, she decided to become an actress and appeared in Paris in a series of great roles.

There were very few people in the large auditorium. The curtain was up and the stage set for the first act. Even in the flat work-lights, I thought I had never seen a lovelier room. The walls were a wonderful shade of blue, and the cornices and moldings perfect in every detail. They were painted in perspective on flat canvas—so that the whole set could be flown—but the artist's execution was so masterly that the effect was one of depth and solidity far superior to any built set I have ever seen. Benois had of course painted it himself. All the furniture, even the smallest accessory, was chosen with exquisite taste, and everywhere—in flat silver bowls, in porcelain vases, in formal bouquets scattered about the room as though received and discarded, as living trees growing in cunningly wrought jardinières of metal or stone—were white camellias, *real* camellias that had been especially shipped from the South of France. It was enough to turn one green with envy! Oh, to be able to play the play in such a setting! I tried to imagine what it would be like—heaven, perhaps?

But just then the director appeared and ordered the stage lights turned on. I was appalled. He flooded that wonderful blue room with amber, and the whole thing immediately turned a rather nasty spinach-green! I thought there must be some mistake, but the director walked up the aisle toward me, beaming with delight and watching for my approbation. I managed to control myself, for the French are touchy, and

I knew foreigners were best seen but not heard. Then the play began.

Madame Rubinstein made her entrance—a very tall, angular woman with a striking, almost Byzantine face. She was superbly dressed, but somehow one couldn't imagine her as Marguerite Gautier, the fragile Lady of the Camellias, whose febrile gaiety and vitality were the result of the illness that consumed her. Mother turned to me and whispered, "She is like a Russian wolfhound!" And it seemed to me a very apt description.

I soon noticed that unless the actors played quite far upstage it was impossible to see their expressions. Whenever they came to within six feet of the curtain line their faces were plunged in shadow. Benois' set was exceptionally tall, which added to the beauty of the proportion, but the first light-pipe had to be flown correspondingly high in order to mask. I looked up at the balcony rail and boxes, thinking they had forgotten to turn on the front spots, but I could see no trace of any. The director and his assistants seemed agitated and were carrying on a lively discussion in what they fondly thought were whispers, much to the evident annoyance of Madame Rubinstein and her supporting cast.

Suddenly the director called a halt to the proceedings, and I heard several exclamations. *"On ne voit rien!"* *"Vous jouez trop près de la rampe! Il faut changer tout ça!"* His solution was to order all the furniture moved upstage six feet, completely spoiling the lovely symmetry of Benois' room, and crowding the action into a narrow corridor of space, where the lights from the first pipe managed to reach the actors' faces. I sat there open-mouthed and wide-eyed while they went on with the play.

During the first scene-change the director came and sat down beside me. He turned to me and asked how I would have solved the problem. How would such a thing be handled *"aux Etats-Unis"*?

I mildly expressed surprise at the absence of all front lighting. With the elimination of footlights, which I agreed was desirable, it seemed to me mandatory to use spots from the house; for, I hastily added, the grouping and general movement had been so right, so beautifully planned, that it seemed a pity to have to spoil it, when that could so easily have been avoided.

This opinion precipitated a violent outburst on the part of the director. He had heard that in Germany and in America such vulgar effects were used to light up the actors' faces. That was all very well in vaudeville or musical comedy, but in a high-class theatre such a thing would be unthinkable! *"Non, non, et non! Jamais!"* The storm swept over me, and I was properly annihilated.

It was time for the second act to begin, and the director strode down the aisle with much waving of arms and shrugging of shoulders. When he rejoined his comrades down front, I heard muttered groans of contemptuous despair. *"Oh! Ces américains!"*

Orders were given to move all the furniture upstage as in the first act, and another of Benois' beautiful rooms was ruined.

Mother leaned over to me and said with a snort of disgust, "Idiotic!" She reminded me of the Queen of Hearts in *Alice in Wonderland.*

We sat on for another act, but that was all I could endure; my sense of theatrecraft rebelled. Also I was afraid that, should the director come and talk to me again, Mother would tell him with Scandinavian forthrightness just what she thought of him. She had plenty of valor, but discretion was never the better part of it.

Mother's visit was a great success. We had a lovely Danish Christmas, much to the wonder and excitement of Marie, Miss De La Mar's maid, who was in charge of the rue Gît-le-Cœur apartment. She had never seen anything like it. In France there is not much fuss made about Christmas; it is the New Year—the *jour de l'an*—that is important. The holly and mistletoe, the tree decorated with tinsel and ornaments, which sparkled in the magical light of real Christmas-tree candles, enchanted Marie.

Mother was always like a child over her presents, and because it was such fun to give her things she always had an immense number of parcels, which she undid with a kind of eager, greedy curiosity, culminating in cries of delight or murmurs of indifference, depending on whether she really liked the present or just made an effort to be polite about it—an effort that was singularly unsuccessful, for her reactions were always vividly transparent. Darling Mother! I do hope one can have fun in heaven. But if not, I'm sure she has set about making the necessary changes.

I stayed on in Paris another six weeks after Mother went back to England. I was beginning seriously to think of the reopening of the Civic Repertory, which was scheduled for October. I had resumed work on my version of *Alice in Wonderland* and, since Irene Sharaff—who has made such a fine name for herself as a top-flight costume-designer—was in Paris on a visit, we had several meetings to discuss the scenery and costumes for *Alice*. Irene Sharaff had been Aline Bernstein's assistant at the Civic for the past couple of years, and this was to be her first solo effort. She was deep in a meticulous study of Tenniel, for the entire production, down to the smallest prop, was to be a faithful reproduction of Tenniel's famous illustrations. My aim was to make these familiar and much-loved pictures come to life on the stage. I had myself devised the technical scheme of production, in which, by the use of trolley platforms and other stage devices, it would be possible to keep the entire action of the play flowing, uninterrupted by curtains or conventional scene-changes, in this way giving the effect of Alice's dream. The various scenes and characters had to come to her without her ever leaving the stage, since they were all figments of her own imagination. It was a difficult problem to work out, and a fascinating one. In her end of the work Miss Sharaff succeeded brilliantly in conveying the Tenniel drawings, down to the tiniest bit of cross-hatching.

I had also been working hard at fencing during my stay in Paris. Dr. Moorhead had advised me to exercise my fingers as much as possible, and since the French school of *escrime* concentrates most importantly on wrist and hand work, I thought it would be very salutary. I found that the old gymnasium on the rue de Vaugirard, which I used to attend twice a week as a child, for general physical training, was still in existence. It looked just the same, only of course much smaller to my grown-up eyes; I had remembered it as a vast place. The same old sign was there over the entrance—"Gymnase Georges"— and Monsieur Georges was still in control. He too looked smaller and of course much older. He remembered my name and looked me up in a dusty old ledger; he seemed very pleased that I had thought of him after all those years. His colleague, who had been my professor of gymnastics and who used to make all our little-girl hearts flutter with his dark wavy hair, lithe slim body, brown eyes, and small carefully waxed mustache, had been killed in the First World War. I arranged to have a fencing lesson every morning at nine o'clock.

The professor Monsieur Georges chose for me was a wonderful teacher. He was an instructor in the army, a short, stout little man, but incredibly light on his feet and with a wrist and fingers of steel. He soon discovered me to be quite an advanced pupil and started me off almost immediately on actual bouts with some of his best students. His great advice was *"Soyez méchante, mademoiselle! Soyez méchante!"* But his jovial grin was so good-natured and disarming that it quite belied the fierceness of his words.

Most of my previous studies in fencing had been in New York with dear Giorgio Santelli, a wonderful man, and one of the kindest and best. He always staged fights for me at the Civic in such plays as *Romeo and Juliet, Twelfth Night,* and *Peter Pan.* He has a great sense of the dramatic and knows how to make a duel that is actually quite simple seem breathlessly exciting. He has become practically indispensable to the New York theatre; whenever a "fight" is called for, Giorgio Santelli is sure to be around. But his form in fencing is definitely of the Italian school, very flamboyant and dependent upon fast legwork and breadth of movement; whereas my little Frenchman depended mostly on the wrist and hand. He taught me a couple of mean, tricky little attacks, demanding great accuracy and meticulous timing; they looked innocuous enough, but if executed with speed and precision they were very "deadly." He made me promise, next time I had a lesson with Santelli, to try one of these on him. I remembered to do this when I returned to New York, and I can still see the gleam of delighted surprise in Giorgio's eye when I touched him. "Oho!" he said. "Where have *you* been studying?" Of course I was never able to touch him again; he was onto my new tricks.

I've always thought fencing one of the most stimulating and fascinating forms of exercise. It's never dull because one's mind is kept just as busy as one's body. And I think that's why it's so good for actors; it develops that precise coordination between thought and action that is such a necessary part of playing. This, I suppose, should be true of dancing too, but I have found that dancing lessons are apt to make a young actor self-conscious about his movements, unless he is a born dancer and instinctively uses movement to express a mood or a thought; but that is of course comparatively rare. And in general movements in dancing are apt to be made for themselves alone, unrelated to any inner compulsion. This, in fencing, is impossible; for without thought there is no reason for movement. The movement is a direct result of a specific intention; the execution of this intention demands complete concentration, and complete concentration eliminates self-consciousness.

From this lecture one may conclude that I advise aspiring young actors to take up fencing. I think I'll ask Giorgio for a commission!

My hands were greatly improved, but I knew that before I

could appear on the stage again a couple of operations would be necessary, and the sooner they could be got over with, the better. So I decided it was time to return home and see what Dr. Moorhead had to say.

Before leaving Paris, however, I naturally had to make a farewell visit to my beloved circus. All the time Mother had been with me, it was obviously impossible for me to go there. The familiarity with which I should surely be greeted would certainly have surprised her and roused her suspicions. But once she was safely back in London I was free to return.

I went there one night with Marcel Achard, the brilliant young playwright. Among his many amusing comedies was one about the circus—*Voulez-vous jouer avec Môa?* While writing it, he had practically lived at the Cirque d'Hiver, and he knew the Fratellinis intimately. I told him about my circus experience, and he was greatly amused.

We had dined at a smart restaurant and were both in evening dress. My circus friends hardly knew me, I looked so respectable. Achard insisted on taking me backstage in the intermission and introducing me to the Fratellinis as myself. He told them all about me and about my theatre in New York; they were as excited as children. Somehow word got around that I was there with Marcel Achard, and that I had turned out to be *"une grande artiste américaine"*—that was the way they delightedly expressed it. The famous dressing room soon became crowded with numbers of my ex-colleagues, and there was much embracing and many cries of wonder and admiration. Even the maestro bowed low and kissed my hand. And dear old George, my "cousin," having drunk several toasts to my happiness and continued success, was seen to wipe away a tear. It was an occasion that only Dickens could describe, and I shall never forget it. Before I left we had evolved elaborate schemes to transform the old Civic into a one-ring circus, so that we might all be reunited there and I should have the honor of presenting the Fratellinis *aux Etats-Unis.* "Ah, youth, youth!" as Chekhov would say.

I sailed in February from Le Havre on the French Line. The boat called at Plymouth just after midnight, and Mother journeyed all the way from London, all by herself, and came aboard from the tender just to have a farewell glimpse of me. I had some sandwiches and champagne for her in my stateroom, and we had a jolly little visit. It was a very stormy night, and Mother was one of very few people who had braved the elements, in spite of warnings from friends and relatives in London. She was not a Viking for nothing! I can still see her now, standing very upright on one of the hatches as the tender made ready to leave, smiling and waving and blinking back her tears. It's a gallant and endearing picture. Julie Le Gallienne-Peter Pan, I thought to myself as the tender disappeared into the night.

CHAPTER SIX

IT WAS wonderful to get home again. There's always something thrilling about arriving in New York. Europe had soothed and calmed me, and I was deeply grateful for the months I had spent there, but the moment I felt the electric atmosphere of the United States I was filled once more with energy and a desire to get back to work.

I often think how different my life would have been had not some obscure instinct led me to the United States. It was really strange that I should have chosen to come when I did. I had just made a big success in London in my first speaking part, and had a great number of offers. My career there seemed assured. No one understood at the time why I insisted on turning my back on what looked like a secure future, to go to a country so far away, so different, and where I would be a complete stranger. It is amazing to me, now I think back on it, that Mother should have let me have my way. I know she would have preferred to stay in Europe, where she belonged; but though I was only sixteen I was already the head of the house in her eyes. I was the breadwinner, and because of that, I think, she felt that my wishes, based on a strong intuition, should be taken seriously. Mother never treated me as a child; she always had great respect for anything I felt deeply, and though it is difficult accurately to remember one's motives of so long ago, it seems to me that the great challenge of this country had a fascination for me. Possibly the prospects of my future in London seemed too clear, too tame; I wanted wider, more difficult worlds to conquer. In any case, whatever power it was that guided me here, I have certainly never for a moment regretted it or wished it otherwise.

Before settling down to the immense amount of work the reopening of the Civic entailed, I had first to consult Dr. Moorhead. On the whole he was pleased with my hands and felt that the time had come when he could operate and improve their looks. Both my little fingers needed his attention; they were imprisoned in webs of scar-tissue that made it impossible for me to straighten them. A few days after arriving home I went to Le Roy Hospital to have them fixed.

I used to say there should be a credit-note on the program: "Miss Le Gallienne's little fingers by Dr. Moorhead." He had planned to operate on both hands at the same time, and I remember how furious I was when I came out of the anesthetic to find that only the right hand was in bandages. My one idea was to get it all over with, so that I would be free to work as soon as possible.

It appeared that the right hand had been so severely burned that the job was more complicated than Dr. Moorhead had anticipated. As far as I could understand his explanation, the main tendon had been almost totally destroyed and had to be freed from the scar-tissue and cut and spliced together again, in order to make it long enough to serve. All this, of course, was delicate and tedious work and took a good three hours. He didn't want to keep me under ether any longer than that, so postponed the left hand until some days later. Eventually, however, both hands were taken care of.

I had to stay in the hospital for a while, which infuriated me since I felt perfectly well otherwise, and the pain of surgery seemed as nothing compared to the pain I had suffered from the burns themselves. But I was again helpless, since I had splints on both hands for over a month.

As soon as I left the hospital I returned to my apartment on Fourteenth Street for a couple of weeks before going home to Westport for the summer. There was much reorganization to be done, and the final plans for our sixth season had to be definitely settled and pulled together.

This apartment of mine on Fourteenth Street was a wonderful place. It was right in the theatre building itself, on the very top floor, up five flights of rather dilapidated stairs.

The first season of the Civic I had lived on West Eleventh Street, but even that short distance was irksome to me. The press of work was great, and I needed to be right on the spot every moment.

The second season we took over the house next door to the theatre. It had been occupied by a number of business firms and offices of various kinds. Their leases ran out in 1927, and we were able to take possession of the building.

I had a door knocked through the dividing wall to the stage, and turned the whole ground floor into dressing rooms and a greenroom. Above this was the huge costume department, which ran the whole depth of the building. Above this again was the play-reading department, students' library, and Mary Benson's and my own offices. The fourth floor was occupied by the press department. There remained the fifth floor. This was cut up into a great many tiny dingy rooms that had been rented out very cheaply to a number of rather peculiar tenants; one old man had kept chickens there—a fact to which the smell and the state of the floor amply bore witness. I decided this would be an excellent place for me to live.

I had most of the partitions removed and divided the large space into a living room, kitchen, library, and bedroom with a bathroom adjoining. I had the entire floor covered with heavy linoleum that successfully concealed all traces of the previous feathered tenants.

It was fun fixing it up, and I made it into a roomy and most comfortable apartment. And it was marvelously convenient; I never had to leave the building.

Each morning at nine o'clock Santelli arrived and we fenced for half an hour. I then had breakfast. After that I gradually descended from one floor to the next, stopping on the way at the various departments that needed my attention, until at noon I found myself at the stage level, ready for the daily rehearsal. We rehearsed every day from noon to five or five-thirty, either on the current new production or on some of the old ones that needed tuning up. Immediately after rehearsal I had dinner, and then slept for an hour before going down to play. After the performance I usually had a few people up to supper for informal conferences—actors, authors, or scenic-designers. These sessions usually lasted till around two a.m.

It was certainly a busy life, and, looking back on it, I can understand why people called me "tireless," for I don't remember ever really being tired. I was too interested, too deeply absorbed, and I suppose I must have been endowed with quite unusual vitality. Also, I have always had the enviable faculty of being able to relax completely during any free moments that come my way; I can stretch out on anything, anywhere, even in a crowded room, a corner of the stage, or the floor of a dressing room, instantly sleep soundly for five or ten minutes, and wake up completely refreshed. This is a tremendous asset, and I advise any young actors not naturally endowed with this ability to cultivate it. They'll find it will stand them in good stead.

At last I was able to go to the country, and during that summer I wrote At 33, all but the very last chapter. The idea of writing the "story of my life" was suggested to me by one of the big weekly magazines. They offered me a considerable sum of money for the serial rights, and since I hadn't been able to work for a year the need of money loomed as a serious problem to me at that time. I worked every day regularly for six hours, and at the end of four weeks I submitted the manuscript. It did not meet with the editor's approval; he had had something more sensational in mind. I was reminded with disgust of a cable Isadora Duncan had shown me years before, from a publisher who had persuaded her to write the story of *her* life. He implied that he was not interested in her ideas of work and asked for an account of her love-life in detail. This prompted Isadora, in a rage, to write the book that we all know as her autobiography, but which, in fact, was the antithesis of what she wished to write and gives a completely one-sided and distorted picture of her.

I was not surprised that my manuscript had been turned down. While writing it, I had read in this same magazine some memoirs of a famous opera singer, which described in lurid detail such choice "memories" as that of D'Annunzio making wild love to her while she was the guest of Eleonora Duse, or of King Edward VII groveling at her feet and drinking champagne out of her slipper—a form of adulation popular in the nineties, which has always struck me as singularly distasteful.

If that's the sort of stuff they want, I thought to myself, I haven't a chance! For even had I been able to summon such juicy episodes from my past, I had no intention of doing so.

Fortunately the *Pictorial Review* liked what I had written and accepted it. *At* 33 appeared first serially in that publication, and later was published in book form by Longmans, Green.

The Civic Repertory Theatre reopened as planned in the fall of 1932. Our first new production was a revival of Molnar's *Liliom*, and I was fortunate in persuading Joseph Schildkraut to join our ranks. He not only repeated his vivid performance in this play but took over Armand in *Camille* and several other roles in the existing repertory, as well as creating a leading part in a new American play about Jane Austen by Eleanor Hinkley, and an unforgettably comic Queen of Hearts in *Alice in Wonderland*.

It was a most interesting experience to play Julie in *Liliom* again after a lapse of ten years. I was amazed to find how short in actual lines the part is—a bare "six sides," as actors say—yet the impact of Julie in Molnar's play is so strong that many people remember her even more vividly than the flamboyant Liliom himself. Her silent presence on the stage can be more eloquent than words. It is the inner performance of the actress, the power of her unspoken thoughts and feelings, that makes the role so telling, and also so tiring. It was good to be playing the part in repertory instead of eight times a week, month after month, as in the original Theatre Guild production. Although I was only twenty-one when I first created the part, after a year of consecutive performances I had a complete nervous breakdown from the strain. Julie's dumb, unexpressed anguish is not comfortable to live with. But interspersed with such varied interpretations as Camille, Juliet, Peter Pan, Hedda Gabler, the gay Mistress of the Inn, and the many other widely different creatures that I portrayed in our large repertoire, Julie was sheer joy to me.

The play met with great success. It is a play that does not date, nor do I think it ever will. When all Molnar's other works, expert and even brilliant though some of them may be, are forgotten, *Liliom* will endure.

Business was good that season at the old theatre, but the continued repercussions of the Wall Street crash were beginning to make it harder than ever to raise the necessary subsidy on which the Civic, with its limited capacity and its bargain prices, had inevitably to depend. Attendance was by now so excellent that there were seldom empty seats for any of the plays, and the box-office returns were sufficient to take care of the weekly running expenses. It was for new productions that subsidy was still imperative. Had it been possible for us to increase our income by even a thousand dollars a week, with our customary forty-week season we could at that time have become wholly independent. But there was no way of increasing our capacity, and I was loath to raise the prices. Our only "weak" performances—irrespective of the play presented—were Monday nights and Wednesday matinees, and I determined to appeal to Equity for permission to replace these by two performances on Sundays. A large part of our audiences was composed of foreigners, to whom Sunday performances had a very wide appeal. We had many requests for them, and there can be no question that both houses would have been consistently sold out. The members of the company were unanimously in favor of this scheme; it made no difference to them whether their weekly night off fell on a Sunday or a Monday, and they were all eager to do anything to insure the continuance of our work. They therefore signed a petition to Equity, backing up my request. Equity saw fit to turn it down. Again I appealed to them, and again they disappointed me. Finally I myself appeared before the Council and explained that the very survival of the Civic Repertory depended, in all probability, on their decision. The Council, however, remained adamant. Ironically enough, a few years later Sunday performances became customary; the pressure of commercial interests had succeeded in overcoming the objections of the Council, where my earnest efforts had so signally failed.

We managed to scrape together enough money to put on two further additions to our repertory: Miss Hinkley's play *Dear Jane*, mentioned above, and the long-awaited version of *Alice in Wonderland*, on which I had been at work for two years.

Alice was a costly production even in those days, involving as it did elaborate mechanics and the services of a fairly large orchestra to interpret Richard Addinsell's entrancing score. Many dress rehearsals were needed to insure the smooth synchronization of all the elements involved. The overtime bills from the stagehands were staggering; nowadays the equivalent bills would be catastrophic. But somehow, largely through the energy and stick-to-itiveness of Mary Benson, who practically held up various still-wealthy patrons at the point of a gun, the production opened in early December and was received with universal acclaim. We found ourselves with a new smash hit on our hands, and were duly grateful.

But our efforts to bring *Alice* to the stage had, we soon found, exhausted all sources of further revenue, and this sixth season proved to be our last at the old Fourteenth Street Theatre of happy memories.

As on the occasions of our other outstanding successes, I was strongly advised to transfer *Alice in Wonderland* uptown to a larger house at regular prices, and this time circumstances forced me, much against my will, to consent to the move. I succeeded, however, in preserving some semblance of repertory by dividing the week between performances of *Alice* and *The Cherry Orchard*, with Madame Nazimova giving her enchanting performance of Lubov Andreyevna.

We played until the middle of May at the New Amsterdam Theatre, and at the close of our season I retired to the country to meditate on our next move.

CHAPTER SEVEN

THIS next move proved to be an extensive tour, which lasted from October 1933 through the following spring. The Civic Repertory Company, with the exception of brief visits to Philadelphia and Boston, had appeared exclusively in New York City. I felt that a long tour would serve to keep our company intact and enable us to stay alive, at the same time giving me an opportunity to explore further possibilities of a subsidy that would assure the continuance of our work at the old Fourteenth Street stand. I sublet the theatre to a new group, the Theatre Union, which produced a series of modern, rather leftist plays, with some success.

The repertory we presented on the road that season included *Alice in Wonderland, Romeo and Juliet,* and three Ibsen plays, *Hedda Gabler, The Master Builder,* and *A Doll's House.*

During our appearance in Washington, D.C., Mrs. Franklin D. Roosevelt came to a performance of *Alice in Wonderland.* She is a Carroll fan and was most charming about our production; she seemed to feel we had succeeded in capturing the real quality of *Alice.* I had never had the honor of meeting Mrs. Roosevelt before, and when I walked out on the stage to greet her after the final curtain, still wearing my grotesque White Queen costume, I was immediately struck by her rare charm of manner and her deep humanity. She seemed to me very tall, and I couldn't help thinking how much handsomer she looked in person than her pictures would lead one to expect. She very graciously invited me to tea at the White House during our stay in Washington. The tea was happily not a social function; we sat upstairs in her sitting room and had a quiet talk. Her daughter and one or two intimates of the family circle dropped in now and then, but beyond that we were left to ourselves. I told her something of the problems I was faced with. She was tremendously sympathetic and seemed genuinely interested in the work we were attempting to accomplish.

She felt the President might be interested too, and suggested that I submit an outline to him, explaining my dream of creating repertory theatres, similar to the Civic, in important key cities throughout the country. She told me of his concern for creating employment, and that in his scheme artists of all sorts, including workers in the theatre, were to be considered. The creating of some ten or twelve permanent repertory companies would involve the stable employment of around a thousand people, particularly as my plan included free schools connected with each of the suggested centers.

I was much encouraged by my talk with Mrs. Roosevelt, and immediately set to work to put on paper a comprehensive outline of this scheme so dear to my heart. I mailed it to the President. Shortly afterward I received an invitation to lunch at the White House. The President himself expressed an interest in discussing my plan with me.

By that time we were playing in Pittsburgh, but, since the matter was so important to our future, I put an understudy into the White Queen in *Alice* for a couple of performances, and made a quick visit to Washington. I felt very young and somehow lonely as I walked up the steps of the White House portico. I was extremely nervous; so much seemed to be at stake.

It was a small informal luncheon. As I remember, there were not more than eight or ten people present. Mrs. Roosevelt received me with great kindness, and I felt more at ease. We waited by the small private elevator for the President to descend. What a charming man he was! As he shook hands with me he spoke of my father, with whose books he was familiar, and whom he had met on some occasion years before.

He preceded us into the dining room, walking with some difficulty, leaning on the arm of his aide. I found that I was seated at his right. Mrs. Roosevelt sat opposite her husband at the oval table, and to my right was a gentleman who was introduced to me as Harry Hopkins.

Mr. Roosevelt spoke of my plan with appreciation and approval, but he told me he did not find it comprehensive enough. He wanted to create employment for many more theatre people—for all the theatre people, in fact, who were unable to find work. At that time the WPA was already functioning in certain fields, and his idea was to expand it to the theatre. He spoke at some length and in considerable detail, and I listened with pleasure to his beautiful voice, noticing the ease with which he clothed his thought with appropriate and compelling words. But I could not bring myself to agree with his point of view. It seemed to me to be the antithesis of mine. His project was primarily humanitarian; his aim was not so much to bring fine theatre to the people but to provide actors and other theatre workers, *regardless of their talents*, with work. He was not particularly concerned with standards of achievement; his concern was to create opportunities for all actors to make a living. It was a fine and noble design, but one, I felt, that would inevitably encourage mediocrity at best. It is obvious that in the theatre, as in all other fields, there is a large proportion of workers, devoid of talent, who, through a pathetic and misguided love for their profession, persist in it, unwilling to face the fact that God has made them totally unfit to serve it.

My dream, on the other hand, was to create people's repertory theatres throughout the country, staffed by the very best craftsmen procurable for their respective jobs. I felt that in order to foster a theatre-mindedness in the American public comparable to that in European countries, it was mandatory to bring them the highest possible standard of performance. The subsidized state theatres of Europe employ only the most efficient workers. It is a hard-won honor to be a member of such organizations as the Comédie Française, the Moscow Art Theatre, the Vienna Burgtheater—even the Kongelige-Teater in little Denmark. Such institutions, far from giving refuge to the incompetent and the unfortunate, are designed as strongholds of the very best standards and traditions in theatrecraft.

Such a point of view must seem hard and ruthless in contrast to President Roosevelt's desire to alleviate hardship and misery. But the service of art in any form cannot be soft or easy; it is a mistake to look for kindness or pity there. *"Aus meinen grossen Schmerzen, mach ich die kleine Lieder,"* says Heine. If one's aim in life is to live in comparative comfort, ease, and contentment, one should not meddle with the arts; they are ruthless masters and demand sterner stuff.

The President listened to what I had to say. I suppose it was temerity on my part to disagree with him, but I felt so strongly in this matter that I had to say what I thought. He referred me to Harry Hopkins, the gentleman on my right, and asked me to think over and discuss with him the possibility of my heading the National Theatre Division of the WPA.

I was aware that the President was doing me a great honor in considering me for such an important post, but, disagreeing as I did with the basic concept of the entire scheme, I felt I would be unable to do a good job in this most difficult and demanding position.

Harry Hopkins and I left the White House together. We were no sooner settled in the taxicab, and had not yet left the White House grounds, when he turned to me and said, "Dear Miss Le Gallienne, you should learn to play politics."

"That's one thing I never *have* learned to do," I answered, "and I'm not sure that I want to."

"If you would just learn to play politics," he continued, "you could get millions out of the old man."

I looked at him in amazement; it seemed such a curious remark to make to a perfect stranger. I have no doubt he was right. I suppose one should learn to compromise and play one's hand with a certain amount of skill and subtlety. Mr. Roosevelt was obviously a trifle irritated at what must have seemed to him the arrogance of a highly opinionated young woman. Like many great men of strong convictions, he preferred people to agree with him. But it would have seemed to me dishonest to conceal what I thought, and even now, with whatever good sense and judgment I have painfully accumulated in the past twenty years, I'm afraid my attitude would have to be the same.

In spite of the fact that I could not bring myself to consider heading the WPA Theatre Division, I felt that, since so many millions were about to be spent on theatre work, it might be possible to arrange for a modest sum to be allocated to the continuance of the Civic Repertory Theatre. There, after all, was a running concern that had cost many hundreds of thousands of dollars to establish; an institution that had been hailed on all sides as a valuable contribution to the culture of the times; an organization that employed close to a hundred people, and that had built up and kept alive a repertory of some forty complete productions; a living theatre that during the six years of its existence had created for itself a large and enthusiastic audience. Also of value was the free school run in conjunction with it, which I had started in 1928. It seemed such a tragic waste to allow all this to founder, when a comparatively small yearly sum was all that was now needed to keep it going and continue its very real service to the public.

I mentioned all this to Harry Hopkins, and he very sympathetically agreed that something should be done to insure the survival of the Civic Repertory. He told me he would call me up in Chicago, where I would be laying-off the week before Christmas, and asked me to be in readiness during that week to return to Washington for a further conference with himself and some of his colleagues in the New Deal. He was most cordial and assured me that I had good grounds to hope for some government aid in my struggle to keep the Civic Repertory Theatre alive.

I rejoined the company in Cincinnati and, the following week, went on to Chicago. Mr. Hopkins was as good as his word; he telephoned me as he had promised, and a few days later I went back to Washington.

I spent a busy day there. In the morning I had a conference with the Secretary of Labor, Madame Perkins. She was interested in learning details of labor conditions in the theatre. I did my best to answer her questions, and some of the facts revealed seemed to surprise and startle her. Nowadays the situation would undoubtedly surprise and startle her even more.

That afternoon I had a long talk with Mr. Hopkins. It was determined that I should ask for a yearly subsidy of one hundred thousand dollars, which I felt would permit me to add four or five new productions each season to our existing repertory and also make one or two improvements I had long had in mind. It was arranged that I should make this request that evening at a dinner at which some of Mr. Hopkins' colleagues were to be present.

This dinner took place in a private dining room at the Mayflower Hotel. I had expected it to be in the nature of a business conference, but, like many similar "conferences" in the honeymoon days of the New Deal, it was more in the nature of a party. There must have been close to twenty people there, prominent members of the Brain Trust, most of them accompanied by their wives, or by secretaries of the female sex. It was a gay and animated gathering. We all had a great number of cocktails before sitting down to a very excellent dinner, and to my surprise drinks were served all during the meal; I had always thought of official dinners in the United States as being strictly washed down with ice-water. I couldn't help thinking of Chekhov's line in the last act of *The Three Sisters*, when the old nurse delightedly tells Irina what a fine life she is now leading: ". . . I have a room to myself, and a bedstead . . . all at the government expense!"

Most of these people were young, all of them eager, excited, enthusiastic, tremendously alive. They felt they were rebuilding the world, and perhaps, in a way, they were. There could be no question of their sense of dedication, their ardent desire to better the lot of their fellow men. Everything seemed possible to them, and anything that promised to distribute the goods of this world more evenly and indiscriminately seemed to them desirable; they did not examine the ways and means too closely.

I have never been what is known as a good mixer. I am not comfortable in a crowd, and at first I got the impression that some of the people present thought me aloof and a bit stand-offish. They all seemed to know each other very well, and I felt rather like the lone outsider at a family gathering. But gradually the conversation got around to the problems of the Civic Repertory Theatre and whether or not it was deserving of New Deal support. The consensus seemed to be favorable, and my answers to innumerable questions seemed to make a fairly good impression. The discussion finally focused on the exact sum of money I would require. I mentioned the hundred thousand dollars a year that Mr. Hopkins and I had decided on as adequate. I explained how I had arrived at this particular figure. Again I answered question after question, some eminently intelligent, others showing complete ignorance of the problem at hand.

Dinner had been over for some time, and Mr. Hopkins went into a huddle with some of his colleagues at the far end of the room, while the rest of us lingered over our coffee and made polite conversation.

At last Mr. Hopkins and the other gentlemen returned and sat down at the table again. I was asked whether I could manage on a subsidy of ninety thousand dollars. I was rather surprised at this sudden desire for economy and wondered, in view of the huge sums of money that had been bandied about in the general conversation, why ten thousand dollars should seem of such great importance. However, I conceded that ninety thousand would certainly enable me to save the Civic from foundering.

I was then told, with much good will and evident pleasure from all concerned, that I could definitely count on this sum, and that I should by all means return to my work with a light heart and make arrangements for the renewal of my lease on the old Fourteenth Street Theatre.

The party broke up, and Mr. and Mrs. Hopkins started to drive me back to my hotel. We were all in rather a convivial mood, and he suggested that we go on to the Maisonette Russe to hear some gypsy music. But the thought of being regaled with "*Ochy Chornaya*" in every conceivable key and tempo was more than I could bear, so instead we went back to the Hopkins' apartment, where Mrs. Hopkins made us some more coffee, and where Mr. Hopkins persuaded me to read aloud Wordsworth's "Ode: Intimations of Immortality," which we had discovered was practically our favorite poem.

When he finally dropped me off at the Carlton Hotel, Mr. Hopkins' last words to me were a solemn promise to send me the very next day an official confirmation of the proposed subsidy for the Civic Repertory Theatre, so that I might in all confidence make arrangements for the continuance of the work.

This was the last I ever heard on the subject. I never received another word from Mr. Hopkins, nor could I succeed in getting an answer to a single letter I subsequently wrote to him.

It is scarcely to be wondered at that, ever since, I have listened to talk of possible government subsidy with a very large grain of salt.

CHAPTER EIGHT

MEANWHILE we found ourselves in 1934. The tour had
been a tremendous success artistically, with rave notices
everywhere and the houses good, but not sufficiently good to
give us the slightest margin of profit. Our expenses, even for
those days, were very high. *Romeo and Juliet* and *Alice in Wonderland* required a huge company; we must have traveled around
sixty people. Unfortunately, in Chicago the Paramount picture
of *Alice in Wonderland* was released simultaneously with our
opening there. Since we were playing during the Christmas and
New Year holidays we had leaned heavily on this attraction and
had arranged our repertory schedule so as to give as many
performances of *Alice* as possible. I think if the picture had been
a good one it would have hurt us less, but it was not a success
in any way, and I believe the public and critical response—or
lack of response—to the story in that medium discouraged people from attending the stage version.

When our *Alice* had opened in New York to tremendous
critical acclaim, the Columbia Pictures Company had evinced
great interest in making a film of it. The negotiations had progressed so far that contracts had been drawn up and were
ready for our signatures. Then Paramount announced its intention of making an *Alice* movie, and Columbia changed its
mind.

The Paramount staff attended many performances of our
production after we moved up to the New Amsterdam, and I
was much amused one day at finding a memo on my desk say-

ing that one of the gentlemen in charge had called up to ask for
John Tenniel's telephone number!

When the picture finally came out I was interested to find
that Paramount had used puppets for the "Walrus and the
Carpenter" scene. They must have been foolish enough to take
this idea from me, since the book gives no reason for handling
the episode in this way. Of course in the picture medium there
was absolutely no necessity for doing so; with the help of trick
photography it would have been simple to scale the oysters
down to proportionate size. I used the device only out of ex-
pediency, since it was self-evident that no human creature could
ever be small enough to portray the Tenniel oysters in correct
contrast to the size of the Walrus and the Carpenter. I remember puzzling for months over this scene; I felt it most desirable
to include it in the play, for it is one of the most famous sections
of the book, but those oysters caused me no end of cogitation.
I finally hit on the scheme of using super-marionettes for the
Walrus and the Carpenter. These huge figures, wonderfully
created strictly according to Tenniel by Remo Bufano, were
over seven feet tall. The little oyster-puppets stood just about
one foot high in their Tenniel boots, and were the most adorable creatures imaginable. The marionettes were worked by
eight puppeteers from a bridge twelve feet high. This scene
turned out to be one of the most effective in the entire show;
I'll never forget the shouts of delight that greeted the entrance
of the oysters. But I've never understood why, with all the possibilities of illusion at its command, the moving-picture company chose to follow the pattern of the stage production in this
sequence. Perhaps, however, since the Paramount staff had expected to reach John Tenniel on the telephone, they also imagined that the use of marionettes was implicit in Carroll's story.

These were very difficult weeks for me. The crushing disappointment at the mysterious collapse of the Washington talks,
combined with unsatisfactory business, were a severe strain on
my faith and courage. I realized it would be financially impossible to continue our tour, which was to take us to the Coast and

back, with productions demanding such large casts and such complicated scenery as *Romeo and Juliet* and *Alice*. With great reluctance and a heavy heart I decided to abandon these two plays and go on to the Coast with the Ibsen repertory alone. It was a great blow to me, as I was particularly proud of these two productions and would have liked the Civic Repertory Company to be seen in them all over the country. It was a sad Saturday night in Detroit when the big company split up, but I could see no other solution, and I could not bring myself to give up the struggle entirely. I still hoped that if I could succeed in keeping a nucleus of the company together and the name of the Civic Repertory Theatre alive throughout this difficult season, I might find a way of continuing the work in New York the following year. I wrote to Mother at the time: "Perhaps, if we can stick together profitably for another year, something may happen during that time that will allow us to preserve the idea and ideals for which we have worked long and hard."

We set out for the West with *Hedda Gabler*, *The Master Builder*, and *A Doll's House*. The difference in running expenses was of course colossal, and those of us who had been playing for bare living expenses in order to keep the larger company going as long as possible were now able to go back on regular salaries again. The relief from the weight of responsibility was very welcome. "One could breathe more freely for a little while," as the Master Builder says. But in spite of that we were a mournful little remnant that worked our way across the country.

The farther west we got, the more stimulating and exciting our audiences became. Business was excellent, and the eager response to these plays, on the part of the young people especially, was heart-warming and immensely encouraging. We began to feel that our work was of some use after all and that all our struggles had not been in vain.

How foolish are actors who refuse to go on tour! They don't know what they're missing. What does it matter where one plays, as long as the work is good and the audience alive and eager? But the work *must* be good. I've heard actors say, "What difference does it make how you play out in the sticks? What do *they* know out there?" I can't understand such an attitude, nor have I any patience with it. I've often found the response of the audiences "out there" far more intelligent, and certainly more exhilarating, than that of the bored and satiated crowd that flocks in half an hour late to a Broadway opening night. Their point of view out there is fresh and keen, alert and unprejudiced. They are quick to sense the phony and the pretentious, and they don't like it. They demand honest work and they deserve to get it; and when they do get it their appreciation is warm and rich and uncluttered; it's a reward that makes an actor feel proud of his job.

Our tour closed in early May, and I returned home to Westport to take stock of things and determine future plans.

I had to have another operation on my right hand. This was the fourth operation and, thank God, the last. I had had the third while playing at the New Amsterdam in the spring of 1933. That too was on my right hand. Dr. Moorhead certainly had a lot of trouble with that one! Since I was only playing the White Queen in *Alice* and Varya in *The Cherry Orchard*, I was able to put an understudy into these parts during the week I had to stay in the hospital. Then I went back to work with my right hand in a cast. In those parts it didn't matter much; after all, the White Queen does "prick her finger," and I always thought Varya the sort of girl who might be accident-prone. But on my return from the tour, in 1934, Dr. Moorhead was still not satisfied with the result of his efforts and decided on one more try. This time he did a graft job on the little finger of my right hand. When he examined it forty-eight hours later the graft was not taking as he had hoped, and he said we might have to start all over again. My heart sank, but I showed nothing and said, "All right," with Scandinavian fortitude. But when he turned at the door and said, "You certainly are a game one!" I burst into tears. Praise and kindness were more than I could stand. The next day, however, showed a marked improvement, and though I had lost the middle joint and never could bend the finger again, I did have a finger of sorts. I soon grew used to it and found it quite serviceable; in fact, I developed a sort of affection for the poor little thing.

When I first started to play again after my accident I was very nervous about my hands. I developed an elaborate make-up for them; by the use of tempera paint I shadowed and high-lighted them so as to give them the necessary modeling, for they were still very thick and clumsy. I made a study of the positions in which they looked best, and concentrated on developing a special technique of using them, with these positions in mind. This was all extremely difficult for me at first, for I have never believed in consciously planning any movement or gesture; but this was a special case and demanded a special solution.

After a while this conscious use of my hands became second nature to me, and I no longer had to think about it. Once I had arrived at this point I decided that the less aware I myself was of my hands, the less aware the audience would be of them; so I forced myself to forget them entirely. I felt that if I lacked the power to rise above this handicap, if I was incapable of holding an audience's attention beyond a morbid curiosity in the state of my little fingers, I had no business in the theatre.

After a year or two an amazing and wonderful thing began to happen: I began to receive letters from the public, praising the beauty of my hands. The people who wrote were unaware that anything had ever happened to them, and were also unaware of the gift they were bringing me. Some of the letters were from artists, sculptors, painters, photographers, asking if they might paint, photograph, or take a cast of my right hand—because it was so beautiful! The first time this happened to me I wept, and I never receive such a letter without feeling deep emotion, wonder, and gratitude.

Before they were burned, no one ever thought my hands were beautiful. They were large strong hands, like those of a worker, and no one had ever wanted to paint or sculpt them. What miracle had happened? I thought of Christ's words: "Except a corn of wheat fall into the ground and die, it abideth alone; but if it die, it bringeth forth much fruit."

I shall not mention my hands again in this book, and I apologize if I have seemed to lay too much stress on their adventures; but I felt it would be impossible for me to write the book at all unless I shared to some extent with my readers this experience that broke my life in two. For it was not only the specific facts of the accident that mattered; the shock to my entire inner life was so great that, if I came out of it at all, I was bound to come out of it a changed creature. Now that it lies well in the past and the inner wounds, as well as the outer ones, have healed, I realize that perhaps this accident, which at the time seemed so tragic and bitter, so hard to understand, was in fact a necessary lesson; without it I might always have remained unaware of selfishness, vanity, ruthlessness, and personal ambition. Now, while I cannot claim to have been purged of these things, being aware of them, I can at least try to temper them a little.

That summer of 1934 was a strange one for me. I had to face the fact that I should be unable to reopen the Civic Repertory in the fall. Those wonderful people who through their generosity and understanding, coupled with their belief in the value of the work, had subsidized our theatre throughout the seven years of its existence, reluctantly had to withdraw their support. The Wall Street catastrophe of 1929 had made even the very rich comparatively poor—at least for a while—and I had no contacts with any "new" money. I tried desperately to interest some strangers, but those I managed to talk to all considered the theatre exclusively as "show business" and felt that unless it paid its own way there was no excuse for its existence. That is of course undoubtedly true of show business, but I have never understood why we should be the only country in the so-called civilized world that fails to recognize the need for another kind of theatre, one that in no way competes with or impinges upon the field of commercial entertainment. The existence in France of the Comédie Française and the Odéon does not interfere with the many playhouses that cater to the myriad tastes of the public on a purely money-making business basis. All the important cities of Germany, Russia—long before the Soviet regime—the Scandinavian countries, Holland, and Czechoslovakia have never limited the theatre to show business. They have also, as a matter of course, people's repertory theatres, permanent institutions that are an integral part of the life of the communities, "libraries of living plays" that enable the public to become familiar with and enjoy the finest dramatic works of all periods and all countries, classic and modern, national and international, played by the best acting talent, and at *popular prices*. In many of these lands such theatres are objects of national pride, and it is an honor for actors to be members of these companies.

We have subsidized opera, symphony orchestras, libraries, and art-galleries. When will we realize that the living theatre is every bit as valuable for the enjoyment, education, and cultural development of the people as these other great forms of art?

Since the year before the Civic opened I had always spent the summer months planning the productions for the following season. While to me these were months of rest and relaxation, since I didn't actually have to play, they were far from idle. As a matter of fact, I have never found rest in idleness, and my work has always been my favorite hobby. I chose the plays, decided on the casting, worked out my schemes of production, set up the entire schedule for the new season.

In this summer of 1934 I had to do none of these things, and I felt strangely lost. The other day I found a letter I wrote to my mother during that time: "All kinds of offers continue to pour in; but I feel like Captain Hook in *Peter Pan*—'in a way it's a sort of a compliment; but I want no such compliments.' I want my Repertory Theatre!"

However, I had to learn—among the many things that I

needed to learn—that for once I couldn't have what I wanted.

Among the many offers of which I wrote to Mother, I finally chose one. A new management, the Messrs. Franklin and Selwyn, were planning several attractions for Broadway that fall. They were to bring over Elizabeth Bergner, Yvonne Printemps, and Lucienne Boyer. They approached me with a plan to present me in "modified repertory." It was decided to open with a production of Rostand's *L'Aiglon*—a play which I had always intended to add to our repertory at the Civic, and which I had always wanted to play.

The existing translations were inadequate, to say the least. That used by Maude Adams many years before seemed particularly hopeless. (As an example of its shortcomings, Rostand's wonderful lines beginning, *"Triste oiseau bi-céphal au cruel œil d'ennui . . ."* began, in English, "Sad double-headed fowl with mournful eye . . ." I always wondered how Miss Adams ever managed that one!) Clemence Dane consented to make a new adaptation of the play for me, for which Richard Addinsell wrote the score.

Later in the summer I made a quick trip to England to talk over the new version with Clemence Dane and discuss casting and production. I was to direct the play myself, and my contract allowed me complete control back of the curtain.

I was pleased with Miss Dane's translation, which was unquestionably head and shoulders above the others I had seen. I disagreed in some respects with her editing of the play. It seemed to me it would have been wiser to eliminate the elaborate ballroom scene, which is not only difficult and expensive to stage, but which has always struck me as somewhat tedious. Instead, she chose to keep that in and sacrifice the episode of the toy soldiers, of which I was very fond, in which Napoleon's son exclaims so tragically, *"Voici les soldats de Napoléon II!"*

We had royal battles and arguments on this point. Miss Dane is not only a powerful artist but a powerful personality, and I was no match for her. She firmly overruled me and had her way—I still think, to the detriment of the production.

On the boat coming home I learned the long and difficult part of the Duc de Reichstadt. For years I had known the play in French, and at first I rebelled against having to speak the words in English. Miss Dane was wise in completely discarding the Alexandrine form of verse. She used a combination of prose and blank verse that was very effective. But the French Alexandrines have a cumulative excitement and glamour; they soar on golden wings, and in spite of Miss Dane's genuinely poetical language, the result in English seemed to me, by comparison, drab and matter-of-fact. French and English are notoriously difficult to translate, one into the other. Shakespeare in French is almost ludicrous, and those who are unfamiliar with the works in the original can never know the glories of Racine, de Musset, Verlaine, or Baudelaire.

Back in New York I was faced with the problems of casting. I had confided to Miss Dane my dream of persuading Miss Ethel Barrymore to play the part of the Empress Marie-Louise, *L'Aiglon*'s mother. She had laughed at me and suggested that I be more realistic. I was certainly not unaware that it might seem presumptuous on my part to ask Miss Barrymore to consider the part. It is far from being a starring role, or one in the least worthy of her; but, to the play, it is vitally important, and I knew that with her incomparable magic she would transmute it into something radiant and glowing. Besides, how many women are there who can realize one's ideal of an empress? And of course, in the theatre, and particularly in Rostand's theatre, only the ideal will serve. The genuine article, even when it still existed, could never have been satisfactory. To me Miss Barrymore *is* an empress, and all the empresses who have ever lived ought to have been just like her!

So, in fear and trembling, with infinite humility and devotion, I approached her and begged her to play the part. I could scarcely believe my good fortune when she finally consented. Her daughter, "little Ethel," and her son Sammy were also in the cast, as well as her cousin Georgie Drew Mendham, who was wonderful in a small character part. Her faithful stage-manager, Eddie McHugh, consented to share the running of the stage with my faithful stage-manager, Thelma Chandler, so all was satisfactorily arranged.

During the final rehearsals Clemence Dane passed through New York on her way to Hollywood. Since I was directing as well as playing the leading part, I felt grateful at the thought of handing over the reins to her for a few days. I had never worked with her before and hadn't realized how different our methods were. Although we all admired and respected her, there were moments when she drove us nearly mad; her boundless energy overwhelmed us. She billowed up and down incessantly, from auditorium to stage, in her flowered chiffon dress, until, as the hours went by, we wilted under her barrage of specific readings and meticulous instructions. We felt like a bunch of awkward, rather naughty children, who were receiving, with inward rebellion, their first lesson in acting. Miss Barrymore was of course exempt from this onslaught, and sat out front fuming.

When Miss Dane's plane left for the Coast we gathered the bits and pieces of our shattered nerves and morale together as best we could, and prepared for the Philadelphia opening.

I was much worried at having to play some of my most important scenes against music. The score was lovely, but I think there was too much of it. There was a fairly large orchestra, and they played in the pit; in the death scene especially I found it hard to project over the music. Had I been able to use a normal healthy voice there would have been no problem, but the boy was dying, and I wanted his voice to be correspondingly weak and feeble.

For the first and only time in our most pleasant association, Dick Addinsell and I had words at the final dress rehearsal. He stalked out in a huff when I, at the end of my nerves and patience, told him in no uncertain terms that the play was not a musical, had usually been played without any music at all, and could be so played again.

No one is quite sane during dress-rehearsal time; only theatre people know the agony of despair one lives through in those hateful last days before an opening night. One glares at one's best friends with passionate hatred or cold fury. To a layman it must seem as though the most agreeable of collaborations, the tenderest of friendships, even the happiest of marriages, must inevitably be wrecked and shattered by the storms that invariably accompany dress rehearsals in the theatre. But after the dreaded first night is over, whether catastrophically or blissfully, all is forgiven and forgotten—if, indeed, it has been even vaguely remembered.

We played at the Forrest Theatre in Philadelphia. This is one among many buildings, designed as playhouses, in which the architects completely forgot that actors require dressing rooms. So the dressing rooms were added hastily in another building across the alley, and in order to reach the stage one has either to go outdoors or to make a five-minute trip through a subterranean corridor that connects the two basements—a most convenient arrangement!

I had naturally given Miss Barrymore the star dressing room, a large room furnished with the usual hideous and uncomfortable furniture reserved for such apartments. This was the only occasion when Miss Barrymore made the slightest protest about anything, and I had a tough time with her. It was only after I had made her laugh by insisting that, since I was her leading man, I should naturally occupy the leading man's room, that she reluctantly gave in.

What a joy it is to play with her! Some actors, particularly youngsters, are scared to death of her—and indeed she can be terrifying. She is justifiably intolerant of bad work and dislikes people without talent; I think she rightly feels that they belong elsewhere. But if she respects you and believes in you as an actor, no matter how young or insignificant you may be, there can be no one more generous, more helpful, or more rewarding to work for. I had discovered this many years back, when, as a girl of eighteen, I was lucky enough to be a member of her company. And in *L'Aiglon* the warmth of her encouragement, the acuteness of her criticism, and the magic of her very presence inspired me and gave me strength.

I shall never forget that death scene in *L'Aiglon*. To see Miss Barrymore's noble, beautiful face, which gets more beautiful with every year that passes over it, bending over me, to feel her tears falling gently on my hair! No wonder people thought I played it well; a stick or a stone could not have failed to play well under such conditions.

There's nothing an actor enjoys more than a good juicy death scene. I have been very fortunate in that respect. I once started to write an article called "Deaths I Have Lived Through." I counted up to twenty-seven of them, of all sorts and varieties. I started on them very early in my career. The first one was quite unpleasant. It was in Maeterlinck's play *Aglavaine and Sélysette*, of which Clare Eames and I gave two special matinees during my run of *Liliom* in 1921. As Sélysette I had to throw myself from the top of a high tower, and I shall never forget the suffocating clouds of dust that rose from the mattress on which I landed. I shot myself in *La Vierge Folle*; died of a broken heart in *Sandro Botticelli*; was burned at the stake as Jeanne d'Arc; died of starvation in Hauptmann's lovely play *Hannele*; committed suicide, again by shooting, many hundreds of times in *Hedda Gabler*, by dagger-thrust as Juliet; was treacherously killed in a duel by Laertes' poisoned foil in *Hamlet*; guillotined as Marie Antoinette; hanged for murder in *Uncle Harry*; died again of a broken heart, and other possible complications, as Catherine in *Henry VIII*. The list goes on. And then, of course, many, many times I have lived through that touching, radiant death of Marguerite Gautier—the immortal Lady of the Camellias. But of them all the death of *L'Aiglon* is my favorite. How could it be otherwise? To die in the arms of Miss Ethel Barrymore—what a privilege!

I would not wish people to think me flippant about these death scenes. They're quite a dangerous business. If one is playing really well—if "God is there," as Madame Sarah would have said—a part of oneself really does die in such a scene. One goes so far out of one's own body that it is sometimes quite difficult to pull oneself back to reality; and there is nothing more painful than to have to receive a lot of visitors backstage after such an experience. People should not be surprised if an actor seems strange and vague after such a scene; he may have come very close to that "undiscovered country from whose bourne no traveller returns," and the readjustment cannot happen in a moment.

We opened at the Broadhurst Theatre in New York. The play was well received and, for a semi-classical revival, had a very respectable run.

After nearly eight years of playing repertory, I found eight performances a week, week after week, in the same play, almost intolerable. The long-run system is infinitely more tiring to me than repertory, and I think that is true of all actors who have been lucky enough to have repertory experience. Repertory of course involves more actual work, more time spent in the theatre, but what actor worth his salt objects to that? Spiritually and emotionally, the strain of a long run in one play, particularly a tragedy, is infinitely greater.

The long run is a part of modern technocracy, like the assembly line. It is stultifying and frustrating. None of the great actors of the past would ever put up with it. I remember Madame Duse saying to me years ago in reference to my long run in *The Swan*, "*Chère petite Le Gallienne, vous allez tuer votre âme!*" I didn't understand what she meant then, but I do now. She advised me to run away and join *les Russes*—meaning the Moscow Art Theatre, which she greatly admired. And then, with characteristic humor, she exclaimed, thinking of my mother's undoubted disapproval, "*Non, non! Je suis folle! Il ne faut pas. Ah! Je suis l'ennemi des mamans!*"

So, instead of running away to the Moscow Art Theatre, I ran away to the Civic Repertory. It was the same impulse toward freedom. People were kind enough to speak of my "sacrifice" in giving up a career of Broadway ease and stardom,

but actually my motives were almost entirely selfish. The kind
of theatre I wanted to play in didn't exist in this country, so
it seemed quite natural to me to try to create one.

The Messrs. Franklin and Selwyn, against their better judgment, tried to live up to the "modified repertory" terms of my
contract by allowing me to put on some extra matinees of *The
Cradle Song* during the run of *L'Aiglon* at the Broadhurst. I
still had all my productions intact at the old theatre on Fourteenth Street, which was rented again to the Theatre Union,
so the technical end of *The Cradle Song* was taken care of.
But modified repertory just doesn't work; you have either to
do it thoroughly or not at all. In a theatre rented on regular
Broadway percentage terms there are endless complications,
and a company selected for a run in a specific play is not easily
adaptable to the repertory system. Besides, adding two special
matinees to the eight performances of the main attraction only
increases the work of all concerned, without really alleviating
the burden of the regular run. We quickly abandoned the attempt by mutual consent, and *L'Aiglon* continued its engagement unmolested.

The firm of Franklin and Selwyn ran into financial difficulties and finally had to dissolve. Mr. Lee Shubert took over the
production of *L'Aiglon* for a spring tour, and I played it in a
number of cities east of and including Chicago till the end of
the season.

CHAPTER NINE

Aᶠᵗᵉʳ a short rest in Westport, I played a week of four-a-day at the Capitol Theatre, in a one-act sketch by Sutro called *The Open Door*. This was an interesting experience, and financially most lucrative.

There were only two characters in the play, and my old friend and colleague Donald Cameron played opposite me. We had a dress rehearsal at nine-thirty in the morning, and our opening performance was at one-thirty that afternoon. We were both exceedingly nervous, as neither of us had ever acted under such conditions. The Capitol Theatre is very large, and the use of an amplifying system is mandatory. There is a floating audience, since the entertainment is continuous, consisting of a feature picture and a selection of vaudeville numbers, of which we were what is sometimes referred to as the "class act." It was a whole new world to me, and I was fascinated by it.

Our playlet was preceded by a Scotch comedian à la Harry Lauder, and followed by that entrancing animal Charlie the Seal. I never tired of watching him and made great friends with both him and his trainer, Mr. Hueling. He—the seal—ended his act by singing "Rocked in the Cradle of the Deep" in a voice that compared quite favorably with those of a number of bassos I have been privileged to hear. He was a real ham, and you could tell by watching his exit just what kind of house there was out front. At the supper show, which was often less well attended than the other three, he would slink off the stage with his head down and every part of his sleek shiny body expressing dissatisfaction with his reception. When the house was full, however, he would literally prance off, head held high, joining in the applause by enthusiastically flapping his fins. He spent his time between appearances in a special cage, which included a water-tank, that was placed in a corner of the wings. He took a good plunge to refresh himself after his labors and then fell quietly asleep on a shelf above the waterline until his next performance. A sensible routine for an actor! Several years later I heard he had been retired and was living down at the old New York aquarium. I went to visit him there. He seemed bored and depressed, and I heard of his death shortly afterward. I expect, like many an old ham, he missed the bright lights and the applause, and life just didn't seem to him worth living without them.

After closing at the Capitol I was asked to play in Washington, D.C., at a large movie-house there—also four-a-day. But this time they requested the balcony scene from *Romeo and Juliet*. We were allowed no dress rehearsal, but fortunately I stopped in at the theatre while they were setting up for the various acts, and discovered to my horror that they had placed an ordinary standing microphone on the balcony, with no attempt to disguise or conceal it—quite an anachronism for fifteenth-century Verona! I persuaded them to remove it from its stand and hide it among the vines with which the balcony was lavishly adorned.

I came across the following in a letter I wrote to Mother during this engagement. "Just a word to say the bicycle race is half over! Only twelve more performances!!! It has been a hard pull and it's been terribly hot. However, it's extraordinary how the scene holds them. . . . It's like wrestling with lions, but we manage to win every time, which is very encouraging."

And, indeed, to have to play the balcony scene four times a day, during one of the hottest weeks I ever remember, with fans revolving noisily overhead (for those were the days before air-conditioning), with the entrance and exit doors opening and shutting incessantly to take care of the shifting crowd, with a sweltering audience fanning itself frantically with programs, handkerchiefs, and hats, with matches being struck constantly all over the house to light the innumerable cigarettes that shone like glowworms in the darkness—besides filling the air with smoke—was quite a challenge. I returned home to Westport completely exhausted, considerably richer, and with my faith in the American public and the magic of Shakespeare suitably enhanced.

During those months I had been working on plans for a tour in repertory in the fall. I decided on two of the Civic plays, *Camille* and the charming Quintero comedy *The Women Have Their Way*. To these I added Ibsen's *Rosmersholm,* which I had always wanted to produce. My idea was to keep the repertory scheme alive, using as many of the old company as possible. The *Camille* and *The Women Have Their Way* productions were intact, and we were able to provide *Rosmersholm* with suitable scenery by adapting some of the many old sets I still had stored at the Fourteenth Street Theatre. Mary Louise Bok was able once more to come to my aid with sufficient backing to launch the tour, which we hoped to continue the whole season, with only a limited engagement in New York City.

I arranged to put up the entire company at a small inn a couple of miles from my home in Weston, and we started rehearsals in late September. It's wonderful how much better one can work in the country than in the hectic atmosphere of New York. It's easier to concentrate, and somehow the simple human values of a play come to life more fully in such informal untheatrical surroundings.

Rosmersholm is fascinating stuff. I had made a new translation from the Norwegian, since this is one of Ibsen's plays that have suffered most from William Archer's Victorianism. We were all of us constantly amazed at the timeliness of the theme: the scenes between Rosmer and Kroll might have been conversations between Roosevelt and Hoover; it was really startling.

The character of Rebecca West is an extraordinary psychological study. How well Ibsen knew the female of the species! It must have been the insight of genius, for, as far as one knows, there were not many women in his life. Yet when one thinks of the remarkable diversity of such characters as Nora in *A Doll's House*, Hilda Wangel in *The Master Builder*, Mrs. Alving in *Ghosts*, Hedda and Mrs. Elvsted in *Hedda Gabler*, Ella Rentheim and Gunhild Borkman in *John Gabriel Borkman*, Gina in *The Wild Duck*, Ellida Wrangel in *The Lady from the Sea*—to mention but a few—his deep knowledge and acute observation of the female heart and mind are little short of miraculous. No wonder so many actresses have been drawn to Ibsen's plays. His gallery of women offers the same satisfying challenge to the actress that Shakespeare's incomparable gallery of men offers to the actor. There is no need for embroidery or invention; these people are living human beings, and the actor has only to open the doors of his mind and allow them to take over; the less he interferes the better. These plays do demand of an actor, however, tremendous concentration, as well as a sensitive, flexible instrument, and he must be capable of really listening and really thinking; merely pretending to listen and to think is not enough. Ibsen's plays are like icebergs; the major substance lies below the surface, and an actor's inner performance is the most important part of it. The line of thought must be kept unbroken—both on and off the stage—from the rise of the curtain to the very end of the play. Actors unused to playing Ibsen find this sustained concentration extremely tiring; yet without it, I am convinced, a successful performance is impossible.

Ibsen requires, it seems to me, a style of acting that might be described as "heightened realism." His plays bridge the gap between the artificial theatricality of Scribe and Brieux and the relaxed naturalism of Chekhov and his numerous followers. Ibsen is always a little larger than life and demands from his interpreters a corresponding stature, but it is a stature perhaps more of the brain than of the heart. Where Chekhov creates a series of moods and relies on the actor to fill them and realize them in tangible form, with all the resources of heart, human understanding, and technical invention at his command, Ibsen presents one with a clear and undeviating pattern, which it is the actor's job thoroughly to understand and absorb and to interpret with the utmost faithfulness.

Of all Ibsen's women Rebecca West in *Rosmersholm* makes perhaps the greatest demands on the player's power of concentration. For the first two acts Rebecca listens, watches, thinks, but rarely speaks. It is not until the middle of the third act that she begins to reveal herself in words, and then the intricate inner pattern is gradually unfolded: her passion for Rosmer; her murder of Rosmer's wife—achieved obliquely and by the use of mental suggestion, of psychological persuasion, but a murder none the less; her horrified realization of her incestuous relations with her own father; the gradual weakening of her will to power, of her almost pathological ego, through constant association with the purity and nobility of Rosmer's spirit, until at last she finds herself no longer capable of using the forces of evil and sees her insane passion, with all its violence and terror, transformed into a pure and selfless love. All these factors suddenly burst through the calm, reserved surface of the woman, and the darkest, most secret corners of her mind and soul are ruthlessly exposed.

But the vociferous turbulence of the last two acts must spring from a constantly sustained line of thought and feeling underlying the brooding stillness of the acts preceding. Without this preparation, Rebecca's sudden outburst seems no more than a display of theatrical fireworks. By far the most difficult part of the job lies in the first and second acts; if the actress has played them well, the rest follows inevitably.

We were much encouraged by the reception of our *Ros-*

mersholm performances outside of New York City. The play
seemed to fascinate and enthrall the public, and the reviews
almost universally spoke of the timeliness of the play and
admired unreservedly the wizardry of Ibsen's craftsmanship,
which enabled him in little more than two hours to state with
economy and clarity, but none the less fully, an intricate
theme, which would have taken some of our contemporary
playwrights seven hours and a dinner intermission to develop.

We were all of us happy to be playing repertory again, to
be able to temper the somber violence of Ibsen with the gay,
ingenuous laughter of the Quintero brothers and the "champagne and tears" of our old friend *Camille*. We opened at
the Shubert Theatre on Broadway with high hopes—but alas,
here the story was very different. Our more erudite New York
critics, while they found kind things to say of my performance
as Rebecca, relegated Ibsen's play to the region of "motheaten
museum pieces" and "dusty relics of a former day." Since we
had played *Camille* and *The Women Have Their Way* so
often at the Civic, and realized that these would not rate renewed critical attention, we had made *Rosmersholm* the main
attraction on our New York schedule, and the uniformly bad
notices were of course disastrous. In the two weeks we played
at the Shubert Theatre we lost every penny of our precious
reserve fund, which would have enabled us to continue our
tour, and I had to accept the fact that this time we were
thoroughly defeated.

I was tired and utterly discouraged. Up to that time I had
kept all the Civic Repertory productions intact, hoping that
by some miracle we might eventually be able to reopen. But
I now felt that this was only wishful thinking on my part, and
I resolved to free myself from all further responsibility, dis-
pose of any disposable assets, disband the company for good,
and continue on my way alone. It was a bitter decision to arrive
at, but once it had been taken and executed I felt as though a
great weight had been lifted from my shoulders. For ten years

I had been "in management"; into ten years I had crammed the work of twenty; and the constant worry and strain it had involved—in spite of all the joy and fun—had told on me quite considerably.

The thing that upset me most was the dreadful waste of it all—to see all those productions, all the costumes, all the myriad accessories of a repertory theatre, practically—and in some cases quite literally—thrown away. I have a certain frugality in my nature; perhaps it is the old Danish blood that rebels at seeing perfectly good scenery burned or dumped: lumber, canvas, even such humble things as hinges, angle-irons, and assorted hardware calmly scrapped. There is something shocking to me in such wanton waste. But of course the expense of storing productions is appalling. I've often thought how sensible it would be if all theatrical producers were to chip in and rent a large storehouse somewhere near New York, where used scenery, costumes, props, and lighting equipment could be preserved and pooled, to be drawn upon when needed. Such a plan, however, would require cooperation—something that seems to be nonexistent in our mad theatre-world. And also it is almost impossible to persuade scenic artists and costume-designers—to say nothing of the members of the craft unions—to make use of existing assets, even when they are in perfect shape and ideally suited to a new production. They have a distinct allergy to that kind of sensible economy; everything must be built from scratch every time. The unnecessary throwing away of vast sums of money under our present producing system is not only foolish but downright wicked. I suppose, like most other evils that exist in our society, this too springs from greed, indifference, and laziness. More money can be made by more people, with less trouble, under the present system. The slogan seems to be "Let's get the most pay for the least work!" And unfortunately this point of view is by no means limited to show business.

During the sad days when the dissolution of the Civic became final I couldn't help thinking with some bitterness of the millions that were being spent on the WPA, and of the modest fraction of those millions that could have prevented the Civic's demise. However, thank God, I am not temperamentally inclined to bitterness, and such thoughts were only fleeting and were soon banished without a trace.

CHAPTER TEN

THE months that followed were quiet, happy months. In giving up the Fourteenth Street building, I naturally also gave up my apartment there, and from that time on my only home has been in Weston, Connecticut—a small township a few miles inland from Westport.

This home has meant so much to me for so many years, and has brought me such comfort, serenity, and peace, that I should like to dwell on it for a few moments and try to express some of the gratitude that fills my heart when I think of how greatly blessed I have been in the enjoyment of it.

I have always loved the country. I love trees, plants, flowers, animals, the earth, the stars, the quiet, the solitude; I am happiest in such surroundings. It has often seemed strange to me that I should have become an actress, for by temperament I am not in the least theatrical. And yet from my earliest childhood this vocation was so clearly marked, and my following of it was so definite, so undeviating, that it seemed inevitable. I have many avocations, a host of other interests that have contributed endlessly to my enjoyment of living, but they have been on the periphery; the sharp focusing point of my life has always been the theatre. Perhaps the very depth and violence of my passion for it caused me, in a kind of self-defense, to withdraw from it at times and seek respite in simpler, more natural, more serene occupations.

In line with my love of the land, I always planned to have a little place in the country that was my very own. During the days of my Broadway successes, culminating with *The Swan*, I managed to put by a small sum of money for this purpose. Several good friends of mine, engaged in big business, tried to persuade me to invest this money in gilt-edged securities, but they might as well have tried to get a French peasant to give up his little hoard of gold.

With this money I bought a tiny little house in Weston in 1926. The house was well over two hundred years old, and about four acres of rocky woodland went along with it. To this haven I fled every week end—rain, shine, or snow—and those few hours of peace helped me immeasurably to sustain my physical and spiritual energy. Shortly after I bought the house, five acres of land adjoining mine came up for sale, and, to insure my solitude, I raised a loan on my little house and added them to my "estate." So, through the years, the place grew.

I built a small house on the new land, and it was here that Sidonie and Marinette lived, as well as other kind people who worked for me from time to time and helped me to look after the place. I myself lived in the tiny old house, which was a couple of hundred yards down the lane, but when I moved out of New York for good I had no room for my books and furniture from Fourteenth Street. These were all things I loved, and I didn't want to part with them. On the other hand, I was afraid of spoiling the old cottage, which in its way is perfect, by adding onto it. So, instead, I decided to add onto the new building and make that my permanent home.

Originally the house was a small box-shaped three-room structure, and it was easy to throw out wings on either side, as well as to add a large room upstairs. Building then, compared with the fantastic prices of today, was unbelievably cheap. And with the help of the "bicycle races," various radio shows, and the surprisingly successful sale of *At 33*, I was able to afford all this. When the alterations were finished I moved all my worldly belongings to the country and settled down.

I think one reason why I love my home so much is that

each room, each fireplace, each bow window, every slightest
addition or improvement, represents a definite piece of work.
One bow window I call the "Molly Pitcher"; another, "The
Girl of the Golden West"—after the radio parts that provided
them. My entire study—the Blue Room, as it is called—was
built out of the Capitol Theatre "bicycle race." It was to this
Blue Room that all my books and my favorite pieces of furniture were moved. Almost every table, sofa, or chair appeared in some play or other at the Civic. Whenever my dear
friend Aline Bernstein, who designed practically all our stage
sets at Fourteenth Street, comes to visit me, she never fails
to greet these familiar acquaintances as she enters the Blue
Room: the sofa from *Camille*; Hedda's armchair from *Hedda
Gabler*; a lovely old Italian Renaissance table from Goldoni's
Mistress of the Inn; the spinet from *Dear Jane*, the play about
Jane Austen; in front of it a fantastic piano stool in the shape of
a shell, that I picked up in Paris, and which we used in Claude
Anet's *Mademoiselle Bourrat*; a huge antique Dutch milk-
pail of copper and brass—always filled with dogwood, apple
blossoms, or lilac in the spring—which appeared in Heijer-
mans' great play *The Good Hope*. A prie-dieu from *The
Cradle Song* exchanges reminiscences with an old Victorian
ottoman that took part in almost every Ibsen and Chekhov play
the Civic Repertory produced. And on the long Provençal table
that I use as a desk—and which "played" in most of the
Quintero comedies—are such personal props as Juliet's dagger,
L'Aiglon's riding-crop, Masha's snuffbox from *The Seagull*,
and the emerald cross that comforted Queen Catherine's last
moments in *Henry VIII*.

The walls of the room are painted a faded Italian blue and
are almost entirely lined with books, from floor to ceiling. In
one panel there is a wonderful poster of Bernhardt as Lorenzaccio by the Czech artist Mucha, who designed all her posters
at the turn of the century. It is a very simple room; there is
nothing magnificent about it, for both my temperament and
my pocketbook preclude magnificence. It is obviously not one

of those perfect rooms designed by a decorator, in which each object is carefully harmonized and blended. There are scarcely two pieces of furniture in it that speak the same language, and yet somehow there is great harmony there; perhaps it is because all these things have been gathered together in such a personal way, each one representing a specific memory, each one a landmark, a symbol of something lived through, of thoughts and feelings pondered over and at last understood.

The large window by my desk looks out over part of the rose-garden, and beyond the rose-bed a mass of lilies blooms in a glory of white and gold. At night their heavy fragrance creeps into the room to rekindle the image of their beauty.

From early spring, when the first snowdrops so delicately and valiantly fight their way up through ice and snow, to the first days of November when Michaelmas daisies, hardy chrysanthemums, and a few late-blooming roses still hold their own against early frosts, and the woods are a flaming riot of color, there is not a day when one is not overwhelmed by the beauty of the world. One stands in silent awe before the exquisite perfection of some tiny blossom, some spray of foliage, the gemlike brilliance of some insect, the free joyous rhythm of a bird in flight. One or another of the myriad miracles of nature, at every moment, fills one with amazement and humility.

So often, as I stand "rapt in the wonder" of such things, the radiant words of Thomas Traherne sing in my head:

Your enjoyment of the world is never right, till every morning you awake in Heaven; see yourself in your Father's palace; and look upon the skies, the earth and the air as Celestial Joys: having such a reverend esteem of all, as if you were among the Angels. The bride of a monarch, in her husband's chamber, hath no such causes of delight as you.

You never enjoy the world aright, till the sea itself floweth in your veins, till you are clothed with the heavens and crowned with the stars: and perceive yourself to be the sole heir of the whole world, and more than so, because men are in it who are every one sole heirs as well as you. Till you can sing and rejoice and delight in God, as misers do in gold, and Kings in sceptres, you never enjoy the world.

Yet further, you never enjoy the world aright, till you so love the beauty of enjoying it, that you are covetous and earnest to persuade others to enjoy it. And so perfectly hate the abominable corruption of men in despising it, that you had rather suffer the flames of Hell than willingly be guilty of their error. There is so much blindness and ingratitude and damned folly in it. The world is a mirror of infinite beauty, yet no man sees it. It is a temple of Majesty, yet no man regards it. It is a region of Light and Peace, did not men disquiet it. It is the Paradise of God.

So those last months of 1935 and the first half of 1936 were healing and fruitful. Relieved of the burden of worry and responsibility that had been a necessary part of my activities for many years, I had time to indulge in occupations that had long been set aside in the press of work. I read avidly; I worked in the garden. I took up weaving and proudly produced linen handtowels, rough, nobbly bathtowels, table-runners, and fine materials to cover chairs and sofa pillows. I made my first attempts at painting. I helped care for the numerous animals that peopled my little domain: a couple of sweet Jersey cows that gave me delicious milk, rich cream, and butter; an old goat, who, in spite of her age, her forbidding horns, and long patriarch's beard, presented me with a couple of entrancing kids for Easter; a robust Western pony, which took me for long rides through the lanes and meadows—for Weston was still wild country then, and many roads were still unpaved. And then, of course, there were cairns and cats, with their various puppies and kittens, not to speak of a motley crew of hens and ducks whose eggs were gratefully consumed but whose happy lives were never haunted by fears of pot or frying-pan.

The theatre seemed so far away I scarcely gave it a thought. Every now and then I went to New York to do a radio show, or went off somewhere to give a lecture—for of course my paradise, being an earthly one, had to be supported—but such work took very little of my time. I wrote to Mother on a note of wonder. "Funny to think that in a few hours' time I can make more than I should probably make in personal profit during a long and arduous tour!" I was referring of course to my work in repertory, and to those last tours under my own management, when the effort to survive was the all-important issue, and the likelihood of personal profit, from a financial point of view, was so remote as to be almost nonexistent. If one behaves sensibly and denies oneself the joys of lunacy, the theatre can be a very profitable place!

That summer my mother came over for a visit. She was delighted with all the improvements, and highly approved of my little home. But to my mother the country was a place to go to for week ends or for a few weeks' holiday during the hot months of the year. She was a city girl by nature and couldn't understand how I could bear to live "out in the wilds" for any length of time. I can see her now, after a day of rural delights, which to her seemed drab and uneventful, pacing solemnly about the Blue Room, ruefully examining the many rows of books through her lorgnette, and finally exclaiming in exasperation, "Good God! There is not a single thing to *read* in this house!" Darling Mother! I think if she hadn't loved me so much she would have found me a very dull companion.

Fortunately things became more amusing for Mother as the summer progressed. Lawrence Langner asked me to appear at his Westport theatre. The play was an amalgamation of the best scenes of Congreve's *Love for Love* and *The Way of the World*. This might sound alarming to a student of Restoration comedy, but Mr. Langner had succeeded in combining the two plays very cleverly, and the result was a gay, amusing entertainment. The cast was a fine one, including Dennis King, Rex O'Malley, Van Heflin, and Fania Marinoff. The director was Richard Whorf.

Mother had always been attracted to the theatre—I think she would have loved to be an actress, and she might have been a very good one too—and never tired of watching rehearsals and superintending costume-fittings. In this she was a great help, as she had an unerring sense of clothes and with a few skillful touches could make a seemingly hopeless dress look chic and elegant. She was pleased with my part in *Love for Love*, as I had really to "dress up" for it, and the powder and patches of the period were very becoming to me. We had great fun with this production. The Playhouse in Westport is a delightful place to work; the stage and equipment are excellent, and the slipshod amateurish atmosphere that pervades so many summer theatres is kept at a minimum. And then, for me, it is particularly pleasant since I can live at home.

My friend Marion Evensen was also in the cast. A fine actress, she had joined my company a couple of years before, playing Aunt Julia in *Hedda Gabler*, Countess Camerata in *L'Aiglon*, and a beautiful Nanine in *Camille*. When I moved to the country I asked her out for a visit. She loved the place and the quiet life so much, we had so much in common and enjoyed such a peaceful companionship, that the visit was prolonged indefinitely and has now lasted for sixteen years. She too has developed avocations that are an excellent complement to mine. She has become one of the finest cooks I ever hope to meet, and it's no thanks to her that I've managed to keep my figure all these years. Her thoughtfulness and care have done much to make my home the happy place it is, and I truly hope that her long "visit" has been as pleasant to her as it has been to me.

It was during the work on *Love for Love* that Mr. Langner and Miss Theresa Helburn suggested that I rejoin the Theatre Guild. Many years had passed since my first association with that organization—that was, of course, in *Liliom*, a play that had meant much both to the Guild and to me personally. They had in mind the part of Mathilde Wesendonk in a new play about Richard Wagner. I was rather disappointed in the script, and the "fair Mathilde" struck me as a decidedly silly woman, but I thought it was about time for me to act again, and since I am so fond personally of Mr. Langner and Miss

Helburn, I felt it would be pleasant to appear under their management.

Rehearsals started in the fall under the direction of Philip Moeller. For the difficult part of Wagner, Wilfred Lawson was imported from England. Lucile Watson played the part of the Comtesse d'Agoult, Evelyn Varden was the unfortunate Mrs. Wagner, and Leo Carroll my stanch but dull husband, Mr. Wesendonk.

While I was never really drawn to the play from the beginning, I had no idea this was to become the one production of my career that I would try to banish from my memory. I have succeeded in this so thoroughly that when people ask me if I ever appeared in *Prelude to Exile* I have to think twice before answering in the affirmative.

Mr. Moeller was a strange director. He had had many great successes and enjoyed a very distinguished reputation. Madame Nazimova had startled me some years before by an account of his methods. She was playing in *The Good Earth* under his direction, and told me that on the first day of rehearsal he had boasted of never having read the book, nor even having looked at the play-script until that moment! According to her, the resulting confusion was ample proof of the truth of his statement. I thought at the time either that he had been joking, or that Nazimova was inventing a tall story; *Prelude to Exile*, however, convinced me that I had done her an injustice.

Mr. Moeller is a kind man, a gentle man, extremely vague, slightly eccentric. I had the impression that he was very self-conscious and, like some other directors I have observed, was more aware of himself than of the play or the actors in it. It was as though he were giving a performance of a "great director" at work.

We rehearsed in a large untidy room on the top floor of the Theatre Guild building. The furniture was a motley collection of derelict old pieces that looked as if they had been salvaged from a particularly unsuccessful junk-shop. Everything was dirty, rickety, and seemed about to fall apart; the

corners of the room were decorated with large heaps of rubbish, and against the back wall stood a row of old costume
trunks in varying stages of disintegration, upon which we
perched precariously when we were not "on the stage." But
for the first week we did nothing but sit around in a semicircle
reading the play. This can be very interesting when the material is provocative and demands discussion and clarification,
but in a "theatre piece" such as *Prelude to Exile*, in which the
values are obvious and fairly shallow, it can be a tedious
process. After a few days we all began to get restless and bored,
and finally Miss Watson gave the signal for rebellion and urged
that we be allowed to start breaking-in the play.

This work was begun the second week of rehearsals, and
we hoped we might be moved onto the stage of the theatre.
This was a vain hope, however, and we actually set foot on a
stage only twice before the dress rehearsal in Princeton.

Mr. Moeller did not impress me as a master of the art of
stage traffic. He had obviously worked nothing out in his own
mind, and the movements and business were left to the improvisation of the moment and were to my mind very far from
satisfactory. Improvisation can be a fine thing—some of the
greatest effects in the theatre have sprung from it—but I think
it is dangerous for a director to depend solely on such happy
accidents.

To set down an arbitrary scheme on paper, from which no
deviation is permitted, is obviously a stultifying method, pre-
cluding any creative contribution on the part of the actors, and
closing the door to sudden flashes of inspiration on the part of
all concerned; but, to guard against confusion and the waste
of much precious time, the director should have a clear pattern
in mind. This may be modified and changed to suit the exigen-
cies of the moment or the temperament of some specific player,
but it should provide a basic over-all line from which the finished performance can evolve. Actors, while they enjoy the
freedom and leeway that a fine director should give them, still

like to feel a sureness of craft and a clarity of conception in the person in charge.

I think it must be difficult, perhaps almost impossible, for a director who has never been an actor himself to understand the precise balance of freedom and authority required in handling players. Ideally a director should never be tentative, vague, or evasive. Actors are nervous creatures—at least good actors are—and they look to the director for confidence and reassurance as well as constant understanding and attention. No two actors can be treated alike. Some need to be flattered, some cajoled; some even need to be bullied. Some like to be told precisely how to read a line or execute a piece of business, while others must be left strictly alone to work out their performance undisturbed. Some must be directed in specifics, others by suggestion. A great director, therefore, must be not only an artist and a craftsman, but, very importantly, a psychologist as well. While he should have complete control and authority over all the elements involved in a performance, his authority should be tempered with humility, for he must serve his actors as well as lead them. If he is immured in his own ego, he will lose contact with his players, and his fruitful communion with them will be broken.

Such were the thoughts that went through my mind as we struggled to breathe life into our unresponsive play.

During the third week we spent one day on the stage. Mr. Lee Simonson, who had designed the scenery, had marked out the measurements on the stage floor, so that we should know precisely where the doors and windows, the stairs and furniture would be. It then became apparent that Mr. Moeller and Mr. Simonson had been working at cross-purposes. Evidently it had not been thought necessary for them to confer on the stage plans, and the sets, built according to Mr. Simonson's designs, in no way resembled those of Mr. Moeller's imagination. Where he had visualized windows, we were now faced with doors, and consequently the furniture had to be entirely rearranged, and practically every movement, so laboriously and gropingly worked out in the preceding week, had to be altered. Quite naturally, actors resent this kind of confusion, and the morale of the company sank to a new low.

Our faith in the play had dwindled rapidly all during the rehearsals. We had been bored, confused, and frustrated in our performance of it, and this final proof of what we considered incompetent leadership filled us with disgust. We were like an army with a bad case of gripes. I felt sorry for Mr. Moeller; my own experience as a director told me he had a rough road ahead.

Our opening in Princeton proved to be our only dress rehearsal, and on the first night in Philadelphia we felt foredoomed to failure. Next day the notices were all bad, and, for once, we actors all agreed we had deserved them.

In the days that followed the play was constantly changed. New scenes were written, old scenes were drastically cut, endings of acts were altered. We rehearsed incessantly. Miss Watson, Mr. Lawson, and I begged the Guild to close the play in Philadelphia, or, failing that, to release us from our parts. I have never seen a company in such a state of revolt and confusion. Mr. Moeller himself accused us of mutiny, and he was right; the trouble was that we had never had a captain.

It was quite extraordinary to see what bad performances actors of the caliber of Wilfred Lawson, Lucile Watson, Evelyn Varden, Leo Carroll, and myself managed to turn out. We were all thoroughly disgusted with ourselves. It was like being in a nightmare.

During the New York engagement—which, alas, lasted five weeks due to the Guild subscription—Miss Watson and I used to take our calls hand in hand, with bowed heads, murmuring under our breath, "In shame we bow before you!" And when the closing night finally came there was universal rejoicing among us actors, something practically unheard of in the theatre, where a closing night is generally an occasion for sobs and tears.

I have dwelt at some length on this production of *Prelude to Exile*, in spite of my wish to forget it, because it is such a vivid example of the unaccountability of the theatre. Here was a play presented by the outstanding theatrical organization of this country, an organization to whom all lovers of the drama are immensely indebted. It was directed by a man who was famous for such great successes as *The Guardsman, They Knew What They Wanted, Ned McCobb's Daughter, The Second Man, Caprice, Strange Interlude,* and *Mourning Becomes Electra.* The scenery was by one of the foremost stage-designers of our time. The five leading players had all of them received high praise for innumerable successful performances. And yet the net result was complete failure, both materially and artistically.

In the last analysis it was probably the play that was basically weak; yet in justice to the author I can't help feeling that he was badly served. The whole venture was "wrong from the beginning to end," as the caterpillar remarks in *Alice in Wonderland.* It was nobody's fault; it was everybody's fault. God just had His back turned.

So I shall once more lock *Prelude to Exile* away in the remotest, darkest recess of my memory—and this time I shall throw away the key.

CHAPTER ELEVEN

During my engagement at the Guild Theatre I had stayed at the New Weston Hotel in New York, going home only for week ends; but as soon as the play closed I returned to my peaceful country life.

I started work almost immediately on a translation of Ibsen's *When We Dead Awaken*. This was the last play that Ibsen wrote, and while many critics consider it the work of an old man at the end of his powers, it has always held a great fascination for me, and I believe that in performance it would hold a similar fascination for an audience. It is impossible to judge the play in the English of Archer's version; many passages in his translation verge on the ludicrous, but these are powerful and arresting in the original.

The play is extremely personal. Ibsen speaks through Rubek, reveals through him all the inner torment, aspiration, and bitter disillusionment that were a part of his genius. It is a terrifying portrait of an artist, stark and uncompromising. It's as though Ibsen looked back over his life and asked himself whether the glory of achievement had been worth the sacrifice of his simple humanity. He seems to feel that the artist must inevitably feed on himself and others, destroying his own and others' joy, freedom, peace, and even goodness in order to create his masterpieces. And in the end he stands spent and empty, wondering in bitter doubt whether the end justified the means.

One senses in this play such ruthless self-revelation on Ibsen's part that one hesitates to attempt its performance; to play it badly would be like betraying a confidence. The physical difficulties of the production would be immense, and an actor really capable of playing Rubek would be hard to find, yet there is something alluring in the very greatness of the challenge. I have never been able to put the play out of mind, though I realize that in our theatre there is small hope of my ever having an opportunity to grapple with it. But the mere fact of struggling, however inadequately, to translate Ibsen's terse, clean sentences into an English that would neither emasculate them nor muddy them was challenge enough for the moment, and I found the work absorbing and stimulating.

I was also deep in the study of *Hamlet*, and, having in mind a production of the play that summer, was kept busy designing and building a model of the settings in which I wanted to present it.

At the age of sixteen, soon after I started work in the theatre, I made a list of the parts I was determined to play before turning forty. It was by no means a modest list, and I kept it strictly to myself. I saw no reason for courting ridicule, but there was never the slightest doubt in my mind that my aim would be achieved. So convinced was I of this that I spent a great part of my time studying these various roles, thinking about them, preparing myself for the day when I should actually be called upon to play them.

The list follows:

> Hilda Wangel in *The Master Builder*
> Hedda in *Hedda Gabler*
> Peter in *Peter Pan*
> Juliet in *Romeo and Juliet*
> Marguerite Gautier in *Camille*
> The Duc de Reichstadt in *L'Aiglon*
> Hamlet in *Hamlet*

At thirty-eight, with only two years to go, I decided to keep faith with myself and tackle Hamlet. All the other parts on the list I had played many times, and Hamlet seemed to me to come under the head of unfinished business.

During the summer of 1936 Mr. Langner had spoken to me about playing it in Westport, but—although I had worked on the part on and off for many years—I didn't feel quite ready for it then, and also the fact of Westport's being so close to New York City deterred me. I knew that for many years there had been no precedent in this country for a woman's playing Hamlet, and realized that the idea might be received with decided skepticism, not unmixed with ridicule. In Europe the situation was different; there had been many women Hamlets in Germany, Scandinavia, Russia, and France. The most famous French woman Hamlet was of course Sarah Bernhardt, but as recently as the early thirties Marguerite Jamois had played the part with great success at Baty's Théâtre Montparnasse in Paris. However, since the idea was foreign to our American point of view, I felt I would rather try it out in a more secluded spot than Westport, where I would be out of range of curiosity-seekers from Broadway and would be able to get a clearer audience-reaction.

Mr. Raymond Moore, at that time manager of the Cape Playhouse at Dennis, Massachusetts, expressed an interest in the production, and plans were made to present the play there in August. As soon as this was definitely settled I set to work in earnest.

Since I had long dreamed of playing Hamlet, I was already very familiar with the lines, but I wanted them to become so part of me that each thought and emotion must find expression in those particular words as simply and inevitably as though they had just sprung from my own consciousness. I wanted to eliminate all sense of having learned them. As a rule I never study the lines of a part beforehand. As the inner structure of my performance grows and takes shape, the words are gradually absorbed and become a part of the whole. And the average words one speaks on the stage are well within one's

own range of expression and vocabulary; the thoughts and
emotions are conveyed in sentences one might easily hit upon
oneself. But Shakespeare speaks with the tongue of angels;
no ordinary mortal could hope to clothe his feelings in such a
cloak of glory. The lines themselves are easy enough to learn,
but it is not enough just to know them; they must become an
integral part of one's way of thinking. One must breathe them,
live them, absorb them into one's very blood, and then one
may perhaps be able to speak them as though they were in
truth one's very own.

If one thinks of Hamlet as a man in his thirties, the idea of
a woman's attempting to play the part is of course ridiculous.
But Hamlet's whole psychology has always seemed to me that
of a youth rather than of a mature man. His melancholy, his
thoughts of suicide, his hero-worship of his father, his mercurial changes of mood, and above all his jealous resentment
at his mother's second marriage, are touching and understandable in a boy of nineteen, whereas in a man of thirty they indicate a weak and vacillating nature in no way admirable or
attractive. In studying Furness's *Variorum*, I was happy to
find ample corroboration of my feelings on this question.

William Minto, for instance, defending his theory of Hamlet's youth against Professor Edward Dowden, who "pro-
nounces that theory incredible which makes Hamlet, the
utterer of the saddest and most thoughtful soliloquies to be
found in Shakespeare, a boy of seventeen," writes:

I venture to say that sad and thoughtful questionings of the mysteries of life are more common among boys under twenty than
among men of thirty. . . . Not only is it possible for sad thoughts
to come to a youth of seventeen, but it is at such an age, when the
character is not deeply founded, that the shattering of first ideals is
most overwhelming. The terrible circumstances that overthrew
Hamlet's noble mind gave a stimulus to the development of his
thoughtfulness apart from an increase in years. The fresher and
brighter our conception of the gay boy-world out of which he was

summoned, the deeper becomes the monstrous tint of the horrible ambition, murder and incest, which appalled his vision and paralyzed the clear working of his mind when he was first called upon to play a man's part in the battle of life. Too much has been said of the philosophic temperament of Hamlet; impulse and passion were more in his nature than philosophy; his philosophy was not a serene growth, a natural development of a mind predisposed to thought; it was wrung out of him by circumstances terrible enough to make the most obtuse mind pause and reflect.

And again:

Hamlet's action is not the weak and petulant action of an emasculated man of thirty, but the daring, wilful, defiant action of a high-spirited sensitive youth, rudely summoned from the gay pursuits of youth, and confronted suddenly with monstrous treachery.

It would be rare indeed to find a young actor in his teens, or even in his early twenties, capable of sustaining and projecting this many-faceted, arduous role. No matter how clearly he might understand it and feel himself akin to it, it is doubtful if his instrument would be powerful and resilient enough to translate his theories into practice. It is undoubtedly mainly for this reason that Hamlet is almost always presented as a mature man; and it is also for this reason that actresses have frequently undertaken to play the part. But it must be remembered that such performances can be acceptable only if the theory of Hamlet's youth is kept in mind. It is possible for an actress at the height of her powers to give the impression of being a boy, while having at her command all the craft, range, force, and subtlety which such great roles require. This has always been true of Rostand's *L'Aiglon*, which, with a few insignificant exceptions, has always been played by women; also De Musset's Lorenzaccio, and—in a very different mood—Barrie's Peter Pan.

I came across a clipping I had sent to Mother during my run of *L'Aiglon* in Chicago, and which may be of some interest here. It was from a review by Ashton Stevens, in which he said:

Well, no critic need resign today on account of conscientiously objecting to Miss Le Gallienne's appearance as the frustrate Napoleon II. She is as believable a lad as ever wore a uniform. She is, as I think I said earlier, as boyish as any actress has a right to be.

Indeed—and this is what I am driving at—she here gives me pleasant visions of an actress's Hamlet, where formerly I saw only nightmares in that dire disguise. Yes, I realize that this is the second Prince of Denmark I have recruited (in my imagination) this season. And even if Dennis King presently responds to the first challenge, I reasonably hope that Miss Le Gallienne will not ignore the second.

It is only living performances on the stage that can prove to the younger playgoers and playactors this finest (and perhaps most modern) of all plays in our language is something more than mere reading matter. And why not a Le Gallienne Hamlet?

Not merely because other women have played this prince, but because here is a young actress who, in this very *L'Aiglon*, proves her princeliness as well as her ability to cancel her sex without either revolting or convulsing us. I'll wager a Hamlet by Eva Le Gallienne would be as virile as a Hamlet by Leslie Howard. Moreover, I think this poet's daughter has the poet's mind for the part, the cerebral graces as well as the physical. And it is a certitude that she has the sense of beauty, without which an impersonation of Hamlet is an obscenity. Besides, Miss Le Gallienne has the imagination exercised by experience for staging the piece as a play as well as a part. I feel that she would make the right fleet scenery serve rather than strangle the noble and witty words; that she would, in a word, give Shakespeare's prince as lovely a break as she gave Carroll's Alice. And if this is Hamlet-baiting, I hope Eva Le Gallienne makes the most of it.

I've often wished Mr. Stevens might have seen my performance of Hamlet. I'd have been interested to know whether he thought his faith had been justified.

Every morning I set off on long rambles through the woods and fields of Weston, with my copy of *Hamlet* in my pocket.

Often Marion Evensen accompanied me on these journeys and patiently cued me hour after hour. The evenings were spent perfecting the stage model. A young scenic-artist, Michael Weightman-Smith, was staying down at my old cottage, and together we worked out every detail of the production. I wanted the play to move swiftly, with no scene-waits and only one intermission. I had evolved a practical scheme that would permit this, and Michael Smith contributed the necessary decoration. The play was to be played in the Viking period; I took this idea from the King's lines in Act IV, Scene 3:

> And, England, if my love thou hold'st at aught—
> As my great power thereof may give thee sense,
> Since yet thy cicatrice looks raw and red
> After the Danish sword, and thy free awe
> Pays homage to us—

To enhance the crudeness and violence of the North of that period, we limited our colors to every conceivable shade of red, set off by black and varying shades of gray. To achieve the desirable roughness and sturdiness of texture, we decided to weave all the materials for the principal costumes ourselves, and both looms were put to work. A professional weaver in the neighborhood was put in charge of the largest loom, and Michael Smith, Marion Evensen, and I took turns at the smaller one, producing countless yards of various kinds of fabric. Some we wove in color, some Michael Smith dyed to the exact shade required. Even had we been able to buy such stuffs ready-made, the cost would have been far beyond the range of our slim budget; and besides, there was something wonderfully satisfying in producing for ourselves these rugged materials that conformed so completely to the ideas we had in mind. When, after weeks of work, we shipped the fruits of our labors to Hélène Pons, who was to execute the costumes, we glowed with pride at her appreciation of them, of the way they responded to her drapes and pleats and folds. Later, when many actors had to wear them on hot summer evenings, the epithets be-

stowed upon them were less flattering; their weight and substance were almost too authentic for modern comfort.

It was not easy to cast a play like *Hamlet*, even adequately,
for a week's engagement in a summer theatre. Some of my old
faithfuls from the Civic rallied round me, and I was lucky in
finding a few talented young people who were eager for the
chance. The problem of an Ophelia was difficult. I have rarely
seen the part well played, even under the best of circumstances; I have seen it played only once to my complete satisfaction. Several young actresses read for me, but none of them
had the quality I sought for, and the few that approached it
were either unavailable or too expensive.

I then remembered a young girl I had seen some months
before; she had written to me early in the year, requesting an
audition. Her father was a professor at the University of Wisconsin; her mother was a singer and a fine musician; and both
were willing that she should take up a stage career, but wanted
the advice of an expert before finally committing themselves to
full cooperation. They promised the child to send her to New
York for a few days if she could persuade me to see her and
give my opinion of her talent.

My first impulse was to refuse. I had given so many hundreds
of auditions in connection with the free school at the Civic,
and there is always a formidable number of young people who
imagine themselves destined for greatness in the theatre, demanding help and encouragement. I was loath at that time to
break my serenity, but there was something about this letter
that intrigued me. The handwriting alone was full of character
and individuality—an increasingly rare thing nowadays, when
most young people seem incapable of writing at all. The phras-
ing of the letter too was striking; it was forthright, honest, and
simple, and the choice of words was intelligent and original;
one felt a personality there. So, in spite of my reluctance, I
found myself answering in the affirmative.

One day in March the girl took the train to Westport and
presented herself at my house. She was very young—only just

seventeen—a tall, rather gawky creature, by no means pretty, but with a face that one remembered, large hands and feet, and the shy ungainly grace of a young colt. She was obviously very nervous but made a gallant attempt to conceal it. She had been born in Germany and spent her early childhood there, so her first selection was a scene from a play of Schiller's, which she spoke in German. I told her I was not sufficiently familiar with the language to judge her fairly in that medium. She then switched to English, which she spoke without an accent, and played the end of the trial scene from Shaw's *St. Joan.*

I was puzzled by her. She spoke Joan's speech quite badly; the effect was artificial and stilted, it was forced and unnatural, and yet I sensed in her an inner truth that very occasionally filtered through in a word or a look. I was disappointed in her reading, but for some reason I felt she was worth giving a little time to. I was ruthlessly honest with her, told her that I didn't believe a word of Joan's speech, talked to her about it, gave her a few pointers, and asked her to think it over for an hour. I left her to herself in the Blue Room and went about my business. At the end of an hour I returned, and she played the scene for me again.

The improvement was startling. Though the execution was clumsy and monotonous, it was no longer a piece of stilted elo-cution. The truth that had glimmered so faintly in the first reading now blazed up strongly, and the over-all effect was strangely moving. I felt that here was a real talent, crude and groping, but obviously sensitive to direction: the immediate change that my criticism had brought about was proof of that. The girl listened gravely to what I had to say, thanked me politely, and went off to catch her train. I watched her as she walked down the path to the taxi that was to take her to the station. There was something touching in that youthful, gallant little figure, so full of purpose.

In 1951 I went to a Theatre Guild opening in New Haven. It was the first night of Margaret Webster's production of *St. Joan* by Bernard Shaw. I had the joy of watching that same girl play that same scene. Her fourteen years of tireless work, her constant development as an artist and as a human being, were revealed in a performance of power and beauty, honesty and radiance, that held the audience spellbound and had them cheering at the end. The name of the girl is of course Uta Hagen, a name which I feel certain will rank among the truly great names of our theatre.

So, back in 1937, it was of little Uta Hagen that I thought when the problem of casting Ophelia threatened to become insuperable. I wrote to her parents and suggested that they allow her to come East and try out for the part. I made no promises, but said I would coach her for a week and then make my decision. She arrived full of eagerness, hope, and determination. What she lacked in experience she made up for in a natural instinct for the theatre, in freshness and sincerity, and above all in a complete singleness of purpose. I made up my mind to take a chance on her and let her play the part.

Several of the principals came out to Westport prior to the official rehearsals, and we did much preliminary work there. My little cottage was completely "sold out"; it was practically a case of "standing room only." A few people, including Uta, stayed at Cobb's Mill, about a mile down the road. It was a busy, happy time. The looms were still hard at work turning out materials, and our professional weaver had quite a time eluding the many offers of unskilled labor thrust upon her; each actor wanted to weave a bit of his own costume. Uta turned out to be quite good at it and actually succeeded in weaving most of the stuff for her own dress.

At last the day came to move to Dennis and start work there. Michael Smith and I had gone up for a couple of days some time before, taking our precious model and blueprints with us. Since the settings involved many different levels, it had been arranged that they should be built two weeks ahead of the opening and set up in a deserted schoolhouse near the theatre, so that we might rehearse in them from the start. This was a great help, as it is almost impossible to explain steps and levels on a flat stage, and it enabled the actors to get accustomed to the use of them.

We had only two weeks of rehearsal, and we worked day and night. We were all of us too eager and excited to pay much attention to such things as Equity rulings; an official of that august body would have found it hard to prevent us from working beyond the eight hours allotted by the law. I'm afraid I've always been something of a rebel as far as that's concerned. I dislike being told how long I may work; if there's a job to be done, and well done, one can't be bothered to count the hours.

Giorgio Santelli had joined us in Dennis, and James Harker, who played Laertes, and I worked for an hour each morning on our duel, under Giorgio's supervision, and another hour each evening. Giorgio had planned a most exciting fight, but it was a tricky one, and he kept us hard at it. It was terribly hot weather, and any superfluous fat we may either of us have possessed rolled off with the sweat, until we were both of us reduced to shadows.

The night of the dress rehearsal came, and it was on this occasion that I, for the first and last time, really "saw Ophelia plain." The sacred fire struck, and the child Uta was transported to a region which I well knew she would not set foot in again for many years to come. The company was electrified by her performance; they crowded round her after the rehearsal and overwhelmed her with excited praise. She seemed dazed, as though just awakened from a trance, and then, quite suddenly, she fainted.

I shared the actors' feelings about her performance, but I understood so well what had taken place that I felt I must prepare her for the certain disillusionment of the nights to come. As Bernhardt would have said, "*Dieu était là*"—God was there. But even with such a great actress as Bernhardt in her prime, such occasions were rare, and, "God" failing, she had infinite resources to fall back on that could make "God's" absence at least endurable. I knew how lonely, helpless, and lost Uta would feel, left to struggle on her own.

She listened patiently and with respect while I told her not
to be surprised and disappointed if her subsequent performances failed to equal, or even approach, her inspired playing
at the dress rehearsal. However, I don't think she believed me.
I knew how she felt; I had often been through the same thing.
I remembered particularly my playing of Juliet's farewell scene
in a preliminary rehearsal at Tree's Academy, at the age of
fifteen. I too had been lifted up by some mysterious power that
swept through me and transformed me and left me dazzled
and bewildered and wildly happy; but it was many years before this magic power took hold of me again. When it happens it is an overwhelming experience; I've often thought it
may be similar to what mystics describe as a "state of grace."
Novices are sometimes favored with this sort of revelation, but
it is only after years of discipline and prayer that it occurs with
any frequency, and only the most spiritually evolved can hope
to summon it at will.

The next night, after the opening, little Uta sat sobbing in
her dressing room. She had given a good performance, indeed
an amazing one for such an inexperienced child. Her father
and mother, and her brother too, were all there from Wisconsin
to see her make her debut; their faces glowed with happiness
and pride. But God had not been there, and, in spite of all
their loving praise, Uta felt alone, abandoned, and discouraged.
The next day she kept saying to me, "What happened? Why
couldn't I do what I did the night before? It seemed so easy
then!" All week she played conscientiously and well; she tried
hard and gave the very best she was capable of giving, but the
heavens were closed, and God remained silent.

That was a thrilling week at Dennis; I shall never forget it.
The theatre was crowded every night. I was aware that many
people came out of curiosity, expecting to see a freak performance, a ridiculous sort of stunt; quite a number, I suspect, came
prepared to scoff. But when the curtain fell at the end of the
play, the silence for several moments was electric, and then
the storm of applause broke loose and the shouts and "bravos"

brought tears to my eyes. I have seldom been so happy, though I found the eight consecutive performances almost unbearably exhausting.

I was proud of the production; it had fire and pace and great excitement. Although the acting was uneven, there were some excellent performances. George Graham was a particularly good Polonius, and later played the part in Margaret Webster's production with Maurice Evans. Howard Wierum was a sympathetic Horatio, Donald Cameron an impressive Ghost, Marion Evensen a fine Gertrude, and I liked Victor Thorley as Fortinbras. Thomas Gomez promised at rehearsal to be a wonderful Claudius, but somehow his actual performance proved disappointing.

In spite of the distance from New York, several theatre managers came up to look us over. Two of them offered to take over the production. Mr. Lee Shubert wanted me to play a limited engagement on Broadway, to be followed by a long tour throughout the country. I shall always be ashamed that I had not the courage to accept this offer. Cowardice has never been among my major failings, but on this occasion I was a coward. I was not afraid of playing the part, could I have been left in peace to play it, and I had no fear of the public's reaction. But the thought of all the fuss and commotion and publicity, the quips of the columnists, the storm of controversy that a "female Hamlet" would in all likelihood provoke, filled me with dismay. I didn't feel strong enough to face it. For the first time in my life I felt vulnerable; perhaps I was growing up. Perhaps the ordeal by fire, while strengthening me in one way, had weakened me in another. Perhaps if both John Gielgud and Leslie Howard had not played Hamlet the preceding season, I might have felt different about it—at this moment it seemed particularly daring for a woman to step in and provoke inevitable comparisons. Perhaps, above all, the prospect of having to play the part eight times a week for several months appalled me, and this was probably the decisive factor in my refusal. If I could have played Hamlet in repertory, I think I might have been persuaded—perhaps, perhaps! At all events, I decided against it, and it is one of the very few decisions in my life that I have occasionally regretted. To play Hamlet for a week and then never again is like having a glimpse of a wonderful country without ever being allowed really to explore it. However, brief as it was, the glimpse was wonderful, and I am eternally grateful for it.

I was back in Westport once again, and there followed a few active and interesting months during which I endeavored to work out an experiment, which Mrs. Bok and I had discussed during the preceding year. She had never ceased to believe in the value and importance of the type of theatre represented for seven years by the Civic Repertory, and to regret its closing. But to start such an organization again from scratch, to secure a building in New York, a first-class company, a staff, and all the basic technical equipment necessary to reopen such a theatre, would have cost a very large sum of money—far more than any amount Mrs. Bok personally was able to allocate to such a purpose. We felt, however, that it might be possible to start in quite a different way.

Our idea was to gather together a small group of actors who would spend the fall and winter in Westport and work on a repertory of plays, which might then be presented at the Westport Playhouse for a spring season in advance of the regular summer season there. We hoped that the intimate sort of work such a scheme would make possible might create the kind of spirit without which a repertory theatre of the sort we dreamed of cannot well function. If we could succeed in welding together such a company, prepared to offer a certain number of plays, it seemed to us that ways might gradually open up which would permit that company to work as a unit, and perhaps, from a small beginning, important results might be achieved.

Mrs. Bok personally assumed the expense of taking over the Cobb's Mill Inn during the fall and winter months, so that the company would be comfortably housed and fed.

She also volunteered to guarantee all of us minimum Equity salaries, above and beyond our living-expenses, during the months of preparatory work. It was a most generous and wonderful gesture, and the idea was full of intriguing possibilities.

With some difficulty I had collected approximately ten people who wholeheartedly welcomed such an experiment. Several of these actors had taken part in the performances of *Hamlet* in Dennis, and when Uta Hagen heard of the plan she too asked to be included in the group.

My great problem was to find a leading actor. It was comparatively easy to discover young potential talent, but to induce an experienced actor of the right age—equipped to tackle such parts as Rubek in *When We Dead Awaken*, Trigorin in *The Seagull*, Jaques in *As You Like It*, Svedenjelm in a Scandinavian comedy I wanted to work on called *The Nobel Prize*, and other great parts of that caliber—to give up Broadway or radio or Hollywood, and bury himself in the country to work on a plan that might or might not lead to tangible results, was a very different proposition. This was understandable: if an actor is really talented, at the age of forty or thereabouts he is in great demand. He usually has responsibilities, and at that age his earning capacity is at its highest and he must make the most of it. He is naturally afraid of leaving the limelight, of missing opportunities, of removing himself from the marketplace. No matter how idealistic he might like to be—or thinks he might like to be—the existing system of our theatre makes such risks too dangerous.

I spoke to many actors who might have filled this gap in our ranks, but, while some of them appreciated the idea in theory, none of them felt they could afford to join us. I should have been realistic and sensible enough to realize that unless this gap could be filled there was no use in even starting on the work, but I was misled by my own enthusiasm and faith. I foolishly expected a miracle to occur to solve our problem. Such, however, was not to be the case. Looking back, I can't help being amazed at my rather touching naïveté.

A couple of exceedingly nice men came out and successively tried to grapple with these great parts that were far beyond them. If only they had been as fine actors as they were fine people, all might have been well. As the weeks went by I became increasingly discouraged. I had to face the fact that I was using a considerable amount of someone else's money on a venture that I now saw clearly could never hope to achieve the kind of standard which alone would have justified the time and expense involved.

At the end of two months I felt morally obligated to go to Mrs. Bok and confess that I had been mistaken, and that the plan would not work out as we had hoped it might—or at least that I was not the person to enable it to do so. As always, she listened to me with the deepest sympathy and understanding; she seemed grateful to me for my honesty, for my refusal to take further advantage of her generosity, when the ultimate results now seemed to me of dubious value. She had visited us in Westport and had listened to some of our rehearsals, and while she felt that some of the young people showed great promise, she agreed that without that one key actor all our work must be in vain.

It was a hard and ungrateful task to break the news to my fellow workers. Many bitter things were said to me that evening. I can understand them now. It's always a hard thing to have one's hopes buoyed up, only to see them shattered—particularly when one doesn't clearly grasp the reason—and the disappointment all the members of the company suffered prevented them from impersonally analyzing the situation. It was natural that they should blame me and resent what they considered a betrayal.

In my own particular logic, it was to prevent a betrayal that I acted as I did—to prevent the betrayal of a trust, the betrayal of a standard.

The child Uta was the only one of them all to appreciate my true motives in this decision and to share with me the feeling that it was necessary and right. Several months later, while I was in Paris, someone sent me a clipping from a New York paper announcing that Uta Hagen was to play the part of Nina in the Lunts' production of Chekhov's *The Seagull*. I was of course delighted, and was once again struck forcibly by the strangely logical pattern life so often follows. *The Seagull* had been one of the plays we had worked on most during those months in Westport. I myself was rehearsing the part of Nina, and Uta was studying it along with me. She was present at all our discussions of the play and knew it by heart. When the Lunts started trying out young actresses for this role—and they tried out a great number—Uta succeeded in persuading them to give her an audition and, instead of the usual reading, was actually able to present them with a real performance. Her knowledge of the play and the part, combined with her natural talent, impressed them so favorably that they decided to let her play it, and it was the first important step in her career.

I cannot bring myself to believe that such things happen by mere chance. There is a curiously definite line of destiny traceable in the lives of nearly all prominent people in any field. I hold the unpopular view that a really great talent cannot be stopped. I do not believe that the woods are full of undiscovered geniuses. Many people, I know, will disagree with me in this, but my own observation through the years, as well as my intensive reading of biographies and memoirs of well-known people in the past, strongly corroborates my firm conviction on this subject.

Actual achievement does not depend on talent alone—though that of course must be the basic ingredient. It is almost as though a combination of natural and occult forces are drawn into play. Solness in Ibsen's *The Master Builder* says, "Do you believe, Hilda, that there exist certain chosen people who are endowed with the power and faculty of believing a thing, wishing a thing, willing a thing, so persistently and so inexorably that at last they make it happen? Do you believe that, Hilda?"

It seems to me that that basic talent must be combined with this ruthless singleness of purpose to become effective. Then, too, there must be a willingness, as well as a capacity, for working longer and harder than anyone else, without question and without complaint, with no specific reward in mind, but simply because one is driven by an inner compulsion that provides no choice; a self-discipline, where the work is concerned, that admits of no short-cuts, no labor-saving devices; an ego so devoid of vanity that over-indulgent praise cannot satisfy, nor deter one from that constant striving for perfection that, of course, one never reaches. Leonardo, in his *Notebooks*, says, "The supreme misfortune is when theory outstrips performance." And success, to an artist, has little to do with money or fame (though these are pleasant things); it has to do fundamentally with the narrowing of that gap between theory and performance, between his vision and what he is able to convey of it.

In these days, when, more and more, "success" means money and "fame" means notoriety, such views must seem old-fashioned, if not downright foolish. They certainly cannot be expected to appeal to "artists' representatives" or press agents; nor will they appeal to the many young people whose ambition is focused on glamorous careers based upon grossly inflated earnings with the minimum amount of effort, and fulsome adulation earned by some happy trick of looks or personality. But those young artists—and thank God they still exist and always will—whose ambition is a vision that compels them to constant effort, a spur that drives them inevitably to "attempt the impossible"—to quote Ibsen again—those free spirits who can never be bribed or bought, who will never consent to exchange their birthright for a mess of pottage, whose joy comes from the work itself and not solely from the profits it involves, whose faith in their own destiny and pride in their own capacity to serve it are so strong that they can afford to be humble—they will understand these views and, I venture to think, will agree with them.

CHAPTER TWELVE

I DID not feel like staying in the country and spending the winter there. I felt restless, disillusioned, and tired, and decided to spend a couple of weeks in New York, seeing some plays and renewing old acquaintances. I had no desire for work; I felt a great need to shake off all sense of responsibility to other people, to be quite free for a while, free to look around and take new bearings. I decided that after my visit to New York I would go abroad. I felt "stale, flat, and unprofitable," and I thought it would be good for me to get a "change of ideas," as the French say, see some new things and make some new contacts.

The other day I came across a diary that I started to keep at that time, and it brought back some of my impressions so vividly that I'd like to use some excerpts from it here.

Oct. 28th. It is nice here at the old Algonquin, and surprisingly quiet for New York; though a political loudspeaker of some sort—"Save this great city by the help of the great Democratic party!"—is blazing away over by the Hippodrome. I notice the Centre Theatre is dark again. What an example of building grand and expensive "Temples of Art" and then finding that one has nothing to put in them!

Oct. 29th. Went to see *Yes, My Darling Daughter.* . . . The second act was an immense improvement on the first. In fact it had one or two extremely amusing and quite original scenes. What it would have been like without the brilliant performance of Lucile Watson, heaven knows. What a deft comédienne! What a sense of timing! She plays with her brain—but there is heart in her work too—and knowledge and understanding of life and people; a sort of shrewd kindliness. A very curious, intensely personal quality, that might not appeal to everyone—particularly if they had no means of appreciating how exquisitely she places her lines, her every movement, her slightest expression. Yes! For her second act alone the play was worth seeing. . . . Went back to see Lucile afterwards. . . . She spoke of Mrs. Pat [Campbell], who is living in a little room at the Hotel Sevilla. Poor old woman! She's made a point all her life of being spectacularly nasty to everyone, and now she is quite alone. Yet I don't believe she's really cruel *at heart*—she made a sort of impudent game of it. She's always been so nice to me; but then I disarmed her the first time we met by saying, "Everyone believes you to be a devil and they're all afraid of you. I'm not afraid of you a bit and I think you're a darling!" She's liked me ever since. Lucile is very fond of her, and has done a lot for her. She worries about her and tries to think up things to help.

Oct. 30th. This morning I went out to try and find a hat. The quest seems as hopeless as ever! I should find it such agony to wear the hats that are now in fashion. I remember as a child Mother putting me into the "latest thing" in children's bonnets; it was a gorgeous affair of pale blue satin with pink rosebuds. I was so acutely miserable in it that the moments I was obliged to wear it stand out as some of the blackest in my life. Now, thank God, I am not "obliged" to wear either a witch's hat by Valentina or a monkey's pillbox by Schiaparelli —and I just *won't!* But where can one find anything one *can* wear that doesn't look like a Girl Scout Mistress?"

This problem seems to have remained insoluble, which is probably the reason why—except in the dead of winter—I am nearly always hatless.

That same day I had lunch with my dear friend Constance Collier. She was pleased to hear, as were most of my friends, that I had abandoned all thought of attempting to start another repertory theatre and intended to concentrate on working for myself for a while. My diary tells me:

She was delighted and remarked enthusiastically that for the first time in all the years she had known me I was talking common sense. She then added, with a touch of malice, that of course there was no knowing how long this welcome change in me would last, but for the moment, at least, I showed some sense!

The diary continues:

She said some very interesting things about herself in relation to her philosophy of life: "I never allow myself to dwell on the past, and look very little into the future. I enjoy the present, and, whatever my work may be at the moment, I do it to the fullest extent of my powers and with great enjoyment. Should anyone comment on the anachronism of my supporting Shirley Temple in *Wee Willie Winkie* and start talking of my great parts at His Majesty's with Beerbohm Tree, I merely remark that I was myself at that time, and at this time I am still myself—but in another period. Life is never static; there is good in all phases of oneself. The world changes; points of view change; values change; and we must not go on clinging to the old and the past. We must go through the present to whatever the future brings us; and in the present state of the world, anyone who thinks that his own little personal life is all-important is a fool!"

A sane, wise way of looking at things. Her complete lack of sentimentality with regard to herself, her genuine interest in other people and their problems—these are the things that have kept Constance so young and so vitally important to her innumerable friends. I'm sure all those who love her as I do will agree with this.

Oct. 31st. Went to the Radio City Music Hall to see *Victoria the Great*. I went in at the very beginning of the program, for I wanted to see the whole show—and it certainly *is* a show! I don't see how they do it—a new one every week. It fills one with such infinite respect for every one of those *really* hard workers. . . . The show began with the lights imperceptibly fading over the huge auditorium, until they were gradually concentrated on the orchestra which rose out of its sunken pit to stage level. They played "Selections from *La Bohème*" to the great satisfaction of the packed house—and it was very good as far as I could judge. After this the huge curtains opened on a very grand hall—a sort of beer-hall—in which were revealed innumerable groupings of gentlemen in very bright blue and gold Hussar uniforms, each with a beer-mug in his right hand. One gentleman, noticeably stouter than the others, had a strong spotlight on him and was obviously the featured tenor. They sang a rollicking song about love and beer, with much harmonizing and rearranging of positions. The orchestra pit, with the musicians playing at full tilt, then proceeded to rear itself up onto the stage, and, with the imperturbable members of Local 802 still performing merrily, traveled toward the back of the stage, where it was suddenly elevated to what seemed like a dizzy height, the lights following it, leaving the fore-stage in shadow. Gauzes fell, drops were let in, chandeliers descended from the skies, and in an instant the stage was transformed into an immense ballroom, with the orchestra (which had never ceased to play) seen through arches in the background. Then came ballerinas dressed in classical tutus—only they were bright candy-pink topped with "candy-blue" bodices. They entered by fours from either side of the wings alternately, each quartet performing classical pas-de-ballets until the stage was quite crowded. When all were in position, eight dancers in Hussar uniforms sprang on and executed a number of divertissements with various ladies in turn. The lights changed incessantly, and the dancers' costumes took on different colors accordingly. Finally two strangely dressed creatures of female sex leaped on from either side of the stage and performed the most complicated steps hitherto seen, to great applause. There was the usual "grand finale," and in a second drops had risen, chandeliers disappeared, and we found ourselves in a courtyard outside a military-looking building of red brick; in a covered porch high up in this building the heroic orchestra still continued to play. Our singing Hussars, minus beer-mugs, marched in from either side, and then—to deafening applause—came the famous Rockettes, also in Hussar uniform with feminine variations. There is something really thrilling about these girls. I don't know why, but I found something poignant and curiously touching about their gallant precision. And when one thinks that each week they learn a new and complicated routine, while performing the current one four times a day, one can't help looking upon them with admiration mingled with awe. I had tears in my eyes and a lump in my throat; it was the same sort of irrational emotion one feels at the sight of a crack regiment sweeping by with flags flying and fifes playing. No matter what other "featured attraction" may be included in this show, the Rockettes remain its star, and always bring it to a climactic conclusion.

Nov. 2nd. Constance asked me to lunch today with Robert Edmond Jones and his wife, but the lunch turned out of course to be a larger one than that; George Cukor and George O'Neil were among the other people present. What a dear Bobbie Jones is—I have always loved him; I had never met his wife, the famous voice teacher Mrs. Carrington, who taught Jack Barrymore to speak the "Queen's English"! She seemed charming, immensely intelligent—a grand woman and full of humor. We sat at the famous "round table," and it was really a most amusing lunch. I liked Cukor so much—he's so

alive and has such a quick clever brain. It was fun to hear
them talking about Hollywood and all its inside machinations
—like another world to me, a world in which I feel I would
find it hard to fit, but it is fascinating to hear about it now
and then, as an outsider. We started talking about Ina Claire,
for whom we all have a very great admiration, and of the
feeling we have long shared that she should play something
really great, like Hedda or Rosalind, or Lubov in *The Cherry
Orchard*. Constance told them how for years I have been
urging Ina, imploring her, to play one of these roles. She always
seems interested, indeed enthusiastic, but she gets scared at
the last moment and changes her mind; she's afraid that
"people won't like her in something different," that it "wouldn't
be a success"—all those fears that prevent one from ever doing
anything but the safe and the obvious. Cukor said an interesting thing in speaking of *As You Like It*; he felt Hepburn
would be a marvelous Rosalind; in his opinion the part is
nearly always played as a coy and ultra-feminine ingenue who
suddenly, for no logical reason, decides to don masculine attire.
He felt she should be the sort of high-spirited, quasi-arrogant
girl for whom to become a boy would be but a "quarter-
step," as he put it; that the moment a disguise was involved
it would be quite natural for her to decide immediately to wear
boys' clothes, having a leaning in that direction. Bobbie Jones
felt that in Shakespeare's time the fact of a male actor playing
first as a girl, then as a girl pretending to be a boy, then as a
girl again (all the time being in *reality* a boy) gave the play
an added fillip that was of necessity lost to us in the modern
theatre. He thought it would be amusing to do a production
of *As You Like It* with a boy playing Rosalind—that only in
that way could one recapture the true values of Shakespeare's
intention. I can see what he means, but I disagree with him,
for after all in Shakespeare's day it was taken for granted that
all girls were played by boys anyhow—whereas now it would
inevitably be regarded as a stunt, and would therefore upset the
values from another angle.

George Cukor has certainly been proved right! Katharine Hepburn was an enchanting Rosalind and broke all records with the play in the Theatre Guild production in 1950. As to Ina Claire, the situation has remained unchanged, and her friends and admirers continue to bemoan the fact. It seems such a waste that this great actress, perhaps the very greatest that we have, should be so seldom seen—and then only in plays totally unworthy of her. It is one more thing that makes one regret our lack of a theatre like the Comédie Française, where a perfect artist like Ina Claire might occasionally appear for our delight, without feeling trapped by the unnerving responsibility of having to deliver a commercial success complete with rave notices and substantial returns to the backers.

Nov. 3rd. This evening I went to see *The Star Wagon.* I hadn't seen Burgess Meredith play since he was with me as the Dormouse in *Alice in Wonderland.* The only leading part I ever saw him do was in a student performance of *Outward Bound* when he was an apprentice at the Civic, so I was very interested in watching him. There can be no question of his *great* talent; he just *is* an actor. If only he would *work*—I have great fears that he is just lacking in genius and will therefore take it easy. He should work *unceasingly,* especially on his voice, if he really thinks of some day (and they mention 1940) playing Hamlet or anything of that type, which *does* require a perfected instrument. He has a very light voice, limited in range, and with very little sustained resonance. That's all very well in the sort of parts he's playing, where his "personality" and natural instincts are 80 per cent of the game. *But*—well, we shall see.

Have we seen?

Nov. 4th. Today the new Garbo picture opened—*Conquest,* about Napoleon and Marie Walewska. I looked forward to seeing Garbo at last playing with a great actor, Charles Boyer. If MGM had deliberately set out to harm Garbo's standing, they couldn't have done a better job than they have done in *Conquest*. She literally has *nothing* to do. Her part constantly reminded me of Mathilde Wesendonk, both in its inconsistency and in its vapid "womanliness." It is perhaps true that in a story in which Napoleon is the central male figure, if the part is well played (and Boyer is superb), no one else really exists. It is especially true in this case, since the part of Marie Walewska is so underdrawn, so negative and underrealized, I defy anyone to do anything with it. Garbo is like a pale, distinguished ghost. Apart from the fact that in this case her material is far beneath her, something seems to have happened to her in the last two years. She made such extraordinary progress as an artist in the years before; each picture showed a definite and exciting advance in sheer mastery of her instrument. She was not just a beautiful woman but a superb and thrilling actress; and now suddenly it's as though she weren't there at all. Perhaps she is ill. She is far too thin—even for beauty—and seems to be robbed of all vitality. Perhaps she is sick of the whole business and has become supremely indifferent—to such an extent that it projects in her work. I have always been such a great admirer of hers, and it makes me sad to see her performances grow less. I wish she would make a great picture in Europe. So many of her performances in the past are unforgettable—one longs for more.

And one still "longs for more"; though fortunately the pale Walewska was followed by the entrancing Ninotchka—but that is too long ago.

Nov. 5th. We went back to the hotel in time to run up and say good-by to Constance, who was supposedly leaving on the 4:20 for Hollywood. The door to the suite was open, and various people kept dropping in, mostly bearing gifts. Constance looking wonderful, pleased as a child—most engaging. Evelyn Laye, Gloria Swanson, Carrie Darling, Mrs. Ben Hecht, etc., and the two faithful Georges—O'Neil and Bergen. It all ended, after much confusion and comings and goings and good-bys and telephone conversations, in Constance putting off her departure till tomorrow! Something wrong at the last minute with accommodations. It was all great fun; I'd forgotten what great actresses were like. What a darling she is really!

Nov. 6th. Went to see *Golden Boy* this evening. By far the best play and performance I've seen for a long time. Odets has come back from Hollywood richer in more than mere money—and I think he's the only one it's possible to say that about! The play is a success; it is cleverly written, cleverly planned—the sort of play that people who *don't* think will enjoy, because of its swift external sense of theatre, and that people who *do* think will enjoy, because of the sober bitter truths expressed throughout. It is a terrific indictment of the "bitch-goddess Success" worship in this country. Its terse, eliminated style is tremendously powerful and moving. I liked it—oh, I liked it so much! And they played it well—with truth, with conviction, with a kind of sober passion. It was *fine!*

Nov. 7th. Have had a marvelous ten days. I can't remember a better time; have seen many stimulating and interesting things and talked with many interesting people. It is good to get away from one's own petty little bits of nonsense and have a look at what's going on in the world, now and then. There is so much to learn, so much to do. Life is "frightfully thrilling," as Hilda Wangel would say!

I sailed November 20 on that charming little French boat the *Champlain*, one of the many, alas, that were destroyed in the war.

This time Marion Evensen came with me. She hadn't been to Europe for ten years and had then visited only France and

England, and as I intended to go to Scandinavia on this trip
she was anxious to go along, being a one-hundred-per-cent
Norwegian born in Wisconsin, and having a number of relatives in Norway whom she had never met.

We first went to England to see Mother, and spent the
holidays there. A typical entry in my diary is the one on December 8:

Pouring rain again! At nine in the morning one would think it
was midnight. How these people can live is beyond me—and
they are all so extraordinarily cheerful! Such fortitude gives me
an inferiority complex. In spite of the rain I walked for miles.
Bought a *stout* pair of walking shoes; really thick soles and
waterproof leather throughout; very useful here—though really
I think the only comfortable outfit would be ski-pants! Had
to go to one of Mother's "teas" this afternoon. Mrs. Alice
Campbell was there, a charming woman called Mrs. Dummit,
and dear old "Auntie Roy" [Mrs. Roy Devereux]. She's a
fascinating old lady. The subject of the Zola picture came up
and started her off talking about *L'Affaire Dreyfus*. She was
in Paris during the whole thing and knew most of the people
involved. The truth is certainly far more dramatic than the
picture. One very interesting twist was the fact that no one
could bear Dreyfus personally—he was greatly disliked. Auntie
Roy remembered Zola saying to her, *"C'est de la pure canaille,
mais il est innocent!"* How much more interesting this makes
Zola, and what a much greater apostle of justice! It would be
fascinating to write a play on the whole thing from this particular angle—something Odets could do brilliantly I should
think.

I evidently escaped as soon after Christmas as I decently
could, and fled to my beloved Paris, for on December 29 I
wrote:

The joy of waking up in Paris! Even though there was no sunshine the day seemed bright after the gloom of London. Quite

cold, but the air is delicious and blessedly breathable. Walked for hours. Stopped and looked at No. 1 rue de Fleurus. My plane trees are still there in front of the window that was mine for so many years—so long ago. How well I know their every aspect. As I looked at them today, bare in the winter cold, I could see them as they look in April, with sticky buds ready to burst—"thrusting forth difficult leaves," then in their full summer splendor, and then the golden-brown of their leaves in autumn, and the round black fruits outlined against the sky. I love these two trees. It must be because of them that *platanes* always fill me with such gentle nostalgia. I entered the Luxembourg Gardens by the rue de Fleurus gate, and my feet automatically tried to take the route to school, to the old Collège Sévigné on the rue de Condé. I controlled them with some difficulty, reminding them that they were years too old for that, and walked straight up the Allée and down the steps to the Bassin Central. Here I heard the shade of my childhood crying out importantly, *"Attention, s'il vous plaît!"* as I led the goat-cart loaded with small fry through the Sunday crowd of a hot summer's day. Then, following the old pattern, I took the path that led to the Orangerie where the goats and the donkey used to have their stable and were fed and put to rest for the night. I remembered with what pride I used to ignore the sign *"Le public n'entre pas ici"* and, ignoring it once more, though now with some trepidation, having no blessed and important business there, went into that sacred precinct, where all the greenhouses of the Luxembourg are concealed from the vulgar eye. The big Orangerie was green and humid and warm, like a jungle. Being winter, all the great palm trees, orange and lemon trees, the many semitropical plants that in summer adorn the parterres of the public park were massed in the huge hothouse, bathed in a fragrant mysterious twilight. Nothing has changed—except that here and there, in an occasional empty space, a small car was parked for the winter. Incongruous blasphemy! But enough of memories—this is 1937 and will soon be 1938, and there is so much beauty in

Paris that in those far-off days I was incapable of appreciating
—or rather, merely took for granted.

This whole trip to Europe was remarkable for the amount
of walking I did. Marion Evensen is a great walker too, and we
went everywhere on foot. It's by far the best way of getting
to know a city. Of course in Paris I was at home, but in a
strange town the first thing I did was to buy a map, find our
hotel on it, and from then on we used our feet. Those stout
walking shoes, my London investment, were well worn by the
time they hit the soil of Connecticut.

Jan. 1st, 1938. We lunched at the little restaurant Chez
Francis [of *Madwoman of Chaillot* fame]. Then on to the
Place du Trocadéro. For the first time we saw the Exposition
buildings at close range. In the bright sunshine, deprived of
the illusion created by cleverly placed floodlights, I thought
they were hideous—like a lot of bad scenery at a first dress
rehearsal with the work-light on—*most* depressing. Dreadful
colors, like the most sickening kind of "modern" painting. The
Pont de l'Alma, normally so graceful with its delicate marble
parapet, swamped and disfigured beneath this fungus growth.
The old horror, the Trocadéro (a relic of the Exposition of
1878), has been torn down and replaced by a huge white
building, the Palais de Chaillot, which is to remain there permanently. It faces the Tour Eiffel, on the same site as the
old Trocadéro—and what a marvelous site it is! From there it
was possible to see at a glance the whole layout of the Exposition, and to walk rapidly over the whole vast territory. The
Soviet Union building, with its gigantic statue of a man and
a woman holding high the hammer and sickle, was by far the
most impressive, though quite terrifying in its exultant power.
There is something menacing about it. One feels that Russia
decided to steal the show, and she certainly succeeded. The two
colossal figures, striding forward with a kind of ruthless joy,
dominated the whole scene. Even the German building op-

posite dwindled into insignificance; the other buildings seemed completely swamped. We went down the endless flight of steps and crossed the bridge to the old Tour Eiffel, which wore a look of surprised and offended middle age. Walked home along the rue de l'Université.

Jan. 2nd. Went into the Louvre for a bit. Being Sunday, there was a frightful mob; better to go on days when you have to pay a few francs, not on a holiday or a Sunday, when it's free. Nice, though, to see how enthusiastically and how extensively the French use their public monuments—with a kind of affectionate possessiveness; they really feel that they belong to them in a very intimate sense. I know of no other country where one has such a feeling of true democracy—a democracy that is part of the very air you breathe, a democracy taken for granted, a democracy without the slightest trace of self-consciousness. . . . What an incredible place the Louvre is! . . . The thought of all that has gone on in those vast rooms and apartments . . . and the never-ending thrill of the *Victoire de Samothrace!* It's like seeing Isadora dance. I always think of her when I look at the *Victoire*—she might have posed for it. . . . From the Louvre we walked along the *quais*, over to the Cité, toward Notre Dame. On the Quai du Marché Neuf, by the rue Lutèce (where Katherine Mansfield lived), we came on the Bird-Market in full swing. It is the most charming sight; I'm surprised K.M. didn't write a story about it! Thousands of birds of all sorts—they seem to have many more varieties than we ever see in our pet-shops at home. French people are notoriously fond of birds, and there is scarcely a French woman "of the people," a concierge or a workingman's wife, who hasn't a little bird of some sort singing away in its cage, which is always hung outside the window on sunny days. Their birds are given the most loving care; all kinds of delicacies are on sale at this market, things we can never find for them at home—a wide selection of herbs and grasses, millet in long ears, in its natural state (this the

birds *love*), innumerable varieties of seed. And then a marvelous choice of cages, all sizes, shapes and styles, from early
Victorian to the latest *art moderne*. And an adorable choice
of nests, to the pattern of every conceivable bird, woven of
straw or twigs, and lined with fine moss. The whole atmosphere
is filled with this touching love of birds; their every need—
one might say their every whim—is foreseen and provided
for. And radiating from this market, as from a joyous center,
come old ladies in black shawls, bearing triumphantly the little
bird or birds they have chosen after much careful thought and
examination; little children, with their fathers and mothers,
gravely carrying home their newly acquired treasure. And everywhere shrill cries of admiration and wonder: *"Oh! Qu'il est
beau!" "Quel plumage!" "Tu entends comme il siffle!" "Quelle
merveille!"* There is much these people know that we have
not thought worth while. They have the wisdom of simple
joys. . . . After dinner, to the Comédie Française. They were
playing *Le Jeu de l'amour et du hasard* by Marivaux, and
Molière's *L'Ecole des maris*. Again I was impressed by the vast
improvement in lighting and *mise-en-scène* generally, over the
productions I saw in 1931. And also by the surprising soberness
of the playing. Nothing overstressed—no shouting or declama-
tion or playing to the gallery. A smooth and excellent ensemble
—perfect workmanship. The Molière play I enjoyed especially.
How well they handle that verse (rhymed couplets, the most
dangerous form of all for the unskillful); in spite of the insistence of the rhyme, how natural they make it sound, how
dexterously they toss the lines about, like clever jugglers. And
with what ease they wear the clothes—they never seem like
costumes. If only our young actors could wear clothes like that
—but where can they ever get the training? What a joy it
would be if someday we could have a theatre like this! It's true
that at the moment—at least from what I've seen so far—they
have no actors that even begin to be *great*, as individuals; the
merit lies in the *whole*, in the spirit that emanates from the
idea of the organization itself. The performances are **perfect,**

but there seems to be no individual at this time capable of breaking that perfection with excitement. It is an even, polished, pleasant perfection—and that is much. There was a very full house, in spite of its being the day after a holiday. Again, it's good to see that the French make use of their advantages; they love this theatre of theirs and really support it.

The next day I wrote of a performance, at Jouvet's theatre, of Giraudoux' *Impromptu de Paris* (suggested, of course, by Molière's *Impromptu de Versailles*):

Renoir remains the best actor in Jouvet's company—a sober actor, with great power and a fine compelling voice. His right hand is withered and useless, yet no one ever notices this; if he were a bad actor one would notice nothing else! Giraudoux can certainly write—what noble, wonderful French! But what an inexhaustible flow of words; it's as if, having expressed a thought in one way, he then found ten other ways, each finer than the last, and couldn't bear to sacrifice one of them! This excess of verbiage is a bit trying at last—especially to a mere Anglo-Saxon. The French, of course, love it; they adore words for their own sake; they are connoisseurs of words as they are of fine wines. The *Impromptu de Paris* interested me very much. It is an informal discussion by the company, in their own persons at a rehearsal, of the theatre, from a thousand different angles: the actor's point of view of the public, of acting, of the state in relation to the theatre, of the theatre in relation to the state; of the playwright; of the scenic-designer; of the weather in relation to the public, and the public in relation to the weather; of the critics; of the evolution of a performance in the actor's mind; of a thousand and one things of immense interest to anyone of the theatre because he knows and understands these things, and to the public because it neither knows them nor suspects them. I'm surprised that this little *Impromptu* has never been played in New York. The *essence* is the same in America as in France—for after all the theatre, in its essence, is universal. A fine thing for a theatre such as the Group or the Mercury to do. Giraudoux is very difficult to translate—still, it could be done.

I believe the *Impromptu de Paris* (though I have not re-read it) might be greatly appreciated in New York now; 1938 might still have been too soon. There is a much larger audience for modern French plays in New York today than there was twenty years ago, or even ten. The Civic Repertory presented the first Giraudoux play ever to be produced—at least profes-sionally—in this country: *Siegfried*. It was enormously inter-esting—though full, certainly, of the aforementioned verbiage —but the critics received it impatiently and called it "dull and wordy." Wordy it certainly was, in Giraudoux' usual style, but dull it was not.

Our repertory also included a tender and provocative play by Jean Jacques Bernard, *L'Invitation au voyage*. This was an example of what came to be known in Paris as the *théorie du silence*, and it was far from wordy. The critics found this one "dull and underwritten." We kept it in the repertory, how-ever, and put it on for a few performances each season, to the delight of a small but immensely enthusiastic audience. Our treasurer, Fannie Levine, used to call it "Miss Le Gallienne's luxury."

Another French play presented by the Civic, *Mademoiselle Bourrat* by Claude Anet—a great success in Paris—was also received with bored indifference by the press. I feel sure that, had *The Respectful Prostitute* or *The Madwoman of Chaillot* been produced at that time, they would have met a similar fate. Modern French plays had not yet become the fashion.

One of the first theatres I visited as soon as I reached Paris was the Théâtre Montparnasse, under the direction of Gaston Baty. They were playing a play called *Madame Capet*. I knew nothing about it. I vaguely suspected from the title that it had something to do with the French Revolution, since I re-membered that the Commune always referred to Louis XVI as "*le citoyen Capet*," and to his widow, Marie Antoinette, as "*la veuve Capet*"—just as I suppose the Russian communards referred to the Emperor Nicholas of all the Russias as "Comrade Romanov." But I had heard nothing definite about the play or the production, apart from the fact that it was a great popular success, and I knew that anything presented by Baty was usually worth seeing.

I got seats with difficulty and found the house packed. The play started slowly. The scenery and costumes were exceptionally elegant for a French production. There was some delightful recorded music that set the mood of the initial scenes —eighteenth-century music of a rather stylized gaiety, which was immediately reflected in a couple of very frivolous, worldly thumbnail sketches of Marie Antoinette in her youth, at the peak of her pampered, thoughtless power. Gradually the play gained momentum and purpose. It was finally revealed as an engrossing and strangely gripping study of Marie Antoinette, illustrating her development as a human being from the year 1777 to the day of her death on the guillotine, October 16, 1793. The play was based on a phrase in one of her mother's letters. Maria Theresa, Empress of Austria, wrote: "*Faudra-t-il le malheur pour vous rendre vous-même!*" And, taking this as her theme, the author, Marcelle Maurette, drew an unforgettable picture of the proud capricious girl, the haughty defiant queen, and finally the bewildered woman deprived of everything—her possessions, her title, her dignity, her husband, her son, and, at last, her life. And through this immense suffering, this terrible retribution, she does find herself, and goes to the scaffold with a nobility and a serenity at which she herself, in her years of insolent prosperity, would undoubtedly have scoffed.

I found the last three scenes almost unbearably moving, and Marguerite Jamois played them beautifully. The entire cast was excellent. It was only after I had seen the play several times, and really studied the program, that I realized that many members of the cast played two and even three different parts, and all so perfectly that it was hard to believe they were the same actors.

I left the theatre in an exhilarated mood. I felt that here was a play I should really like to work in, and decided to try and buy the rights for this country. In my diary I describe my first efforts in this direction:

Jan. 4th. This morning I called up Alfred Bloch at the Société des Auteurs Dramatiques and arranged an appointment for four p.m. . . . . When I arrived punctually at 9 rue Ballu, there was no sign of Mr. Bloch. A lady who was, I suppose, meant to be a secretary knew nothing about anything—so I waited. At the end of half an hour I got a bit mad, and told said lady I had something else to do besides hanging about offices. Whereupon, with many groans, and the certainty that she would catch her death owing to the changes of temperature through which she would have to pass to reach Mr. Bloch in another part of the building, she suffocated herself in a shawl and disappeared. Presently she returned, groaning more than ever, and announced that Mr. Bloch would descend; and indeed, in another five minutes or so he appeared. A little fat French Jew—like a benevolent toad. I informed him that I wished to talk to him about *Madame Capet*; I understood it was not yet sold for America. I explained that a film was in the process of making, with Norma Shearer as Marie Antoinette; that it was bound to be a very important film from the standpoint of fanfares and hallelujahs, and that I was sure it would be difficult to persuade a manager that the appearance of this film would not necessarily damage the chances of a play on the same subject. I therefore proposed to take a personal option for a three- or six-month period. He must have imagined me to be an innocent creature, devoid of all knowledge of theatre business, for he seemed to think I expected to receive this option for nothing! He explained kindly and patiently, as though talking to a rather silly child, that it was impossible to give me such an option. But when I told him of the French plays I had produced, and made it clear that I knew something of theatrical terms, he became interested— though still incredulous. However, I finally convinced him that I meant business, and we parted most amicably, with the understanding that I was to put my offer in writing and he would then submit it to the author.

As it happened, that very same evening, and quite by chance, I met the author in person at a supper given in celebration of the hundredth performance of a play by H. R. Lenormand. I had had the pleasure of knowing Lenormand for some years and had always admired his work. He sent me an invitation to see this play of his and attend the supper afterward.

They gave me seats on the second row. Alice Cocea is the star and is also presenting the play—with the assistance of her current admirer. I thought it very bad—a bewildering mixture. Poor Lenormand has evidently tried to compromise and has deliberately tried to write a popular success. At times the innate poetry and sensitive feeling that are the true Lenormand shone through incongruously in a curious Oriental hodgepodge of snake-dances and rather inferior sentimental ballads. A most peculiar show. A sad, frustrated kind of show. It succeeded in *nothing*. It wasn't good cheap theatre, for the serious moments prevented that; on the other hand, these moments seemed grotesque in the tawdry frame that surrounded them. The performance left me uncomfortable and vaguely unhappy. Afterward a huge buffet supper was served in the foyer of the theatre. There were literally hundreds of people—what is known as *tout Paris*. An amazing crowd. I've never seen so much make-up—and not only on the women! It made one feel quite naked! Marguerite Jamois came in late after her performance, and I had the pleasure of telling her how much I admired her in *Madame Capet*. I told her I should so much like to play the play in New York. She was quite excited at the idea and dragged me over to meet the author, Marcelle Maurette. I was surprised to find her so young—still in her twenties, I should think—very chic, very brilliant, very intellectual—the real French bluestocking. She introduced me to her husband, who bears the disconcerting name of Mr. Bec-de-Lièvre. We had a very nice talk, and I was glad of this—for if Mr. Bloch proves tiresome I've a feeling Maurette will be on my side. She seemed genuinely pleased at the idea of my playing the play *aux Etats-Unis*.

That next day I went to visit my friend Madame Simone, the famous actress-producer. I wanted to ask her advice on the technical wording of my letter to Mr. Bloch. Though it was five o'clock in the afternoon, I found Simone ensconced in her comfortable bed, surrounded by papers and documents of all sorts. She was busy writing a scenario of *Adrienne Lecouvreur* for a French film company. She told me she was getting very tired of the theatre and found writing much more agreeable. As she put it, "If you develop into a real human being as you grow older, reach a real state of identity, which of course few actors do, the fact of having to allow the public to look you over and more or less possess you for two or three hours out of the twenty-four is decidedly unpleasant. It offends one's sense of *pudeur*." At that time I didn't agree with her at all, but I'm beginning to see what she meant now.

She was most helpful to me in the *Madame Capet* matter. She is a superlatively good businesswoman, as well as a great actress. I have a feeling Mr. Bloch must have suspected an alien, Machiavellian influence when he came to read the masterpiece of shrewd logic I wrote at Simone's dictation!

We had a most interesting talk. Simone told me some quite fascinating things about Madame Sarah, whom she knew very well. She said the nicest thing about Sarah was that you could always tell her the truth about her work. One day Sarah asked Simone what she thought of her performance in *Phèdre*. As it happened, Simone liked it least of all Sarah's roles, and told her so. Sarah agreed with her at once and said, "Yes, I do not play Phèdre well. That is because I have never felt physical passion." An astonishing statement from one who was supposed to be a veritable tigress of passion—both on and off the stage. Simone said Sarah admitted never having loved anyone but herself. What a delightfully honest person—no pretense or chi-chi about her!

I remember Sarah as being overwhelmingly great as Phèdre. It's true that I was only a child of twelve when I saw her play it, and was perhaps not a very reliable judge of *la grande passion,* but at that age one is apt, if anything, to be hypercritical, and certainly very quick to sense the untrue or the phony. Phèdre was always considered one of Sarah's greatest roles. There are moments of her performance that I can still see vividly, and certainly Madame Sarah generated an excitement in a theatre that I have never seen equaled.

At last the *Madame Capet* deal was consummated—largely, I'm sure, due to Simone's letter—and I sent off a script of the play to my lawyer and agent in New York, Arthur Friend. Anyone who knew Arthur will agree with me that he was well named; he was indeed a loyal and valuable friend and is greatly missed. I suggested that he go to work immediately to find a manager interested in producing the play for me in the fall.

Meanwhile I made frequent visits to the Théâtre Montparnasse, and my enthusiasm grew with each performance I saw there. Mr. Baty was most helpful and cooperative, and allowed me to watch the work from backstage on several occasions. I was particularly impressed with the fine spirit of comradeship that existed in his organization. There were no stars; everyone worked for the good of the play and the whole, with no sense of self-importance; and there seemed to be none of those exhibitions of arrogance and bad temper often falsely dignified by the name of temperament. I was envious of the freedom from petty union rules and regulations that these people enjoyed. In a quick change, actors were actually allowed to lend a hand, something I've often longed to do! If a piece of furniture was "off the mark" an actor could replace it without feeling he was committing a crime of lèse-majesté to Local Number 1. The musical interludes, which had been recorded especially for this performance prior to the opening, were most effectively handled by a *régisseur*, without the aid of a totally unnecessary extra electrician. Nor were there four live musicians sitting in the basement playing poker and drawing salaries each week for music they didn't play. These reprehensible and unfair labor conditions would naturally never be tolerated by such high-minded guardians of labor ethics as Mr. Petrillo or Messrs. Goodsun and Pernick; but the poor French people just don't know any better, I guess—and it's surprising what fine work they do, and how greatly they enjoy doing it.

Mr. Baty warned me that the production had been ruinously expensive. From the figures he showed me I gathered it had cost just under ten thousand dollars—a very high price indeed for a Paris production. I wonder what he would have said if he could have seen the American figures!

I began to read everything I could lay my hands on about Louis XVI and Marie Antoinette: about their background, their childhoods, their upbringing, the influences that shaped their lives; a great deal about the Revolution, its causes and its development, the different phases it went through. I had read a lot about this period in studying to play *L'Aiglon*, for I wanted to know all about "my father's" life. I owe any slight knowledge I have of history to the various historical characters I have played: Jeanne d'Arc, Simonetta (Botticelli's famous model), *L'Aiglon*, Marie Antoinette, Elizabeth, Catherine of Aragon—even poor Mathilde Wesendonk caused me to find out a good deal about Wagner and his times.

Between the periods with which I am somewhat familiar lie vast lacunae of ignorance. My education has been what one might call untidy. My formal schooling came to an end when I was fifteen, and though the Collège Sévigné, which I attended in Paris, was an excellent school, I was never a good scholar, though I gave the impression of being one and my marks were usually good. But I'm afraid they were won mostly by quick cramming and by a shrewd appraisal of my various teachers, which enabled me to bamboozle them into thinking I knew far more than I in fact did. What I learned was never well grounded, and after I had managed to pass the necessary examinations I allowed the knowledge to leave my memory as speedily as it had entered it. I have never been able to retain dates or specific facts, and in my theatre work, while I am a very quick study, I forget a part as quickly as I learn it. But I have always found it fascinating, in preparing a part or a play, to find out all I possibly can about the social history of the period, the climate of the times: what people were thinking; what great writers, painters, architects, musicians—as well as statesmen and politicians—dominated the scene; why people wore certain clothes or used particular types of furniture and accessories. This kind of study is perhaps not actually essential to the playing of a period piece, but it does help one to understand the atmosphere in which the characters lived, to wear the clothes naturally and correctly, to move and speak and think in a rhythm akin to theirs. And, above all, it's fun! It becomes an absorbing kind of game.

I made many pilgrimages to the places that had known Marie Antoinette, spent many days roaming about Versailles, through the little private theatre where she performed as a royal amateur and basked in the flattery of the courtier-spectators, and around the Petit Trianon, where she played at living the "simple life" made fashionable by Jean-Jacques Rousseau. Then I roamed through the Louvre, St. Cloud, the Temple, and the Conciergerie, scenes of the grim last years that swept her to her inevitable destruction. I described one of these expeditions in my diary:

Jan. 6th. . . . along the rue de Rivoli toward the popular quarter of St. Antoine. It was from this quarter that the most turbulent mobs set out on their missions of vengeance and destruction. Up the rue de Sévigné to the Musée Carnavalet. It is such a lovely old house, and at the hour we went—the

sacred hours between *midi* and two o'clock—it was deserted.
The great trouble with all the museums here is that the lighting is appalling. Some of the cases, especially on a gray day,
are plunged in shadow. One should carry a flashlight! I love
this museum with all its tragic souvenirs of the Revolution
and the Commune. The everyday trivial possessions of Louis
XVI and poor Marie Antoinette—a handkerchief, a drinking-
glass, a pair of silk stockings carefully mended—the poor little
possessions left them during their days of terror in the Temple.
And then the grim statutes and proclamations that drove them
gradually and inexorably to their death, proclamations signed
with the showy, self-conscious signatures of the egomaniacs,
the tyrants of the Commune, the *amis du peuple*. From the
Carnavalet we walked over to the amazing Place des Vosges.
It had scarcely changed since the seventeenth century, except
that now the district is very poor and the great old houses,
once occupied by the aristocracy, are shabby and unkempt—
but still beautiful. In one corner of the square Victor Hugo's
old house stands, now a museum consecrated to his memory.
I hadn't realized how much he painted and drew. The place
is full of engravings, designs, and drawings by his hand. One
gets a sense of his incredible vitality, of the great wealth of
ideas that poured from him like a torrent. I couldn't help
wondering whether he had been familiar with Blake—I should
think it doubtful—but so many of his watercolors remind one
astonishingly of Blake. All his political activities, too, are
interesting. Several proclamations written in his most flamboyant style; some of them would not seem out of place at this
very moment—as always, the fight between the intellectual
idealist, nursing dreams of Plato's *Republic*, and the rule of
the Communist rabble. The eternal fight between the raisers
up and the knockers down! I suppose it will never end.

After several weeks I had word from Arthur Friend that
Eddie Dowling was enthusiastic about *Madame Capet* and
had agreed to produce it. He had hopes of persuading Margaret

Webster to direct the play. This prospect delighted me as I had greatly admired her production of *Richard II* with Maurice Evans, under Eddie Dowling's management.

I had known Peggy Webster for years. Her parents, Ben Webster and Dame May Whitty, were great friends of the Favershams, and we often used to meet at Chiddingfold in the old manor house that had once briefly been my home, and which the Favershams had taken off my father's hands when he found a poet's earnings insufficient to support so large an establishment. It was always a joy to go back there for a visit. William Faversham and his beautiful wife, Julie Opp, spent their summers there, with their two boys, Billie and Philip. The place was always full of interesting people. Every year my mother and I were invited to spend some blissful weeks there.

I didn't pay much attention to Peggy in those days—she was among the small fry and beneath my notice. The first clear memory I have of her is when I was twelve and loftily engaged in my Girl Guide activities. I can see her now, a very small child of six, rather plain, with her hair plaited into two tight pigtails, her eyes looking very large and round behind a pair of very large and round spectacles. She always seemed to be hanging about, staring at me with admiring awe as I blew up a bicycle tire or saddled Will Faversham's pony, wearing the hideous uniform of a Girl Guide of the period, complete with badges, insignia, whistles, knives, hatchets, and frying-pans—the four last-mentioned objects hanging from various hooks and rings on my belt and making me look rather like the White Knight's horse in *Alice in Wonderland*. All these clanking accoutrements were a source of endless interest and envy to Peggy and the "Favvy" boys, and endowed me with an aura of glamour in their eyes. In order to escape their adoring attentions, on the days when I was not at the Girl Guide camp some ten miles distant, I used to perch at the top of the tallest tree in the garden and sit there for hours, engrossed in some large tome, which I carried up strapped to my back so as not to interfere with my climbing prowess, which was considerable.

In the years that followed I occasionally saw Peggy in London. Once, during the days of the Civic, I magnanimously offered her the part of Lady Montague in *Romeo and Juliet*, which she had the good sense to refuse. But it was not until she came to New York to direct *Richard II* that we really became friends. By that time the superior, self-important Girl Guide of twelve no longer looked down with condescending toleration on the shy, inarticulate child of six; the years had bridged the gap between us.

Our ideas on the theatre, on acting, and on the work in general are very similar, yet sufficiently different to make our conversations lively and stimulating. At times we disagree violently and vociferously—but rarely in essentials. The suggestion that Peggy Webster should direct *Madame Capet* filled me with confidence. Unfortunately, prior commitments prevented her from accepting Dowling's offer.

As soon as plans for *Madame Capet* were settled I took a trip through Italy. I hadn't been there for many years and, as usual, found it enchanting. I visited my cousin Mogens Nörregaard, the painter, in Assisi. He had become a convert to the Roman Catholic faith and lived an austere and solitary life in that wonderful old town, studying the works of Giotto and Cimabue in the church there, himself painting beautiful pictures that found their way to many churches in various parts of the world. We toured the hill towns together—Siena, Perugia, and my favorite of all, San Gimignano—and ended up with a few days in Florence. Mogens was a perfect companion and guide, imbued as he was with an intimate knowledge of that whole region. This tall, blond, typically Danish man somehow seemed to belong there; his love and understanding of these places and their people enabled him to bring their past to life, and he made it glow with a thousand fascinating comments and anecdotes.

I went on to Rome, Naples, Pompeii, Pisa, Venice—so

much beauty everywhere! I think one appreciates it more as one gets older; one is no longer driven by mere curiosity, by a desire to see things with one's outward eyes. It's as though the rhythm and color, the harmony and proportion, sink into one's inner being and become absorbed there, to remain a part of one forever. I felt like a well-fed plant, ready to send out new leaves, green shoots, finer flowers.

Before leaving Italy I went to Asolo, the little town just north of Venice where the Brownings lived, and which is the scene of his poem "Pippa Passes." It is a tiny village, undisturbed by modern civilization. The nearest railroad station is Bassano, about ten miles away; from there one follows a winding dirt road up into the hills. To me it is a hallowed place, for it was there that Duse spent her years of retirement before she returned to the theatre in 1923, and there she is buried. Her companion of many years, Désirée, has often described to me Duse's last journey to Asolo; how the country folk from miles around streamed down from the hills and accompanied her on foot all the way from Bassano to the little cemetery, piling the coffin high with spring flowers and strewing branches of blossoms in her path.

I stood a long time by the plain marble slab that marks her grave, on the slope of a hill facing the violet-tinged mountains that she loved.

I had promised Mother to meet her in Copenhagen early in March. We were to celebrate her seventy-fifth birthday there.

I hadn't been to Denmark since I was a child, and I'd forgotten what a warm, gay, friendly place it is. I stood on the balcony of my room at the Hotel d'Angleterre and looked out over Kongensnytorv. From innumerable flagpoles the bright Danish flag, the Dannebro, scarlet and white, streamed gallantly in the stiff breeze, giving the town a festive air. On the other side of the square the Kongelige-Teater—the Royal

Theatre—was every bit as impressive as I had remembered it. The city had grown a lot since my last visit many years before, but only on the outskirts. The core of the old town had remained unchanged, and later, as I walked about the narrow crooked streets with their colorful houses, their churches and public buildings crowned with copper roofs that had turned soft green with age, I felt pleasantly at home. The language too, I was happy to find, was easy and familiar to me.

That first day we had lunch out at Frederiksberghave. Under the great beech trees the lawns were embroidered with drifts of snowdrops and aconites, shining white and gold in the sunshine, although it was still very cold. Everything was sparkling and bright and bracing. The coffee tasted better than any other coffee in the world, and the famous Danish open sandwiches—the *Smörrebröd*—were delicious and of infinite variety. A long stay in Denmark would certainly be hard on one's figure!

On her birthday, March 16, Mother was given a big party by *Politiken*, the newspaper for which she had been correspondent for forty years. There was a huge cake, much champagne, and many speeches. Most of the prominent people in the artistic, literary, and journalistic circles of Copenhagen were there. Mother was in her element. In fact the whole visit was what might be called a "round of festivities."

We went to the theatre several evenings. At the Kongelige we saw an interesting play by Kai Munk (later murdered by the Nazis). This "Royal Theatre" is a beautiful old house. Over the proscenium arch in great gold letters are the words *"Ej blot til Lyst"*—"not only for amusement"—for the Danes look upon the theatre as a source of enlightenment and inspiration as well as a place of entertainment. Betty Nansen, the famous Danish actress and one of Mother's old friends, was playing *Elizabeth, femme sans hommes*, translated from the French success, at her own theatre. A fine young actress, Else Skovboe, was starring in a delightful comedy at the Folketeater. Also at the Kongelige we saw a splendid performance of *Jean*

de France by Holberg (the "Danish Molière"); afterward
Johannes Pavlsen—one of the leading lights of the Kongelige,
a flamboyant, engaging actor of the old school, full of fun and
fireworks—took me around backstage, introduced me to the
other players, and showed me the various departments of the
vast building. Everywhere I was greeted with the utmost
cordiality and hospitality.

One afternoon, at one of the endless teas given for Mother,
I met Ibsen's granddaughter. It was fun to meet a descendant
of the wonderful old man. She told me, among many interesting things, that Ibsen had written *A Doll's House* to please his
wife, who was a great feminist—I should think the only occasion on which he wrote anything to please anybody! But
what really fascinated him about the play was not so much
Nora's emancipation; it was the basic difference in the masculine and feminine concepts of honor. Nora could see no harm
in forging her father's signature in order to save her husband's
life. In her scene with Krogstadt in the first act she says, "Hasn't
a daughter the right to shield her dying father from worry and
anxiety? And hasn't a wife the right to save her husband's
life? I don't know much about the law, but I'm sure that,
given the circumstances, it could never condemn one for that!"
Since her motives are good, she can see no harm in her actions.
And in the last act, when Helmer says, "No man would sacrifice his honor, even to the one he loves best," she answers,
"Hundreds and thousands of women have done so!" It was this
theme in the play that Ibsen found most engrossing, and it
is this theme in the play that still remains undated. The problem of woman's freedom has been largely solved. Her right
to be a human being is supposedly unquestioned now, and
this side of the play may seem to us obsolete. But the ethical
question of behavior remains alive and challenging. In those
of Ibsen's plays that seem to deal only with social conditions
of the moment, there is usually some element that remains
timeless and universal.

Leaving Mother in Denmark, Marion Evensen and I went

on to Norway for a couple of weeks. The difference in the two countries is quite startling. There is a feeling of austerity and frugality in Norway, both materially and spiritually. The Danish gaiety and charm seem frivolous by comparison. Norway has a starkness and a strength that might impress one as dour at first acquaintance. The people are reserved and lacking in the easy social graces of their cousins to the south. But they are wonderful people. One still feels in them the proud, fierce spirit of the Vikings. Their honesty is almost disconcerting. Never ask a Norwegian his opinion unless you can stand the truth!

I met with great kindness on all sides. I was surprised at how much they knew about me there. We spent a couple of days in the little town of Skien—Ibsen's birthplace as well as that of Marion's mother. On the wall of the dining room in the hotel was hanging an antique plate with Ibsen's portrait on it—quite a hideous object, but curious. As I left, the proprietor took it off the wall and presented it to me with a flourish: "To the great Ibsen-interpreter of America!" I was very amused and touched. It now hangs on the wall of my dining room in Westport, accompanied by another similar trophy. In Oslo I was given a whole set of Ibsen's first editions, by the editor of one of the newspapers there; these occupy a proud position in my library.

Marion found several first cousins in Skien, and, although she didn't think she spoke the language, she found herself understanding most of it. Several large stores bore the name of Evensen, and she was quite pleased to see it spelled correctly —something which seldom happens over here, where she is usually addressed as Evans, or, at best, Evanson.

We went as far north as Bergen, and at a little station high up in the mountains we were thrilled to see a sleigh arrive to fetch some passengers; it was drawn by a reindeer with magnificent antlers topped with bells. It was like being in a fairy tale.

The old theatre in Bergen where Ibsen worked as a stage manager, and where his first two plays were presented, is a fascinating place. We were allowed to examine all his prompt-scripts there. I wish some of our stage managers could see them —every direction, every movement, every piece of business meticulously written out in his small clear handwriting. It made me think of that singularly foolish aphorism of Oscar Wilde's: "Genius is an infinite capacity for not taking pains." How clever that sounds, and how basically false and silly it is!

One of the most thrilling things I saw in Norway was the new building near Oslo that houses the three great Viking ships. It is built in the shape of a T. The largest ship lies in the stem of the T, the two smaller ones on either side of the crossbar, and at the intersections of the letter are circular staircases leading to a gallery from which one can look down into the interior of the vast open boats. The entrance door is at the foot of the T, and when one opens it one is faced with the prow of the largest ship. I have rarely seen anything more breathtaking. The pure, clean line soars like a phrase from some heroic symphony; here is functional beauty that puts our modern streamlining to shame. In spite of its immense size, its rugged power, the ship yet has a sureness of proportion that gives it an almost lyrical delicacy. It is like a "greyhound of the sea"—the phrase is apt. I felt as if I were gazing at the whole spirit of the North.

I thought of another door I had opened on this visit to Europe. Then, too, I stood overwhelmed with wonder—the doors to St. Peter's in Rome. There one's senses are intoxicated with the lavish wealth of color and detail. A thousand intricate forms, fantastically elaborated and embroidered, weave an intricate pattern drenched in vivid hues of gold, scarlet, crimson, purple, blue, and silver; it is like stepping into a pagan temple built all of jewels. There I felt I was gazing at the whole spirit of the Latin world. D'Annunzio and Ibsen, I thought—the two poles.

We returned to Copenhagen, where I again spent a few days with my mother. One very windy afternoon Mother decided to make a pilgrimage to the main cemetery to pay her respects to her parents, her brother, and other relatives who were buried in this beautiful park. I can't imagine any place in the world as windy as Copenhagen in the spring. Wind, especially in a city, always makes me nervous and bad-tempered. Mother, of course, had on her trusty veil, but in those days I wouldn't have been caught dead wearing such an object; now, at "plus twenty," I'm beginning to find veils comforting and friendly things.

Inwardly cursing, clutching my hat, my hair streaming in the wind, laden with large bunches of flowers to be deposited at the various graves, I struggled after Mother toward the "best" side of the cemetery; for it seems that in death too one can be on the right or wrong side of the railroad tracks.

I found it hard to summon the appropriate mood of reverence as I stood reading the familiar names on the family tombstones. Mother stayed there a long time, deeply moved and lost in memories. I began to despair of ever dragging her away. My ears and nose were frozen, and tears streamed down my face, but I'm afraid they were due to the wind rather than to any commendable grief. At last I could bear it no longer and tugged at Mother's arm in an effort to lure her back to the entrance gate, but she refused to be robbed of her excursion into the past. She set out resolutely in precisely the opposite direction, and with slow, determined steps started on a tour of the more aristocratic regions of the cemetery. We passed slowly through long avenues of tombs. At every other step Mother would pause and stand in contemplation before some hideous monument. "So that's where dear Admiral Sorensen lies," she murmured. "How well I remember the day he proposed to me after my first big ball. I couldn't have been more than fifteen at the time. Well, fancy!" A few steps further on: "Good Heavens! That poor Chamberlain Scavinius! Never shall I forget how madly in love with me he was!" A few more steps; then: "Chancellor of the Exchequer Gyldendahl! He wanted to leave his wife for my sake. What a time I had with him!" One after another, the tombs opened to release some memory: Commander Ericson, General Bodenhof, Count Flensdorf, Baron Rosenstjern, Ambassador Bott-Hansen—the ghosts rose from their graves and bowed low at Mother's feet. The belle of Copenhagen was once more receiving her admirers.*

It was an incredible afternoon. I felt as though I were living in a story by Katherine Mansfield—and what a story she could have made of it! My feelings of impatience, exasperation, and discomfort were so strong at the time that they prevented me from adequately appreciating the strange mixture of eeriness, pathos, and slightly macabre humor in the situation. But in retrospect I find that afternoon indelibly etched on my memory, like an engraving by Daumier.

It was a couple of hours before Mother tore herself away from this spell of the past. I looked at her curiously as we rode back in the cab to the hotel. Daughters are notoriously skeptical and unsympathetic when it comes to imagining their mothers in the flush of romantic youth; but I feel now as though I had actually had a vision, that afternoon, of that "Sphinx of the North," as Father used to call her, that elfin, fascinating wisp of a woman, with her pale translucent skin, her ash-blond hair, her blue eyes, her pert nose, and her long thin-lipped mouth, which caused such havoc among all the admirals and generals, the counts and the barons, now safely sheltered by their imposing mausoleums.

At the time, however, I was too relieved to be out of the wind, out of the cold, away from that icy city of the dead, to indulge in such flights of fancy. I gave Mother a hug, and we went off and had a jolly evening among the living.

---

* For obvious reasons, the names used in this paragraph are fictitious.

CHAPTER THIRTEEN

IT WAS fun to return to New York with the prospect before me of interesting work on a play in which I so firmly believed. Arthur Friend met me at the boat, and the following day took me to meet Eddie Dowling in his offices at the St. James Theatre.

There the contract was signed, a lengthy and involved document, the fruit of many conferences between Arthur Friend and Dowling's lawyers. Ah! These legal minds! What a genius they have for complicating life! I examined the many pages of typewritten clauses and whereases and wherefores with some distaste. My idea of a contract is to write on a half-sheet of paper what I require and what I intend to give, in language that a child of five could understand. But what would become of the legal profession if such ideas prevailed?

I found Eddie Dowling to be a man of considerable charm. He has a disarming way of seeming very ingenious, simple, and frank, a rather boyish warmth of manner—quite engaging.

Our first problem was to get the play adequately translated. Dowling suggested that we try to interest Paul Vincent Carroll in this difficult task. His play *Shadow and Substance* had been successfully produced under Dowling's management, and their relations most cordial. Paul Vincent Carroll came out to Westport and spent the day with me discussing the play, going over the script. We got on wonderfully well, and he seemed fully decided to undertake the job. I was pleased, for I admired his writing and felt he would give the play in English

153

the same elegance and lucidity of style that marked the original. Also I liked Carroll personally. We had a grand afternoon together, and I looked forward to working with him. I felt sure the feeling was mutual—such things usually are—and was therefore surprised and disappointed to receive a rather ambiguous letter from him a few days later, excusing himself and expressing his regrets at being unable after all to take on the assignment.

I then thought of my dear friend George Middleton, who had made so many fine translations from the French, notably some of Sacha Guitry's plays, which are notoriously difficult to put into English. Dowling thought well of the idea, and George Middleton consented to do the work.

I had first met George Middleton in my early days in New York. He was working on a Guitry play for David Belasco—*Une petite main qui se place*. Belasco had seen me in one of my early parts, before I ever aspired to a leading role. He had sensed something in me that intrigued him, and felt I had "the makings of a star." He sent for me and offered me the lead in the Guitry play. I remember the sensation his interest in me caused among my theatre friends. Here was the great opportunity. At that time every young actress's dream was to become a Belasco star.

I was ushered into the master's presence and left alone with him in his ornate and cluttered apartment on the top floor of the Belasco Theatre. The lights were very dim, and the rooms filled with an amazing collection of bric-a-brac of the most varied sort. The atmosphere troubled me; there was incense burning somewhere. I felt as if I were about to have my fortune told by an expensive soothsayer.

Mr. Belasco was a rather short man, at that time inclined to stockiness. His curly, gray hair, worn quite long, the clerical collar he affected, his carefully tended hands, white and soft as a woman's, gave him a definitely theatrical appearance. His voice was so soft and low that I had difficulty in understanding what he said. He sat on a straight chair facing me, and so close that his presence made me uncomfortable. He fixed me with his black, piercing eyes as though he were about to hypnotize me, and indeed his personality was strongly hypnotic. He spoke at great length in a purring gentle tone. He asked me innumerable questions about myself, and I had the feeling he wanted to take possession of my whole personality. I was too shy and nervous to say much. After the first few minutes I had to struggle hard to control a wild impulse to rise and make my escape, but my brain kept telling me that this was my great chance and that this suave, civilized gentleman was doing me a great honor by his faith in me and would help make me the fine actress I dreamed of becoming someday. I thought of how thrilled Mother was at this interview, and the Favershams and Constance Collier—all those wonderful people who believed in my future and wished me well. Yet somehow my whole inner being rebelled. I felt as though I were being swamped, suffocated, trapped in some strange way. My instinct told me that if I succumbed to this man's influence I would have to abandon my precious freedom of spirit. I had a vision of a heavy door closing behind me, imprisoning me in a world over which I would have no control, where I would be a slave to the rules and regulations, both of thought and conduct, imposed by a powerful and relentless master. I was too young to express my fears in words, too insecure to assert my feelings of independence and fight for them. I sat there quietly, but with a furiously beating heart, and gave no inkling of the doubts that rose up in me like danger signals.

At last the interview came to an end. I thanked Mr. Belasco for his offer and left the room. There was nothing in my behavior to indicate anything but grateful acceptance, and Mr. Belasco was quite naturally convinced that I would return the next day and sign the contract. Anything else would have seemed to him inconceivable.

Once out in the good light of day, I walked rapidly away from the Belasco Theatre, without knowing where I was going, the feeling of panic rising in me. I found myself in Central

Park. I strode along, taking deep breaths of the cold air, and trying to assemble my thoughts. I didn't want to go home to Mother, for I knew I would be unable to explain my feelings to her; they would have seemed vague and illogical, and she would certainly have thought them very foolish, for indeed they had no logical basis in fact. Mr. Belasco had treated me with great kindness; there had been nothing questionable in his behavior, nothing concrete that could explain the sense of revulsion I had at the thought of putting my career into his hands. But I suddenly saw quite clearly that I must refuse his offer. I felt ashamed of this decision, but I knew it was inevitable. I decided that I must settle the business at once, before discussing it with anyone. I must make my refusal definite and irrevocable.

I walked all the way down Fifth Avenue to Washington Square and rang the bell of George Middleton's house on Waverly Place. The door was opened by a small woman with fair hair and very blue eyes, and a face that radiated such simple truth and goodness that I loved and trusted her at once. This was Fola La Follette, George Middleton's wife. She told me George was not home just then, but, seeing the look of disappointment in my eyes, and, with her rare sympathy, no doubt sensing the deep trouble in which I found myself, she asked me to come in and talk to her. I somehow knew that she would understand, and poured out the whole story to her. I explained that I knew how foolish and ungrateful I must seem, but that some strong and irrefutable instinct warned me of danger and made it impossible for me to work under Mr. Belasco's direction; I would wreck my career, abandon all my hopes of success, rather than submit to his powerful authority.

Fola La Follette listened with great patience and understanding to this outburst. She must have thought me pathetically young and silly, but she gave no hint of that. To my infinite relief she agreed that I was right, that in spite of all worldly reasons to the contrary, if I felt I would be jeopardizing my freedom of spirit I must refuse and be strong enough to take the consequences. She gave me tea, fed me, soothed me, and promised to explain matters to George Middleton and make things right with him. When I left her house I felt confident, settled, and at peace. She had helped me through my first great spiritual battle and had won my devotion and gratitude forever.

It was many years before Mr. Belasco forgave me. He was not used to having his plans thwarted by insignificant little actresses, and his vanity was outraged. I understand very well how he must have felt, but, for right or wrong, I had done what I had to do; I had no choice.

Thanks to Fola's persuasive tact, George held no grudge against me, and we have been friends ever since; so it was a joy to me to work on *Madame Capet* with him. During the summer he made frequent visits to Westport. He is a huge man, full of ebullient vitality, and there were times when I thought my little house would collapse under the strain of sheltering him. He knows French thoroughly but speaks it with a strong American accent, and it made me laugh to hear him massacre the delicate music of the French language in his booming, hearty voice. He would suddenly burst into the room, like a big overgrown boy, his face pink with triumph as he announced the solution to some particularly tricky phrase; the play was full of them. It was a difficult task indeed to put it into English, and I think George succeeded admirably.

Another great friend of mine, José Ruben, was engaged to direct the play. Though a Frenchman by birth, he had spent many years in this country, had played many important parts in English, and had perfect command of both languages.

In the late summer we started on the important job of casting. This presented many serious problems. There were a great number of interesting and demanding parts, but none that could strictly be termed leads. Marie Antoinette was the only character that appeared in the play throughout. Each scene called for several fine actors, but their parts were comparatively short. It is difficult to persuade actors of reputation and consequence to play short parts, no matter how effective. In Paris this problem was solved by doubling or, in some instances, even tripling, but this practice is not customary here and is looked upon with a certain amount of contempt; and our deplorable tendency to type-cast has robbed our actors of the necessary pliancy and versatility. The leading actor of the Théâtre Montparnasse had played Mirabeau—the most telling male role in the play—but he had also appeared in a small part in the first scene, and in one of the last scenes he gave a gem of a performance as an old peasant. He didn't seem to feel that these minor excursions in any way detracted from his dignity or his importance in the great part of Mirabeau. But we were faced with the dilemma of persuading actors to play what seemed to them minor parts—and, judged in terms of length, they might have been called so—without, naturally, any reduction in their regular salaries. This, had the play been ideally cast, would have made the operating costs prohibitive, and we were forced to make many compromises from which the performance undoubtedly suffered.

My association with Eddie Dowling continued pleasantly enough. I dare say he found me difficult at times, since I had been my own boss for so long and was used to my own way of doing things. On the other hand, I found some of his methods rather disconcerting. I remember very clearly one incident that caused me acute distress. Between the second and third scenes of the play there was a sort of interlude performed by the dressmaker to the queen. It was practically a monologue, quite a showy tour-de-force, and demanded great skill and personality on the part of the actress. Since the part was not that of a young woman, Eddie Dowling suggested we might persuade some older star to emerge from retirement and lend the glamour of her name and prestige to this very special role. This seemed a good idea, and we had endless discussions on whom we should approach. One morning, as we were all sitting in Dowling's office, he became greatly excited and told his secretary to get him the Actors' Home on the telephone. There was an old actress there, he enthusiastically explained, a "great star," who would be superb. This would give her a splendid comeback and would inject a thrilling element of surprise into the proceedings. His secretary got him the connection, and soon he was describing the part in glowing terms to the old actress on the other end of the wire. "It'll be a great comeback for you, darling," he said. "You'll make a sensation in it! I'll be in touch with you!" He hung up, and a few seconds later, to my amazement, he turned to us and said, "No! I guess she wouldn't be any good anyway!"

My heart stopped beating. I had such an overwhelming picture of what that old actress was doing at that moment. I could see her, flushed with excitement, rejoining her companions and telling them that she was about to return to the stage, in a splendid part, under Eddie Dowling's management. I could imagine the congratulations, the flattering speeches, the envious glances, the dead hope revived. "Hadn't you better call her right back and tell her you've changed your mind," I said, "before she gets too happy?"

"That's all right. I'll write her a note," was Eddie Dowling's reply. I only hope he did, and perhaps that was the best way to handle it. He seemed quite undisturbed at the time, and I feared he had no conception of the possible results of his well-meant but thoughtless impulse. How can a man with so little imagination be a good actor? I thought to myself. For the first time a faint cold doubt crossed my mind and made me wonder how long our present amicable relations would endure.

Eddie Dowling chose Watson Barratt to do the scenery and costumes for the play, and for this I owe him a debt of gratitude, since Watson Barratt is one of the most delightful people I know, and it was through *Madame Capet* that we met. Watson Barratt looks like an eighteenth-century marquis. I always have the feeling he is living in the wrong period; he should have been a *grand seigneur*, a patron of the arts. His taste is impeccable and exquisite and his appreciation of beauty sensitive and discriminating; he always seems to me singularly out of place in the confusion of our modern scenic studios, coping with productions for Shubert musicals, of which he has designed countless numbers. Yet his gracious charm, his patience, and his gentle manners make him at home anywhere and win the respect and cooperation of even the roughest customers. I had brought back many pictures of the French production, and, since it could scarcely be improved on, we decided to approximate it as closely as possible. I thought Watson Barratt's costumes a great improvement on the originals and, executed by Hélène Pons, they were extremely beautiful and a joy to wear.

We started rehearsals with hope and confidence. Our high spirits, however, were considerably dimmed by the increasing gravity of the world situation. The Czechoslovakian debacle cast a gloom over us all. There was a feeling of foreboding in the air. In France I had been acutely conscious of an atmosphere of cynicism, a kind of fatalistic indifference, in the rapidly deteriorating morale of the French people. Everywhere one heard men say, with a characteristic shrug of the shoulders, *"Que voulez-vous? Nous sommes pourris!"* But no one attempted to do anything about it.

As the threat of a European war grew more and more imminent, I decided to try to persuade Mother to join me in this country. She was still a British subject, while I was an American citizen, and the thought of her being marooned in England at her age, should war break out, filled me with anxiety. She was loath to make the trip. To the last she was optimistic that the incredible folly of war would somehow be averted, and it was indeed hard to believe that, only twenty-five years after the horrors of World War I, mankind could be rash enough and wicked enough to embark upon another holocaust. She gave in eventually for my sake, and it was arranged that she should come to New York in October and be present at the opening of *Madame Capet*.

We were booked into the Locust Street Theatre in Philadelphia for three weeks prior to the New York première. The Locust is an abominable theatre, the stage shallow and grossly inadequate, the auditorium large and cold and remote from the players, the dressing rooms indescribably inconvenient and uncomfortable. I believe it was built as a movie house and converted to the use of legitimate attractions. It's sad to think of the many delightful old theatres Philadelphia once boasted —the Broad, the Garrick, the Lyric, and the Adelphi—all torn down. One used to look forward to playing in this charming city; now it has become a dubious pleasure.

The star dressing room at the Locust is a cubbyhole about six by seven feet, stuck in a corner of the stage. The noise is nerve-racking. There is no sense of privacy; it is impossible to relax or concentrate. There is just space for a dressing table and one chair. I had many quick changes in *Madame Capet*— seven costume changes and three wig changes. There was no room to hang the ample dresses of the period; they had to be brought me one by one from the wardrobe department in the basement. In order to put on the elaborate court-dress of the Louvre scene, I had to stand half outside the room, and, once I had it on, it was impossible to get inside the room again. There was no chance of checking one's appearance in a mirror; one just had to hope for the best. It is intolerable that actors should have to put up with such conditions. The nearest of the other dressing rooms is up two long flights of steps and has been aptly named "the cave of the winds." Few actors who have ever dressed there in winter have escaped without bad colds. The remaining rooms, up other endless flights, are equally menacing to health and well-being. The usual agonies and horrors of final dress rehearsals were enhanced by these added irritations, and I have rarely lived through such misery and despair.

We had a rough opening night. The cramped stage made the numerous scene-changes extremely difficult, and the scenery, while supposedly following the French pattern, was so clumsy and heavy that it took three times as many stagehands to shift it as should have been necessary. This of course added considerably to the production costs, while robbing the performance of the necessary smoothness.

Immediately after the first dress rehearsal Eddie Dowling grew increasingly nervous and irritable and communicated his fears to everyone concerned. He began insisting on cast changes, on changes of direction, and even proposed some fantastic alterations in the script itself. He made the mistake of attacking José Ruben bitterly in front of the whole company, and Ruben, catching this note of hysteria, became hysterical himself. Through strain and exhaustion he began to lose control, and shouted and screamed at the actors and the crew until his voice was reduced to a hoarse whisper.

The rumor started to spread that the play was doomed to failure. Disturbing reports reached me that Eddie Dowling was heard in various Broadway restaurants already bemoaning his inevitable losses. I had no way of verifying this, but his attitude around the theatre was certainly not calculated to inspire confidence. Yet the response of the public became increasingly favorable as the performance grew in stature and authority. We needed a calm firm hand at the helm, but our director was "shot," and our manager seemed to have a bad case of the jitters.

I had one very cogent proof of the aura of failure that had grown around the play. The Lunts were playing in *The Seagull* at the Forrest Theatre, and asked me over to the Hotel Warwick to have supper with them one evening after our respective performances. They had played *The Seagull* in New York for a respectable run the previous season, and Philadelphia was their first stand on a tour of considerable length. But they had never been satisfied with the performance, and it is typical of the integrity and insistence on perfection of these great actors that they wished to work on the play afresh and improve their interpretation of it. As we sat in their suite in the hotel, enjoying one of Alfred's delicious suppers—for he is a master chef as well as a master player—I was told how unhappy they were in Chekhov's play, how uncomfortable and ill at ease. They felt there must be something basically wrong in their approach to it which prevented them from enjoying the work, and asked me, as one who had had considerable experience in playing Chekhov, whether I would redirect the play for them. I felt, naturally, deeply honored and touched by this great compliment. I had seen their performance and had been somewhat disappointed in it, but had put this down to the almost insuperable difficulties of producing a Chekhov play under ordinary Broadway conditions. I was somewhat dubious of my powers to succeed where Lynn and Alfred felt they had failed, but even had I been willing to accept such a responsibility, I pointed out, I was playing and would be opening in New York in less than two weeks. The Lunts didn't seem to think this would present any difficulty. "But *Madame Capet* will close in a week," they said, as though that were a foregone conclusion. This estimate proved optimistic: *Madame Capet* lasted four days!

I got to the theatre early the Wednesday night of our New York première—it must have been about seven o'clock. As I entered my dressing room I saw an envelope lying on my make-up tray. It contained a notification that the play would close the following Saturday. This was the first and last time in all my theatre experience that a management has seen fit to announce the closing of a play before it has even opened!

The reception the public gave us on that New York first night was so thrilling, so heart-warming, that it made up for all the unpleasantness we had struggled through. I thought the applause would never end; the cheers and bravos continued long after the house lights went on, and I had to return to the stage repeatedly from my dressing room for added curtain calls. An enthusiastic crowd of typical New York first-nighters fought their way backstage, all loud in their praises, all hailing the "great success" that was unquestionably ours. Most indicative of all was the eagerness with which several representatives of the big radio agencies pursued me to my dressing room, vying with one another to make appointments with me within the next few days to discuss big radio deals. The insistence of this elite of the "bandwagon" almost had me fooled, and I thought perhaps we might be "in" after all.

The next day I didn't read the notices; I seldom do, unless I'm involved in the management and have to study them for business reasons. Whether they are good or bad, I find them disturbing. I never think of myself in connection with the parts I play, and I dislike reading my name in the papers. But I soon learned from my friends that, with the exception of the *New York Times*, the reviews had all been disastrous. Business had been brisk at the box office all morning, but as soon as the afternoon papers appeared, containing the worst attacks on the play, the lobby gradually became deserted, and the advance sale all but ceased. The following day the papers announced that *Madame Capet* would close that Saturday night.

The unmistakable enthusiasm of the public, for both the play and the performance, made the decision to close seem overhasty and tragic. Actors are glad to abandon a play that obviously has no appeal, but in this case the thought of so lightly giving up the fight made us all unhappy. The entire company, myself naturally included, offered to continue playing for the bare minimum, but even this would not induce Eddie Dowling to hold the play over even for one extra week. It is true that in Philadelphia he had asked me, through Arthur Friend, to take a very drastic cut in my salary. This Arthur advised me not to do, since he felt, and I agreed, that such a demand was premature. A manager should be amply prepared for out-of-town losses, and no doubt Arthur felt that to abrogate his elaborate contract at the very beginning of proceedings would be slightly ludicrous. However, I made it quite clear, even at that time, that, should dire necessity arise, I would be more than willing to cooperate to the fullest possible extent. Since dire necessity had arisen, I was ready to keep my word.

After every performance there were enthusiastic crowds at the stage door, but after the closing announcement appeared the crowds became so large that a mounted policeman was needed to clear the street for traffic. When I left the theatre I was mobbed by bewildered and indignant people, protesting the closing and begging me to keep the play on. But the decision was out of my hands, and I was powerless.

In Paris too the play had received bad notices; it evidently didn't appeal to the sophisticated taste of the critics. But in France the public is less influenced by the press. It insists on making its own decisions, and *Madame Capet* ran nine months to packed houses. In New York it is more difficult to combat unfavorable criticism, and it is very probable that our efforts to keep the play alive would have been useless in the end, but we were all of us eager to make the attempt. The cheers and applause that greeted us at each performance were unmistakable proof that the general public in no way agreed with the critics and found the play absorbing, exciting, and full of dramatic and emotional impact. No one could understand what made the management so willingly, so almost casually, give up the struggle. Indeed this seemed so remarkable that it gave rise to the most incredible rumors. I was even told "on good authority" that the producers of the picture *Marie Antoinette*, starring Norma Shearer, had something to do with the decision. I naturally paid no attention to such flights of fancy; it would have been ludicrous to suppose that even the most successful play on the same subject could in any way influence the fate of a lavish picture backed by all the power and money of Hollywood.

Mother arrived on Friday, too late for the New York première. When I met her at the boat I exclaimed gaily, "Well, darling! You missed the opening, but you're just in time for the closing!" She came to see our last three performances. The play moved her profoundly, and on the last night she came backstage with tears pouring down her face, flushed and excited by the amazing ovation the audience gave us, and refusing to believe that this was to be the end of a production that could rouse people to such a pitch.

But the end it was, and *Madame Capet* was no more.

CHAPTER FOURTEEN

I FELT thoroughly depressed and discouraged by the whole
Madame Capet experience. The ways of Broadway did not
seem to be my ways. While at that time I still enjoyed playing,
I could not bring myself to enjoy the hectic, almost hysterical
method by which plays are harried and hurried onto the New
York stage. Producing a play there is just like betting on the
horses: the opening night assumes the importance of life or
death; actual worth and true values seem not to matter; either
you "click" or you "flop," and the reasons for either are often
highly mysterious.

So I was pleased to receive an offer from a new firm called
Legitimate Theatre, Inc., under the management of Gallo
and Oberfelder, for a long tour to take place in the fall of
1939. They asked me to play *Hedda Gabler* and *The Master
Builder* in repertory. Their plan was an excellent one and was,
I believe, the first of its kind. They offered three attractions as
a package, to be sold beforehand to various organizations
throughout the country, and presented at suitable intervals
on guaranteed booking. The other plays they had chosen were
Golden Boy and *On Borrowed Time*. In my case the buyers
were given the choice of either *Hedda* or *The Master Builder*,
or they could take both plays if they so wished. The scheme
of course entailed a vast number of one-night stands, since the
idea was to bring the living theatre to towns from coast to coast
that had been deprived of it for many years. This appealed to
me strongly; I have always felt that the theatre, in order to

remain healthy, must become decentralized, as it used to be in the old days—and one-night stands have never held any terrors for me. I was to have complete artistic control of my own unit, and the tour was to be guaranteed for the entire season, which made me confident of securing a good company. Without any hesitation I signed the contract, since I felt this would be useful and constructive work along the lines I most enjoyed.

I then went back to Weston, to my plants, my animals, and my books, doing an odd job now and then to keep the home fires burning.

One of the oddest of these odd jobs was another excursion into vaudeville, again playing my old friend the balcony scene from *Romeo and Juliet*. This was in a venture directed and sponsored by Frank Fay, in which he assumed the role of master of ceremonies. He had implicit faith that the lost form of vaudeville must come into its own again, but he planned to present the bill on an eight-performance-a-week basis, rather than the customary two-a-day. He engaged Elsie Janis as the headliner, myself as the "class act," Smith and Dale for the comics, the Chester Hale Girls for pulchritude. He himself contributed one of his inimitable turns, and Maxine de Shone, a strip-tease artist, was thrown in for good measure.

In order to make the "class act" even classier, he secured the services of Robert Milton to direct the balcony scene. This seemed to me a waste of time and money, since I had played *Romeo and Juliet* so many times, and was afraid that Mr. Milton, the original exponent of the "pear-shaped tone," would only confuse me.

We had only a week's rehearsal and held our first reading at Mr. Milton's studio. Frank Fay had picked us out a Romeo; he was a beautiful young man to look at, but agonizing to listen to. The sounds that came out of his mouth had only the remotest connection with the English language, and none whatsoever with that of Shakespeare. Mr. Milton and I exchanged troubled glances. After the reading we discussed the feasibility of teaching our Romeo to speak English, even adequately, in the short time at our disposal. We thought of sending an SOS to Mrs. Carrington and persuading her to attempt to work this miracle. Then we put the young man on his feet, to see if movement would help to make his speech seem more human. But, alas, his body was just as stiff and awkward as his reading, and we began to despair. We both felt it would be fatal to let him play the scene. Frank Fay at first refused to consider changing him. I think he had rashly promised to give him this opportunity. It was an awkward situation. Mr. Milton and I worked very hard for another couple of days to help the young man, but it was obviously hopeless. I finally called Frank Fay and told him he would have to find another Juliet if he insisted on this particular Romeo. Fortunately Mr. Milton heartily agreed with me, and Frank Fay at last gave in. We had only a few days left before the opening, and I suggested getting Richard Waring for the part, as he had played it with me for several months on the road with the Civic Repertory and was one of the best Romeos I have ever seen. Luckily Waring was free at the time and gladly consented to take over.

The assurance that Elsie Janis was to be in Frank Fay's show was the determining factor in my accepting the job. Elsie and I had been friends for many years. I first met her in England, before I came to this country, in 1914, when she was the darling of London. She was playing at the Palace Theatre in *The Passing Show*, and the English people went mad over her. Many a night after the performance the crowd at the stage door mobbed her car, refused to let the chauffeur start the engine, and insisted on pushing the car themselves in a triumphant procession all the way down Shaftesbury Avenue, through Piccadilly Circus, and down the Haymarket to the Carlton Hotel, where the Janises lived.

When mother and I came to New York in 1915, Elsie and Mrs. Janis were on the same boat, and our friendship dates from then. The omnipresent Mrs. Janis was often a sore trial to Elsie's many friends and admirers. I remember once some of us got together and composed a rhyme of protest. It began:

Nous sommes les Ambitieux.
Nous sommes ceux
Qui désirent voir Elsie seule.

But none of us ever succeeded!

Elsie was always kindness itself to me. I remember one time, when Mother and I were desperate for money, I nerved myself to ask Mrs. Janis to lend us two hundred dollars. How I hated having to do it! Elsie was wonderful about it. "How disgusting of me not to have thought of it myself!" she said. It took me several years to pay it back, and when I finally managed to save up the money I was embarrassed as to how to give it to her. I put ten twenty-dollar gold pieces in a pretty little box— this was in those fabulous and well-nigh forgotten days when gold pieces were still available—and tied it to a toy ship in full sail. I left it at the Palace Theatre, where Elsie was playing at the time, with a note in which I said, "This ship has been a long time bringing back its treasure, but here it is at last!" Mrs. Janis was so impressed she called me up immediately to say it was the first time such a thing had ever happened to them. She had never expected to see the two hundred dollars again!

The loss of her mother must have been a terrible shock to Elsie. They had never been separated, and Elsie depended on her for everything. She must have felt completely bewildered and adrift when her mother died. She hadn't appeared in New York for quite a while, but during the fall of 1938 she gave a series of special performances on Sunday nights at the Hudson Theatre. She was of course the chief attraction, but with characteristic generosity she introduced a number of young people to the public, singers and dancers mostly, in whose talent she believed; quite a number of them owe their subsequently successful careers to Elsie Janis.

I went to the first of these Sunday programs. The house was

packed with theatre people, and we all gave Elsie a rousing welcome. It was wonderful to see her again in her inimitable imitations; no one that I know of has ever compared with her along those lines. These were no ordinary imitations; by some curious process of self-hypnosis Elsie actually seemed to become these other people, and she never imitated them in things they had done or were ever likely to do. She would give an unforgettable impression of Eddie Foy in Hamlet's "To be or not to be," or Ethel Barrymore interpreting "Yes! We Have No Bananas!"; and without the slightest change in make-up or costume she would succeed in twenty minutes in looking like George M. Cohan, Sarah Bernhardt, Eddie Cantor, Jack Barrymore, Fannie Brice, and half a dozen other celebrities. It was positively uncanny. I looked forward with joy to being on the same bill with her.

Since our vaudeville dress rehearsal was fairly hectic, I saw very little of the show that night, but once we started playing I often watched the other acts from the wings. I loved Smith and Dale; I've always had a penchant for clowns and found these two hilariously funny. Though they must have played their famous "Dr. Kronkheit" for well over twenty years, it seemed as fresh and spontaneous as though they had just thought it up. I admired the skill and craftsmanship that made this possible.

Since the balcony scene finished the first half, I was usually out of the theatre and on my way home to Westport by ten o'clock. I had decided to commute, for since it was early spring, there was much to do in the garden. On Friday nights, however, I stayed in town, since we had matinees Saturday and Sunday. During the performance the first Friday evening Dick Waring came to my dressing room in a glow of excitement and told me I simply must stay and watch the strip-tease artist from the wings. "She's absolutely *marvelous!*" he said, his blue eyes shining like a child's. I hadn't even known we had such a thing as a strip-teaser on the show; she had been kept a deep dark secret and technically wasn't even supposed to exist, for reasons of possible censorship. Frank Fay handled the whole act so subtly and so wittily that many people sitting out front weren't even sure of what they had been watching.

Not being familiar with the art of stripping, I was curious to see how it was done. I sat on the floor in the wings with Dick, waiting to be introduced to his new flame. A small piano was placed well over on stage-right, and Frank Fay started to sing various hackneyed songs, interrupted by a series of rude quips from his accompanist. I wondered what he was up to. After a good deal of amusing patter, Frank finally began on "My Boy Joe," only he had changed the lyrics to "My Girl Jo." He sang with great sentiment and sweetness of this girl whose rosy lips were unsullied by tobacco or liquor, whose innocence was like a dove's, whose modesty put violets to shame, and whose unassailable virtue was the despair of her admirers. I was just about to turn a bewildered look in Dick's direction when he suddenly seized me by the arm and hissed in my ear, "Look! Look over on the far side of the stage!"

Frank Fay stood in a sharply focused spotlight on stage-right, and my eyes had been concentrated on him, so I hadn't noticed that an arc-light had picked up the entrance on stage-left, and that a very tall young woman of ample proportions, modestly dressed in a long black velvet gown, had made her appearance. She glided about on her side of the stage in a kind of dance, accompanied by Fay's singing. He paid not the slightest attention to her but stood leaning in the curve of the piano, with his back to her. She was a dizzy blonde, heavily made up; her face wore a vapid though dazzling smile, and she seemed extraordinarily remote, as though moving in a pleasant dream of her own. At the very end of the first chorus she turned her back to the audience for a second and, without breaking the rhythm of her smooth, gliding steps, with an absent-minded air unzipped a long zipper skillfully concealed in her skirt and revealed a pair of quite wonderful legs and one naked thigh. She then disappeared. There was scattered applause from a few hep customers who began to realize that there was more to this than had as yet met the eye.

Frank Fay beamed and said to his pianist, "You see! Didn't I tell you they'd love that song! I'll sing them another chorus." No sooner had he begun than the blond lady appeared again and in the same absent-minded manner unzipped a few more hidden fastenings, so that by the end of this chorus a considerable expanse of her naked beauty was freed from its black velvet prison. This time her disappearance was followed by vociferous applause on a note of eager anticipation.

Once again Frank Fay pretended to be delighted with the reception of his song, and embarked on the third and last chorus.

Maxine de Shone, for that was the blond lady's name, immediately reappeared. This time she had very few zippers left to cope with. Remote, cool, immensely at ease, she paced about on her side of the stage like some beautiful animal, and on the very last note of the song, with a movement so slight and so deft that it was scarcely noticeable, she released the last fastening of what costume still remained, and, for a split second before she vanished, stood completely naked. The moment was so brief that it left me wondering whether after all it had not been an illusion. Frank Fay accepted the prolonged applause with grateful bows and smiles. Not for an instant had he ever given the slightest inkling that he was aware of Miss de Shone's presence; and since she, quite properly, didn't return to take a call, she might never have been in the theatre at all as far as he was concerned. It was a very clever piece of showmanship, and handled with such taste and discretion that no one in his right senses could possibly have felt anything but amusement at it. The only person I know of who took offense was Elsie's old Negro maid, Hally, who indignantly exclaimed, "If Mother Janis had been alive she never would have allowed Miss Elsie to appear on the same bill with one of them strip-teasers! The idea!"

Dick Waring had to put up with a lot of ribbing over Maxine

de Shone. He was quite infatuated with her. However, she was strictly unattainable. Off the stage her behavior in the theatre verged on the prudish. "If they wanna see me, let 'em sit out front and pay!" she said with excellent logic.

I had great fun in this company. Dick told me that all the real vaudevillians had been highly suspicious of me at first; they thought of me as a highbrow actress and expected me to be very lofty and distant. But gradually, as they realized my profound admiration for a job well done, and my genuine interest in their work, and observed that I treated them with the respect that they richly deserved, they began to think of me as a human being like themselves, and showed me a friendliness mixed with a kind of awe. At every performance many of them crowded into the wings and listened to the balcony scene with an appreciation that was very like reverence. Several Chester Hale Girls were there at every single show, and I don't think it was solely for the sake of Dick's blue eyes and curly hair. Smith and Dale were frequently in our backstage audience and expressed an admiration for my work which I told them was entirely mutual. One sensed a warm comradeship that is all too often lacking in some of the more highbrow companies. I felt very happy with them all.

I gathered the notices for the show had been pretty good, yet Fay seemed worried about the business. The second week he asked Elsie and me if we would wait for our salaries. He promised to settle with us in a day or two, but when the time came he was only able to give us half of what he owed us. The third week we received even less—a sort of token salary. Elsie and I began to wonder what to do. We both liked Frank Fay and wanted to help him. We couldn't bring ourselves arbitrarily to walk out on him; he'd had some tough years, and we felt he was entitled to a break. He gave us to understand that if he paid us in full the rest of the company would suffer, and that, if we would just be patient for a while, he was sure business would pick up, and in any case he had some funds coming to him which would enable him to catch up on the arrears.

After our third week's token salary Elsie and I never received another penny. We played the next four weeks literally for nothing. Neither of us could explain precisely why we did it; we decided we were just being "fools for Fay's sake," and it somehow appealed to our sense of humor. As each Friday came around we would say to each other, "Did you get any money?" "No, did you?" "No!" And then we just laughed our fool heads off. It was a fantastic situation. I think we sort of egged each other on and waited to see which of us would endure the longest.

At last, after seven weeks, Fay decided to close in New York, and begged Elsie and me to go on a short tour, but this we balked at. After much persuasion, however—and Frank Fay is certainly a good persuader!—we consented to play Boston for two weeks. Fay told us he had raised a considerable sum of new backing, and guaranteed to pay us for the Boston engagement at a higher scale and also promised to reimburse us for the weeks of free performances we had, for some unknown reason, made him a present of. He gave full vent to his Irish charm, and Elsie and I once more succumbed.

We both discovered on the opening night in Boston that, without taking us into his confidence, Fay had greatly cheapened the show. There were many substitutions in the cast, and the magnificent Miss de Shone had been replaced by a journeyman strip-teaser of such inferior quality that the act became dull, embarrassing, and almost vulgar. It made one realize what a fine art stripping can be, and our respect for Miss de Shone's skill was greatly enhanced.

The Janis-Le Gallienne humor suffered an eclipse during these Boston weeks. The Saturday of the first week we received half-salary with many apologies, but when, on the closing night, Fay presented us each with two hundred dollars in cash, we felt the joke had gone a bit too far. But we had only ourselves to blame and accepted the situation with the philosophy common to fools and angels.

While in Boston, at Fay's request, I had coached a young actress in the part of Juliet, for he was determined to carry on with his mad venture. Dick stayed with the show. They struggled through another couple of weeks and then collapsed.

Poor Frank Fay had not only put all his own available resources into this ill-starred venture, but had run deeply into debt. I believe several people sued him. Elsie and I, of course, never did. Apart from my natural loathing for legal procedure, I could see no point in suing someone who was obviously incapable of producing a nickel.

Several years later, when raising funds for the American Repertory Theatre, I wrote Frank Fay, who had been performing most lucratively with his imaginary rabbit for many months, and asked him to put the money he owed me into the ART. I got no answer to my letter. Just before the final break-up of the American Repertory Theatre, Actor's Equity had very magnanimously presented us with five thousand dollars, a gesture which was hotly resented by several members of the Council. The person who voiced the loudest protest was Frank Fay. On hearing of this I again wrote him a note and suggested that if he objected so strongly to Equity's supplying the sum, he had an easy remedy within his power: he need only pay me my back salary, and I pledged myself to turn it over to Equity as soon as I received it. I got no answer to this proposition either. I was evidently no match for Frank Fay as a persuader!

Preposterous as this whole Fay saga turned out to be, I have never been able to summon up either resentment or anger when I think back on it.

In recent years, Frank Fay's behavior has often made me angry, but for reasons that were in no way personal. Charming irresponsibility is one thing; fanatical bigotry is quite another. I find nothing persuasive about that.

Thanks to my Frank Fay escapade, the home fires were burning pretty low when I got back to Weston toward the middle of May. However, I didn't worry; my own personal needs are quite frugal and I always have faith that, with a little help from my own energy and resources, God will provide. But I was faced with the necessity of doing some work during the summer to tide me over until fall and the beginning of my tour.

One day Rex O'Malley came to see me with the suggestion that we should make a package of Noel Coward's *Private Lives* and play a few of the summer theatres. The idea of playing a comedy intrigued me. I reread the script and found it much better than I had remembered; indeed, I think it is probably the best play Coward ever wrote—with the possible exception of *Design for Living*.

Rex was very familiar with *Private Lives*. I think he had followed Noel in it at some time in England. He undertook the direction and secured an excellent cast. Since so many of the scenes are duets, he and I did a lot of preliminary work in Westport. We had a lot of fun with it. It was very exhilarating to me to have a fling at comedy again; I always enjoy it and am really quite a good comedian, but for some reason theatre managers are apt to think of me as an exponent of what my friend Noel Coward once termed the "Oh, the pain of it!" school of acting. I have always been irritated by this, for I believe that a real actor should not be limited to any particular type of performance. At the Civic I played a great deal of comedy: Goldoni's *Mistress of the Inn*, the Marquise in Molière's *Would-be Gentleman*, *Peter Pan*, Viola in *Twelfth Night*, the White Queen in *Alice in Wonderland*, and many small character-comedy bits in other plays. My debut in the theatre was in a broad comedy part in *The Laughter of Fools*, and my first real Broadway hit was in a delightful comedy by Arthur Richman, *Not So Long Ago*. But this side of my talent has been consistently ignored by the majority of managers and critics, and they persist in remembering me exclusively as a tragedian. It seems that in our theatre one has to be thrust into a pigeonhole.

We opened in Spring Lake, New Jersey, in a charming little theatre run by Watson Barratt. He made things very pleasant for us, and we had a most successful engagement there. The other parts were all well played, and I was particularly delighted with that entrancing actress Michelette Burani as the comic French maid in the last act.

Rex O'Malley was easy to play with; his performance was witty and deft. The audience seemed to enjoy the play immensely. We played it with a light touch. We saw no valid reason for turning it into the raucous circus it has sometimes become. It seems to me to be more high comedy than farce; its humor is based on human foibles and caprices, not on grotesque and arbitrary slapstick. There are occasional moments that strike an almost poignant note. To treat it as one long rowdy brawl between two impossible people is to rob the play of the overtones that give it value.

Watson Barratt was so delighted with the business that he asked me to come back to Spring Lake in a couple of weeks to play *Hedda Gabler*. I decided to do this before continuing with *Private Lives*, as I thought it would be a good opportunity to try out various actors I had in mind for the forthcoming tour. It was a daring gesture on Barratt's part, for most summer-theatre managers are inclined to think of Ibsen as box-office poison. We were both much gratified when *Hedda Gabler* proved even more successful financially than *Private Lives*, and broke all previous records for the house.

Rex and I resumed our *Private Lives* activities in Lawrence Langner's Westport Playhouse, and also played it at the Paper Mill Theatre in New Jersey. By then it was time for me to start preparations on *The Master Builder* and *Hedda* for the Legitimate Theatre, Inc., engagement.

My great casting problem was of course Halvard Solness. To explore the depths and reach the heights of this tremendous part requires an actor of rare stature. John Barrymore would have been my ideal, but I was forced to be more realistic! To find an actor good enough to play *The Master Builder* even adequately for the salary I was empowered to offer, and under circumstances that could not fail to be arduous in the extreme, was no easy task. Ever since I had signed the contract with Gallo and Oberfelder, I had been cudgeling my brain for a solution.

At last I thought of Earle Larimore—his name at least rhymed with Barrymore! I had seen him give many excellent performances in a number of contrasting roles while he was a member of the Theatre Guild acting company, during the years of the Guild's finest achievement. Physically he seemed a little lightweight and delicate for the part, but I knew him to be sensitive and intelligent, and I thought his understanding of the inner workings of Solness would more than compensate for any lack of heft. Moreover, he was also to play Eilert Lövborg in *Hedda Gabler*, and his slim distinguished figure would be an asset to him there.

Larimore was not happy in the regular Broadway theatre. He too had been spoiled by the opportunity to play a wide variety of parts in consistently great plays, during his long association with the Theatre Guild. He listened with a favorable ear to my offer and quickly decided to join me.

I engaged Matthew Smith, whose work had impressed me in *Private Lives*, for Tesman and Ragner; Peter Capell, who has since won a fine position for himself in radio and television, for Judge Brack and Dr. Herdal; Katherine Squire for Mrs. Elvsted and Kaia; Alice John, a favorite of mine since the days of *The Swan*, for Berta in *Hedda Gabler*; and Marion Evensen came with me to play her old part of Aunt Julia and to give one of the finest interpretations of Mrs. Solness I have ever seen. Also in the company was a young girl who had been an apprentice at the Civic, Louise Svecenski. She was to understudy and play the piano for Hedda in the last scene, since piano-playing is unfortunately not one of my accomplishments. Her fine musicianship, combined with her actor's talent, enabled her to give just the right attack to the wild piece of music Hedda plays in a kind of frenzy just before she mercifully shoots herself.

For the difficult position of stage manager we had a young

man called Jules Racine, who handled the innumerable complications that arise on such a tour with outstanding competence and good humor.

Three heads-of-departments, a company manager, and an advance agent completed our little unit.

Lawrence Langner very kindly allowed me the use of his Westport Playhouse for rehearsals, and in three weeks we were ready to embark on our long trek.

I had decided to travel by car. I have always much preferred this way of touring; it frees one from the tyranny of train schedules and greatly eases the baggage situation. Also one can evade welcoming-committees at ungodly hours in dreary stations. Such delicate compliments are none too welcome when one arrives exhausted and disheveled from a night in a Pullman.

My maid, Dorothy Murray—whom I had nicknamed Dot Doolittle, to her great delight—sat in front with a friend of hers, a very large and very black Negro whom she had recommended as chauffeur. Marion and I sat in the back with the two dogs: a young-lady cairn, Heather, and a delightful little creature, part Chihuahua and part miniature terrier, called Chico.

The company traveled by train. They had a company car, and since there were so few of them they managed to be fairly comfortable.

We left Mother in charge at Weston. War had, alas, at last broken out in Europe, and I thanked God that she was on this side of the ocean. I used to call her up every Sunday morning, no matter where we were, so that she shouldn't feel too isolated and abandoned.

I came across a copy of the itinerary in an old diary the other day. It was so staggering it made me catch my breath and wonder how we ever survived. In seven months we played in thirty-eight states and covered over thirty thousand miles.

We opened in Hartford, Connecticut, on October 23 with *The Master Builder*. This play, perhaps the greatest Ibsen ever wrote, has meant a great deal to me in my life. While I was playing in *The Swan*, on the several miraculous occasions when Madame Duse sent for me and we sat talking for hours, she constantly referred to it; I think it was one of her very favorite plays. *"C'est pour vous, chère petite Le Gallienne,"* she used to say. *"Vous devez jouer la Hilda Wangel!"* *The Master Builder* became a sort of "twelve-pound look" to me, for it gave me my freedom. Out of the special matinees I gave of it under my own management in 1925 grew the Civic Repertory Theatre.

The Master Builder has always appealed to youth. Much of it is a hymn to youth with all its ruthless, ecstatic, confident striving; and it is this facet of the play that young people find so exciting. Even if they don't understand its full implication, they are instinctively attracted to it and thrilled by it. Hilda seems to them a symbol of themselves.

When the Civic opened, *The Master Builder* took its place among the four plays in our initial repertoire, and was given many performances each season for the seven years of the theatre's existence. I remember the first time a group of youngsters was herded to see it by an English teacher of the Washington Irving High School. They came reluctantly, filled with apprehension at the thought of having to sit for two hours in the presence of a "classic." They left filled with surprise and enthusiasm; to them it was a revelation that a great play could make them laugh and cry and cheer. From then on their English teacher had no peace; they insisted on attending the Civic regularly, and became happily familiar with Chekhov, Shakespeare, Molière, Goldoni, and a long list of other great playwrights whose plays came to life for them in that old building on Fourteenth Street.

Again, throughout this tour, I was constantly amazed and delighted at the eager response of the young people. Their appreciation, their almost passionate gratitude at being given the chance to see great theatre, were infinitely rewarding. And I was again poignantly reminded of the shocking lack of opportunity there is in this country for them to receive the kind of mental and spiritual recreation so many of them obviously long for.

The best Halvard Solness I ever had was the man who first played it with me at the matinees, and who remained one of the mainstays of the Civic Repertory Company until its close: Egon Brecher. Perhaps he was not a great actor, but I know of few men today with his power, his versatility, and his sense of invention. He was a wonderful comic; his Toby Belch in *Twelfth Night*, his Mr. Jourdain in *The Would-Be Gentleman*, and his old doctor in *The Cradle Song* would be hard to match. In parts like Solness, John Gabriel Borkman, and Vershinin in *The Three Sisters*, he had a rugged strength combined with a shrewd understanding of the author's meaning that were invaluable. He had been trained for twenty years in the State Repertory Theatres of Germany, and there wasn't much about acting he didn't know.

In Earle Larimore I was faced with a totally different Solness, and I had to modify my Hilda Wangel considerably to keep the play in balance. Where Egon had power and drive and a harsh bitterness, Larry gave the part a nervous, almost neurotic quality. The fear of madness, the sense of disillusionment were convincing enough, and there was a febrile mental energy there that was definitely arresting, but there was little physical vitality. In *Hedda Gabler*, in which he played Lövborg, this lack of physical strength was not so noticeable, but I soon realized that the part of Solness was a great strain on Larry, and I was glad that, of the two plays, *Hedda* was the more heavily booked. Indeed, all during rehearsals I had been much concerned for Larry's health. He was far too thin and was troubled by a constant cough—a "tickling in the throat," he called it. I noticed that, although he was very pale, there were sometimes feverish patches of color at his cheekbones. I felt worried and insisted on his consulting Dr. Stewart Craig about his throat, and also begged him to have his lungs examined.

I knew that for the next seven months his life would be very strenuous, and he would need a sound constitution to stand up to it. He assured me that the doctors found nothing wrong with him, that I mustn't be influenced by his delicate looks, for actually he was "as strong as an ox." Dear Larry! He managed to overcome my fears, but later on they were to be only too tragically realized.

Our first ten days were spent in northeastern states—Connecticut, Massachusetts, Rhode Island, and Pennsylvania. Then we started south. From the very beginning we ran up against difficult working conditions. My diary is full of entries like the following:

Norristown, Penn. The "million-dollar" auditorium has no dressing rooms, no running water backstage, no way of hanging any spotlights—in short, *nothing* except a huge capacity for taking in money. . . .

Winston-Salem, N.C. The auditorium was huge and the acoustics bad. . . .

Rockhill, S.C. Went to rehearse at the auditorium. This one seats 3500. Entirely sold out. I went out front. From the back of the house the stage looks the size of a fireplace. All nuance out of the question in such a place. . . .

Little Rock, Ark. The "theatre" was a huge basketball court (the stage), in a vast auditorium. No dressing rooms, no lights, no running water, *nothing* for the actors! . . .

St. Cloud, Minn. Conditions at the "theatre" simply incredible. They had to hold the scenery in place with sandbags—no stage-screws. No lines. Could only use three spots in X-ray border. Only one small dressing room for all the women and a similar one for the men. No running water. They finally procured me a bucket of water to wash my hands in.

Now and then there are joyful entries on the few occasions when we struck an old theatre that somehow had managed to escape the wreckers:

. . . a very old house, *lovely* to play in—one could *embrace* the audience and really give them a performance. The dressing rooms are all in the cellar and *completely* lacking in ventilation —but I don't mind that; the pleasure of playing on the old stage made up for it. We all felt happy and relaxed.

But, no matter what the circumstances, constantly reiterated are the sort of entries that made the whole tour worth while:

The warmth and enthusiasm of these audiences are *wonderful*. It certainly repays you for any effort.

. . . and yet the audience was marvelous—warm, intelligent, and eager; deeply enthusiastic and grateful. *There* is the great reward! . . .

I don't believe I've ever struck such an audience. The house was jammed. My reception was unbelievable. One might expect it at an opening night in New York—but *here!* It went on so long that it was quite disturbing. They were so quick on the trigger—every laugh went over tremendously, every slightest point. There was an atmosphere of excitement that reminded me of the free performances of *Peter Pan* we used to give at the Civic at Christmastime.

In view of the great interest in the living theatre that undoubtedly exists all over the country, especially among the young people, and which has if anything increased in the years since the above entries were set down, it does seem a pity that so few adequate theatres exist. It is not the personal discomforts one objects to, and actually many of these vast auditoriums have luxurious backstage trimmings. My entry for Kansas City, Missouri, for instance, runs as follows:

Dressing-room *suite*, complete with blue-tiled bathroom! Felt like a Rockette! Would prefer to dress in a rat-hole and play in a *theatre*. Impossible to make any contact.

That is the point. One is completely out of touch with the audience in these huge buildings. The element that more than any other distinguishes real theatre from the mechanical forms of entertainment, the living communion between the public and the players, is almost entirely lost in such conditions. These houses that seat anywhere from three thousand to five thousand people may be all very well for opera, operetta, musical comedy, or great spectacles, but for plays that depend on delicacy of shading, on subtle transitions, on fragile moods, they are lethal. One might as well present a Bach suite in Madison Square Garden. It is unfair to the author, unfair to the actors, unfair to the public.

In most of these so-called theatres the use of an amplifying system is mandatory. But the voice of a great actor is not merely a machine for speaking words audibly; it is a rare instrument that, by the precise use of a thousand delicately graded tones, expresses the slightest nuance of thought and feeling. To subject such a voice to the harsh, metallic medium of the loudspeaker is to rob it of its human magic. In order to do his best work, a craftsman needs good tools—tools suited to the job at hand—and the theatre in which he plays can help or hinder an actor, according to its suitability.

Of course, if one thinks only in terms of "grosses" these oversized auditoriums are heaven-sent. How often have I read the proud boastings of press-agents announcing an intake— for some legitimate attraction—of nine thousand dollars for a single performance at the Des Moines auditorium or twenty thousand dollars for two performances in the Kansas City Music Hall, and wondered to myself just how much the performance itself was worth. The theatre at its best is a fine art and cannot be fostered by such circus methods.

If the American public is to be brought back to a genuine love for, and a fine appreciation of, the living theatre, there must first be adequate playhouses throughout the country in which such theatre can be seen and heard. With the advent and increasing range of television, many old theatres that for years have been used as moving-picture houses may again become available to touring companies; and any city that is planning to build a huge auditorium could include under the same roof, at little added expense, a smaller playhouse seating anywhere from one thousand to fifteen hundred people, to be used for the more intimate attractions.

"But what will happen to those delicious grosses?" I can hear some voices say. And indeed, in these days of murderous costs, the desire for large receipts is not necessarily mere greed on the part of the management, though that is frequently a potent factor. But the present system can never succeed in building up a healthy demand for living theatre on the road. The audience must be given the chance to appreciate the finer aspects of theatre art. To witness performances of plays of the type of *The Glass Menagerie, A Streetcar Named Desire,* or *Death of a Salesman*—to say nothing of the works of Ibsen, Chekhov, and Shaw—in buildings adapted to automobile shows, prizefights, or skating carnivals, is to miss, or at best dangerously to weaken, their impact.

The solution, it seems to me, lies in building up in each community a solid group of theatre-minded people who would undertake the sponsorship of traveling companies on a guaranteed basis. But the success or failure of such a scheme depends, in the last analysis, on the high standard of the entertainment provided, and on the possibility of its being shown under conditions that will not negate its excellence.

The Council of the Living Theatre is at last becoming really active along these lines, and it has the power to prepare the ground. It will then be up to the managers and the players to

keep faith with the expectations of the public; they may have
to be prepared to give more and take less. The astronomical
grosses occasionally possible under existing conditions will have
to give way to a less spectacular but more consistent intake.
The craft unions will have to come to their senses and use their
powers constructively. And stars will have to resign themselves to travel and to work for salaries which, while still
princely, are not fantastic. They will find a rich reward in the
gratitude and enthusiasm of audiences all over this vast country, which will more than repay them for their efforts.

The idea behind the Legitimate Theatre, Inc., was a good
one and appealed to my pioneering nature, but the organization defeated its own purpose by the low caliber of the majority of its attractions. I had been assured that the standard
of the other two productions would be at least as high as that
I strove for in my own unit. *Golden Boy* had opened first, but
for the initial weeks of the tour my unit covered territory in
which *Golden Boy* had not yet made its appearance. We were,
at that time, the trail-blazers, and the reports of our performances were everywhere most satisfactory and, in some instances,
ecstatic. Later, however, we started to follow in *Golden Boy's*
footsteps and began to meet with skepticism and mistrust on
our arrival in the towns we visited. The impression left by
the preceding offering was lamentable. On all sides I heard
complaints of shoddy acting, incompetent direction, and scenery that was disgraceful in its shabbiness. The two young
"stars" of *Golden Boy*—chosen for their "movie names"—had
apparently, even with the aid of a P. A. system, been inaudible
beyond the fourth row. This general dissatisfaction was most
disturbing to me, and created an atmosphere of doubt that we
had to work doubly hard to dispel. The reports that came to
me about *On Borrowed Time* were equally distressing. Gallo
and Oberfelder should have engaged a general artistic super-
visor whose business it was to insure the over-all excellence of
the productions. This they failed to do, thereby jeopardizing
their whole scheme. The only unit that came through with

flying colors was my own, but the ratio of one to three was not high enough to permit the continuance of their plan beyond this first and only season.

Once we hit the South, and as we went west across Texas, we started to have great trouble over the Negro members of our party. Besides my Dot Doolittle and the chauffeur James, there was Larimore's Negro valet. We had been warned that they might have a difficult time, but we none of us believed it could be as bad as it turned out to be. I hadn't played the South since my first touring engagement with Miss Barrymore. I was only eighteen at that time and was blissfully unaware of such responsibilities as maids—white or colored—let alone chauffeurs. But during the weeks we spent in this difficult territory I was constantly shocked and outraged at the treatment our Negro friends received. Not only could they not stay in the hotels—they had to live in rooming houses for Negroes, under conditions that no human being should be asked to tolerate—but they were refused service in even the cheapest and dirtiest lunchrooms, and no store would consent to wait on them. In many of the places where I stayed Dorothy was not permitted to come to my room, though my breakfast was served by a coal-black waiter in the employ of the hotel. This seemed to me singularly illogical. I finally discovered that, by means of indignant interviews with the various hotel managers, I was usually able to secure a "pass" for Dorothy, whereby she was graciously allowed to use the service elevator and join me upstairs to attend to her duties. On one occasion, though she had been given her "pass" the night before, she was prevented from coming to my apartment the next morning and was refused permission even to call me up on the house telephone to explain her absence. I waited for her for nearly an hour, thinking she had mistaken the time. At last there was a knock at my door, and when I opened it Dorothy was standing outside, in floods of tears, accompanied by a young whippersnapper of a bellboy who greeted me with "This nigger says she's supposed to come up and help with your baggage."

For a moment I was so angry I literally saw red, and I heard myself say in an ominously quiet tone, "What was that word you used? How dare you talk to me like that? Get out! And send the manager here immediately!" I must have looked terrifying, for the boy ran down the passage with the speed of a frightened rabbit. I rarely lose my temper, but when the manager appeared he received a most unpleasant welcome.

In one college town in Texas, when I got to the theatre I found Dorothy in hysterics and poor James with his shiny black face gray with anguish. They had been quite unable to find a place to sleep that night, and it was only due to the kindness and humanity of the college president, who invited them to stay at his own house, that they were able to find shelter at all.

I realize, of course, that there are deep-seated reasons for these things, and that the situation is complicated and delicate, but nowadays it seems inexcusable that such conditions should be allowed to persist. I know that to all Americans of intelligence and good will such practices are abhorrent, and, thank God, in recent years particularly, great strides have been made to eradicate this blot on our democracy.

I had so many interesting experiences on this trip that it would take a whole volume to describe them thoroughly. I shall mention only one or two that I remember with especial vividness.

It was in Abilene, Texas, that I received my one and only telephone call from Alexander Woollcott; he was stranded there with a bad cold, on his way to the Coast—and I suppose even the prospect of my company was better than enforced solitude! Although I had met Woollcott on one or two occasions, I was never a member of the "Woollcott set"; I am too shy and nervous to be anything but a damper on such brilliant gatherings. Groups of witty and scintillating people, all so clever and self-assured, give me a terrible inferiority complex and fill me with a vague uneasiness, and I'm sure that to them I must seem infinitely dreary. Knowing him to be abandoned and alone on this occasion, I would have enjoyed talking to Woollcott, but when he called I was about to go to the theatre for my performance and was scheduled to leave the town immediately afterward. He seemed quite annoyed with me at being unable to join him, and professed great disappointment.

My first meeting with Woollcott had taken place some years before at a supper party given by Constance Collier at the Algonquin. The Civic was still running, and, since Woollcott also lived downtown, he escorted me home to Fourteenth Street. We got on very well in this tête-à-tête, though I remember we had a violent discussion about *Hedda Gabler*, which grew so animated and enthralling that we sat in the taxi for at least an hour in front of the Civic stage door. We disagreed on every aspect of the play and held precisely opposite views on every performance we had seen of it. He was an admirer of such exotic and neurotic interpretations as those of Nazimova and Emily Stevens, while I insisted that Mrs. Patrick Campbell and Clare Eames were the only real Heddas I had ever seen. The smoke-filled air of the taxi became even thicker with our vituperations. With great good humor and enjoyment we hurled insults at each other, and when, in a final disrespectful outburst, I informed him that he knew nothing at all about the play—couldn't be expected to, since he was capable of reading it only in the grossly inadequate English translations—he flung his arms round my neck and gave me a resounding kiss, much to the bewilderment of the taxidriver, who must have thought we were nearer to murdering each other than embracing. We parted the best of friends. From that time on Woollcott never gave me a bad notice. I've often wondered whether, to judge by that experience, it might not be a good plan to insult critics before they have a chance to insult you.

From Texas we went on west into Arizona—next to my home state of Connecticut, my favorite state in the Union. I fell in love with it when, as a youngster of seventeen, I played some one-night stands there with old William H. Crane in *Mr. Lazarus*, prior to our West-Coast engagement in that play. The amazing combination one finds there of desert and verdant valleys; the never-ending pageant of mountains that change their shapes and color with the varying light so that the landscape has the fluidity and shifting moods of the sea; and above all the air, so clear and light that it pours into one's lungs like some healing invigorating elixir—these give Arizona a quality unique and magical.

After the performance in Tucson, which boasts a charming intimate theatre, built on Spanish lines and beautifully equipped, an actor friend came back to see me. He was on location, making a picture with Gary Cooper, and invited me to stop over for a couple of hours the following day on my way to Phoenix, and watch the shooting. Since Gary Cooper is one of my screen heroes, I accepted with delight.

The location was some twenty-five miles outside the town. We found it without any trouble and presented our pass at the gate guarded by state troopers. We made our way along the fringe of a cotton plantation and at last came to an immense cornfield. The corn had been harvested, but the stalks were still standing; rough paths had been cut through them, leading to a large clearing where the shooting was taking place. On one side was a big tent, which sheltered the numerous personnel from the broiling sun, and opposite stood a tall scaffolding on which were set up the cameras and the director's chair and loudspeaker. Hundreds of supers milled about, some on horseback, some driving crude wagons crowded with women and children. They were rehearsing one of the big sequences, in which the cornfield was to catch fire and the inhabitants were to fly in terror before the rapidly spreading flames. William Wyler, the director, was organizing the flight down to the smallest detail, so that all would be in readiness when the fires were started.

My actor friend saw me arrive and came over to guide me

to the welcome shelter of the tent, and there I was introduced to Gary Cooper. He was sitting on a rough bench before a trestle-table, surrounded by other members of the cast. They were having coffee and sandwiches and waiting to be called for the big take, which seemed to be imminent. Gary Cooper rose to his full, wonderful height. His high-heeled cowboy boots made him seem immensely tall, and I felt a mere shrimp as I gazed up at him. He greeted me with that quiet, modest charm that is world-famous. "His eyes are like fringed gentians," I said to myself as I shook his friendly hand. We sat and talked and smoked cigarettes and drank coffee for several hours—for the "imminent take" was constantly postponed by one mishap after another. I should think this endless waiting around must be the most tiring part of picture-making. I was glad of the delay, for I was much more interested in Gary Cooper than in watching a prairie fire with its customary stampede.

I asked Gary Cooper if he had ever thought of playing in the theatre. His face lit up with that slow smile of his, and he admitted that he had often dreamed of it but felt that he was really not an actor, in the theatre sense of the word, and would probably be incapable of playing anything but himself.

"You should have a play written for you," I said.

He muttered shyly that he thought he'd be too scared, and I believe he meant it. Everything about this man seems sincere and completely genuine; he has a modest sort of reticence that is immensely engaging. He speaks slowly in a low deep voice, and seems to ponder seriously over every word he says; yet there's an occasional gleam in those blue eyes that betrays a boyish sense of fun. No wonder the world has fallen in love with him. There are times when I think the world has queer tastes in its sweethearts, but in this instance I couldn't agree with it more heartily.

Dorothy and James were beside themselves with excitement at the news that I was actually going to meet Gary Cooper. They begged me to try and procure his autograph and armed me for this purpose with two pieces of paper and a pencil. As

I reluctantly rose to leave—for I had a performance in Phoenix that evening—I caught sight of Dot and James gesticulating frantically from the entrance to the clearing, where they had been told to wait. I then remembered my mission and produced the papers and pencil as I explained to Gary Cooper the joy his signature would give them. He duly signed and then walked over to the entrance with me and shook hands cordially with Dot and James. I thought my Dot Doolittle would faint with delight; it took her days to recover from her ecstasy, and I think this friendly gesture on Gary Cooper's part did much to wipe out the miseries she had endured in the past weeks.

Later, when the picture was released, I went to see it. It was fun to recognize the location where I had spent such pleasant hours. That particular sequence proved to be quite brief, and I couldn't help thinking of the days of preparation, the infinite care, the meticulous attention to every detail that had gone into the making of it. How seldom audiences stop to think of the grueling work that goes into these entertainments that they accept so casually.

We were to lay off the week before Christmas, and to our great joy this welcome rest took place in San Francisco, where we were to open for a week's run on Christmas Day. This meant that we could actually spend a fortnight in the same place. It seemed too good to be true!

I stayed at a delightful hotel, the Huntington, high up on Nob Hill. My apartment had a magnificent view over toward Sausalito. The luxury of being able to unpack one's things and get reorganized! The relief of not having to travel anywhere from one hundred to three hundred miles a day! And what a wonderful city San Francisco is!

Since I had a whole week without performances, I was really free to enjoy it. I've often thought that, if I had to live in a city, I'd like to live in San Francisco. It is such an individual, such a personal town; it has its own unmistakable flavor. Many of our great cities are singularly amorphous; one is much like another. They seem to have sprung up for utilitarian purposes only; they are extensions of the factories that brought them into being. But San Francisco is a living entity. Its vibration is rich and subtle; it is full of shifting moods and sudden caprices, like a mysterious, fascinating woman. I wish someone would start a real repertory theatre there and let me come and direct it!

My friend James, the chauffeur, in no way shared my enthusiasm. The steep hills baffled and terrified him, and of course I would elect to live at the top of the very highest! The first time we started up the last steep incline to the hotel entrance the back of James' neck turned pale gray with fright, and I was sure we were going to hurtle backward down the hill and land in a heap of wreckage at the bottom. From then on he always took the long way round and ascended to the hotel by a series of moderately graded hairpin turns that he was able to negotiate in comfort. Nothing would induce him to try the direct route again.

After this wonderful respite we once more took to the road, and drove up the West Coast, playing small towns and large, through Oregon and the state of Washington, all the way to Vancouver. Here we began to encounter snow and ice, and James frequently landed us in a ditch. He was not a resourceful driver!

At this point in our travels we were to make our first crossing of the Great Divide (due to the peculiarities of the booking we were to cross it five times in the course of the next two weeks!), into Montana. My faith in James' prowess was by this time anything but firm, and I decided that Marion Evensen, Dorothy, the dogs, and I would take the train to Butte and leave poor James to struggle over the mountains alone and join us in Helena three days later.

Helena, Montana, is Gary Cooper's home town, and, on hearing we were to play there in January, he had warned me to expect cold weather. How right he was! It was twenty below zero when we got off the train early in the morning. There was a wool-growers' convention on in the town; the hotel was filled with tall, narrow-hipped men, wearing ten-gallon hats and chaps, who teetered about comically on their high heels. There was also, prominently displayed in the center of the lobby, a pen containing several live sheep, whose presence added considerably to the stifling atmosphere and deafening noise of the place.

As we drove from the station on the icy roads, I resolved that James must be shipped East. The prospect of the next few weeks of travel, with him at the wheel, filled me with foreboding. The look of relief that came over his face when I broke this news to him was comical as well as touching. Poor James! I'll bet he was a happy man when he got safely home to New York.

Through the manager of the hotel in Helena I found a local youth, Jack Veach, who was highly recommended as an excellent driver and an honest and reliable person. He was anxious to see the world and was only too eager and willing to act as my chauffeur for the rest of the tour. Early the next morning he was all packed and ready to start off on what was to him an exciting adventure. He was very young and hadn't a nerve in his body. The more difficult and dangerous the road, the more he seemed to enjoy it. He sped along at breakneck speed round icy curves, and, while my heart was often in my mouth, I realized his skill and was grateful for his intrepid spirit.

Our route took us back to the state of Washington, then into Idaho, then back to Washington again, this time to Walla Walla (a name familiar to me from old vaudeville jokes— "when I rolled them in the aisles in Walla Walla, Wash."). For the fifth time we crossed the Great Divide and proceeded through Idaho, Utah, Wyoming, Colorado, Oklahoma, Missouri, Kansas, Nebraska, Iowa (here, for some mysterious and lunatic reason, we jumped to Illinois for two stands and right back to Iowa again), South Dakota, Minnesota, North Dakota, Wisconsin, Michigan, Indiana, and Kentucky.

By then it was early April, and in Louisville, Kentucky, my

fears about Larry's health were at last tragically realized. In spite of all his assurances to the contrary, I became more and more convinced that he was very far from being a well man. I got into Louisville around four o'clock in the afternoon and found an urgent message telling me to call Larry's room immediately. The telephone was answered by a doctor, who asked to speak to me in private. From him I learned that within the last two hours Larry had had three serious hemorrhages, and that in this doctor's opinion he was in the last stages of pulmonary tuberculosis.

It was naturally out of the question for Larry to play that night. The doctor advised keeping him in Louisville for a few days and then sending him to a sanatorium in Saranac, where he thought there was a slight chance of recovery, providing Larry resigned himself to staying there for a couple of years.

This terrible news filled us all with dismay. We all loved Larry, we had been worried about him frequently, but he had put on such a gallant front that this sudden revelation of his true condition came as a hideous shock.

Being at the head of my unit, and responsible for it, I had to take steps without a moment's delay to insure the continuance of the tour, which still had three weeks to run.

I first called up the New York office and told Gallo to cancel all performances of *The Master Builder* and substitute *Hedda Gabler*. I felt there was some possibility of securing an adequate replacement in the role of Lövborg, but to attempt to find a Solness at such short notice would have been impossible. I fortunately thought of Staats Cotsworth, who had been an apprentice at the Civic and had remained with us subsequently as a member of the acting company. I managed to trace him to Chicago and succeeded in getting him on the telephone. He agreed to fly down to Louisville immediately.

Meanwhile I was faced with the problem of protecting the performance for the Louisville engagement of *Hedda Gabler* that very night. Our stage manager, Jules Racine, was the official understudy for Lövborg, and as soon as I had made the arrangement with Staats we rushed over to the theatre and I took Jules through the part. He was a good-looking young man and he knew the lines, but his ability as an actor was in no way comparable to his excellence as a stage manager. It's curious what bad actors most good stage managers are. Now, under the new Equity contract, they are no longer permitted to act. Could Equity have been protecting the public as well as the stage managers when it thought up that ruling? In any case, I decided it would be wiser for Jules not to attempt a real performance, and I made a dramatic speech to the audience, informing them of the tragic circumstances and announcing that Jules Racine had very nobly offered to read the part of Lövborg for us that evening, in order to prevent the disappointment of a cancellation. This put Jules in a much better position; it gave the public no opportunity of criticizing his acting, and they thought of him simply as a brave young man who gallantly stepped in to save the day. Jules received quite an ovation at the end of the play, in token of the audience's gratitude.

Having solved this immediate problem by these somewhat Machiavellian methods, I went back to the hotel, where Staats awaited me, and we worked half through the night. The next day we had a 250-mile drive to Huntington, West Virginia. This didn't leave us much time for rehearsal, so Staats drove with me, and we worked on his scenes all during the trip. Jules Racine read the part again that night, and Staats watched the play from the front. The following day we mercifully had only a sixty-mile run to Charleston, West Virginia, and were able to fit in a rather sketchy rehearsal on the stage when we arrived. Staats went on and played that night; how he ever did it I shall never know. He was outwardly calm and poised and gave a really remarkable performance. I shall always be grateful to him for so promptly and efficiently coming to our rescue.

It was awful to have to leave poor Larry all alone in the hotel in Louisville, but somehow the tour had to go on. He subsequently went to a veterans' hospital in Saranac, and a little over a year later I was delighted to receive a call from him telling me he was completely cured. Unfortunately this turned out to be only a temporary respite, for he had a relapse, and by the time he returned to the sanatorium his condition was beyond remedy. He died shortly afterward, still a young man, and his many friends were deeply saddened by his loss.

We arrived home in Westport the last week in April. It didn't seem possible that the long trek was over. I felt exhausted, and the tragic circumstances of the final weeks had been hard to bear. But the tour had been a stimulating and glorious adventure; I was immensely encouraged by the results and felt more strongly than ever the value of such work. There can be no question of the existence all over this great country of an audience eager and hungry for fine theatre. But one should not make the mistake of thinking of this audience as easily satisfied. They are proud enough, intelligent enough, and perceptive enough to know a good thing when they see it; and this pride, intelligence, and perception form a challenge to the good faith and respect of players and managers alike.

If we expect to bring back the road to its former glory, we must be prepared to give wholehearted service in exchange for reasonable profits.

CHAPTER FIFTEEN

IN APRIL of 1940 the Germans invaded Norway and Denmark. My mother was overwhelmed with grief. Although devoted to her adopted country, England, she always remained a Dane at heart. She was born in Flensborg, which at that time belonged to Denmark, where her father held some sort of government position. She was still under a year old when Germany invaded and took over Schleswig-Holstein, and her parents had to escape to Copenhagen. In 1914 she left her home in Paris, when the fall of that city seemed imminent, to join me in London, where I was studying at Tree's Academy. For the third time in her life, in the Second World War, she saw the German war-god on the rampage. Her contemptuous hatred for Germany as a predatory force for destruction was one of the keynotes of her nature.

In June Paris fell, and it was my turn to weep. I can still hear the dreadful silence that blotted out the radio station atop the Tour Eiffel, and in a few moments the strains of the *"Seine et Marne"* were replaced by German waltzes played on a note of triumph.

My sister Hesper and her husband, Robert Hutchinson, were living in England. As soon as war broke out they started the Eagle Club in London, a club-canteen for the twenty thousand American volunteers in the British services. Hesper and Bobbie were in the very thick of the terrible air raids of 1940, and Mother and I lived in constant terror at the thought of their danger, though we were filled with pride at the fine work they had voluntarily undertaken.

After Pearl Harbor orders came that no agency other than the American Red Cross was to do military welfare work for our troops, and "Hep" and Bobbie offered the Eagle Club to the Red Cross in London. It became the first Red Cross recreation center and served as a model for the many others set up all over England. Hep and Bobbie themselves joined the Red Cross as volunteers and were assigned to the Palace Hotel in Birkdale near Liverpool, where they organized a club for GIs —one of the largest in the country. In the spring of 1943 they were transferred to Bournemouth and put in charge of a large officers' club there. Here they received officers before and after D-Day. They worked on right through to 1946, when the clubs were closed. They were both awarded the Medal of Freedom in recognition of their pioneering job in 1940–41. Many thousands of our young men think of "Hutch" and his wife with gratitude and affection. Now, as I write, the Hutchinsons are back in this country and have just bought a charming old house in West Redding, only ten miles away from me. It is a great joy to have my dear Hep so near.

I fought the Second World War on the battleground of my own tormented spirit. In World War I, I had been too young to take an active part, though at that time I longed to do so. Had I been a boy, I have no doubt I should have lied about my age, as so many did, and somehow found my way into the thickest fighting. World War II found me in a totally different frame of mind. Had I been a man, I should undoubtedly have preferred the despised heroism of the conscientious objector to taking part in the senseless and inexcusable carnage of modern warfare. On the other hand, how could one permit the forces of evil to prevail? The horrifying part about war, it seems to me, is that the forces of evil do prevail, no matter which side wins the so-called victory. I think of Susan Glaspell's lines in her great plea for a better life, *Inheritors:* "Have we brought mind, have we brought heart up to this place—only to turn them against mind and heart?"

Thousands of people, men and women, must have shared with me this spiritual struggle, particularly those who remembered, as I did, the grandiloquent phrases of the 1914 disaster —"War to end war," "War to make the world safe for democracy"—and saw the pitiful results of that first bloody "victory." I could find in my heart no enthusiasm, no sense of exaltation, nothing but horror, revulsion, and pity.

Now, when the term "World War III" is bandied about fatalistically, as though such a disaster were inevitable, I am more and more convinced that nothing but a great spiritual revival can save mankind from self-annihilation. I do not believe this spiritual revival will come in the form of organized religion, for organized religion has succumbed too greatly to the "practical," commercial, efficient trend of these times. It must come through a growing awareness of the universal core of all religion; through a sense of personal, individual responsibility, on the part of all men, to the best that is in them.

Each in his little way can contribute to this rising tide that will eventually sweep away greed, cruelty, vanity, corruption from this beautiful world, and allow man to realize the God within him. It may be a thousand years or more—as Chekhov says, "Time doesn't matter"—and perhaps our present civilization must be destroyed to allow a better life to rise from its ashes. Who knows? But I am certain that we should all of us raise our sights and aim high. Despair and skepticism are bad masters; love and faith can still work miracles; it is everybody's job to strengthen the spirit of love and faith.

In the fall of 1940 I set off on a lecture tour through the country. I had found no play I cared to act in or direct; and in any case I felt that to try and bring to young people a realization of what the theatre could mean to them, to foster in them a taste for it and an understanding of its power to enrich and embellish their lives, would be of more value than to work on Broadway in something that would merely contribute another hit or flop to the local scene.

I had never lectured before and found it infinitely more difficult and tiring than playing a performance. To appear as a character on the stage is to forget oneself completely, and I always find that restful. But to hold an audience "in person," to stand there all alone on a platform and put into one's own words one's own thoughts and convictions, to be acutely aware, as one never is in playing a part, of being the focus of all those eyes, was to me a terrifying experience.

As my confidence grew, I gradually became more accustomed to this kind of work, and in recent years I have done a great deal of it, but I have never reached the point where I can take it casually. Some of my friends laugh at these perennial "crusades" of mine; they know how I dread them, and think it foolish of me to persist in them. Perhaps they are right. There are times when I doubt; when I wonder if anything is accomplished by them, but in my heart I know there has been value in this work.

I spoke mostly in schools, colleges, and universities, with an occasional women's club or town forum thrown in. I preferred to talk to students; I felt it was important to "catch them young" and start them thinking along theatre lines. Again the great reward, the thing that made me know there was a reason for these long and sometimes wearing pilgrimages, was the eager interest, enthusiasm, and response of youth.

I continued these lectures into 1941 and then settled down at home for a while.

As usual I was busy formulating plans for ways to bring the living theatre to the people who want it most, not to the "limousine trade," which arrives late to a play after a dinner party and looks upon seeing the latest successes as a social duty, paying little regard to the high cost of tickets. The people I have always wanted to reach—and this was my purpose in starting the Civic Repertory—are those who patronize Carnegie Hall and the Metropolitan Opera House in the peanut gallery or as standees; those who make constant use of our great museums and public libraries; those who find in the theatre the same recreation and stimulus that are found in music, ballet, great painting, and fine literature, but whose low budgets make theatre-going under existing conditions a luxury in which they can seldom indulge. If this public could be reached and served, the "fabulous invalid" would be an invalid no more, but would grow strong and flourish in spite of all opposition from mechanized entertainment.

I talked over my plans with Margaret Webster, and we had endless discussions as to ways and means. We enlisted the interest of Uta Hagen and her then husband, José Ferrer, and the Blue Room was the scene of many conferences. There was no dearth of ideas, no confusion of purpose; the one insuperable obstacle was, as usual, the lack of money.

To launch, on a successful and permanent basis, the kind of theatre we had in mind, one that we all firmly believed would fill a great need in the cultural life of our country, would require solid financial backing; for such a theatre must, above all, be freed from the necessity of depending on immediate box-office returns and the favor of the critics, on whom these returns, almost without exception, depend. The consideration "Will it make money?" which prevents so many fine plays from ever coming alive, must be eliminated from one's way of thinking and be replaced by the sole question "Is it worth doing?" It was useless to approach the usual run of backers, the "angels" of Broadway, on such a basis, for their interest in the theatre is the interest of those who gamble solely for profit. We needed to discover a group of wealthy men and women who wholeheartedly shared our views and looked upon the work as a public service. To bring great theatre to the people at *popular prices* seemed to us so eminently worth while that we were all of us prepared to donate the major part of our earning capacities to achieve this end, but this in itself was insufficient. We needed a sum of money large enough not only to start the theatre but to insure its continuance for at least three years, by which time we felt it would have proved its worth and might very possibly become self-supporting.

During that summer, at the height of these discussions, which were fruitful in everything except the necessary cash, the Theatre Guild made me an offer which sounded interesting and promised to achieve something along lines similar to those we had been considering. The Guild proposed to present a series of revivals at popular prices. The plays were to be chosen from among the best productions of both the Theatre Guild and the Civic Repertory Theatre. The Guild asked me to serve as director of this scheme. It was not the Guild's intention to play these plays in repertory, since its aims, while often idealistic, are nevertheless directed toward financial solvency, and the true repertory system cannot, in my opinion, exist in this country without at least initial subsidy. However, the idea of popular prices attracted me strongly, and my admiration for the Guild's achievements, as well as my personal regard and affection for its two guiding lights, Lawrence Langner and Theresa Helburn, prompted me to accept their offer. Since there seemed to be no immediate likelihood of our acquiring the means to start our own theatre in the near future, Peggy Webster and my other colleagues felt that this would at least be work in the right direction and approved my decision.

The first job at hand was the choice of a play for the initial offering. I was presented with copies of all the plays the Theatre Guild had produced since its inception in 1919. With my car weighed down by this mountainous load of scripts, I returned to Westport for a week of steady reading.

I often feel, and it was brought home to me most vividly at that time, that the Guild is seldom given enough credit for its truly remarkable contribution to the American theatre. The Guild was the first organization in this country to present, with high professional standards, the kind of plays that, in the days before its existence, were considered by all theatrical managers way above the heads of our good American public, and therefore sure death at the box office. The Guild alone, at that time, had faith in the intelligence and perception of our audiences and could see no valid reason why they should be considered inferior to the audiences of Europe. It dared to present plays of the caliber of *Liliom, He Who Gets Slapped, St. Joan, Peer Gynt, The Tidings Brought to Mary, The Dance of Death*, as well as the major works of Eugene O'Neill, Sidney Howard, S. N. Behrman, and Maxwell Anderson. It is impossible for young people to realize how deeply the Guild revolutionized the New York theatre scene, and we older people are all too apt to forget it. As we do all good things that manage to endure, we are inclined to take the Guild for granted and to deny it its due of appreciation and gratitude.

I have always found it difficult to work on a board of directors. I'm afraid I am somewhat of an autocrat—though I hope a benevolent one—and I have never done my best work when constrained to share decisions and responsibilities. It is not that I am violent or difficult when working in a group— quite the contrary. I simply give up, and cease to function creatively. I can take orders or I can command, but I find it difficult to act jointly. This, in our present world of committees and board meetings, is a definite handicap.

In this particular work with the Theatre Guild I naturally held the minority vote, since I was the only outsider. On such matters as choice of plays and decisions on casting I was constantly overruled. The Guild, very understandably, wished to start this season of revivals with an O'Neill play, since its destinies had been so deeply influenced by his work. In this wish of the Guild I wholeheartedly agreed, but I was violently opposed to the choice of *Ah! Wilderness*. It was only six years since the original production of this play, with the unforgettable George M. Cohan in the leading role. I felt one of the older plays would have been preferable, and begged the Guild to consider *Desire under the Elms*, which had not been seen for nearly twenty years and which I have always considered one of O'Neill's most powerful dramas. They refused to listen to me, and *Ah! Wilderness* it was.

For the difficult part of the father they determined to use Harry Carey, who was chiefly known for his work in moving pictures and had had little stage experience. When I first met him I could see the logic of this casting, for he was a perfect type for the part: a breezy, lovable, warm personality, the typical head of a middle-class American family. There was something "folksy" about him; he was the kind of boyish-elderly male ever popular in our American scene. But a natural, temperamental kinship with the part is not enough. The big scene between the father and son in the last act, particularly, calls for immense skill. The actor must possess great crafts-manship, infinite technical resources, successfully to project the wonderfully human blend of pathos and comedy inherent in the situation. It is one of those scenes that seem so simple till you try to act them. This Harry Carey found out to his dismay and bewilderment.

It was fortunate for us both that we took a great liking to each other from the start. Carey's frank dependence on my help was touching and engaging, and I did my honest best to feed to him in three weeks some semblance of the stage actor's craft. Often he and I would remain on the stage for several hours after the general rehearsal was dismissed, and we would both go home confident that at last he "had the scene licked." But alas, the next morning there would be little im-provement to show for our joint efforts.

The other great casting problem in the play is the part of the son. Indeed, O'Neill always considered this the all-important role. We held innumerable auditions; I should think a good eighty per cent of all available juveniles from coast to coast must have suffered the agonies of a reading in the Guild re-hearsal room. With a good deal of trepidation, and after end-less arguments, we chose a young man called William Prince, now one of our most successful leading men. I have seen him do much fine work since, and I always feel proud that I should have been instrumental in giving him his first break. At the time of Ah! Wilderness Bill Prince was totally without experience, but he certainly made up in determination and hard work for what he lacked in knowledge. He absorbed every suggestion, every piece of direction, every lesson in timing and coordination like a thirsty sponge! He was immensely rewarding as a pupil and succeeded in giving a performance on opening night that won him general critical praise and started him off on his acting way with flying colors.

Another young man we "discovered" in this production, and who made quite a hit in a small comedy part, was Walter Craig. If anyone had told me then that a few years later Hollywood would transform him into Tony Dexter and select him to reincarnate the great Valentino, I would have had them searched for marijuana—but such are the mysterious ways of show business.

We assembled an excellent cast for this revival: Ann Schumacher, Enid Markey, Tom Murphy, Dorothy Littlejohn, and an alluring young creature named Dennie Moore, who was very amusing as the "temptress" in the café scene. As the bartender in this same café, the Guild insisted on my using (much against my will, for he was utterly miscast in this particular part) a most attractive young man whom they had under contract— Zachary Scott. He too was destined for Hollywood fame.

Our revival of Ah! Wilderness was, on the whole, well received by the press, and the performance was generally good, but it suffered, as I had anticipated, from following too closely on the heels of the original production, and Harry Carey could not stand comparison with George M. Cohan, whose expert showmanship and outstanding personality in the part of the father brought to the play the warmth and humanity vital to its success. In spite of popular prices, business was disappointing, and the Guild took this as an indication that the policy—in which I have always so strongly believed—was a mistake. It decided this policy created the impression in the minds of the public that the product must of necessity be inferior, a sort of bargain-basement offering. I have heard this argument used constantly as an excuse for high prices, but I cannot agree with its validity. I do believe, however, that it takes more than a couple of weeks to test out this policy and convince the public of the management's integrity of purpose; and I never felt there would be sufficient demand for *Ah! Wilderness* to gauge the ultimate success of the whole scheme by this one attraction. If the Guild had persisted in its original idea and had had the faith and patience—as well as the money!—to continue this series of revivals throughout the entire season, instead of being discouraged by the lack of immediate response, I believe it would have succeeded in gaining the support and gratitude of the public. Such plans take time to become established, and there must be consistency on the part of the planners. But after the disappointing results of *Ah! Wilderness* at the box office, the Guild changed its whole approach to the project, and little was left of those aspects that had originally attracted me to it.

For the second time I was overruled in the choice of plays. I pleaded for a revival of *The Cradle Song*, one of the Civic's outstanding successes, but the Guild did not think favorably of this idea. Instead it decided to present Sheridan's comedy *The Rivals*. This decision in itself was contrary to the basic scheme, since neither the Guild nor the Civic had ever produced the play; but I am no great upholder of the letter of the law and would certainly have had no objections on that score. The reasons for this choice, however, seemed to me unconvincing. Mary Boland had appeared at Lawrence Langner's Westport Playhouse the previous summer in *Meet the Wife*, and various people, impressed anew by her talents as a comédienne, had suggested that she would be hilariously funny as Mrs. Malaprop. The idea appealed to Lawrence Langner and Theresa Helburn and now prompted them to put on *The Rivals* and present her in the part. I had not seen Miss Boland in *Meet the Wife*, and, apart from a few moving-picture performances, her work was unfamiliar to me, but I saw no particular reason why her success in that type of modern farce-comedy should necessarily insure her fitness to play Sheridan's famous caricature. Such material requires a breadth of style, a kind of Hogarthian exaggeration of deportment and manner, a robust vitality, and a very definite sense of period, which Miss Boland struck me as lacking.

A most happy suggestion of the Guild's was the casting of the incomparable Bobby Clark in the role of Bob Acres, and I remember this otherwise highly unsatisfactory experience with affection, since it gave me the chance to get to know—and inevitably to love—this genius of comedy.

For the part of Sir Anthony Absolute the Guild chose Walter Hampden, a fine actor and an even more wonderful person. However, I was not in entire agreement with the wisdom of this casting. Although *The Rivals* is classical comedy, it does not, it seems to me, demand the finesse and delicate elegance of touch required by Sheridan's masterpiece *The School for Scandal*—a type of acting in which Mr. Hampden excels. *The Rivals* is much lustier, much more grotesque; its comedy is not wit but broad farce that appeals to our sense of fun rather than to our sense of humor. I feel it must be played in this key in order to succeed. It should have the flavor of Rowlandson's paintings, with their bold strokes and monstrous comment on the foibles of those times. Neither Miss Boland nor Mr. Hampden consented to play along these lines. I think they felt that I favored gross overplaying of their respective parts, and they politely differed. Bobby Clark alone caught the spirit of the play as I conceived it, and his portrait of Bob Acres was a constant delight to me, to the audience, and to the critics.

At the first rehearsals I had the feeling that Bobby Clark was slightly apprehensive as far as I was concerned, and he later confided to me that he had feared I would cramp his style and prevent him from giving full play to his inventive genius. He had no doubt been misled by my "oh, the pain of it!" reputation. He anticipated objections on my part to his bawdy, boisterous, uninhibited antics; but when he saw that, far from discouraging him, I happily egged him on to even greater liberties, he seemed to enjoy working under my direction. Not that I would ever claim to have "directed" Bobby Clark. My contribution to his unforgettable performance was limited to becoming a sort of traffic cop. I cleared the stage for him in the Bob Acres scenes, and arranged the action so as to feed and enhance his comic extravagances. And the miraculous thing about his portrayal was that it interpreted perfectly the spirit of the period; there was no anachronism there. The great American clown of the twentieth century was, by some curious alchemy of mind, perfectly translated into Sheridan's bumpkin of eighteenth-century England. Even the famous Bobby-Clarkian growls assumed an eighteenth-century air, and he wore his breeches and boots, his frills and periwig, as though his wardrobe had never known such objects as raccoon coats and pork-pie hats.

Like most great artists, Bobby Clark is a painstaking, meticulous worker. He was constantly bombarding me with questions as to the manners and customs of the Sheridan world, and I had to prepare myself for this onslaught by an intensive reading course of Fielding, Richardson, and Smollett. Fortunately, and somewhat to my surprise, I found such books as *Tom Jones*, *Roderick Random*, and *Peregrine Pickle* vastly amusing; I recommend them as entertaining companions that make much of our modern fiction fade, by comparison, into modest and respectable dullness.

Bobby Clark also demanded to know what every other actor who had ever played Bob Acres had done in the various scenes, and I spent many hours in the public library, looking up old prompt-copies and making notes of the different business indicated. Bobby would listen to the results of these researches with great attention. Every now and then his little bright blue eyes would twinkle as he recognized the comic value of some traditional gag, but his own sense of invention was so original, so personal, and so prolific that, as far as I remember, he

made use of none of this material which he nevertheless insisted on examining. I was thankful for my own vitality, for
working with Bobby Clark was far from being a restful experience. I have never known anyone so avid for rehearsals; even
I occasionally groaned when, at the end of a long day, he
would insist on going over some tiny point "just once more"
before disbanding.

Apart from our disagreement on points of policy and occasionally on casting, my relations with the Guild in this venture were most pleasant. Friendship and business are often bad
mixers, but such was not the case in this particular instance. I
was allowed a fairly free hand at rehearsals, and in *The Rivals*
Lawrence Langner was a real help to me. He has a great love
and knowledge of this type of English comedy, and his sug-
gestions were well worth listening to. We agreed that the gaiety
of the proceedings would be enhanced by the interpolation of
a number of songs, and we were fortunate in having some excellent voices in the cast—notably those of Donald Burr, who
played young Absolute with dash and charm, Helen Ford as
the soubrette, and Philip Bourneuf as Sir Lucius O'Trigger.
Bourneuf's wife, Frances Reid, was attractive and graceful in
the thankless part of Julia, and Haila Stoddard was a pert and
amusing Lydia Languish. I found the whole cast, with one or
two exceptions, cooperative and delightful to work with, and
was most happy with them all.

Since the salaries of the three stars were very considerable,
the running costs of this production were high, but the very
caliber of the cast promised good returns at the box office, and
the Guild decided to tour the production for several weeks. I
had hoped they would bring the play to New York for Christmas, as I felt it should make a good holiday attraction, but business on the road was good, and the Guild kept it out of town
till the middle of January.

December 7, 1941, found us on a train bound from Pittsburgh
to Toronto. The Bourneufs had a small portable radio, and it
was over this that we heard the fateful news of Pearl Harbor.

We listened in shocked silence to the details of this incredible
disaster. We were now in the war, and the importance of our
little theatrical venture was swallowed up in the overwhelming
drama of world events.

Still, the show had to go on, and the Toronto week was spent
in constant rehearsal and improvements. Lawrence Langner
had sent us a new song he wished me to put in for Lucy and
Sir Lucius O'Trigger. The lyrics were very funny, but they had
a number of rude things to say about Mrs. Malaprop, and
when Miss Boland heard them for the first time at the mid-
week matinee she was filled with ire.

I was having dinner at my hotel between performances when
John Fearnley, the stage manager (now production manager
for Rodgers and Hammerstein), called up in great excitement
to tell me that Miss Boland refused to go on that night unless
the offending song was withdrawn. I hurried over to the theatre
to deal with the situation.

This protest of Miss Boland's clearly illustrates her attitude
toward her part, and I think explains her unsatisfactory playing of it. Much against my will she had insisted on choosing a
most becoming costume in pastel shades of blue, and this,
combined with an exceedingly flattering powdered wig and a
peaches-and-cream make-up, gave her the appearance of a
Dresden-china shepherdess—a slightly mature one, perhaps,
but still attractive. This did not, in my opinion, conform with
Sheridan's description of Mrs. Malaprop as a "weatherbeaten
old she-dragon." On several occasions I had expressed to Lawrence Langner my disapproval of this costume, but, while he
agreed with me in principle, he was no match for Miss Boland
and allowed her to have her way. Since the "weatherbeaten old
she-dragon" lines were *echt* Sheridan, they had to be tolerated,
and no doubt Miss Boland felt that her charming appearance
sufficiently refuted them, but, when faced with a new song
which devoted two whole verses to a further unflattering description of the character she represented, she rebelled and
presented us with the aforementioned ultimatum.

I entered her dressing room determined to equal her in obstinacy. I hadn't the faintest intention of giving in to her; my "bosses" had given me specific instructions, and it was my business to see that those instructions were carried out. Besides, I felt no sympathy with Miss Boland's stand. An actress playing Mrs. Malaprop, far from seeking compliments on her appearance, should welcome insults and endeavor to deserve them by the faithfulness of her portrayal.

I'm afraid Miss Boland took an active dislike to me that night, but it is not a director's function to curry favor from his actors by betraying the values of a play. Miss Boland played that night, and the song was retained.

A few weeks later, and quite unwittingly, Miss Boland had her revenge. By then *The Rivals* was playing in St. Louis. I had been spending a few days in New York; I felt it would be salutary to leave the company alone for a while, and I wanted to gain a fresh perspective on the performance. I rejoined them in St. Louis on Monday, December 29. On Tuesday I called a rehearsal to straighten out a few points that I felt needed attention. Miss Boland was not feeling well; she had had a cold for the past few days, and I told her to rest. She seemed tired, and we naturally wanted her to be in good shape for the New York opening, which was scheduled for January 14. On Wednesday we again rehearsed for a couple of hours, but since Miss Boland still felt ill she was excused.

Theresa Helburn had arrived on Tuesday night to see the show, and Peggy Webster also turned up on her way to the Coast to visit her mother. On Wednesday, New Year's Eve, we all three were sitting in my room at the hotel, around six-thirty, having dinner. The telephone rang, and Miss Helburn answered it. She was perfectly calm, but I could tell by her manner that the call was important. She hung up the receiver and said very quietly, "Mary Boland has just been taken to the hospital with a temperature of a hundred and six—pneumonia!"

There was complete silence in the room, and my heart sank

as I realized the thought behind the two pairs of eyes that were expectantly focused on my face. The house was completely sold out for that night's performance; there was no adequate understudy; and the prospect of refunding over four thousand dollars of good St. Louis cash was grim indeed. Without a word I rose to my feet, put on my hat and coat, and headed for the theatre. I knew I was in for it!

Although I had been so close to the play for many weeks and, as director, was familiar with every line of it, as an actress I was totally unprepared to play the part of Mrs. Malaprop. Her lines are particularly hard to learn, since the sense of what she says constantly contradicts her meaning, and the famous malapropisms not only are frequently tongue-twisters but have to be delivered with great speed, assurance, and conviction. It's like trying to sing a tune off-key when you are naturally endowed with true pitch; it requires practice to execute with precision.

However, there was no time for thought, no time for doubt, no time for cowardice. It was then seven o'clock, and at eight-thirty that curtain had to rise and that four thousand dollars had to be properly earned.

Terry and Peggy were both magnificent; their complete confidence in my ability to save the day was a healthy challenge. They followed me to the theatre. Not a word was spoken.

The question of clothes and make-up troubled me greatly. I would have to use Miss Boland's costume and wig. There was no chance of finding any others, since all shops were naturally closed for the holiday.

I was determined somehow to live up to that "weather-beaten old she-dragon," but how to do this in the beautiful outfit Miss Boland had chosen for herself was quite a problem. I was somewhat younger than she, and the dress of that period has always been particularly becoming to me. I knew that if she looked attractive in it I would look positively ravishing. Fortunately her dress was several sizes too large for me, and in-

stead of allowing the wardrobe mistress to take it in I im-
provised some padding and succeeded in completely ruining
my figure. This result achieved, I concentrated on uglifying
my face. I was handicapped by having no make-up of my own,
and since it was impossible to buy any I borrowed some from
Bobby Clark, for Miss Boland's supply consisted only of aids
to beautification. While I was hard at work evolving a suitable
Malaprop exterior, Peggy sat holding the script and cued me
in the Malaprop lines. Luckily my scenes were separated by
substantial offstage waits in which other characters held the
stage, so I decided to concentrate on the first one and catch
up with the others one by one during the course of the evening.

Terry Helburn informed the audience of the change of cast
in a delightful speech which put everyone in the best of humor.

I emerged from Miss Boland's dressing room looking like
anything but a Dresden-china shepherdess, and was encouraged
by the shouts of mirth with which the rest of the cast greeted
my appearance. But as I stood in the wings ready for my entrance, still casting frantic glances at the script which Peggy
held before my eyes, I felt for all the world like poor little
Dumbo at the top of his burning tower, and was not at all sure
whether my ears would prove large enough to keep me from
being dashed to pieces in the ring below.

Then came the cue, and on I went. I was relieved to hear
much laughter mingled with the applause at my entrance, and
the response of the audience throughout the evening was so
warm and generous that I could have hugged them all for
the help they gave me. The house was so packed, and in such
good spirits, that under cover of the constant roars of laughter
I was able to catch many a needed prompt from the wings and
gave no sign of faltering or hesitation. During my first wait
offstage Peggy cued me for the second scene, and, after that
was safely over, for the third. And so I managed to get through
the evening without mishap.

When the final curtain fell, and I knew it was all over, I almost collapsed with relief and exhaustion. What I would have done without Peggy and Terry I can't imagine; if they had shown the slightest trace of nervousness or doubt, I'm sure I would never have had the courage to go through with it. It was certainly the maddest New Year's Eve I've ever spent!

CHAPTER SIXTEEN

IT WAS a fortunate thing for poor Miss Boland that the miraculous sulpha drugs had just been discovered, though penicillin was still unknown. But with the help of sulpha drugs her temperature dropped almost to normal within twenty-four hours, and the doctors assured the Guild she would be well enough to play at the New York opening. Meanwhile the tour had two more weeks to run, and they asked me to continue as Mrs. Malaprop for that period.

Once having overcome the terrifying hurdle of that first unexpected performance, I was able to enjoy the part. It was quite different from anything I had hitherto tackled—it would never have occurred to me to cast myself in the role—and I had a lot of fun with it.

I was glad for Miss Boland's sake that she was spared the strain of those final road engagements. It was bitterly cold, and we hit a blizzard going into Milwaukee that held up our scenery and costumes for several hours. The old Pabst Theatre was crowded with customers waiting for the curtain to rise as our scenery was being hauled onto the stage. I conferred with Miss Margaret Rice, the manager of the house, and suggested that we raise the curtain and allow the audience to watch the setting up of the show. This proved to be an excellent idea, and people were so interested in watching the backstage mechanics that the two-hour wait became a kind of added attraction instead of a boring inconvenience.

Our New York première fell on a Wednesday, and on the

Monday and Tuesday we held technical and dress rehearsals. Miss Boland seemed fully recovered, though naturally weak after her illness, and we spared her as much as possible to save her strength for the opening night. The play was fairly well received, and Bobby Clark made a huge personal success, much to my delight.

Due to the high running expenses, *The Rivals* played at the regular Broadway top, and the Guild decided at this point to abandon its plan of revivals at popular prices. I returned home to Weston to await further developments.

I had become absorbed in a production scheme for *The Tempest* and set to work in my studio to try to realize it in model form. Margaret Webster was much excited by my idea. *The Tempest* was a play she had often wished to direct, and the scheme that I evolved seemed to her an interesting solution to the difficult technical problems it presents. The weather continued bitterly cold, and my studio was none too well heated. I became so engrossed in the work that I often spent hours in the chilly room and would emerge from there shivering and nearly frozen. Whether this was the cause of my particular siege of pneumonia, or whether I picked up Miss Boland's germs from using her clothes and dressing-room accessories I shall never know, but the fact remains that her "revenge" was complete!

I felt so ill that I went to New York to consult Dr. Irving Somach. He instantly ordered me to bed, and Margaret Webster very kindly put me up at her Tenth Street apartment. Within twenty-four hours I grew rapidly worse, and at last Dr. Somach had me moved to Mt. Sinai Hospital in an ambulance. I remember very little of the next four weeks; most of the time I was in high delirium, and for forty-eight hours, during the crisis, I was given up for lost. I have never been one for halfway measures, and I had succeeded in catching the worst kind of virus pneumonia, which refused to yield to any of the sulpha drugs. I just had to battle my way out by the sheer strength of my own constitution.

It was Dr. Somach who really saved my life. For one whole night he never left my bedside. He had sent for two specialists, who pronounced me as good as dead, but he refused to give me up. Knowing the soundness of my heart, he followed a hunch and filled me full of immense and unprecedented quantities of aspirin. To his own surprise and joy this broke the fever, and I lay in such a bath of perspiration that the imprint of my soaking body went right through to the underside of the mattress. I remember none of this, of course, but Dr. Somach, and the three nurses who worked so indefatigably to pull me through, triumphantly described these critical hours to me during the long days of my convalescence.

I finally emerged from this terrible ordeal as weak as the proverbial kitten. When I was able to see my friends again, and darling Mother, I could see in their faces the ghastly strain they had been through. My mother looked so frail and drawn, she seemed positively to have dwindled, and I was filled with anxiety for her own health. Marion Evensen told me she had behaved with her usual wonderful gallantry; but I've always felt that the immense effort she made to control her emotion, the fight she put up to preserve her outward calm and not go to pieces in her terror of losing me, did much to bring on the illness that a few months later caused her death.

Dr. Somach advised me to spend some time in a more favorable climate, and I instantly thought of my beloved Arizona. Peggy Webster was planning a return to the West Coast and volunteered to take me by plane to Phoenix and install me at the famous Arizona-Biltmore Hotel.

I spent over two weeks, through the end of March, in this veritable paradise. The beauty and quiet of the place, the warm sunshine, the delicious air fragrant with the perfume of sweet peas, stock, petunias, and lemon and orange blossoms, soon brought me back to health and strength. Though the large hotel was very crowded, I soon discovered that, by avoiding the usual timetable, I was able to live in near-solitude. Everyone lunched at one p.m. I lunched at noon, and when the crowd

streamed from the swimming pool to the dining room, I moved
in exactly the opposite direction and lay on the hot sand by
the pool, completely unmolested, for two hours. While the
others took their siesta I took my walk—at first this consisted
of a feeble half-mile, but gradually I was able to get up into
the hills and spent many hours there, watching the ever-shifting
play of light and color on the surrounding mountains. My spirit
as well as my body felt renewed and strengthened by this magical interlude. I should have liked to stay there for months,
but, alas, it is an expensive paradise, and I was forced to turn
my mind to more practical matters.

I had been home only a little over a week when my darling
"Pepkin," Joseph Schildkraut, called me up. He had just read
a play that seemed to him a good vehicle for us both. Would I
consider it? If so, it would go into rehearsal almost immediately
under the management of Clifford Hayman, and was to be
directed by a young director in whom Pepi had great faith, Lem
Ward. He sent me the script; the play was *Uncle Harry* by
Thomas Job.

On reading *Uncle Harry* my reaction was not one of unal-
loyed enthusiasm. I could see that it had good theatrical possibilities (though they were rather too full of "corn" for my taste)
and the part of Letty—particularly her really fine scene in the
last act—quite intrigued me; but I doubted that the play would
achieve much success. However, I felt it would be fun to act
with Pepi again—we play well together—and his eagerness to
win my consent was so warm and friendly that I succumbed to
it. Pepi can be a very persuasive fellow.

I still felt a bit on the frail side, but both Pepi and Lem Ward
made things so easy for me, and were so careful to guard me
from all unnecessary exertion, that the rehearsals were comparatively restful. It never occurred to me that the play would last
beyond a couple of months, and then I planned to spend the
rest of the summer peacefully at home. How wrong I was!
Uncle Harry ran for over a year in New York, and for six
months on the road after that.

We opened cold in New York, after several previews. I was amazed at the way the play went over. Immense enthusiasm! The next day, rave notices. We were evidently a hit.

But that "next day" holds for me only sad memories. On my return from Arizona I had been much shocked at the change I saw in my mother; she had lost thirty pounds and seemed like the shadow of herself. I insisted that she be examined by Dr. Somach. The day after the *Uncle Harry* first night I went to see him to hear his verdict. It was a grim one. He told me that Mother had perhaps three months to live—four at most. It was cancer of the lungs, and nothing could be done to save her. His great hope was that she might not suffer much.

He had not told Mother the truth and begged me to conceal it from her. This struck me as a terrible responsibility. I tried to imagine myself in her position, and I couldn't help feeling that I should want to know. In my heart I believed that Mother would agree with me in this; the one thing she could never endure was not to know the truth. It seemed to me that she might wish to settle various things in her life, in her spirit, before going away. I thought of *L'Aiglon's* wonderful line: "*Vous n'avez pas le droit de me voler ma mort!*" Dr. Somach was firmly convinced that it would be cruelly wrong to tell her the facts. He based this conviction on long and varied experience, and I felt I must bow to his superior knowledge, but I can't help hoping that if ever I am in a similar situation someone will have the courage, and the faith in my courage, to let me have the truth.

It was mainly for Mother's sake that I was so grateful for the success of *Uncle Harry*. She was so happy and proud that opening night, and she looked lovely. I like to think of her as she looked then.

She had taken a little apartment in New York, having no great love for the country, and often dropped in to my dressing room and saw a bit of the performance. She was very fond of Pepi, and he was always sweet to her. After a matinee, looking pale and beautiful, he would escort us through the crowd of stage-door fans and with old-world courtesy seat us in a taxi, gravely kissing our hands and bowing low in farewell. It was a charming performance and, while quite genuine, well calculated to melt the hearts of the young ladies who stood gazing at him with soulful eyes.

For the first month after I heard Dr. Somach's verdict I noticed little change in Mother's condition. The doctor gave her several medicaments to take, mostly innocuous vitamin pills. He told her that she was extremely anemic and must try to build up her strength. She took the pills conscientiously and I think was quite surprised at their not working an immediate miracle. She had no pain, was aware only of a persistent slowing up of energy; she tired easily, and to one of her amazing vitality this was acutely annoying. Every now and then I saw in those blue Danish eyes of hers a puzzled look. I believe her instinct sometimes warned her that she was slowly declining and perhaps hadn't long to live, but her brain always rejected this vague premonition.

At the approach of the hot summer days, Mother decided she would like to get out of the city for a while, but she longed for the sea. She felt sure that the sea air would definitely restore her health. In accordance with Dr. Somach's instructions, I agreed with anything and everything Mother suggested. He advised me to let her have her way in everything, as nothing could make any difference to the inevitable outcome. Mother found an advertisement of a small hotel situated in Old Greenwich and asked Marion Evensen to go and look it over with her. Marion reported to me that she thought it a dreary place, but it was on the water, and Mother seemed to have taken a fancy to it. We drove her down one lovely day in early July. I had a talk with the proprietor and made all possible arrangements for Mother's comfort, but I didn't like the place and hated leaving her there. I went to see her as often as my work would allow, and it was unbearably sad to see the gradual but constant deterioration in her condition.

After a few weeks the poor darling had to admit that the

sea air did not seem to be having the salutary effect she had anticipated, and I realized the time had come when we should move her home to Weston; there I knew she would be surrounded by the love and care she needed. I applied to the local gas-rationing board for extra coupons to make it possible for me to commute. When I explained the situation to them they were most kind and gladly granted my request. In this way I was able to drive in to the performance of *Uncle Harry* in the late afternoon and return most nights after the show; on Tuesdays and Saturdays I had to stay in town, since we had matinees on Wednesdays and Sundays.

Marion Evensen stayed in Weston to look after Mother. I can never be thankful enough to her for her care and devotion. Mother was a dreadfully difficult invalid. Like most people who have enjoyed perfect health during a long life, she was impatient and resentful of her increasing feebleness; she fought against it stubbornly every inch of the way. It was most painful to watch the efforts she made to appear perfectly normal. Often, when Marion would bring her her breakfast in bed, she would be studiously reading her morning *Times*—but she would be holding it upside down. She insisted on trying to get up, and Marion would spend two hours getting her dressed and ready to sit out in the garden for "a breath of air," but by the time she reached the door she was exhausted and had to be put back to bed again.

Mother had an absolute horror of nurses, and Marion insisted on looking after her herself as long as possible, but at last I decided that the strain on her had become intolerable—by this time Mother was so weak that she literally couldn't stand on her feet—and I made up my mind to call in a nurse. I was immensely fortunate in securing the help of my precious Greenie. She had just come off a case the night before I telephoned, and moved out to my house that very day.

Still Mother had no pain; Dr. Somach said it was a most merciful miracle. For long stretches she would lie in a semiconscious state, and she had no awareness of time. She never seemed to know whether I was leaving or had just come home. She was so feeble that Greenie had to treat her like a child, and it was a godsend to know she was in such capable and gentle hands.

Mother lived at least a month longer than any doctor had conceived possible; her heart would not give in. She just faded away gradually, slowly, inevitably. One morning, about four o'clock, she quietly went to sleep for the last time.

I stood looking down at Mother as she lay in the little funeral chapel surrounded by masses of gay vivid flowers sent by her many friends, and thought I had never seen anyone look so serene and happy.

It was the first time I had been in the presence of death, and I had dreaded it, but it was not at all as I had expected. Suddenly I thought of those simple and profound words in the Wisdom of Solomon, and at last sensed their truth:

But the souls of the righteous are in the hand of God, and there shall no torment touch them.
In the sight of the unwise they seemed to die: and their departure is taken for misery,
And their going from us to be utter destruction: but they are in peace.

CHAPTER SEVENTEEN

IT WAS hard to go back that evening and play my part in *Uncle Harry*. The company were all wonderfully helpful and very kindly left me to myself. I think they were surprised that I turned up as usual, but, apart from the strict discipline the theatre imposes on one, I felt Mother would have wanted me to carry on; she was never a shirker herself and would have been disappointed had I not followed her example.

It was impossible for me to believe Mother was really gone; it still is. I think of her as being somewhere in Europe, and that I ought to write to her. It's strange how one misses having to perform those little duties that may have seemed burdensome at times. When there is no longer any need for them, one realizes how precious they really were and what a privilege it was to have to do them.

I felt the need of new work; the long run of *Uncle Harry*, which promised to be endless, was beginning to make me restless. Pepi Schildkraut and I were eager to put on some special matinees of other plays. We discussed presenting a series of dramatic works representative of the various Allied countries, as war-benefits; but the insuperable obstacles put in our way by the rules and regulations of the craft unions forced us to abandon such a plan.

That summer I gained a small companion who proved a great comfort to me and has remained so to this hour. On the last day of July one of the cairns, Sally, gave birth to a fine litter of four plump, furry little babies. Sally was a "wheaten" cairn—a real platinum blonde. I had her mated with a red-head, a champion dog from the famous Tapscot cairn kennels. Days before her own eyes even opened I recognized my little friend. She was red like her father, for all the world like a tiny fox cub, so I called her Vixen. As soon as she was weaned she and I became inseparable. Since the death of my old dog Tosca—who had been part and parcel of my life for fifteen years—although I had many cairns around the place, as well as the adorable little Chico, and loved them all, I had had no "personal dog," no little shadow that was an extension of myself. This Vixen became. At eight weeks old she started coming with me to the theatre and soon became a veteran of the dressing room. Now she is a slightly portly lady, getting on for ten, and at this moment is lying near me in a disreputable old chair whose broken springs form a neat hollow that exactly fits her plump little body—I dare not have it reupholstered for fear of interfering with Vixen's comfort. Each time I write her name she flicks an ear in my direction and looks at me with her sharp brown eyes, as much as to say, "See that you do me justice!" But how could I ever possibly do that? What hostages to fortune such creatures are—and yet, one wouldn't be without them. Anyone who has really had a personal dog—and I pity those who haven't—will understand what Vixen means to me.

All that fall and winter Vixen and I walked from our Twelfth-Street apartment to the Hudson Theatre, where *Uncle Harry* persistently endured, and sometimes all the way home again. The staunch, chunky little figure, with its bristling red hair, ferocious whiskers, black shiny nose, alert ears, and formidable bark accompanied me everywhere. I was immensely grateful for that trusting little presence.

Uncle Harry ran right on into its second summer, and we then mercifully closed for a couple of months before setting out on tour. Pepi Schildkraut and I were already searching about for another play we might do together when *Uncle Harry* should be no more, and I suggested a revival of *The Cherry*

Orchard, with Pepi as Gaev and myself as Lubov Andreyevna. But we were not satisfied with the Constance Garnett version, and, during July and August, Margaret Webster and I set to work on making a new one with the help of an old friend of mine, Irina Skariatina. I had met Irina years before in Chicago, while I was playing there in *The Swan*. I was studying Russian at the time, and Irina volunteered to give me lessons. I felt she would have a rare understanding of this particular Chekhov play. She herself belonged to the old Russian aristocracy and had for many years been an exile from her country. She had written several successful books on Russia, mostly memoirs of her youth under the old regime, but since in these writings she had shown a deep love for the country itself—regardless of its government—and had avoided the usual bitter diatribes against the Soviet Revolution—in spite of the fact that it had deprived her of wealth, position, and motherland—the Soviet government had permitted her to return there for occasional visits, so that she was also familiar to some extent with the "New Russia" that Chekhov so strangely anticipates in certain passages of his great play.

We spent hours in that summer of 1943 sitting out in the garden, Irina reading aloud from the Russian text and giving us the absolutely literal translation of the meaning, which Peggy and I would put into what we hoped were suitable English phrases. In the evenings we tried the result of our labors out on Marion Evensen, who contributed helpful comment and criticism. We had great fun working in this way, and the gentle, compassionate, humorous spirit of Chekhov seemed to hover round us, encouraging us with good-natured tolerance.

By the time we started rehearsals for the tour of *Uncle Harry* our script of *The Cherry Orchard* was ready, and we submitted it to Mrs. Carly Wharton, who had indicated an interest in producing it.

The first *Uncle Harry* engagements were in the vicinity of New York City, and one week end Carly Wharton arranged a reading of *The Cherry Orchard* for potential backers. This business of auditions to lure money from Broadway angels was new to me, and I found it strange and rather unpleasant, but Carly handled the situation with her usual tact and made it as easy as possible for me. I read the play aloud to some dozen people, who were all extremely nice, and most of whom agreed to take part in the financing. The tour of *Uncle Harry* was booked until late December, and we decided to put *The Cherry Orchard* into rehearsal immediately thereafter.

My association with Carly Wharton was most delightful. I have referred to her ever since as "my favorite boss." There is something so honest and direct about her. She is a real gentle-woman, and the atmosphere of her office reflects her own courtesy and integrity. It is a pleasure for actors to be inter-viewed by her. She avoids assiduously the usual managerial practice of keeping people waiting for countless hours; her appointments run strictly according to schedule. She never brushes an actor off with vague, ambiguous promises or eva-sions; if she knows she has no intention of using someone, she tells him so quite frankly, and in this way rouses no false hopes and saves both his time and her own. Her warmth, humanity, and good nature endear her to everyone she has dealings with and make even her adverse decisions comparatively painless. And it is such a comfort, in the devious world of the theatre, to meet someone who honestly means what she says. There is no hanky-panky about Carly Wharton; she is one of the finest human beings it has ever been my privilege to work for.

Carly and I, with the invaluable help of Peggy Webster, assembled a fine cast for our production. Stefan Schnabel played Lopahin; Edward Franz, Trofimov; Katherine Emery, Varya (the part I originally played at the Civic Repertory). Lois Hall was a charming little Anya, Carl Benton Reid a fine Pishchik, and Pepi and I insisted on Leona Roberts for Char-lotta, the eccentric German governess. Miss Roberts, known as Robbie among her friends and colleagues, was playing the im-portant part of Nona, the maid, in *Uncle Harry*. During her long association with the Civic, she created the part of Char-

lotta with great success. She was an invaluable member of the
Civic Repertory Company. Her long list of characterizations
at the old Fourteenth Street Theatre forms a gallery of portraits of such range and variety that I can think of no other
character actress in this country with a comparable record. And
in none of these vivid creations was there ever a trace of Robbie herself; she had the rare faculty of completely transforming
herself to suit the demands of the various roles. It was not only
a question of make-up either—she seemed to *become* these
other people: the Nurse in *Romeo and Juliet,* fat, bawdy,
unctuous; the Vicaress in *The Cradle Song,* crotchety yet
somehow lovable; Prudence in *Camille,* raucous and predatory;
the grandmother in *Inheritors,* dry, humorous, and shrewd;
Truus in *The Good Hope,* stark and tragic. These are only a
few of the many women Robbie brought to life on the stage,
and I can still see them all as clearly as though I had known
them as human beings. Her talent was purely instinctive, and
woe to the director who tampered with it and tried to clutter
it up with elaborate analyses and "motivations." To one unfamiliar with Robbie's way of working, the results at early
rehearsals might well be disappointing and somewhat puzzling,
but gradually the part would take hold of her and claim her for
its own, and her impact on an audience was nothing short of
miraculous.

I could see a dubious look in Carly Wharton's eye as she
watched Robbie during the early stages of our work on *The
Cherry Orchard.* I begged her to have patience and faith in
my knowledge of the ultimate result, and when she heard the
delighted laughter of the New Haven first-nighters, and the
burst of applause that followed Charlotta's difficult scene in
the second act, she had to admit that I had not misled her.

For the important part of the old servant, Firs, we engaged
"Bogie" Andrews, an entrancing little gnome of a man, then
eighty-six years of age. During our first interview with him in
Carly's office, Bogie suggested, with a twinkle in his eye, that
we postpone the production for six months, as he was still

rather young for the part—Firs is supposed to be eighty-seven! At the dress rehearsal I had quite a tussle with Bogie over his make-up. He felt it necessary, no doubt in order to make up for his lack of age, to cover his cute little rosy face with heavy lines and shadows. I told him I felt that eighty-six-and-a-half might be sufficiently convincing.

This was my first experience of directing a Chekhov play under regular commercial conditions, and, as I had expected, it was by no means easy. A group of actors accustomed to working together over a period of years, and familiar with one another's methods and those of their director, have a distinct advantage over a company assembled for the one play only, strangers to one another, and restricted to a bare three and a half weeks of rehearsal time. The quality of a Chekhov production depends so tremendously on what goes on beneath the lines, on the almost casual interplay between the various characters, on a truth and simplicity so thoroughly understood and digested that it becomes effective in a subtle unobtrusive way in no sense dependent on the usual theatrical externals. It is a sort of flavor that permeates the whole ensemble—a mood, an aura so delicate and special that the slightest false note on the part of even the most seemingly insignificant player in the cast can ruthlessly dispel it. In Chekhov's plays it is essential that each unit serve the whole, with no regard for its own separate interests. I believe it is for this reason that most "all-star" productions of Chekhov so frequently betray his intention. Whenever I read a set of notices praising to the skies the acting, the scenery, the costumes, and the direction, and dismissing Chekhov as a depressing, ineffectual dreamer whose play, like a museum piece, has no relation to life as we know it, I know that once again he has been betrayed. Such performances may seem brilliant, colorful, glamorous, if you like, but they are not Chekhov. The stars of the stage may shine in all their box-office glory, but the true, modest, enduring star of Chekhov will have suffered a temporary eclipse.

It is difficult, in the short time at one's disposal, to make this clear to actors unfamiliar with the material. Chekhov makes rare and unusual demands on his players, and the tools he provides, as far as words and "effective" scenes are concerned, seem disconcertingly elusive. Pepi Schildkraut, who was new to Chekhov, was often sorely puzzled. The heartbreaking farewell to the old house in the last act, when Lubov and Gaev stand in the nursery weeping silently, bereft of words, is a case in point. Pepi would often exclaim, "But, Evale, how does one *play* this scene? I have nothing to *say*—nothing to *do*." He was right; Chekhov provides no words, no specific action. Instead of doing, one must simply be, and that is no easy matter. There are no shortcuts, no props, no half-measures. Chekhov creates the mood, and it is up to the actor to succumb to that mood so completely, so uncompromisingly, that all "acting," in the usual sense of the word, is unnecessary. The situation simply is. It is for this reason that Chekhov's plays should, ideally, be presented under the repertory system, for to demand of the actor eight times a week the intense concentration that will stimulate his imagination to this essential pitch of truth is demanding the impossible. The performances inevitably vary; such powers are not responsive to assembly-line methods.

In the days of the Civic we were able, from the very first rehearsal, to surround ourselves with the furniture, properties, even an approximation of the lighting, in which we were to live these plays before the public. On the Broadway of 1944 we had to work right up to our only dress rehearsal, in New Haven, on a bare stage, with the usual allowance of straight-backed chairs inadequately indicating the old-fashioned, well-worn comfortable furniture to be used at performance—furniture that should give the sense of having been lived with for a lifetime and thus contribute to the ease and familiarity of the actor's playing—with no properties of any sort, under the harsh glare of the thousand-watt regulation rehearsal light, which is a torment to actors and director alike.

Gaev spends most of the first act reclining on a chaise-longue. His use of this piece of furniture is an essential part of his whole character; one should feel that he has reclined there with indolent grace, sucking on his ever-present caramel, only vaguely aware of the general conversation around him, for years. That chaise-longue has become molded to his body; he is familiar with every threadbare spot in its upholstery, with every detail of its carving. It is an old friend that welcomes, understands, and condones his idiosyncrasies, his incorrigible ineffectuality. At our rehearsals two straight chairs placed side by side had to suffice.

Old Firs dies, in the last moments of the play, on a dilapidated sofa in the abandoned nursery. In this overwhelmingly touching scene, so simple and eliminated, every line of the actor's body must express the gentle, nostalgic mood. He goes to sleep there like a faithful old dog that has been left behind by its masters. Bogie Andrews had to try to work this out on one of the same straight-backed chairs, with his feet precariously propped up on a packing-case which the stage manager had triumphantly unearthed from a pile of rubbish in the basement. This sort of thing means that all the "fining-up" of one's performance has to be done before the public, during the out-of-town try-out. There is never any opportunity to stop and experiment with various positions, various movements, to repeat certain passages over and over again until one achieves the pattern that seems exactly right; for once the curtain has risen on the opening night one is never permitted to rehearse in the furniture, or make use of the properties, reserved for the actual performance, without calling the stage crew. This naturally means overtime, and few managements ever have the financial margin that would permit such extravagance. To attempt to evoke the myriad moods and nuances of this great play under such handicaps is indeed a challenge. I often wonder how we ever succeed in our theatre in achieving even passable artistic results. Existing conditions are obviously designed to benefit everyone but the artist.

But to our great joy, in spite of these many obstacles which prevented the performance from achieving the quality of perfection which was our aim, *The Cherry Orchard* met with great success and acclaim wherever we played it. I was at first very nervous at attempting Lubov Andreyevna, and was most grateful to Peggy Webster, who, at my request, relieved me, for the latter part of rehearsals, of my duties as director and so left me free to absorb Lubov in peace.

Although we were appreciative of *Uncle Harry*, Pepi and I couldn't help being delighted that *The Cherry Orchard*, on its pre-Broadway appearance in Boston, drew far greater box-office returns than the Thomas Job opus. Pepi loved playing Gaev and was most engaging in the part. I am always happy to play with Pepi Schildkraut. He has the reputation for being "difficult," and in the old days he *was* a bit of a scoundrel in the theatre! But with me he has always been a darling. I think this is due more to his devotion to his father than to any feeling he has for me personally. His father—that great actor!—had a deep affection and respect for me and always told Pepi to listen to me and follow my advice. There is much of the child in Pepi, and that is what makes him so endearing. His naughtiness is no more significant than that of a spoiled boy, and is just as easily dispelled.

A few items of typical Schildkrautiana will illustrate my point. The first Saturday night of our Boston engagement of *The Cherry Orchard*, the house was completely sold out. When I arrived at the theatre a couple of hours before curtain time I was met at the stage door by a frantic company manager, who informed me that "he" (Pepi) had sent word he was ill and wouldn't play that night. At the matinee he had been in perfect health, and I was sure this was just one of Pepi's little bits of nonsense. I immediately went to his apartment at the Touraine, unannounced—for I didn't want to give him any warning—and found him calmly lying in bed, reading a book, looking serene and peaceful. The moment he caught sight of me he started playing the invalid and in a weak voice announced how ill he was.

"Have you a temperature?" I coldly asked.

"Oh, yes, Evale! Indeed I have!"

"How high is it?" I said unsympathetically.

"It's ninety-nine, Evale!" he answered. I greeted this fearful news with rude laughter, and it didn't take me long to rout him out. In a few seconds he was following me to the theatre as meek as a lamb. He played beautifully that night, as I knew he would, and after the performance he told me how "much better" he felt and how grateful he was that I had insisted on his working. People make the mistake of taking Pepi seriously on such occasions. They don't know that his bark is so much worse than his bite!

If Pepi had been playing *The Cherry Orchard* in repertory, his performance would have been consistently excellent. As it was, he found it immensely tiring to force himself to the same truth eight times a week, and he missed being able to rely on the actor's tricks of which he is a past master.

After we had been running in New York for several weeks, I was puzzled to see the floods of tears that poured down Gaev's face when he made his entrance at the end of the third act, bringing news of the sale at auction of the old estate. Such an abundance of tears—they flowed from his eyes like water from a faucet—struck me as excessive. They disturbed me, and their uncalled-for extravagance broke into my mood, making it very hard for me to play the end of the scene. On Gaev's entrance in the last act I noticed the same phenomenon. It seemed to me unlike Pepi to go to such lengths of preparation before stepping onto the stage. Even the most ardent disciple of the Group-Theatre-neo-Stanislavski method would have had a tough time producing such an alarming inundation. Then one night, quite by chance, I discovered the answer to this mystery.

I was pacing up and down in the wings, waiting for my own cue before my last-act entrance, when I caught sight of Pepi sitting very quietly behind a stack of scenery. In front of him stood the property man. With the care and solicitude of a doctor performing some delicate operation, the man was blow-

ing menthol into Pepi's eyes! It was all I could do to play the
rest of the performance without going into gales of laughter.
Pepi knows me so well, it didn't take him long to realize that
I was on to him, and after the final curtain, when I jokingly told
him I didn't think Chekhov would approve of such Hollywood
customs, he was all ready with an explanation. It was not the
actual tears he cared about, but the fact that his eyes were
really streaming "put him in the mood" and helped him to
play better! I begged Pepi to deprive himself of this form of
inspiration, for my sake. Now that I knew the secret, I found
it harder than ever to look into those streaming eyes and keep
my mind on my work. But I pleaded in vain. Knowing Pepi
to be something of a hypochondriac, I hit upon a plan that
proved effective: I told him I had consulted a doctor, who had
assured me that the constant use of menthol would be most
damaging to Pepi's eyesight. In pictures the situation was different, since the need for tears was infrequent, but consistently
—eight times a week—to submit his eyes to this treatment
was definitely dangerous. This fable had the desired result,
and from then on the menthol-tears only appeared when someone very special was out front.

Darling Pepi! When we act together I often feel like a
combination of governess and jailer. I'm constantly amazed
and touched at the way he lets me bully him; I suppose it's because he knows I really love him, and I think he really loves
me. "Why didn't we get married, Evale?" he sometimes asks
me. "We wouldn't be the good friends we are if we had!"
I answer sensibly.

The critics were warm in their praise of our production of
The Cherry Orchard, and, to my great relief, spoke of the play
itself in glowing terms. There were no references to "museum
pieces" or "dusty relics," and this made me feel that we had
managed to serve Chekhov with some degree of faithfulness,
although there were many things in the production that I was
far from pleased with. I'm still convinced his plays can best
be realized in the repertory of a permanent acting company.

The greatest interpretations of his work we have ever seen in this country were of course those of the Moscow Art Theatre. The only performances in English that came near to conveying his true quality were those of the Civic Repertory, and the superlatively fine production of *Uncle Vanya* which the Old Vic brought to New York in 1946, and which met with such frigid disapproval from the press. Many people agree with me that this was far and away the best of the Old Vic's presentations, and I was amused only recently to see that Laurence Olivier, in an interview, spoke of Dr. Astrov in *Uncle Vanya* as not only his favorite part but the one in which he felt he had achieved his finest work.

Our *Cherry Orchard* met with such success that we settled down at the National Theatre with every prospect of a long run. Unfortunately, in the late spring I was forced to undergo a sudden operation and had to leave the cast at a couple of days' notice. Peggy Webster took over my part, much to my relief and that of the company, and finished off the season.

Early in September we set off on tour. Everywhere business was excellent. Our angels all got their money back, somewhat to their own and our surprise, and even made a modest profit. This delighted us all; we felt that our faith in the good taste of the public had been vindicated.

Traveling conditions, due to the war, were difficult—not to say disagreeable. Hotels everywhere were so prosperous that they made a point of rationing courtesy along with the butter. To make things worse, practically every member of the company carried at least one dog; at the railroad stations people stared at us curiously and decided we must be members of an animal act. Pepi and his wife Marie had two Chihuahuas that made up in noise what they lacked in size; Thelma Chandler had a fox terrier; my understudy, Cavada Humphrey, was accompanied by a black poodle; Carmen Mathews, who had taken over the part of Varya, boasted a dachshund; Marion Evensen had the beloved little Chico; and of course Vixen came with me. On a couple of trips Peggy Webster joined us with her dog, a lovely little cairn, Susie, sister to Vixen. Then there was the small gray poodle, whose presence was purely professional, since it played the part of Charlotta's dog who "eats nuts too." This extensive menagerie was not calculated to make traveling easier!

One journey I remember with especial amusement. All the dogs had been successfully smuggled onto the train in their various containers, and managed to escape the vigilance of a particularly ornery conductor. They were all quiet as mice and seemed to understand the situation perfectly. Only Pepi's Chihuahuas grew restless toward the end of the trip, and let out a barrage of shrill barks from their tiny prison. The conductor insisted on Pepi's sending them to the baggage car. Pepi indignantly protested and managed to prolong the argument in the corridor until we arrived at our destination. He left the train, pursued by the irate remarks of the conductor. The rest of us, as we climbed off the car onto the platform, opened, one after another, the boxes and bags that concealed the larger dogs, who triumphantly emerged under the amazed and increasingly apoplectic eye of this guardian of the law. At the sight of the gay and impertinent procession making its way jauntily to the station exit, the conductor was struck dumb with impotent fury and could only shake his fist in the laughing faces of actors and dogs alike as the train glided by us.

Another time we were less fortunate and we all spent an entire day in the baggage car, since we were unwilling to trust our pets to the tender mercies of the train personnel.

Many of the hotels refused to give us shelter. In Chicago the managements had made a general rule to refuse dogs for "the duration." Marion Evensen and I finally located a veritable dump, situated under the El in the heart of the Loop. There were no private baths, not even private showers or toilets; no closets, no room-service, no telephone connections, no elevator —but they consented to accept our precious pets! When my friends expressed their horror at such lodgings, I philosophically remarked that if the people of Dover found it possible to live in caves for several years, it couldn't hurt me to spend three weeks in the comparative comfort of Chicago's worst hotel.

We wound up our tour at Christmastime with a wonderful engagement in Washington, D.C., and played the first week of 1945 at the City Center in New York. We had spent nearly a year in our beloved *Cherry Orchard* and were sad to leave it. Thanks to the play, the unusually pleasant and efficient management, a congenial company, and the response of hundreds of enthusiastic theatre-goers, this whole experience was a most happy one, and I look back on it with affectionate appreciation.

CHAPTER EIGHTEEN

URING the summer of 1944, prior to our departure on
the *Cherry Orchard* tour, Cheryl Crawford decided on a
fall presentation of Shakespeare's *The Tempest* with Peggy
Webster directing.

Cheryl was much intrigued by the production scheme I had
evolved for the play, and it was this primarily that caused her
to undertake the venture. The fact that I was not a member of
the Scenic Artists' Union, and was therefore barred from ex-
ercising any talents I might have in this field, created a serious problem. But Cheryl Crawford is not one to be deterred
by obstacles and at once set about finding a solution. I built a
scale model of my set, and Cheryl persuaded the well-known
scenic-designers the Motleys to execute it, with such decorative
embellishments as they saw fit to use, but with the understanding that the basic scheme was in no way to be altered. The
Motleys expressed great enthusiasm for my plan and undertook the production. My name, of course, was not to appear
in connection with it. The costumes were designed after a set
of Bernacini drawings I had in my library, which conveyed
miraculously the quality of fantasy, both poetic and comic, inherent in the script. But this way of working is far from satisfactory to either party. The first model the Motleys evolved in
no way resembled my original conception. I was in no position
to be dictatorial, since I had no real authority. Cheryl Crawford, however, insisted that my scheme be used. I was playing
in Chicago at the time, and one of the Motleys came to see

me there for a final conference. I had the embarrassing feeling that they did not really approve of my model, in spite of their first wholehearted acceptance of it, and would have been glad to see me and my ideas at the bottom of a very deep ocean.

The production of *The Tempest* did not actually open until early in January. Since I had just closed in *The Cherry Orchard*, I went to Boston to be on hand at the final dress rehearsals. Cheryl and Peggy had assembled a most interesting cast. For Ariel they chose Vera Zorina, whose pale ethereal beauty gave an other-worldliness to this strange sprite of Shakespeare's imagination that was most effective. In contrast, Canada Lee played the tragic monster Caliban. Arnold Moss was the magician Prospero, and for the two clowns, Trinculo and Stephano, Peggy had the brilliant idea of casting Wierek and Voscovec, a team of comedians famous in their own Czechoslovakia. The "comics" of Shakespeare can be unutterably dreary, but these two great artists brought a spontaneous invention to the roles that was sheer delight.

I had no sooner arrived in Boston than I received an SOS from the Colonial Theatre: would I please come immediately to give my advice on the flying equipment?

Peggy had thought it would be most effective if Ariel, when given his freedom at the end of the play by Prospero, could make a flying exit instead of just bounding off the stage. This was a splendid idea in principle, but there are very few people in this country expert in the fine art of "flying" actors. I know of no one except the famous Schultz family capable of handling this difficult mechanical process. The Schultzes had "flown" people for years, ever since the days of the flying ballets at the old Hippodrome and Maude Adams' original production of *Peter Pan*. When I put *Peter Pan* into the repertory at the Civic I was fortunate enough to secure their services, and they were responsible for the famous "audience fly" I inaugurated, in which Peter, instead of taking an ordinary mortal bow at the end of the play, flew over the heads of the audience in the orchestra seats, right up to the first balcony and back to the stage, leaving the children speechless with delight and wonder.

Cheryl Crawford, however, had not succeeded in locating the Schultz family. An assortment of stage carpenters and engineers were trying to dope out a way to provide Ariel with the necessary wings. When I reached the theatre they were busily experimenting with a large sandbag, which alternately fell with a thump to the floor of the stage or jerkily disappeared aloft into the rigging of the fly-gallery.

My arrival was greeted with enthusiasm, since my *Peter Pan* experiences had given me the reputation of being something of a flying expert. When the efforts with the sandbag used as Ariel's stand-in had produced results that seemed more hopeful, I daringly volunteered to put on Zorina's flying-harness and leotard and lend myself to further experiment, since I knew from experience that the dead weight of a sandbag cannot take the place of a living body on the end of the wire, and we all wanted to spare Zorina, who was nervous enough with the opening night before her, from the enervating hazards of these first clumsy attempts.

I mounted a high stool, gave the flying signal, and in a second found myself biting the dust of the stage groundcloth. After much vociferous argument among the men, and much rearranging of ropes and pulleys, we started again. Once more I climbed up onto the stool, once more I bit the dust. Three times we went through the same disastrous performance. I then discovered that the man who was supposed to cause the "elevation" was assiduously pulling the wrong rope and was precipitating me each time to the floor. Once this important point had been straightened out, we decided to try again. This time I mounted the stool, gave the signal, and found myself jerkily but rapidly ascending straight up into the air, where I was left hanging on a level with the first light-pipe. Here I dangled precariously for several minutes while the stagehands below carried on a heated altercation as to which rope would pull me down again. This decided upon, I landed on the stage with a resounding bump.

Cheryl Crawford and Peggy Webster had been out front during these terrifying experiments, and now came backstage, resolved to put an end to any further attempts. They were scared to death at what might happen to me at the next try. As they came through the pass-door onto the stage, they overheard one of a group of stagehands who were watching the proceedings exclaim, "Gee! She's certainly a good-natured dame!" This accolade I felt I richly deserved. As I picked myself up, my hands and face as black as my dusty leotard, I earnestly advised that Ariel should be content to make a bounding exit, for not only did I fear for Zorina's life and limbs, but I felt that the probability of such a hilarious ending to the play would be detrimental to the lyricism and beauty that Shakespeare intended. Cheryl and Peggy cordially agreed with me.

I shall never forget this production of *The Tempest*; it was one of the loveliest things I have ever seen in the theatre. David Diamond wrote a haunting, elusive score that successfully captured the essence of this most enchanting fantasy. As the huge turntable moved and the different facets of the magical island of Shakespeare's dream came successively into view, with no drop of the curtain to break the sustained mood of the fairy tale, I was filled with pleasure at seeing my crude little model transformed into this living reality. It was a daring production and, during the try-out weeks in Boston and Philadelphia, caused much controversy. But in spite of financial losses on the tour and gloomy predictions on the part of some wiseacres, Cheryl Crawford's faith remained unshaken, and she had the joy of launching *The Tempest* with great success at the Alvin Theatre on January 25.

Thelma Chandler, the stage manager, told me an incredible story about that opening night. Before the curtain rose Caliban had to take his place behind a rock over which he was to climb for his entrance; otherwise he would have been seen from the balcony as he emerged from the wings. Thelma checked to make sure Canada Lee was at his post, and, having seen him safely ensconced behind his rock, she rang up the curtain. There were about ten minutes of dialogue before Caliban's appearance. A few seconds before his cue something warned Thelma to check again, and to her amazement she saw that Canada Lee had fallen fast asleep and was snoring away blissfully in his hiding place. She had no way of reaching him, since he was a good eight feet from the shelter of the wings. She hurriedly fetched the master carpenter, and with the aid of a long stage-brace they managed to prod Canada Lee awake just in time for his entrance. Such lack of concern on a New York opening night is something of a record and fills one with a combination of astonishment and envy. Thelma added a note to her prompt-copy: "Look to see if Canada is awake one minute before cue."

Peggy Webster and I had been much impressed by Cheryl Crawford's handling of this whole production. Not only did she prove herself a shrewd businesswoman, but her calm and her consistent good humor, her firmness in the face of trials that would have made most managers lose faith and abandon the struggle, had been invaluable in preserving the high morale of the company and guiding the venture to its ultimate success. Peggy had been associated with Cheryl before, in *Family Portrait*, but *The Tempest* was my first introduction to her. I now agreed with Peggy that we should discuss with Cheryl Crawford the possibility of starting a repertory theatre of which she should be the executive director. When *The Tempest* was safely launched we started the many conferences that led to the creation of the American Repertory Theatre in the fall of 1946.

I spent the spring and summer of 1945 blissfully at home, working in the garden, reading plays, and making plans for our proposed repertory theatre. I did a good deal of radio work from time to time—I always enjoy this, providing the material is worth while. If I were not so insistent on that point I should undoubtedly have worked a great deal in this medium, but unfortunately the good programs are few and far between, and I have a foolish distaste for entering people's homes bearing unworthy gifts.

During this summer I began to paint in oils and found it an absorbing and fascinating occupation. There is nothing so profoundly restful, and as long as you don't inflict your "masterpieces" on the world at large, it is an innocent enough pastime. How I envy artists who can create in solitude and retirement—painters, writers, composers. They alone are responsible for the results of their labor, for their failures and their triumphs. Work in the theatre is always a collaboration. A performance is dependent on such a multitude of factors. It is only as strong as its weakest link, and often the carelessness of the least important member of the team can wreck a whole carefully planned production.

That spring and summer I designed several productions for which I built scale models: *The Merchant of Venice*, *The Three Sisters*, and *John Gabriel Borkman*. The last two were ultimately used in production and turned out very successfully. I was urged by some of my scenic-designer friends, notably Watson Barratt, to try to pass the examination that would have made me a member of the union, but it sounded so formidable that I was scared to attempt it. There was so much academic knowledge involved, and for that reason I felt sure I would flunk it.

In the late spring I signed a contract to appear that fall in a production of *Thérèse Raquin*, a dramatization by Thomas Job of Zola's famous novel. It was to be produced by Victor Payne Jennings, directed by Peggy Webster, and my co-stars were to be Dame May Whitty (Peggy Webster's mother) and Victor Jory.

We started rehearsals in August and opened in New Haven early in September. Thomas Job had fashioned a grim melodrama out of Zola's powerful book, but it was not really a good play. However, I found the association interesting; it was the first time I had had the pleasure of working with Dame May.

I had of course known her since I was a child, but we had never played together. What an extraordinary old woman she was! At eighty she had an energy and a vitality that put us younger people to shame. In the last act of *Thérèse*, as Madame Raquin, she was confined to a wheel chair, completely paralyzed, incapable of speech or movement, yet with her small piercing eyes she dominated the entire scene. She was really the star of the play. Jory and I did all the hard work, but she reaped the benefit of it; he and I often looked at each other ruefully and decided that "wheel-chair parts" were hard to compete with, especially when the wheel chair was occupied by such a bundle of concentrated will.

A Boston engagement followed the New Haven opening, and I'll never forget an adventure Dame May and I went through there, which brought us very close together and filled us with a sense of profound mutual respect.

Peggy Webster has a small house on Martha's Vineyard. She is devoted to it, and indeed it is a wonderful little place, very wild and remote, at the far end of the island, Gay Head, with the most magnificent view over the sea. Her mother had never seen the house, and Peggy was anxious to introduce her to it. On the second Saturday of our Boston run Peggy took the morning train to go to the Vineyard, and Dame May and I drove to Falmouth after our performance that night. We slept at an inn in Falmouth and took the boat to Oak Bluffs the next morning. Here Peggy met us and drove us to her house, where we spent a pleasant day. At that time of year there are very few steamers running, so Peggy hired a small boat to take Dame May and me back to the mainland, where I had left my car in a parking lot. The sea was quite rough, and there was a bitterly cold wind. However, apart from some caustic remarks on the temerity of a director's subjecting her two stars to such hazards, Dame May took it calmly enough. We settled ourselves comfortably in the car and set off on our three-hour trip, expecting to reach Boston by midnight.

At first all was well, but I soon noticed an ominous dimming and flickering of my headlights. I said nothing, but drove on, praying that they would right themselves. Dame May said nothing either, and I hoped she hadn't noticed anything amiss. Then suddenly, as we were driving at about fifty miles an hour on the dark highway just beyond Falmouth, the lights went out altogether. For a moment I was blinded by the glare of cars coming in the opposite direction, but I cautiously steered in to the side of the road and tried to find out the trouble. We had no flashlight, and even had I had any knowledge of where to look or what to do I would have been helpless. As it was, my ignorance was as dense as the darkness in which we sat. I tried to signal for help to the numerous cars passing us in both directions, but it was a Sunday night and people were all hurrying home after the holiday, in no mood to play the Good Samaritan. There was nothing to do but to crawl carefully along the side of the road and hope to find a service station open in the next village.

After about an hour of this painful progress we reached Buzzards Bay. The garages were all tightly closed, but by the railway station I located a taxi stand, and one of the drivers very kindly volunteered to come to our assistance. He didn't really seem to know what to do, but fumbled about under the dashboard and, with the help of a piece of metal wire, he managed to produce a faint gleam from the headlights. This he seemed to consider a major achievement, deserving a handsome reward, and, having pocketed it, left us to continue on our crippled way. The faint gleam lasted for ten miles or so and then suddenly failed. While it had been grossly inadequate, it was better than the total darkness in which we again found ourselves.

It was by now very late, and there was no sign of life from any of the houses or gas stations we crept past. My concern for Dame May prompted me to knock at one or two doors where I thought I detected a glimmer of light, but in most cases I got no response, and the one time that I did I was greeted by such unpleasant expressions of annoyance that I hastily retired.

We resigned ourselves to crawling along at a maximum speed of ten miles an hour all the rest of the way.

Dame May was wonderful! She kept up a cheerful and fascinating conversation, as cool and unruffled as though she were presiding over a delightful party—not a word of complaint or reproach. I learned innumerable interesting details about the theatre in England and Ireland in the days of her youth; listened entranced to her vivid descriptions and shrewd analyses of the work of the many great actors she had seen; was constantly amazed at her penetrating comments and acute understanding of every phase and facet of the art of playing.

I became aware of a smell of burning that troubled me mightily. In my ignorance and fear of engines, I had visions of the car suddenly exploding, but decided to say nothing and crept along, seemingly unconcerned, hoping Dame May's sense of smell was less alert than her other faculties.

At last dawn broke and found us on the outskirts of Boston. As we looked at each other in the cold light we burst into uncontrollable laughter and proceeded to exchange compliments on our good sportsmanship. I left Dame May at her apartment at six in the morning, seemingly none the worse for her nerve-racking night, and that evening at the theatre she was as spry as ever. "The one thing that worried me was that smell of burning," she said with a twinkle in her eye. "It was good of you to try and keep it from me." You couldn't put anything over on that old lady!

From that time on, though Dame May and I often disagreed, we shared a mutual admiration for each other's character and fortitude that nothing could destroy.

For the first time, in *Thérèse*, I had the privilege of working under Peggy Webster's direction. The play was not a particularly grateful subject for a director, but I was impressed—as most players who work for Peggy are—by her clean, precise theatrecraft, her honesty, her rare understanding of the actor's problems, and her unfailing kindness and good nature. Later on I was to have the joy of taking part in her production of

Henry VIII for the American Repertory Theatre, one of the finest jobs of creative direction it has ever been my good fortune to see.

Another pleasant outcome of the *Thérèse* engagement was our discovery of Victor Jory, one of the nicest of men and the most cooperative of actors. He became immensely enthusiastic over the idea of our repertory theatre and wholeheartedly agreed to join our company.

Thérèse opened at the charming little Biltmore Theatre on October 9 and had a moderately successful run to the end of the year. The critics didn't like the play—for which no one could blame them—but Victor Payne Jennings had sold a great number of theatre-parties on the strength of the distinguished names involved, and these kept us going profitably for three months.

CHAPTER NINETEEN

ALL during this time Cheryl Crawford, Peggy, and I were kept constantly busy on preparatory work for the American Repertory Theatre, which was now definitely scheduled for the fall of 1946. The work of raising the necessary funds was left largely in Cheryl's capable hands, though Joseph Verner Reed, who had been associated with Peggy Webster in her successful productions of *Richard II* and *Hamlet* with Maurice Evans, contributed through her a princely sum which definitely assured the realization of our repertory dream. We had many small contributions from all over the country, and these filled us with especial appreciation, as they seemed indicative of a widespread interest in furthering the establishment of the type of theatre we had in mind.

We made many appearances at various clubs and organizations, at which we described our aims, and usually our ideas met with tangible proofs of public enthusiasm. Often, however, we came up against discouraging indifference. I remember in particular one luncheon we attended, at an exclusive club whose members included some of the wealthiest businessmen in New York City. These gentlemen listened to us with exquisite courtesy but with firmly closed checkbooks. The only men there who, with typical generosity, promptly opened theirs were three actors—among those present, probably the least equipped to be extravagant—Bobby Clark, Edmund Gwenn, and Leo Carroll, who bought a thousand dollars' worth of shares apiece.

Next to the task of raising the required capital, our two greatest problems were to assemble an acting company and to find a suitable theatre in which to start our venture. On both of these points we met with considerable difficulties.

Actors frequently express a passionate desire to work in a repertory theatre—no amount of effort would be too much, no amount of sacrifice would be too great. But when they are presented with a hard-and-fast proposition their enthusiasm all too often vanishes, and, though they are still loud in their protestations of sympathetic agreement as to the desirability of creating such a theatre, "much as they would *love* to be a part of it," the reasons for their ultimate refusal suddenly become legion.

The search for an adequate home for our theatre often seemed hopeless. Most of the Broadway playhouses not only command rentals of astronomical proportions but provide hopelessly inadequate stage space for a repertory of plays. To be forced to haul scenery to and from a storehouse between performances, with the assistance of the Teamsters' Union, would insure bankruptcy within a week.

We examined innumerable abandoned theatres off the beaten Broadway track, but they were either unavailable or completely unsuited to our project.

I was convinced then, as I am now, that the whole purpose of our undertaking would be defeated unless we were able to charge popular prices. For this an ample seating capacity was mandatory. Such a repertory theatre should be a people's theatre and should in no way depend upon the support of the smart set or the carriage trade. In this view Peggy Webster agreed with me, but, while I think Cheryl Crawford agreed in theory, her sense of showmanship inclined her toward making the American Repertory a success, even if that meant sacrificing the essential idea of service to the public, which in my opinion was the crux of the whole venture.

My feelings in this matter were so definite that I strongly advocated a tie-up with the City Center. Although this theatre

has countless drawbacks and is abominable to play in, due
mostly to its unwieldy size and faulty acoustics, I felt that
there at least we would be able to reach the type of audiences
to whom great plays at popular prices, presented with the high
standard which was our aim, would be a veritable godsend.
Negotiations, with this tie-up in view, were started and continued for some time, but prior booking commitments on the
part of the City Center Board of Managers created obstacles
that prevented a satisfactory collaboration. Also some members
of our advisory committee, organized by Cheryl Crawford, felt
that our prestige would suffer by such an affiliation, and feared
it might cause a loss of interest on the part of certain pro-
spective backers.

Prestige be damned! I thought to myself as I remembered
my old dump on Fourteenth Street with nostalgia.

At last we learned that the International Theatre on Colum-
bus Circle, owned by the Marquis de Cuevas, might be available. On the day that we made an inspection of this house I
stood on the stage and looked out into the auditorium that had
been so beautifully decorated and appointed by the Marquis
for the presentations of his fine ballet company. In my mind I
went back to 1916, when I had played a dress rehearsal there,
prior to the out-of-town try-out of Mr. Lazarus. At that time
this theatre, then known as the Park, was dusty and dilapidated, but it boasted a high gallery, and its capacity as well as
its acoustics were unimpaired. As I admired its present white-
and-gold elegance, its handsome crystal chandelier, and its
graceful balcony, I fervently wished it were possible to bring
that old gallery back again. In its old form this theatre would
have been ideal for our purpose; its former capacity of sixteen
hundred seats would have allowed us to charge those low prices
I have never ceased to dream of. The removal of this vast gallery has not only adversely affected the acoustics of the house,
but has reduced its capacity to little more than eleven hundred
seats.

However, the charm of the building, its feeling of gracious

tradition, combined with a more than ordinarily adequate stage
and dressing-room facilities, greatly attracted us. The rent too
was comparatively reasonable—a mere seventy thousand dollars a year! Before deciding on it definitely, troubled as we were
by the small number of seats, we combed every other possibility;
but in the end we found ourselves with no other reasonable
choice and determined to adopt it as our home.

Almost every week we held auditions. We must have seen
and heard hundreds of young men and women eager to become members of the repertory company. We gradually assembled a small group of those that seemed to us especially
talented. Some of these youngsters have done well for themselves since, though not always in the legitimate-theatre field.
Efrem Zimbalist, Jr., for instance, went into management and
met with great success in his presentations of Menotti's provocative operas *The Medium* and *The Consul.* Mary Alice
Moore has devoted herself mostly to television. William Wynd-
ham abandoned the theatre for a while to become an insur-
ance broker, but has recently, happily, returned to his first love.
Dion Allen has continued to do good work in several of Peggy
Webster's companies. Ann Jackson, now married to Ely Wallach and the proud mother of a son, has appeared in many
Broadway plays, and her work has always been received most
favorably. Ely Wallach himself made quite a name in *The
Rose Tattoo,* under Cheryl Crawford's management. These
are only a few of the fine young players we were fortunate to
discover through our weekly auditions.

Our search for leading members of the company continued
unabated. The list of actors and actresses we hopefully approached gives proof of the high standard we aspired to achieve.

Peggy Webster made a trip to the Coast in the late fall of
1945 and thoroughly explored the possibilities of Hollywood.
Among many people she talked to out there was Greer Gar-
son, who appeared greatly interested in joining us, and for
whom we thought of producing Shakespeare's *Antony and
Cleopatra* and Sheridan's *School for Scandal,* among other

plays that we hoped might lure her away, at least temporarily, from pictures. But she succumbed to a new long-term contract with M-G-M, and our efforts in that direction failed. Lee Cobb was approached—we had Shylock in *The Merchant of Venice* in mind, as well as other roles—but he was too involved in picture work to give us a favorable answer. One of the first people I thought of was, of course, my dear Pepi Schildkraut, but he too turned us down. We were hopeful that Tyrone Power might join us; several years before he had played in *Liliom* at Lawrence Langner's Westport Playhouse, and spent a whole afternoon at my house discussing his dreams and ambitions. His heart seemed to be set on a career in the theatre, and he made me promise that if I ever started another repertory company I would allow him to be a member of it. He was much distressed that picture commitments prevented his taking part in our 1946 adventure and did all he could to help us in our efforts. We were deeply disappointed at his inability to join us; his warm, glowing personality and his great gifts as an actor would have been invaluable assets.

Remembering our former talks with José Ferrer back in 1939, Peggy asked him to come to her Twelfth-Street apartment and discuss the possibility of his coming in with us; but by this time he had ambitious plans of his own and firmly informed us that he "didn't want to come into our house."

Montgomery Clift, Sam Jaffe, and Henry Hull were among the other people who played with the idea of joining us but for various reasons decided against it.

Among the young actresses we talked to were Barbara Bel Geddes and Beatrice Pearson—but they were both packing up to go to Hollywood. We had a pleasant interview with Geraldine Fitzgerald, who was strongly tempted by some of the parts we offered her, but domestic entanglements complicated her life at the moment and prevented her from devoting the necessary time to such strenuous work. Wendy Hiller (who we felt would be a perfect Maggie in *What Every Woman Knows* as well as an enchanting Lady Teazle in *The School for Scandal*) was loath to leave her family in England for the necessary length of time.

Mary Martin, who had just appeared with such success in Cheryl Crawford's production of *One Touch of Venus,* was very definitely intrigued with the idea of having a fling at the legitimate theatre. Cheryl suggested that instead of Shakespeare's *Antony and Cleopatra* we produce Shaw's *Caesar and Cleopatra* with Mary as the kitten-queen. Rosalind in *As You Like It* was another possibility discussed, and perhaps Lady Teazle. Though these entrancing prospects, alas, never materialized, I shall always be grateful that these talks gave me the opportunity of getting to know Mary Martin. She is just as wonderful a person as she is an artist, and that's saying a lot!

Among the many other players we approached were Richard Hart, Vincent Price, Jessica Tandy, Hume Cronyn, Alexander Knox, Michael Chekhov, Susan Hayward, and Paul McGrath. But in every case there were obstacles: Hollywood contracts, prior commitments, children, husbands, wives—yes, even dogs! It is not so easy to assemble a repertory acting company as some people seem to think.

In late February I went to see a performance of *Truckline Café.* I wanted to see Richard Waring, who was playing in it, and also an old friend of mine, David Manners. The audience and I were not particularly impressed by the play and we were giving it no more than a polite and somewhat bored attention, when suddenly in the last act we were all electrified by a remarkable young man who played a scene with such violent and uncompromising truth that on his exit we all applauded for at least two minutes. On looking at my program, I saw the name of Marlon Brando and left the theatre convinced that here was one of those rare talents that very occasionally emerge full-fledged from the hand of God.

Some weeks later I saw this same boy play Marchbanks in one of Miss Cornell's revivals of *Candida.* For the first time I felt I had seen the part really come to life; and it was impossible to believe that this was the big, clumsy, rough, rather brutal young man of *Truckline Café*. In *Candida* he seemed small and slender, mercurial and possessed of an almost lyrical beauty. Yet this transformation was achieved by no external means; it came solely from a change within.

Rarely have I been so excited by a young player's potentialities. I felt that here was a boy with the spark of true genius, who might, given the right opportunities and training, become one of the really great actors of our time. I found myself wishing that he might be quickly removed from the Broadway scene, to some place where he would be allowed to develop and grow and stretch; where he might have the chance to play a wide variety of parts and learn to use all the various facets of his actor's temperament—some place where he might, securely sheltered from premature "success," perfect his instrument, so that his potential range and stature might not be impaired or limited. But, alas, the machinery of show business was already in action: Brando was doomed to the only kind of success we recognize.

We had deliberately left our choice of plays open until we were sure of the composition of our company. I therefore begged Cheryl and Peggy to try and persuade Brando and his agent to postpone the chance of big money and featured billing for a while and allow him to work in repertory for a year or two. I suggested putting on Chekhov's *The Seagull,* in which Brando would have been an extraordinary Kostya; or Ibsen's *Ghosts,* so that he might have a chance at Oswald; and that for the rest he should content himself with playing smaller parts in repertory, in the various plays by Shakespeare, Sheridan, Shaw, and Barrie we had in mind, which would give him an opportunity to master several different styles of acting. I think he himself might have thought well of the idea, could we have reached him a little earlier; but I must confess that at that time Marlon Brando was such an uncouth, inarticulate youth that it was almost impossible to know what was in his mind.

Dick Waring had got to know him and like him while

playing with him in *Truckline Café,* and volunteered to bring him down to Twelfth Street to see Peggy Webster and me one night after the *Candida* performance. Marlon Brando greeted us with grunts, and thereafter for two solid hours sat completely speechless, slumped down on a low chair, with his feet, encased in rather dirty socks of a hideous shade of green (one of his first acts on arriving was to kick off his shoes), firmly planted on an adjacent table. Every now and then he took a handful of grapes from a bowl at his elbow and chewed them solemnly and vigorously, punctuating his silence by occasionally spitting out a seed. Yet in spite of these incredible manners—or rather, lack of them—my heart went out to him. I find one can forgive genius much—though I am disinclined to condone the belief prevalent among many of our young moderns that rudeness, sloppiness, and an unsavory personal appearance are its inevitable attendants.

The French have a word *sauvage,* which constantly came to my mind that night as I watched Brando. They use it about animals—and people too—who are wary and shy of the approach of strangers. It implies a fear of being caught, of being tamed, of the encroachment of another creature on one's inner privacy. It is a feeling I understand very well from personal experience, but my upbringing and the discipline of the years have enabled me to cloak it with some semblance of graciousness. To be natural is certainly engaging, but it seems to me there should be some slight difference between the naturalness of a human being and the naturalness of a dumb animal. I suppose I'm old-fashioned, but I fail to see anything attractive or clever in reverting to the manners and customs of the jungle.

I have watched Brando's astronomical rise to fame with a touch of wistfulness. Not that I have any objections to fame or success or prosperity—they can all be good things when rightfully earned, and are delightful and even necessary—but in our present cockeyed world, and especially in this country, they come so prematurely and so swiftly that a young immature artist is in danger of being overwhelmed and robbed forever of the opportunity to ripen and fulfill his early promise. All gardeners know the danger of permitting a rare plant to grow unpruned and untrained, overfed and overpampered. In its first wild exuberance it will put forth mighty leaves and powerful tendrils, but the flowers and the fruits will suffer.

Fortunately our search for actors willing and free to do more work for less money, out of a true love for the theatre and a belief in the essential rightness of our aims, was not always so unsuccessful. We finally managed to assemble a company of which we were genuinely proud. Walter Hampden, Victor Jory, Ernest Truex, Richard Waring, Philip Bourneuf, and myself headed a cast of players that any manager might have envied and few could have afforded. But we still had to find a talented young actress, and we continued to be frustrated in this all-important quest by either Hollywood contracts or matrimonial entanglements.

At last Clifford Odets came forward with a suggestion that seemed promising. Some time before, he had directed a picture which he himself adapted from Richard Llewellyn's book None But the Lonely Heart. In it Miss Ethel Barrymore gave one of the greatest screen performances of recent years, and a young actress, June Duprez, contributed a remarkable characterization of a cheap, sexy floozy, whose charms were a veritable menace to any male that strayed within her orbit. I remembered her work in this picture very well, but her impersonation was so convincing that I assumed it to be the result of the usual type-casting, and it would never have occurred to me to imagine her in the kind of parts we had in mind.

Clifford Odets, however, assured us that June Duprez had nothing whatsoever in common with the girl of Llewellyn's imagination, and that her performance was due entirely to her great talents as an actress. His enthusiasm was so glowing, and we naturally had such faith in his judgment, that we decided to follow his advice and find out if Miss Duprez would be interested in joining us. Clifford Odets very kindly arranged for None But the Lonely Heart to be privately run off for us, since neither Cheryl nor Peggy had seen the picture. They were both greatly impressed by June Duprez' work.

We had word from the Coast from Miss Duprez' agent that she reacted favorably to our proposition, and I was dispatched on a brief visit to Hollywood to meet her and discuss the matter further.

Dame May Whitty graciously invited me to stay at her house in Hollywood for a week, and after our initial meeting June Duprez came there every day and read over with me some of the parts destined for her. She proved to be a charming, simple person, utterly unpretentious and eagerly cooperative.

This problem solved, we were able to concentrate on the final crystallization of our program and put the various productions into work. Our plan was to present six plays during our first season, and since we were to play real repertory from the start, three of them had to be prepared and rehearsed simultaneously.

It would have been easy for us to choose the more hackneyed and popular classics, and, in view of subsequent criticism, we might have been wiser to do so. But we all agreed that part of the purpose of such a theatre lay in presenting to the public great plays that they would be unlikely to see under regular commercial auspices. It was for this reason that we decided on *John Gabriel Borkman* rather than on *Hedda Gabler*, and on *Henry VIII* rather than on *Macbeth*. Peggy and I strongly advocated *The Merchant of Venice*, but Cheryl and her advisers feared this play might be considered anti-Semitic and would antagonize our Jewish public. In my opinion, the gentiles in the play behave so much like Nazis, and Shylock has so many aspects of nobility, that unless the production is deliberately twisted into anti-Semitic channels there could be little cause for offense. However, Cheryl was so definite on this point that Peggy and I gave in, and *Henry VIII* won the day.

Our first trio of plays also included Barrie's delightful comedy *What Every Woman Knows*, and four or five weeks later Shaw's *Androcles and the Lion* was to be added to the repertory. To follow this we hoped to find a new American play, and the final production of the season was to be Sheridan's *School for Scandal*.

Cheryl was most anxious to establish as early as possible the approximate running costs of our program, but in order to do this it was necessary to find out from the stagehands' union, Local Number 1, what conditions it intended to impose on us. We were told that the rulings in effect during the repertory season of the Old Vic company had been extremely onerous, but we had hopes that since ours was an American organization whose members had agreed without exception to serve at great personal sacrifice, some special consideration might be shown us. We were not so naïve as to expect comparable sacrifices on the part of the stagehands, and had no intention of asking for anything of that nature, but we felt we had the right to anticipate some small measure of cooperation and good will.

Early in the spring Cheryl had already approached the executive board of Local Number 1, but was advised to postpone seeking for a decision until after the union election. She was informed that the delegates would be inclined to be "tougher" in their demands prior to this event, since any signs of "weakness" on their part in their dealings with us might result in their being voted out of office.

By the middle of May, however, these internal politics having been settled, the union delegates made an appointment to meet with me and our business manager, John Yorke, at the offices of the League of New York Theatres, where Mr. Reilly, secretary of the League, was to preside over the discussion.

I was chosen to represent the three of us at this meeting, since I was the only one among us who had had previous experience in running a repertory theatre in New York City, and although we were all well aware that conditions had immensely changed since 1933, we assumed that some of the problems imposed by the repertory system might be solved by methods similar to those adopted at the old Civic.

After an exchange of civilities with the union delegates, I proceeded to outline our aims and ideas to them, and expressed the hope that we might count on their sympathetic understanding. I immediately received the impression that, far from appreciating our willingness to put ideals before profits, they condemned it as mere foolishness. I hastened to make clear to them that we had no thought of urging them to share in our folly, but only asked them not to be too arbitrary in their demands. They listened to me in silence and gave no inkling of any reaction, favorable or otherwise.

This meeting took place on May 20, and on June 10 I was again summoned to Mr. Reilly's office. This time we were hopeful of reaching some decision that would enable Cheryl to organize her budget. But after two hours of completely futile argument the delegates once more evaded the issue. At the end of the conference one of these gentlemen slapped me on the back and jovially exclaimed, "If we want you to have your little theatre, you'll have it, and if we don't want you to, you won't—see?"

I think I have never in my life prayed for self-control as I did at that moment.

It was not until some months later, in October, just before our New York opening, that Cheryl was finally informed of the working conditions decided upon by Local Number 1. By then, of course, it was too late to do anything but accept them.

CHAPTER TWENTY

THAT summer of 1946 was a happy one for all of us. There was not a member of the company who did not share a feeling of joyful enthusiasm at the thought of the work ahead.

Richard Waring and Victor Jory were installed at my little cottage, and Peggy Webster worked with them on their respective parts in *Henry VIII*. Vic Jory and I also spent many hours delving into the problems of *John Gabriel Borkman*.

The first week of August, June Duprez arrived from the Coast, and we put her up at Cobb's Mill Inn for several days. Peggy worked with her and Dick Waring on their scenes in *What Every Woman Knows*.

The first time Peggy drove Miss Duprez up from New York the lock on the car trunk jammed, and June was in despair, as her precious bag of "medicines" was inaccessible until the following afternoon, when a locksmith was called in to the rescue. Like many inhabitants of Hollywood, June was full of "allergies" and "deficiencies" and religiously consumed vast quantities of assorted pills and vitamins, also meekly submitting to daily shots of some mysterious nature. We were all amused to see the speed with which her various "ailments" vanished—along with her bag of medicaments—as she became more and more engrossed in her work.

We were happy to find that Actor's Equity, ever anxious to help the legitimate theatre in all possible ways, gave us the cooperation that the stagehands' union so persistently with-

held, and allowed us six weeks of rehearsal time. But thanks
to the careful preparation with which our first three productions had been planned, as well as to the preliminary work in
Westport, we found five weeks sufficient. Regular rehearsals
started at the International on August 13, and we opened
Henry VIII in Princeton on September 20.

The costumes and scenery had been put into work in early
June. David Ffolkes designed the production of *Henry VIII* and
the costumes for both this play and *What Every Woman
Knows*—now familiarly referred to as "Wewk"—for which
Paul Morrison provided the sets. It had been decided to use
my scheme for *John Gabriel Borkman*, which Paul Morrison
"ghosted" for me, and he also designed the *Borkman* costumes.
The clothes were executed by Edith Lutyens with her customary skill, and the scenery was built at Barney Turner's
studios at Fort Lee.

As the weeks went by it was thrilling to see our productions gradually come to life. Peggy Webster's treatment of
Henry VIII was a masterpiece of showmanship. By judicious
cutting of the occasionally unwieldy text, and the clever use of
interpolations from Holinshed's *Chronicles* read by two nar-
rators in the persons of Philip Bourneuf and Eugene Stuck-
mann, she fashioned out of this material a swiftly moving
drama, full of humanity, color, and excitement, that held
the audience spellbound. Lehman Engel's music and David
Ffolkes's magnificent settings and costumes lent it an added
glamour, and we were all of us proud to be a part of this wonderful production.

We suffered greatly at our dress rehearsals and opening in
Princeton from Indian-summer weather that sent the temperature into the eighties. David Ffolkes had not only realized the
clothes of the period with an unerring sense of beauty, but with
such a rigid adherence to correctness that at times we thought
we could never survive their heaviness and volume. The first
time I started up the steps to my throne, in the council scene,
I staggered and was almost pulled backward off the platform

by a train that must have weighed in the vicinity of eighty pounds. The men, particularly poor Vic Jory as Henry, agonized in their velvets and brocades worn over thick padding. We all decided that costume-designers should themselves be forced to live in their own creations before so light-heartedly inflicting them on innocent actors. The golden angels who were to have appeared in Queen Catherine's vision just before her death, and who were called upon to perform a kind of ritual dance around her throne, were rendered literally incapable of movement by their gorgeous but unyielding robes. David Ffolkes's refusal to lighten their burden resulted in the suppression of the angels altogether, and a thousand dollars' worth of labor and material was accordingly wasted.

Altogether the fantastic expense of these *Henry VIII* costumes shocked and dismayed us. The simplest of my dresses cost five hundred dollars, and nothing Jory wore cost less than seven hundred and fifty. Even the soft black velvet caps worn by the judges at Catherine's trial, and which we could have made ourselves for a mere song had such a thing been allowed, came to twenty-five dollars apiece; they had to go through the hands of three different unions before completion. The—to us —staggering bill of forty thousand dollars for the costumes of this production alone would undoubtedly be considerably higher today. This bill in no way represented a large profit for Edith Lutyens, who did her best to help us keep down the budget, nor was it due to excessive extravagance in the choice of materials; rather it was the result of the customary exorbitant demands on the part of New York's theatrical labor unions. Anywhere else these clothes could have been made with equal excellence at one-third of the cost.

We opened in Philadelphia on September 23 with *Henry VIII* and on the following Friday put on *What Every Woman Knows*, continuing with these plays in alternation for the two weeks of our engagement there.

We were all of us anxious for the success of our two young stars, June Duprez and Richard Waring, in the Barrie comedy.

Walter Hampden and I, who played the supporting roles of Venables and the Comtesse de la Bruyère, listened eagerly in the wings and smiled at each other happily as the audience gave definite signs of taking our "children" to their hearts.

Our reception in Philadelphia, both from press and public, had been most encouraging, and it was with high hopes that we moved on to Boston, where we looked forward to three weeks at the old Colonial Theatre.

Our *Borkman* rehearsals continued during the Philadelphia run, and this play was added to the repertory our second week in Boston. While Paul Morrison had in most respects adhered faithfully to my production scheme, on the bad advice of our master carpenter he had consented to some slight technical modifications which, far from lessening the difficulty of the scene changes, gravely enhanced them.

John Gabriel Borkman is a short play, and the action is continuous, though laid in four different locales: Mrs. Borkman's drawing room, John Gabriel's study, the exterior of the house, and a promontory on the Borkman estate. We played this play at the Civic with two intermissions, and I always felt that these arbitrary interruptions in the sweep of Ibsen's drama were definitely detrimental. I had therefore designed our present production on a turntable, the use of which eliminated all necessity of scene waits and carried the action straight through to its great climax without a break. When the drama was thus played, the running time was just over an hour and forty minutes, and I felt that audiences accustomed to watching moving pictures of far greater length without the need of a respite would be willing to give similarly sustained attention to Ibsen's powerful story. In this I was not mistaken, and, to my great joy, *John Gabriel Borkman* was hailed by many as the finest of all the American Repertory Theatre's presentations.

But to achieve the technical smoothness inseparable from the success of such an experiment was by no means simple. I have never lived through moments of such acute despair as during the dress rehearsals and opening night of this play in Boston.

Our own men—the members of our production crew—were most willing and cooperative, but their work was constantly hampered by the carelessness and inefficiency of their local assistants.

One could face with comparative equanimity the high wages and countless petty rules and regulations which the unions impose, if only one could be sure of even adequate service. But the callous indifference of the great majority of stagehands, their complete lack of regard for standards of workmanship, the cynicism with which they view the deplorable results of their badly performed tasks are enough to make one weep.

A work of art in the theatre is the product of careful collaboration, and without it the finest of actors, the greatest of directors, the most skillful of stage managers find themselves helpless. Our final dress rehearsal in Boston was technically so unsatisfactory that, in spite of the added overtime, which we could ill afford, I found it imperative to call the complete working crew for a thorough scenic run-through on the day of the Borkman opening. For six hours, tired as we were, we practiced the entire routine with full lights, scenery, furniture, props, and music, until our men and I were satisfied that the show that night might be worthy of our aims. That evening the local union saw fit to send us a completely different set of stagehands to work the show, not one of whom had taken part in the painstaking work of that afternoon; we might just as well have saved our time and money. There was nothing our own men could do in such a situation but struggle to the best of their ability to run the changes themselves, and prevent the new men, completely ignorant of their several duties, from misguided efforts that were more of a hindrance than a help. That opening was a nightmare to us all, and I felt ashamed and humiliated that the critics and first-nighters should blame the many mishaps of the performance on any lack of care or proper respect for the public on the part of myself and my colleagues.

I left the theatre that night without seeing a soul. I didn't dare trust myself to speak to anyone, my heart was so filled with rage and despair. After an hour's walk round and round the Common, I regained sufficient control of myself to go back to the hotel.

I was amazed the next morning at the kindness and understanding of the Boston critics. During this whole engagement they gave us the most cordial encouragement and help. They seemed genuinely aware of the validity of our purpose and highly appreciative of what they felt was fine work on the part of a distinguished company. Had we met with similar cooperation from the New York press, the fate of the American Repertory Theatre might possibly have been different.

Our out-of-town expenses were so heavy that we suffered considerable losses during the five weeks prior to our New York opening, but we were prepared for this contingency and were not too deeply discouraged by it.

Cheryl reported that there was great interest in our venture in New York and seemed pleased with the prospects there. She was in favor of presenting the plays one at a time, over a period of weeks. In this she was probably wise, since the distaste of stagehands for the repertory system, involving as it must more work and trouble than that of the long run, entails such heavy penalties that operating costs become prohibitive. Peggy shared with me the feeling that, since it was our intention to create a repertory theatre, we should play repertory from the start. Cheryl agreed that ethically we were right, but her business sense warned her there was danger in adhering too faithfully to our much-publicized ideal.

A compromise was arrived at, which, like most compromises, was not completely satisfactory to either Cheryl or myself. A schedule was arranged whereby our plays were to rotate on a half-weekly basis, reducing the change-over of scenery to a minimum, yet preserving some semblance of the repertory scheme. This solution, however, did not reduce the costs of operation enough to please Cheryl, while to me presenting one play for alternate blocks of four or five performances was very different from the constant nightly rotation which is the essence of the real repertory idea.

Since opening on the road, Peggy and I were of necessity completely absorbed in our acting and directing tasks; we had left all business matters and decisions in Cheryl's hands. Before leaving New York we had discussed at length the scaling of the house. Due to the small seating capacity of the International, I realized that a compromise on our dream of popular prices would also be inevitable, but I experienced an unpleasant shock on reading our preliminary ad and seeing the New York opening announced at a $7.50 top. This was indeed a far cry from the policies of a people's theatre. It seemed to me such a grave psychological error that I turned to Peggy and said, "That is the end of the American Rep. We might as well all go home!" For subsequent performances the scale dropped to a mere $4.20, with $4.80 on Fridays and Saturdays, but these prices were no different from those charged by the majority of Broadway attractions at that time. The really low-priced seats were kept at a minimum and consisted of a couple of rows at the back of the balcony.

I have no doubt that this policy would have met with the approval of every single manager in New York City, and in view of the high standard of our productions, the expense of our acting company—which, in spite of unselfish concessions on everyone's part, was still considerable—and the smallness of the house, Cheryl could scarcely be blamed for adopting it, but that did not alter the fact that the policy was in every way contrary to our professed aims. I think Cheryl cherished the hope, which neither Peggy nor I shared, that the American Repertory Theatre would become the fashion. And if the Old Vic company could play to exalted prices, why shouldn't we? But in London the Old Vic had won its reputation as a people's playhouse and it was not its purpose to set itself up in opposition to the commercial theatres of the West End.

I was also troubled at this time by the realization that the

American Repertory Theatre was doomed to be labeled in all press-releases, publicity, and reviews as the ART. It was by pure accident that the letters of its title boiled down to this most unpopular word, and the unfortunate coincidence had, stupidly enough, escaped us all; we had always referred to it as the American Rep, or the Rep, for short. Had anyone pointed out this danger in time, we should certainly have shunned it as we would the plague. In this country any sincere effort to embark on what is often drearily called a "high-minded attempt" to establish the equivalent of an art-theatre is sufficiently discouraged and ridiculed without having its instigators gratuitously brand it with a name so favorable to sneering wisecracks. There is nothing in the world I hate more than "artiness," and I had the uncomfortable feeling that malicious people might find vast amusement in the thought that we had chosen the name ART deliberately.

However, I was so happily engrossed in the luxury of playing three such wonderful and contrasting parts as Queen Catherine in *Henry*, the Comtesse in *What Every Woman Knows*, and Ella Rentheim in *John Gabriel Borkman* that I was able to thrust aside all gloomy thoughts and join in the general excitement of the New York opening.

And indeed that Wednesday evening, November 6, 1946, was a thrilling occasion.

We chose *Henry VIII* as our initial offering, since we were all particularly proud of it and felt it to be a good indication of the kind of theatre we wished to stand for. Certainly its lavishness and sheer beauty must safeguard us from the stigma of dull frugality so often associated with ventures of this sort. *Henry VIII* in Margaret Webster's glowing production was above all else a wonderful show, with all the dash and color and glamour that term implies, and the audiences reacted accordingly.

There was a distinct feeling of success in the theatre that night, and the company and its many friends were jubilant. But knowing that, far from being a subsidized theatre, we were only too dependent for our ultimate survival on the critical reception accorded us, and having often seen the cheers and applause of the public translated into the cold, grudging terms of a newspaper column, I was more skeptical. The next morning the critics were far from helpful.

The following Friday we gave *What Every Woman Knows*. For some reason we were all much more nervous than on the Wednesday night; I think the lukewarm notices unaccountably vouchsafed to *Henry* had taken some of the heart out of us. The performance suffered accordingly, and our young stars seemed unable to rise above the situation. I myself played abominably and remembered, as I often do on such occasions, Mrs. Fiske's remark to Alexander Woollcott: "No critic has ever seen me act!" It is comforting to realize that even such a great artist as Mrs. Fiske could be paralyzed by nerves.

The reviews the next day consisted almost entirely of panegyrics in praise of Maude Adams and Helen Hayes, both of whom had played the part of Maggie with eminent success, and bemoaned the fact that June Duprez was in no way comparable to them. Miss Duprez would herself be the first to admit that she was undoubtedly inferior to these great ladies, but we all felt that the critics were unnecessarily hard on her. She was a talented young actress, just starting her career, and the play, in Margaret Webster's production, was not handled as a star vehicle. It is, on careful examination, an ensemble play, and that was one reason for our choosing it. Miss Duprez' performance may not have been startling, but it fitted, with charming sincerity, into the general excellence of the whole.

The following Tuesday *John Gabriel Borkman* took its place in the repertory. Whether from the indifference of despair, or whether "God was there," I managed to play well that night and was so happy that no amount of critical abuse could possibly have touched me. Knowing the reviewers' unconquerable allergy to Ibsen—which, incidentally, is far from being shared by the public—I expected the worst and was agreeably surprised at the comparative kindness of most of our journalistic friends.

I have no reason to resent the critics; they are usually quite amiable to me personally—with the exception, of course, of that lone wolf George Jean Nathan, who, perhaps out of a misguided sense of chivalry, often praises those abhorred by most of his peers, while condemning others who are fortunately well able to dispense with his support. His attacks on me have often been so virulent that "kind friends" have cut them out and sent them to me with solicitous inquiries as to what I could possibly have done to Mr. Nathan to rouse him to such a pitch of contemptuous fury. I have no answer to this question since, to the best of my knowledge, Mr. Nathan and I have never met.

Mr. Nathan has every right to think me the worst actress in the world, and, far from resenting it, there have been moments when I have cordially agreed with him. My faith in his judgment and good taste falters somewhat, however, when I read excerpts like the following:

Why these extravagant hymns to Madame Sarah Bernhardt because she possesses the courage to appear on the stage with a wooden leg? A leg is approximately not a one-sixth part of the human body. There are therefore any number of star actresses amongst us who, in the matter of woodenness, have the Madame beaten six to one. . . .

Chaplin moves as he has always, without much variation of any kind, moved. He is still the fundamentally proficient zany that he was years ago, but so inelastic in his technique that his every movement, every grimace . . . is foretellable a second or two ahead of itself. . . .

We accordingly find Mrs. Fiske's performance [of *Ghosts*] to be of a piece with a vaudeville comedian's recitation of *The Raven*. . . .

In view of such opinions, it is not surprising that many actors and theatre people, of whom I am definitely one, find a pleasure amounting almost to pride in being among his damned rather than among his blessed. I am reminded of a remark André Gide makes on certain critics in his *Journal:* "*Ils ont à ce point galvaudé leurs éloges, que l'artiste qui se respecte tient pour encens leurs imprécations.*"

I have always felt that to quarrel with critics over their judg-
ments—highly controversial though they often seem to experienced theatre workers—is not only in bad taste but downright foolish. The critics unquestionably have a perfect right
to their opinions, and one can thank God that in our country
these opinions are never for sale, as they frequently are in
other theatrical worlds. In the case of the ART the critics saw
fit to damn us with faint praise, and, more importantly, they
undoubtedly succeeded in creating around the name of the
ART an aura of dull worthiness that prevented many people
from coming to judge us for themselves. Still, if that was how
we impressed them, it was their privilege, and indeed their job,
to say so. My quarrel with them lies in their failure to show
any real understanding of the issues involved, and their conse-
quent failure to help make these issues clear to the public.

After the appearance in this country of some foreign acting
company, whether it be the Moscow Art Theatre, the Abbey
Players, The Old Vic, or that of Louis Jouvet, the critics are
prone to bewail at great length the lack of similar companies
here at home, and roundly scold us theatre people for making
no attempt to provide the United States with comparable organizations. They neglect to take into account certain primary
facts:

1. These companies have had the opportunity of working
together consistently for many years, thus achieving a confidence, a versatility, and a smoothness of ensemble that only
such long association can provide.

2. The endurance of such foreign organizations was made
possible by subsidy of various kinds, which enabled the players
to continue in their work and gradually achieve the perfection
that makes them famous.

3. In the rare instances where such companies are not subsidized, the labor conditions in their respective countries are
such as not to deprive them, by unreasonable demands and
handicaps, of the possibility of survival.

4. The public in these foreign lands is definitely theatre-

minded; it is accustomed to the repertory system and looks upon the theatre in the same way that we look upon music, opera, ballet, and the fine arts. The theatre is not, with this public, limited to show business. In order to develop similar feelings in our own audiences, time is above all necessary. While the Civic Repertory cannot be judged on a basis of profits or even solvency—since it was designed from its inception as a subsidized institution—the growth in its percentage of attendance was indicative. Starting with houses averaging forty-five per cent of capacity, the figure gradually increased with every season, until in its last two years the percentage of attendance rose to ninety-five. The public cannot be expected immediately to respond to something it has never known. It must have time to discover and enjoy the advantages of a repertory theatre, to become familiar with its aims and functions.

The critics might have helped us greatly to clarify our purpose had they deliberately stressed the repertory angle. Instead, their criticisms were no different in tone or form from those accorded single productions presented under the regular Broadway format. The company was judged each time on the basis of its work in the particular play under review, with no relation to its work in general. The fact that within a week an actor like Ernest Truex, usually limited to farce-comedy, played the Chamberlain in *Henry VIII*, Maggie's lovable father in *What Every Woman Knows*, and the pathetic Foldal in *John Gabriel Borkman*, passed unnoticed. Nor was any consideration given to the contrasting styles of Hampden's Cardinal Wolsey and his Venables in the Barrie play, or Jory's flamboyant King Henry and the grim Borkman of Ibsen's imagination. My widely divergent parts of Queen Catherine, the Comtesse de la Bruyère, and Ella Rentheim might have been played by three different actresses to judge by the three different sets of notices.

Perhaps this attitude was largely inevitable, for the critics too work under intolerable handicaps in our theatrical system.

It can be no easy task to write, in the few minutes at their command, a review taking intelligent account of the various elements that make up even a single performance, and it would be even harder exhaustively to analyze the relative merits of a group of actors and directors in terms of three successive plays. The natural inclination would be to stick to the old routine and judge each separate unit with no relation to the whole. This inclination was almost universally followed by the press.

I feel sure that no one could accuse Cheryl Crawford of being a bad businesswoman. She is both realistic and efficient, as well as courageous and resourceful; the record of her successes in the theatre gives ample proof of this. Her careful budgeting, handicapped though it was by the persistent refusal on the part of the craft unions to give her a clear picture of their intentions, gave her cause to hope we would break even at seventeen thousand a week. Such receipts, while high for a theatre of this type, were still within the realm of possibility. But when we were finally faced with the full demands of stagehands and musicians combined, this figure rose to a sum perilously close to twenty thousand. In view of this we had little hope of survival.

In the days of the Civic, Local Number 1 had allowed me to employ a basic number of permanent stagehands. This number was augmented—in some instances very considerably—in accordance with the various plays performed. It is obvious that such productions as Peter Pan, Romeo and Juliet, and Alice in Wonderland require more men to run them than Hedda Gabler or The Cradle Song. This was an eminently fair arrangement, and we were hopeful that the ART would meet with similar consideration. In this we were disappointed. In the case of the ART the ruling was reversed, and our permanent crew, instead of being based on the minimum of men required, was based on the maximum. Since Henry VIII was an elaborate show, the union judged that twenty-eight men were necessary to run it, and a permanent crew of twenty-eight was therefore imposed on us. This was a severe penalty and, in my opinion, quite unjustifiable.

I regret having to speak unkindly of theatrical unions. Having started work in this country long before the majority of them came into being, I know from personal experience how sorely they were needed. The abuses of unscrupulous men made their creation a matter of necessity. But how far in the opposite direction should one go? The increasing demands on the part of the now triumphant unions threaten to create abuses just as dangerous and formidable as those they so rightly abolished. The professional theatre in this country is already so shackled by rigid labor rules and regulations, so crippled by excessive labor costs, that all chance to experiment, to seek new forms, to grow in peace and freedom, is reserved for those theatre workers still outside all union jurisdiction. Such groups—some of them amateurs in the best sense of the word —while of great value, are unfortunately generally lacking in knowledge and experience, and their performances can never be wholly satisfactory. Our best talents in the fields of acting, playwriting, and direction are limited by inexorable conditions to playing safe, and such a limitation is not conducive to the full development of any art. Our theatre has become a formidable game of chance, concerned exclusively with high stakes and huge profits. There is no longer any joy in it, or any place for those who think of it in other terms than these.

Among the members of the various craft unions there are many who feel as I do. Some of my best friends have been stagehands, and these I think of with deep gratitude and affection; the help and cooperation they gave me at the Civic were incalculable. Such men as Henny Link, the electrician, John Ward and Ralph Phillips, the carpenters, and dear Joe Roig, the property man, worked with pride and care and were just as deeply concerned for the welfare of our old theatre as I was. Our own heads of departments at the ART were equally understanding and anxious for the success of our venture. The carpenter, Johnny Norel, the property man, Bunny Moorhead, and Harry Abbott, the electrician, all gave of their best and worked with commendable zeal, but they were vastly outnumbered. Such men nowadays are rare. How could it be otherwise? Games of chance are not apt to encourage the virtues of discipline and loyalty. A sage once said, "The care of discipline is love." Perhaps when we care enough about discipline to bring love back, we'll once more have a theatre; but as long as our code is "Give me, give me!" we may have the greatest "show biz" in the world, but our theatre will be limited to occasional foreign importations, memories of the past, and dreams of a better future.

Our fourth production, *Androcles and the Lion*, went into the repertory on December 19. It was received with considerable favor from the critics, but our financial situation was rapidly deteriorating, and it became evident that drastic measures must be adopted if we were to survive through the rest of the season.

My plea for a cut in prices was overruled, perhaps rightly, for such a step would now be indicative of failure rather than of any basic policy. It was, however, decided, in order to stress the repertory idea, to sell tickets for all four plays at a considerable reduction, while the price for a single play remained unchanged. This was a good plan and should have been adopted from the start.

Equity came to our rescue and actually granted us the five thousand dollars to which Frank Fay had so strenuously objected. ANTA, though itself low in funds, made efforts to collect money for us and also contemplated sending the ART on a cross-country tour under its auspices.

Miss Helen Hayes personally donated a thousand dollars, as did Miss Dorothy McGuire and other important theatre people. We welcomed these evidences of friendship to our cause not only because they enabled us to carry on a little longer, but because they gave concrete proof that people who had the general good of the theatre at heart realized the value of our work and were loath to see it fail.

In spite of our frantic efforts to save it, it soon became obvious that the repertory system would have to be abandoned. No sooner was this decided than people began to rally to our assistance. On all sides the news was greeted with dismay and astonishment. Even the stagehands now came forward with belated concessions, and the press suddenly seemed aware of the importance of our aims and bemoaned the thought of losing us. We ourselves explored every possible avenue that seemed to offer hope, but we were all by now convinced that the ART was doomed.

It was with many regrets that we said good-by to repertory and presented *Androcles and the Lion* for a run while preparing further attractions. We had unfortunately been unable to find a new American play suited to our company, and now decided to revive Sidney Howard's *Yellow Jack*. We entrusted the direction to Martin Ritt, since we felt that a new approach might be welcomed by the critics and salutary to our actors. This experiment was not particularly successful.

For the past year I had been approached on several occasions by Miss Rita Hassan, who was interested in presenting a revival of my production of *Alice in Wonderland*. I had been too involved with my repertory work to consider this, but I now suggested that Miss Hassan join forces with the ART and present the play at the International. There were advantages to both sides in this plan: Miss Hassan would have the use of our theatre, company, and stage facilities, while *Alice in Wonderland* seemed to us a good Easter attraction with which to round out the season. Cheryl and Miss Hassan arrived at a satisfactory business arrangement, and I started work immediately on the production.

Alice opened at the International with great success on

April 5, the night before Easter, and was subsequently moved to the Majestic, where it ran throughout the summer.

If I have seemed to blame the failure of the ART to some extent on the critics and the unions, this does not mean that I am oblivious to our own mistakes. Our choice of plays was perhaps unfortunate, our prices were certainly too high, and it may be that as actors we were none of us sufficiently exciting. Perhaps our partnership itself was largely to blame. Although Cheryl, Peggy and I all sincerely believed we had the same aims in mind, I think there were certain underlying differences. Cheryl alone might quite possibly have made a success of the enterprise because she would have compromised more. I might have made a success of it because I would have compromised not at all—in pioneering work I've always found there is no middle way; it must be all or nothing. Peggy was always a kind of moderator between the two, agreeing now with one, now with the other; her fair-mindedness made her see reason on both sides. Many people felt that three women were bound to disagree, but this we never did—quite the contrary. Out of mutual respect and friendship we each made concessions in an effort to harmonize our different points of view, and this perhaps gave a synthetic quality to the whole venture. But the fact remains that the skill and industry that enabled us, in spite of difficulties usually termed "insurmountable," to present in New York, within a week, superior productions of three such contrasting works as those of Shakespeare, Barrie, and Ibsen might, it seems to me, have merited a little more understanding and recognition on the part of men who profess to love the theatre.

We ourselves, while justly proud of some aspects of our work, were acutely aware of our shortcomings, but we felt that, given time and a chance to grow, these would gradually be corrected, and we might succeed in contributing something of value to the American scene. There can be no doubt that the failure of the ART will discourage any other similar efforts for a long time to come. Its fate is also conclusive evidence of the impossibility of establishing a permanent repertory theatre in this country without the aid of subsidy. Subsidy is imperative to overcome the initial allergies of press and public, to prevent expenses from sinking such a venture before it can become established, and to enable a company of actors to weld itself into a smooth and perfect ensemble.

Government subsidy is not only remote but probably undesirable. Private subsidy is desirable but, in these days of dwindling fortunes, probably remote. What then? A logical answer might be found in the resources of our numerous cultural foundations, but the theatre is not generally thought of as an instrument of culture. I have often wondered why some of our great business corporations, instead of subsidizing soap operas or vaudeville shows on radio and television, do not invest some of their advertising money in subsidizing a great repertory theatre for the American people. As a public service such a gesture would do more for their products than all the radio and television commercials put together. It would be a long-range proposition, perhaps, but the prestige and fame of such an institution would travel round the world, and its sponsors would reap the respect and appreciation of the public. The performances of such a theatre could be televised and broadcast on a weekly basis, in that way assuring the product its customary network audience; and eventually, as the theatre grew in stature and renown, it could not only tour all over the United States, but visit foreign countries and do much to further international understanding and friendship.

Ours is above all a commercial civilization; perhaps the only way we shall acquire the kind of people's theatre enjoyed in other countries is through some such tie-up between art and industry. Let us hope some businessman of vision may suddenly realize the practical possibilities in prestige and publicity of such an innovation and be bold enough to adopt it.

CHAPTER TWENTY-ONE

I HAVE known many *Alice* fans in my day, but never one so devoted as Rita Hassan.

From the first day of rehearsals, as she watched the performance gradually take shape, her smiling face was a joy to behold. She loved every word of the script, every note of the music, every trick of the production, and sat out front like an eager child, radiating satisfaction. Her devotion was touching and endearing and prompted us all to work with affectionate zeal to make the show a success, if only for her sake.

Our search for a suitable Alice was finally rewarded. Josephine Hutchinson, who created the part at the Civic Repertory, had been so perfect that I looked forward with some trepidation to the thought of anyone else playing it. But Bambi Linn ran her a close second.

When I first met Bambi, a couple of months before the opening, I was troubled by her speech. Alice is such a British child, and her expressions are so typically English, that the rhythm of an American accent is more than usually disturbing. Bambi, however, is blessed with a remarkably quick ear and was able to assimilate the English inflections with lightning speed.

Many pretty little girls, some crowned with Hollywood laurels, had been suggested for the part, but Alice is not a "pretty little girl." Apart from the desirability of suggesting Tenniel's drawings, Alice's whole personality, as indicated in her lines and actions, is solemn, intensely proper, at times verging on the priggish. Alice is a character part, not a child ingenue. Bambi's little face seemed to me exactly right; at times stubborn and serious, it could suddenly light up with surprised wonder and a kind of radiant untouched loveliness that were extraordinarily engaging.

Since Mrs. Hassan had greatly admired the original production at the Civic, she was anxious to have it reproduced as closely as possible. I therefore tried to assemble as many members of the old gang as were available. Richard Addinsell came over from England to supervise his score; Ruth Wilton once more attended to the choreography; Remo Bufano took charge of the masks and puppets; and Thelma Chandler, already one of the ART stage managers, ran the stage. Irene Sharaff was busy in Hollywood, so Robert Paddock was commissioned to execute the scenery and costumes. He was completely faithful to my production scheme and to the Tenniel drawings, and turned out an excellent job.

Any theatre engaged in preparations for *Alice in Wonderland* gradually acquires the atmosphere of a happy lunatic asylum. The conversation of all concerned soon became almost entirely Carroll. We "gyred" and "gimbled" through the days. Like all Carroll devotees, we found there was scarcely a contingency that could not be covered by a quote from his inspired chop-logic. Such lines as the White Queen's "I wish I could manage to be glad—only I *never* can remember the rule!" and "Jam tomorrow, and jam yesterday, but *never* jam today!" seemed to express with remarkable accuracy our feelings at that time, while the Red Queen's famous pronouncement, "A slow sort of country! Now *here*, you see, it takes all the running you can do, to keep in the same place. If you want to get somewhere else, you must run at least twice as fast as that!" is almost uncannily descriptive of our modern world. And the Cheshire Cat's dialogue with Alice—"We're all mad here. I'm mad. You're mad." "How do you know I'm mad?" "You must be or you wouldn't have come here"—was greeted each time by the entire ART personnel with shouts of acquiescent laughter.

We were all relieved, for Rita Hassan's sake, at the critical raves that greeted this revival. I had been afraid it might be compared unfavorably with the original. In some respects I felt we had improved on it, though there were a few aspects of the first edition that I preferred. Robert Paddock was a better technician than Irene Sharaff but he was not himself an artist, and while he had meticulously followed the letter of Tenniel, it seemed to me that she had somehow managed to catch more of the spirit and succeeded, while never for a moment betraying the incomparable drawings, in lending the production the imprint of her own personality. Hers was a brilliant interpretation rather than a careful copy.

I personally greatly missed Pepi Schildkraut's mad Queen of Hearts and Nelson Welch's fantastic Gryphon. Burgess Meredith's Dormouse and Howard da Silva's White Knight were also hard to equal, but on the whole the revival was well played. Peggy Webster as the Red Queen was immensely right and funny, Henry Jones was incredibly good as Humpty-Dumpty, and the smallest of our White Rabbits—in the person of Julie Harris—was destined for great things.

We left the International Theatre at the end of May; it was a sad leave-taking. In spite of all our trials and tribulations, the memories that remain of our season there are happy ones. The experience of repertory had been a revelation to those of the company who had never known it, and the young people all felt that those months had taught them more than they could have learned in as many years of ordinary theatre work.

We played an additional six weeks of *Alice* at the Majestic Theatre and then disbanded for the summer. During that time we recorded the show for RCA Victor in an hour-length album. While everyone agreed on the excellence of these recordings, RCA, for some obscure reason which they alone can fathom, shrouded their existence in such profound mystery that I doubt if more than a dozen people have ever heard them. Now, of course, they have been supplanted, and the American child no longer thinks of *Alice* in terms of Carroll and Tenniel but in those of Disney and Hollywood.

Rita Hassan was determined to send the production on the road. In spite of repeated warnings on my part that the high operating costs would defeat her, she opened in Boston at the Opera House in early September, only to find that in spite of weekly grosses in excess of twenty-five thousand dollars, the tour had to be abandoned.

One morning during that Boston engagement I opened the paper and read of my father's death. It was a strange feeling to see his picture looking at me from the front page and to read the columns reviewing his life and works. Although we had seen so little of each other, I felt deeply bound to him.

In *At 33* I scarcely mentioned him, for while both he and Mother were alive I was afraid of touching on things that might cause embarrassment or pain. But now that they are both safe and at peace, I should like to pay a small tribute to his memory.

The first time Mother saw him, at one of his lectures in the London of the nineties, she turned to her companion and firmly announced, "That is the man I shall marry!" It was, for her, love at first sight, and, although she found it impossible to go on living with him, there is no doubt that no other man ever meant to her what Father did. They were neither of them very young—they were both close to forty when I was born; at that time Father was at the height of his fame and beauty. A couple of volumes of poems and several collections of *Prose Fancies* had brought him into prominence in literary circles, and with the appearance of his *Quest of the Golden Girl* his reputation was firmly established with the public. Of this book he used somewhat ruefully to say, "The publishers got all the gold and poor Richard got the girls." And "the girls" certainly played a great part in Richard's life. Mother's friends warned her repeatedly that "Richard Le Gallienne was *not* the sort of man one married," but she would have her poet, and marry him she did.

I once had an Icelandic friend who used to tell me an old legend about "the Biskop and the Daymon," as he called them in his quaint accent. These two creatures lived in the soul of one man and fought incessantly for dominion over him. Sometimes the Biskop won the battle, but then the Daymon rose up again and reigned triumphant for a while; the struggle was unending. My father was like that man. When the Biskop was victorious no one could have been gentler, wiser, more loving-kind—a quiet scholar, a patient worker, an understanding friend. But all this disappeared when the Daymon got the upper hand; then Richard would be transformed into a mercurial being, violently alive, brilliant, cruel, fascinating, and dangerous, like Hedda's Lövborg—beautiful, "with vine leaves in his hair." The girls, of course, were dazzled by the Daymon, and the poor Biskop had a hard time struggling to survive. That the Biskop did survive and constantly grew stronger is a tribute to the fundamental fineness of my father's nature.

My parents separated when I was only four, and Mother gave my father a divorce when I was eight, in order that he might remarry. The third Mrs. Le Gallienne (for my mother was Father's second wife, his first having died shortly after my sister Hesper's birth) was the ex-wife of the sculptor Roland Perry, and her daughter by this first marriage is the Gwen Le Gallienne whom many people think of as my sister, though we are not related and scarcely know each other. This third marriage was a successful one, and lasted to the day of Father's death at eighty-four. I am grateful to the third Mrs. Le Gallienne for her patience and loving understanding, which must have contributed greatly to the final conquest of the Daymon.

When we first came to this country my mother did nothing to prevent my seeing Father, but I didn't "meet" him until a couple of years later. I was eighteen when one day I decided to go and call on him. He always worked away from home, and I went to his study on the top floor of a fine old house at 1 Washington Square. Father was well over fifty then, but I thought him the handsomest man I'd ever seen, and the most charming. He was of medium height, with a slim, sturdy, well-proportioned body. When Mother married him he wore his dark hair very long, and his pale face and blue eyes gave him the romantic appearance expected of a Pre-Raphaelite poet. He used to describe himself in those days as a "crescent moon in a forest of fir trees"! But by the time I met him his hair was gray and conventionally short, and he looked more of the scholar than the poet.

That first visit lasted for six hours; we had a grand time "discovering" each other. Father was wonderful to listen to; there was nothing he didn't know about poetry and literature, and he had the kind of student's mind I've always envied, a rich storehouse of beauty and knowledge. We had great fun too. Father told me of the first time he went to see me play, in *Mrs. Boltay's Daughters*, my first New York job, in which I appeared as a colored maid, looking most peculiar in rather smudgy blackface. This was Father's introduction to his "lovely" daughter! How we laughed!

And so, through the years, we met from time to time, and though we missed the comfortable, familiar routine of a father-daughter relationship, we shared a comradeship that was rare and close.

It was during my visit to Paris in 1931 that we saw most of each other. By one of those queer tricks of chance that make life so much stranger than fiction, Father was living at the very address, 60 rue de Vaugirard, that Mother and I lived at when she first left him and brought me to Paris as a child of four. But Father worked in a wonderful garret-studio on the rue Servandoni, up seven flights of stairs, which he mounted with the ease of a boy. It was here that he wrote his weekly articles for the New York *Sun*—"From a Paris Garret," afterward published in book form. It was here that one day I saw the Daymon. I felt as though I were in the presence of a stranger; his eyes were wild, almost evil, yet so tragic that my fear turned to a passion of pity, and I would have given my life to help him.

Dear Father! I'm glad I caught this one glimpse of the Daymon, for it made me understand the bitter struggle, the constant effort of will, the falling down, bruised and defeated in spirit, and the gallant climb upward again. To those who have no Daymon in their souls life must be a simple thing, yet there's a kind of glory in the battle and victory my father won, which gave to his face the melancholy radiance of those who have struggled out of hell.

In my Blue Room there is a whole shelf filled with my father's books. He was not a facile writer; he was a hard worker, a perfectionist, a true lover of beautiful words, a superb craftsman, perhaps, rather than a great poet. He is truly representative of the nineties; and his work no doubt appears old-fashioned now, when clarity and exquisite imagery are frowned upon and craftsmanship is cast aside impatiently as a bar to "inspiration."

I am grateful to have inherited my father's love of words, for while I only speak their patterns, while he created them, beautiful words are best spoken with love.

I suppose it's natural to be proud of one's parents, and I am very proud of mine. They lived their long lives fully, with courage and awareness, and they both went to sleep quietly at the end, like tired workers whose job has been well done.

CHAPTER TWENTY-TWO

I WAS thankful, at the close of the *Alice* engagement, to return to the peace and tranquillity of the country. After this active year I felt the need of solitude and devoted myself with joy to my various avocations in the garden, at the loom, or in the studio.

Late in November my peace was broken by the advent of Mr. Louis J. Singer. Ever since the closing of the ART, Mr. Singer had toyed with the idea of salvaging the venture. He appeared to feel that by certain modifications and adjustments, by the kind of sane business management which he felt competent to provide, as well as by the use of further capital at his command, its survival in some form might be assured.

Wise woman that she is, as soon as the collapse of the ART seemed imminent, Cheryl Crawford resigned herself to her very genuine disappointment and quickly turned her back on failure. She returned to her Broadway activities, and her production of *Brigadoon* was the first of many distinguished successes.

Peggy Webster and I, however, were less sensible. Apart from our unshaken belief in the work's intrinsic value, we felt a loyalty to those of the company who still looked to us with hope, as well as to the people whose faith had prompted them to invest money in the enterprise. It was obvious that this investment, even under the best of circumstances, could never be redeemed, but it might still pay dividends in terms of honorable achievement.

For these reasons, on our return from Boston, Peggy and I had several meetings with Mr. Singer, in the hope of arriving at some constructive agreement; but our aims and opinions were basically so different that an association between us seemed inadvisable.

In November, however, Mr. Singer approached me again and proposed a short spring engagement in a repertory of Ibsen. He suggested this might serve as a sort of trial partnership and, if it proved agreeable to all concerned, might lead to a further collaboration the following season.

Incorrigible Ibsen fan that I am, I allowed myself to be prodded out of my serene retirement and succumbed to the temptation of once more playing *Hedda Gabler* and having a try at *Ghosts*. I was reminded of a telegram we received at the ART after our repertory schedule was abandoned; it was from a group of students at a Southern university and read: "Please put in performance of *John Gabriel Borkman* during spring vacation stop would rather see Ibsen than eat." Well, I would rather play Ibsen than eat—and that's often just what it amounts to!

I can't imagine what prompted Mr. Singer to ally himself with Ibsen. Perhaps he was attracted to him for the reasons so pungently expressed many years ago by a famous manager who told Madame Nazimova, "If you only need one set and six actors you can go on playing your Isben [sic] as long as you like!"

In any event Mr. Singer did present *Ghosts* and *Hedda Gabler* for a pre-Broadway try-out, followed by a short season at the Cort Theatre in New York. I am kindhearted enough to prefer to draw a veil over this Singer-Ibsen saga.

It did, however, serve two good purposes: it proved beyond the shadow of a doubt that an association between Mr. Singer on the one hand and the Webster-Le Gallienne ART on the other would have been disastrous; it also gave me the opportunity of meeting Mrs. Alving in *Ghosts*—with whom some day I hope to become better acquainted under happier circumstances.

Since, as was only natural, my work in the cause of ART had not been particularly remunerative, I made arrangements to tour in 1948 and 1949 in a series of recitals, starting in late October and continuing to the first of April. This having been settled, I resumed my peaceful life at home.

The summer was an eventful one for me, for during those months I wrote my first work of fiction. I'm afraid I am not one of those unselective child-lovers who drool and gurgle sympathetically with every baby they lay eyes on. Children to me are very much like other creatures—some of them are very, very nice, while others are very, very horrid—so I was astonished and somewhat dismayed to find I had written what is peremptorily called in "the trade" a "juvenile."

I had planned that summer to start on a series of prefaces to those plays of Ibsen's that I had translated and produced, somewhat along the lines of Granville-Barker's *Prefaces to Shakespeare*. Every day I went over to my studio, which is situated in an old barn next to the chicken-house, and, while pondering over the problems of Ibsen's tragic heroine, I found myself frequently gazing out of the window and casually observing the activities of the barnyard.

I had never been especially drawn to poultry; indeed I had thought of hens as rather insignificant silly creatures, but as I watched them I began to notice patterns of behavior that struck me as extraordinarily similar to those of certain human beings. My mind kept veering away from *Hedda Gabler* and roaming along quite different paths.

Two little Bantam hens having shown an obstinate determination to raise families, I set some fertile eggs from the large hens under them—five under one and four under the other—and as I watched the development of this experiment I became more and more fascinated by the individual traits and differences of temperament that, on closer acquaintance, became apparent in all the inmates of the henhouse.

By the time the chicks were hatched and the two proud mothers were marshaling their respective broods around the garden, my thoughts of Hedda grew vaguer and more elusive, and my pen suddenly acquired a life of its own and dashed over the pages, setting down words and sentences that certainly had nothing to do with Ibsen's grim drama.

This state of affairs continued for over two months. At the end of this time I found myself somehow possessed of a sizable manuscript entitled "Flossie and Bossie: A Moral Tale." No one could have been more surprised than I was. When it came back from the typist I gazed at it with amusement and wondered where on earth it had come from.

I diffidently showed it to one or two friends, explaining somewhat sheepishly that I had had no intention of writing anything of the sort—it had, in fact, written itself. Their reaction was most enthusiastic, and, thus encouraged, I put the manuscript to a severer test and gave it to a literary agent in whose judgment I had confidence. Her opinion was equally flattering; it was one of the best juveniles since *Alice in Wonderland*, she said. I swallowed this pleasant news with a large grain of salt and proceeded to read the story through myself. I must say I enjoyed it, but the term "juvenile" rather puzzled me; it would never occur to me to call *Alice* a "juvenile." Children are supposed to love it, of course, and many of them do, but I think it takes a grown-up fully to appreciate its humor and wisdom. The same is true, it seems to me, of many of Hans Christian Andersen's satirical fantasies, and of La Fontaine's wise fables. All these works are, somewhat erroneously, classed as children's books, and for this reason many grown-ups never bother to read them. I know that in this age of specialization precise labels are the custom; I suppose in our busy lives they are necessary conveniences, but I think it is frequently a pity.

I certainly haven't the arrogance to compare *Flossie and Bossie* with the great classics mentioned above—and indeed arrogance could scarcely enter into the question, since I never had the remotest feeling of having written it myself—but as I reread it I was strongly convinced that it should not rightfully be limited to the field of juvenile literature. The basic story is of course artless and childish, and if taken literally could appeal only to a childish mind, but I saw it also as a satirical fable—which the subtitle, "A Moral Tale," clearly indicates.

In 1949 I had the honor of having this little book published by Harper and Brothers. It was, inevitably perhaps, classified and reviewed solely as a juvenile, and, to my regret, Harper's saw fit to suppress the revealing subtitle, "A Moral Tale." In 1950 Faber and Faber presented *Flossie and Bossie* in London, and in the English edition "A Moral Tale" smiles ironically from the title page. The book is immensely enhanced in both editions by Garth Williams' amusing illustrations, which, to my infinite gratitude, unmistakably catch the satirical implications of the story.

The great Mr. Ibsen having thus been rudely thrust aside by two determined little hens, the preface to *Hedda Gabler* was postponed till the following spring.

These two little hens became the most wonderful pets. Poor Flossie was killed a year ago by the neighbors' dog. She was defending a tiny newborn chick and refused to run away— so she lived up to her reputation in the book and became a "hero." Bossie is still with us, a trifle portly, somewhat matronly, but ever beautiful. This summer she hatched out ten of her own eggs and produced the "perfect brood" she dreamed of in the story. Through the industry and care of Flossie and Bossie our little Bantam flock has become a source of endless pleasure and amusement. It now consists of Bossie and one of Flossie's descendants, Lilliput; two very proper young hens, Dorcas and Tabitha, hatched by Bossie and Lilliput jointly; the two "Lillipets," Dum and Dee; Bossie's five girls, Buffy, Buffa, Do, Mi, and Sol, and the one boy she was allowed to preserve, Coqto. He, poor wretch, has rather a frustrated existence since his father, 'Ti-Coq, will tolerate no intruder in his harem.

Maybe one of these days my pen will run away again and write the sequel to the "moral tale"; if I should begin on my preface to *The Master Builder* there's no telling what might emerge. Perhaps I'd be surprised again!

Ever since my first venture in the lecture field the bureau had from time to time urged me to resume these activities; but somehow lecturing is such a lonely, forlorn sort of business, and I suggested a different kind of program. Knowing how few companies manage to survive the increasingly difficult conditions and ever-soaring expenses of travel, it occurred to me that more and more of our young people throughout the country never catch even a glimpse of the living theatre. They hear about it, they read about it, but they never see it. I proposed to combine a brief talk with selected scenes from great plays. I felt that if the acting and the material were good enough they could stand alone without the impediments of scenery and costumes. For the first experimental tour I decided to use only duologues—famous high spots from the classical repertory, such as the *Romeo and Juliet* balcony scene, the Macbeth-and-Lady-Macbeth sequences, some Hamlet soliloquies and his advice to the players, the Mirabell-Millimant scene from *The Way of the World*, the Wagram scene from *L'Aiglon*, a brief excerpt from *The Cherry Orchard*, Camille's death, and part of the last act of Anderson's *Elizabeth the Queen*. Later, if this initial tour proved successful, I planned to extend the scope of the program to include a much wider range of scenes, requiring the presence of several players, but still using a bare stage and dispensing with elaborate costumes.

I was fortunate in finding a helpful and effective colleague in Jon Dawson, who not only gave me excellent support in his capacity of actor, but looked after me with such patient, gentle care, such unfailing good humor, that I managed to survive this really grueling trip with comparative ease and, thanks to him, preserved both my health and sanity.

To describe in detail our many adventures would require a whole separate volume. The first part of our tour was comparatively uneventful and was limited to the eastern territory but, after a brief respite at Christmas, we embarked on eight weeks of unremitting travel that took us literally round the entire United States. We were hurled from train to plane to bus to taxi to private car—even on one occasion to a boat. The only vehicles we escaped were sleighs, jeeps, and helicopters. We took the bare minimum of luggage, not only on account of so much flying, but because in the majority of the college towns porters were unheard of and we usually had to carry our own bags. On one trip, from Lansing to Granville, we had to change four times, and since all four trains were late we arrived at our destination just half an hour before our program, having had nothing to eat since nine in the morning. We were caught in a blizzard on the way from Fargo, North Dakota, to Portland, Oregon, where we were supposed to catch a morning plane to Stockton, California, for a recital that same evening. The train was marooned for twenty-four hours at Spokane, and the Stockton date had to be canceled. But apart from this one engagement we managed to keep faith, and felt we were entitled to carry a banner proclaiming proudly, "Neither snow nor rain, nor heat nor gloom of night, stays these couriers from the swift completion of their appointed rounds." The United States Post Office had nothing on us!

The success of these programs proved conclusively that scenery and costumes are by no means essential to the audiences' enjoyment of great drama, and on my return to New York I booked a further tour for the season of 1950–51—but with the understanding that I would travel by car and that the distances between engagements should not exceed two hundred miles. Much as I enjoy the work, I love my life too much to wish to cut it short by reckless and unnecessary hardships.

In the interval between my two recital tours I spent much time at home, and at last finished the preface to *Hedda Gabler*, which, I am happy to say, will be published shortly by Faber and Faber, together with my translation of the play. This will be the first of a series to include *The Master Builder*, *Rosmersholm*, *John Gabriel Borkman*, *A Doll's House*, *Ghosts*, and *When We Dead Awaken*. I have already made the translations of these plays, but have yet to write the accompanying prefaces. I'll have to keep away from the barnyard if I ever expect to get those finished!

That summer of 1949 I had the pleasure of playing *The Corn Is Green* for ten weeks on the summer circuit. Jane Broder and Richard Waring organized this tour on a package basis, and Dick played his old part of Morgan Evans. We carried a company of eight—all the principals—several of whom had played in Miss Barrymore's production, notably Eva Leonard Boyne, who was wonderful in the part of Mrs. Watty, and Darthy Hinkley, who was excellent as her nasty daughter.

I loved playing Miss Moffat; it gave me great joy. She's so clear and honest and true, and such a very human human being. So I was delighted when Maurice Evans asked me to play her for two weeks at the City Center during his winter drama festival.

Herman Shumlin, who first presented *The Corn Is Green* in New York, graciously consented to supervise the City Center production. I had never met Mr. Shumlin but had heard rather alarming things about him as a director from actors who had worked with him. I think he must have heard equally alarming things about me, for the first time Maurice Evans introduced us we sat cautiously eying each other, our fur ready to bristle and our claws at attention. I think, if anything, I behaved worse than Mr. Shumlin, and the two of us gave Maurice a bad half-hour. We both firmly announced our conviction of never being able to work together, but Maurice—with the success of his season in mind—skillfully poured oil on the troubled waters, and Mr. Shumlin and I magnanimously promised to try to tolerate each other for his sake.

Never have two people been more frigidly polite than Mr.

Shumlin and I were at those first rehearsals; the temperature was positively arctic! But before the week was over I found myself, like most women, quite in love with this strange, complicated man—so gruff and tender, so shy and arrogant, so homely yet so attractive. I don't think I ever really wholeheartedly agreed with anything he wanted me to do in the part, but I found myself meekly obeying him—greatly to my own discomfort, and somewhat to the detriment of my performance.

One day when we were laughing about our first cagey meeting, we came to the conclusion that we were both "lambs in lions' clothing." I'm not sure how Mr. Shumlin feels about me, but I know that I now count myself one of his many devoted friends.

My second bout of recitals started in October of 1950, and this time I was accompanied not only by Jon Dawson but by Kendall Clark, Frederick Rolf, and Sylvia Farnham. This small but excellent company enabled me to play a much wider variety of material, and the work was not only received with great enthusiasm by our audiences, but was also immensely stimulating and interesting to us all.

We had no fixed program but selected scenes from our repertory in accordance with working conditions and the wishes of each particular group. We were a congenial little band of strolling players, blissfully free to do the work we loved, untrammeled, and happy to earn an honest living in exchange for valuable service.

There is no doubt that this vast school and college field offers immense opportunities to acting companies, and even to single players, whose activities have been curtailed by present theatre conditions. It is to be hoped that unscrupulous elements will not be allowed to creep in and, through greed for the money and disregard for the service, spread distrust and disillusionment in the hearts of these young audiences, whose eager faith and intelligent enthusiasm deserve only the best.

I had protected us all by a clause in my contract against social engagements of any kind. The constant travel, added to the exertion of a two-hour program, made any such extra strain inadvisable, but we were always glad to receive visitors backstage after the performance, and a great number of students as well as members of the faculties took advantage of this invitation. We enjoyed these informal meetings and were happy at the great interest our work inspired. We found that a large percentage of the young people had stage aspirations, and I grew to dread the constantly repeated question, "What ought I to do to become an actor?" It is so hard to find a satisfactory answer! In nine cases out of ten the answer should be "Just don't attempt it!" for in nine cases out of ten there is insufficient talent. But in those rare cases where great talent unquestionably exists, what can one say? Where can these young people find the chance to learn and develop? There are innumerable dramatic schools all over the country, a few of which are excellent; but where does our young talent go from there? You can learn acting only by acting; too much theorizing and work in "study-groups," particularly those that imagine themselves to be followers of the "Stanislavski Method," can be positively harmful. Stanislavski, like most great teachers, has been ludicrously betrayed by well-meaning disciples. I have seen countless young actors of promise hopelessly warped, confused, and stunted by an eight-week course of "Moscow Art Theatre" training. To begin with, to the Moscow Art Theatre an eight-week course would seem the most incredible nonsense; but we are always in such a hurry! The training that Stanislavski and Danchenko had in mind would stretch over a period of several years; there are no shortcuts to it, you cannot take it in capsule form. Then, too, most exponents of this "method" dwell on only one aspect of it: the search for truth. That in itself is a splendid thing, and no one could be a greater believer in truthful acting than I am, but there are many sizes, shapes, and forms of truth. You cannot generalize about acting; all plays cannot be attacked alike.

You cannot paint a mural with the same brush, the same stroke, the same restraint with which you paint a miniature— yet both mural and miniature may be equally true in essence. In the same way the truth of Joan of Arc about to be burned at the stake is larger in size than the truth of a young girl disappointed in love. We must train our imaginations to encompass these larger truths if we are ever to play anything that transcends our common everyday experience, and we must train our bodies—the only instruments we actors have to play on—to keep pace with our imaginations and not hamper, weaken, or betray them. But where are young actors to learn the ways of doing this? In television? In the movies? By playing small parts in our modern "realistic" shows? It's easy enough for a talented young American with sloppy speech and still sloppier manners to play a truckdriver—but what of Hamlet? What of Romeo? And, make no mistake, young talent still longs to play such roles. What then?

Many of our youngsters go to England for a year or two of training. At least it is still possible there to acquire a sense of style in speech and movement, a grace of manner, a clarity of language. But this opportunity is given to few, and I often feel the British way seems superimposed on an American. We should have theatres of our own throughout the country, where our young people could work and learn and stretch themselves.

Lawrence Langner's idea of creating an "American Stratford" in Westport is a hopeful sign, and if he only half succeeds in attaining his ideal it should prove an invaluable help to preserving in this country the rapidly disappearing traditions of style and beauty indispensable if the classical theatre is to survive.

If our young people were content with playing tarts and truckdrivers all this might not be so important. But the great majority of them are not. They long to tackle the great parts, to work in great material. In the final analysis, I think it's up to them. They should have the courage and initiative—yes, the daring—to start theatres of their own. Their tendency now is to play safe, to be cautious, to be jealously careful of "hurting their careers." Most of them have "personal representatives" who do their thinking for them in terms of money, of shrewd business moves, of star billing and Hollywood contracts. Great actors do not grow out of such limitations. Let them shake off Broadway and Hollywood for a while. What does it matter where they play if the work is good? Let them throw caution to the winds and really learn their jobs and have some fun!

Some young people have now and then, in recent years, made gallant attempts along these lines—but never those who are successful. It is the successful ones who should set about this work if it is to carry any weight. When I started the Civic Repertory my greatest asset was my success; without that I could have accomplished nothing. I had just finished starring in *The Swan*; I had triumphantly won the Battle of Broadway, and every manager was eager to secure my services; my position was exactly analogous to that of Uta Hagen or Julie Harris at the present day. If Uta Hagen and Julie Harris, having legitimately won stardom and all that goes with it, were deliberately to turn their backs on it, take an old burlesque house in Brooklyn or the Bronx, transform it into the kind of theatre they profess to believe in, and play in it for a hundred dollars a week —then people might sit up and take notice!

I know it will be said, and with some truth, that conditions today are far more difficult than they were in 1926; but I believe that with sufficient faith, youthful energy, talent, vision, and guts, they might still be overcome. The word "impossible" should not be allowed to play too dominant a part in one's vocabulary.

Of course nothing can destroy the living theatre—nothing ever has and nothing ever will—but I sometimes get impatient when I hear young people talk about "How wonderful it would be if . . . !" Why don't they *do* something, or at least *try* to do it? It's a job for youth. What does money matter when you're young? Time enough for caution when you reach "plus twenty"; and as far as I'm concerned—"plus twenty" and all—I still think a bit of daring is a healthy thing.

It's because I love and admire young people that I feel so strongly. I rejoice when I see them do good work—all our young players, so full of splendid promise. I love them and admire them and I want them to be the "most they can be." I want them to be great, not merely prosperous; I want them to be rich in more than money; I want their lives to be filled with something rarer than just "success."

Now who says I'm not *"l'ennemi des agents"*!

CHAPTER TWENTY-THREE

M Y LONG fight for the establishment of classical repertory
theatres has often been misunderstood. I have been
accused of having a contempt for the great popular shows, of
gazing with lofty disdain at the best-sellers of Broadway. Nothing could be further from the truth. No one enjoys a good
show more than I do, and I look with pride and wholehearted
admiration on the skill and imagination that make our entertainment industry the finest in the world. But I see no reason
why our theatre should be limited to that one facet. There
should be room not only for classical repertories but for children's theatres and, very importantly, for the type of experimental playhouses known in France as *théâtres d'avant-garde*.
None of these would be in competition with show business and
should receive quite different treatment at the hands of the
craft unions and the critics.

There exists in this country a large group of people that
might well be called "the forgotten public." These are the
people who have reluctantly given up theatre-going, not only
because their means are usually limited, but because they find
little there to satisfy their tastes. For the same reason they
seldom go to movies or listen to the radio, and their houses
are unadorned by television aerials. They represent perhaps
the most enlightened and cultivated section of our population,
yet they are almost completely ignored by those who control
all branches of our entertainment world. These are the people
the kind of theatres I have in mind would serve. They are un-

questionably a minority group—though perhaps not to the extent generally believed—but a group large enough to be important, and it is wrong that their needs should be denied. In the fields of mechanical entertainment particularly, the product is geared deliberately to the lowest grade of mentality. I have been told repeatedly by the powers that be, in pictures, radio, and television, that the average intelligence of our fellow citizens is that of a child of twelve. Apart from the folly of such generalizations, even if this were true, is it necessary to lower intelligence still further—to force the figure down to eight instead of perhaps raising it to sixteen? The answer to such questions is invariably, "It's not our job to educate the public; we're in business to make money." The sole aim seems to be to "make the unskillful laugh" even though this often makes "the judicious grieve." I feel this situation to be a great, a tragic pity. But of course if the theatre, along with its mechanical offspring, is considered solely as a means of getting the most money out of the public, and all thought of service and desire for giving is brushed aside as so much nonsense, that is the logical procedure.

In the summer of 1951 I had a radio program for some sixteen weeks. It was a sustaining show and therefore cost the network very little. While the standard of the broadcasts seemed pleasingly high, it didn't strike me as in any way remarkable; yet the flood of letters I received from all over the country, expressing gratitude, relief, and praise, was touching and revealing. For a while I tried to answer these letters personally, for they in no way resembled the general run of slightly sophomoric fan-mail; they were letters from thoughtful, appreciative people, all welcoming with almost pathetic joy a program that they considered "adult" and that was free from singing commercials and glowing, ecstatic panegyrics to soap, coffee, or laxatives. But after the announcement that these broadcasts were shortly to be discontinued, the flood of letters became so overwhelming that I was forced to abandon all attempts to acknowledge them, except through the microphone. I personally received over two thousand communications, and thousands more were addressed directly to the station, bemoaning the prospect of losing the program and begging for its continuance. But the station could find no time for our modest offering, and we were supplanted by entertainment which, in the opinion of our masters, was more to the public's taste.

I was genuinely sorry about this decision, for it is nice to give pleasure to so many people, and the radio is a medium I greatly admire and value. It is a force so powerful that its misuse can be calamitous, while its right use can be of immeasurable benefit to all mankind.

It remains only for me to say a few words in farewell, and, if you have followed me throughout these twenty years, to thank you for your companionship.

I cannot tell whether there is any longer a place for me in the American theatre. There are times when I doubt it. I say this with no feeling of dismay or bitterness—I have never been one of those "theatre-apes" who find life empty and meaningless away from the smell of greasepaint or the glare of the footlights—and if the thought brings with it any tinge of regret, it is only because of my desire to share the store of skill and knowledge that has come to me through long searching and constant practice. My powers as an actress are now greater than they have ever been, and I should like to be able to use them in the service of the American public, for which I have ever had high regard and warm affection, and which has always given me, in return, ample proof of similar sentiments.

The fact that I find it increasingly difficult to do this is no doubt partly due to my own intransigence, but perhaps mainly to the rapidly changing values in the theatre world. I am not alone in my feelings of dislike for some of these new values. I know of at least half a dozen other artists equally endowed— some of them far more greatly than I—whose careers have been similarly acclaimed and rewarded, who feel as I do that the theatre we loved—which, in spite of frequent hardships, struggles, and disappointments, was still a joyous place—has become for the moment a grim and ruthless game of chance, where the players watch with feverish anxiety the turn of that fateful wheel which will bring them either triumph or disaster.

Too many whimsical and wayward forces nowadays control the destinies of plays and players; the race is no longer always to the swift. This situation may have existed before to some extent, but at no time in my experience has the theatre been subject to such capricious turns of fortune.

In trying to compete with the all-powerful mediums of moving pictures, radio, and television, our theatre is so busy frantically searching for the new, the startling, the sensational, the lurid—yes, even the obscene—that it is losing sight, it seems to me, of the power that, above all, makes it unique and will, if nurtured and cherished, preserve it unscathed and unconquered; its power—and I now quote from *At 33*—"to spread beauty out into life." And not only beauty but truth, wisdom, compassion, gaiety, and magic, and, above all, by the theatre's special quality of living contact, a greater, and in these troubled days so necessary, understanding of our fellow men.

This is the theatre I have loved and wish to serve, and, wherever I may find it, always shall.

It need not necessarily follow an old format; new times create new forms, and I am not yet old enough to shy away from innovations, providing they are good ones. My intransigence chiefly lies in a refusal to work in any medium without joy, without pride, and without freedom of spirit. "Man does not live by bread alone"—at least this creature cannot. Form doesn't matter; what counts is the spirit that creates it.

I have loved every moment of my life and I thank God for it. I have been greatly blessed. I have been blessed with a good mind and a sound body, with talents and countless opportunities to make use of them. I have been greatly loved and have loved greatly in return. I have been blessed with enduring friendships and have received far more than my share of admiration and praise. There is no trace of bitterness in my heart toward any creature living or dead, and that is perhaps the greatest blessing of them all.

I have enjoyed the past, I find the present good, and I look to the future with a quiet heart.

Weston, Connecticut, 1952

INDEX

The Temptation of Your Touch

Center Point
Large Print

**This Large Print Book carries the
Seal of Approval of N.A.V.H.**

The
Temptation
of Your Touch

TERESA
MEDEIROS

CENTER POINT LARGE PRINT
THORNDIKE, MAINE

This Center Point Large Print edition is published
in the year 2013 by arrangement with Pocket Books,
an imprint of Simon & Schuster, Inc.

The text of this Large Print edition is unabridged.
In other aspects, this book may
vary from the original edition.
Printed in the United States of America
on permanent paper.
Set in 16-point Times New Roman type.

ISBN: 978-1-61173-710-3

Library of Congress Cataloging-in-Publication Data

Medeiros, Teresa, 1962–
  The temptation of your touch / Teresa Medeiros. — Center Point Large
Print edition.
     pages cm.
  ISBN 978-1-61173-710-3 (Library binding : alk. paper)
  1. Aristocracy (Social class)—Fiction. 2. Master and servant—Fiction.
     3. England—Fiction. 4. Large type books. I. Title.
  PS3563.E2386T46 2013
  813′.54—dc23
                                                     2012050820

To Luanne, my sweet sister of the soul.

And for Michael, the man who
made all of my dreams come true.

Acknowledgments

I'd like to thank Garnet Scott, Stephanie Carter, Tina Holder, Gloria Staples, Veronica Barbee, Diane Alder, Richard Wimsatt, Janine Cundiff, Ethel Gilkey, Nadine Engler, Nancy Scott, Elliott Cunningham, Tim Autrey, and all of my tennis buddies for keeping me smiling (even when I'm on deadline).

And my heartfelt thanks to the city of Metropolis, Illinois, for keeping the dreams of Superman alive and for being my home away from home whenever I need to rediscover my creative soul.

Chapter One

Maximillian Burke was a very bad man.

He watched a tendril of smoke rise from the mouth of the pistol in his hand, trying to figure out exactly when he had embraced the role of villain in the farce his life had become. He had always been the honorable one, the dependable one, the one who chose each step he took with the utmost care to avoid even the possibility of a stumble. He had spent his entire life striving to be the son every father would be proud to claim as his own. The man any mother would want her daughter to marry.

At least that's what everyone had believed.

It was his younger brother, Ashton, who had gone around getting into brawls, challenging drunken loudmouths to duels, and facing the occasional firing squad after stealing some price-less relic—or woman—from a Middle Eastern potentate. But now Ash was comfortably settled in the family's ancestral home of Dryden Hall with his adoring wife and their chattering moppet of a daughter. A daughter, according to gossip, who had been blessed with her mother's flaxen hair and laughing green eyes. A daughter who should have been his.

Maximillian briefly closed his eyes, as if by doing so he could blot out the image of the niece he would never see.

While Ash enjoyed the domestic bliss that should have been Max's with the woman Max had loved for most of his life, Max stood in a chilly Hyde Park meadow at dawn, his expensive boots coated in wet grass and the man he had just shot groaning on the ground twenty paces away. Ash would have laughed at Max's predicament, even if a drunken slur cast on Max's sister-in-law's good name had prompted it.

Max could not seem to remember Clarinda's honor was no longer his to defend.

When he opened his gray eyes, they were as steely as flints. "Get up and stop whining, you fool!" he told the man still writhing about in the grass. "The wound isn't mortal. I only winged your shoulder."

Clutching his upper arm with bloodstained fingers, the young swell eyed Max reproachfully, his ragged sniff and quivering bottom lip making Max fear he was about to burst into tears. "You needn't be so unkind, my lord. It still hurts like the devil."

Blowing out an impatient sigh, Max handed the pistol to the East India Company lieutenant he had bullied into being his second and stalked across the grass.

He helped the wounded man to his feet,

gentling his grip with tremendous effort. "It's going to hurt more if you lie there whimpering until a constable comes to toss us both into Newgate for dueling. It will probably fester in that filth and you'll lose the arm altogether."

As they crossed the damp grass, the young man leaned heavily on Max. "It wasn't my intention to give offense, my lord. I would have thought you'd have thanked me instead of shooting me for being bold enough to say aloud what everyone else has been whispering behind your back. The *lady* in question did jilt you at the altar. And for your own brother, no less!"

Max deliberately stripped his voice of emotion, knowing only too well the chilling effect that always had on his subordinates. "My sister-in-law is a *lady* of extraordinary courage and exceptional moral fiber. If I should hear you've been speaking ill of her again, even in so much as a whisper, I will hunt you down and finish what we started here today." The lad subsided into a sulky silence. Max handed him off to his white-faced second and the hovering surgeon, relieved to be rid of him. Resting his hands on his hips, Max watched them load the young fool into his rented carriage.

If Max hadn't been so deep in his cups when he had overheard his unfortunate dueling opponent loudly tell his friends that legendary adventurer Ashton Burke had married a sultan's whore, Max would never have challenged the silly lad to a

11

duel. What the boy really needed was a sound thrashing before being sent to bed without supper.

Despite his regrets, Max had to admit that relinquishing his heroic mantle was almost liberating. When you were a villain, no one looked at you askance if you frequented seedy gambling halls, drank too much brandy, or neglected to tie your cravat in a flawless bow. No one whispered behind their hands if your untrimmed hair curled over the edge of your collar or it had been three days since your last shave.

Max gave the sooty stubble shadowing his jaw a rueful stroke, remembering a time when he would have discharged his valet without a letter of recommendation for letting him appear in public in such a disreputable state.

Since resigning his coveted chair on the Court of Directors of the East India Company in the aftermath of the scandal that had sent the society gossips into a feeding frenzy for months, he was no longer forced to make painfully polite conversation with those who sought his favor. Nor did he have to suffer fools graciously, if not gladly. Instead, everyone scurried out of his path to avoid the caustic lash of his tongue and the contempt smoldering in his smoky gray eyes. They had no way of knowing his contempt wasn't for them but for the man he had become—the man he had always secretly been behind the mask of respectability he wore in public.

He would rather have people fear him than pity him. His ferocious demeanor also discouraged the well-meaning women who found it unthinkable that a man who had been one of the most eligible catches in England for over a decade should have been so unceremoniously thrown over by his chosen bride. They were only too eager to cast him in the role of wounded hero, a man who might welcome their clucks of sympathy and fawning attempts to comfort him, both on the ballroom floor and between the sheets of their beds.

Shaking his head in disgust, Max turned on his heel and went striding toward his own carriage. He needed to get out of London before he cast an even greater stain over his family's good name and his own title by killing someone. Most likely himself.

The lieutenant returned the pistol to its mahogany case before trotting after Max. "M-m-my lord?" he asked, his stammer betraying his nervousness. "W-where are you going?"

"Probably hell," Max snapped without breaking his stride. "All that remains to be seen is how long it will take me to get there."

Chapter Two

"Annie! Annie! I've something you must see!"

Anne Spencer withdrew her head from the cast-iron oven as young Dickon came racing into the kitchen of Cadgwyck Manor, all gangly limbs and boundless enthusiasm. With its low ceiling, exposed rafters, massive stone hearth, and scattering of faded rag rugs, the kitchen was by far the most cozy chamber in the drafty, old manor and the one where its residents chose to spend most of their free time.

"Mind your tongue, lad," Anne scolded as she slid a large wooden paddle from the stove and swung it toward the sturdy pine table, depositing two loaves of freshly baked bread topped with buttery, golden crusts on the table's scarred top.

Having never dreamed she would excel at such a domestic pursuit, she could not resist sparing a moment to admire her handiwork. Most of her early efforts at baking had resulted in the ancient stove's belching black clouds of smoke before it coughed up something that looked more like a smoldering lump of suet than anything fit to be consumed by humans.

By the time she returned her attention to Dickon, he was bouncing up and down on his

heels with excitement. "How many times have I told you how important it is to stay in the habit of addressing me as Mrs. Spencer?"

"Even when there's no one around to hear?"

"Beer? There's no beer, lad, and if there was, you'd be too young to drink it."

They both turned to look at the old woman rocking in a chair in the corner of the kitchen. Nana squinted at them through her rheumy eyes, the merry click of her knitting needles never faltering despite her gnarled fingers and swollen knuckles. They had long ago stopped trying to guess what she could be knitting. It might have started out as a stocking or a scarf, but now it trailed behind her wherever she shuffled, growing longer each time Anne scraped aside a few pennies to buy another skein of wool at the market.

Anne exchanged an amused look with Dickon before saying loudly, "Don't fret, Nana. Our young Dickon here has always preferred brandy to beer."

Harrumphing her amusement at Anne's jest, Nana returned to her knitting. Her hearing might be failing her, but her mind was still sharp as the proverbial tack.

Setting aside the paddle and dusting the flour from her hands, Anne nodded toward the rotund pooch napping on the rug closest to the hearth. "Nana might be too deaf to hear you, but what

about dear old Piddles over there? He's always been an insatiable gossip." Piddles, the rather ill-favored and ill-tempered result of a sordid tryst between a pug and a bulldog, lifted his grizzled head just long enough to give them a disdainful snuffle through his flattened nose before curling himself back into a ball. Anne pointed at the calico cat who was treating the threadbare cushion of the other rocking chair as if it were his own private throne. "And then there's Sir Fluffytoes. Who knows what secrets the rascal might reveal to his numerous ladyloves to coax them out of their drawers?"

Dickon wrinkled his sun-freckled nose at her. "Now you're just being silly. Everyone knows cats don't wear drawers—only bibs, boots, and mittens."

Laughing, Anne gave Dickon's already hopelessly tousled tawny hair an affectionate rumple. "So what treasure have you brought for me today? Another dinosaur egg perhaps or the mummified corpse of a shrew that met its tragic fate at the merciless claws of Sir Fluffytoes?"

Dickon gave her a reproachful look. "I never said that was a dinosaur egg. I said dinosaurs had a right number of things in common with birds."

As the lad reached into his jacket, Anne recoiled out of habit. She had learned from bitter experience to check his pockets for snakes, frogs,

mice, or any other reptile or rodent likely to send Lisbeth or one of the more squeamish house-maids into a fit of shrieking hysterics. Her smile faded as Dickon's freckled hand emerged with an expensive-looking square of vellum sealed with a daub of scarlet wax. "It was waiting for us in the village."

Anne took the letter from his hand, almost wishing it *were* a snake.

In her experience, the post rarely brought good news. A quick perusal of the exclusive Bond Street address on the outside of the missive confirmed today was going to be no exception to that rule.

Just as she had expected, the letter wasn't addressed to her but to Mr. Horatio Hodges, the butler and de facto head of the household whenever the manor's current master was not in residence.

Ignoring that small fact, Anne slipped one chipped fingernail beneath the wax seal and unfolded the cream-colored sheet of paper. As she scanned the letter's contents, her face must have revealed far more than she intended for Dickon immediately snatched the missive from her unsteady hands, his lips moving as he struggled to decipher the elegant handwriting. Anne had patiently been working with him on his letters, no easy feat when he much preferred to be out roaming the moors or scouring the steep cliffs for

long-forgotten smugglers' caves or cormorant nests.

Even with his limited reading skills, it didn't take Dickon long to understand the gravity of their situation. When he lifted his eyes to her face, dismay had darkened their caramel-colored depths. "We're getting a new master?"

"Disaster?" Nana echoed loudly, her needles still clicking. "Is there a disaster?"

"So it seems," Anne replied grimly, swiping a smudge of flour from her flushed cheek. Given that she had sworn no man would ever be her master, the irony of their predicament did not escape her. "I was so hoping they would leave us to our own devices for a while."

"Don't look so worried, Annie—I mean, *Mrs. Spencer*." At the exalted age of twelve, Dickon considered himself a man full grown and more than capable of looking after them all. Anne wondered if she was to blame for forcing him to grow up too fast. "I doubt the gent will be here long enough to trouble any of us. We made short enough work of the last one, didn't we?"

A reluctant smile canted Anne's lips as she remembered the sight of their former *master* bolting over the hill toward the village as if the Beast of Bodmin Moor were snapping at his heels. Since he had publicly sworn he would never again set foot on the property, she had anticipated he might sell the manor or foist it off

18

on some unsuspecting relative. She just hadn't expected it to be so soon.

"And then there was the one before that," Dickon reminded her.

They'd barely avoided an official inquiry over that one. The village constable still looked at Anne askance when she did her shopping at market on Fridays, forcing her to don her most guileless smile.

"That one wasn't precisely our doing," she reminded Dickon. "And I thought we all agreed we would speak of him no more. God rest his lascivious soul," she muttered beneath her breath.

"Well, if you ask me," Dickon said darkly, "the rotter got just what he deserved."

"No one asked you." Anne plucked the note from Dickon's hand to give it a more thorough reading. "It seems our new master is to be a Lord Dravenwood."

Something about the very name sent a shiver of foreboding down Anne's spine. Once, she might have recognized the name, would have known exactly who the gentleman's mother, father, and second cousins thrice removed were. But the noble lineages immortalized between the covers of *Debrett's Peerage* had long ago given way in her brain to more practical information, like how to beat a generation of dust out of a drawing-room rug or how to dress a single brace of

scrawny partridges so they would feed ten hungry servants.

She squinted, trying to read between the lines, but nothing in the letter from the earl's solicitor gave a clue as to their new master's character or whether the man would be arriving with a wife and half a dozen pampered bratlings in tow. With any luck he'd be some potbellied, gout-ridden sot in his dotage, already half-addled from decades of overindulging in too many overly rich plum puddings and after-dinner brandies.

"Oh, no," she whispered, dread pooling low and heavy in her breast as her gaze fell on the date neatly inscribed at the top of the page. A date she'd overlooked in her haste to read the rest of the letter.

"What is it?" Dickon was beginning to look worried again.

Anne lifted her stricken eyes to his face. "This letter is dated nearly a month ago. The post must have been delayed in reaching the village. Lord Dravenwood isn't scheduled to arrive at the manor a week from today. He's scheduled to arrive . . . *tonight!*"

"Bloody hell," Dickon muttered. Anne might have chided him for swearing if his words hadn't echoed her own feelings so precisely. "What are we going to do?" the boy asked.

Gathering her scattered composure, Anne tucked the letter into the pocket of her apron, her

mind working frantically. "Fetch Pippa and the others immediately. We haven't a second to squander if we hope to give our new master the welcome he deserves."

Chapter Three

The journey to hell was much shorter than Max had anticipated. It seemed the abode of the damned wasn't located in the stygian depths of the underworld but on the southwest coast of England in a wild and windswept place the unbelievers had christened Cornwall.

As his hired carriage jolted its way across the stony sweep of Bodmin Moor, rain lashed at the conveyance's windows while thunder growled in the distance. Max drew back the velvet curtain veiling the window, narrowing his eyes to peer into the night beyond. He caught a brief glimpse of his own scowling reflection before a violent flash of lightning threw the bleak landscape into stark relief. The lightning vanished as quickly as it had come, plunging the moor back into a darkness as thick and oppressive as death. Given how ridiculously overwrought the entire scene was, Max wouldn't have been surprised to hear the ghostly hoofbeats of King Arthur and his knights as a spectral Mordred pursued them or to see the

Bodmin Beast, the phantom creature who was said to haunt these parts, loping along beside the carriage, eyes glowing red and teeth bared.

Letting the curtain fall, he settled back on the plush squabs, feeling an unexpected rush of exhilaration. The rugged terrain and ferocious weather perfectly suited his current temper. If he had sought to banish himself from the comforts and charms of civilization, he had chosen well. The bone-rattling journey from London alone would have been penance enough for a less sinful man.

There had been a time when his father might have tried to talk him out of leaving London. But when the gossip about Max's duel had reached the duke's ears—and the society pages of the more sordid scandal sheets—the duke had been forced to admit it might be in everyone's best interests if Max took a brief *respite* from polite company. His father still hadn't recovered from the blow of Max's resigning his prestigious position with the East India Company. Even Max's mother, who had yet to give up on her cherished hope that Max would find a new—and far more suitable—bride, had managed no more than a token protest when informed of his plan to manage the most remote property in the family's extensive holdings.

If it had been within his power, Max would gladly have relinquished his title along with his

career. Ash had ended up with everything else Max had ever wanted. Why not just hand him the earldom and make him heir to their father's dukedom as well?

As his parents had bid him an affectionate farewell in the drawing room of their London mansion, neither of them had been able to meet his eyes, plainly fearing he might recognize the relief within their own. Since his past transgressions had come to light on the day his bride had jilted him, proving he wasn't the perfect son they had always believed him to be, Max had become a stranger to them both—dangerous and unpredictable.

Despite his determination to embrace the rigors of his exile, he felt a flare of relief when his carriage traded the rutted road for a cobbled courtyard. He wasn't immune to the temptation of stretching his long legs after being confined to the cage of the vehicle for hours—and days—on end.

He was gathering his hat, gloves, and walking stick when the coachman flung open the carriage door. Rain dripped steadily from the drooping brim of the man's slouch hat.

"Have we arrived at our destination?" Max was forced to practically shout to be heard over the rhythmic slap of the rain against the cobblestones.

"I have," the man said shortly, his long face looking as if it would shatter completely if it dared to crack in a smile. " 'Tis as far as I'll go.

You'll have to hire one o' the locals to take you the rest o' the way."

"Pardon? I was under the impression you'd been engaged to take me to Cadgwyck Manor."

"I was hired to take you to the *village* of Cadgwyck," the man insisted.

Max sighed. His diplomatic skills had once been the stuff of legend, but of late the reserves of his patience had been all but exhausted. "If this is the village, surely the manor can't be that much farther. Wouldn't it make more sense to press on than to go to all the trouble of unloading my baggage just so it can be reloaded into another conveyance? Especially in this weather."

" 'Tis as far as I'll go. I'll go no farther."

Max wasn't accustomed to having his will defied, but it was rapidly becoming clear the taciturn coachman was not to be swayed, either by logic or threats. Since Max didn't have a stockade, a firing squad, or even a dueling pistol at his immediate disposal, he found himself with no recourse but to exit the man's carriage.

"Very well," he said stiffly, yanking on his gloves.

He climbed down from the carriage, tugging the brim of his hat forward to shield his face from the wind-tossed gusts of rain. He straightened to find himself standing in the cobbled courtyard of a ramshackle inn. He half-expected the inn to be named Purgatory, but a splintery sign suspended

on creaking chains over the door proclaimed it the Cat and Rat. Max could only hope it was a tribute to the faded black cat with a rat hanging out of its mouth painted on the sign and not what they served for supper.

The establishment had plainly seen better days, but the cozy glow of the lamplight spilling through the windows promised a haven for the weary—and wet—traveler.

Max watched as the coachman's outriders piled his trunks beneath the overhang of the inn's roof, where they would at least be out of the worst of the weather. He supposed he should be grateful the lunatic hadn't dumped him and his baggage in the middle of the moor.

The coachman scrambled back up into the driver's seat, drawing an oilcloth hood up over his hat to shelter his dour countenance. *He must be in a great hurry to escape this place,* Max thought. He wasn't even lingering long enough to change out his team or allow his outriders a bit of refreshment.

As the man gazed down at Max, shadows hid everything but the sharp glint of his eyes. "God be with you, m'lord," he said before muttering beneath his breath, "You'll have need o' Him where you're goin'."

With that enigmatic farewell, the coachman snapped the reins on his team's backs, sending the carriage rocking away into the darkness.

Max stood there in the rain gazing after him, not realizing until that moment just how weary he was. This weariness had little to do with the hardships of his journey and everything to do with the thirty-three years that had preceded it. Years spent chasing a single dream only to have it slip through his fingers like a woman's sleek blond hair just when it was finally within his grasp.

Max's expression hardened. He wasn't deserving of anyone's pity, especially his own. Forcing himself to shake off his ennui along with the droplets of rain clinging to the shoulder cape of his greatcoat, he went striding toward the door of the inn.

Max entered the inn on a tumultuous swirl of wind, rain, and damp leaves. The common room was far more crowded than he had anticipated on such an inhospitable night. Well over a dozen patrons were scattered among the mismatched tables, most of them nursing pewter tankards of ale. Max hadn't seen any other coaches in the courtyard. Since it was the only establishment of its kind in these parts, the local villagers probably assembled there nightly to indulge in a pint—or three—before seeking out the comfort of their own beds.

A thick haze of pipe smoke hung over the room. A cheery fire crackled on the grate of the stone hearth, making Max wish he were an

ordinary man who could afford the luxury of drawing off his damp gloves and warming his hands by its flames before settling in to enjoy a pint and some companionable conversation with his mates.

He tugged the door shut behind him. The wind howled a protest as it was forced to retreat. An awkward silence fell over the room as the gaze of every man and woman in the place settled on him.

Max returned their gazes coolly and without a trace of self-consciousness. He had always cut an imposing figure. For most of his life, he had only to enter a room to command it, a trait that had served him well when negotiating peace treaties between warring factions in Burma or assuring Parliament the interests of the East India Company were also the interests of the Crown. He could feel the curious stares lingering on the plush wool of his greatcoat with its multilayered shoulder capes and brass buttons, the ivory handle of the walking stick gripped in his white-gloved hand, the brushed beaver of his top hat. The last thing the patrons of the tavern had expected to blow through their door on this night—or any other—was probably a gentleman of means.

He gave them ample time to take his measure before announcing, "I'm looking for someone to transport me to Cadgwyck Manor."

Suddenly, no one would look at him. Instead, they exchanged furtive glances with one another, lifted their mugs to their lips to hide their faces, or gazed into the steaming depths of their mutton stew as if the answers to the mysteries of the universe could be found there.

Baffled by their odd behavior, Max cleared his throat forcefully. "Perhaps you misunderstood me." His voice rang with an authority honed by years of snapping out orders to brash young lieutenants and chairing board meetings attended by some of the wealthiest and most powerful men in England. "I'm seeking to engage someone to carry me and my baggage the rest of the way to Cadgwyck Manor. I'm willing to pay. And pay well."

The silence grew even more tense, broken only by an ominous rumble of thunder. Now the villagers wouldn't even look at each other. Max studied their drawn profiles and hunched shoulders, fascinated against his will. He could easily have dismissed them as a provincial and unfriendly lot with an instinctive mistrust of strangers. But as a man well acquainted with battle fatigue in all of its incarnations, he recognized that their nervous twitching and averted gazes were not a result of hostility but fear.

A woman Max assumed must be the innkeeper's wife came bustling out from behind the bar, wiping her hands on her ale-stained apron.

Judging by the fetching dimples in the dumplings of her cheeks and the alarming way her heavy breasts threatened to overflow the front lacings of her bodice, she had probably been quite the buxom beauty in her day.

"Now, m'lord," she crooned, her smile a shade too friendly, "why would ye want to go back out on such a foul night as this? Especially when ye've got everything you need right here. Why, we've even a mattress ye can let in a private room!" Her smile deepened to a leer. "Unless, of course, ye'd like someone to share it with ye."

The woman seized a scraggly-haired young barmaid by the elbow and thrust her in Max's general direction. The girl gave him a flirtatious smile, which might have been more alluring if both her front teeth hadn't been missing.

Suppressing a shudder at the thought of sharing some flea-infested mattress with a barmaid who probably also had fleas—or worse—Max offered both women a polite bow. "I appreciate the hospitality of your fine establishment, madam, but I've already come all the way from London. I've no desire to waste another night on the road, not when I'm this close to my destination."

The woman cast the man polishing a pewter tankard behind the bar a desperate glance. "Please, sir, if ye'll just wait till morning, we'll have our boy Ennor take ye up to the manor.

And I won't let him charge ye so much as a ha'penny for his trouble."

Ignoring her offer, Max swept his gaze over the room, assessing its occupants with a jaded eye. "You there!" he finally said, settling on a hulking giant of a man with a shiny melon of a head and a homespun shirt stretched taut over the slabs of muscle in his shoulders. The man was hunched over a bowl of stew and did not look up as Max strode over to his table. "You look a strapping sort, not inclined to let a little rain or a bit of thunder and lightning keep you from making a tidy profit. Have you a conveyance?"

"Won't go." The man spooned another heaping mouthful of stew into his mouth. "Not afore the sun comes up. She wouldn't like it."

"She?" Max cast the innkeeper's wife a bewildered glance. Although the woman looked perfectly capable of wielding a mean rolling pin, she hardly looked menacing enough to hold an entire village hostage.

"Her." The man finally lifted his head to meet Max's gaze, his voice a rumble even deeper than the thunder. "The White Lady o' Cadgwyck Manor."

Chapter Four

An audible gasp went up from the other patrons of the inn. Catholicism had fallen out of favor in these parts over three centuries ago, after King Henry VIII had decided it would be simpler to divorce Catherine of Aragon than to behead her, but from the corner of his eye, Max saw a man sketch the sign of a cross on his breast.

As understanding slowly dawned, an emotion he hardly recognized came bubbling up inside of him. Throwing back his head, Max did something he hadn't done for months and had suspected he might never do again.

He laughed.

It was a deep, ripe, full-bodied laugh, as out of place in the tense atmosphere of the tavern as a baby's cry would have been at the undertaker's.

"She won't like that, either," the bald man warned dourly before returning to his stew.

Max shook his head, still grinning. "I can't believe all of this nonsense is over a ghost! Although I don't know why I should be so surprised. It's not as if I'm a stranger to native superstitions. In India it was the *bhoot* who wear their feet backward and cast no shadow. In Arabia, the cunning *efreet* who can possess a man's body

and then trick others into doing its will. And what crumbling manor or castle in England doesn't come equipped with its own spectral hellhound or Gray Ghost? I did a fair bit of reading after I decided to come here, and it seems Cornwall is so rife with spirits of the dead it's a miracle they aren't stumbling over each other's chains." He began to tick them off on his fingers. "There's the Bodmin Beast, of course, along with the shades of all the sailors lured into dashing their ships on the rocks by unscrupulous wreckers out to salvage their cargo. Then there are the ghosts of the wreckers and smugglers themselves, doomed to wander the mist as flickering lights for all eternity as punishment for their terrible crimes."

He shook his head ruefully. "But if I'm to have a ghost, naturally it would be a White Lady. Because God knows I haven't already wasted enough of my life being haunted by a woman!"

The villagers were beginning to eye him askance, as if he were the one making mad assertions. Even to his own ears, his voice had a wild edge to it, just shy of violence.

The innkeeper's wife planted her hands on her generous hips, her disapproving scowl warning him just how quickly the villagers could turn on him. "Ye might not be so quick to dismiss our words as a bunch o' rubbish—or be so bloody smug—if ye'd have seen the face o' the last master o' the house on the night he came runnin'

into the village a little after midnight, half-dead from fleein' whatever evil lurks in that place."

"Why, he wouldn't even speak o' the things he saw!" the barmaid added, her face growing even paler beneath its curtain of lank, lemon-colored hair.

"Aye," said an old man with leathery skin and a patch over one eye. "Unspeakable they were."

The other villagers began to chime in, growing bolder with each word. "He swore he'd never set foot in that cursed place again, not for all the money in the world."

"At least he escaped with his life. The one before him weren't so lucky."

"Took a tumble out a fourth-floor window, he did. Found him in the courtyard, his head twisted clean round on his neck."

A hush fell over the common room once again. The rain had subsided, and for a long moment there was no sound at all except for the eerie whistle of the wind around the eaves.

When Max finally spoke, his voice was soft, but edged with an authority that dared anyone within earshot to defy him. "I've spent the last twelve years of my life journeying to places most of you will never see, not even in your darkest dreams. I have seen men do unspeakable things to each other, both on the battlefield and off. I can assure you ample evil lurks in the hearts of men without conjuring up phantoms and monsters from the

shadows of our imaginations. Now," he said briskly, "I've no intention of squandering any more of my time or yours." He reached into an inner pocket of his greatcoat and withdrew a leather pouch. He tossed it toward the nearest table, where it landed with an impressive clunk. "Twenty pounds to the man who possesses the backbone to get me to Cadgwyck Manor before the rain sets in again."

The eyes of the inn's patrons gleamed with avarice as they gazed upon the pouch.

Max wasn't playing fair. But if he hadn't tried to play fair for most of his life to atone for the one time he hadn't, he wouldn't have ended up stranded in this miserable tavern at the mercy of a bunch of overly superstitious rustics. The men in the tavern were fishermen, shepherds, and farmers living a hardscrabble life on whatever scraps the sea and the land deigned to toss them. Twenty pounds was more than most of them could hope to earn in a year.

Still, no one moved to accept his offer.

Until a scrawny young man rose slowly to his feet. Ignoring the dismayed gasps of his companions, he drew off his cap in a gesture of deference before wadding it up in his tense hands. "Derrick Hammett, sir. I'm yer man."

Max eyed him thoughtfully, taking in the sunken hollows of his cheeks and the way his clothes hung loosely on his rawboned frame,

before retrieving the pouch and tossing it to him. "Very well, lad. Let's make haste then, shall we? I'm sure this White Lady of yours is only too eager to meet the man who will be her new master."

Max had envisioned arriving at the gates of his new home in the dry, cozy comfort of a carriage, not while perched stiffly on the bench of a rattletrap cart with chill rivulets of rain trickling beneath his collar and down the back of his neck. Despite his young driver's best intentions, the lad had been unable to make good on his promise to get Max to Cadgwyck Manor before the rain returned.

As they passed between two stone gateposts, one of them leaning crazily to the left, the other to the right, the sky hurled violent gusts of rain at them, rendering the brim of Max's hat utterly useless. Twice during their journey up the long, twisting drive he was forced to climb down from the cart to help the boy dislodge its wheels from jagged ruts carved by the rushing water, an exercise that ruined his expensive gloves and left both his boots and his temper much the worse for wear.

The weather in this place was as perverse as its people. Just as they reached the top of the hill and the promise of shelter, the wind gathered speed, whipping away the last of the rain. It carried on its breath the salt-tinged scent of the

sea and the muted roar of angry waves breaking against the cliffs on the far side of the house.

Setting his jaw in a rigid line to keep his teeth from chattering, Max peered through the gloom, struggling to catch his first glimpse of his new home.

A pale splinter of a moon materialized from behind a wisp of cloud, and there it was, perched at the edge of the towering cliffs like some great hulking dragon.

Max's father had informed him he had picked up the property from a distant cousin for a song. *If that were so,* Max thought grimly, *it must have been a very sad song indeed. Perhaps even a dirge.*

It was difficult to believe the manor had seen better days, although he might be convinced it had seen better centuries. An abandoned stone tower crowned one corner of the structure, complete with crumbling parapets and a lopsided turret. A glistening curtain of ivy had clawed its way up the weathered stones and through the gaping black holes of the windows, making it look like a place where Sleeping Beauty might dream away the years while waiting for a prince's kiss that would never come.

The front door was set like a rotting wooden tooth in the mouth of an ancient gatehouse that must have been part of the original castle charged with the duty of guarding these cliffs.

The various descendants of that castle's lord had haphazardly slapped Elizabethan wings on each side of the gatehouse, then adorned the entire monstrosity with several deliciously droll Gothic touches—gables pitched at dizzying angles, lancet windows set with cracked panes of jewel-toned glass, impish gargoyles spitting streams of rainwater on the unsuspecting heads of anyone reckless enough to pass below them.

A tragic air of neglect hung over the place. Shutters hung at awkward angles over the grimy windows. The roof sported several bald spots, where slate shingles had been hurled into the night by the gleeful fingers of the wind and never replaced.

Had the village lad not been with him to confirm this was indeed their destination, Max might have mistaken the manor for a ruin. The house looked as if it would do them all a great favor—especially Max—by completing its inevitable slide over the edge of the cliff and into the sea.

Despite its dilapidated state—or perhaps because of it—Max felt a curious kinship with the structure. The two of them might just suit after all. The manor looked less like a home and more like a lair where a beast might go to lick its self-inflicted wounds in privacy and peace.

The wind sent a fresh veil of clouds scudding across the moon. Darkness reared up to cast its shadow over the house once more.

That was when Max saw it—a faint flicker of white in the window of the crumbling tower, gone as quickly as it had appeared. He frowned. Perhaps he had been wrong about the tower being abandoned. Or perhaps a broken pane of glass still clung to a splintered window frame, just large enough to pick up a reflection.

But a reflection of what?

With the moon cowering behind the clouds, there was nothing but an endless stretch of moor on one side of the manor, and jagged cliffs and churning sea on the other. The flash of white came again, no more substantial than a will-o'-the-wisp against that solid wall of blackness.

Max glanced over to see if his companion had noticed it, but Hammett was using every ounce of his attention to keep his team from bolting back down the hill. Both horses were tossing their heads and whinnying nervously, as if they were as eager to depart this place as their young master. By the time Hammett got them under control and brought the cart to a lurching halt, the tower was once again shrouded in darkness.

Max gave his eyes a furtive rub with the palms of his hands. He was hardly a man given to fancy. Those spectral flashes must simply be a symptom of his own exhaustion—a trick of his weary eyes after the grueling journey. Due to the run-down state of the house, a man was more

likely to be murdered by a loose chimney pot or a rotted banister than a vengeful ghost.

"Are ye sure they're expecting ye, m'lord?" Max's young driver blinked the last of the rain from his ginger lashes as he gazed anxiously up the hill toward the manor's forbidding edifice.

"Of course I'm sure," Max replied firmly. "My solicitor sent word over a month ago. The household staff has had ample time to prepare for my arrival."

Despite Max's insistence, he couldn't blame the young man for his skepticism. Except for that mysterious flash of white, the house looked as deserted and unwelcoming as a tomb.

Max gathered the single portmanteau he had salvaged from his baggage and climbed down from the cart. He had decided to leave the rest of his bags at the inn and risk the villagers picking through them rather than transport them in the back of the cart, where they would have been soaked through in minutes.

"It's nearly ten o'clock," he pointed out. "The lateness of the hour must be taken into account. And I can hardly expect even the most devoted of servants to be lined up in an orderly row on the front steps to greet their new master in this foul weather."

Although Hammett still looked dubious, he managed an encouraging nod. "I'll bring the rest o' your baggage at first light, m'lord. I swear I will."

Reaching into his coat, Max drew out a second purse and tossed it to him. "In my years with the East India Company, I came to believe a young man should always be rewarded for both his bravery and his gallantry."

"Oh, sir!" Hammett gaped down at the purse, a disbelieving grin splitting his gaunt face. "Why, thank you, sir! Me mum and me sisters thank you, too. Or at least they will once they see this!" Although he was plainly itching to go, he shot the house another reluctant glance. "Would ye like me to wait until ye're safely in?"

"I appreciate the offer but that won't be—"

Just like that, Hammett snapped the reins, wheeled the cart around, and went careening down the hill.

"—necessary," Max finished on a whisper heard only by his ears. The rattle of the cart wheels quickly faded, leaving him all alone with the desolate wail of the wind.

Gripping his portmanteau in one hand and his walking stick in the other, he turned toward the house. Once, he had imagined returning from some long journey to a far different scenario. One where a loving wife ran out to greet him, trailed perhaps by a towheaded moppet or two, all eager to leap into his arms, smother his face in kisses, and welcome him home.

Squaring his shoulders, Max went striding toward the door, ruthlessly banishing that vision

from both his imagination and his hopes. As he climbed the stone stairs leading up to the make-shift portico tacked onto the gatehouse, the wind tossed a few fresh droplets of rain into his face.

Drawing off his hat, he hesitated at the top of the stairs. He was at a complete loss as to how he should proceed. He was accustomed to being greeted with deference wherever he went, not left standing outside a closed door like some beggar at the gates of heaven.

Should he use the tarnished brass knocker to alert the servants to his arrival? Should he test the doorknob himself? Or should he just go striding into the place as if he owned it?

Which, of course, he bloody well did.

He was lifting his walking stick to give the door a firm rap when it began to swing slowly inward, its unoiled hinges creaking in protest.

Chapter Five

Max stood his ground, half-expecting to be greeted by a swirl of mist or some chain-clanking ghoul. A stocky, stoop-shouldered man with a snowy white mane of hair appeared in the doorway, bearing a single silver candlestick. The candle's flame cast wavering shadows over

the man's downcast face, a victim of his unsteady hand.

Without a word of explanation or greeting, the man turned toward the interior of the house, as if it were of no particular import to him whether Max chose to follow.

Max cocked a questioning eyebrow but didn't hesitate for long. While the musty smell and flickering candlelight could hardly be called cozy, it was a definite improvement over the darkness and damp of the night.

The two-story entrance hall of the manor was covered in some sort of burgundy velvet-flocked paper. Sections of it had peeled away in moldering strips to reveal the unpainted plaster beneath. Max suspected some valuable wainscoting was buried beneath it as well. Despite enduring the abuses of more recent centuries, the ancient gatehouse had sound structural bones.

His gaze drifted upward as they passed beneath a grand chandelier. Cobwebs draped the fixture's tarnished brass arms, and its once-graceful tapers were melted down to beeswax nubs. On the far side of the entrance hall, a broad staircase climbed up to a second-story gallery shrouded in shadows. A handsome longcase clock hugged the wall at the foot of the stairs, its pendulum hanging still and silent. Its gilded hands were frozen, seemingly forever, at a quarter past midnight.

Max's silent escort led him through a pair of

open pocket doors and into the drawing room. A handful of oil lamps scattered on various tables battled the gloom. Despite their valiant efforts, it wasn't difficult to see why the manor had looked so dark and inhospitable from the drive. The house had been graced with ample windows, but dusty velvet drapes guarded every one of them.

Remembering with a pang of longing the crackling good cheer of the fire at the Cat and Rat, Max noted that a fire hadn't even been laid on the drawing room's marble hearth to welcome him. Could the manor's staff be so provincial they were ignorant of even that basic courtesy? He lowered his portmanteau to the faded Turkish carpet. The butler—or at least Max assumed it was the butler, given that there had still been no proper introduction—set his candlestick on a low-slung pier table, shuffled over to the wall, and gave an unraveling bellpull a feeble yank. A cloud of dust spilled down upon his head, sending him into a violent fit of sneezing.

The man was still snuffling and dabbing at his eyes with the cuff of his shirt when the door at the far end of the drawing room swung open. It seemed Max had done his staff a disservice. They had turned out to greet their new master after all.

They paraded into the drawing room, only managing to arrange themselves in a proper row after a fair amount of elbowing, giggling, muttering beneath their breath, and treading on

each other's feet. Max felt his anger melting to dismay. No wonder the manor was in such sorry neglect. There wasn't nearly enough staff for a house of this size. Why, his town house on Belgrave Square had twice the number of servants!

It hardly strained his advanced mathematical skills to count the still wheezing butler, five housemaids, and a lad wearing footman's livery plainly tailored for a grown man. A powdered wig that looked as if it had been rescued from the head of some unfortunate French aristocrat just *after* his trek to the guillotine sat askew on his head. Max blinked as a moth emerged from the wig and fluttered toward one of the oil lamps.

While the maids quickly averted their gazes to their feet, the lad settled back on his heels and gave Max a look rife with insolence.

There was no sign of a cook, a wine steward, or a groom of the chambers. Max was already beginning to regret not forcing his valet to share his exile. He had just assumed there would be a manservant in the house he could recruit for the position.

Just when he had given up any hope of receiving a proper welcome, a woman glided through the door and took her place at the end of the row, her lips curved in a dutiful smile. "Good evening, my lord. I am Mrs. Spencer, the housekeeper of this establishment. Please allow me to welcome you to Cadgwyck Manor."

In Max's experience, the butler customarily did the welcoming when one was needed. But his new butler was currently occupied with plucking bits of dust from his moth-eaten coat, the faint tremor in his hands even more pronounced now that he'd divested them of the heavy candlestick.

Max inclined his head in a curt bow. "Mrs. Spencer."

Despite the rather motley appearance of the rest of the staff, Mrs. Spencer appeared to be all that was proper in an English housekeeper. Her posture was impeccable, her spine more ramrod straight than that of most military men of Max's acquaintance. A crisp white apron offset her stern black dress.

Her brown hair had been drawn back from her face and confined in a woven net at her nape with a severity that looked almost painful. Her pale skin was smooth and unlined, making it difficult to determine her age. Max judged her to be close to his own thirty-three years, if not older.

She was a plain woman with nothing striking or unique about her features to draw a man's eye. Her chin was pointed, her cheekbones high, her nose slender and straight, though a shade too long to be called delicate. She smiled with her mouth closed as if her lips were accustomed to holding back as many words as they spoke. Or perhaps she was simply seeking to hide bad teeth.

The only feature that might tempt a man to take

a second look were her eyes. Their dark-green depths sparkled with an intelligence that could easily have been mistaken for mischief in a less guarded woman. Her sole concessions to vanity were the delicate tatting peeping out of her collar and the thin chain of braided silver that disappeared beneath it. Max's natural curiosity made him wonder what dangled at the end of it. A cheaply painted miniature of Mr. Spencer perhaps?

"I trust you had a pleasant journey," she said, lifting one delicately arched brow in an inquiring manner.

Max glanced down. Water was still dripping from the hem of his greatcoat to soak the carpet beneath his feet, and fresh mud was caked on the once-supple calfskin of his favorite pair of Wellingtons. He returned his gaze to her face. "Oh, it was simply divine."

Just as he had expected, his sarcasm was wasted on her. "I'm so very pleased to hear that. I'm afraid there are some who find our climate less than hospitable."

"Indeed," he said drily, his words underscored by a fresh rumble of thunder. "That's certainly difficult to imagine."

"If you'll allow me, I shall introduce you to the rest of the staff."

If he hadn't been distracted by the velvety timbre of her voice, Max would have informed

the housekeeper the only thing he was interested in being introduced to at that moment was a tumbler of brandy and a warm bed. The cultured note in her speech shouldn't have surprised him. The upper servants of a household might hail from the local villages, but they commonly affected the accents of the ladies and gentlemen they'd been hired to serve. Most were talented mimics. It seemed his new housekeeper was no exception.

"These are the housemaids," she informed him, gesturing toward the row of young women. "Beth, Bess, Lisbeth, Betsy, and Lizzie." Mrs. Spencer had just reached the end of the row when a sixth maid came racing into the drawing room, skidding to a halt at the far end of the row. "And Pippa," Mrs. Spencer added with somewhat less enthusiasm.

While her fellow maids had at least taken the time to pin up their hair and don aprons and caps, young Pippa looked as if she had just stumbled out of bed. Her gown was rumpled, its collar gaping open at the throat, and she hadn't even bothered to hook the buttons on her scuffed half boots.

The other maids bobbed dutiful curtsies; Pippa yawned and scratched at her wild, dark tangle of hair before mumbling, "Your grace."

"*My lord* will be sufficient," Max said. "I won't be *your grace* until my father dies, and the man

is in such vigorous health he may very well outlive me."

"If we're lucky," the young footman muttered beneath his breath.

"Pardon?" Max shifted his frown to the boy.

Mrs. Spencer's smile tightened as she reached to give the lad's ear a fond tweak. "Our head footman, Dickon, was just saying how fortunate we are to have a new master here at Cadgwyck Manor. We've been quite adrift since the last one took his leave in such haste."

"Aye," Dickon muttered, rubbing his ear and giving her a resentful look from beneath his tawny lashes. "I was just saying that, I was." As far as Max could tell, the lad wasn't just the head footman. He was the *only* footman.

"Called back to London on some urgent bit of business, was he?" Max was not yet willing to let on that he knew the last master of the house had fled the premises in terror, pursued by some dread specter from his own imagination.

"We can only assume," Mrs. Spencer replied, calling his bluff with an unruffled stare of her own. "I'm afraid he didn't linger long enough to give us any reason for his abrupt departure." She turned away from Max, her voice softening. "I would be quite remiss in my introductions if I left off the captain of this fine ship we call Cadgwyck Manor—our esteemed butler, Mr. Hodges."

A muffled snore greeted her words. Max craned

his neck to discover the man who had let him in the door had slumped into a faded Hepplewhite chair and dozed off. His chin was tucked against his chest like a plump pigeon resting its beak in the feathers of its breast.

"Mr. Hodges," the housekeeper repeated, much louder this time.

The butler started violently, shaking himself awake. "Teatime, is it? I'll just go fetch the cart." He sprang to his feet and went bolting from the room, leaving the rest of them staring after him.

Max arched one brow. Apparently the man wasn't a mute as he had first feared, but simply a garden-variety lunatic.

In the time it took for Mrs. Spencer to turn back to Max, she had recovered both her composure and her smile. Folding her hands in front of her like some sort of beatific Buddha, she said, "You must be terribly weary after such a long journey, my lord. Dickon would be delighted to show you to the master chamber."

Judging by his sullen scowl, the young footman would be even more delighted to shove Max over the nearest cliff. Or out the nearest open window.

"That won't be necessary, Mrs. Spencer," Max said. "I'd prefer that *you* escort me to my chamber."

Although Max would have thought it impossible, Dickon's scowl darkened.

Mrs. Spencer's expression remained carefully bland. "I can assure you young Dickon is perfectly capable of—"

Max took a step toward her, using the advantage of his size and his physical presence to underscore his words. "I insist."

The housekeeper's crisp smile wavered. Although Max could tell it displeased her, she had no choice but to respect his wishes or risk defying him in front of the other servants, which would set a poor example indeed.

Her smile returned. As her lips parted, he was reminded of a cornered creature baring its teeth at him. Teeth that weren't bad after all, but were small and white and impressively even except for the winsome gap between the two in the front.

"Very well, my lord," she said stiffly, retrieving from the pier table the heavy candlestick the butler had abandoned. For some reason, Max had a sudden image of it coming down on the back of his head.

She started toward the entrance hall, tossing a look over her shoulder that could easily have been mistaken for a challenge had they met as equals instead of master and servant. "Shall we proceed?"

Max followed his new housekeeper up the shadowy staircase toward the deeper gloom of the second story. He knew he ought to be ashamed

of himself. He had always had his autocratic tendencies, but he had never been a bully. So why was he taking such mean-spirited pleasure in baiting a stranger—and an inferior at that?

He could hardly fault Mrs. Spencer for trying to foist him off on Dickon. Max had been a willing slave to propriety for most of his life. He was well aware there was nothing proper about a lone woman escorting a man to his bedchamber, especially a man she had just met. Perhaps he had simply wanted to see if the composure the woman wore like a suit of armor had any chinks.

Judging by the stiff angle of her neck, the rigid set of her shoulders, and the almost-military cadence of her half boots on each tread of the stairs, it did not. Her determination was so unyielding she might have been marching along behind Hannibal and his elephants as they crossed the Alps during the Second Punic War.

Max's gaze strayed lower, finding a vulnerability he had not anticipated in the subtle sway and roll of her hips. Something unsettling lay in imagining any hint of womanly softness beneath those crisp layers of starched linen. She stole a glance over her shoulder at him; he jerked his gaze back to her face. He was also not in the habit of ogling women's derrieres, especially women in his employ.

"Am I to assume that was the entire staff on display down there?" he asked, hoping to remind

them both of his new role as lord of the manor.

"I should say not!" Mrs. Spencer exclaimed, as if the very notion was nonsense. But her next words quenched Max's swell of relief. "There's also Nana the cook. I saw no need to disturb her since she has to rise so early to prepare breakfast. And on the second Tuesday of every month, Mrs. Beedle comes up from the village to assist with the laundering of the linens. I believe you'll discover we run a very efficient household here at Cadgwyck, my lord. One that is quite beyond reproach."

Max trailed his fingertips through the thick layer of dust furring the banister, wondering if she might not be as mad as his new butler.

During that awkward silence he noticed a most peculiar trait—his housekeeper jingled when she walked. It took his weary brain a minute to trace the musical sound to the formidable ring of keys she wore at her waist.

"That's quite a collection of keys you have there," he commented as they approached the second-story landing.

Without missing a beat, she replied, "Someone has to mind the dungeons as well as the pantry."

"Must be a challenge for you to sneak up on people. Rather like a cat wearing a collar with a bell on it."

"*Au contraire*, my lord," she purred, surprising Max anew with the graceful way the Gallic

syllables rolled off her tongue. "When one expects a cat to wear a bell, removing the bell only makes the cat that much more dangerous."

This time the smile she cast over her shoulder at him was sweetly feline. When she returned her attention to the stairs, Max narrowed his eyes at her slender back, imagining her slinking through the halls of the manor in the dead of night, up to any manner of mischief. He would be wise not to underestimate her. This kitty might yet have claws.

The swish of her hips beneath her staid skirts seemed even more pronounced now, as if she were deliberately baiting him. As they reached the second-story gallery, the wavering shadows fled before the gentle glow of her candle. A halo of light climbed the wall, illuminating the portrait hanging directly across from the top of the stairs.

Max's gaze followed it, as irresistibly drawn as a hapless moth might be to a deadly flame.

His breath caught in his throat. Mrs. Spencer was forgotten. His desperate desire to collapse onto a warm, dry mattress was forgotten.

Everything was forgotten except for the vision floating before his eyes.

Chapter Six

"My God," Max whispered, taking the candlestick from Mrs. Spencer's hand and holding it aloft.

The housekeeper did not protest. Her sigh was resigned, almost as if she had been anticipating such a reaction.

Max had been entertained in some of the finest homes in England, had toured countless museums in Florence and Venice during his grand tour, and seen hundreds of such portraits in his day, including many painted by masters such as Gainsborough, Fragonard, and Sir Joshua Reynolds. Dryden Hall, the house in which he had grown up, was home to an entire gallery of his own stern-faced ancestors. But he'd never before been tempted to forget they were anything but flecks of dried paint on canvas.

The artist of this portrait, however, had captured not just a likeness, but a soul. To even the most insensitive eye, he had obviously been madly in love with his subject, and his intention was to make every man who laid eyes on her fall in love with her, too.

He somehow conveyed the illusion that he had caught her in the wink of time just before a smile.

One corner of her lips was quirked upward, leaving one to wait in breathless anticipation for the dimple that would surely follow. Those ripe, coral lips might tease with the promise of a smile, but her sherry-colored eyes were openly laughing as they gazed boldly down at Max beneath the graceful wings of her brows. They were the eyes of a young woman tasting her power over men for the first time and savoring every morsel of it.

Her curls were piled loosely atop her head, held in place by a single ribbon of Prussian blue. A few tendrils had escaped to frame full cheeks tinted with a beguiling blush no amount of expensive rouge could duplicate. Her hair was no ordinary brown but a rich, glossy mink. She wore a dress the sumptuous yellow of buttercups in the spring—a marked contrast to the gloom of the gallery. The pale globes of her generous breasts swelled over the square-cut bodice of her high-waisted gown.

Something about both her beauty and her manner of dress was timeless. She might have been imprisoned in the faded gilt frame for a decade or a century. It was impossible to tell.

"And just who would you be?" he murmured. A brief glance down the gallery confirmed that the rest of the portraits had been removed, leaving darkened squares on the wallpaper where they had once resided.

The housekeeper sniffed, reminding Max of

her presence. "The rest of the artwork was sold, but *she* comes with the house. It's a stipulation of the sale agreement. No matter how many hands the property passes through, the portrait must remain."

Max could easily understand why the house's past masters might not have grumbled about such an eccentric entailment. Most men would be happy to pass the portrait every day and pretend such an enchanting creature were his wife.

Or his mistress.

"Who is she?" he asked, oddly reluctant to relegate the woman in the portrait to the past, where she undoubtedly belonged.

"Another time perhaps, my lord. It's late and I know you're exhausted. I wouldn't wish to bore you."

As Mrs. Spencer started to turn away, Max's hand shot out to close around her forearm. "Bore me."

She froze in her tracks at his imperious command, her startled gaze flying to his face. Only seconds before he had nearly forgotten her existence. Now he was keenly aware of how near she was to him in the flickering candlelight. Of each shuddering breath that passed through her parted lips. Of the uneven rise and fall of her breasts beneath the starched linen of her bodice. Of the faint, clean scent of laundry soap and freshly baked bread that clung to her the

way expensive perfumes clung to other women.

Her bones felt almost delicate beneath the tensile strength of his hand. He had wrongly assumed she would be forged from something cold and unbreakable, like granite or steel. His gaze lingered on her lips. When not curved into a closemouthed smile that was no smile at all, they looked surprisingly soft and moist and inviting. . . .

The candlestick in his other hand had listed, and the steady drip of the melted candle wax against the toe of his poor beleaguered boot finally broke the peculiar spell that had fallen over them.

Removing his hand from her person as if it belonged to someone else, he said gruffly, "It wasn't a request, Mrs. Spencer. It was an order."

Mrs. Spencer smoothed her wrinkled sleeve; the look she gave him from beneath her fawn-colored fringe of lashes made it clear exactly what she thought of his order. "Her name is . . . *was* Angelica Cadgwyck."

Angelica.

Max's gaze strayed back to the woman in the portrait. The name suited her. Despite her impish charms, she certainly had the face of an angel. "I gather her family was the namesake for both the manor and the village?"

"Up until little more than a decade ago, they were the closest thing the county had to royalty.

And from what I understand, Angelica was their crown princess. Her mother died when she was born, and her father, Lord Cadgwyck, doted upon her."

"Who could blame him?" Max muttered beneath his breath, bewitched anew by the sensual promise in those sparkling brown eyes. "What happened to her?"

Mrs. Spencer's elbow brushed the sleeve of his coat as she joined him in front of the portrait, gazing up at it with a distaste equal to his fascination. "The same thing that always happens when a young woman is raised to believe her every whim should be satisfied without giving any thought whatsoever to the consequences. Scandal. Disaster. Ruin."

Intrigued by the note of scorn in her voice, Max stole a sidelong glance at the housekeeper's disapproving profile. He should have known such a woman would have no sympathy for those who fell prey to temptations of the flesh. She had probably never experienced even the most harmless of them.

"What manner of scandal?" he asked, although he could probably guess.

"At a fete given in her honor on her eighteenth birthday, she was caught in a compromising position with a young man. The artist of this very portrait, I believe." The housekeeper shrugged. "I don't hail from Cadgwyck so I

wasn't privy to all the sordid details. All I know is that her brother was rumored to have shot and killed the young man without even the benefit of a duel. Her father suffered an apoplexy and went mad with grief. The brother was carted off to prison—"

"Prison?" Max interrupted, engaged against his will by the lurid tale. "I thought murder was a hanging offense."

"The Cadgwyck name was still a powerful influence in these parts, so the young man managed to escape the gallows and was deported to Australia. Apparently, her father had made some ill-advised investments prior to all this. Scenting blood in the water, the creditors descended and the family lost everything—their fortune, their good name . . . even this house, which had been in Cadgwyck hands since the original castle was built five centuries ago."

Max returned his gaze to the portrait. "What became of her?"

Mrs. Spencer shrugged, as if the fate of one foolish girl was of little to no import to her. "What was there left for her to do after bringing ruin upon everyone she loved? On the night before they were to vacate the premises, she flung herself over the cliff and into the sea."

Since losing Clarinda to Ash, Max had grown accustomed to the dull, heavy ache in his heart. The piercing pang he felt in that moment caught

him off guard. He had no reason to grieve for a girl he had never met. Perhaps it was simply impossible for him to imagine that such a vivacious young creature would surrender her life without a fight.

"Was there an investigation? Any suspicion of foul play?"

"None whatsoever," Mrs. Spencer said flatly. "The girl left behind a note that made her intentions quite clear."

"Notes can be forged."

The housekeeper slanted him a wry look. "In overwrought theatricals and gothic novels perhaps. But we are not so clever or diabolical here in Cornwall. I suspect her suicide was simply the impulsive action of a rash young girl steeped in a morass of guilt and self-pity."

Max gazed up at the portrait, in danger of forgetting the housekeeper's presence once again. "I should have liked to have made her acquaintance."

"Don't despair, my lord. You may yet get your chance."

Mrs. Spencer retrieved her candlestick from his hand and went sweeping away toward the staircase on the opposite end of the gallery, leaving Max with no choice but to follow or be left behind in the darkness.

As the full import of her words sank in, he could not resist stealing one last look over his

shoulder to watch the portrait of the irrepressible Miss Cadgwyck melt back into the shadows.

At the far end of the third-floor corridor of the east wing, Mrs. Spencer used one of the keys from her expansive collection to unlock the master suite. As she pushed open the door, Max felt his spirits sink. The spacious chamber still bore traces of its former splendor, but the marble hearth was just as dark and dusty as the one in the drawing room. Nor was any supper laid before it.

A single lamp burned on the side table next to the canopied four-poster, casting more shadows than it dispelled.

Had Max known he was going to receive such an inhospitable welcome, he might have at least lingered at the inn for a bowl of stew. Apparently, he was expected to content himself with the maddening aroma of bread wafting from Mrs. Spencer's hair. As savagely hungry as he suddenly was, it was all he could do not to lean down and gobble her right up.

She had stepped aside to let him pass, making it clear she had no intention of placing so much as the pointy little toe of her half boot across the threshold of his bedchamber. Did she truly believe herself in danger of being ravished? Did he appear so desperate for female companionship that he would toss the first female domestic

who crossed his path down on the musty mattress and force himself upon her?

Max could feel his temper rising. He had spent so much of his life holding it in rigid control he almost didn't recognize the danger signs until it was too late.

When he finally spoke, his jaw was clenched so tightly his lips barely moved. "Would a fire in the hearth be too much to ask? And perhaps a bite of supper as well?"

His housekeeper's smile lost none of its infuriating serenity. "Of course not. I'll send Dickon up right away with a tray and your portmanteau." She started to turn away, then looked back at him. "Have no fear, my lord. We'll be here to see to your every need."

The woman's husky voice, completely at odds with her starched appearance, played over Max's strained nerves like crushed velvet. Her innocent promise sent an image flitting through his mind, an image more shocking than any other he had contemplated on this night . . . or perhaps for a long time.

Still smiling, she gently drew the door shut in his face, leaving him to wonder if he had chosen a punishment even he did not deserve.

Anne made it as far as the second-story gallery before collapsing against the balcony rail, her breath coming quick and hard. She felt as if she'd

just run up a dozen flights of stairs instead of walking down one. She lifted a hand to smooth her hair, the tremor of her fingers betraying her. The unflappable Mrs. Spencer had vanished, leaving Anne to pay the price for her composure.

"I daresay his lordship is not quite what you expected."

The mocking voice came out of the darkness, making Anne jump and grab at her heart. It might not have startled her so badly if the sentiment hadn't echoed her own thoughts with such eerie accuracy.

Pippa came gliding out of the shadows, grinning at her. "What's wrong? Did you think I was a ghost?"

Still clutching her heart, Anne glared at the girl. "Keep springing out at me like that and you'll be one before your time. Why aren't you back in bed? I barely managed to rouse you out of it to greet our illustrious new master."

Pippa had just turned sixteen, but when she wrinkled her pert little nose at Anne, she looked as if she were seven again. "Don't be such a scold. I was just making sure His-High-and-Mighty didn't try to take any liberties with his new housekeeper."

"And just what were you going to do if he did?"

"Hit him over the head with a poker."

Anyone else would have assumed Pippa was joking, but Anne wasn't even surprised when the

girl's slender hand emerged from the folds of her skirts to reveal the implement in question. Given the bloodthirsty glint in her eye, Pippa might have undertaken the task with more relish than was strictly necessary.

"Dear Lord, Pippa!" Anne exclaimed. "You're going to get us all hanged for murder. There's no need for you to play knight in shining armor to my damsel in distress. I'm quite capable of looking after myself."

"And Lord Scowlywood looks quite capable of ravishing a housekeeper and perhaps a scullery maid or two, all without removing his greatcoat or wrinkling his cravat."

Remembering how his powerful hand had closed over her arm with such startling intimacy and how close that simple touch had come to undoing her, Anne blew out a disheartened sigh, conceding Pippa's point. "He's certainly no doddering old fool inclined to drink too much port and mistake a sheet on a broom handle for a shrieking portent of doom."

Pippa's observation also forced Anne to relive the shock of walking into the drawing room to find him standing there, glowering beneath those heavy, dark brows and dripping all over the Turkish carpet brought back to the original castle by some marauding Cadgwyck ancestor after the final Crusade. As she had gazed upon his forbidding visage for the first time, it had been all

she could do to keep Mrs. Spencer's congenial smile pasted on her lips.

The earl stood well over six feet, but it wasn't his height—or even the intimidating breadth of his shoulders beneath the shoulder capes of his greatcoat—that was so imposing. It was his effortless command of the room and all who were in it. Another man might have looked ridiculous standing there with hat in hand and mud-caked boots, but Dravenwood looked more inclined to bellow "Off with their heads!" while the potential victims scurried away to fetch him an ax.

Perhaps both his barber and his valet had met with just such a fate. The thick, sooty waves of his hair weren't artfully trimmed as was the current fashion but were long enough to brush the collar of his greatcoat. Striking threads of silver burnished the hair at his temples, and his beautifully sculpted jaw was shadowed with at least two days' worth of stubble.

His dark-lashed eyes were gray, as gray as the mist that swirled over the moors. Anne had always thought gray to be an ordinary color, but his eyes had the disconcerting habit of flashing like summer lightning when he was displeased. The greatest threat to them was the glint of intelligence in those eyes. He was not a man who missed much, and that, more than anything else, could prove to be their downfall if they weren't careful. When she had introduced herself, his

gaze had flickered over Anne, taken her measure, then dismissed her for what she was—a menial, an underling, his inferior. He didn't find her wanting; he simply found her beneath his notice.

Which was exactly where she needed to stay.

"Well, you have to admit dispatching him with a poker would have solved most of our problems," Pippa suggested cheerfully. "Or at least bought us a bit more time to continue our search before the next master arrived."

"Not if we all ended up in the village jail, awaiting a visit from the hangman. But you are right about one thing: the sooner Lord Scowly— Lord *Draven*wood," Anne corrected herself, "is in a carriage and on his way back to London, the sooner things can go back to normal around here."

"Normal? We've spent the last four years combing the manor from the cellars to the attics for a treasure that may not even exist. I'm not even sure I remember what normal is."

Hoping to hide her own misgivings from Pippa's bright, dark eyes, Anne said firmly, "The treasure exists and it's only a matter of time before we find it. Once we do, we can leave this place forever and make a home of our own far away from here."

"But what if it's nothing more than a family legend? A fairy tale trotted out to entertain children and stir the imaginations of dreamers? Dreamers have been searching for Captain Kidd's

buried plunder for over a century now and not a single coin has been found."

Anne touched her fingertips to the familiar shape of the locket that always hid beneath her bodice, and never strayed far from her heart, reminding them both of why they had no choice but to keep searching. "I stopped being a dreamer a long time ago. Which is why I know the treasure is real and that we're going to find it. We simply have to send Lord Dravenwood on his way as quickly as possible so we can get back to the business at hand. Preferably without the assistance of any hearth tools." Sweeping the makeshift weapon from Pippa's hand, Anne started down the gallery, her steps once more brisk with confidence. "The earl may appear to be invincible, but he's already proved he has the exact same weakness as any other man."

Pippa trotted along behind her. "And just what would that be?"

Anne stopped in front of the portrait that faced the descending staircase, holding her candle aloft. *"Her."*

Angelica Cadgwyck gazed down upon them from her exalted perch, her lush lips quirked as if she were hiding some delightful secret that could only be coaxed from her with a kiss.

"Ah," Pippa said softly. "So our lady has already added another heart to her collection. Her appetites really are insatiable, aren't they?"

"Up until the moment Lord Dravenwood saw the portrait, I would have sworn the man didn't have a heart."

Anne had seen the look on the earl's face often enough on the faces of other men. Men who stopped in their tracks and gaped at the woman in the portrait as if they had been struck both mute and blind to everything but the beauty before them.

As Anne had watched their new master succumb to that same old spell, she had felt herself disappear, winking out like a star at the approach of dawn. She should have been pleased her efforts to make herself invisible had met with such success.

Instead, she had felt a sharp twinge of disappointment.

For the briefest blink of time, she had allowed herself to believe this one might be different. That he might be immune to such superficial charms. She couldn't imagine what had prompted her to entertain such an absurd and dangerous notion. Perhaps it was the cynical curl to his lip, his droll sarcasm, or the way the grooves bracketing his mouth deepened when other men might have smiled.

But the second she'd seen him surrender his heart—and his wits—into Angelica's lily-white hands, she had known he was no different from any other man.

As she gazed up into Angelica's knowing eyes, she felt a pang of something even sharper than disappointment, something more akin to jealousy. Now she was being truly ridiculous. Angelica would serve them well, just as she always had.

"Come, Pippa. I need to send Dickon up with some supper for our new master. The sooner he takes himself off to bed, the sooner he can make the acquaintance of the woman of his dreams." She lowered the candle, robbing Angelica of her halo of light. As she herded Pippa toward the stairs, Anne stole one last glance over her shoulder at the portrait, barely resisting the childish urge to poke her tongue out at Angelica's smug visage. "And his nightmares."

Angelica Cadgwyck stood gazing down at the stranger who had invaded her home. Even with his unshaven jaw and unruly hair, there was no denying he was a beautiful man. But she had learned the hard way that a beautiful face could hide a dark and destructive heart.

She had hoped to catch a glimpse into that heart by coming here tonight, but he was no less guarded in sleep than he had been in wakefulness. His lips were pressed into a forbidding line, and the faint furrow between his brows made it look as if he were still scowling, even in his dreams. She was seized by a peculiar urge to touch him, to see if she could soothe that furrow

69

away with the tender caress of her fingertip.

But he was flesh and she was nothing more than a dream, deliberately fashioned to haunt the hearts of men.

She was already beginning to suspect this man was no stranger to ghosts. He muttered something beneath his breath, then gritted his teeth and stirred restlessly, sending a lock of dark hair tumbling over his brow.

Angelica reached out a pale hand toward him, yearning only to touch something warm and solid and surging with life before she had to go drifting back into the cold, lonely night.

Max had never been a man who dreamed. When he had confessed that to his fiancée, Clarinda had looked up at him with her dazzling green eyes and exclaimed, "Don't be ridiculous! Of course you dream. All men do. You just don't remember what you dreamed."

He'd given little credence to the notion until late that night in his bed at Cadgwyck Manor when he felt a woman's cool fingers tenderly brush the hair from his heated brow. He groaned and shifted restlessly in the bed. That simple touch was somehow both soothing and arousing, stirring his body and his soul. He longed to capture her slender wrist in his hand, to bring those finger-tips to his mouth and kiss them one by one as a prelude to tasting the softness of her lips.

70

Determined to do just that, he reached for her. But his hand closed on empty air. He opened his eyes and gazed up into the shadows gathered beneath the canopy of the unfamiliar bed, finding himself exactly as he had expected to.

Alone.

How was it that such a simple dream could seem more vivid and real to him than the waking fog he'd been wading through in recent months? Even if he willed himself to do so, he didn't think he would be able to forget it.

It might have been easier to do so if he weren't still fully aroused and aching for a woman's touch on some far more provocative spot than his brow.

Despite the cool façade he presented to the world, Max's appetites were stronger and more driving than those of most men. That was exactly why he had vowed never to lose control of them. If his brother had taught him anything, it was just how much damage a man could do when he selfishly indulged his lusts without stopping to count the cost to those around him.

Of course, Max hadn't exactly lived as a monk, either. He had always been too much of a gentleman to pay for his pleasures, but he was not above satisfying his baser needs with some discreet widow looking for a bliss more transitory than matrimonial.

All of that had ended when Clarinda had finally accepted his suit. Temptations were far less

difficult to resist when he was anticipating sharing a marriage bed with the woman he had adored for most of his life. He had been confident marriage to Clarinda would fulfill his every desire, both emotional and carnal.

Bloody fool, he thought, kicking away the tangle of bedclothes and throwing his long legs over the side of the bed. As he emerged from the bed curtains, shoving them aside as he did so, the damp chill hanging in the air struck his overheated flesh like a dash of icy water.

The fire the surly little footman had laid still languished on the grate, its soft glow bathing the ancient mahogany armoire crouched in the corner and the tray of nearly untouched food on the Pembroke table. After the tray had been delivered, Max had discovered he was too exhausted to eat after all. He had listlessly pushed the bland bits of beef and potato around on the plate until tossing down his fork in disgust and taking himself off to bed.

An unexpected draft played over the crisp hairs furring his naked chest. With its chill caress stirring gooseflesh wherever it touched, Max slowly turned his head to find the French windows leading to the balcony standing wide open, as if to invite in whatever the night had in store for him.

Chapter Seven

The lace panels adorning the French windows fluttered in the breeze like a bride's tattered veil. Max's scowl deepened along with his bewilderment. Those windows had been closed when he had retreated behind the musty velvet curtains of the bed. He would be willing to swear his life on it.

He reached to the foot of the bed to retrieve his dressing gown, thankful he'd had the foresight to pack it in his portmanteau since the rest of his baggage wouldn't be arriving until morning. Knotting the robe's silk belt around his waist, he rose and padded over to the windows.

The rain had stopped but the moon was still huddled behind a towering bank of clouds, leaving the night beyond the balcony shrouded in darkness. Thinking that perhaps the windows had blown open, Max examined both the latches and their moorings. They seemed perfectly sound, but that didn't mean they were strong enough to withstand a particularly violent gust of wind.

Accepting the irrefutable logic of his own deduction, he reached to close the windows and return the night to its proper place. But before he could, an unexpected scent drifted to his nose.

A scent quite distinct from the clean fragrance of the rain and the briny tang of the sea.

A scent that was delicate and floral and unmistakably feminine.

Max's nostrils flared as he drew the heady elixir into his lungs. It stirred long-buried memories of sultry summer nights and velvety, white petals too shy to bloom while the sun was still up.

Jasmine.

Lured by the irresistible aroma, he stepped out onto the balcony, barely feeling the chill of the rain-soaked tiles beneath his bare feet. Had it not been the wrong time of year for such a tender and fragrant flower to bloom, he might have been able to convince himself that a pergola or a trellis was nearby beneath his balcony. With the wind whipping his hair from his eyes and snatching at his dressing gown with greedy fingers, he found it difficult to believe anything but the hardiest of plants could survive this harsh climate.

The wind also dispelled the lingering hint of perfume, leaving him to wonder if he had imagined it. Shrugging off the scent's intoxicating effects, he started for the balcony windows. He might as well return to the dubious comfort of his bed, where he could blame any other such ridiculous fancies on dreams he would not remember in the morning.

That was when he heard it—the distant tinkling of a music box playing a melody that was

hauntingly beautiful and yet just off-key enough to make the tiny hairs on the back of his neck shiver to life.

He slowly pivoted on his heel, his narrowed eyes searching the night. The east wing had been built at just enough of an angle to the gatehouse to give him an unobstructed view of the tower standing sentinel over the far side of the manor. Without the moon to give it an air of tragic romance, the structure was nothing more than a crumbling ruin—a darker shadow against a sea of turbulent clouds. The tower's windows were vacant eyes with no mysterious flashes of light to bring them to life.

Yet Max would have sworn the eerie waltz wafting to his ears on the wings of the wind was coming from that direction. He drifted to the edge of the balcony, his hands closing around the damp iron of the balustrade.

The music ceased abruptly, almost as if spectral hands had slammed the lid of the music box.

Max released a breath he hadn't even realized he had been holding. He stood there for a long time but there was no repeat performance, no sound at all except for the muted roar of the wind and the distant crash of the waves against the rocks.

Another man might have doubted his senses, but a mocking smile tugged at one corner of Max's mouth. "I've been haunted by the best," he

murmured. "If you want to be rid of me, sweetheart, you'll have to do better than that."

Leaving his challenge hanging in the air, he turned his back on the night and returned to the master chamber, gently but firmly drawing the French windows shut and latching them behind him.

Since their previous master had rarely risen before noon, Anne fully expected Lord Dravenwood to spend most of the morning languishing in bed. She was caught off guard by the staccato tap of his bootheels crossing the second-floor gallery at only half past eight. She tossed the broom she'd been using to judiciously apply fresh cobwebs to the entrance hall chandelier behind a rusting suit of armor and scurried over to the wall to give the ancient bellpull a hearty yank. She could only hope someone was on the other end to hear its jangle of warning.

She smoothed her hair out of habit as she hurried back across the floor. She had risen before dawn to choose her garments with deliberate care—no easy feat when faced with a cast-off armoire containing only a handful of black and gray gowns, all cut from serviceable linens and wools. She had finally settled upon a sturdy merino the same misty-gray shade as Lord Dravenwood's eyes. A freshly starched apron

completed her ensemble. The apron was the identifying badge of the domestic, its purpose to ensure none would embarrass themselves by mistaking her for a lady of the house.

Anne checked to make sure her locket was tucked safely into the bodice of her gown. She knew she would have an extra second or two to prepare as Lord Dravenwood approached the painting at the end of the gallery. No man had ever made it past Angelica Cadgwyck without slowing to pay homage. Still, she couldn't resist rolling her eyes when his footsteps paused at the top of the stairs. He was doubtlessly searching Angelica's exquisite face, trying to determine if the arrival of dawn had broken the spell she had cast over him in the night.

By the time he started down the last flight of stairs, Anne was standing at the foot of them, her hands clasped in front of her as she dutifully awaited her master's pleasure.

Or displeasure, it would seem, judging by the way he was glowering at her from beneath his thick, dark brows. Shadows brooded beneath his eyes, making it look as if he'd slept little. Or perhaps not at all. Anne pressed her lips together to suppress a smirk of triumph.

Perhaps only one night at Cadgwyck was enough to make him realize his mistake in coming here. With any luck, he was coming down to inquire just how quickly she could arrange for

his passage back to London. That would be one order she would hasten to obey.

Stepping off the last stair, he scowled at the frozen hands of the longcase clock. "How is one ever supposed to know what time it is around here? Make a note to get the bloody thing fixed." He must have seen her eyes widen for he shifted his scowl to her. "I hope you're not easily offended by the occasional oath. I'm afraid I spent more of my career with the East India Company in the presence of ruffians than ladies."

"Ah, but I'm no lady," she gently reminded him. "I'm your housekeeper. And I do believe the clock is quite beyond repair. From what I understand, it hasn't worked since the night . . ."

As she trailed off, he arched one eyebrow in a silent demand for her to continue.

She sighed sadly, seeking only to whet his curiosity. "For a *very* long time."

His thoughtful grunt warned her he wasn't satisfied with her answer, but was willing to content himself with it. For now.

"I trust you slept well?" she offered, watching his face carefully.

"As well as can be expected in an unfamiliar bed. Although you'd think by now I would be accustomed to sleeping in strange beds."

Now it was her turn to arch an eyebrow at him.

A glimmer of unexpected amusement warmed his cool gray eyes. "My position on the Court of

Directors of the Company required a great deal of travel. To climes far more inhospitable than this one." He peered around the drafty entrance hall, the lines bracketing his mouth deepening a degree. "Although that might be hard to imagine."

"How very fortunate you were! Most people around here will go their entire lives without ever traveling more than a league away from the patch of ground where they were born."

"I never cared for it. I've always been a man who preferred the simple charms of hearth and home to the unpredictability of the unknown."

"So will your lady be joining us at Cadgwyck Manor after you're properly settled in?" Anne carefully inquired.

A fresh shadow crossed his face. She didn't realize she was holding her breath until he said shortly, "I have no lady." He reached up to give the stubble darkening his jaw a rueful stroke. "At the moment I find myself more in need of a valet."

His current appearance certainly lacked the polished edges expected of a gentleman. His wavy, dark hair was tousled as if he'd raked his fingers through it instead of a brush. He had taken enough care to don a claret waistcoat of watered silk and a black coat, but he wore no cravat. His shirt was laid open at the collar to reveal the strong masculine lines of his throat.

Something about his artless disarray made Anne suddenly feel as if her own collar were

choking her. She touched a hand to her throat to make sure one of her buttons wasn't about to spring free of its mooring without her leave. "Perhaps Dickon could—"

Lord Dravenwood's glower returned. "I have no intention of letting that surly little brat near my throat with a straight razor. Is there no one else in the household who could assist me for a time in the morning and evening? The butler perhaps?"

"Oh, no," Anne said swiftly. "I'm afraid Hodges's duties are far too demanding. We couldn't possibly spare him."

Another skeptical grunt. "What about that lad from the village who brought me up here last night? He wouldn't have any formal training, of course, but he seemed the sort who would be quick to learn and eager to please."

"Derrick Hammett?" She nodded toward the leatherbound trunks piled up in a corner of the entrance hall. "He delivered the rest of your baggage to the front stoop shortly after sunrise and departed before anyone could so much as thank him or offer him a shilling for his trouble. I sincerely doubt he'd be interested in the position. Most of the villagers won't come within shouting distance of the manor. Even Mrs. Beedle, the laundress who comes once a month, won't set foot in the house, but insists we carry all of the soiled linens out to her kettle in the courtyard."

Scorn laced the earl's deep, resonant baritone.

"I suppose it's because of that superstitious twaddle about the ghost."

"I gather you don't believe in such apparitions?"

He lifted one broad shoulder in an indifferent shrug. "We're all haunted in one way or another, are we not? If not by spirits, then by our own demons and regrets."

"Are you speaking from experience, my lord?" Anne could not resist asking.

The chill returned to his eyes, giving them a frosty glint. "What I am doing, Mrs. Spencer, is speaking out of turn. If the local villagers refuse to serve at Cadgwyck Manor, where did you find the staff you have? Such as they are," he added, eyeing the chandelier, which appeared to be in imminent danger of collapsing beneath the weight of the cobwebs drifting from its spindly arms.

"They were engaged from other areas. With Mr. Hodges's expert assistance, of course."

This time he didn't even bother with a grunt. He simply studied her face through narrowed eyes, his penetrating gaze threatening to breach all of her defenses. Anne had forgotten how it felt to have a man look at her that way. She honestly wasn't sure *any* man had ever looked at her that way.

She couldn't help but wonder what a man like Lord Dravenwood saw when he looked at her. She had no Milk of Roses to smooth out her

complexion, no rice powder to dull the faint sheen of her nose, no paste mixed with lampblack to darken her lashes to a sooty hue. The greatest luxury she allowed herself these days was tooth powder, which she used to polish her teeth upon rising and before bed each night.

Did he even realize a woman's heart beat beneath the cloth-covered buttons of her staid bodice? Did he suspect that some nights she woke up tangled in her sheets, her body aching with a yearning she could not name? A yearning that was beginning to bloom again beneath his steady gaze.

Reverting to the stiff formality that always served her so well when dealing with his kind, Anne said, "I've already rung for your breakfast, my lord. If you'll allow me to escort you to the dining room, I'll see to it that you are served immediately."

She was turning away from him, seeking to escape that dangerous gaze, when his hand closed over her arm. It was the second time he had touched her, but that didn't lessen the delicious little shock that danced along her nerves. She hadn't felt delicate or feminine for a long time, but it was difficult not to with Lord Dravenwood's dark form looming over her, his large hand easily encompassing her slender forearm. The back of his hand was roped with veins and lightly dusted with crisp, dark hair. Drawing an uneven breath through her parted lips, she reluctantly lifted

her gaze to his face, half-afraid of what she might find there. "My lord?"

"Your eyes . . ." he murmured, his harsh expression softened by bewilderment as he gazed down into them.

Chapter Eight

Anne had to use every ounce of self-control she possessed not to lower her lashes, but to continue to boldly meet Lord Dravenwood's gaze. She had never expected him to be *that* observant. "Pardon?"

"Your eyes," he repeated more forcefully. "Last night I would have sworn they were green, but now they seem to be brown."

She offered him her most soothing smile. "My eyes are a quite ordinary hazel, my lord. They can appear different colors in different light—sometimes brown, sometimes green, sometimes a mixture of both."

This time she didn't wait for him to relinquish his hold on her. She simply slid her arm neatly out of his grasp and started toward the dining room. She didn't even spare a glance over her shoulder to make sure he was following. Her only desire was to escape before the bewilderment in his eyes could harden into suspicion.

Max sat all alone at the head of a long mahogany table that could easily have accommodated thirty guests, feeling more than a little ridiculous. The only other furniture in the room was a dusty sideboard sporting a silver tea set in desperate need of a sound polishing.

The moldering velvet drapes had been drawn back from the impressive wall of windows overlooking the cliffs, inviting in the meager rays of what passed for daylight in this place. The wavy panes of glass were nearly as grimy as the curtains, making the choppy, gray sea beyond the cliffs look even grayer.

As he awaited the arrival of his breakfast, Max caught himself cocking his head to listen for the telltale jingle of Mrs. Spencer's keys. The merry sound that accompanied her every step was completely at odds with her oh-so-proper appearance. When he had found her waiting for him at the foot of the stairs, her every button and hair had been in place, as if secured with the same starch she used on her collar and apron.

Apparently, the only thing unpredictable about the infernal woman was the color of her eyes.

He was already regretting that awkward moment when he had seized her arm. He couldn't imagine what had possessed him to put his hands on her not once, but twice, since his arrival

at the manor. He'd never been inclined toward manhandling the help. Of course, nor was he in the habit of engaging in personal conversation with them. In his father's household, and later in his own, servants had always been treated as if they were of no more consequence than the furniture—necessary, but hardly worthy of notice.

But who else was he supposed to talk to in this accursed place? Himself? The ghost? A derisive snort escaped him. A few more lonely nights in this mausoleum and he might find himself doing just that.

There was no reason why he shouldn't be perfectly content with his situation. After all, hadn't he come here to the ends of the earth because he wanted to be left alone?

As the dining room door came swinging open, he sat up eagerly. The tantalizing aroma of freshly baked bread drifted through the doorway, making his stomach quicken with anticipation.

The young footman ducked through the door, a tray balanced in his hands. His scrawny chest was swallowed by the oversize coat of his faded blue livery. The legs of his trousers had been pinned up at the ankles so they wouldn't trip him. His powdered wig was canted at an even more precarious angle than it had been the previous night.

The boy slapped the tray down on the table in front of Max, rattling the china dishes, then with a

85

grudging flourish whipped away the silver lid shielding Max's meal.

Although Max's disappointment was keen, he could find nothing to complain about. It was standard English breakfast fare—a pair of poached eggs, a bowl of watery porridge, a limp kipper, three rashers of overcooked bacon, a piece of underdone toast. The food looked every bit as tasteless as it did colorless. There was no sign of the buttery, golden loaf that had haunted his culinary fantasies ever since he had caught the aroma of it clinging to Mrs. Spencer's hair.

Without a word, the footman took his place next to the sideboard, staring straight ahead like one of the king's guards.

The boy's truculent silence was going to make for a long meal. A *very* long meal. Max took a sip of his lukewarm tea, wishing it were something much stronger, before asking, "Have you any newspapers I might peruse while I breakfast?"

The boy blew out a disgusted huff, as if Max had requested the Holy Grail be located without delay so his tea could be served in it. "I'll see what I can find."

Max had finished his bacon and was poking listlessly at his eggs with his fork when Dickon returned with a yellowing broadsheet tucked beneath his arm. Max unfolded the brittle pages to discover it was a copy of the *Times* . . . dated October 1820. Since Max had no desire to read

what Queen Caroline had been wearing at her husband's coronation sixteen years ago, he tossed the useless thing aside. It seemed he had escaped not only London but the modern world altogether.

He managed to choke down a few spoonfuls of the lumpy porridge before a combination of boredom and curiosity prompted him to speak again. "Dickon? It is Dickon, is it not?"

The boy shot him a suspicious glance. "Aye, sir . . . um . . . m'lord."

"How long have you been in service at Cadgwyck?"

"Nearly five years now, m'lord."

Max frowned. "Just how old are you?"

"I'm seventeen," the boy said staunchly.

What you are, Max thought, *is lying through your teeth.* The boy didn't look to be more than a day over thirteen. And that was a generous estimation. "Were you hired by Mr. Hodges?"

"No, it was An—Mrs. Spencer what gave me my place here."

"Your Mrs. Spencer seems to wield an uncommon amount of influence for a mere housekeeper," Max remarked thoughtfully.

"She's not *my* Mrs. Spencer. She belongs to no man."

"Not even Mr. Spencer?" Max asked, amused against his will by the unmistakable note of pride in the lad's voice.

"Oh, there is no Mr. Spencer," the lad blurted out. When he saw Max's eyebrow shoot up, a flicker of alarm danced over his face. "At least not anymore. Mr. Spencer died in an unfortunate . . . um . . . accident. Crushed by a . . . a wagon, he was. A very large, very heavy wagon."

"How tragic," Max murmured, wondering just how long the unflappable Mrs. Spencer had been a widow. Based on the way her breath had quickened and her lips had parted both times he had put his hand on her arm, it must have been a long time indeed. If the mere touch of his hand had stirred such a response, he couldn't help but wonder how she would react if a man actually tried to kiss her. Shaking off the absurd and dangerous notion, he said, "It's no wonder she ended up as a domestic. There are very few avenues open to a woman who must make her own way in the world without the protection of a man."

Dickon didn't even try to disguise his snort. "If any man crosses Mrs. Spencer, he'll be the one in need of protection."

Before Max could stop himself, he had returned the boy's cheeky grin, making them compatriots for the briefest of seconds. Then, as if realizing he was guilty of consorting with the enemy, Dickon jerked himself back to attention, staring straight ahead with his face set in even more sullen lines than before.

Sighing, Max returned his attention to his breakfast. Since he had no idea if anything more nourishing—or flavorful—would be forthcoming for lunch, he forced himself to finish every bite of the pallid fare before rising and leaving the boy to clear his place.

When he emerged from the dining room, he nearly collided with his stalwart housekeeper, who was hovering over a potted ficus tree just outside the door, watering can in hand. She might have been more convincing in her task if the tree had sported a single living leaf. Or if her watering can had so much as a drop of water in it.

Had she been lurking outside the door all along listening to every word of his conversation with young Dickon? Perhaps Max should have paid more heed to her warning about the cat and the bell. As long as she was relatively still, her ring of keys would not betray her.

Determined not to be drawn into yet another inappropriate exchange, he offered her a curt nod and continued on his way.

She fell into step behind him, her dogged pursuit shredding what was left of his frayed temper. "I wasn't sure what you had planned for your first morning at Cadgwyck, my lord. If you'd like, I could take some time out of my duties to go over the household schedule and accounts with you."

"That won't be necessary," he said without

slowing his strides. "You've managed this long without me. Just continue doing whatever it is you're doing."

If she was taken aback by his words or the dismissive wave he aimed in her direction, the cheery jingle of her keys did not betray her. "I trust you found breakfast to your satisfaction, my lord. Will you be requiring—"

He wheeled around to face her, forcing her to bring herself up short or risk colliding with the immovable expanse of his chest. "What I require, Mrs. Spencer, is some decent coffee with my breakfast and a newspaper published in the current decade. Beyond that, all that I require is to be left to my own devices. If I'd have wanted to have my every need anticipated by some well-intentioned, yet interfering, female, I would have remained in London."

With that, he turned on his heel and went stalking toward the nearest set of French windows, determined to escape both the house and his meddling housekeeper.

Behind him, he heard nothing but silence.

It took Max only a brief turn about the grounds of Cadgwyck Manor to discover they were as neglected and unkempt as the interior of the house. Clumps of weeds had sprung up between the cracked flagstones of the terraces, while scraggly, untrimmed shrubs and dangling vines

transformed every walkway into a shadowy maze. The lawn had long ago surrendered to the same rambling ivy that had clawed its way up the walls of the crumbling tower. An ornate bronze birdbath crowned by a mossy statue of Botticelli's *Venus* sat in the center of what must once have been a handsome garden, its basin choked with stagnant water. An air of deserted melancholy hung over it all.

Although he stalked from one end of the grounds surrounding the house to the other, Max encountered no gamekeeper, no gardeners, no stable boys. Of course, why would stable boys be required to tend a stable populated only by rustling mice and the swallows that had darted in through the gaping holes in the roof to build their nests in its sagging rafters? For the first time, it occurred to him he was practically a prisoner in this place.

His restless ramblings finally led him to the edge of the cliffs. Savage gusts of wind tore open his coat and whipped his hair away from his face. Propping one booted foot on a rock, he leaned into its battering force, grateful to finally find a worthy opponent with whom he could do battle. Someone besides himself.

At the foot of the cliffs far below, the wind churned the peaks of the waves into foaming whitecaps before driving them to their death against the jagged rocks. The ceaseless roar of the

sea was much louder here. A towering wall of clouds brooded on the horizon, their ever-present threat sharpening the very air with the scent of danger.

Despite his growing misgivings about coming to Cornwall, Max had to admit the landscape had a raw, seductive beauty, a wildness that was as stirring to the blood as a swallow of fine whiskey or a beautiful woman. It was as if he were standing on the edge of a storm that could break at any minute, sweeping away everything in its path and making all things new.

Off to the left, he could see a shallow cove cut into the cliffs, where the rocks grudgingly gave way to a half circle of sandy beach. When he was a boy, such a sight would have sent his imagination soaring with dreams of smugglers and the shuttered glow of lanterns dancing along the beach beneath a moonless sky, of secret passageways winding their way deep into the stony recesses of the cliffs, and heaps of shimmering treasure buried in long-forgotten caves. But those dreams had long ago been replaced with ledgers full of endless columns of figures and long, dull board meetings where he presided over a bunch of gouty old men more interested in fattening their own coffers than in steering their company—and their country— toward the future.

The back of Max's neck prickled. Even with

his gaze fixed on the sea, he could feel the inescapable shadow of the manor behind him, its windows gazing down upon him like watchful eyes. He wondered if other eyes were watching him as well—mercurial eyes with a maddening tendency to shift when a man least expected it from the glossy green of leaves in deep summer to the rich brown of burled walnut.

He hadn't lingered long enough to see if his curt rebuke had made those eyes darken with hurt.

Seized by a fresh restlessness, Max turned away from the sea and began to stalk along the edge of the cliffs. As he studiously banished his house-keeper from his thoughts, another woman intruded. And not the woman he had expected—the woman who was now happily wed to his brother.

No, this was a mocking little minx, her lustrous brown hair piled carelessly atop her head, her lightly blushed cheek poised on the verge of dimpling. Max slowed his steps as he picked his way over the rocks, wondering just how many times Angelica Cadgwyck's dainty feet might have trod this very path.

And at precisely which spot she had chosen to end her life.

As he reached the very tip of the rugged promontory that jutted out over the sea, his question was answered as surely as if he'd spoken

it aloud. Here, the wind was even more relentless. Nearly staggering against its force, Max drew close enough to the edge of the cliff to watch the roiling sea break over the jagged, glistening blades of the rocks below.

Had moonlight glinted off those same rocks on the night Angelica died? Or had clouds shrouded the moon and tricked her into believing that if she took flight off the bluff, she would drift gently down into the arms of the sea?

Max lifted his eyes to the distant horizon. He could almost see her standing there—a young woman blinded by tears, about to be cast out of the only home she had ever known. The ruthless wind would have stripped the pins from her hair like the fingers of a jealous lover until it danced in a cloud around her beautiful, tear-stained face.

Her lover was dead, her brother carted off to prison, then banished from these shores, never to return, and her father driven mad by grief. Which one of them had she mourned the most in that moment? Had she given the brash young artist both her body and her heart or held one in reserve for some future love? A love she would never live long enough to meet.

In the fraction of time before she had stepped off the edge of that promontory, had she been fleeing her destiny or rushing forward to embrace it with open arms?

Without warning, the thin shelf of rock beneath Max's feet began to crumble. He jumped backward just in time to watch what was left of the shelf tumble toward the sea in a dizzying spiral before shattering against the rocks below like so many grains of sand.

Chapter Nine

As Max watched the swirling sea swallow the pulverized rocks just as it must have swallowed Angelica Cadgwyck's broken body all those years ago, his chest heaved with delayed reaction. Despite the violent pounding of his heart—or perhaps because of it—he hadn't felt this alive for a long time.

When he had arrived at Cadgwyck last night, he had foolishly assumed the chief dangers a man might encounter in such a place were a loose chimney pot or a rotted banister. He had never dreamed the cliffs themselves might try to lure him to his doom. Had he been possessed of a more suspicious—and less practical—nature, he might even have suspected foul play. But common sense told him the shelf of rock at the tip of the promontory had simply been weakened by time and the elements. He had no one to blame for his near fatal plunge into the sea but

himself. He should never have wandered so close to the cliff's edge.

Shaking his head, Max turned to give the windows of the house a rueful look, wondering if anyone else had witnessed his folly.

He half-expected to see Angelica herself laughing merrily down at him from some shadowy attic dormer, but there was nothing ghostly about the flicker of movement he glimpsed in a second-story window.

As Lord Dravenwood's sharp-eyed gaze swept the back of the manor, then returned with eerie precision to the exact window where she was standing, Anne ducked behind the velvet draperies. Her mouth was dry, her heart still racing madly beneath the palm that had flown to her chest when he had stumbled back from the edge of the cliff, only inches away from a plunge into nothingness.

She fought to steady her breathing before peeping around the edge of the curtain again. To her keen relief, Dravenwood had already turned away from the house and was beginning to make his way farther along the cliffs, this time remaining a safe distance from their treacherous edge.

"This one's going to be trouble, isn't he?" Pippa observed, setting down her ash bucket to join Anne at the window of the cozy second-floor study.

Pippa had made a more concerted effort to embrace her role of maidservant on this day, taming her flyaway dark curls into two proper braids coiled neatly above her ears and donning an apron with only a few faded chocolate stains marring its snowy-white surface.

Anne watched their new master pick his way over the rocks, unaccountably angry at him for frightening her so badly. "They're all trouble, dearest," she said darkly. "It's just a matter of degree."

Despite her reassurances, Anne knew Pippa was right. Trouble was written in every line of Lord Dravenwood's bearing—in the stiffness of his broad shoulders, the way he carried himself as if he were nursing some mortal wound no one else could see. It was etched in the shadows that brooded beneath his eyes and in the way his coat hung loosely on his tall, rangy frame, as if it had been tailored for a different man.

A man who hadn't forgotten how to smile.

But those were just warning signs. Even without them, he was the sort of man who could cause trouble for a woman with little more than a smoldering glance from beneath the thick, sooty lashes veiling his quicksilver eyes or the casual brush of his hand against the small of her back. And if such a man should choose to employ the full range of his seductive skills, he could easily go from being trouble to being a full-fledged

disaster. At least for the woman foolish enough to grant him access to her vulnerable heart—or her body.

Anne could feel Pippa's worried gaze lingering on her face. "Whatever is the matter with you, Annie? Why, you're as white as a ghost yourself!"

"And why wouldn't I be?" Anne replied with a lightness she was far from feeling. "I was afraid the careless fool was going to tumble headlong over the cliff, leaving us to explain yet another unfortunate *accident* to the constable."

"What do you suppose ails the man?" Pippa's smooth brow puckered in a quizzical frown as she watched Lord Dravenwood stalk along the edge of the cliffs, the tails of his coat blowing out behind him. "Do you think he's recovering from some terrible illness? A brain fever or some exotic malady he picked up on one of his journeys perhaps?"

Anne would have wagered Lord Dravenwood was suffering from a sickness of the heart, not the body. She knew its signs only too well, having nearly died from it herself once.

"Whatever ails him, it's none of our concern." As the earl turned and began to make his way back toward the manor, she yanked the drapes shut. "If I have anything to say about it, he'll be gone soon enough, just like all the others."

Pippa hauled her bucket over to the hearth and dumped its contents on the pristine iron grate. A

dark cloud of ash shot up into the air, forcing her to wave it away from her watering eyes. "If we succeed in driving him away, won't they just send another pompous nobleman in his place?"

"Perhaps," Anne said firmly, hoping to hide her own doubts. "But thanks to our diligent efforts, the infamy of the White Lady of Cadgwyck is beginning to spread beyond the borders of Cornwall. If her legend continues to flourish, it's going to grow ever more difficult for them to find a buyer or overseer for the property. With any luck, they'll leave us to our own devices just long enough for us to find what we've been looking for."

"What if they should decide to close down the house altogether? *Before* we can find the treasure?"

"I don't believe they'll do that as long as they have a household of loyal servants willing to remain in this cursed place. After all, we're the only ones standing between the manor and utter ruin." Anne wagged her eyebrows at Pippa. "At least that's what we're allowing them to believe."

Pippa set aside the bucket. "Just what manner of mischief are you proposing this time?"

"Nothing too extreme. I suspect all his lordship really needs is a little nudge toward the door."

"A nudge or a shove?"

Anne lifted her shoulders in a noncommittal shrug. "Whatever will serve us best."

99

"Promise me you'll take care, won't you?" Pippa urged, her dark eyes absent their usual teasing spark. "I fear he might be more dangerous than the others."

Anne wanted to dismiss the warning. But she knew far more about the dangers a man such as Dravenwood could present to a woman than Pippa did. Dangers lurking behind longing looks and stolen caresses and pretty promises never intended to be kept.

Mustering up a reassuring smile, she marched past Pippa and to the fireplace. Kneeling on the hearth, she reached up into the chimney and fumbled blindly about until she located the grimy iron key that controlled the flue.

She gave it a sharp twist, then rose, briskly dusting ash from her hands. "Try not to fret so much, my dear. Lord Dravenwood might be a threat to me, but I can assure you Angelica is more than his match."

"Mrs. Spencer!"

To Anne's credit, she didn't even flinch when that thunderous shout came echoing through the halls of Cadgwyck Manor later that night. The convivial conversation she and her staff had been enjoying around the long pine table in the kitchen ceased abruptly. Lisbeth seized Betsy's hand in a white-knuckled grip while the other maids exchanged wide-eyed glances of alarm over

their steaming bowls of bisque prepared with lobsters Dickon had trapped for them just that morning.

Hodges lurched halfway to his feet, snatching up the wicked-looking knife they'd used to cut the bread. Dickon clapped a hand on the old man's shoulder, easing Hodges back into his chair before gently removing the knife from his clenched fist and sliding it out of harm's reach. Pippa buried her pert nose even deeper in the dog-eared copy of *The Castle of Otranto* she had filched from the manor's library.

In an ominous silence broken only by the cheery click of Nana's knitting needles and Piddles's snoring, Anne took one more sip of the succulent soup before laying down her spoon. She dabbed delicately at her lips with her napkin, then rose from her chair. "If you'll excuse me, it seems the master is in need of my services."

As she started for the door, the rest of them eyed her as if she were marching off to the gallows. She forced herself to maintain her even pace as she climbed the stairs and crossed the second-story gallery, keenly aware of Angelica Cadgwyck's mocking gaze following her every step. Her composure wasn't tested until she passed the third-floor staircase at the far end of the gallery and saw the man barreling down the long corridor. Heading straight for her.

Lord Dravenwood looked as if he'd just marched

out of the gates of hell. Soot blackened his face, making the whites of his eyes gleam that much more vividly. His hair was wild and his coat missing entirely. Each of his furious strides left a blackened footprint on the shabby carpet runner. A billowing cloud of smoke trailed behind him.

Another man in his predicament might have looked comical. But perhaps one had to have a sense of humor to look comical. He just looked murderous.

Ignoring her instinctive urge to snatch up the hem of her skirts and flee in the opposite direction, Anne donned her most unflappable expression as he halted in front of her. His broad chest was still heaving, although whether with rage or from exertion she could not tell.

Given the sparks of unholy wrath shooting from his eyes, it seemed only fitting that he smelled of fire and brimstone as well. His ash-smudged shirtsleeves had been shoved up to reveal muscular forearms generously dusted with curling, dark hair.

"You bellowed, my lord?" she inquired, jerking her gaze away from that rather riveting sight and its unanticipated effects on her composure and back up to his face.

His sharp eyes missed nothing. "I do hope you'll forgive my shocking state of undress, Mrs. Spencer," he said with scathing courtesy. "I had to use my coat to fan the smoke out of the

study before it choked me to death." His eyes narrowed in an accusing gaze. "When you informed me the study would be a pleasant place to enjoy an after-dinner brandy, you neglected to mention it would turn into a death trap the minute I lit the fire that had been laid upon the hearth."

"Oh, dear." Anne touched a hand to her throat in what she hoped was a convincing display of dismay. "Are you quite all right?"

"Fortunately, I was able to smother the flames and wrestle the windows open before being overcome by the smoke. When was the last time that chimney was cleaned? Seventeen ninety-eight?"

Anne shook her head, heaving a bewildered sigh. "I don't understand what could have happened. Why, I checked the damper myself only this morning when Pippa and I were airing out the room! I would have sworn the flue was—" She stopped abruptly, lowering her eyes before casting him an uneasy glance from beneath her lashes.

Dravenwood folded his arms over his chest, an expression far too cynical to be called a smile quirking one corner of his lips. "Let me guess. You think the ghost was the one who tampered with the flue."

"Don't be ridiculous, my lord! You said yourself there was no such thing as ghosts."

His jaw tightened. "What I said was that men are perfectly capable of creating things to haunt them without the aid of the supernatural."

"And quite right you are about that, I'm sure. Perhaps it was simply a malfunction of some sort. I'll send the maids to clean up the study and have Dickon check the flue right away."

"Very well. Then you can send Hodges to my chambers. As you can see, I'll be requiring some assistance with my bath."

A flutter of panic stirred in Anne's throat. She had not anticipated this complication. "Perhaps Dickon can check the flue in the morning. I'm sure he'd be more than happy to assist you in the bath if you'll just give me a moment to—"

"Send Hodges," Dravenwood commanded. "Unless, of course"—he leaned toward her in an unmistakably menacing manner, his stern voice betraying not so much as a hint of humor—"*you'd* rather assist me."

Unfortunately, the earl's raw masculinity was made even more potent by his savage appearance. With his gray eyes smoldering with a fire of their own, his hair tousled as if by a lover's fingers, and his bared teeth dazzling white against the soot-darkened planes of his face, he looked like a man capable of anything. Anything at all.

A dangerous little flame uncurled low in Anne's belly, bringing a kindred rush of heat to her

cheeks. She wouldn't have been surprised to see smoke rising from her own flesh.

She took an awkward half step backward before saying stiffly, "I'll have Lisbeth and Betsy draw a bath and send Hodges up to assist you."

"Thank you," he replied with exaggerated formality.

Through narrowed eyes Anne watched him stride away from her, almost wishing she had armed herself with Pippa's poker.

Max sank deeper into the copper hip bath, resting the back of his head against its rim. He had to cock his knees up at an awkward angle just to partially submerge his long legs, but the warm water lapping at the muscled planes of his chest almost made up for the inconvenience. He made a mental note to have Mrs. Spencer order a tub more suited to a man his size.

A reluctant half smile curved his lips at the memory of his housekeeper's outraged expression when he had suggested she attend him in his bath. He didn't know why he took such delight in taunting the stiff-necked woman, but there was no denying it gave him a naughty little thrill of satisfaction. One he hadn't felt for a long time.

For a brief time as boys, he and Ashton had endured a tyrant of a German nanny they had taken equal delight in tormenting. He could still remember her guttural screams on the night she

had rolled over on the hapless lizard they had slipped into her bed. Max's smile slowly faded. That was when he and Ash had been inseparable, long before their love for the same girl had torn them apart.

The German nanny and Mrs. Spencer were probably equally deserving of his scorn. He was beginning to suspect the White Lady of Cadgwyck Manor was nothing more than an imaginative attempt to excuse the incompetence of her staff. He had a good mind to dismiss the lot of them and replace them with a capable household of servants summoned directly from London. Servants who would never dare to challenge his authority or gaze up at him with a faintly mocking sparkle in their fine hazel eyes.

Somehow, the thought didn't hold as much appeal as it should have. If he sent for his London staff, they might know nothing about the house or its resident ghost, but they would know everything about him. He had come to this place to escape the prying eyes he could feel following him every time he entered a drawing room, the whispers he could hear even when they thought he wasn't listening. Mrs. Spencer and her motley little crew might tax his patience, but at least they didn't scurry out of his way as if he were some sort of ill-tempered monster or, worse yet, shoot him pitying glances behind his back.

He retrieved the cake of bayberry soap floating

in the water and ran it lazily over his chest to wash away the lingering taint of the soot. What would he have done if Mrs. Spencer had called his bluff and taken him up on his offer to assist him with his bath?

As he closed his eyes, he could almost feel her pale, cool hands gliding over the heat of his damp flesh. Could imagine himself reaching up to pluck the pins from her hair one by one until it came tumbling around her face to reveal its mysteries. Could see himself wrapping his hand in that silky skein and tipping back his head as she leaned over and touched her parted lips to his, enticing him to run the very tip of his tongue over the winsome gap between her teeth before plunging it deep into the hot, wet softness of her—

"Holy hell!" Max swore, shooting straight up out of the water and shaking off the dangerous daydream along with the droplets of water beading in his hair.

Where in the bloody hell had *that* come from? He'd never once entertained such naughty notions about the German nanny. Of course the German nanny had been shaped like the bulwark of a warship and had a deeper voice and a more impressive pair of mustaches than Max's father. Still, the very thought of his prickly housekeeper welcoming his kiss or his advances was beyond ludicrous. She was far more likely to grab him by

the scruff of the neck and shove his head under the water until the bubbles stopped rising.

A timid knock sounded on the door. Had he somehow succeeded in summoning up the object of his unseemly fantasies?

"Enter," he commanded gruffly, sinking back into the water to disguise the telltale heaviness of his groin.

The door creaked open, the soft glow of the lamplight revealing Hodges's snowy-white head. The butler minced gingerly into the room, his gaze darting from side to side as if to search for potential assailants. He had a thick towel draped over one forearm.

At first Max feared Hodges had been struck mute again, but after an awkward silence the butler said, "Mrs. Spencer sent me, my lord. She said you had need of assistance with your bath."

"You have excellent timing, Hodges. The water was just beginning to cool."

Hodges hesitated for a second, as if confused about what should happen next, then dutifully hastened to the side of the tub. Spreading the towel until it formed a curtain between them, the butler politely fixed his gaze elsewhere while Max climbed out of the bath.

Max took the towel and began to rub it briskly over his head and chest, as unself-conscious in his nakedness as any man who had been dressed by

someone else for as long as he could remember. "My apologies for the inconvenience, Hodges. I realize this task is beneath your position. We really must look into finding me a proper valet."

"I'm sure Mrs. Spencer will see to it."

Max wrapped the towel around his waist, eyeing Hodges's broad, blank face thoughtfully. The man's cheeks and nose were a little ruddy, as if he'd done his share of drinking in his day. "You're the butler of this household, are you not? Don't you have any concerns about Mrs. Spencer usurping your authority?"

"Mrs. Spencer is quite good at what she does." Hodges's words had a stilted quality, almost as if he were some Drury Lane actor practicing his lines for a Saturday matinee. "I am more than happy to defer to her wishes."

Max snorted. "A sentiment Mr. Spencer shared, no doubt. At least if he knew what was good for him."

"Mr. Spencer?" Hodges echoed, the glazed look returning to his eyes.

"Mrs. Spencer's dearly departed husband? Dickon told me all about the tragic accident that claimed the man's life."

Hodges blinked several times as if striving to remember something he'd been told long ago. "Ah, yes!" Relief brightened his face. "The wagon!"

"From what Dickon said, it sounded like a

terrible tragedy. I daresay the good widow was prostrate with grief."

"From what I hear, she was inconsolable! She was devoted to the man, you know. Utterly devoted."

While Max digested that bit of information, Hodges retrieved Max's dressing gown from the hulking armoire in the corner and held it open so Max could step into it.

Max let the damp towel fall to the carpet and accepted the butler's invitation, knotting the sash of the dressing gown around his waist.

Hodges beamed at him, plainly proud his efforts had been so well received. "Will that be all, my lord?"

"I do believe it will." Taking Hodges by the elbow, Max gently steered him toward the door.

Before the butler's hand could close on the doorknob, Max snatched the door open himself, half-expecting his housekeeper to come tumbling headfirst into the room. But the shadowy corridor was deserted. Max poked his head out the door and looked both ways. Not a soul was in sight—either living or dead.

"Your services have been very much appreciated," he assured Hodges. "You have no idea how helpful you've been."

As the butler went bobbing off down the corridor, humming cheerfully beneath his breath, Max closed the door behind him and leaned his

back against it. Pondering everything he was learning about his rather enigmatic housekeeper, Max murmured, "Very helpful indeed."

That night Max dreamed again.

Despite his many trips to China, Max had never visited an opium den. But he had always imagined it would feel something like this—his limbs weighted to a bed or a couch in a pleasant stupor while his mind drifted away, unfettered by the chains that bound it during his waking hours. Chains he had forged himself with his single-minded devotion to duty and his slavish adoration of a woman whose heart had always belonged to another man.

Leaving his body behind, he soared through the open French windows of his bedchamber and into the night. The wings of the wind carried him straight to the dizzying height of the cliffs. A woman stood at the very tip of the promontory, her back to him. She wore the same dress she had worn in the portrait, its voluminous skirts rippling in the wind. The dress was the color of buttercups ripe with the promise of spring.

A spring that would never come if she took one more step.

Max ached to gather her shivering body into the warmth of his arms, stroke her wind-tossed hair, and tell her that, although it seemed impossible now, her broken heart would mend. He would

see to it himself, even if he had to gather the scattered shards of it with his bare hands and piece them together one by one.

But he'd left his body paralyzed on the bed. All he could do was watch in helpless horror as she spread her graceful arms into wings and disappeared over the edge of the cliff.

Max sat straight up in the bed, his breathing a harsh, painful rasp in the darkness. Only seconds ago he would have sworn he wouldn't be able to budge if someone set a lit match to his mattress, but now a terrible restlessness seized him. He threw back the sweat-dampened sheets and shoved open the bed curtains, desperate to escape their smothering confines.

His dream was no less vivid to his waking eyes. He could still see that forlorn figure standing at the edge of the cliffs. Could feel his own helpless anguish as he watched her make a decision she would never be able to take back. He swung his legs over the edge of the bed and stared at the shadowy outline of his own hands in the darkness, despising how powerful they looked, yet how powerless they felt in that moment.

Cool night air spilled over his heated flesh. He slowly lifted his head. For a dazed moment, he thought he must surely still be dreaming because the windows leading to his balcony were standing wide open.

An icy chill danced down Max's spine. He had

secured the windows himself before retiring, checking and double-checking their latches, then giving their handles a stern shake to test them. He had even locked his bedchamber door to ensure none with mischief on their minds could sneak into the room while he slept. A quick glance confirmed the door was still closed, the brass key still visible in its lock.

As he turned his gaze back to the windows, a gentle breeze caressed the frozen planes of his face. There was no storm on this night, no violent gusts of wind he could blame for wrenching the windows open. They had either opened of their own accord or been opened by some unseen hand.

As he watched, a ribbon of mist came drifting into the room, bringing with it the haunting fragrance of jasmine—dense and sweet and seductive enough to drive a man's senses wild. For the briefest instant, the mist seemed to coalesce into something more substantial—a human form with long, flowing hair, a rippling, white gown, and gently rounded curves. Max blinked and the illusion vanished as quickly as it had appeared.

Biting off an oath, he reached to the end of the bed for his dressing gown. He yanked on the garment, then strode through the open windows and onto the balcony. The fragrance of jasmine was weaker there but still potent enough to make his groin tighten with longing.

Gripping the balustrade, he turned his fierce

gaze toward the abandoned tower, half-expecting to see a spectral flash of light or hear the tinkling notes of a music box. The tower remained dark and all he heard were the waves breaking over the distant rocks, a wistful murmur on this peaceful night instead of a roar.

The tension slowly seeped from his body. Hadn't he accused the last master of Cadgwyck of being chased from the premises by his own imagination? Yet he was no different. He had allowed an overwrought dream and melodramatic tales of an old tragedy to stir his fancies in a way they hadn't been stirred since he was a boy.

Angelica Cadgwyck was nothing more than a stranger to him. No matter how wretched her fate, he had no reason to give her a foothold in his imagination . . . or his heart. There was probably some perfectly sound explanation for why the windows kept slipping their latches. Come morning, aided by the bright light of day and his refreshed wits, he would find it.

Shaking his head at his own folly, he rubbed a hand over his tousled hair and padded back inside. The scent of jasmine had completely dissipated, making him wonder if he had conjured that up from some long-buried memory as well.

He had slipped out of his dressing gown and was poised to climb back into the bed when he glanced over his shoulder and saw the door to his bedchamber standing open.

Chapter Ten

The brass key was still in its keyhole, right where Max had left it, but the door stood ajar. The corridor beyond was as dark as an underground tunnel.

Max stood there in a misty wash of moonlight, his every sense tingling with awareness. Then he heard a sound even more disconcerting than an off-key tune ground out by the rusty gears of a music box—a rippling echo of laughter, feminine and sweet.

He might have been able to dismiss some maudlin specter weeping into her invisible handkerchief. But something about that girlish giggle was irresistible. It was like the taunting laughter of a child playing hide-and-seek while actually longing to be found.

His lips twisted in a grim smile as he tossed aside the dressing gown, strode over to the wardrobe, and yanked out a pair of trousers and a shirt. He donned the trousers and tugged the shirt over his head but didn't waste time securing it at the throat. His hands were unnaturally steady as he located the tinderbox and lit the candle sitting on the side table. Taking up the brass candlestick, he headed for the corridor.

The wavering flame of the candle did little to penetrate the darkness. Max hesitated just outside his chamber, cocking his head to listen. All he heard was the peaceful hush of the sleeping house. He was beginning to wonder if he had imagined the laughter just as he had the scent of jasmine, but then it came again, faint but unmistakable.

Now that he was actually in the corridor, the ghostly echo seemed to be coming from even farther away, as if it were traveling not just through the shadowy passageways of the house but through the corridors of time itself. Dismissing the absurd notion, Max moved toward the sound with the fleet grace of a born hunter.

He slipped silently down the stairs to the second floor, his senses heightened by a strange elation. He had felt the same way standing on the edge of the cliff earlier in the day, only seconds before the world had crumbled beneath his feet. Perhaps it wasn't Angelica Cadgwyck's intention to drive him away, but to drive him mad. Or perhaps he was already mad. Most men would flee from a ghost, yet here he was, eagerly pursuing one.

He crossed the second-floor portrait gallery, his candle casting flickering shadows over the empty walls where the Cadgwyck ancestors had once resided. By the time he reached Angelica's portrait, he wouldn't have been surprised to find

the ornate gilt frame empty and its occupant romping gleefully through the entrance hall below. But when he lifted the candlestick, Angelica was still gazing down her slender nose at him, her eyes knowing, her lips poised on the verge of a smile, as if she were about to reveal some terribly amusing secret she could only share with him.

A draft as warm and sweet as a woman's breath breezed right past him. The candle's flame guttered once, then went out, leaving him alone in the darkness with her. He stood there, inhaling the acrid smell of snuffed wick, and waited for his eyes to adjust to the meager moonlight drifting through the grimy arched window above the front door.

A new sound penetrated the gloom. It took a minute for Max to place the rhythmic ticking, to recognize it as the sound of a pendulum swinging back and forth in a graceful arc, measuring each second as if it would be his last. Max slowly turned, a fresh chill dancing down his spine. It was the longcase clock at the foot of the stairs, the clock with its hands frozen at a quarter past midnight. The hollow ticktock seemed to echo each heavy thud of his heart.

The warning of the innkeeper's wife echoed through his memory: *Ye might not be so quick to dismiss our words as a bunch o' rubbish if ye'd have seen the face o' the last master o' the house*

on the night he came runnin' into the village a little after midnight, half-dead from fleein' whatever evil lurks in that place.

If Max had thought to check his pocket watch before he left his bedchamber, what would he have found? That it was rapidly approaching the moment when something so terrible had happened in this house even time had stopped to mourn it?

He *had* ordered Mrs. Spencer to have the clock fixed. Perhaps in her eagerness to please him, she had done just that.

A skeptical snort escaped him as he dropped the useless candlestick and went speeding down the stairs, rounding the ornately carved newel at the bottom of the staircase to bring himself face-to-face with the clock.

The ticking had ceased. Wan moonlight bathed the clock's impassive face, revealing its motionless hands dutifully stationed at the twelve and the three. Max's heart was left to beat on all alone.

Curling his hands into fists, he swung away from the clock and swept his gaze over the entrance hall. He was shocked to realize he wasn't the least bit afraid. He was angry. He didn't care for being toyed with, not by any man or woman and certainly not by some chit of a ghost who still fancied herself mistress of *his* house.

As if to taunt him, a sweet ripple of girlish

laughter danced through the entrance hall. Max strode to the center of the hall, then slowly turned, holding his breath to listen. Too many rooms and corridors led off the hall to determine from which direction the laughter was coming.

The moon drifted behind a wisp of a cloud, bathing the hall in shadows. That was when he saw it—the briefest flash of white down a darkened corridor, like the trailing skirts of a woman's gown as she darted around a corner.

Spurred on by the thrill of the hunt, Max broke into long strides. As he rounded the corner where he had seen the flash of white, he sensed a presence in the darkness ahead of him, moving quickly.

But not quickly enough.

Another corner loomed at the end of the corridor. He quickened his pace. He had no intention of letting his prey escape, not when he was this close to getting his hands on it. As he swung around the corner, his arms shot out to seize whatever they found in front of him.

He was half-expecting them to close on empty air. Which was why it was such a shock to his senses when the bundle he hauled against his chest turned out to be warm, soft, and ever so human.

As his captive squirmed against him, panting with frustration, it wasn't the haunting scent of jasmine that tickled his nose but another aroma—

one that made his stomach clench with hunger and reminded him just how bland his supper of overcooked beef and underdone potatoes had been. Puzzled, he wrinkled his nose. Could a ghost smell of something as mundane, yet irresistible to a man's appetites, as freshly baked bread and cinnamon biscuits?

The bundle in his arms abruptly stopped squirming. After a moment of silence, an acerbic voice came out of the darkness. "The next time you need something in the middle of the night, my lord, you might try simply ringing the bell."

Chapter Eleven

Anne held her breath as she awaited Lord Dravenwood's response, resisting the dangerous urge to relax against the broad expanse of his chest. For such a cold man, he was incredibly warm. He radiated heat like a cookstove on a blustery December day.

Once he had seized her, it hadn't taken her long to realize her struggles against his unyielding arms were futile. He seemed to be exceptionally well formed for a man who had probably spent much of his career seated behind a desk.

Despite holding herself as stiffly as she could, there could be no denying the shocking intimacy

of his makeshift embrace. One of his muscular arms was cinched around her waist while the other was wrapped firmly around her shoulders, just above the swell of her breasts. He'd planted his feet apart to balance them both, leaving her legs to dangle between his splayed thighs, the tips of her toes barely brushing the floor. His hips cradled the softness of her rump as if they'd been designed by their Maker for just such a provocative purpose.

The awkward silence only made the rasp of his ragged breathing more obvious. His chest hitched unevenly against her back while his heated breath caressed the back of her neck. A helpless shiver of reaction danced over her flesh. Anne almost wished she'd left her hair unbound to protect her vulnerable nape from that tantalizing assault instead of dividing it into two precise braids.

She had assumed identifying herself would win her freedom.

She had assumed wrong. Although Lord Dravenwood's grip had softened a nearly imperceptible degree, his arms showed no sign of relinquishing their prize. He lowered his head next to hers in the darkness, his brandy-scented breath grazing the side of her throat.

Her eyes drifted shut as if even the darkness was too much for them to bear. She could feel both her muscles and her will softening of their own accord. Could feel her head listing to the

side to expose the tingling curve of her throat to his lips.

It had been so long since a man had touched her . . . kissed her yearning lips. If he turned her in his arms and used his weight to bear her back against the nearest wall, would she have the strength to resist him? Or would she twine her arms around his neck and draw his warm, seeking lips down to hers?

"Honey. Sugar," he murmured, his husky baritone a seduction all its own. His breath danced over the delicate swath of skin behind her ear. "Cinnamon. Nutmeg. Vanilla. Fresh cream."

His words slowly penetrated the languorous haze threatening to overcome her. She frowned in bewilderment. He wasn't whispering endearments but ingredients. And it wasn't his lips gliding toward the curve between her throat and shoulder but his nose.

Her eyes flew open. The man wasn't trying to seduce her; he was *sniffing* her!

"My lord," she snapped, having no difficulty whatsoever striking just the right note of exasperation, "have you any intention of unhanding me before morning?"

This time her words had the desired effect. Dravenwood released her so abruptly she stumbled and nearly fell. She was surprised by how chilly the air felt without his arms to shield her from it.

She slowly turned to face him. He loomed over her, a faceless silhouette against the deeper shadows.

"Why do you always smell like that?" he demanded, his voice deepening to a near growl.

"Like what?"

"Like something that just came out of the oven. Something warm and freshly baked."

Although it certainly wasn't the accusation she had expected, Anne still felt oddly guilty. "As housekeeper, I spend a fair amount of my day in the kitchen planning the weekly menus and overseeing the cook."

"I've yet to see anything emerge from the kitchen of *this* house that smells like *that*. Except for you, that is."

"Is that what drove you to accost me? You mistook me for a warm cross bun?"

"I mistook you for"—he hesitated—"an intruder. It's a risk you run when you wander about the manor in the dead of night . . . without your clothes," he added pointedly.

Anne could almost feel the heat of his gaze sweeping over her. Apparently, his night vision was much keener than hers. She touched a hand to her throat, reassuring herself there was no need to stammer or blush in embarrassment. Her modest nightdress shrouded her from throat to ankle. Of course, now he knew exactly what it was shrouding. He had felt the softness of her

curves mold to the hardness of his own body, had felt the wild patter of her heart as she writhed against him.

"I thought I heard a noise so I came to investigate," she said primly.

"Without a lamp? Or even so much as a candle?"

"I would think you'd be more in need of a candle than I would. I'm far more familiar with the house and less likely to bark my shins or tumble down a flight of stairs."

"Or out a fourth-floor window," he said coolly, reminding them both of the fate another, less fortunate, master of the house had met.

Anne's mouth fell open, then snapped shut. She could feel him studying her again, but was grateful she couldn't see his expression. She would do well to guard her sharp tongue. If she goaded him into dismissing her, all was lost.

"I left my chamber with a candle," he finally admitted. "But it was lost to a draft."

"Old houses do tend to have an abundance of those."

"Among other things. Aren't you the least bit concerned about roaming around the manor in the dark yourself when it's been rumored there's a vengeful ghost on the loose?"

Anne shrugged. "We seem to have reached a mutual agreement with our White Lady. We don't trouble her and she doesn't trouble us."

"Aha!" He drew a step closer to her, bringing

his triumphant features into focus. "So you do believe in ghosts!"

"It's impossible to live in this house and not believe in spirits of some sort. The past can be a very powerful influence on the present."

"Only for those who insist on dwelling in it." His words had a bitter edge, as if he had recognized the irony in them even before they were out of his mouth. "You claimed you heard a noise. Just what did you hear?"

"Nothing of consequence. Probably just a loose shutter banging against a window."

"I heard a woman laughing."

His stark confession hung between them, a shimmering thread of truth cutting through the darkness.

It pained her to neatly sever that thread with her next words. "What you most likely heard was a pair of housemaids giggling over some nonsense in their beds. The girls rise early and work hard during the day. I try not to deny them their simple pleasures."

He was silent for so long Anne knew he hadn't believed a word of her explanation. But he'd been a diplomat long enough to recognize a standoff when he saw one. "What of yourself, Mrs. Spencer?"

"Pardon?" she asked, confused by his question.

"Do you deny yourself your simple pleasures? Or do you prefer the more complicated ones?"

For a long moment Anne found it difficult to breathe, much less formulate a coherent answer. When she finally did, the arid formality had been restored to her tone. "I trust you can find your way back to your bed, my lord. I'll strive to see you pass the rest of your night undisturbed."

As she turned away from him, she would have almost sworn she heard him mutter beneath his breath, "Pity, that."

She started down the darkened corridor, still feeling the prick of his suspicious gaze against her back. She forced herself to measure each step, though she was nearly overcome by the absurd notion that he was going to seize her again. That he was only a breath away from closing the distance between them so he could wrap a powerful arm around her waist and draw her back against the seductive heat of his body. She'd resisted the temptation to melt against all of that enticing masculine strength once, but she wasn't sure she'd have the fortitude to do it again.

She waited until she'd reached the shelter of the servants' staircase before giving in to the overpowering impulse to flee.

By the time Anne reached her attic room, she had a stitch in her side and was gasping for breath. She slipped inside the room and closed the door, twisting the key in the lock with trembling fingers.

Pippa and Dickon had helped her install the lock before their last master had arrived. The three of them had laughingly celebrated their efforts, knowing all the while it would be a feeble defense against a powerful shoulder or a booted foot.

Anne pressed her ear to the door but heard no sign of pursuit. She sagged against it, going limp with relief. She had certainly never intended to end her evening in her employer's arms. She had only her own carelessness to blame. She knew every cranny and nook of this house. If she had anticipated his pursuit, she could easily have eluded him.

She'd grown accustomed to men fleeing her company, not seeking it. She certainly hadn't expected Lord Dravenwood to plunge headlong into the darkness, turning the hunter into the hunted.

She pushed herself away from the door. She'd left a candle burning on the washstand, and as she crossed the floor, she caught a glimpse of her reflection in the looking glass that hung over it.

Mesmerized against her will, she drew closer to the mirror. She expected to see what she saw every morning when she arose—an ordinary face, not unpleasing, but certainly not worthy of praise or adulation. But tonight her breasts were rising and falling unsteadily beneath the plain, white linen bodice of her nightdress. Her eyes were

sparkling, her cheeks flushed a soft rose, her lips slightly parted as if awaiting a lover's kiss. She lifted her hands as if they belonged to someone else and raked her fingers through her braids, releasing her aching head from their pressure. Taming the thick mass was a constant struggle, usually requiring a wealth of pins that stabbed her scalp every time she turned her head. Her hair spilled around her shoulders in a rippling cloud, and she was left staring into the face of a stranger.

Her lips tightened. No, not a stranger at all but a face she knew only too well, a face she had hoped never to see again except as a distorted reflection in the eyes of those too foolish to recognize it had never been anything more than an illusion.

Leaning forward, she blew out the candle, banishing that creature to the past where she belonged.

Chapter Twelve

Anne stood at the head of the long pine table in the kitchen the next morning, her gaze traveling the circle of faces turned expectantly toward her. Each of those faces was desperately dear to her, but she still felt the burden of their need weighing down her heart. Sometimes she didn't

know if her heart would be strong enough to bear it.

Nana had already finished her porridge and retreated to her rocking chair in front of the hearth to rescue Sir Fluffytoes from the hopeless tangle the cat had made of her yarn. Hodges was rocking back and forth in his chair and humming the singsong notes of a nursery rhyme beneath his breath, the front of his white waistcoat already dappled with various food stains.

Anne sighed. She had hoped to send Hodges back to the cellar to do some more excavating while Lord Dravenwood was occupied elsewhere, but in his current condition, Hodges probably wouldn't be able to find the cellar, much less any treasures that might be hiding there.

Pippa and Dickon sat directly across from the maids, who had managed to stop giggling and chattering just long enough to give Anne their attention.

Anne had found the five young maids on the streets of London, living from one crust of bread to the next. They shared one thing in common with her—they had all been left to fend for themselves after being betrayed by a man. Or in some of their cases, by many men.

When Anne had first brought them to Cadgwyck, they had slunk around the manor like a pack of feral cats, shying away from every sudden movement and loud noise. Their hair had

been stringy and dull, their features pinched by a combination of hunger and mistrust.

Now their hair was shiny, their faces full and glowing with good health and good humor in the cozy light from the kitchen fire. To them, Cadgwyck Manor wasn't a pile of crumbling stones, but the only true home they'd ever known.

Anne had deliberately chosen the window of time before the earl would rise to address them all.

"I don't wish to alarm any of you," she said, pitching her words at a volume even Nana could hear over the steady creak of her rocking chair, "but I'm afraid we're going to have to endure Lord Dravenwood's company for a little longer than we anticipated."

"And just why is that?" Pippa demanded, looking alarmed.

Anne bit her bottom lip. "I fear I have only myself to blame. In my haste to be rid of the man, I may have overplayed my hand last night."

"Oh, dear!" Betsy's cheerful little pumpkin of a face went as pale as the starched folds of the mobcap perched atop her yellow curls. "He didn't catch you, did he?"

If she closed her eyes, Anne could still feel Dravenwood's arms enfolding her, hauling her against the hard, ruthless planes of his body as if she weighed no more than a feather from one of his pillows. "In a manner of speaking, yes. But I

told him I'd left my bed to investigate a mysterious noise myself."

"And he believed you?" Lizzie asked hopefully.

Anne could still see the skeptical gleam of the earl's eyes shining down at her out of the darkness. "I'm not sure Lord Dravenwood believes in much of anything. Since his suspicions have already been stirred, I think it would be best if we try a more subtle approach from this day forward."

Pippa blew an errant curl out of her eyes, her expression sulky. "Just how long must we put up with the insufferable man?"

Anne took a deep breath. "A fortnight at least. Perhaps as much as a month."

Dickon groaned. "I can't wear that silly wig for a fortnight. It itches something fierce!"

"You're just going to have to bear up. He'll be gone soon enough, just like all the rest," Anne assured the boy. "We don't want to make him *too* comfortable, of course, or he might stop pining for his London luxuries and decide he fancies it here. We'll keep feeding him uninspiring meals and making sure the house is as inhospitable as possible. But for the time being there will be no more peculiar noises in the night or mysteriously closed chimney flues. I think it would be best if Angelica didn't put in any more appearances for a while."

"She won't care for that," Pippa warned. "You

know what a brat she can be when it comes to getting what she wants."

"I've often thought the two of you were kindred spirits in that respect," Anne shot back, earning an appreciative chuckle from Dickon. Pippa made a face at him.

"Angelica has always been a good girl," Hodges said softly to the remains of his porridge. "If she is overly indulged, it is only because she deserves to be."

Anne gazed down at his snowy-white head, forced to swallow around the sudden tightness in her throat. "Yes, darling. Angelica *is* a good girl. If not for her, none of us would be here right now."

Dickon still didn't look convinced. "How are we supposed to keep hunting for the treasure if he's always lurking about, ordering us to fetch his gloves or lick his boots clean or glowering at us as if we'd accidentally gelded his favorite stallion?"

"We'll simply have to take more care," Anne replied. "Once the earl has relaxed his guard a bit, we'll have a much better chance of—"

"Mrs. Spencer!"

Chapter Thirteen

Anne froze right along with the rest of them as the echo of that familiar roar slowly faded. After a stark moment of silence, one of the rusty bells strung over the door began to jangle with undeniable violence.

"Do you hear the cathedral bells?" Hodges clapped his pudgy hands, his eyes shining like a child's. "Why, it must be Christmas morning!"

Lizzie gazed up the inscription above the bell, her eyes as round as saucers. " 'Tis the master's bedchamber."

Pippa gave Anne a wide-eyed look, but Anne shook her head in answer to the girl's unspoken question. Neither Anne nor Angelica had had a hand in this bit of mischief. Anne was as bewildered as the rest of them by their master's abrupt summons. Keenly aware of their anxious gazes following her every move, Anne forced herself to walk calmly from the kitchen. She waited until she was out of their sight to quicken her steps to a run.

When Anne arrived at the east wing, Dravenwood was pacing back and forth in the corridor outside his bedchamber in shirtsleeves and trousers, his

untied cravat hanging loose around his throat. He wasn't trailing smoke or reeking of fire and brimstone, but he did appear to be in a devil of a temper.

As she approached, he wheeled around and stabbed a finger toward the closed door. "There is a creature in my room!"

To Anne's credit, she managed to keep a straight face. "What is it this time, my lord? A ghost? A bogey? Or perhaps a werewolf?"

Scowling at her from beneath a brow as dark and forbidding as a thundercloud, he reached down and flung open the door. Anne gingerly peered around the door frame, unsure of what she would find.

Piddles was curled up right in the middle of his lordship's bed, chewing on a piece of mangled leather. As they crept into the room, the dog bared his pronounced underbite and let out a low growl, as if to warn them away from attempting to wrest his prize from him so they might chew on it themselves.

A smile slowly spread across Anne's face. "That is not a creature, my lord. *That* is a dog." She squinted at the shiny leather tassel dangling from one corner of the dog's mouth. "And what is that? Is it . . ."

"It *was* one of my very best boots," Dravenwood said morosely. Piddles gulped, then swallowed. The tassel disappeared.

As the dog went back to gnawing on what was left of the boot, the earl glared at him. "I discovered him when I came out of the dressing room. How do you suppose the little wretch got in here?"

"Was the door secured?"

Dravenwood snorted. "Why should that matter in this house? He probably just walked right through it."

"If it wasn't locked, he may have nudged it open with his nose."

"Such as it is." Dravenwood eyed a squashed black button disparagingly, as if it couldn't possibly have any useful purpose.

"I'm afraid it's a long-standing habit of his."

"Along with ingesting wildly expensive footwear?"

Sighing, Anne nodded. "As well as stockings, straw bonnets, and the occasional parasol. I'm terribly sorry, my lord. I'll be more than happy to remove the dog from your chamber, but I fear your boot is quite beyond repair." She marched over to the bed and snapped her fingers. "Piddles, down!"

The dog uncurled himself and obediently descended the bed stairs, landing on his stocky legs with a decided thump. He sank down on his squat haunches, the remains of the boot still hanging from his mouth, and looked up at her expectantly.

Dravenwood frowned. "Every time I got anywhere near the bed, the beast snapped at me like a baby dragon. I was afraid I was going to lose a finger, if not an entire hand."

"Dickon is the one who trained him."

"Well, that explains it. Why do you call him—"

As if anticipating the question, Piddles strolled to the foot of the bed, hiked up his leg, and proceeded to ruin the earl's other boot.

Anne held her breath. Their last master would probably have kicked the cantankerous little dog out the nearest window for such a slight.

But after a short pause, Lord Dravenwood simply sighed. "Well, it wasn't as if I was going to have need of one boot."

Unmindful of his narrow escape, Piddles trotted from the room, his stub of a tail wagging proudly as he displayed his trophy for all the world to see.

"Did you never have a pup when you were a boy, my lord?" Anne could not resist asking.

Dravenwood shook his head. "My father had hunting hounds, of course, but he believed such beasts were for sport, not for pleasure."

"And what did you believe?"

He frowned as if no one had ever asked him such a thing before. "One winter, when I was a very small lad, I found a litter of kittens that had been abandoned by their mother in a corner of

the hayloft. They were tiny, mewling creatures . . . so very helpless. I wrapped them up in my woolen muffler and carried them back to the house, thinking I might be able to coax my father into letting me keep them in my bedchamber until they grew old enough to thrive on their own. He informed me that animals had no place in a house and I must give them to one of the footmen for safekeeping." Dravenwood's voice remained almost painfully expressionless. "I found out later he ordered the footman to drown them in a bucket."

Anne gasped. "How unspeakably cruel! How could he do such a wretched thing to those poor, innocent creatures?" *And to his own child,* she thought, her heart going out to that eager little boy who had hurried back to the house in the cold with his precious bundle.

"I'm sure he thought he was teaching me a valuable lesson about life."

"What? Not to trust a footman?"

"That only the strong are worthy of survival." Judging by the cool look he gave her, it was a lesson he had learned only too well.

Effectively reminded of her place, Anne smoothed her apron and said stiffly, "I'll send someone to tidy up right away, my lord."

Eyeing the puddle spreading around his remaining boot, Dravenwood's eyes narrowed to silvery slits. "Dickon. *Send Dickon.*"

. . .

Having left Dickon on hands and knees, muttering beneath his breath as he grudgingly scrubbed the floor of the master bedchamber, Max sat all alone at the head of the massive dining-room table. He was wearing his *second* favorite pair of boots and feeling no less ridiculous than he had the day before.

As he waited for his breakfast to arrive, he was forced to smother a yawn. His midnight encounter with both the ghost and his housekeeper had kept him tossing in his bedclothes until the wee hours of the morning.

He should never have mentioned hearing the ghostly laughter to Mrs. Spencer. She and the other servants were probably gathered in the kitchen at that very moment, having a hearty laugh at his expense.

The dining-room door swung open and two of the maids came bustling in. One of them made a beeline for the sideboard, while the other came around the table and set a plate in front of him. His breakfast appeared to be identical to the one he'd suffered through yesterday, except today the toast was burned to a blackened crisp and the rashers of bacon limp and undercooked.

The girl stepped back and beamed at him, plainly awaiting some sign of his approval.

"Thank you, Lizzie," he said wanly.

"You're welcome, m'lord," she replied,

blinking at him with her big brown eyes. "But I'm Beth."

"Well, then, thank you, Beth."

The girl's smile began to falter. "I'm not Beth. I'm *Beth*."

Max blinked at her, utterly confounded.

The girl at the sideboard cast a glance over her shoulder. "She's Bess, my lord, but she has a slight lisp. Beth is the scullery maid."

He scowled at the second girl, mainly because she had been arranging extra dishes on the sideboard just in case—God forbid—he would care for more of the unappetizing fare on his plate. "Then I suppose you must be Lizzie."

The girl blushed so furiously the smattering of freckles across her snub nose disappeared. "Oh, no, m'lord, I'm Lisbeth. Lizzie is the upstairs maid."

"A hopeless endeavor," Max muttered beneath his breath. "Suppose I just call you all Elizabeth and be done with it."

"Very good, sir," the two maids said in unison, bobbing curtsies in such perfect synchronization they might have been choreographed.

As Beth . . . *Bess* joined her companion at the sideboard, Mrs. Spencer appeared with a tall Sevres pot. Max hadn't thought it possible for her to smell any more enticing than she had when he had held her in his arms last night, but that was before a whiff of rich, dark coffee drifted to his

nostrils. As he inhaled the bracing aroma, he was tempted to jump up and press a lusty kiss to her tightly pursed lips out of pure gratitude. He couldn't help smiling to himself as he imagined her reaction to *that*.

"My lord," she murmured in way of greeting as she leaned over his shoulder to fill his cup.

He took a sip of the potent brew, closing his eyes for a moment to savor its bitter smoothness. Although he had dutifully hosted tea every afternoon for his commanders and their wives during his time in India, it was this irresistible concoction he craved.

"I wouldn't drink too much if I were you," Mrs. Spencer whispered, her velvety voice dangerously close to his ear. "I've heard it can deprive a man of his sleep."

He whipped his head around to give her a suspicious look, but she had already retreated to the sideboard, where she was placing the pot next to the chafing dishes, her profile a study in innocence. Before he could catch her eye, Hodges came marching into the room and dutifully placed a folded newspaper next to Max's plate.

Max glanced at the date inscribed at the top of the *Times*. The edition had been published a fortnight before he had left London for Cornwall. He had already lazily perused its pages over a delicious breakfast in the plush comfort of his dining room in Mayfair.

But, per his request, the newspaper *was* from the current decade, so he had no choice but to accept the small token with grace. "Thank you, Hodges."

As Max unfolded the newspaper, his nostrils recoiled from another, far more unpleasant, smell—the stench of scorched paper.

"I took the liberty of pressing the paper for you," Hodges explained.

Max held up the newspaper, peering at the butler through the iron-shaped hole in the middle of the financial page. "Yes," he said drily. "I can see that." He snapped the paper shut, sending a cloud of crisp ash fluttering through the air to settle over the top of his poached eggs like flakes of pepper. "I do appreciate the effort, Hodges, but you might try using a slightly cooler iron next time."

"Very good, sir." Looking quite pleased with himself, Hodges marched back out of the room, adding an odd little skip just as he reached the door. Max slanted a glance at the sideboard, but Mrs. Spencer had slipped out as well when he wasn't looking. She must not have been wearing her infernal ring of keys.

Backing out of the room and bobbing curtsies all the way, the Elizabeths quickly followed suit, leaving Max all alone with his singed newspaper and his bland breakfast, the coffee his only comfort.

• • •

After breakfast Max went up to the second-floor library, where he hoped to find a book to while away the long, dreary morning. But when he entered the gloomy chamber, he found the little dark-haired maid perched on a stool in front of the towering floor-to-ceiling bookshelf on the far wall, her back to the door.

Although the room looked as if it hadn't been properly cleaned since Elizabeth sat on the throne, Max assumed she must be working. But as he watched, she tugged a single book forward to the edge of the shelf, then slid it back into its place. She repeated the process with the next book and then the next, until she was teetering for balance on the stool. Each time she slid a book out, she would cock her head to listen, almost as if she was waiting for some sort of resulting reaction. When she reached the end of the shelf, a dejected sigh escaped her.

Max leaned one shoulder against the door frame and drawled, "Looking for something?"

She swung around so quickly she nearly went tumbling headfirst off the stool. With her bright, dark eyes and pointed chin, she had the face of a charming little fox, and as Max watched, it flushed a dusky pink. "Oh, no, my lord. I was just dusting."

He gave the feather duster protruding from her apron pocket a pointed look. The duster's glossy

feathers looked as if they'd just been plucked from the fowl that morning.

If he expected the girl to express remorse at being caught in such a blatant lie, he was doomed to disappointment. Instead, she heaved a martyr's sigh as she descended from the stool. "I suppose you'll be wanting the truth now."

"Please don't trouble yourself on my account," he said, his voice dripping sarcasm.

"If you must know, I was searching for something I might read in my bed tonight. After all of the drudgery of the day, it's such a pleasure to curl up beneath the blankets with a rousing story." As if to prove her point, she snatched a book from the nearest shelf and cradled it to her chest.

Max strode over and plucked the book from her hands, turning it so he could peruse the cover. "Ah, *The Mechanization of Plowing in an Agrarian Society*. Yes, I can see how that might make for rousing bedtime reading after a vigorous day of not dusting."

Pippa snatched the book back, returned it to the shelf, and grabbed another one, taking the time to read the title first as she did so. She held the clothbound book up to reveal the title—*A Sicilian Romance*. "Have you read any of Mrs. Radcliffe's work?" she asked, inching her way around him and toward the door. "This one is absolutely thrilling! My favorite scene is the one where

poor Julia finds her presumed-dead mother imprisoned in the haunted dungeons of the Mazzini castle while fleeing the debauched overtures of the dastardly Duke de Luovo!"

Before Max could open his mouth to point out that it was *his* library and *his* book she was stealing while she was supposed to be working, she was gone. He stood blinking at the empty doorway for a minute, feeling a bit like the dastardly Duke de Luovo himself, then turned toward the bookshelf.

After casting a look over his shoulder to make sure he was still alone, he drew a book to the very edge of the shelf, then quickly pushed it back into its slot. He waited expectantly, but the hearth didn't swing open to reveal a secret passageway, nor did a trapdoor open up beneath his feet to swallow him.

He shook his head, a rueful snort escaping him. If he didn't get a grip on his imagination, he would soon be as dotty as the rest of the inhabitants of this house.

Max quickly discovered *The Mechanization of Plowing in an Agrarian Society* made for equally dry reading during the daylight hours. Which is how he found himself back on the second-story landing later that morning, gazing up at the mysterious Miss Cadgwyck's portrait. She seemed determined to haunt his waking hours as well as

his dreams. He still couldn't understand why a stranger would stir such sympathy in his heart.

She had chosen her fate just as surely as he had chosen his.

He locked his hands at the small of his back, striving to view her through dispassionate eyes. There was no denying her face was striking enough to drive a man to all manner of folly. To win the favor of such a woman, a man might lie, steal, cheat, duel, or even murder.

He'd spent most of his life believing Clarinda to be the most beautiful woman he would ever lay eyes on. But even when the two of them were at their closest, hers had been a beauty as cool and unattainable as the moon. Angelica's charms were far more warm and approachable.

"Shall I fetch you a chair, my lord, so you'll be able to make calf's eyes at Miss Cadgwyck in comfort?"

That dry, familiar voice jolted him out of his reverie. Was that a hint of pity he heard in it? Or contempt?

He turned to find his housekeeper climbing the stairs, a pile of clean linens in her arms. In another time, another place, he might have chided her for not using the servants' staircase. But he was oddly glad to see another face. Especially a living one. "Should I be embarrassed to be caught mooning over a portrait of a girl long dead?"

Mrs. Spencer joined him on the landing. "I

wouldn't waste the effort if I were you. You're certainly not the first gentleman to be ensnared by her spell."

His housekeeper was garbed all in black on this day, and as she tilted back her head to give the portrait a jaded look, she resembled nothing so much as a drab crow gazing up at a vibrant canary. There was no sign of the warm, soft woman Max had held against his body in the dark. The woman who had stirred him with her scent and the provocative press of her curvy little bottom against his groin.

Trying desperately to forget that woman, he returned his attention to the portrait. "What became of Miss Cadgwyck after the . . . accident? Does she rest in the family crypt or is she buried somewhere else on the property?" Max knew that some zealots would never stomach a suicide being interred with their esteemed ancestors, many of whom had probably committed far more damning sins.

"Her body was never recovered. All they found was her yellow shawl tangled around one of the rocks."

The housekeeper's words struck Max's heart a fresh blow. As he scowled up into Angelica's laughing eyes, it was nearly impossible for him to imagine all of that vitality, all of that charm, reduced to bones at the bottom of the sea—stripped of their flesh by tide and time.

He almost welcomed the anger that surged through him. "I can't help but think her story might have had a different ending if there had been even one person who cared enough to follow her out onto that promontory. Someone who could have wrapped their arms around her and pulled her back from the brink."

He must have imagined Mrs. Spencer's sharply indrawn breath, for when she spoke, her voice was flatter than he had ever heard it. "There was no one to save her. She was all alone."

Max gave her a sharp look. "If there were no witnesses, how do you know that?"

"Servants' gossip. Whenever a scandal rocks the nobility, tongues will wag, you know."

"Was it those wagging tongues who resurrected the unfortunate young lady from her watery grave to terrorize the future masters of Cadgwyck?" As he remembered the haunting hint of jasmine that had made his groin ache with longing, his scowl deepened. "Although I suppose there are some shades a man might welcome into his bedchamber in the lonely hours between midnight and dawn." He slanted his housekeeper a mocking glance. "Why, Mrs. Spencer, I do believe I've managed to shock you. You're blushing."

"Don't be ridiculous," she said tartly, the flush of rose tinting her delicate cheekbones giving proof to his words. "I'm not some green girl who

blushes and simpers at the mere mention of romantic entanglements."

"Ah, yes, I forgot that as a widow you're no stranger to what takes place between a man and a woman in the privacy of their bedchamber."

Their eyes met, giving Max a jolt he hadn't expected and a reason to regret his mockery. Especially when he was assailed by a vivid image of what would never happen with *this* woman in the privacy of *his* bedchamber.

Still, she was the first to look away. "That may be true, but that doesn't mean I wish to discuss it with my employer." Brushing past him, she continued down the gallery, her steps crisp with purpose.

"What do you think she desires?" he called after her.

Mrs. Spencer stopped and slowly turned to face him, her expression even more wary than usual. "Pardon?"

"Isn't that the popular notion? That souls who have been somehow wronged are doomed to roam the earthly plane in death until they find what they were denied in life? If Angelica *has* returned to this house, what could she be searching for? What do you think she wants?"

"Perhaps, Lord Dravenwood, she simply wants to be left alone." Clutching the pile of linens to her breast like a shield, Mrs. Spencer turned and left him there in front of the portrait, her

impertinent rump twitching beneath the black linen of her dress.

Max watched her go, Angelica's spell momentarily broken.

In the days that followed, Max had no more visits to his bedchamber from Angelica, Piddles, his housekeeper, or anyone else. Oddly enough, the long, peaceful nights made him feel *more* restless instead of less. After tossing and turning in the tangle of his sheets for what felt like hours, he would throw open the French windows and stride out onto his balcony, his nostrils flared to detect any lingering hint of jasmine. He would stand gazing across the courtyard at the crumbling tower on the far side of the manor until the night's chill sank deep into his bones. But no matter how long or how patiently he waited, he heard no off-key tinkling of a music box or haunting echoes of girlish laughter. The muffled roar of the sea was the only sound to reach his ears.

The days were even longer than the nights. When he had fled London, he had dreamed only of escape, not of what he might do to occupy his mind and his hands during the interminable hours between dawn and dusk. Until he had resigned from the Company, his every waking hour had been consumed by board meetings, appointments, teas, balls, delicate treaty negotia-

tions, and speeches before Parliament. Even during the longest, dullest sea voyages, there had been figures to study, memorandums to dictate to his secretary, languages to master, and business ledgers to fill with his precise scrawl.

Now he spent his days stalking along the cliffs, trying to convince himself it wasn't too late for the salt-edged wildness of the wind to blow the cobwebs from his brain. He would walk for hours only to find himself standing once again on the very spot where Angelica had taken flight, gazing down at the churning whitecaps and the sea crashing against the rocks below.

After nearly a week of such aimless ramblings, he made a rather startling discovery. For the first time since losing Clarinda, he was hungry. No, not just hungry . . . he was bloody well famished. Yet whenever he returned to the house for lunch or supper, he was met with fare even more bland and tasteless than what he had endured for breakfast.

It wouldn't have been so galling if his housekeeper didn't walk around smelling like a bakery. Mrs. Spencer might be cool and distant, but the aroma clinging to her was warm and irresistible.

Max was seated at the head of the dining-room table one night when Dickon lurched clumsily through the door, a silver tray rattling in his hand. Max took a sip of sherry to hide his disappoint-

ment. If Mrs. Spencer had delivered his supper, he might at least have been able to steal a whiff of something that smelled like actual food.

As Dickon leaned over to place a plate in front of him, Max caught himself staring at the boy's powdered wig. No . . . it wasn't his imagination. The wig was most definitely on backward.

Max waved a hand toward it. "Do you like wearing that ridiculous thing?"

Dickon straightened, eyeing him mistrustfully. "No, m'lord."

"Then why do you?"

"Because Annie . . . um . . . Mrs. Spencer says if I'm to be a proper footman, I have to wear the proper attire. It's only proper."

Hunger had sharpened Max's temper to a dangerous edge. "From this day forward, I'm the one who will decide what's proper around here, not your Mrs. Spencer. Please remove it. At once."

"Very good, sir." Dickon dragged off the wig, looking so relieved he forgot to scowl for a minute. His hair was a tawny brown, plastered to his head by sweat except for an irrepressible cowlick at the crown.

The boy bowed his way from the room, leaving Max all alone with a plate containing a few shriveled potatoes and a kidney pie. Max pierced the pie's crust with his knife. Not a single enticing tendril of steam emerged. Why should it when everything in this accursed house was served at a

lukewarm temperature that was somehow less appetizing than if it had been served cold?

Max had yet to lay eyes on the mysterious Nana. He was beginning to wonder if he had inadvertently done something to offend the cook—like defiling her daughter or murdering her firstborn offspring. Why else would the infernal woman torture him day in and day out with her appalling dishes? Or perhaps they were all in cahoots and had decided that slowly starving him would leave less evidence for the constable than shoving him out a window.

Max picked at the pie's dry crust with his fork, growing both hungrier and angrier by the moment. He finally summoned up the courage to try a forkful of the meat but was forced to spit it out with his next breath—not because of its taste but because it had none.

Deciding it was far past time for Nana to make the acquaintance of her new master, he tossed down his napkin and went storming from the room.

Max had no trouble locating the basement kitchen. All he had to do was follow the cheerful clink of silver against earthenware and the sound of voices raised in happy chatter. As he approached the doorway, a husky ripple of female laughter assailed his ears, infectious and irresistible.

"Oh, do go on, Dickon!" someone else cried, clapping her hands in anticipation.

Max arrived in the doorway of the kitchen to find his staff gathered on benches around a crude pine table. Mrs. Spencer sat on the far side of the table, a genuine smile exposing that fetching little gap between her front teeth, making her hazel eyes sparkle, and erasing a decade from her age. As another throaty giggle escaped her, he realized with an all-too-pleasant shock that it had been her laughter he had heard.

He made no attempt to disguise his presence, but they were all too engrossed in the proceedings taking place in front of the stone hearth to take notice of him.

Dickon was holding court there, his powdered wig once again perched precariously on top of his head. Piddles sat at the boy's feet, gazing up at the boy as if equally mesmerized by his performance.

"So then he said"—Dickon fixed his face in a ferocious scowl and deepened his voice to a menacing upper-crust drawl—" 'Do you like wearing that ridiculous thing?' to which I replied, 'Of course I like wearing it, my lord. Who wouldn't want to wear a deceased hedgehog on their head?' "

Two of the Elizabeths collapsed in fresh titters while another was forced to wipe a mirthful tear from her eye with the hem of her apron. Hodges

pounded his open palms on the table, chortling like some great overgrown baby.

"What happened next?" Pippa demanded. "Did he insist that you be carted off to the dungeons or thrown to the dogs?"

Tucking his thumbs in the waistband of his breeches, Dickon puffed out his scrawny chest to a ridiculous degree. "That was when he said, 'From this day forward, *I'm* the one who will decide what's proper around here, not your precious Mrs. Spencer. Please remove it. At once!' "

With that, Dickon swept the wig from his head with a flourish and dropped it on Piddles's head. The dog endured the indignity with grace, looking exactly like a jowly barrister Max had once debated in Parliament.

Max waited until the fresh round of laughter had died out before putting his own hands together in a slow round of applause. "A creditable impersonation, young master Dickon. Your talents are obviously wasted here. You should be treading the boards at the Theatre Royal."

Chapter Fourteen

Max's staff whipped their heads around as one, their faces reflecting a mixture of horror and alarm at finding their employer leaning against the door frame, surveying them through dispassionate eyes.

Dickon immediately snatched the wig off Piddles and thrust it behind his back, ducking his head sheepishly. The only one who seemed unfazed by his appearance was an ancient woman rocking to and fro in a cane-backed chair in the corner. Judging by the heaps of multi-colored yarn piled at her feet, she had spent the last hundred years knitting a scarf for a giant. Since Max had never laid eyes on her before tonight, he could only assume she must be the elusive Nana, the author of all his culinary misfortune since arriving at Cadgwyck.

Mrs. Spencer rose, her charming smile replaced by the tight-lipped expression he was coming to hate. The smile that wasn't a smile at all, but something designed solely to placate others. "Why, Lord Dravenwood, is there something you require?" She gave the row of rusting bells over his head an accusing look. "We didn't hear you ring."

155

As Max's gaze traveled the circle of wary faces, he recognized his staff for the first time for what they truly were—a family. When his own family had gathered for supper, it had been in a formal dining room much like the one he had just left. Conversation had been limited to his father's bombastic pronouncements on whatever politician had most recently provoked his ire and their mother's sympathetic murmurs. Most meals were eaten in a tense silence broken only by the clink of silverware and the muted breathing of a battalion of servants standing behind their chairs, waiting to attend to their every need.

Occasionally, when their father would turn red and start to sputter, Ash would kick Max under the table and pull a funny face, but Max would keep his eyes carefully fixed on his plate, knowing he would be the one to suffer for their insolence should the duke take notice of it.

Max had vowed to himself that when he was master of his own house, his family would gather around a table much like this one to eat and talk and laugh and savor the pleasure of one another's company. But that dream was done now. He might be master of this house, but he would never be anything more than an outsider in the eyes of those gathered around this table—an intruder on their happiness.

The bench across from Mrs. Spencer had an empty place, and for one crazy moment Max

wanted nothing more than to ask if he could join them. But he simply straightened and said stiffly, "I was wondering if you might have some salt."

"I'll have Lisbeth bring it to you," Mrs. Spencer promised, relief evident on her face. Apparently, she thought him heartless enough to sack them all just for having a bit of fun at his expense.

He was about to beat a less than graceful retreat when he spotted it—a loaf of freshly baked bread sitting in the middle of the table. The golden loaf must have emerged from the oven right before his arrival. Steam was still rising from its crusty, perfectly browned top, taunting him with the very scent that had been driving him mad since his arrival at Cadgwyck. A small earthenware crock of freshly churned butter sat next to it, just waiting to be slathered over all of that warm, yeasty goodness.

It was nothing but a humble loaf, perfectly suited to a tenant's cottage, not the master's table. Yet the mere sight of it made Max feel savage with want.

His hands curled into fists. He was the master of this house. The bread belonged to him. He slowly lifted his eyes to meet his housekeeper's wide-eyed gaze.

Everything in this house belonged to him.

Something dangerous must have been in his expression. Her lips parted as if she was suddenly

having difficulty drawing breath. One of her pale hands fluttered nervously to the scrap of lace at her throat.

If he hadn't had a lifetime of practice denying himself the very thing he wanted the most, Max might not have been able to muster up the fortitude to turn his back on both her and her damned bread.

But after taking only two steps, he stopped. Without a word, he pivoted on his heel, marched straight back to the table, and snatched up the enormous carving knife resting next to the bread. One of the Elizabeths squeaked in alarm, and another shrank back in her chair as if he were going to murder them all. Giving his housekeeper the same look Hades had probably given Persephone before sweeping her away to his underworld lair to have his way with her, he brought the blade of the knife down in a shining arc, impaling the loaf of bread with a single savage motion.

He made it as far as the door with his prize before returning for the butter and a plump sausage. The servants were all gaping at him as if he'd gone stark raving mad, but in that moment he didn't care what anyone thought of him as long as his appetites were satisfied.

He paused in the doorway just long enough to give his housekeeper a curt nod. "Thank you, Mrs. Spencer. That will be all."

• • •

In the months since Clarinda had jilted him at the altar, Max had grown accustomed to paying the price for embracing dissipation. He would wake at midday with a pounding head and unsteady hands, his gullet still burning from all the brandy he'd poured down it the night before. He would stagger out of bed and to the convenience, one hand raised to shield his bleary eyes from the merciless rays of the sun. Then he would crawl back into the bed and wait for dark to fall so he could do it all over again.

What he was not accustomed to was waking at dawn with a full belly and a smile curling his lips. He rolled to his back and stretched like a tomcat after a night of successful prowling, a satisfied groan escaping him.

After sitting at the dining-room table all by himself and gorging himself on bread, butter, and sausage, he had retired early and slept like a babe. During his years with the Company, he had dined at the tables of both lords and princes, but none of their exotic delicacies could compare to the hearty goodness of that simple meal.

Hoping to steal a few more hours of sleep, he drew in a deep, contented breath redolent with the scent of baking bread. At first he thought the enticing aroma had clung to him, but as the haze of sleep faded, he shot to a sitting position,

yanked open the bed curtains, and poked his head out, sniffing at the air.

Five minutes later, Max was hastening down the stairs, tying his cravat as he went. He soon found himself leaning against the kitchen door frame, his gaze drinking in all the details he'd been too hungry and angry to notice the night before.

The kitchen was tucked away in the basement of the manor, but a high row of windows along the far wall welcomed in the hushed glow of the dawn light. Here, there was no sign of the dust and decay that seemed to plague the rest of the manor. A cheerful fire crackled on the grate, its warmth smoothing the edge off the morning chill. Gleaming copper pots and bunches of dried herbs tied up with frayed ribbons hung from iron hooks set in the exposed rafters. The flagstone floor and low ceiling made the room feel like a large, cozy cave.

Piddles was curled up on a faded rag rug in front of the stone hearth, his chin resting on his paws while a plump calico cat with tufted, white feet dozed in the cushion of the rocking chair in the corner.

It wasn't his cook but his housekeeper bending over to peer into the open door of the cast-iron oven. Max sincerely doubted Nana's rump had ever been that shapely. For once Mrs. Spencer didn't look as if she'd been dipped into a vat of

starch. A large white apron protected her skirts, and her face was flushed pink from the heat of the stove. Several strands of hair had escaped the net binding her chignon and tumbled down to frame her face. Max watched in reluctant fascination as one of them began to curl in the moist heat.

Despite her dishevelment, she looked happier than Max had ever seen her. She was even humming some tuneless ditty beneath her breath.

Just as she closed the door of the oven with a rag-wrapped hand, he said, "An early riser, are we, Mrs. Spencer?"

Straightening so fast she nearly bumped her head on a copper stew pot, she spun around to face him. She looked as guilty as if he'd caught her in flagrante delicto on the kitchen table with some strapping young gardener, an image that gave Max more pause than he had planned.

The rag slithered to the floor. Her hand darted up to tuck a strand of hair back into the net, but met with little success. "My lord, even in London I'm sure it is customary to ring when you need something, not creep up on your servants and frighten them half out of their wits."

"What do you think you're doing?" he asked flatly.

She glanced at the table. It was covered from end to end with sacks of meal and flour, crocks of butter and lard, a basket of brown-speckled eggs,

bottles of spices, stoneware bowls, and a slew of other utensils and ingredients, many of them unidentifiable to Max's untrained eye.

Her mouth took on a faintly insolent cast. "Cooking."

Max advanced on her. "I was under the impression that Nana did the cooking for the household."

"Nana is feeling a bit under the weather today." As if to remind him someone was within screaming distance, Mrs. Spencer nodded toward the door. "She can't manage the stairs any longer so she sleeps in a room just down the corridor instead of in the servants' quarters."

Max moved around the end of the table. She turned with him as he stalked her, following him warily with her eyes as if he were a snarling hound and she a wounded fox. "And just how many days of the week is Nana under the weather?" he asked. "Four? Six? *Seven?*"

"She is getting on a bit in years. We don't mind lending a hand when we can."

"*We?*" Max looked around the kitchen pointedly. "*You* seem to be the only one here."

Mrs. Spencer lifted her stubborn little chin. "I've discovered that if I rise early, I can work undisturbed for a while before the others awaken."

Max could almost feel her exasperation with him growing. He might be master of the house,

but this was *her* kitchen. *Her* territory. He was the interloper here. She would probably like nothing more than to pick up the flour-dusted rolling pin from the table and chase him from the room.

"Is there something you need?" she asked.

As he gazed upon her proud visage, Max was surprised to feel a dangerous surge of desire uncoil within him. He needed many things, none of which she could supply.

"If not," she said, turning away from him with a defiant flounce of her apron, "I have other matters to—*Ow! Damn it all!*"

He'd gotten her so flustered she had forgotten all about the fallen rag and seized the stove door's handle with her bare fingers. As she cradled her wounded hand to her breast, gritting her teeth to keep another cry from escaping, Max quickly closed the distance between them. Helpless tears sparkled in her hazel eyes, making them look larger and more luminous.

Cursing himself for distracting her, he gently tugged her hand into his own. "Let me see," he urged when she kept her fingers tightly curled.

Her breath escaped in a near sob. "There's no need. I don't require a nursemaid."

"It wasn't a request. It was an order."

She sniffed. "That's very high-handed of you. I hope you know I plan to mock you mercilessly over supper tonight, and my impressions are even more spot-on than Dickon's."

"Make sure and include the part where I sack you for disobeying a direct order."

Still glaring at him, she reluctantly unfolded her hand. Each of her slender fingers had an angry red mark on it.

"Fortunately, you let go of the stove before the skin could blister. But it must hurt like the very devil." He glanced up to catch her biting her lower lip. "You may cry if you like."

"How very magnanimous of you. Must I seek your permission for that as well?"

Despite her sullen expression, she didn't protest when he led her over to the basin resting on the long table beneath the row of windows. He cranked the pump, then gently guided her wounded hand beneath the spigot. As the cool water cascaded over her fingers, she moaned. Her eyes fluttered shut, her face going slack with relief.

Max was strangely transfixed by the sight. Her mink-colored lashes weren't particularly long but they were lush and curled lightly at their tips. She didn't appear to be wearing a trace of powder, yet her skin had the smooth purity of fresh cream. His gaze strayed to her lips. When not flattened into a dutiful smile or puckered into a disapproving moue, they were surprisingly ripe and rosy with an enticingly kissable little Cupid's bow at their top. She opened her eyes and he yanked his gaze back to her hand before she could catch him staring.

"Come," he said gruffly, tugging her over to one of the benches flanking the table. He eased her into a sitting position, then straddled the bench and sank down in front of her. "I've just the thing for your burns."

Thankful he hadn't gobbled down every bit of butter in the house during his culinary orgy, he dipped his fingertips into an earthenware crock and began to dab a bit of the stuff onto each of her wounds. Most women of his acquaintance wouldn't leave the house without elbow-length gloves to protect their lily-white skin. But her hands were lightly tanned with fingertips that sported a callus and shallow nick or two. They were the hands of a woman who was no stranger to hard work.

"How did you know the butter would help?" she asked, casting him a shy glance from beneath her lashes.

"I had a baby brother who used to get into a great deal of mischief as a lad. He was always knocking down beehives or swiping hot mincemeat pies out from under Cook's nose and scorching his fingers. I had to play nursemaid to his wounds more than once so our parents wouldn't find out what havoc he'd been wreaking and give him a sound thrashing."

"*Had* a baby brother?" she echoed softly, plainly fearing the worst.

Max couldn't quite keep the bitter edge from his tone. "He's no longer a baby."

"What about you? Didn't you get into any mischief of your own?"

A rueful snort escaped him. "Very little. But only because I didn't dare. Before I could stand up in my cradle, it was drummed into my head that I was the eldest son, my father's heir, and the hope of all who worshipped at the Burke altar. Mischief was a pleasure afforded to lesser mortals, not to solemn little boys in short pants who would someday be dukes."

"It sounds like a heavy burden for a child to bear."

"I'm not sure I ever was a child."

"Did your father approve of your career with the East India Company? I thought noblemen were expected to do little more than lounge about at their clubs with other gentlemen of means, sipping brandy and discussing their tailors and their triumphs at the faro tables."

Max shuddered. "A pursuit for which I was singularly ill suited. My father nearly had an apoplexy when I announced my intention to join the Company. But once he saw that my influence would imbue the Burke name with even more prestige and power, he embraced my choice as if it had been his fondest ambition for me."

"Didn't you ever tire of being the perfect son? Didn't you ever want to escape the shackles of duty and do something really . . . wicked?"

A reluctant half smile canted his lips as he

lifted his eyes to meet her inquisitive gaze. "With my every breath."

Only then did he realize he had finished smoothing the butter over her burns, but was still cradling her hand. His thumb was absently stroking the center of her palm, tracing lazy circles over the satiny skin he found there.

His smile faded. This was an impossible situation. She was an impossible woman. Yet in that moment, with her hand cupped trustingly in his and the sweetness of her peppermint-scented breath fanning his lips, the world seemed ripe with possibility.

It suddenly occurred to him that this might be his chance to break the chains of duty. What could be more wicked than stealing a kiss from the lips of his housekeeper? Why, it was practically a rite of passage, wasn't it? Nefarious gentlemen had been seducing their housekeepers and parlor maids for centuries.

Max's body had already hardened in anticipation, urging him to do something wild and impractical for once in his life, consequences be damned.

He lifted his other hand toward her face, half-expecting her to flinch away from his touch. But when he brushed his thumb over the softness of her cheek, she held as steady as her gaze. One of her stray curls tickled the backs of his fingers as his thumb strayed into even more dangerous

territory, grazing the velvety warmth of lips no longer pressed together, but parted in invitation. Testing the softness of those lips with the firmness of his thumb only deepened his hunger until all he could think about was how sweet they would taste beneath his own.

As Max leaned forward, Mrs. Spencer's lashes swept down to veil her luminous eyes, almost as if to deny what was about to happen. Their lips were a breath away from meeting when the first tendril of smoke came wafting between them.

Chapter Fifteen

Both Anne's and Dravenwood's gazes flew to the stove to discover thick, acrid clouds of smoke billowing around the cracks in the cast-iron door. Crying out with dismay, Anne sprang to her feet and rushed for the stove. This time she remembered to grab both a rag and a wooden paddle before throwing open the door. Her rescue effort came too late. The paddle emerged from the oven topped with a smoldering lump.

She dumped it on the table. Dravenwood joined her, gazing down at the blackened bread with a dismay equal to, if not greater than, her own.

"Forgive me," he said, his voice still husky with an emotion that could have been either chagrin

or desire. "I should never have distracted you."

"The blame is entirely mine," she replied, her fingertips absently straying to the familiar shape of the locket beneath her bodice. "I allowed myself to forget that only a few careless seconds of inattention can ruin everything."

He nodded curtly, then strode from the room without another word.

Anne watched his broad shoulders disappear through the door, recognizing with a treacherous stab of regret that neither of them would be foolish enough to make that mistake again.

"The master wishes to see you in his study."

Anne glanced up from her task of halfheartedly grinding some fresh garden dirt into the drawing room carpet with the heel of her boot to find Lizzie standing in the doorway. The young maid was wringing the hem of her apron in her hands, looking nearly as anxious as Anne felt.

Anne had been halfway expecting this summons since her encounter with Lord Dravenwood in the kitchen that morning. She had hoped finally receiving it might loosen the knot of dread in her stomach, not tighten it into an inescapable vise.

She had spent the past ten years desperately trying to prove she was no longer the same girl she had been. But all it had taken was a tender caress and the tantalizing promise of a kiss from Dravenwood's beautifully sculpted lips to shatter

that illusion. What might she have done if their lips had actually touched? Wrapped her arms around his neck and climbed into his lap? Would he have stolen her heart as deftly as he stole her kiss? Was she even capable of giving one without the other?

"Thank you, Lizzie." Tucking a flowerpot half-full of dirt beneath the ruffled skirt of a chaise longue, she managed an encouraging smile for the girl before climbing the stairs to meet her fate.

The door to the study had been left open a crack. Anne slipped into the room to find Lord Dravenwood seated behind the dusty cherrywood desk, surrounded by towering stacks of ledgers with mildewed covers and yellowing pages. He was making notations in one of the open ones, his concentration absolute.

She stood there, waiting for him to acknowledge her presence. That morning in the kitchen she had discovered just how intoxicating—and how dangerous—it could be to have his attention focused on her with such intensity.

A wavy, dark lock of hair had fallen over his eyes. He brushed it back impatiently, his pen still flying across the page. Something about the boyish gesture unleashed an odd tenderness in Anne's heart. Knowing it was wrong to spy on him in such a craven manner, she cleared her throat.

He glanced up immediately, his pen ceasing its motion. He didn't say anything but simply took her measure from beneath the thick, dark wings of his brows. She was no longer the vulnerable woman who had allowed him to nurse her wounds and nearly steal a kiss. Her apron was freshly starched, her hair neatly dressed and confined to its tidy little net.

They were once again master and housekeeper, each knowing their places and which boundaries were not to be crossed.

Ever.

Striving to keep her expression as free of emotion as possible, Anne returned his gaze evenly. "You had need of me, my lord?"

His eyes narrowed ever so briefly before he closed the ledger with an audible snap, making it clear *she* was now the business at hand. "I believe it is you who have need of me, Mrs. Spencer. After our *discussion* this morning, I realized I was being completely remiss in my duties."

"You? Remiss? In *your* duties?"

"If I hadn't been remiss, you wouldn't have been attempting to do the work of an entire day before the sun had so much as crested the horizon."

"I am the housekeeper of this establishment. It's my job to make sure everything runs smoothly."

"That may be true, but it's not your job to do

everyone else's job." He leaned back in his chair, steepling his fingers beneath his chin.

His hands were everything a man's hands should be—strong, powerful-looking, with a light dusting of dark hair on their backs and long, elegantly tapered fingers. They were the sort of hands a woman could easily imagine caressing . . . gliding . . . stroking . . . Anne jerked her gaze back to his face, horrified by the wayward direction of her thoughts.

"From what I've observed since I've been here, you're saddled with a daft butler, an ancient cook, several affable but supremely incompetent maids, and an ill-tempered footman who doesn't know a silver salver from a dormouse. If you keep trying to compensate for the shortcomings of your staff, all you'll succeed in doing is working yourself into an early grave."

Before Anne could stop it, a bitter laugh bubbled from her lips. "Perhaps I'm simply trying to work my way *out* of an early grave."

"I'm confident you're doing the best you can, but one woman can only do so much. It was evident to me from the first night I arrived that the manor's staff wasn't adequate to care for an estate this size. Yet I did nothing to rectify the situation. Which is why I've decided to send to London for some help."

Anne felt her lips go numb at the thought of a horde of strangers traipsing about the manor,

digging into things that were none of their concern. Things long buried that desperately needed to stay that way. And other things that must only be unearthed by her and her staff.

"I can assure you that won't be necessary," she said, fighting to keep a note of hysteria from creeping into her voice. "I'm the one who allowed the other servants to grow lax in their duties when there was no master in residence. Once I explain what's required of them, they'll work harder. I swear it."

"I might be able to believe that of the younger ones, but what about Hodges? And Nana? You're supposed to be running a household here, Mrs. Spencer, not a home for the elderly and the mentally infirm."

"Nana and Hodges would be devastated if deprived of their positions. Neither of them have any family left to look after them. They have nowhere else to go. Hodges has only recently started exhibiting signs of a mental decline," she lied. "I fear it's the result of an injury he suffered in the war."

Dravenwood scowled suspiciously at her. "Which war?"

"The one with Napoléon," Anne replied, hoping that would cover most wars of the past several decades. "It would hardly be sporting to shunt him aside after he so valiantly served his country and king."

Dravenwood grunted. "And what of Nana? Was she a gunner in the Royal Navy?"

"Nana faithfully served a local family for most of her life," Anne said, hoping a morsel of truth would placate him. "But when she started losing her hearing, they insisted she be replaced and gave her notice. Her only desire now is to live out the rest of her years here at Cadgwyck—in the place she has come to call home." Anne drew close enough to lay her palms on the desk, willing to sacrifice her stiff-necked pride on the altar of his mercy. "Please, my lord. If the others agree to work harder to lighten my load, may Nana and Hodges stay?"

"Of course they may stay." He frowned up at her, looking genuinely insulted. "What did you think I was going to do? Cast them into the hedgerows to fend for themselves?"

She straightened, sighing with relief since that was exactly what she had feared. "Thank you, my lord. Will there be anything else?"

"There is *one* more thing." The lascivious glint in his eyes made Anne's stomach tighten all over again.

"Yes, my lord?"

"I don't care what other slop you feed me, but I want some of that bread you bake on my table. Every day. For breakfast." After a moment of thought, he added, "And supper."

Anne could feel a smile flirting with her lips. "I

believe that can be arranged. Will *that* be all, my lord?"

"For now." The innocent words sounded oddly provocative on his beautifully chiseled lips. Lips that had been a breath away from claiming hers just that morning.

She had almost reached the door when he said, "Mrs. Spencer?"

She turned, eyeing him warily.

"Has it ever occurred to you that I may not be the heartless ogre you believe me to be?"

"No, my lord," she said solemnly. "I'm afraid it hasn't." But just before she slipped out the door, she flashed him a genuine smile, not her usual tight-lipped one.

"Impossible woman," she heard him mutter beneath his breath as he returned to his ledgers.

"I demand an increase in my wages!" Pippa exclaimed as she and Dickon struggled to wrestle a rolled-up Turkish rug out of the drawing room and through the entrance hall the following afternoon.

"You don't receive any wages," Anne reminded her. Anne was perched on a rickety ladder in the middle of the hall, using a broom to swipe the thick veil of cobwebs from the tarnished brass arms of the chandelier. Every twinge and throb of her muscles only served to remind her that she was the one who put them there.

"All the more reason to demand an increase." Heaving an exhausted sigh, Pippa dropped her end of the carpet and plopped down on it. She'd covered her dark curls with a linen kerchief to keep the dust out of them.

Dickon rolled his eyes. "I don't know why *you're* in such a foul temper." The boy gave the open front door a longing glance. "I could be out on the moor right now hunting for supper or catching a wild pony to ride. Instead, I'm stuck in this miserable house doing women's work with the likes of you."

"Don't grumble, dear," Anne chided from her swaying perch. "You'll get plenty of fresh air when you're out in the courtyard beating a decade of dust from that rug."

Muttering something beneath his breath that would doubtlessly have gotten his ears boxed if Anne could reach them, Dickon gave his end of the rug a hard yank, dumping Pippa in the floor. As she sprang to her feet, rubbing her rump and glaring after him, he dragged the rug the rest of the way out the door.

Anne tossed down the broom, then descended from the ladder. She dusted off her grimy hands, surveying the results of their handiwork with a satisfied smile.

She'd wasted no time in fulfilling her promise to Lord Dravenwood. A sneezing Beth and Bess had spent most of the morning dragging the

moldering draperies down from the tall, arched windows and were now diligently scrubbing years of grime from the wavy panes of glass. Betsy was slopping a mop around the floors, while Lisbeth dipped her rag in a container of linseed oil and beeswax to buff the mahogany of the banister to a rich luster. Lizzie was upstairs whisking old sheets off the furniture and stuffing handfuls of fresh feathers purchased from the local goose girl into all of the mattresses. Even Hodges and Nana had insisted on doing their part. Hodges was gleefully collecting every bit of tarnished silver in the house and dragging it to the kitchen so Nana could her set her gnarled hands to the task of polishing it.

With their limited resources, there was no way for them to restore the house to its former glory. All they could do was hold up a dim mirror to reflect what once had been. But even those modest efforts had stirred up more than just dust. If Anne tilted her head just right, she could almost hear the graceful notes of a waltz drifting out from the deserted ballroom, the merry clink of champagne flutes hefted in a teasing toast, the muted murmur of conversation, and laughter from voices long gone. Angelica gazed down upon them from her haughty perch at the top of the stairs. It was impossible to tell from her cryptic smile if she approved of their efforts or was mocking their foolishness.

Pippa followed the direction of Anne's gaze. "Our White Lady hasn't made an appearance in almost a fortnight. And now you're making the manor so comfortable Lord Imperious won't ever want to leave. I'm beginning to suspect you're not in as great of a hurry to be rid of the man as you'd like us to believe."

"Don't be absurd," Anne replied, her voice sounding oddly unconvincing even to her own ears. "Of course I am. But I thought we agreed it would be in all of our best interests to tread carefully with this one. He's no fool like the rest."

"I wasn't implying *he* was a fool," Pippa replied, giving Anne an arch look before heading out the side door to join Dickon in the courtyard.

"Saucy little baggage," Anne muttered, knowing it was probably only a matter of time before Pippa and Dickon stopped using their paddles to whack the rug and started whacking each other.

Despite what Pippa believed, the last thing she wanted was for Dravenwood to linger at Cadgwyck. They were wasting precious time that could better be spent looking for the treasure. Plus, the longer he stayed, the harder it was going to be to dislodge him. All Anne was doing now was humoring the man, allaying his suspicions and waiting for him to relax his guard. Once he did, she would gladly step aside and let Angelica have her way with him.

She was assailed by a shocking image of

Dravenwood sprawled on his freshly stuffed mattress beneath the canopy of his bed, wearing little more than a silk sheet draped low on his narrow hips and a come-hither smile.

"Mrs. Spencer!"

Had Anne still been atop the ladder when that deep, masculine voice interrupted her wicked little fantasy, she would probably have tumbled off and broken her neck. Drawing a handkerchief from the pocket of her apron and dabbing at her flushed cheeks, she hastened toward the stairs. How had her wayward imagination produced such a ridiculous notion? She'd never seen the earl wear a genuine smile, much less a come-hither one.

She arrived at the corridor outside Lord Dravenwood's chamber to find it deserted. She gave the door a tentative knock.

"Enter," he commanded gruffly.

Anne cautiously eased open the door, half-expecting to find Piddles devouring another pair of boots or Sir Fluffytoes tangled up in the earl's finest cravat. But the earl was all alone, sitting on a stool in front of his dressing table, glowering at his reflection in its beveled looking glass.

He shifted his gaze, his smoky gray eyes meeting hers in the looking glass. "I'm sorry to pull you away from your duties, but I have need of you."

I have need of you.

That bold confession made Anne wonder what it would be like to be truly needed by such a man. To hear those same words whispered in her ear in the dark of night in a lover's hoarse tones.

She stepped forward, deliberately sharpening the brisk edge of her voice. "How may I be of service, my lord?"

He swiveled on the stool, revealing the flash of the shears in his hands and the handful of glossy, dark locks littering the hardwood floor around him.

"Oh, no!" she exclaimed, unaccountably dismayed by the sight. "What have you done?"

"I was starting to look like a savage. Or an American. I've become much more adept at looking after myself since arriving at Cadgwyck, but I need you to help me trim my hair. As you can see, I'm making quite the muddle of it."

Anne's gaze flew back to his hair. She felt a ridiculous surge of relief. He hadn't yet done irretrievable damage to it, although the right side was decidedly longer than the left.

She took another step into the room, then hesitated. An intimate task like cutting a man's hair was far more suited to his valet or barber. Or his wife.

"Why don't you let me summon Dickon, my lord?"

"If I'm not going to let the lad near my throat

with a straight razor, what makes you think I'd trust him with a pair of shears?"

Growing ever more desperate, she said, "Then Hodges perhaps . . ."

He cocked his head and gave her a reproachful look.

She huffed out a sigh. "Very well, then. If you insist . . ."

Donning her most imperturbable air, she marched across the room to his side. She brushed the fallen hair from his shoulders, that simple contact making her fingertips tingle with awareness. Her hands lingered of their own volition, measuring the impressive breadth of his shoulders until she realized what she was doing and jerked them out of harm's way.

As she removed her apron and swept it around his shoulders to protect his coat from further insult, she could not resist asking, "Are you certain you should let *me* near your throat with a sharp instrument?"

"Not entirely. But convincing the local magistrate I tripped and fell directly onto the blades of a pair of shears would no doubt tax even your considerable resources." Casting her a darkly amused look, he offered her the shears, handles first.

She accepted them, her lips compressed to a thin line. As she leaned over him to assess the damage he'd already done, the warm, masculine

spice of bayberry soap drifted to her nostrils. An answering warmth purled low in her belly.

He held himself as still as a marble statue beneath her hands as she captured a thick lock of his hair between her fingers and gave it a tentative snip. She was clever enough to realize her power over him in that moment was nothing but an illusion, easily shattered by nothing more than a look or a touch.

"Was this the sort of task you once performed for Mr. Spencer?"

She glanced down to find him surveying her face, his expression inscrutable. "On occasion," she replied, her hands slowly gaining in confidence as she moved around him.

"And was yours a happy union?"

"For a time. As are most."

"Just how long have you been on your own?"

Forever, she almost blurted out before remembering it only felt that way. "Nearly a decade."

A frown touched his brow. "That's a very long time for a woman to make her own way in this world. Was there no one to look after you after you lost your husband?"

"I'm quite capable of looking after myself, and I've found all the family I need right here at Cadgwyck. What of you, my lord?" she asked, hoping to shift the attention away from herself. "How long have you been *on your own?*"

She expected him to chide her for her impertinence, but he simply shrugged and said, "All my life, it seems."

Their eyes met for the briefest of seconds, then she continued snipping gently away at the right side of his hair until its length matched that of the left. She shied away from cutting it any shorter than the rugged line of his jaw. His sooty locks tended to wave and curl even more without the extra weight bearing them down.

"There," she said when she had finished, guiding him around on the stool so they could both admire her handiwork in the looking glass. "I believe that should do it. At least until you get to a proper barber."

Without thinking, she reached down and feathered his freshly trimmed hair between her fingers, much as she would have done Dickon's. Their gazes met in the looking glass and her hand froze in midmotion. No matter what duty he required of her, she had no right to touch him in such a familiar manner.

She moved to jerk her hand back, but he caught it in his own, his powerful fingers curling around hers, steadying the faint tremble he found there. He held both her gaze and her hand captive, and for a breathless moment she thought he would bring her hand to his lips or use it to inexorably tug her into the warm shelter of his lap.

Instead, he gave it a gentle squeeze. "Thank you, Mrs. Spencer."

Assailed by a curious mixture of relief and disappointment, she slid her hand from his, then whisked her apron from his shoulders. "Will there be anything else, my lord?"

Still watching her in the looking glass through hooded eyes, he opened his mouth, then closed it again before saying softly, "No, Mrs. Spencer. I believe that will be all."

Anne drew the door shut behind her, then sagged against it, her breath escaping her in a wistful sigh. Pippa had been right all along. Their new master *was* more dangerous than all the rest.

But for all the wrong reasons.

Chapter Sixteen

"Please, dearest . . . I have faith in you. I just know you could remember if you'd only try a bit harder."

Max was crossing the entrance hall the next morning when he recognized his housekeeper's voice drifting out of the drawing room. He froze in his tracks. He'd never been given to eavesdropping, but something about the soft, coaxing note in her voice—a voice that was usually crisp and edged with pride—was riveting.

"I tell you, I can't remember!" Max recognized Hodges's voice as well, though he'd never heard the butler sound quite so petulant. "I've wracked my brain until my head aches but it won't come to me!"

"Perhaps if you gave it just one more go?" Mrs. Spencer urged.

Max eased close enough to the arched doorway to peer into the room.

Hodges was seated in a Sheraton chair that had one splintered leg propped on a book. Mrs. Spencer was kneeling beside him with a hand resting on his thigh. She was peering up into his red-rimmed eyes, hope and desperation mingled in her expression. "You mustn't give up. You're our only hope and we're running out of time. Oh, please, darling . . ."

Max stiffened. If she begged him like that, he wasn't sure he could refuse her anything.

"It's just not there! Can't you see I'm doing the best I can?" Hodges wailed, burying his ruddy face in his hands.

"Of course you are." She gently patted the old man's leg, her shoulders slumping in defeat. "There, there, dear. It's all right. I'm so terribly sorry. I shouldn't have pushed you so hard."

Max cleared his throat.

Hodges jerked up his head, and both of their gazes flew to Max's face. The sheen of tears in the butler's eyes was unmistakable, just as was

the frustration and guilt on the housekeeper's wary face.

"Is there something amiss?" Max asked. "Perhaps I can be of assistance."

Mrs. Spencer rose to her feet, her shoulders once again ramrod straight. "Dear Mr. Hodges has simply forgotten where he put the key to the wine cellar. I'm sure he'll remember before we have need of it."

Max glanced at her waist, where her ever-present ring of keys still hung. She was lying to him. Her gaze might be bold, even challenging, but all that meant was that she had been lying for so long she had become fluent in the language. Max had lived a lie himself for almost a decade. He knew just how easily that could happen.

Hodges had averted his eyes and was gripping the carved arms of the chair in a futile effort to hide the palsied trembling of his hands.

Aside from threatening to dismiss the both of them, Max had little recourse. And if he did that, he might never learn what they were hiding. "Don't overtax yourself, Hodges," he said, returning his thoughtful gaze to Mrs. Spencer's face. "Sometimes things that go missing have a way of turning up where you least expect them."

Max awoke the following morning to the patter of rain against the French windows of his bedchamber. He considered braving the cliffs for

his usual morning walk, but by the time he finished breakfast, the rain was falling in relentless gray sheets past the wall of windows in the dining room, obscuring even the tempestuous tossing of the sea.

Another man might have found the hushed gloom and the steady drumming of the rain on the roof cozy. It would have been a perfect opportunity to return to the study, light a fire to burn off the damp, and continue to review the account ledgers and correspondence left by the former masters of Cadgwyck Manor. He had come here ostensibly to manage the estate, not haunt it himself. But the very idea of spending the day trapped behind a desk, devoting himself to the same inconsequential drivel that had consumed his attention for most of his life, suddenly seemed unbearable.

He was passing a window in the stairwell after breakfast when the rain abated just enough to allow him to catch a glimpse of the tower standing sentinel on the other side of the courtyard. He ducked his head, peering through the curtain of gloom. The mere sight of the tower quickened his senses in a way no dusty ledger ever could. He hadn't realized until that moment just how much he had missed Angelica's visits.

An unexpected smile tugged at one corner of his mouth. If his White Lady wouldn't come to him, then perhaps it was time to go to her.

It took Max nearly half an hour to make his way across the house to the west wing. He could simply have thrown on an overcoat and hat, slipped out one of the terrace doors, and crossed the wet cobblestones of the courtyard, but he wanted to avoid the prying eyes of the servants. Their efforts to set the house to rights hadn't yet progressed this far. Along the way he passed darkened rooms crowded with furniture slumbering beneath ghostly white sheets. A pair of towering doors decorated with peeling gilt opened onto a cavernous ballroom where Angelica Cadgwyck must once have danced in the arms of her adoring suitors. After Max was forced to detour around his third locked door, he began to regret not bringing his housekeeper's ring of keys with him.

Or perhaps his housekeeper herself.

He finally reached a windowless corridor with rotting floorboards that groaned ominously beneath his boots. The gloom grew so thick he was forced to feel his way along the walls for the last few steps of his journey until the corridor ended in a door.

After fumbling about for a minute, cursing himself for not having the forethought to bring a candle, he finally located an iron handle and gave the door a shove. It resisted for a moment, as if reluctant to yield its secrets, then surrendered with a gusty sigh.

Max found himself standing on the first floor of the tower, blinking with relief to discover he was no longer in darkness. Just as he had suspected, the tower had most likely been the keep of the original castle. Murky light stole through arrow slits set at intervals in the stone walls. The winding stairs hugging the exterior wall were crumbling in spots and slick with the rain blowing through the arrow slits and trickling through the cracks in the wall. Despite that it would be only too easy to slip, break his neck, and remain undiscovered for days, Max's steps were strangely confident as he started up the stairs.

They wound their way up to an iron-banded, oaken door that looked far older than anything else Max had encountered in the house. Unlike the door at the foot of the stairs, this one gave easily beneath the cautious push of Max's hand.

Before he had a chance to get his bearings, a white shape flew directly at his face.

Chapter Seventeen

Letting out a guttural cry, Max instinctively threw up his hands to protect his eyes. From the frantic beating of the wings about his head, he quickly realized it was not some wailing banshee accosting him but a confused egret that had

darted in through one of the broken window-panes. Once the bird realized Max wasn't a threat, it quickly lost interest in him and went soaring up to land on one of the rafters, where it sat prettily preening its feathers.

Bemused by his own reaction, Max shook his head, thankful his acerbic housekeeper hadn't been around to see *that*.

As his surroundings reclaimed his attention, he turned in a slow circle, gazing about him in rapt fascination. Because of its dilapidated state, he had assumed the tower would have been unoccupied for generations. Instead, it was as if he'd stumbled upon the abandoned abode of some fairy-tale princess who had just stepped out for a decade or two and would soon return in a flourish of satin and silk and a cloud of perfume. Max moved deeper into the room, beguiled against his will by the romance of it all.

The round chamber occupied the entire top floor of the tower. Dirt and mold stained the stone walls, but at some point they had been white-washed and decorated with an intricate pattern of ivy eerily similar to the real ivy now creeping through the shattered windows.

A tarnished brass bed sat between two of the lancet windows, the rotting lace adorning its half-tester drifting in the rain-scented breeze. A delicate cherrywood harpsichord sat nearby. Max could easily imagine a young girl's graceful

fingers tripping lightly along its keys, charming forth some timeless melody from Bach or Handel. He wandered over and touched a finger to one of its yellowing keys, striking a wheezing note that made him wince.

A tall, oval looking glass with a jagged crack down the middle of it hung in a frame designed so it could be tilted to reveal the one gazing into it at the most flattering angle. As Max reached up and adjusted it, he almost expected to see another face gazing back at him. But all he saw was his own countenance split in two by that crack, expressionless and draped in shadow.

Turning his back on the looking glass, he wandered over to one of the windows over-looking the cliffs and the sea. The cushions of the window seat had rotted away long ago, but Max could still see a young woman curled up on them with a book in her hand, while the rain beat against the diamond-paned windows on a day just like this, as cozy and secure as the egret would be when she returned to her nest.

A skirted dressing table sat directly across from the bed with a broken stool sprawled on the floor in front of it. Max's steps slowed as he approached it. He was already trespassing, but somehow invading the sacred domain of a young woman's dressing table made him feel even more like a marauder.

There was something irresistibly feminine about

the dusty items scattered across the marble top of the dressing table—an ivory-backed mirror with a silver handle; a pair of amber hair combs; a cachou box of lip salve; an assortment of bottles labeled with promising names like *Milk of Roses, Olympian Dew,* and *Bloom of Ninon;* a faded ribbon rosette that might have been plucked from an elaborate coiffure and carelessly tossed on the table in the wee morning hours after dancing the night away at some magnificent ball.

And a single bottle of perfume.

Max drew the cut-crystal stopper from the elegant bottle, then lifted the bottle to his nose, already knowing what he would find. Its contents had dried up long ago, but as he inhaled, the subtle notes of jasmine filled his lungs—sultry, erotic, yet strangely innocent. He was carefully returning the bottle to its place when he saw the heart-shaped silver box adorned with pearl plating sitting on the corner of the table.

He hesitated, knowing just how Pandora must have felt when presented with such an enticing temptation. He picked up the box, cradling it in a hand that suddenly seemed far too large and clumsy to be entrusted with such a treasure.

Fighting a mixture of dread and anticipation, he gently lifted the hinged lid to reveal an empty interior lined in ruby velvet. A handful of familiar, slightly off-key, notes drifted through the room

just as they had drifted through his balcony door on his first night at the manor.

Unable to bear their piercing sweetness, he slammed down the lid. If anything could summon up a spirit that wished only to be left alone, then surely it was that haunting melody. Restoring the music box to its rightful place, he turned to survey the rest of the room, growing ever more desperate to find some clue to the mystery that was Angelica Cadgwyck.

He was facing a tall mahogany armoire almost identical to the one in his room. He crossed the timber floor with a determined stride, hesitating only when his hands closed over the ivory knobs on the twin doors. One of the doors hung askew on its hinges, leaving a narrow crack between door and frame. Bracing himself for some grinning skeleton to come tumbling into his arms, he threw open both doors at once.

All he saw were the remains of an extravagant wardrobe that had gone unprotected from the elements for years—shredded satin, shattered silk, moth-eaten merino. The floor of the armoire was littered with delicate slippers in faded pastel shades with frayed ribbon laces and curling toes. When he nudged one of them with his boot, a squeak of protest warned him a family of baby mice had taken up residence there.

Leaving the doors of the armoire hanging open, he swung back around to face the room, finally

forced to admit that his was a fool's errand. If Angelica was guarding any secrets, she had taken them over the edge of that cliff with her.

A row of dolls gazed down their noses at him from a shelf carved into the stone wall itself. Hairline cracks marred their pale porcelain faces, but did nothing to detract from their haughty demeanors. Even their daintily pursed lips looked disapproving. Oddly riveted by the sight, Max drifted across the tower toward them. Their satin skirts were stained with mildew but still arranged in precise folds. They had obviously been placed there with tender care by the hand of a girl too old to play with them any longer but too young to relinquish their cherished place in her heart.

He reached up to draw one of the dolls from the shelf. She didn't resemble her young mistress, yet something was oddly familiar about her. Her painted lips didn't seem to be pursed in disapproval, but to hide a smile. Her brown eyes were lit with a mocking twinkle. Unable to place the resemblance, Max shook his head ruefully, wondering if he was losing his wits completely. He was starting to see ghosts everywhere he looked.

He was returning the doll to her perch when he noticed something odd. He had believed her to be sitting on a Prussian-blue velvet cushion befitting her exalted station, but closer inspection revealed it wasn't a cushion at all but a velvet-

bound book. Max shoved the doll carelessly into the corner of the shelf and drew the book into his hands.

A gentle ruffle through the fragile pages confirmed that it was a journal—the sort a young girl might use to preserve her musings and dreams.

And her secrets.

Still holding the journal, Max wandered over to one of the windows, where the light was marginally better. He gazed blindly out over the rain-slicked cobblestones of the courtyard. Despite his romantic fancies, Angelica hadn't been some captive princess abiding in this tower. And even if she had been, he had come too late to rescue her. If he had even an ounce of integrity left in his soul, he would return the journal to its hiding place and do what Mrs. Spencer had suggested—leave Miss Cadgwyck to rest in whatever peace she had managed to find.

Before Clarinda had walked away from him and back into his brother's arms, that's exactly what he would have done.

Propping one boot on the splintered remains of the window seat, Max opened the journal to its first page. It began with the usual mundane meanderings of any child enchanted with dolls and ponies and fairy cakes. But between the lines of those simple yet charming sketches of daily life at Cadgwyck, a portrait far clearer than the one on the landing began to emerge.

Angelica had been overly indulged perhaps, but still keenly aware of those around her. She was the first to notice when her childhood nurse was suffering from a toothache and required a poultice to relieve it. Nor was she above mourning when the young son of one of her father's grooms suffered a fatal injury after being kicked by an ill-tempered horse. The ink on the page where she recounted that incident was splotched and the paper wrinkled, as if it had been forced to absorb more than one tear.

She clearly adored her father and looked up to her older brother, Theo, even as she despaired of his constant teasing and tweaking of her curls. She envied him the freedoms he enjoyed as a boy and seized every opportunity she could find to sneak out and run wild on the moors alongside him, even if it meant risking a stern scolding from her papa when she returned. But apparently the man couldn't stay angry at her for long because he would relent every time she crawled into his lap and fixed her small arms around his neck.

Max skimmed through the pages, discovering long gaps between the dates as she grew older. She'd probably been too busy living life to record it. As the years danced past, the script grew more flowery, the clumsy blots of ink replaced with the elegant penmanship of an educated young lady.

After a drought of several months, he found this entry:

March 14, 1826

Papa has decided to commission a portrait of me for my eighteenth birthday. Although I know it will please him, I am dreading the prospect of sitting for hours on end for some stuffy old artist without twitching so much as an eyelash. However shall I survive such torture?!

A smile touched Max's lips. Like any girl of seventeen, she was prone to fits of drama and overembellishment. But as he read her next words, his smile faded.

April 3, 1826

I can be silent no longer. I must now make a confession fit for no other ears but yours: I am in love! It has come upon me like a storm, a fever, a sweet, yet terrible, madness! Upon our very first meeting, he brought my hand to his lips and pressed a kiss upon it as if I were already the sophisticated young lady I so often pretend to be for my other suitors. I fear sitting for this portrait may prove to be a sort of torture I had not anticipated.

April 14, 1826

You cannot know how difficult it is for me to strive to appear calm and collected as he arranges me for his pleasure, commands me to tilt my head this way or that, scolds me ever so gently when I fidget or fail to smother a yawn. The merest touch of his fingertips against my cheek makes me a stranger even to myself. As he leans over me to correct the angle of a curl or a ribbon, I am terrified he will hear my heart beating like the wings of a captive bird in my breast and discover all. It is almost as if those piercing blue eyes of his are peering into my very soul. I dare not be so bold as to hope for his affection, but in those moments I fear I would do anything to win the slightest crumb of his approval. Anything at all.

April 28, 1826

Oh, woeful day! The portrait is finished! Where once I was counting the seconds until my birthday ball with joyful anticipation, now I dread the day of its arrival. Every tick of the clock brings me closer to the moment when

he will be gone from here, taking my still-beating heart with him.

May 3, 1826

He is teasing me mercilessly by refusing to let me see the portrait until its public unveiling at the ball. I tremble at the prospect. What if it should reveal the besotted creature I have become? Would he be so cruel as to expose the deepest yearnings of my heart to the mockery of the world?

May 6, 1826

All is not yet lost! He sent me a note, begging me to meet him in the tower after the unveiling of the portrait. What if he should try to steal a kiss? He cannot know he would not have to steal it for I would give it freely. How could I do any less when he already has my heart?

Max's brow furrowed in a thoughtful frown. So Angelica and her beloved artist had not yet been lovers when she agreed to meet him in the tower that night. She had still been an innocent, yet ripe for seduction. Especially by some cunning

lothario whose every word, smile, and touch had been calculated to lay bare the heart of a young woman undone by the joy and anguish of first love.

Even as he felt his frown deepening to a scowl, Max knew he was being unfair. If the portrait was any indication, the artist had been just as enamored of Angelica as she was of him.

He was about to turn the page when another realization struck him. If their final rendezvous had taken place in the tower, then chances were that this was where the man had died. Max studied the timber floor, every stain and shadow now suspect. Angelica's lover might have breathed his last right beneath Max's very boots. For some reason, Max abhorred the notion of Angelica's nest, her charming refuge from the harsh realities of the world, being forever tainted by such violence.

The next page of the journal had no date, just six stark words, absent of dramatic flourishes and exclamation marks:

I am ruined. All is lost.

Dread uncurled low in his gut as Max slowly turned the page. He already knew what he would find—blank pages, all that remained of a life unlived. He began to frantically flip through them, almost as if he could will the words to appear.

Words that would reassure him Angelica had given herself enough time to realize that as long as she could draw breath, all was *not* lost. There was still hope.

But her voice had fallen silent, leaving him with nothing but empty pages and the hushed whisper of the rain.

The journal fell shut in his hands. He was still gazing down at it, dazed by his journey into the past, when a furious female voice cut through the quiet.

"What in the devil do you think you're doing?"

Chapter Eighteen

For an elusive moment, Lord Dravenwood looked so guilty Anne thought he was going to tuck Angelica's journal behind his back like a schoolboy caught perusing a book of naughty etchings. Before she could fully appreciate just how oddly beguiling that was, the expression vanished, leaving his eyes hooded and his face as inscrutable as always.

He was the last thing she had expected to find when she'd climbed the stairs to the tower. None of the former masters had been bold enough to beard the White Lady in her lair.

She had been standing there paralyzed in the

doorway for what felt like an eternity, watching him handle the journal with a touch so tender it was almost reverent. The sight of his strong, masculine hands ruffling through those fragile pages had sent a delicious little shiver through her, almost as if he were touching *her*.

Desperate to shake off the lingering sensation, she stormed across the tower and snatched the journal from his hands, earning a raised eyebrow for her trouble. "Men! Always interfering where they're not welcome or wanted! I suppose you thought you could just march up here and begin rifling through things that are none of your concern as if you hadn't been taught any better. Why, you ought to be ashamed of yourself!"

He continued to survey her with infuriating calm.

"Why are you looking at me like that?" she demanded when she realized he was not responding to her fit of pique.

A grave smile slowly spread across his face. It was the first smile he had given her that didn't contain so much as a hint of mockery. The smile transformed his face, deepening the grooves around his mouth and making her heart stutter. "I was just thinking that I haven't been scolded like that since I was in short pants. Actually, I was so eager to please as a child I'm not sure I've *ever* been given such a magnificent setdown. Except by my little brother, of course."

For a dangerous moment, Anne had allowed herself to forget this man was not her equal but her employer. Seeking to escape the havoc his smile was still playing with her heart, she turned toward the window, absently hugging the journal to her breast as she gazed out at the falling rain. "Forgive me. I shouldn't have been so passionate in my protest. It's just that the young lady in question has been the subject of sordid gossip for over a decade now. She's had her life dissected and her honor impugned by complete strangers who would denounce her as a strumpet just so they might appear more virtuous." She could feel her temper rising again. "I'm not saying the girl is without blame, but it's far more difficult for women who are embroiled in scandals than men. The women's reputations are destroyed, while the men get to go off scot-free to seduce the next innocent they encounter, boasting about all their conquests along the way."

"From what you told me," he gently reminded her, "the man who seduced Angelica didn't exactly walk away unscathed."

"Well, he proved to be the exception to the rule," she admitted, thankful Dravenwood couldn't see how hard her face must have looked in that moment. "All I'm saying is that the girl doesn't deserve to have her belongings pawed through by strangers. She already lost so much.

Couldn't we at least leave her some small measure of privacy and dignity?"

She sensed rather than saw Dravenwood come up behind her. He was standing so close she could feel his warmth, could smell the scent of the bayberry soap that clung to his freshly shaven throat and jaw. Could remember how warm and safe she had felt when he had held her against his body in the dark and how she had shuddered with anticipation when she had believed he was going to kiss her.

Reaching over her shoulder, he gently but firmly tugged the journal from her grip. She turned to face him, deeply disappointed that he would so callously dismiss her wishes.

He was already crossing the tower. As she watched, hugging herself with her now empty arms, he tucked the book back into its hiding place, then placed the doll on top of it. He even took the time to fan the doll's mildewed skirts out in precise folds so they would shield Angelica's secrets from any other prying eyes.

"There." He turned back to face her. "Satisfied?"

She nodded, although watching his capable hands handle the doll with the same tenderness he had used when handling the journal had stirred such a deep yearning in her she wasn't sure she would ever be satisfied again.

More to distract herself than him, she wandered

over to the bed and trailed a hand over the tattered lace hanging from the canopy. It drifted through her fingers like cobwebs. "After seeing this chamber, it's probably not difficult for you to understand how Angelica grew up to be such a brat. According to local lore, her father sent to Paris to have all of those ridiculous dolls specially commissioned just for her."

"Sounds like your ordinary doting papa to me." A corner of the earl's mouth curled in a droll smile. "If ever I was blessed with a daughter, I'd probably be tempted to do the same thing."

Trying not to imagine a laughing Dravenwood with a little girl with sooty-dark curls and misty-gray eyes perched high on his shoulder, Anne said, "From what I've heard, the tower hadn't been fit for habitation for centuries, so Angelica charmed her father into bringing in an army of workmen and spending a fortune renovating it just so she could preside over her own little kingdom. She probably fancied herself some sort of long-lost princess." Anne shook her head, a helpless, little laugh escaping her. "And who could blame her, given how hopelessly indulged she was?"

"Some children can be spoiled without being ruined. I suspect she was one of those."

Anne gaped at him, unable to hide her surprise. "Why would you say such a thing?"

Dravenwood jerked his head toward the

journal. "Because when she was only seven years old, she already understood her birthday was also the anniversary of her mother's death and sought to cheer her father by doing a watercolor of her mother with a harp and angel wings as a gift to him. Because when she was eleven and several of her father's tenants were stricken with cholera, she defied his express wishes and slipped out of the house to deliver baskets of food to their cottages. Food she'd been scavenging from her own plate by skipping dinner and going to bed hungry for nearly a week."

Unable to bear any further recitation of Angelica's virtues, Anne snapped, "It's easy to be generous when you lack for nothing yourself."

"You're being rather hard on the young woman, aren't you? Especially after making such a passionate plea on her behalf."

"I was defending her privacy, not her character."

Dravenwood's eyes narrowed to smoky slits as he studied her. "Perhaps your own staunch moral character makes it difficult for you to sympathize with the failings of mere mortals."

Anne would almost have sworn he was mocking her. His penetrating gaze seemed to peel away her thin veneer of respectability, to see straight through to all of the subterfuge, all of the lies she'd told to accomplish her aims.

He'd already given her a taste of just how persuasive he could be. How he might tempt a

woman to spill her secrets just by drawing her into his arms and brushing his mouth ever so lightly against her lips.

Armoring her heart against the power of that gaze, she said, "And are you including yourself among the mortals or the gods?"

His harsh bark of laughter was edged with bitterness. "It probably won't surprise you to learn that I've spent most of my life sitting high upon Mount Olympus, gazing down my nose at those I considered less virtuous than myself." His expression darkened. "But I can assure you it's a very long fall from Mount Olympus. And a *very* hard landing."

Not if you have someone waiting to catch you in their arms.

The thought sprang unbidden to Anne's mind. She inclined her head, hoping the shadows would hide her blush. Unfortunately, her reticence only fueled Dravenwood's curiosity.

"You chided me for invading Miss Cadgwyck's *kingdom,* as you call it, but just what were *you* doing here?"

Anne couldn't very well tell him she'd come here intent upon doing the same thing she'd been doing for the past four years whenever she had a free moment—searching, always searching, wracking her brain and the chamber for any clue to the location of the only key with the power to free her from this tower forever.

So instead she told him the closest thing to the truth she could manage. "Sometimes I come here to be alone. To escape. To think." The cozy patter of the rain only seemed to confirm her words. "But I should get back before the others miss me." She gestured toward the door, inviting him to precede her.

Visibly amused by her high-handedness, he started for the door. She followed, but just as they reached the landing, he turned back, eyeing her thoughtfully. "Since you found me here, you haven't once addressed me as 'my lord.' I rather like that."

"What would you prefer I call you? *Master?*"

As their gazes met, some infinitesimal shift in his expression gave her reason to regret those mocking words. A dangerous ember smoldered deep in those cool gray eyes of his, threatening to make her *staunch moral character* go up in a poof of smoke. "My Christian name is Maximillian."

Trying not to imagine how satisfying the name would sound rolling off her tongue, she blinked innocently at him. "Very good, my lord."

"Do you have a Christian name? Or is *Mrs.* your Christian name?"

"Anne. My name is Anne." Even though his face revealed nothing, it wasn't difficult to imagine what he was thinking—a plain name for a plain woman. "Do watch your step on the stairs, my lord," she cautioned. "Yet another reason for

you to stay clear of this place. The stairs are crumbling and could be quite dangerous to anyone not familiar with them. Why, you might have fallen and—"

"Broken my neck?" he volunteered helpfully.

"Turned your ankle," she said stiffly.

He pondered her warning for a minute, then stepped aside. This time there was no mistaking the challenge in his mocking smile as he graciously extended a hand toward the stairs. "After you, Mrs. Spencer."

Late that night Max found himself once again standing before Angelica's portrait. He lifted his candle higher, bathing the portrait in its loving light. He might never know the woman she would have become, but his trip to the tower had enabled him to steal a glimpse of the girl she had been.

He leaned closer to the portrait. He'd been too busy mooning over Angelica's winsome face to pay any heed to the signature scrawled in the corner of the canvas. So *this* was the man whose merest touch had set her heart to "beating like the wings of a captive bird" in her breast. Max's eyes narrowed. He was certainly no stranger to the gnawing pangs of jealousy; he just hadn't expected to suffer them over a woman who had died a decade ago.

Committing the artist's name to memory, he

straightened. Now that he'd read Angelica's diary, he was even more curious about what exactly had happened on the night the portrait was unveiled. Perhaps he had been looking for answers in the wrong places. Tomorrow he would send Dickon to the village with a dispatch for London. If answers were available within the annals of London society gossip, he knew just the man to find them.

Anne wove her way through the market, paying little heed to the cacophony of voices and noise drifting around her. She'd already nabbed a handsome goose, freshly plucked, and a new skein of yarn for Nana from one of the traveling vendors who set up rickety wooden stalls along the main street of the village each Friday morning. She always kept a large store of supplies at the manor, but before she made the long walk home that afternoon, the basket hooked over her arm would be laden with any extras they would require for the week to come.

As she passed the fox-faced magistrate, she spared him a cool nod. She could feel his beady little eyes following her as she moved on to the next stall. Once, such scrutiny might have tempted her to tug the brim of her homely black bonnet a few inches lower in the hope its shadow might hide her face. But now she held her head high, having learned that most people in the world saw

only what they expected to see. And what they expected to see when she strolled by was the plain and pious visage of Cadgwyck Manor's housekeeper.

The brisk autumn air was redolent with the aroma of roasted chestnuts. Unable to resist the enticing scent, Anne stopped at the next stall to purchase a bag for Dickon from her own pin money.

"Nearly shot the poor fellow dead, he did. That's what me cousin Molly heard. Had to flee London before they arrested him for duelin'."

As Anne moved on to the next booth, toying with some pretty silk ribbons she knew Pippa would adore, she paid little heed to the nasal tones of Mrs. Beedle, the village laundress. The woman was a notorious busybody. Anne had little patience for such gossip herself, having discovered firsthand just how much havoc it could wreak on a life.

"I thought he had the look of a rogue about him—marchin' into *my* Ollie's tavern, tossin' 'round purses of gold in that high-handed manner o' his and orderin' everyone about as if he owned the place."

Anne jerked up her head, a lavender ribbon slipping through her fingers. There could be no mistaking the braying voice of Avigail Penberthy, the innkeeper's buxom missus. Nor could there be any mistaking the identity of the high-handed

rogue who went marching about as if he owned every inch of land beneath his shiny leather boots.

Unable to resist the temptation, Anne sidled closer to the two women, adding eavesdropping to her burgeoning catalog of sins.

Mrs. Beedle lowered her voice. "Molly heard he was the perfect gent till his fiancée threw him over. Jilted him at the altar and ran off to marry another just as they was about to say their *I do*'s!"

As both women sighed in chorus, their sympathies shifting, Anne felt a stab of empathy in the vicinity of her own heart. She could only imagine what a terrible blow such a slight must have been to a man of Dravenwood's unyielding pride. Now she understood why he had arrived at Cadgwyck looking as if he were haunted by his own ghosts. He must have loved his fiancée very much for her abandonment to have cut him so deeply.

"I didn't think he'd last a night at the manor, much less more than a fortnight. He must have made a deal with the devil hisself to survive livin' in that tomb," Mrs. Penberthy suggested, a shudder rippling through her voice.

"The devil?" Mrs. Beedle whispered. "Or the devil's mistress?"

Normally Anne would have been thrilled to hear evidence that Angelica's legend was growing, but on this day, the women's nonsense was grating on her nerves. Refusing to listen to another word

of it, she brushed past them, giving Mrs. Penberthy's ample bottom a hearty bump with her basket as she did so. "Pardon me," she murmured.

Both women started, then exchanged a guilty glance. "Why, Mrs. Spencer, we didn't see you there!"

"No, I gather you didn't." Anne fixed the laundress with an icy stare. "Mrs. Beedle, I expect we'll be seeing you at the manor next week?"

The laundress gave her a lukewarm smile. "Aye, Mrs. Spencer. I'll be there."

Leaving them with a cool nod, Anne continued on her way, feeling their eyes follow her all the way to the end of the street.

"My lord?" Anne tentatively poked her head around the door frame of the library later that afternoon to find her employer reclining in a leather wing chair, his long, lean legs in their skintight trousers propped on an ottoman and crossed at the ankles.

"Hmmm?" he said absently, turning a page of the book he was perusing.

Anne barely resisted the urge to roll her eyes when she saw it was *An Inquiry into the Nature and Causes of the Wealth of Nations* by Adam Smith. She allowed herself a moment to covertly study the clean, masculine lines of his profile, the inky sweep of his lashes, the hint of beard darkening his jaw, even though he'd shaved only

that morning. Remembering the gossip she'd heard in the village, she could not help but wonder what sort of woman could break the heart of such a man.

"I checked the post while I was in the village today. This was waiting for you." Crossing to him, she dutifully held out the missive.

Laying aside the book, he sat up and eagerly took the square of folded vellum from her hand. But it was apparently not the piece of correspondence he had been hoping for. He made a sound beneath his breath that sounded suspiciously like a *harrumph* before sliding his thumb beneath the wax seal. As he unfolded the vellum and began to read the letter, his face went pale beneath his tan.

"What is it?" Anne asked, her heart stuttering with alarm. The last letter that had arrived at Cadgwyck Manor had delivered *him* to her doorstep.

As he slowly lifted his head, his expression dazed, she drew closer to him without realizing it. The letter slipped through his long, aristocratic fingers and floated to the floor. "It's my brother."

Anne felt a pang of dread in her own heart at his words. "Is it ill tidings? Has something terrible happened to him?"

"No. Something terrible has happened to me." Dravenwood raised his stricken eyes to her face. "He's coming here. With his family."

Chapter Nineteen

Anne fought to swallow back her own dismay. The last thing she needed was more meddlesome Burkes running around the manor, snapping out orders and poking their handsome aristocratic noses into matters that were none of their concern. "I suppose we can make ready some more rooms," she said reluctantly.

The earl shot to his feet, forcing her to take a stumbling step backward. Raking a hand through his unruly hair, he began to pace back and forth across the room like a caged tiger. "You don't understand. We have to write him back immediately. We have to stop them."

"And just how do you propose to do that?"

"I don't care how we do it. We'll tell them the manor isn't fit for habitation. We'll tell them there's a daft butler. And a surly footman. And a ghost. And an incontinent dog!"

Anne took advantage of his frenzied pacing to rescue the letter from the floor. As she scanned the remainder of it, she almost wished she had left it there. Hoping to soften the blow, she gently said, "I'm afraid it's too late for that, my lord. As we learned when we received word that you were scheduled to arrive at the manor, the post

is notoriously slow in getting to Cadgwyck. According to this letter, your brother and his family left Dryden Hall nearly a week ago. They're scheduled to arrive here in less than two days."

Dravenwood groaned. "Two days?" He abruptly changed direction, forcing her to quickly nudge the ottoman out of his path before he fell over it. "Damn him," he muttered through clenched teeth. "Damn them both."

"I take it you don't welcome their arrival?" she ventured cautiously.

"Of course I do," he drawled with scathing sarcasm. "The same way I would welcome taking afternoon tea with Attila the Hun. Or a recurrence of the Black Plague." He began to mutter again, more to himself than to her. "It's just like him, isn't it? Believing he can come here and somehow charm his way back into my good graces." Dravenwood stopped in his tracks, as if struck by a new thought. "He may very well be coming here to kill me."

"Have you done something that warrants killing?"

He gave her a sharp look. "You don't look as if that would surprise you very much."

Anne kept her face carefully blank. "What would you have me do, my lord?"

Rubbing the back of his neck, he sighed. "Your job, I suppose. Make ready their chambers," he

ordered, his dismay hardening into grim resignation. "As much as I'd like to, we can't very well turn them away. I wouldn't give him that much satisfaction." His face brightened. "Perhaps if we feed them some of that slop you feed me, they won't linger very long. But whatever you do"—he gave her such a threatening look she took an involuntary step backward—"do *not* give them any of your bread."

Anne hesitated outside the closed study door. She had been dreading this moment all day, but there was no longer any way to put it off. She dried her damp palms on her apron before giving the door a gentle rap.

"Enter."

Obeying the clipped command, she eased open the door and slipped into the room. Lord Dravenwood was seated behind the massive cherrywood desk. The ledgers containing the household accounts, both past and present, were no longer scattered haphazardly across the desk but had been organized into neat stacks. One of them lay open on the leather blotter. As she watched, he dipped his pen into a bottle of ink, turned the page, and began to make a fresh notation.

She had never before seen him look quite so composed. One would have sworn he'd been dressed and groomed by the most competent valet

in London. His jaw was freshly shaven, his silver-and-gray-striped waistcoat buttoned beneath his coat, his snowy-white cravat neatly tied. His hair was the only thing that had resisted taming, its sooty ends still curling in open rebellion around his starched collar. Anne sensed that this was her first glimpse of the real Maximillian Burke, the cool and contained man who had ruled his own private empire for years from behind a desk much like this one.

When the tip of his pen continued to scratch its way across the page, she cleared her throat awkwardly. "I'm sorry to disturb you, my lord, but Dickon has spotted a private conveyance crossing the moor. I believe it can only be your brother."

He glanced up, giving her a look so mildly pleasant it made her stomach curdle with alarm. She would have much preferred one of his ferocious scowls. "And just what would you have me do about it?"

"Aren't you going to come greet them?" she asked tentatively.

"I shall leave that to you." He returned his attention to the ledger, dipping his pen in the inkwell once more. "As I recall, you rose to the task with admirable aplomb the night I arrived at Cadgwyck Manor."

"But, my lord, he's your *brother*." As both her bewilderment and her dismay deepened, Anne

sought comfort by tracing the familiar shape of the locket beneath her bodice. "If you haven't seen each other for a time, I thought you might want to—"

"I don't pay you to think, Mrs. Spencer," Dravenwood said without looking up.

Anne stiffened as if he had slapped her. "No, my lord," she replied, her tone edged with frost. "I don't suppose you do."

Refusing to give him the satisfaction of asking if she could be dismissed, she turned on her heel and started for the door.

"Mrs. Spencer?"

She turned back, eyeing him warily.

"Once they arrive, my brother will doubtlessly want to see me. You may send him in after he and his family have dined. *Alone*."

"As you wish, my lord."

Anne left him there with his ledgers, forcing herself to gently draw the door shut behind her when all she wanted to do was slam it hard enough to rattle both the door frame and him.

Anne stood under the portico at the top of the crumbling stairs, watching the coach jolt its way up the rutted drive. This was a private coach, not a rented conveyance, with a handsome team of six matched grays, four liveried outriders, and a scarlet-and-gold ducal crest emblazoned on its shiny lacquered door. For the first time, she

stopped to wonder why her employer—the current Earl of Dravenwood and future Duke of Dryden—hadn't arrived in such regal splendor.

Dickon waited beside the drive in his own ragged livery, but no wig, playing the roles of both footman and groom. The afternoon wasn't exactly fair, but nor was it as damp and chill as recent days had been. The balmy wind threatened to tease a few stray tendrils of hair from Anne's chignon.

As the coach rolled to a halt, Dickon shot her an uncertain look over his shoulder. She made a subtle shooing motion. He hurried over to the coach to whisk open the door.

Anne had no idea what to expect, but the man who descended from the coach was as fair as their master was dark. He was the same height as Dravenwood and had equally broad shoulders, but he was slightly leaner. His caramel-colored hair was straight and cropped close to his head.

His boots had barely hit the ground when he was forced to spin around and catch a flaxen-haired toddler before she went tumbling out of the coach headfirst like an exuberant puppy.

"Whoa, there, Charlotte!" he called out, a dazzling grin splitting his sun-bronzed face. "You do love to keep Papa's reflexes honed, don't you, sweetheart?"

Holding the squirming little girl in the crook of his arm, he offered a hand to his wife. Tucking

her gloved hand in his, a woman emerged from the coach, all but the graceful curve of one cheek hidden beneath the shadow of her beribboned hat brim.

Dickon directed the coachman and outriders toward the tumbledown stables as the trio started up the broad stone stairs. The adorable moppet tucked a thumb in her little pink rosebud of a mouth and laid her head on her father's breast, suddenly overcome with shyness. She had been dressed with all the care of one of the dolls in the tower, but a smudge of dirt darkened the knee of one ivory stocking, and sugary biscuit crumbs were scattered across the bib of her pinafore.

As Lord Dravenwood's brother reached the top of the stairs, Anne pasted a dutiful smile on her lips just as she had done on the night her new master had arrived. "I'm Mrs. Spencer, the housekeeper of this establishment. Welcome to Cadgwyck Manor, my lord."

The man's brow furrowed in a mock scowl that was an impeccable imitation of his brother's real one. "*Mr. Burke* or *sir* will do, Mrs. Spencer. Didn't Max warn you?" He leaned down, lowering his voice to a conspiratorial whisper. "I'm one of those ill-mannered commoners he so disdains."

Anne had to bite back a genuine smile. The man's lazy grin and the mischievous sparkle dancing in his amber eyes were nearly irresistible.

Those eyes crinkled when he smiled, as if he had spent much of his life squinting into the bright sun.

A rich ripple of laughter escaped his wife. "Don't let my husband fool you, Mrs. Spencer. There's nothing common about Ashton Burke. He's as unconventional as they come."

As Mrs. Burke tipped back her head to reveal one of the most beautiful faces Anne had ever seen, Anne felt a curious twinge in the region of her heart. She had never felt so plain or so envied another woman her potions and powders and curling tongs.

The icy edges of the woman's Nordic blondness were softened by the irresistible warmth of her smile. Her green eyes were tilted upward at their outer corners like the eyes of some exotic cat.

She surprised Anne by taking her hand. "Thank you so very much for your hospitality, Mrs. Spencer. It was rather impulsive of us to come here. I do hope we haven't put your staff to any extra trouble."

"None whatsoever," Anne lied. She'd had the maids working nearly around the clock ever since she had learned of their impending visit. Even a grumbling Pippa had pitched in. For some unfathomable reason, Anne didn't want Dravenwood's brother to find him living in a pigsty.

Mr. Burke looked around, his expression going from playful to cautious. "So where is that devoted brother of mine?"

Anne had been dreading the question. "I'm afraid Lord Dravenwood is otherwise occupied at the moment."

Burke exchanged a knowing glance with his wife. "That's just about what I would have expected of dear old Max. So how does he occupy his time these days? Counting his gold? Conducting mock battles with his tin soldiers as he used to do with me when we were lads?" Burke wagged his eyebrows at Anne. "Flogging the peasants?"

Anne had even more difficulty hiding her smile this time. "I can assure you Cadgwyck Manor has no shortage of pursuits to keep your brother's attentions engaged. Now, if you'll allow me to show you to your rooms . . ."

She turned only to run smack-dab into the door. *Bloody hell,* she thought. Hodges must have locked it behind her as soon as she exited the house. She reached to her waist for her ring of keys only to discover she must have left them on the kitchen table.

Casting an apologetic look over her shoulder at their guests, she called out cheerfully, "Hodges! I seem to have accidentally locked the door. Would you mind unlocking it?" When her gracious request met with only silence, she

leaned closer to the door and hissed, *"Hodges! Open the door this minute!"*

After a muffled "Very good, ma'am," the door swung open to admit them.

Hodges stood there, beaming at them like a demented cherub, his hair nearly as wild as his eyes. Praying their guests wouldn't notice his odd demeanor, or would at least be too polite to comment upon it, Anne ushered them through the entrance hall.

As she led them up the stairs and past Angelica's portrait, she stole a glance at Mr. Burke, curious to see if his reaction would mirror his brother's and that of every other man who had ever laid eyes on it.

Strangely enough, Mrs. Burke noticed the portrait first. "Oh my! What an enchanting creature she is!"

Her husband cast the portrait a brief, disinterested glance before slipping an arm around his wife's waist and murmuring something in her ear. She laughed aloud and smacked him playfully on the arm. Apparently, the earl's brother only had eyes for his wife, a realization that left Anne with a strangely wistful ache in her heart.

"My lord, Mr. Burke is here to see you." Anne stood in the doorway of the study, fully prepared to duck should her employer hurl a ledger, an

inkwell, or perhaps a globe of the world at her head.

She had done exactly as instructed—seen to it that the earl's brother and his family were served a mediocre supper, sans bread—shown Mrs. Burke and her daughter to their rooms, and then informed Mr. Burke his brother would see him in the study.

"Very well. Show him in," Dravenwood said without looking up, his tone clipped but civil. He was still seated behind the desk, surrounded by his moat of ledgers. Anne was beginning to suspect he used the desk as a barrier to keep everyone at arm's length.

She ushered Mr. Burke into the room, then turned to go.

"Stay."

Caught off guard by his command, Anne turned back to find Dravenwood glowering at her from beneath the raven wings of his eyebrows. She didn't dare defy him, not with his looking at her as if she were a peasant who might just require a sound flogging as soon as they were left alone.

Fascinated against her will by his desire to keep her close, she moved to stand dutifully in the corner of the room. The earl's brother gave her a curious look before sinking into the worn leather wing chair situated at an angle to the front of the desk with a negligent grace that had probably always escaped his more formal brother. With

the two men facing each other across the desk, both their similarities and their differences stood out in stark relief.

Dravenwood surveyed Burke through eyes as cool as Anne had ever seen them. "So to what do I owe the dubious honor of this visit?"

To Mr. Burke's credit, he didn't waste time on pleasantries that would neither be appreciated nor returned. "We came to inform you that we're leaving England. We decided early on that we didn't belong at Dryden Hall, but were waiting for Charlotte to grow old enough to travel. It probably won't surprise you to learn the life of a country lord and his lady doesn't suit either one of us."

Although the earl struggled to hide it, he appeared to be more surprised than his brother had anticipated. "But where will you go?"

"To Morocco first to visit Farouk and Poppy. Poppy is expecting their first child and would like Clarinda to remain with her until the babe is born. Then it's on to Egypt. Now that I've somehow managed to convince Father I'm not a *complete* wastrel, he's expressed interest in funding an archaeological expedition just outside of Giza."

"And just what will Clarinda do while you're out digging for buried treasure? Do you really believe that to be a suitable environment for a wife and child?"

"Clarinda wouldn't have it any other way. I'm afraid she developed quite a taste for adventure and the exotic while a *guest* in Farouk's harem. And besides, I don't think she ever intends to let me out of her sight again." Burke's crooked smile freely admitted he wasn't entirely displeased with that development.

Dravenwood leaned back in his chair, surveying his brother through hooded eyes. "Why did you really come here, Ash? To rub my nose in your wedded bliss? I know I deserve it—and far worse—but if you're seeking to punish me for what I did to the two of you, I can promise you there's no need. I'm quite capable of punishing myself."

Anne frowned, wondering what transgression Dravenwood could possibly have committed against his brother and his brother's wife.

All traces of humor fled Burke's face, leaving it uncharacteristically somber. "We didn't come here to gloat, Max. We came here to say good-bye. We have no way of knowing how long we'll be gone from these shores. And Clarinda had some sentimental notion that you might want to meet your niece before we left. She could very well be a woman grown before you'll have another chance to see her." When his brother continued to survey him through dispassionate eyes, Burke sat up on the edge of his seat. "I have to confess that I also wanted to make my own good-byes. I realize things between us have been a little . . .

227

um . . . *strained* in the past few years, but I can still remember a time when it was you and me doing battle with the rest of the world. Our swords may have been nothing but a pair of tree branches, but I always knew I could depend on you to protect my back. No matter what has transpired since then, you're still my brother. You'll always be my brother." As Burke extended his hand across the desk, inviting Dravenwood to take it, Anne held her breath without realizing it.

Leaving his brother's hand hanging in midair, Dravenwood asked, "When will you be leaving Cadgwyck?"

"Early tomorrow morning. Our ship departs from Falmouth on Thursday."

"Very well, then. I wish you Godspeed." With that, Dravenwood went back to jotting down figures in his ledger, rejecting his brother's offer of reconciliation with no further fanfare.

Yanking back his hand, Burke surged to his feet, looking even more like his older brother now that he was angry. He stood there, glaring at the top of his brother's head. "I had hoped time might have softened your heart, but I can see you're still the same intractable ass that you always were."

With that, Burke turned and stormed out of the room, slamming the door behind him with satisfying force. Dravenwood lifted his head to

stare at the door for a moment, his face curiously blank, then rose from the desk and moved to gaze into the leaping flames on the hearth, his broad back to Anne.

She crept out of her corner, beset by an almost overwhelming urge to ease the stiffness of his stance with a comforting word or a smile. After all, there must have been some reason he'd asked her to stay and witness such a painfully private exchange.

"My lord?" she said softly. "I may be speaking out of turn, but I hate to see you at such painful odds with your own brother." She cleared her throat, choosing her words with care. "I had a brother once, you see. He used to drive me mad with his bossiness and his teasing. But I always knew in my heart that if anyone dared to wrong me, he would knock them flat. I never thanked him for that or told him how much he meant to me. I just assumed that if I reached out, he would always be there." She swallowed, a familiar heaviness weighting down her heart. "Until the day he wasn't."

Dravenwood continued to contemplate the flames, showing no sign that he was considering her words, or even that he had heard them.

"I'd give anything to have my brother back, to hear his laughter or be able to take his hand in mine." Anne crept closer, addressing that unyielding back. "What I'm trying to say is that

229

you shouldn't let pride make you wait until it's too late to reconcile with Mr. Burke. We can never know what the morrow might bring."

Dravenwood was silent for a long moment before finally saying, "You're right, Mrs. Spencer." Anne's heart surged with warmth. She was about to ask him if he wanted her to fetch his brother back when he continued, "You *are* speaking out of turn, and in the future I'd appreciate it if you would strive to remember your place. That will be all," he added, making it clear he had no further need of her or anyone else.

Anne was standing beneath the portico the next morning, watching Mr. Burke and his family prepare to climb into their waiting coach, when her employer emerged from the house and stalked right past her, his handsome face grim with determination. The shadows beneath his eyes bespoke of a sleepless night, much like Anne's own had been.

"Where are you going?" she called after him, too startled to add *my lord* or to remember his affairs were none of her concern. He had made that abundantly clear last night in the study.

"To bid my brother and his family a proper farewell," he growled, starting down the stairs at a rapid clip. "I would hardly be a gracious host if I didn't." He shot her a virulent look over one shoulder. "And as you were so kind to remind me,

we never know what the morrow might bring."

Anne picked up the hem of her skirts and hurried down the stairs after him, fearful it wasn't reconciliation but murder that was about to be done. As the earl's long strides carried him toward the coach, his brother froze while offering his wife a hand to assist her into the vehicle. Mr. and Mrs. Burke exchanged a cautious glance, but before either of them could react, their little girl wiggled her way out of her mother's grip and slid to the ground.

"Charlotte!" her mother cried out.

It was too late. Charlotte was already barreling her way back up the drive on her fat, little legs, shrieking, "Unca Max! Unca Max!" at the top of her lungs.

Dravenwood stopped in his tracks, looking like a man about to be crushed beneath the hooves of a team of runaway horses. The little girl skidded to a halt and began to bounce up and down on her heels, holding her arms up to him. She was obviously accustomed to being greeted with open arms wherever she went. Much like Angelica Cadgwyck must have been.

Anne had never seen such a powerful man look so helpless. She held her breath, fearing for a moment that he wasn't even going to acknowledge the child's presence. But he slowly bent down, folding his tall frame to scoop her up into his arms.

As he straightened back to his full height, Charlotte wrapped her arms around his neck, clinging to him like a baby spider monkey for a minute before leaning back and giving him a chiding look from green eyes that were a mirror of her mother's. "Don't look so sad, Unca Max. We be back soon." She pressed a noisy kiss to his cheek, then rested her head on his shoulder, her silvery-blond hair looking even fairer next to the darkness of his own.

By that time, her parents had caught up with her.

Burke held out his arms for the child, but Dravenwood showed no sign of relinquishing her. "I don't understand," Dravenwood said, the bewilderment reflected in his eyes tugging at Anne's heart. "How does the child know who I am?"

"Oh, I told her *all* about you," his sister-in-law confessed, a smile touching her lips. "How you used to help me with my sums when I was a little girl so my governess wouldn't rap my knuckles with her ruler. How you bandaged up my stuffed bear after he lost an eye because I had left him out in the rain all night. How you rescued me from that feral dog when I was twelve and carried me all the way home in your arms."

Burke folded his arms over his chest, looking dangerously sulky. "And I told her how your toy soldiers always bested mine in battle when we were lads and how you used to sink my wooden

battleships in the tub while that awful German nurse was making me wash behind my ears."

The earl glanced down at the flaxen head resting so comfortably against his shoulder before lifting his eyes to his sister-in-law's face. "You're as shameless as ever, aren't you, Clarinda?" he said softly. "You knew that if I ever laid eyes on her, I'd be helpless to resist her charms."

"Come, Charlotte," Burke said gently, holding out his arms to his daughter. "It's time for us to go."

Dravenwood cradled the child close for a moment, burying his face in her sleek hair, before reluctantly surrendering her to his brother.

Before Burke could turn away, Dravenwood awkwardly thrust a hand toward him. Burke gazed warily down at it, then lifted his eyes to his brother's face. Although Dravenwood's scowl was as ferocious as ever, Anne would have sworn she saw a flicker of uncertainty in his eyes.

She was afraid Burke was going to reject his brother's offer just as his brother had rejected his. But Burke shifted Charlotte to the crook of his other arm and seized Dravenwood's hand in a hearty grasp. Then Burke turned and carried his daughter toward the waiting coach, leaving his wife and his brother facing each other in the drive. For some reason she could not fathom, Anne began to feel like even more of an intruder. But it was too late to creep back up to

the portico without attracting notice to herself.

Dravenwood gazed down at his sister-in-law, his expression once again inscrutable. "Are you going to give me another well-deserved slap before you go as you did at our last meeting? Sometimes I fancy I can still feel the sting of it."

The woman reached up to touch her gloved fingertips to his cheek, then stood on tiptoe and pressed a gentle kiss to the exact same spot. "That's all in the past now, Max," she murmured. "All I wish for you is the same happiness I have found. I'll never forget all you've done for me. Or why you did it."

She was turning away from him when she spotted Anne standing awkwardly off to the side. Giving her brother-in-law a sly sideways glance, she crossed to Anne and whispered in her ear, "Look after him, won't you, Mrs. Spencer? He's always been too proud to admit it, but he needs it very badly."

Stunned by the woman's candor and keenly aware of her employer's scrutiny, Anne could only nod.

As Dravenwood watched Clarinda Burke turn and walk away to join her husband and child, Anne felt her own heart wrench. She would almost have sworn she had seen that look in his eyes before.

Off for adventures unknown, the handsome young family crowded into the coach, leaving

their host standing stiffly in the middle of the drive. As the coach began to jolt its way down the rutted drive, his niece leaned out the window, frantically waving her little, white-gloved hand. "G'bye, Unca Max! G'bye!"

Dravenwood lifted a hand. He didn't lower it again until the coach rolled out of sight, swallowed by the sweeping grasses of the moor. He stood there staring after them for a long time after they'd gone, his dark hair dancing in the wind.

Emboldened by her unspoken promise to Mrs. Burke, Anne drew closer to him and gently touched the back of his coat sleeve. He turned to give her a narrow look. "Just what did my sister-in-law say to you?"

Anne's hand fell back to her side. She briefly considered lying, but the challenge in his gaze stopped her. "She asked me to look after you."

"How very charitable of her. But I'm afraid I don't require looking after. I'm quite capable of looking after myself." Without another word, he went stalking toward the weed-clotted breeze-way separating the main section of the house from the east wing, heading for the cliffs.

"Then why did you command me to stay in the study last night while you were speaking to your brother?" she called after him.

He hesitated for the briefest second, then kept walking as if she hadn't even spoken.

He was her employer. She was obligated to respect his wishes. Her duty was to meekly return to the house and find something to sweep or dust or polish so he could brood in privacy and continue to mourn his lost fiancée and punish himself for whatever terrible transgression he believed he had committed against his brother and sister-in-law.

Anne lifted her chin, feeling her temper start to rise. For the first time in a long while, she had no intention of doing what she *should* do. Contrary to what she'd let everyone believe for the past several years, she was not a woman who would so easily be dismissed.

Chapter Twenty

When Anne emerged at the back of the house, it wasn't the spectacular view from the cliffs that made her steps slow and her breath catch in her throat, but the man standing at their edge.

Dravenwood stood with one boot propped on a large rock, gazing out to sea as if transfixed by what he saw before him. Something about his stance was irresistibly timeless and masculine. He could have been a pirate king, waiting to board a ship so he could sail the high seas to ravish and plunder. Or one of Arthur's knights,

dreaming of the lady fair he had left behind in Camelot to pine for his return.

"You might have warned me," he said without turning around as she approached.

Anne would have sworn she hadn't so much as kicked a pebble to betray her presence. She was quickly learning he was a difficult man to catch unawares. She joined him at the cliff's edge. "About what?"

He swept a hand toward the breathtaking vista stretched out before them. *"This."*

The coastline had undergone a magical transformation beneath the kiss of the autumn sun. Cottony wisps of cloud drifted across an azure sky. The moss furring the broad rocks along the top of the cliffs was no longer cast in drab shades of gray, but was revealed to be a shade of green somewhere between emerald and jade. Beams of sunlight shattered against the diamond-sharp crests of the waves, brightening the water to a blue-green intense enough to make a man—or woman—dream of Barbados and tropical breezes and swaying palms. Far below them at the foot of the cliffs, the sand of the cove shimmered like gold dust.

"It does rather take one's breath away, doesn't it?" Anne couldn't completely hide her pride as she surveyed the view.

He slanted her a mocking glance. "There was no need for you to follow me out here, you

know. I have no intention of flinging myself off the cliffs in a fit of pique like your impulsive Miss Cadgwyck."

"Well, that's certainly a relief." She seated herself on the opposite side of the rock, ignoring her first inclination to hug one knee to her chest as she might have done when she was a girl. "I suspect you would make a very intolerable ghost, always slamming doors and groaning and rattling your chains. I daresay we'd never get another decent night's rest." As the wind tugged her shawl from her shoulders, she tilted her face to the sun, wishing she could pull the pinching pins from her hair and let it ripple free as well.

"You wound me with your dour assessment of my character. It would no doubt surprise you to learn that for a very long time I was considered the most eligible catch in all of England."

Anne remembered the words of the women in the village: *He was the perfect gent till his fiancée threw him over.* "And why should that surprise me? What woman could resist a gentleman with such a delightful temperament and affable wit?"

He snorted. "As you've probably already guessed, I was pursued more for my title and my fortune than my charms."

Stealing a glance at the rugged purity of his profile and the shadows his long, sooty lashes cast on his beautifully sculpted cheekbones,

Anne doubted that was entirely true. "It's been my experience that charming men tend to think even more highly of themselves than they want others to do. I've never cared for them myself."

"Then you should be *very* fond of me."

May God help her if she was, Anne thought. She dragged her gaze away from his profile and returned it to the sea, feeling suddenly dizzy in a way that had little to do with the height of their perch. "You certainly weren't very charming to your brother and his wife. Especially not after they came all this way just to bid you farewell."

The distant look in his frosty gray eyes deepened, as if he were staring at something far beyond the sea. "I shall have to beg your forbearance for my ill manners. Their visit came as something of an unwelcome shock. I hadn't seen Clarinda since our wedding day."

Anne frowned in bewilderment. "Don't you mean *her* wedding day?"

He gave her an arch look.

"Oh!" Anne breathed, thankful she was already sitting down. So Clarinda Burke was the woman who had jilted him at the altar, the woman who had broken his heart and given his lips their cynical curl. She remembered the look she'd glimpsed in his eyes as he had watched his brother's wife walk away from him, possibly for the last time. Now she knew *exactly* where she

had seen that look before—whenever he gazed up at Angelica's portrait.

"Needless to say, it came as quite a shock to society when my bride tossed me over at the altar so she could marry my brother. All of London was abuzz with the gossip. I'm surprised it didn't travel as far as Cadgwyck."

Not wanting him to know that it finally had, Anne forced herself to say lightly, "Ah, but you forget—we have our own scandals to gossip about in Cadgwyck. Why did she toss you over? Did you do something to earn the slap the two of you spoke of?"

His laughter was edged with bitterness. "I was fortunate it was no more than a slap. Had there been a pistol handy that day, she might have very well shot me."

"Were you unfaithful to her?"

"Once she agreed to wed me? Never." Dravenwood swung around to face Anne, the frost in his eyes extinguished by a fierce fire. "Not in word or in deed. Not with my body or in my heart."

Mesmerized by the passion in his eyes, Anne felt her own heart skip a beat. She had always dreamed of having a man look at her that way.

But not while he was thinking of another woman.

He returned his gaze to the sea, his jaw set in a rigid line. "Clarinda and my brother fell in love

when they were very young. They had a rather . . . *tempestuous* relationship, and when Ash went off to seek his fortune, leaving her behind, it broke her heart."

"And you were there to pick up the pieces?"

"I tried. After she was forced to accept that Ash wasn't coming back for her, she collapsed and became very ill. I"—he hesitated—"I helped to look after her for several months. Until she was well enough to manage on her own."

While a wealth of information was in that simple explanation, Anne sensed he was leaving out large chunks of the story, not to protect himself, but to protect his sister-in-law. Anne had become quite adept at doing that herself.

"Once Clarinda recovered, I offered for her. But she refused me. Since I was Ash's brother, she was afraid she would never see me as anything more than a reminder of the love she had lost. It took me nine years to finally convince her we would suit."

"Nine years?" Anne echoed in disbelief. "Well, no one can accuse you of being fickle, can they?"

"You don't know how many times I wished they could! Wished I was the sort of man who could tumble a different woman into my bed every night without ever once stopping to count the cost to their hearts or mine."

His frank confession made Anne feel oddly

breathless. "After finally agreeing to marry you, what made her change her mind?"

A sardonic smile curved his lips. "Since I was the one fool enough to save Ash from a firing squad and bring him back into her life, I have only myself to blame. On the day we were supposed to be wed, she found out that all those years ago I'd had a hand in keeping them apart because I didn't believe Ash was good enough for her. So she slapped me across the face and walked right back into his arms. She got the man she had always loved while I got exactly what I deserved—a lifetime of regrets and a crumbling manor haunted by a spiteful White Lady."

Anne pondered his confession for a moment. "Just how old were you when you committed this terrible crime of the heart?"

He shrugged. "Two-and-twenty, I suppose."

A ripple of laughter escaped her, earning a puzzled scowl from him. She rose to face him. "You say your brother and Clarinda were very young when they fell in love, but you were little more than a babe yourself—a young man in the first flush of passion. You lashed out because your heart was wounded. Because you couldn't accept that the woman you loved might never come to love you back. But now you seek to condemn that impulsive young fool with the wisdom and experience of a man full grown. Tell me—would you be so merciless and unbending

toward any other soul who made such an error in judgment?"

Dravenwood drew closer, glowering down at her. "Are you mad, woman? I don't deserve any mercy. I robbed my own brother and the woman he loved of ten years they might have spent in each other's arms!"

"Perhaps you did them an unintended service. You said yourself their young relationship was very tempestuous. Their love might have needed time to season and gain in maturity so they could truly embrace the happiness they've found today."

"What I did was unforgivable!"

"It might have been wrong—even wicked perhaps—but was it truly unforgivable? Is any sin unforgivable if the heart is genuinely repentant?"

There was no way for Anne to let him know how desperately she needed him to agree with her. Especially while standing at the edge of those cliffs where another life had ended because a young girl had been too foolish and proud to forgive herself. A pleading note softened her voice. "There's a difference in being sorry for what you did and throwing away the rest of your life because you feel sorry for yourself."

He took a swift step toward her, his hands closing over her upper arms. Even through her shawl she could feel their fierce strength, their irresistible heat as he drew her toward him. He

gave her a sharp, little shake, his scowl a fearsome thing to behold. "I didn't come to this place looking for absolution. And I certainly don't need *your* absolution, Mrs. Spencer."

"What do you need, my lord?" she asked, feeling her breath quicken, her moist lips part in reckless challenge.

His smoldering gaze strayed to her lips, giving her a dangerous glimpse of exactly what he needed. Not forgiveness, but forgetfulness, if only for a night or perhaps even just a few hours. What he needed was the chance to be the sort of fickle man who could tumble a woman into his bed just because he desired her, not because he had loved her for half his life.

She could almost see the effort it took for him to drag his gaze from her lips, to gentle his grip and firmly set her away from him. Instead of the relief she should have felt, her heart ached with disappointment.

"I need the same thing Angelica needs," he said hoarsely, unable to completely purge the passion from his voice. "To be left the bloody hell alone."

With that, he turned and went stalking away from her, skirting dangerously close to the edge of the cliffs as he followed them around to the promontory.

Anne hugged her shawl around her as she watched him go. The wind snatched the sigh from her lips as she whispered, "As you wish, my lord."

The rogue had dared to put his hands on her.

Hodges stood at the corner of the window in the second-floor study, his temple pulsing with fury as he watched Cadgwyck's new master turn his back on Annie and stride away. She stood there gazing after him, hugging herself through the flimsy protection of her shawl.

She looked so small standing there at the edge of those towering cliffs, so terribly vulnerable—as if it would take little more than a gust of wind to blow her right over them.

Hodges touched his fingertips to the window-pane, his face drooping in a mask of sorrow. He never could bear it when she was sad. All he wanted to do was coax a smile back to her lips, to hear her merry laughter ringing through the halls of the manor once again.

The butler's eyes narrowed as they followed the rogue's path along the cliffs. *He* was the one who had stolen her smile. The one who had left her there all alone to be buffeted by the winds of fate.

The man was a fraud, an impostor, a shameless seducer of all that was pure and virtuous. Hodges drew his shoulders back, standing so straight and true that few who had known him in recent years would have recognized him.

There could only be one true master of Cadgwyck. Once the impostor was banished, that master could return to take his rightful place.

Hearing the door behind him creak open, Hodges whirled around, tucking both hands behind his back like a guilty child.

Dickon's freckled face appeared in the crack between frame and door. "Pardon me, sir, but have you seen the good shovel? I thought I'd head down to the caves and do some more excavating while the earl's out on the cliffs."

"Haven't seen it, lad," Hodges replied, his shoulders settling back into their natural slump. "But you might ask Nana."

"Will do. Thanks!" Dickon set off on his errand, his cheerful whistle drifting back to Hodges's ears.

Hodges drew his hands out from behind his back. He stood there for a long time, gazing down at the brass-handled letter opener gripped in his trembling fist. For the life of him, he could not remember how it had gotten there.

Chapter Twenty-one

For the first time in their brief acquaintance, Mrs. Spencer did precisely what Max had ordered her to do. She performed her duties and supervised the other servants without so much as a hint of impropriety in her actions or her words.

Max was surprised by how much he missed

being flayed by her sharp tongue or being offered some opinion he had not solicited and did not welcome. His every request, no matter how trifling, was met with polite subservience. After a few days of this, he began to have wicked fantasies about requesting her to do something utterly outrageous. Every time she asked, "Will there be anything else, my lord?" he had to bite his tongue to keep from blurting out "Take down your hair" or "Lift the hem of your skirt so I can steal a peek at your garters." He was no longer sure of what he would do if she responded with a dutiful "As you wish, my lord" while slowly raising her hem to tease him with a glimpse of a trim ankle or a shapely calf.

Even brooding about Clarinda would have been a welcome distraction from his growing obsession with his housekeeper. But his brother's wife seemed to occupy his thoughts less with each passing day. It was almost as if Clarinda's kiss and her benediction had finally broken the spell she had cast over him when he had been little more than a boy. When his hikes along the cliffs no longer relieved the peculiar tension gathering like a storm in him, he took to walking to the village each afternoon, hoping to receive a reply from his inquiry into Angelica's precious artist. But as his housekeeper had warned him, the post was notoriously slow in reaching Cadgwyck. Although it had been nearly a month

since he had posted the inquiry, there was still no word.

The villagers had begun to eye him as if something were suspect about any man who could survive sharing a house with a ghost.

He supposed his ferocious demeanor and barked requests didn't help. Before long, they were crossing both themselves and the street whenever he came stalking down it.

His patience—or lack thereof—was finally rewarded on a sunny Thursday afternoon. As the squat postmistress handed over the thick package tied in string with his name neatly inscribed on the front, she seemed as relieved as he was.

Max tore open the package and began to scan the first page. He'd read only a few lines when a grim smile began to spread across his face. This was one discovery even his unflappable house-keeper would not be able to ignore.

Anne was in the kitchen, chatting with Nana and nursing a copper kettle of crab stew over the fire, when one of the bells strung over the door began to jingle. Ignoring the treacherous leap of her heart, Anne glanced up to discover it was the bell for the master's study.

She was tempted to ignore it or to send Hodges or Dickon to answer the summons purely out of spite. But after a morning spent scouring every inch of the attic for what had to feel like the

millionth time, Dickon had gone out for a well-deserved romp on the moors. And the last time she'd seen Hodges, he had been merrily waltzing through the ballroom with an invisible partner on his arm and a tea cozy on his head.

Anne traded her gravy-stained apron for a clean one, then leaned down to bellow into Nana's ear, "I don't suppose I could talk *you* into going to see what his lordship wants?"

Nana grinned up at Anne from her rocking chair, baring her toothless gums. "If I was but a few years younger, I'd be more than happy to give that man whatever he wanted."

Anne recoiled in mock horror. "Why, Nana! I had no idea you were such a shameless little hoyden!"

Nana cackled. "The right man can turn any woman into a shameless hoyden."

Anne sobered, remembering the dangerous desire she had glimpsed in Dravenwood's eyes before he had set her away from him on the cliffs. "What about the wrong man, Nana? What can he do?"

Nana caught Anne's sleeve in one of her bony claws, urging her down so the old woman could whisper in her ear, "Give her what *she* wants."

"You rang, my lord?"

Anne stood stiffly in the doorway of the study, trying not to think about Nana's words or how

249

beguiling Lord Dravenwood looked as he sat behind the desk, his coat draped carelessly over the back of his chair while he worked in a waistcoat of copper-colored silk and dazzling-white shirtsleeves.

This time he did not leave her waiting while he tended to his ledgers, but immediately rose and came around the desk. "I just returned from the village. I received something in the post that I thought might be of interest to you."

"Have you been summoned back to London?" she inquired hopefully, blinking at him with all of the innocence she could muster.

He leveled a reproachful look at her before nodding toward the leather chair in front of the desk. "There's no need to hover there in the doorway like a raven portending doom. Do sit."

"Is that a request or an order?"

"It's an invitation. Please?" The husky note in his voice gave her a jarring glimpse of just how dangerous he could be to her resolve when he wasn't ordering her about in that high-handed manner of his.

Anne approached the desk and gingerly sat, clasping her hands primly in her lap.

Dravenwood propped one lean hip on a corner of the desk, an ember of excitement flaring in his smoky eyes. "I've always believed every mystery is nothing more than a mathematical equation that can be solved if you find the right variables

and apply them in the correct order. The one variable we already have in Angelica Cadgwyck's mystery is the name of the artist who seduced her. So I decided if I wanted to find out what *really* happened on the night of her birthday ball, I needed to learn more about the man."

Anne kept her face expressionless with tremendous effort. She could only pray he hadn't noticed the blood drain from it.

"While I was perusing Miss Cadgwyck's portrait, it occurred to me that any man who could paint with such undeniable skill must have left *some* mark on society. So I enlisted the help of a certain investigator the Company has done business with in the past—an extremely tenacious Scot named Andrew Murray. Mr. Murray has a gift for ferreting out the one grain of truth in even the most sordid and convoluted nugget of gossip." Dravenwood stopped abruptly, tilting his head to study her. "Aren't you going to scold me for prying into matters that are none of my concern?"

"I wouldn't dare to be so presumptuous. As you so aptly reminded me, *you* are master of Cadgwyck now. It's your house. Your painting." She hesitated for the briefest instant. "Your ghost."

Nodding his approval, he retrieved a thick sheaf of papers from the desk behind him and shook them open with a crisp snap. "As you probably

already noted from the signature on the portrait, the artist's name was Laurence Timberlake."

"Laurie," Anne whispered before she could stop herself.

Dravenwood frowned at her. "What was that?"

"Oh, nothing. I once had a childhood friend named Laurence."

He went back to scanning the papers. "Murray was able to locate several of Timberlake's paintings scattered throughout London and the surrounding countryside and agreed he was a most remarkable talent. Murray was as surprised as I that the man hadn't attracted the attention of some wealthy patron and achieved greater fame."

"Perhaps being shot to death curtailed his career opportunities," Anne offered drily.

"On the contrary, meeting a tragic end at such a young age should have only enhanced his reputation and made the artwork he left behind that much more valuable to a collector. There's nothing society adores more than a love affair gone wrong. Trust me . . . I should know," he added, flicking a wry glance in her direction.

"So why does this Murray fellow believe Timberlake's talents were overlooked?"

"When he was tracking down the portraits, he noticed something peculiar. All of the paintings were of young women, and very few of them had remained with the families who had commis-

sioned them. Most had been sold or wound up stored in an attic somewhere."

"But why?" Anne was thankful she didn't have to hide her growing bewilderment. "Why would anyone wish to bury such treasures?"

"That question wasn't answered until Murray was able to track down a young woman from one of the paintings. She's a marchioness now and the mother of three small children. She agreed to speak to him only if he promised her his utmost discretion. She was the one who revealed that the majority of Timberlake's income wasn't derived from his art, but from something far more sinister—blackmail."

Chapter Twenty-two

"Blackmail?" Anne echoed through lips that had gone suddenly numb.

Tossing the papers on the desk behind him, Dravenwood nodded. "The scoundrel would choose his victims with care—usually some beautiful young girl with a promising future about to make her debut." Anne could tell he was thinking of Angelica by the distant look in his eye. "He would deliberately seek out girls who came from wealthy and prominent families

whose continuing fortunes and good names might depend on her making a first-rate match. He would accept the commission to paint her portrait, then worm his way into her family's home and her affections. From what I understand, it was no great challenge for him. He was young, handsome, charming, well-spoken."

"Everything a naïve young girl might desire," Anne said softly. "Especially after he immortalized her on canvas, making her believe she was everything she wanted others to see in her."

"Precisely. After the painting was finished, he would complete his seduction. Then he would go to her father and threaten to expose their sordid little affair to all the world unless her father paid him a handsome sum to buy his silence."

Anne's growing agitation made it impossible for her to sit still any longer. She rose and paced over to the window, drawing back the drape to gaze blindly out over the churning waves of the sea. "How can you prove any of this is true? For all you know, the woman your man spoke to might have simply been a scorned lover, out to destroy what was left of Timberlake's reputation."

"With her help, Murray was able to track down two more of the women in the portraits. One of them had been cast out in the streets by her family after Timberlake ruined her and was

plying her wares on the streets of Whitechapel." They both knew there was only one sort of ware a woman might be plying on the streets of Whitechapel. The grim note in Dravenwood's voice deepened. "When Timberlake painted her portrait, she was only thirteen."

Anne turned to face him, her voice a ragged whisper she barely recognized. *"Thirteen?"*

"She was the one who told Murray that when Timberlake's seduction failed, he would sometimes resort to more"—Dravenwood's brow darkened—"*forceful* measures."

Anne slowly drifted back across the room, tugged toward him by the fierce emotion in his eyes and the unmistakable ring of conviction in his words.

"It's awkward to speak of such an unspeakable failing of my own sex to a woman. Men are supposed to cherish women, protect them, even at the cost of their own lives. The thought of a man using brute strength to overpower any woman— especially an innocent girl—in such a way makes me ill. If you ask me, shooting was too good for him." Dravenwood curled his powerful hands into fists, his eyes narrowing to smoky slits. "I'd like nothing more than the chance to beat the bastard to a bloody pulp myself."

Anne might be able to shield her overflowing heart from him, but she could do nothing to hide the warm rush of tears in her eyes.

Dravenwood straightened, gazing down at her with a mixture of alarm and dismay. "Forgive me. I shouldn't have spoken of such things to you. Since you'd expressed an interest in Angelica, I thought you'd want to know that whatever happened to her that night might not have been through any fault of her own."

What Anne wanted in that moment was to bring one of his clenched fists to her lips and soften it with a kiss, if for no other reason than that he was everything Laurence Timberlake had never been. But all she could do was whisper a heartfelt "Thank you."

He retrieved the sheaf of papers from the desk, thrusting them toward her as if they were a handkerchief to dry her tears. "Would you care to take the report to your room and look over it?"

"Yes, my lord. I do believe I would." She accepted the document from his hand, handling it as if it were a pardon from the hand of the king himself. Although she was desperate to escape his scrutiny, she could not resist pausing at the door to give him one last look. "For a man so reluctant to accept absolution for his own sins, you certainly seem eager enough to dole it out to others."

"Perhaps I simply believe others are more deserving of it."

"Isn't that the point of absolution? That we sometimes receive it even when we don't deserve it?"

Leaving him with that to ponder, she gently drew the door shut behind her.

Anne stood on the landing gazing up at Angelica's portrait, Murray's report still clutched in her hand. It had been a long time since the two of them had talked.

"He's determined to prove you didn't deserve what happened to you," Anne said softly. "But you and I know differently, don't we?"

Angelica gazed down at Anne, her enigmatic half smile hiding secrets even the most tenacious investigator would never unearth.

"He's half in love with you, you know. Perhaps more than half. But you could never truly appreciate a man like him. You'd rather squander your affections on some glib charlatan who would steal a child's innocence just to line his own pockets with gold. All the earl did was prove you were even more of a fool than anyone will ever know."

Was that a pout she detected playing around Angelica's full lips?

"You needn't waste your pretty sulks on me," Anne warned her. "Save it for some starry-eyed swain who will appreciate it. I don't feel sorry for you. Not one whit."

Anne wasn't being completely truthful. Like the hands of the longcase clock in the entrance hall, Angelica was frozen in time, unable to

travel back to the past to undo what had been done or move forward to embrace the future.

Just like her.

As Max started down the stairs the next morning, he was still thinking about his housekeeper. He was beginning to wonder if this house was driving him well and truly mad. He'd never even flirted with a pretty parlor maid as a young man. He had always felt it would be unsporting of him to prey on women who depended on him and his family for their livelihood. Yet now all he could think about was his housekeeper and what might lie beneath her starched apron and staid skirts.

She'd jarred him even more when he had shown her the investigator's report. Her unexpected compassion for Angelica and all the other young women Timberlake had betrayed had caught him off guard. When he had seen the tears well up in her luminous hazel eyes, he'd nearly been overwhelmed by the urge to draw her into his arms and kiss them away.

As he reached the turn in the landing between the third and second floors, he braced a hand on the newel as he always did to slow his momentum. The ball snapped off in his hand, sending him hurtling toward the banister.

Thanks to reflexes honed while sailing some of the roughest seas in the world, he ended up

teetering on the edge of the next step instead of pitching forward over the banister in a tumble that would have left him lying broken and bleeding in the entrance hall below.

Or dead.

His heart was thundering against his rib cage just as it had in the moments after the shelf of rock had crumbled beneath his feet on the promontory. He turned the ball over to examine it. Far too much rot was in the wood to determine what had caused the break.

If the ball had deliberately been severed from the post, this was no harmless bit of mischief like a closed chimney flue or ghostly giggles in the night.

He frowned down at the jagged edges of the post. What if something more sinister than a ghost was at work at Cadgwyck? He'd been so intent upon solving the mysteries of the dead that he'd been ignoring the secrets of the living. He was reasonably sure Mrs. Spencer was hiding something. He hadn't forgotten the desperate conversation he'd overheard between her and Hodges in the drawing room or the untimely death of Cadgwyck's previous master.

Not wanting anyone else to fall into the trap that might have been set for him, Max slipped the ball into the pocket of his coat. Since he didn't have Mr. Murray's resources to reply upon, perhaps it was time he did a little sleuthing of his own.

He was not trespassing.

That's what Max told himself that afternoon as he climbed the back staircase leading up to the fourth-floor servants' quarters. The manor belonged to him. He was free to roam wherever he liked. And besides, if someone should spot him, he had a perfectly valid excuse for bearding his housekeeper in her den. She wasn't in any of her usual haunts, and he wanted to take her up on her offer to go over the household accounts with him. For some reason, spending the afternoon closeted in his study with her in front of a cozy fire wasn't the unpleasant prospect it had once been.

Of course, he could simply have rung for her, but then he wouldn't have had any excuse to . . . well . . . not trespass.

He emerged at the top of the stairs in an uncarpeted corridor flanked with doors. He could still remember his horror as a boy when his father had drolly informed him servants were always to be housed on the highest floor so they would be the first to burn to death in the event of a fire while the family made their escape. The observation might have been more amusing if his father had been joking.

Since all the doors were standing wide open, Max didn't even have to feel guilty about stealing a look inside each room as he passed. It didn't

require any detective work on his part to deduce who slept in the first room. Books pilfered from *his* library were scattered all over the room in untidy piles. Although it was the middle of the day, he wouldn't have been surprised to see Pippa sprawled across the bed, munching on an apple with her nose buried in a book.

The occupant of the next room was just as easily identified. An ancient hornets' nest dangled from the ceiling, and the table beside the bed sported a collection of interesting rocks and something that looked suspiciously like a mummified toad. They were exactly the sort of treasures Max might have collected as a lad had he been allowed to roam the woods and meadows as Ash had been instead of attending to his lessons.

The next room was slightly larger and looked quite cozy with its neatly made bed and faded leather chair drawn up in front of the coal stove. Max assumed it must belong to his butler.

The last chamber off the corridor was a long dormer room with five beds where the Elizabeths must sleep. Mrs. Spencer had claimed Max had heard their giggles on the night he had left his bed to chase a ghost. He still didn't believe her. Angelica might not have paid him any more visits, but the echo of her laughter continued to haunt his dreams.

He had reached the end of the corridor. Baffled, he turned in a circle, but there was still no sign

of his housekeeper's room. He was about to give up on his quest and retreat before someone discovered him when he noticed the steep staircase tucked into the corner.

The narrow stairs were more forbidding than inviting, yet Max could not seem to resist them. Shadows enveloped him as he climbed, the risers creaking beneath his boots with each step. At the top of the stairs was a plain wooden door.

He gave it a soft rap. "Mrs. Spencer?"

When there was no response, he tested the knob. The door was fitted with a lock, but it opened easily beneath his hand. Max might have believed he was still in the wrong place if he hadn't recognized the plain black shawl draped over the foot of the bed. After stealing a furtive glance over his shoulder, he slipped into the room and closed the door behind him.

Now he was trespassing.

The first thing he noticed was the cold.

The weather had turned on them during the night, almost as if the coming winter sought to punish them for enjoying those all-too-brief sunny autumn days. The wind was whistling around the eaves of the attic room, its perch at the peak of the house providing little defense against drafts.

His original mission forgotten, Max wandered deeper into the room, growing more dismayed with every step. A single window set into a

recessed dormer let in just enough daylight to reveal how Spartan the room was. It seemed to have been stripped of even the most basic of human comforts. The rooms on the floor below had all been fitted with coal stoves, but this room had only a bare hearth with no hint of recent ash. The other servants' beds were outfitted with feather ticks and piled high with thick, colorful quilts, but the bed in the attic was little more than a narrow cot with a thin mattress covered by a single worn wool blanket.

Aside from the bed, the furniture consisted of a washstand topped by a chipped porcelain pitcher and basin, a side table, and a battered wardrobe that was obviously the castoff of some distant Cadgwyck ancestor. It wasn't difficult to imagine the water in the basin icing over on frigid winter mornings.

A pewter candlestick with a nub of a tallow candle, a tinderbox, and a book rested on the table next to the bed. Max picked up the book, shaking his head as he read the title on the clothbound spine—*Pilgrim's Progress*. Why should that surprise him? If this room was anything, it was the cell of a penitent.

Max tossed the book back down in disgust, then strode over to the window, half-expecting to find iron bars fixed over it. The window overlooked a desolate sea of moorland with endless waves of gorse and grass swaying in the wind. He

shoved it open and leaned out, struck by a dizzying rush of vertigo as the flagstones of the courtyard below seemed to rise up to meet him.

He jerked his head back into the room and slammed the window. As he turned to sweep a despairing look over the bleak little chamber his housekeeper called home, he could not help but compare it to Angelica's tower with all of the lavish luxuries it must have once afforded a pampered child.

A burst of girlish laughter drifted to his ears. There was nothing spectral about those giggles. His despair shifting into anger, Max hastened down the stairs, his bootheels clattering against the wood.

Two of the young maids had just emerged from the back staircase and were heading for their dormer room, their heads together as they tittered over some private jest.

"Elizabeth!" he snapped.

Both girls jerked to attention, visibly shocked to discover their master had invaded their humble domain. Max could only imagine how thunderous his brow must have looked in that moment.

"Where is Mrs. Spencer?" he demanded.

The maids exchanged a furtive look that made Max want to grind his teeth in frustration. Why did everyone in this house always look so bloody guilty?

"It's Friday, yer lordship," one of them finally provided. "She goes to market every Friday. She won't be back until it's time to prepare supper."

He pondered the girl's words for a moment. "Good. Then I need to set you both to a task. But first you have to promise me something."

"What, m'lord?" asked the other girl, looking even more apprehensive.

"That you know how to keep a secret." With that, Max drew the two wide-eyed girls into the circle of his arms and began to murmur his instructions.

Anne trudged up the back staircase, bleary-eyed with exhaustion. She could hardly wait to sink down on the edge of her bed and tug the boots from her aching feet. She'd been up on them since before dawn, and the long walk to the village and back had spread the ache from her feet to her calves.

She had returned from her errands to find Dickon on hands and knees desperately trying to coax Hodges out from the cabinet in the dining-room cupboard before Lord Dravenwood discovered him. Hodges had crawled into the cabinet shortly after lunch and had been cowering there ever since, wild-eyed with fright because he believed the authorities were coming to cart him off to the asylum. It had taken Anne so long to lure him out that she'd had to prepare

supper in a terrible rush. She'd been so frazzled she'd inadvertently stomped on Sir Fluffytoes's tail, nearly broken her neck tripping over Nana's never-ending scarf, and snapped so sharply at Pippa for leaving a strip of peel on a potato that the usually unflappable girl had burst into tears.

Then she had been forced to play the role of perfect housekeeper as she had helped the maids serve Lord Dravenwood his supper. It might have been her imagination, but he had seemed even more smug than usual. She had turned more than once to catch him watching her from beneath those ridiculously long lashes of his, a speculative gleam in his smoky gray eyes.

Performing her final duties of the day had sapped the last of her strength. She'd helped the maids clean up the kitchen, then sent them off to bed while she prepared the dough for the next morning's bread. Leaving the loaves to rise beneath a clean cloth, she'd made one last circuit of the downstairs to make sure every candle and lamp had been extinguished.

As she passed through the servants' quarters, the sound of bellicose snoring drifted out of Hodges's room. When he had refused to come out from the cabinet earlier, she had wanted nothing more than to strangle him with her bare hands. But as she peeked into his room to find him tucked safely in his nest of quilts with just a tuft

of white hair visible, she was flooded with a rush of helpless tenderness.

By the time she reached the steep stairs that led to her own attic room, her eyelids were already drooping. On nights like this, it seemed as if she could climb forever and the staircase would never end. The wind was moaning mournfully around the eaves, and the chill hanging in the air seemed to deepen with each step she took. Hoping to lessen the time it would take to wash up and crawl beneath her blanket, she unbuttoned the first three buttons of her bodice, tugged the net from her hair, and began to pull out her hairpins, dropping them into the pocket of her apron.

Just as she pushed open the door, an enormous yawn seized her. She covered her mouth and closed her eyes. When she opened them, she was standing on the threshold of a dream.

Chapter Twenty-three

Anne blinked in wonder, thinking for a dazed instant that she must somehow have stumbled into the wrong room. But there was no room like this in Cadgwyck Manor.

There hadn't been for a long time.

A cheerful fire crackled on the grate, sending out waves of warmth to envelop her and draw her

deeper into the attic. The wooden bedstead was the same as it had been that morning when she had stiffly climbed out of it, but her ancient mattress had been replaced with a fluffy feather tick draped in a plush down comforter. The pewter candlestick on the side table had been shoved aside to make room for an oil lamp. The lamp's cut-glass, ruby-hued shade cast a rosy glow over the room. A stack of handsome, leatherbound books with gilt-edged pages now accompanied her worn copy of *Pilgrim's Progress*.

A luxurious Turkish rug had been laid beside the bed, as if to protect her feet from the cold when she first arose, while a pair of green velvet drapes had been hung over the window to keep the worst of the drafts at bay. A small, round table fitted with a single chair sat in front of the hearth—the perfect place to enjoy a private supper after a long day of work. There was even a plump ottoman where she might prop her aching feet.

Anne recognized almost every item in the room. They had all been pilfered from other chambers in the house. The attic now looked more like a lady's sitting room than a housekeeper's quarters.

But she was no lady.

She drifted toward the washstand, bewitched by the tendrils of steam she could see wending their way into the air. As if in a trance, she lifted the ceramic pitcher and poured a stream of heated water into the basin. She would have liked nothing

more than to splash the water on her face, to surrender to the tantalizing temptation of having someone look after her after so many years of looking after herself and everyone around her.

But as she lifted her eyes from the basin, she realized one thing in the room had not changed. The oval looking glass still hung behind the washstand. Steam misted the looking glass, softening her reflection, turning back the clock and erasing all of the lonely years until the only features she recognized were the eyes gazing back at her.

And the helpless longing within them. A longing only intensified by the spicy, masculine scent of bayberry soap still lingering in the air.

When Anne reached her employer's bedchamber, she didn't even bother to knock. She simply shoved open the door and stormed inside. Fortunately, Lord Dravenwood's bed curtains had been tied back with gold cords to welcome in the heat from the fire crackling on his grate. She didn't even have to whisk them aside or rip them clear off the canopy to find him.

He was propped up on the pillows reading by candlelight, a pair of incongruous wire-framed spectacles perched low on his nose. He glanced up, his gaze mildly curious, as she closed the door behind her so as not to rouse the rest of the house.

She marched across the chamber and halted at

the foot of the four-poster. "How *dare* you go into my room without my leave?" she demanded, her chest heaving with fury. "I suppose it wasn't enough for you to paw through the belongings of some poor dead girl. You had to go and poke your aristocratic nose into *my* business as well. Tell me—are you so very arrogant, so very presumptuous, so very convinced of your own natural-born superiority, that you believe those in your employ aren't entitled to even a dollop of privacy? Some humble space they can call their own?" He opened his mouth, but closed it again when he realized she had only paused to suck in an outraged breath. "If that's what you believe, you are sorely mistaken. You may own this house, my lord. *But you do not own me!*"

He cocked one eyebrow, calmly surveying her over the top of the spectacles. "Are you quite through, Mrs. Spencer?"

An icy-hot wave of horror and despair washed over Anne as she realized what she had done. She had allowed herself to fly into a full-blown tantrum, losing the temper she'd fought so hard to keep for so long.

And now everyone she loved would suffer for her failings.

"I suppose I am," she said stiffly, her voice stripped of all emotion except for regret. "There's no need for you to dismiss me, my lord. I shall tender my resignation first thing in the morning."

Dravenwood drew off the spectacles and laid them aside, along with his book. "Had I wanted to be rid of you, I'd have continued to let you sleep in that inhospitable crypt you insist upon calling a bedchamber. I'm sure it would have only been a matter of time before you succumbed to consumption or a fatal ague. Then you and Miss Cadgwyck could have taken turns haunting me."

Anne's ire had subsided just enough for her to realize she was standing in a gentleman's bedchamber in the middle of the night. A gentleman who didn't appear to be wearing anything but the sheet drawn up to the taut planes of his abdomen. A silk dressing gown was draped over the foot of the bed, confirming her worst suspicions.

With his naked chest hers for the ogling, there didn't seem to be anywhere else to look. Anne had heard some gentlemen were forced to pad their coats and wear a corset of sorts to achieve the broad-shouldered, narrow-waisted look so favored by fashion these days. Lord Dravenwood was *not* one of those men. His chest was well muscled and lightly furred with the same dark hair that dusted the back of his hands. Anne's hands itched with the pagan desire to rake her fingertips through it, to see if it felt as soft, yet crisp, as it looked.

He cleared his throat. She jerked her gaze back up to his face, her cheeks heating with mortification to have been caught gawking.

271

He might be a guarded man, but there was no mistaking the gleam of amusement in his eyes. "I'm afraid you have me at a disadvantage, Mrs. Spencer. Had I known I would be receiving a female caller who hadn't been dead for a decade, I would have dressed—or undressed—with more care."

He was eyeing her with frank appreciation. She had forgotten all about yanking the pins from her hair and unbuttoning the first few buttons of her bodice as she climbed the stairs to her room.

Her hair was half-up and half-down, a thick, curling rope of it hanging over one shoulder. Her gown was no longer buttoned up to her chin, but was gaping open to reveal the worn lace of her chemise and a creamy slice of cleavage. She probably looked as if she'd just crawled out of a man's bed.

Or was about to crawl into one.

She snatched her collar closed at the throat with one hand, hoping to hide the silver locket nestled between her breasts from his piercing gaze. "I should have knocked. But then again," she added sweetly, "I'm sure you can understand just how much easier it is to barge in where you haven't been invited and aren't welcome."

"Just so you know, I did knock when I came to your room."

"When no one answers, it's customary to go

away and return at another time, not refurbish their abode to your own tastes."

A dangerous glitter dawned in his eyes. "I would have refurbished it to your tastes, but I was fresh out of sackcloth and ashes."

Anne swallowed. If she hadn't let her anger get the best of her, she would have recognized coming here would be a terrible mistake. "Some of us are not so easily seduced by creature comforts."

"You have a lot of nerve reproaching me for wallowing in my self-condemnation when you've confined yourself to a cell like some sort of criminal or penitent nun. Tell me, Mrs. Spencer, just what terrible sins have you committed that would require such sacrifice? Are you hoping to atone for them by freezing yourself to death?"

Stung by the sharp lash of truth in his words, she snapped, "My sins are of no more concern to you than where I sleep at night. You had no right to meddle. I was perfectly content with things the way they were."

"Is that all you believe you deserve from life? Contentment? What about satisfaction? Joy?" Dravenwood tilted his head to survey her, his voice deepening on a husky note that sent a treacherous little shiver cascading through her. "Passion? Pleasure?"

"All luxuries reserved for those of your class, my lord. We humble servants are expected to find

our satisfaction in duty, loyalty, sacrifice, obedience."

"Obedience?" A skeptical bark of laughter escaped him. "No wonder you seem so dissatisfied."

Anne could feel her temper rising again. "You're a fine one to lecture me on the benefits of joy and pleasure. I'd wager you can't remember the last time you experienced either one. You squandered your youth loving a woman who could never love you back just so you could keep your heart safely walled behind the blocks of ice you've built to protect it. All Angelica did was replace that golden idol in your heart. You'd rather pine for a ghost than risk loving a woman fashioned from flesh and blood."

A woman such as her.

Shaken by that treacherous whisper of her heart, Anne spun around and retraced her steps to the door. "I should have never come here. I should have known reasoning with you would prove to be impossible."

The rustle of Dravenwood tossing back the sheets and yanking on his dressing gown was Anne's only warning. Before she could open the door more than a crack, he had crossed the chamber with the same predatory grace he had used to capture her on the night he'd gone ghost hunting. He slammed both palms against the door on either side of her head, shoving the door closed and leaving her with no choice but to stand there

trembling in the circle of his arms as he embraced her without laying so much as a finger on her.

"You have every right to berate me for invading your privacy." His mouth was so close to her ear the warmth of his breath stirred the invisible dusting of hair along its lobe. "But you were wrong about one thing."

"And what would that be, my lord?" she whispered tautly, thankful he couldn't see her face in that moment.

"As long as I am master at Cadgwyck, you do belong to me." His bold claim sent a wicked little thrill shooting through her. "Your welfare is my concern and my responsibility. If you want to spend your nights lying in your lonely bed reading *Pilgrim's Progress* by candlelight until your eyesight fails, then by God you'll at least do it in warmth and comfort. Do we understand each other?"

Mustering every last ounce of her courage, Anne turned to face him. Still held captive by those muscular forearms and the imposing wall of his chest, she gazed up into the passion-darkened planes of his face. "Yes, my lord. I think we understand each other very well."

She didn't realize just how well until he cupped her face in his hands and brought his mouth down on hers. Hard. Her lips melted beneath his, softening the punishing force of his kiss with the aching tenderness of her surrender. His tongue

accepted the invitation of her parted lips, licking into her with a sinuous hunger that coaxed a helpless little whimper from her lips.

Her hands drifted upward to clutch at his upper arms, sliding over the silk sleeves of his dressing gown to explore the firm swell of muscle beneath. She knew she should push him away, but all she wanted to do was tug him closer. To be enveloped in the heat radiating from every unyielding, masculine inch of him.

As his lips blazed a searing path from the corner of her mouth to the pulse beating madly at the side of her throat, she whispered, "Maximillian," cursing and blessing him in the same breath. If he had never come to Cadgwyck, she would never have known how lonely she'd been. How desperately she'd been craving a man's kiss, a man's touch. But not just any touch, she realized with a mingled thrill of joy and despair.

His touch.

"Anne." Her own name was a shuddering growl against the satiny skin of her throat. "My sweet, stubborn Anne."

Then his mouth was on hers again, the rough velvet of his tongue coaxing hers into joining the pagan dance until their mouths were as one. He wrapped an arm around her waist while his other hand combed the remaining pins from her hair, sending it tumbling around her shoulders in decadent disarray.

"You don't know how long I've wanted to do that," he muttered against her lips before seizing her mouth once more for a deep, drugging kiss that seemed to have no end.

Anne might have slid right into a puddle of desire at his feet if he hadn't used his hips to bear her back against the door. She could feel the rigid outline of his arousal pressed against the softness of her belly even through her skirts and petticoats, showing her just how desperately he wanted her. She felt her womb clench at the primal power of it.

This had to stop. *She* had to stop.

But instead she lifted a hand to his hair, sliding her fingers through his thick, dark locks just as she had longed to do for so long. His hand drifted downward, tracing the graceful curve of her throat and the delicate arch of her collarbone before finally dipping into her unbuttoned bodice to claim the softness of one breast.

Anne gasped into his mouth. She had accused him of denying himself pleasure, but he certainly knew how to give it. That much was evident in the deft brush of his fingertips against the throbbing little bud of her nipple. He gently tugged, knowing just how much pressure to apply to keep pleasure from turning into pain.

That irresistible surge of delight shocked Anne back to her senses. She'd been fool enough to trust herself to a man's hands once before. She could

277

not afford to do it again. Not when so much was at stake.

"I have to go, my lord," she murmured against his lips. "Coming here was a terrible mistake."

Dravenwood's hand went still against her breast, his long, masculine fingers still cupping its weight ever so gently. "I've made far more damning mistakes in my life. With far less reward."

She leaned back to peer up into his face. "What would you have me do? Sneak into your bed each night after the others are asleep? Slip away in the morning before the sun rises?"

He lifted both hands to smooth her hair back from her face, his quicksilver eyes heavy-lidded with passion, his voice hoarse with need. "At the moment I can think of nothing in all the world that I'd like more."

"I'm sorry, my lord. I'm not that woman. I can't be that woman." She closed her eyes and pressed her cheek to his chest to block out the sight of his hopeful face before whispering, "Not even for you."

His arms tightened around her, binding her to his heart with a fierce tenderness. For one bittersweet moment, it was enough to pretend that would be enough for them. That a simple embrace would satisfy the craving in both of their souls.

Even when they both knew it would never be enough.

"Are you certain this is what you want?" he

asked, burying his mouth in the softness of her hair.

Anne nodded, her throat too tight with longing and regret for speech. For a breathless moment, she was torn between fearing he wasn't going to let her go and praying he wouldn't.

But then he stepped away from the door and her, setting her free to flee back to the cozy comforts of her lonely room.

From that day forward, Anne would return to her attic each night to find a cheery fire crackling on the grate and a pitcher of hot water steaming on the washstand. Other treasures began to appear as well: a thick pair of new woolen stockings; some little cakes of French soap carved into the shapes of seashells; all three volumes of *Sense and Sensibility*, one of the novels she had adored as a young girl.

Had Dravenwood been any other man, she would have suspected him of trying to seduce her. But she had grown to know him well enough in the past few weeks to recognize that his gifts were given freely, without a price attached. He would never know how high their cost was to her yearning heart.

Anne's only satisfaction came when she would catch Beth or Betsy scurrying guiltily down the attic stairs as she trudged up them so she could mutter, "*Et tu, Brute,*" at them beneath her breath.

Unfortunately, neither of them spoke Latin. There was no need for a translator to interpret her accusing glare.

"We're never going to be rid of His Gracelessness, are we?" Pippa said darkly as they all gathered in the kitchen to prepare supper late one afternoon.

With every lamp and candle lit, the kitchen was even more cozy than usual. Clouds had been rolling in from the sea all day, bringing with them an early twilight and a gusty breeze scented with the threat of rain.

Pippa was wielding the pestle she was using to grind up some fresh parsley as if it were a cudgel. "He's going to die of old age right here in his bed. A bed whose linens *I* was forced to change."

"Oh, I don't know," Dickon said, an amiable grin lighting his freckled face. He was perched on the edge of the kitchen hearth, an iron kettle propped between his knees. He was in such good spirits he hadn't even complained about being tasked to scour out the kettle with handfuls of sand. "I'm starting to think he's not such a bad sort after all. Why, just yesterday he asked if I'd take him down to the cove and show him the sea caves. And he's talking about having the stable repaired and bringing in one of them fancy phaetons and some horses. *Real* horses, not just wild moor ponies."

Anne kept her attention studiously fixed on the

plate she was preparing. "I wouldn't grow too attached to him if I were you, Dickon. Even without our *encouragement,* he'll doubtlessly tire of the provincial country life soon enough and long to return to the excitement of London."

Pippa shot her a resentful look. "Angelica certainly hasn't been of much help lately. I'm beginning to think she fancies him for herself."

"Angelica has had ten long years to learn patience," Anne replied tartly. "She simply knows how to bide her time."

What Anne couldn't tell Pippa was that she didn't think they would even need Angelica to drive Dravenwood away. She was perfectly capable of doing that all on her own. By denying him the thing he most wanted, she had made it nearly impossible for him to stay at Cadgwyck.

She could not quite squelch a thrill of pride as she gazed down upon her creation. She'd given up trying to starve Dravenwood out of Cadgwyck and started feeding him the same dishes she prepared for the rest of them. Tonight's meal consisted of a miniature hen Dickon had snared in one of his traps, its succulent skin browned and crisped to perfection, roasted potatoes swimming in a sea of butter, and a salad of greens she'd grown herself in the manor garden.

"Have you finished filling up the saltcellar?" she asked Hodges.

"Almost!" he sang out. He was hunched over

the end of the long table, pouring a stream of salt into a chipped crystal bowl. His childlike smile made Anne's heart clench.

There was no denying his condition was deteriorating. Rapidly. Anne had learned that assigning him some simple task served the twofold purpose of making him feel useful and keeping him out of mischief.

Bess and Lisbeth came bustling into the kitchen. "The master's at table," Lisbeth informed Anne, while Bess fetched a silver tray from the cupboard and set it in front of Anne.

Anne placed the china plate on the tray, then arranged some freshly polished cutlery and a snowy-white linen serviette to compliment it. The last addition was a loaf of bread fresh from the oven.

"Just a minute!" she cried as Lisbeth held open the door so Bess could carry the heavy tray through it. Anne hurried over to whisk the saltcellar out from under Hodges's nose, then plunked it down on the tray.

As the maids disappeared through the door with their burden, Anne sank down on one of the benches flanking the table, wondering what Dravenwood would make of her meal.

For reasons she didn't care to examine, it was a pleasure to imagine him eating the food she had prepared—his strong, white teeth sinking into the crisp, juicy skin of the hen, his tongue

curling around the buttery goodness of the potatoes.

She was still lost in that agreeable image when Hodges said, "I've always heard there's only one way to rid one's home of vermin."

Distracted by her wayward thoughts, Anne murmured, "Hmm? What was that, dear?"

"Won't be any rats dying in their beds of old age in *my* house."

Pippa's pestle froze in midmotion. Dickon slowly stood, his grin fading. Anne turned to look down the length of the table. Hodges was dusting off his hands, looking extremely pleased with himself.

Only then did Anne spot the glass bottle sitting in front of him—a brown medicine bottle with a black skull and scarlet crossbones emblazoned on its label.

"Dear God," she whispered, horror chilling her blood to ice. "It's not salt."

Chapter Twenty-four

Dickon took off for the door at a dead run, but Anne still beat him to it. Lifting the hem of her heavy skirts to keep them from tripping her, she went pelting down the endless corridors of the basement and up the stairs to the main floor of

the manor. In her mind's eye, she could already see Dravenwood slumped over his plate, his mighty heart laboring harder with each sluggish beat, his piercing gray eyes slowly losing their focus. By the time she finally reached the dining room, her own heart was on the verge of imploding in her chest.

Lisbeth and Bess were just returning through the dining-room door with empty hands, laughing and talking among themselves. Ignoring their startled cries, Anne shoved her way past them and into the dining room.

Dravenwood was gazing down at his meal with obvious pleasure, his fingers poised to add a generous pinch of salt to it. As the crystals rained down from his fingers to dust his food, Anne lunged across the room and used one arm to sweep everything in front of him off the table.

It hit the floor with an explosion of china and crockery, spattering food everywhere, including over the freshly polished leather of his boots.

Silence descended over the room. Lisbeth and Bess stood frozen in the doorway, gawking at Anne as if she'd gone stark raving mad.

Dravenwood slowly lifted his gaze from the carnage on the floor to her face. "Is there something I should know, Mrs. Spencer?" he inquired, the gentleness of his tone belied by the suspicious gleam in his eyes.

Fighting to steady her breathing, Anne tucked

a fallen tendril of hair behind her ear, then wiped her sweat-dampened palms on her apron. "Nothing of any import, my lord. Dickon just realized there was a chance the hen might be rancid."

"Indeed."

Anne hadn't even known it was possible for a single word to convey such withering skepticism. Fixing a shaky smile on her lips, she frantically beckoned the maids back into the room. "Don't mind the mess. Lisbeth and Bess will get it all cleaned up while I fix you a nice mutton sandwich."

Although he didn't utter another word, Anne could feel the steady weight of his gaze following her from the room, as inescapable as the coming storm.

It wasn't his housekeeper who visited Max in his bedchamber that night, but his ghost.

Max had almost given up on her. He had been on the verge of being forced to accept Angelica Cadgwyck was no more real than the naughty nymphs and big-bosomed mermaids who had haunted his boyhood fantasies.

But that was before he felt her lips gently brush his brow, then drift lower to graze the corner of his mouth with bewitching tenderness. He turned his head to fully capture her kiss. He had no intention of letting her escape him this time.

Wrapping his arms around her, he tumbled her into his embrace and his bed. Rolling over, he trapped her beneath him, breathing in the sweetness of her sigh in the heartbeat before his lips descended on hers. She tasted like warm, ripe berries on a hot summer day. Like cool rain watering the parched sands of the Moroccan desert.

He tangled his fingers in the silky skein of her curls, thrusting his tongue deep into the lush sweetness of her mouth. His hips were already moving against hers in an ancient rhythm. The heat roiling off his naked flesh melted away the gauzy skein of silk she was wearing until nothing was left to keep them apart. Not fear. Not time.

Not even death. He entered her in one smooth thrust, his soul singing in tune with his body.

She was here. She was real.

And she was his.

Until a gunshot rang out, snatching her away.

Max sat straight up in the bed, biting off a savage oath to find himself alone. He had been dreaming again. A dream so real it had left his body hard and aching for a woman who had died a decade ago.

He shoved aside the bed curtains and swung his legs over the side of the bed. Ever since he had learned about Timberlake's treachery, he had been haunted by another image of Angelica as well—Timberlake shoving her down on the window

seat of the tower, his cruel fingers biting into her tender flesh. Timberlake's sneering mouth descending on hers to smother her screams for help.

He had wanted answers, but those weren't the answers he had wanted. He would rather continue to believe Angelica had simply succumbed to the artist's seduction, that she had stepped off the edge of that cliff still believing Timberlake was a romantic hero who had died adoring her.

Max dropped his aching head into his hands. He supposed he ought to be grateful he had slept long enough to dream. Ever since Anne had come barging into his bedchamber, he had spent most of his nights tossing and turning until the wee hours of the morning. His sulking body still hadn't forgiven him for letting her go. His body didn't seem to care that she was his housekeeper, only that she was warm and alive and had more substance than a wisp of mist.

He had previously discovered she was capable of delivering a fine scold, but he hadn't realized until that night that she could work herself into such a magnificent fury. Her ire had brought a most becoming sparkle to her hazel eyes and a healthy flush of color into her alabaster cheeks. With the soft swell of her breasts straining to overflow the confines of her bodice and that provocative curl tumbling out of its pins and over one shoulder, she had borne little resemblance to

the prim and proper housekeeper with starch in her spine and vinegar running through her veins. He might have been able to dismiss her dramatic transformation if he hadn't been fool enough to leave his bed and corner her at the door.

He was still unsettled by her peculiar behavior in the dining room. Angelica might not be real, but the panicked guilt in Anne's eyes most definitely was.

Perhaps the time had come for him to admit he didn't belong in this place. There was nothing to hold him here, nothing to stop him from packing his valise and slipping away before daybreak. Wouldn't it be better to let the villagers mock him as a coward driven from his own house by a ghost than to waste another minute of his life being haunted by not one, but *two* women, neither of whom he could ever have? Somehow Anne and Angelica had become inextricably bound in his imagination.

And his heart.

He could send for the rest of his things in the morning, then return to London and his position with the Company. He could allow his parents to choose a suitable bride for him and settle down to produce an heir and the requisite spare. He could sleep soundly through the night, never again troubled by mysterious laughter or dreams that left him aching for a passion he would never know.

How would Anne feel when she found his bed empty and his things gone? he wondered. Would she rejoice? Would she gather the other servants around her to celebrate vanquishing another unwanted master? Or would she miss him just the tiniest bit? Would she lie in her narrow bed with the cold winter winds moaning around the eaves of her attic and remember the man who had wanted only to warm her?

A sullen rumble rattled the house. Max slowly lifted his head. It wasn't the ghostly echo of a pistol being fired that had robbed him of his dream lover after all, but a sharp crack of thunder heralding the arrival of the storm that had been brooding over the manor all day. Fat drops of rain began to pelt the French windows. A flash of lightning illuminated the room.

Max's breath froze in his throat. Angelica hadn't abandoned him after all.

Although the French windows remained closed and latched, a sinuous ribbon of mist was twining its way through the room. Max watched in open-mouthed fascination as it drifted this way and that before rising to coalesce beside the bed.

As he waited for the lithe female curves to gain shape and substance, he drew in an uneven breath, expecting it to be perfumed with the sultry aroma of jasmine. Instead, a choking cloud filled his lungs with the acrid stench of gunpowder and brimstone.

A wracking cough doubled him over. He blinked away a stinging rush of tears, realizing it wasn't mist seeping steadily beneath his bedchamber door, but deadly ribbons of smoke.

Chapter Twenty-five

Max sprang out of the bed and rushed across the room to snatch a shirt and a pair of trousers out of the armoire. There was no time to seek out the source of the fire and try to extinguish it. As ancient and as full of rotting wood as the manor was, it could go up like a tinderbox in minutes. He grabbed a monogrammed handkerchief from his dressing table. He dipped it into his washbasin to soak up as much water as it could hold, then pressed it over his mouth and nose before yanking open the door.

Billowing clouds of smoke crowded the corridor. A flickering glow emanated from the direction of the entrance hall. Ignoring his instinctive urge to sprint down the two flights of stairs and straight out the front door, Max took off in the opposite direction, heading for the back staircase leading up to the servants' quarters. The smoke made the darkness even more impenetrable, but the fitful flashes of lightning striking the windows guided his steps. Perhaps a

bolt of it had struck the house and ignited the fire.

He shot up the steps, his father's smug voice echoing in his ears: *Servants should always be quartered on the highest floor. Should the house catch fire, they won't be underfoot while you're trying to collect your valuables and escape.*

In his mind's eye, all could see was Anne nestled beneath her cozy down comforter, enjoying a blissful slumber with no idea her attic room was about to be engulfed by a raging inferno from which there would be no escape.

By the time Max reached the fourth floor, the smoke had thinned out a little. He shoved the damp handkerchief in the pocket of his trousers. The steady drumming of the rain on the slate shingles could easily drown out the sound of crackling flames from below.

He made a beeline for Dickon's room. He snatched the boy up by his shoulders, yanking him out of the bed and clear off his feet. "Listen to me, lad! There's a fire downstairs. I need you to get the girls up and out of the house. I'll meet you by the back gate to help you with Nana. And Tinkles. And Mr. Furryboots," he added, thinking how displeased Anne would be with him if he let her precious pets perish.

Dickon's head bobbed up and down like a rag doll's, his eyes as wide as saucers. "Yes, s-s-sir . . . I mean, His Graciousness . . . I mean . . ."

"Go!" Max shouted, lowering Dickon to his

feet and shoving him in the direction of the door.

Dickon took off for Pippa's room while Max strode toward the steep stairs at the far end of the corridor. As he passed the other rooms, he noted that the Elizabeths had already began to stir, but Hodges's rumpled bed was empty.

Max took the attic stairs two at a time. He gave the door at the top of the stairs an impatient push, expecting it to swing open at his touch as it had before.

The door was locked.

Swearing out loud, he lifted one bare foot and kicked the door clean off its bottom hinge. As it listed crazily, Anne bolted upright in the bed.

Max crossed the room in two long strides and scooped her into his arms, comforter and all.

Still half-asleep, she blinked up at him, her tousled braids making her look even younger than Pippa. "Forgive me, my lord. I didn't hear you ring."

He gave her a brief, but fierce, squeeze, cherishing the solid feel of her weight in his arms. "The manor is on fire. I need to get you downstairs."

"Fire?" Panic flared in her eyes as she came fully awake. "What about Dickon? Pippa? Hodges? Put me down this instant! I have to warn the others!" She began to struggle against his embrace, fighting to get to her feet.

"They're all safe," he promised, feeling a twinge

of conscience as he remembered Hodges's empty bed. "Just hang on to me, damn it all, and you will be, too! Please . . ." When she continued to struggle, he added fiercely, "Anne."

She stilled, blinking up at him in obvious surprise. He expected her to argue, as was her nature, but after a brief hesitation, she looped her arms around his neck, holding on for dear life. Her trust in him gave his heart a curious little wrench.

They were halfway down the stairs when she cried, "Wait! My locket!" When he glared at her in disbelief, she gave him a beseeching look. "Please . . . Maximillian."

"Where is it?" he growled, infuriated to discover he had no defenses against that look or the sound of his name on her lips.

"Back of the door."

Max snatched the locket from the peg on the back of the dangling door, dropped its chain over her head, then carried her swiftly down the attic stairs. His confidence in Dickon had not been misplaced. The servants' quarters were deserted, the doors standing open to reveal scattered bedclothes abandoned in desperate haste.

They descended the back stairs to the third floor to find the smoke much thicker and blacker than when Max had climbed them. A fit of coughing wracked Anne's slender body.

Bracing her weight against the wall with one

arm, Max tugged the handkerchief from his pocket and shoved it into her hand. "Press it over your mouth and nose."

"What about you?"

"I'll be fine," he promised her grimly, hoping he was right.

Since he didn't care for the idea of hauling her blindly down that narrow back staircase into a potential inferno, he started across the third floor, heading for the main stairs. If he could get a clear look at the entrance hall, at least he would know what they were up against.

Thunder cracked and lightning flashed as Max sprinted across the length of the house. The smoke seemed to pursue them, snaking through the corridors and down the stairs to the second-floor gallery like a dragon's tail looking for an ankle to seize. Time seemed to swell until it felt as if it had been hours instead of only minutes since Max had bolted up the stairs to rescue Anne.

The view from the gallery brought Max up short. There could be no mistaking the hellish glow or the hungry crackle of flames coming from the drawing room. Smoke was billowing through the arched doorway and into the entrance hall, but a clear path from the foot of the main staircase to the front door still remained. When Anne lowered the handkerchief and tried to peer over the banister, Max cradled the back of her

head in his hand, gently urging her face into his chest, and took off at a dead run.

The second-floor gallery seemed to grow longer with each jarring step, but they finally reached the landing. From her gilt frame Angelica watched them fly past her and down the steps, her gaze as coolly amused as ever. Max felt a sharp stab of regret at the thought of leaving her to perish in the flames. But all that truly mattered to him now was the woman clinging to his neck.

They were almost across the entrance hall when a tremendous crash of glass sounded from the drawing room, followed by a rousing cheer.

"What the hell?" Max muttered.

He swept open the front door just in time to see a heap of flaming draperies go sailing through the drawing-room window to land in the over-grown courtyard. They lay there, hissing and steaming as the pouring rain quickly squelched the worst of the flames.

Max and Anne exchanged a baffled glance. Since the smoke had ceased its billowing with no sign of any fresh flames leaping through the window, Max slowly retraced his steps until they stood in the doorway of the drawing room.

Dickon and Pippa were hanging half out the window, admiring the results of their handiwork, while the maids hugged one another in the corner behind the settee, their faces wreathed in smiles of relief.

Max cleared his throat.

Dickon and Pippa swung around to face him, the soot blacking their faces making their triumphant grins seem that much more dazzling. Stray embers had scorched holes in their nightclothes. They looked like a pair of cheeky chimney sweeps.

Max glared at Dickon. "What in the bloody hell did you do, boy? I thought I told you to get the women out of the house."

Dickon's grin lost none of its cockiness. "We were running past the drawing room when I saw it was the drapes all ablaze. We thought if we could get them out the window, the rain would douse the flames. So Pippa hurled a coal bucket through the glass, then I used a poker to drag down the drapes and stuff them through the hole."

Max surveyed the carnage through the lingering haze of smoke hanging over the room. The window frame had already began to buckle from the heat. The flames had shot up the wall above the drapery rod, blistering the paint and blackening the crown molding and a large section of ceiling. Another few minutes and the entire room would have gone up in flames, taking the rest of the manor with it.

Anne began to wriggle in earnest. This time there was no stopping her and she slid out of his arms and went rushing across the room to Dickon and Pippa, leaving Max holding the empty

comforter. "You fools! You silly, brave little fools! Why, I ought to box both your ears and send you to bed without supper!"

Dickon and Pippa exchanged a glance before saying in unison, "We've already had supper."

"Then I ought to send you to bed without breakfast!"

Max watched in fascination as Anne burst into tears, threw her arms around them both, and took turns smothering their ash-flaked hair with kisses. He'd never seen a housekeeper quite so devoted to her staff.

When Anne finally lifted her face, it was streaked with both tears and ashes. She gazed up at the charred ceiling, shaking her head in disbelief. "I don't understand. How could such a thing have happened?"

Dickon crouched down, using the poker to sift through the still-smoking debris beneath the window. With a dull clang the poker struck something heavy. A blackened silver candlestick came rolling slowly across the floor toward Max's feet.

The bewilderment in Anne's expression deepened, mingled with burgeoning horror. "But I snuffed all the candles before going up to bed. I swear I did! Checking the lamps and candles is the last duty I do each night before I retire."

"I left it burning for her." They all turned as Hodges came drifting through the door that led to the shadowy dining room, looking like a ghost

himself with his unfocused eyes and long, white nightshirt. His snowy hair was standing straight up around his head in a disheveled halo. "I told her not to go walking along the cliffs on such a night, but she wouldn't listen. She was always so headstrong. I thought if I left a candle burning in the window, she'd be able to find her way back. I've been waiting so long for her to return. So very long . . ." His voice trailed off in a mournful sigh and he began to hum.

Max's nape prickled as he recognized the off-key notes of the melody from the music box in the tower.

"Oh, darling," Anne whispered, her face crumpling into a mask of pity and pain. She went to the old man, gently folding him into her arms. He buried his face in the crook of her neck, his slumped shoulders beginning to heave with silent sobs. "There, there," she murmured, patting him on the back. "It was just an oversight. I know you didn't mean to hurt anyone."

Struck by the full enormity of what might have happened if the thunder hadn't awakened him from his dreams of Angelica, Max felt his compassion ebbing and his anger rising. Tossing the comforter aside, he said, "I want that man out of here."

Hodges lifted his head. He and Anne both stared at Max as if he had just suggested they sacrifice a kitten on the front lawn.

"You can't mean it," she said. "It was nothing but a simple mistake. I'm sure he had no intention of—"

"He almost killed you!" Max's shout echoed through the drawing room, louder than any clap of thunder. "Us," he amended, feeling the curious gazes of the others settle on him. "He almost burned us all to death in our beds. He's a danger to himself and to everyone around him. I want him out of this house first thing in the morning."

Hodges cowered in Anne's arms, his quivering lower lip making Max feel like the worst sort of bully. But he wasn't about to relent this time. Not when so much was at stake, Max thought, his gaze straying to Anne's pale, ash-streaked face.

She gently extracted herself from Hodges's grip and stepped in front of the butler, drawing herself up as if she were armored in far more than just a soot-stained nightdress and a disheveled pair of braids. She lifted her chin, her gaze openly defiant. "If he goes, I go."

Max knew exactly what was expected of him then. It had been ingrained into his character from the day he'd been born. He was master of this house. He might be able to tolerate a bit of teasing insubordination, but a full-out mutiny—especially in front of the other servants—was grounds for immediate dismissal. His housekeeper had left him with no choice but to send her packing along with his butler and without so much as a letter of

recommendation to guarantee her a chance at another position.

He opened his mouth, then closed it again, glowering at her for a long moment before snapping, "In my study. *Now.*"

Chapter Twenty-six

Lord Dravenwood turned on his heel and strode from the room, the beautifully carved planes of his face making him look positively demonic in the flicker of the lightning dancing through the broken window. Anne could already feel her courage starting to falter.

She gave Hodges a gentle shove in Pippa's direction, her eyes silently pleading with the girl. "Look after him."

Pippa nodded, looking far more worried about Anne's fate than the butler's.

Anne followed Dravenwood up the stairs, each measured step making her feel more as if she were following a black-hooded executioner to the gallows. Her alarm mounted when he didn't even waste a yearning glance on Angelica as he strode past her portrait.

When they reached the door of the study, he stood aside to let her pass, still every inch the gentleman despite his bare feet, sleep-tousled hair,

and murderous expression. His ivory shirt was unfastened at the throat, and Anne felt her cheeks heat as she brushed past him and noted that the top two buttons of his trousers were also undone.

He followed her into the room. She expected him to slam the door behind them, but he closed it with such deliberate care it sent a delicate shiver of foreboding down her spine.

She stood awkwardly in the middle of the room while he lit the lamp sitting on the corner of his desk. The drapes were drawn, giving them a cozy reprieve from the jagged bursts of lightning and pouring rain.

Anne was halfway hoping he would retreat to his favorite sanctuary behind the desk, placing an impenetrable shield between them. Instead, he leaned against the front of it, folding his arms over his chest and crossing his feet at the ankles. The cool and composed Mrs. Spencer seemed to have deserted Anne, leaving her standing before this powerful man in nothing but her nightdress, her hair escaping from her braids in untidy brown wisps.

She forced herself to meet his level gaze. "Perhaps it would be best if we spoke of this in the morning after tempers—and passions—have cooled."

"Ah, but I think we both know there's not much chance of that, now is there, Mrs. Spencer?" he drawled.

So she was back to being Mrs. Spencer again, was she? When he had begged her to remain in his arms, her Christian name had sounded like a promise on his lips.

"I'm certain Hodges didn't mean any harm," she began, choosing her words with care. "It was nothing but an accident."

"It was the careless act of a maniac. If you're not worried about your own well-being—or mine—then perhaps you should stop and think about what would have happened had that fire cut off escape from the servants' quarters. Or if Pippa and Dickon had failed in their foolish efforts to extinguish it and set themselves ablaze instead."

Anne could feel her face blanch. She'd never seen Dravenwood's striking features set in such pitiless lines. "I'll give Hodges a stern talking-to first thing in the morning," she vowed. "We'll all be more vigilant in the future when it comes to keeping an eye on—"

"Just who was keeping an eye on him tonight when my supper was being prepared?"

A blade of ice pierced Anne's heart as she relived that terrible moment when she had seen the skull and crossbones on the bottle and feared it might be too late to save Dravenwood. "How did you know it was poison?" she whispered.

The corner of his mouth curled in a victorious little smile. "I didn't. Until just now."

Infuriated by his trickery, she glared at him. "It was an honest mistake on Hodges's part. He thought we'd charged him with ridding the manor of rats."

"How do I know it was all Hodges's doing? If you hadn't knocked my supper off the table in such a timely manner, I might suspect you were willing to let the poor deranged fellow do your dirty work for you. For all I know, you simply suffered a belated qualm of conscience. Or didn't want to risk your pretty little neck being stretched on the gallows."

She was so caught off guard by the unexpected compliment it took a minute for his words to sink in. "Are you accusing me of trying to *murder* you?"

"Don't try to tell me the thought hasn't crossed your mind."

Exasperated beyond bearing, she snapped, "I'm sure the thought has crossed the mind of everyone who has ever made your acquaintance!"

A muscle in his jaw twitched, although whether from fury or amusement she could not tell. "I'm growing weary of your secrets and lies, Mrs. Spencer. While I'm deciding whether or not to fetch the constable, perhaps you'd like to share if it was you or Hodges who shoved your former master out the window? Or did Angelica do it in a fit of the sulks?"

Anne's mouth fell open as he continued.

"I've never given much credence to rumors, having been the subject of them more often than not. But after suffering so many near-death experiences since my arrival at Cadgwyck, I'm beginning to think the villagers might be either more or less superstitious than I first believed."

Tearing her guilty gaze away from his accusing one, Anne sank down in the chair in front of the desk. She was fully prepared to offer up some easily digested lie, but to her own surprise, when she opened her mouth, the truth emerged. She'd become such an accomplished liar that her voice sounded rusty and unconvincing, even to her own ears. "I'm afraid Lord Drysdale fancied himself quite the lothario. Apparently, a doting mama had convinced him at a very young age that no woman in her right mind could resist the charms of a bandy-legged, overgrown toad. From the moment he arrived at the manor, he was a bit . . . how shall I say it? . . . overly *friendly* with his hands. He was always patting Lizzie on the rump when she bent over to add a log to the fire or peeping up Bess's skirts when she climbed on a stool to dust the top of a bookshelf."

Anne stole a look at Dravenwood from beneath her lashes. He was watching her intently, his face revealing nothing.

"One night after indulging in a few too many after-dinner cordials, he climbed the stairs to the servants' quarters after everyone was abed and

decided to creep into my room. I awoke with the stench of his breath in my face and shot up out of the bed, screaming at the top of my lungs. Startled out of his not particularly considerable wits by my less than welcoming response to his advances, he went stumbling backward, bleating like a stuck sheep. Unfortunately—for Lord Drysdale, that is—it was a warm spring night and my bed-chamber window was standing wide open. We all agreed it was best just to tell the constable he rose in the middle of the night to use the convenience and took a wrong turn."

Rubbing her chilled arms through the thin sleeves of her nightdress, Anne gazed into her lap and waited for Lord Dravenwood's response. And waited. And waited. She was beginning to wonder if he had dozed off on his feet when she heard a strange sound.

She had expected him to express shock, horror, outrage, perhaps even sympathy, but the last sound she had expected was a deep rumble of a chuckle.

Her gaze flew to his face. He was openly laughing now, his grin making his eyes crinkle at the corners just as his brother's had done and erasing a world of care from his face. Anne's heart did a helpless little somersault. If the man believed women were only after him for his fortune and title, he was madder than Hodges.

When his mirth showed no sign of waning, she

surged to her feet with an indignant sniff. "I'm glad you found my sordid little story so amusing."

"I'm not laughing at you. I'm laughing because the poor fool had the audacity to try to crawl into *your* bed."

That only made Anne feel *more* insulted. "You needn't mock me, my lord. I'm perfectly aware I'm no legendary beauty like Angelica Cadgwyck or your precious sister-in-law."

"Oh, I wasn't mocking you." His grin faded, the sparkle in his eyes deepening to a thoughtful glint that almost made her regret her indignation. "I was mocking him for being so foolish as to try to storm the bastion of our Mrs. Spencer's unassailable virtue." Dravenwood pushed himself off the corner of the desk, bringing them entirely too close to one another. "I've already learned what an impossible feat that is."

Anne knew it was her responsibility to put a more proper distance between them, but her feet seemed to be rooted to the floor. As he reached down to gently swipe a smudge of soot from her cheek with the broad pad of his thumb, she drew in a shuddering breath.

His palm lingered against her cheek while his thumb strayed into far more dangerous territory, grazing her parted lips, testing their softness. She gasped against the firmness of his flesh, unable to hide the devastating effect his touch had on her. He was a most difficult man. Yet he caressed her

with an irresistible ease, as if he had been born to the task.

His sooty fringe of lashes swept down to shutter his eyes as he leaned forward and touched his cheek to her hair. "Mrs. Spencer?" The smoke had left his smooth baritone even deeper and more husky than usual.

"Anne," she corrected, her voice a tremulous sigh.

"If you're going to shove me out the window, you'd best do it now."

Anne's hands closed over his upper arms as if to push him away. But her hands were no more cooperative than her feet had been. All they would do was cling to him. "I didn't shove Lord Drysdale. He tumbled out quite of his own accord."

Dravenwood nuzzled her temple with his nose, breathing deeply of her scent as if she didn't smell of ash, but of some potent aphrodisiac he'd been seeking all his life. "I'm afraid I haven't the strength left to tumble out of my own accord. You'll have to do it for me."

Anne was tired of being the strong one. In that moment all she wanted to do was surrender to a strength and a will greater than her own. She wanted to be weak and wanton and foolish enough to make deplorable mistakes that would haunt her for the rest of her life.

And she wanted to do all of those things in this man's arms.

"I forgot to open the window, my lord."

"Max," he breathed into her mouth in the heartbeat before he touched his lips to hers.

That gentle, grazing caress was nearly her undoing. If she hadn't been able to dig her fingertips into the bunched muscles of his upper arms, she might have slid to her knees at his feet. Sipping softly at her lips only seemed to whet his thirst. He deftly deepened his kiss, coaxing the pliant petals of her lips apart with a tender, insistent mastery. She gasped as the warm, sleek velvet of his tongue swept through her mouth, claiming the nectar he found there for his own.

Without warning, the study door came crashing open. The two of them sprang apart. Anne could only pray she didn't look as flushed and guilty as she felt.

Pippa stood in the doorway, her agitation so great she probably wouldn't have noticed if Anne and the earl had been rolling about naked on the desk.

"What is it?" Anne demanded, her chagrin replaced by alarm.

Pippa's entire body was trembling and her dark eyes were brimming with tears. "It's Hodges. He's gone."

Chapter Twenty-seven

Dravenwood swore.

"Gone?" Anne echoed frantically. "What do you mean he's *gone?* I told you to look after him."

Pippa drew in a shuddering breath. "He slipped away while I was helping Betsy roll up the drawing-room carpet. I only took my eyes off him for a moment. I swear it! I had no idea he would bolt the second I turned my back."

Anne struggled to digest the information, her mind racing. "How do you know he's not hiding somewhere in the house? Have you checked the dining-room cupboard?"

"He left the front door standing wide open."

Anne flinched as a violent clap of thunder shook the house, as if to remind them all that a storm still raged outside.

"Oh, dear God, the cliffs," she whispered. She didn't realize she had swayed on her feet until Dravenwood cupped her elbow to steady her.

Pippa shook her head. "He didn't head for the cliffs. Dickon is almost positive he saw him running toward the moors during a flash of lightning. He's getting ready to go looking for him now."

"Like hell he is," Dravenwood growled, striding toward the door.

Pippa glared at the earl through her tears. She was crying in earnest now, her chest hitching with ragged sobs, her pretty face splotched with red. "This is all your fault! You're the one who said you wanted him gone! How could you be so heartless and cruel? Did you think he was deaf as well as daft?"

"You'll have ample time to berate me for my heartlessness later, child," Dravenwood said grimly, taking Pippa by the shoulders and setting her gently out of his path. "At the moment we have more important matters to attend to."

By the time the three of them reached the entrance hall, Dickon was fully dressed and seated on the bench of the coat tree. He was tugging on a pair of careworn boots with a jagged hole in one toe, his lean face taut with determination.

The storm had only just begun to unleash the full force of its fury.

The rain had deepened to a torrential downpour while the wind hurtled rattling fistfuls of hail at the arched window above the door.

It made Anne's heart twist with helpless terror to imagine Hodges out there somewhere, wandering lost and alone.

"Fetch my overcoat and boots," Dravenwood commanded Betsy when he spotted the white-faced maids and Nana huddled in the doorway of the drawing room. When she hesitated, casting

Anne a questioning look, he shouted, "Now!"

Betsy scurried past them and up the stairs to do his bidding.

Dickon rose to face them, squaring his thin shoulders and giving them all a fleeting glimpse of the man he would become. "Don't blame Pippa for letting him go. He was mine to watch as well. That's why I'm going to fetch him."

"Don't be ridiculous." Anne rushed to his side. "I can't bear to lose the both of you. He's my responsibility. I'll go."

Pippa sniffled. "I'm the one who lost him. I should be the one to go."

Dravenwood's voice cracked louder than the thunder. "In case all of you have forgotten, *I* am the master of this house. If anyone is going out in this hell's spawn of a night to look for Hodges, it's me."

"But I know the moors like the back of my own hand," Dickon protested. "I might even be able to catch one of the wild ponies and—"

"The only thing you're going to catch in this weather is your death of a cold," Dravenwood said.

Betsy came rushing back down the stairs with the earl's boots in hand and his overcoat draped over her arm.

"Dickon is right," Anne said, her heart swelling with panic. "You don't know the moors. They can be deadly during a storm."

Dravenwood sank down on the second stair to tug on his boots. "I survived a cholera outbreak in Burma, a sandstorm in the Tunisian desert, being jilted by my bride for my brother at the altar, and nearly being poisoned and burned to death in my bed by you and your motley little crew of minions. I have no intention of letting a little thunder and lightning or your blasted moor finish me off."

Dickon said, "But I—"

"*You* are not setting foot outside this house, young man." Max rose to yank on his overcoat. "You're going to stay right here and look after the women. *That's an order.*" Max turned to Anne. "If he tries to slip out after I'm gone, use those keys of yours to lock him in the pantry. Or the dungeon."

Dickon flung himself back down on the bench, returning the earl's glare with one of his own. Pippa moved to stand beside the boy, placing a hand on his shoulder in a rare show of solidarity.

By the time Max reached the door, Anne was waiting for him there.

Since she didn't dare touch him in front of the others, all she could do was reach up to correct the angle of his shoulder cape. "Take care, my lord. *Please.*"

He gazed down at her, the dangerous gleam in his eye warning her he was on the verge of doing something completely mad. Like drawing

her into his arms in front of them all for a long, passionate kiss. "I'll bring him back to you. I swear it."

Leaving her with that vow, he swept open the door and ducked out into the storm.

Anne perched on the sill of the attic window, straining to see through the inky curtain of rain lashing the windowpanes. She had retreated to her bedchamber when she could no longer bear the stillness of the longcase clock in the entrance hall or the way everyone looked at her expectantly at every brief lull in the storm or noise from outside the manor. Noises that inevitably turned out to be the banging of a loose shutter or a splintered branch slamming into the side of the house.

The storm's rage was even more virulent up here. The attic shuddered and groaned beneath the battering fists of the wind. Anne could clearly hear each time a slate tile gave up the fight and went skittering off the roof.

But her window also provided the best view of the moor. As she watched, a jagged bolt of lightning rent the sky, illuminating the landscape for a precious fraction of a second. She pressed her nose to the glass, her pulse quickening with excitement. She would almost have sworn she had seen two figures in the far distance, grappling against the storm. But by the next flicker of lightning they were gone, leaving only the gnarled

corpse of a tree and a standing stone where they had been.

Anne sank back against the window frame and gazed down at the candle flickering on the windowsill. Her eyelids were growing heavier, but every time she closed her eyes, she saw Dravenwood or Hodges lying facedown in some overflowing brook or flooded gully. She had ordered the maids to set a lamp in every window of the manor to serve as beacons, all the while knowing that anyone bold or foolish enough to brave the moor on a night such as this probably couldn't see more than a hand's length in front of their face.

She had briefly occupied her trembling hands by exchanging her soot-streaked nightdress for a plain gray gown and pinning up her hair, almost as if those commonplace rituals could help to temper the capricious nature of the storm. She lifted a hand to her throat, instinctively seeking comfort from her locket. She almost wished she had pressed it into Lord Dravenwood's hand before he had disappeared into the storm. He could have carried it as a knight would carry his lady's favor, using it as a talisman to guide him and Hodges back to Cadgwyck.

And back to her.

Anne awoke with a guilty start and a painful crick in her neck. She must have dozed off without

meaning to. The candle on the windowsill next to her had burned down to a stub. Its wick was on the verge of drowning in a pool of melted wax.

It took her a dazed moment to recognize the sound that had awakened her—silence.

Rubbing the crook between her neck and shoulder, she lifted her gaze to the window. The rain had departed with the night, taking the howling winds with it, but not the towering banks of clouds. Her mouth opened in a silent gasp. The destruction the storm had left behind was almost more terrifying than the storm itself. The somber dawn light revealed that one of the crumbling gateposts had tumbled the rest of the way over to block the drive. The drive itself was almost completely washed away, reduced to muddy ruts overflowing with rushing water. Roof tiles were scattered everywhere she looked, and a window shutter torn clean away from the house lay splintered on the ground. Even the veils of ivy had been ripped away from the tower windows.

It was hard to imagine how anything—or anyone—could have survived such a night.

Refusing to surrender to such grim thoughts, Anne scrambled off the windowsill to fetch her cloak so she could go out hunting for Hodges and the earl herself. If she had to, she would throw herself on the mercy of the villagers and beg them to send out a search party. But then she

caught a flicker of movement out of the corner of her eye.

She turned slowly back to the window, afraid to breathe, afraid to hope.

At first she thought it was a lone figure staggering toward the house. But then she realized it wasn't one man, but two. The taller of the pair had his arm braced beneath the shoulders of the second man and was all but carrying him. The taller man's tousled dark head hung between his broad shoulders. The visible effort it was taking for him to plant one foot in front of the other warned that any step could be his last.

Anne's heart leapt into her throat. Casting a silent yet fervent prayer of thanksgiving heavenward, she blew out the candle and headed down the stairs.

The distance between the attic and the entrance hall had never seemed so great. By the time Anne reached the front door, Dickon was already sweeping it open. They all poured down the portico steps, through the courtyard, and onto the front lawn. Even a beaming Nana joined them, Bess supporting the old woman's lumbering steps.

The thick mud sucked at Anne's half boots as she lifted the hem of her gown and went sprinting past Dickon, reaching the two men lurching their way up the remains of the drive before anyone else.

Dravenwood lifted his head to give her a weary but triumphant smile. Mud smudged his face, and a rapidly purpling bruise marred his temple. "I couldn't catch a pony but I did manage to catch a butler."

"Where in the name of God was he?" Anne asked, torn between laughter and tears.

"I searched for most of the night and finally found him near dawn curled up in a hollow tree less than a stone's throw from here, none the worse for wear."

Hodges was half-asleep on his feet and mumbling beneath his breath. As Dravenwood staggered beneath the butler's weight, Anne rushed forward to relieve him of his burden. She cradled Hodges in her arms while the rest of the servants gathered around them, laughing and chattering and slapping the bewildered butler on his shoulders and back.

All but forgotten by the others, Dravenwood stood there, still swaying on his feet. Anne hadn't realized just how much he had been depending on Hodges's stout form to balance him. Handing Hodges off into the waiting arms of Lizzie and Lisbeth, Anne gave Dickon a frantic hand signal. To her surprise, the earl didn't even protest when Dickon wrapped one lanky arm around him, supporting Dravenwood's weight much as Dravenwood had supported Hodges's.

Hodges might be none the worse for wear, but

she couldn't say the same for the earl. He was soaked through to the skin. His hair was curled into sooty ringlets by the rainwater still dripping from its ends. The expensive doeskin of his trousers was torn to reveal a nasty gash on one shin. Although he was doing his best not to shiver in the dawn chill, the blue cast of his lips matched the shadows beneath his eyes.

Anne wanted nothing more than to wrap her arms around him and tuck him into a warm, dry bed herself, but instead she forced herself to briskly say, "Betsy, Beth, help Lord Dravenwood up to his bedchamber immediately. See that he gets a hot bath and some dry things before retiring."

"No," Dickon said resolutely, standing even taller than usual. "His lordship needs a man-servant right now. I'll look after him."

Anne nodded. She had never before been quite so proud of the boy.

As he guided Dravenwood past her, she could not resist reaching out and catching the earl's hand in hers. His usually heated flesh felt cold and clammy to the touch. "Thank you for everything . . . my lord."

He nodded down at her, the ghost of a mocking smile playing around his lips. "Happy to be of service . . . Mrs. Spencer."

As the others drifted back toward the house, she stood there gazing after him. Her every breath

seemed to draw her deeper into his debt. It was growing more and more difficult to convince herself the emotion she felt swelling in her heart every time she looked at him was simply gratitude.

Since they were all exhausted by the excitement of the fire and the storm and from keeping vigil through the long hours of the night, Anne gave the rest of the servants leave to sleep the morning away. As soon as Hodges and the earl were safely tucked in their beds, she stumbled up to her attic to do the same.

By afternoon, all of them except Lord Dravenwood were up and gathered around the table in the kitchen to enjoy some warm cocoa and discuss the storm. Humbled by his misadventure, Hodges seemed perfectly content to sit with Nana beside the fire, holding a skein of yarn wrapped around his hands while the old woman added another foot to her knitting.

Darkness was falling when Anne ordered Bess to take a tray of sandwiches up to Lord Dravenwood's bedchamber. When Bess returned to report that her knock on the earl's door had received no answer, Anne felt a wave of tenderness wash over her. "Leave him be, then," she told the girl. "It won't do any harm to let him sleep through the night."

Taking his new duties as the earl's manservant

seriously, Dickon marched up the stairs first thing the next morning to see if his master would require any assistance with bathing and dressing.

He returned to the kitchen a short while later, looking somewhat nonplussed. "I knocked and knocked and he didn't answer for the longest time, but then he finally groaned and shouted at me to go away."

Anne frowned, her concern growing. She was tempted to look in on him herself, but ever since the night when she had stormed into his chamber only to end up in his arms, she had done all she could to avoid being alone with him in any room that contained a bed. "Perhaps he just needs a bit more time to recover. I'm sure he'll ring when he's ready to rejoin the world."

That evening, after a long day spent helping the maids scrub the ash from the drawing-room walls and supervising Dickon and Pippa while they cleaned up the debris from the yard, she sent Betsy up with another tray, this one topped with the one thing she knew Dravenwood couldn't resist—a steaming loaf of her freshly baked bread.

Anne turned around a short while later to find Betsy standing in the kitchen doorway, still holding the untouched tray. The look on the girl's kind, broad face made Anne's heart cringe with dread. "It's the master, ma'am," Betsy said reluctantly. "When he didn't answer my knock, I looked in on him to see if he'd be wantin' any

supper, just like you said, but I couldn't rouse him."

"What do you mean you couldn't rouse him? Was he still sleeping?"

"At first I thought he was just sleepin'. But he was moanin' something fierce. And when I touched his arm, it was burnin' up."

Before Betsy could even finish speaking, Anne was through the doorway. She didn't even realize she had knocked the tray from the girl's hands until she heard it clatter to the floor behind her.

Anne yanked back the bed curtains of Lord Dravenwood's bed to find him caught in the grips of a full-blown chill. She touched the back of her hand to his brow. Despite the audible chattering of his teeth, her worst fears were confirmed. He was burning with fever.

His breathing had deepened to a painful rasp. He'd probably inhaled far more of the smoke than he'd realized when rescuing her from the attic, then compounded that insult to his lungs by spending the night in the cold, pouring rain.

Betsy hovered in the doorway, anxiously wringing her apron in her hands and looking nearly as helpless as Anne felt. "What should I do, ma'am? Should I run to the village and fetch someone?"

"Who would you fetch?" Anne asked grimly. "There's no doctor there, and even if there were,

you'd never be able to convince him to come here." She glanced out the window at the gathering shadows, fighting a bitter surge of despair. "Especially not after nightfall."

Eyeing the earl's shivering form, Betsy asked, "Shall I fetch some more blankets, then?"

"No." Shaking away the paralysis of her fear, Anne briskly tore the bed curtains clean from their moorings, then whipped away his down comforter, leaving only the thin sheet draped across his waist. "He doesn't need to be warmed. He needs to be cooled." She marched over to the French windows and swept them open, welcoming in a rush of chill evening air, before returning to the bed. "Go to the kitchen and tell Nana to brew me up a pot of yarrow tea. Then find Lisbeth and Bess and bring me as much cool water as the three of you can carry."

"Should I fetch Dickon to tend to him?"

Anne shook her head, her heart contracting with helpless tenderness as she gazed down upon the earl's violently trembling form. "Not this time. This time I'll be the one tending to him."

Chapter Twenty-eight

Anne did not have to keep her vigil alone. As night melted into day and day into night and one day into another, the other servants took turns finding some excuse to join her at Lord Dravenwood's bedside.

Dickon was there to brace his shoulders while Anne tried to spoon some warm broth between his lips, spilling more of the stuff down his chest than down his throat. Bess and Lisbeth were there to lend their efforts to hers when his delirium deepened and Anne had to throw herself across his chest to keep him from harming himself as he thrashed about, shouting in a language none of them recognized until both his strength and his voice gave out. Lizzie was there to witness Anne's relieved tears at finding him alive after she'd woken from a brief nap in the chair beside his bed to discover him so still and waxen she'd thought he had died while she slept. Beth and Betsy were there to painstakingly arrange the sheets to protect Anne's modesty as she bathed him, her hands tenderly trailing the soapy cloth over the muscled planes of his chest.

On the third day of her vigil, Anne looked up from reading the same passage from *Pilgrim's*

Progress for the tenth time to find Nana hobbling into the room.

Secretly relieved to be rescued from her own Slough of Despond, Anne leapt up from her chair, dislodging a disgruntled Sir Fluffytoes from her lap. She rushed over to assist the old woman, speaking directly into her ear. "Nana! However did you manage the stairs?"

"The same way I been managin' 'em for the last fifty years, girl. By puttin' one foot in front o' the other."

Nana shuffled over to the bed, shaking her head as she gazed down at Lord Dravenwood's prostate form. "There's nothin' worse for a woman than to see such a powerful man laid so low."

"I despise feeling so helpless," Anne confessed, swallowing around the tightness in her throat.

Nana slanted her a chiding look. "Don't give up on him yet, girl. And don't give up on yourself. If there's anythin' you've always excelled at, it's gettin' your own way. I'm guessin' you could still wrap fate 'round your little finger if you set your mind to it."

"At the moment it feels more like fate has its fingers wrapped around my throat." Anne noticed the colorful garment draped over the old woman's arm. "Why, Nana, did you finally finish your . . ." Anne hesitated, at a loss as to what to call the voluminous creation.

"These old knuckles of mine are gettin' too

stiff to work the needles, and half the time I can't see what color I've picked out. Someone might as well get some use out of it while I'm still here to see it." The old woman carefully unfolded her gift and draped it across Lord Dravenwood's chest.

"Oh, Nana, it's beautiful!" Anne breathed. The garment's rainbow of hues did brighten the room considerably, even giving the illusion of color to Dravenwood's pallid cheeks.

"There's a bit o' love woven into every strand." Offering Anne a toothless smile, Nana tenderly stroked the knotted yarn with her gnarled fingers. "Never forget, girl. Love is still the most powerful medicine of all."

"If he dies, the constable will swear we murdered him," Pippa said glumly from her rocking chair on the other side of the bed, peering over the top of her much-read copy of *The Mysteries of Udolpho* at Anne.

Anne leaned forward in her chair to smooth the earl's sweat-dampened hair away from his brow. He had been drifting in and out of delirium for most of the day. "Perhaps we did."

"You mustn't blame yourself. It was his choice to go after Hodges. We didn't force him to play knight in shining armor."

Anne remembered how Dravenwood had told her about saving his brother from a firing squad,

how he had looked after Clarinda when she had fallen ill, his determination to prove Angelica had no part in her own downfall, how he'd charged up the attic stairs to rescue Anne from the fire without giving a thought to his own welfare. "I don't think he had any other choice. He may be loathe to admit it, but I suspect it's the role he was born to play." A rueful laugh escaped her. "He even rescued Dickon from that ridiculous wig." Anne's smile faded, her fingers lingering against the hot, dry skin of his cheek. "He just hasn't figured out yet that he can't save everyone. Perhaps not even himself."

Late that night Anne found herself alone with Dravenwood at last. After watching Pippa nod off into her book not once, but three times, Anne had finally coaxed the girl into going to bed by promising to don a nightdress and curl up on the divan for a nap once she was gone.

Anne had slipped into Dravenwood's dressing room to change into the nightdress and tug the pins from her hair, but instead of curling up on the divan, she had claimed the rocking chair Pippa had vacated and drawn it even closer to the bed.

At some point in the past few days, she had stopped worrying about the impropriety of spending the night in a gentleman's bedchamber, much less spending the night in a gentleman's bedchamber in her nightdress.

She glanced at the French lyre clock on the mantel. It was just after midnight. Even though she knew its voice had been silenced forever, sometimes she still caught herself listening for the hollow bong of the longcase clock in the entrance hall.

Sleep held little attraction for her. Every time she drifted off, she would feel herself slipping beneath the surface of the waves, feel the strangling cords of silk tightening around her ankles, making it impossible for her to kick her way toward freedom. Then she would begin to sink . . . down . . . down . . . down into the darkness of utter oblivion before yanking herself awake with a start.

She couldn't sleep and Dravenwood couldn't seem to wake up. His fever had finally broken, but except for the shallow rise and fall of his chest, he was as still and pale as a carved marble effigy on a tomb. Anne would almost have preferred delirium to this. At least when he was raving and thrashing, she didn't have to touch her ear to his lips just to hear the whisper of his breathing.

If he didn't survive, she would have to gather pen and paper and write to inform his parents of his death.

Would they mourn the man he had been or would his father grieve because he'd lost his precious heir? How long would it take for word to travel across the distant seas to reach his

brother? Would Ashton Burke remember the difficult man Dravenwood had become or would he fondly recall the boys they had once been together—the boys who had played at toy soldiers and fought mock naval battles in the bath? Would Clarinda shed a tear for the man who had loved her so long and so faithfully? Would she regret scorning a loyal heart another woman might have cherished? Would little Charlotte even remember her "Unca Max," the man who had scooped her up in his big, strong arms and held her so tenderly, no doubt thinking that she might have been his if circumstances had been different?

Anne hugged her woolen shawl tighter around her shoulders. None of Nana's medicinal teas or poultices seemed to be working. They hadn't been able to get so much as a drop of broth down his throat since dawn. All she could do was bathe him, shave his jaw, keep his sheets fresh, gently polish his teeth with her own tooth powder, and accept that he was probably never going to wake up. She would never again see his brow furrow in one of his infuriating scowls or hear him snap out some order she had no intention of obeying.

His face blurred before her eyes as she caught his hand in a fierce grip. "Damn you, Dravenwood! You survived cholera in Burma, a sandstorm in the Tunisian desert, and a broken heart! How dare you let a little rain finish you off? If you're planning on dying just so you can spend eternity

flitting hand in hand around the manor with your precious Angelica, then you're wasting your last breath. She won't have you! I'll see to it!"

The irony wasn't wasted on Anne. If he died, she would be the one haunted until her dying day. She would be the one who would awaken in the middle of the night, aching for a touch she would never know, craving a kiss she would never taste again.

Still clutching his hand in both of hers, she glared at him through her tears. "Pippa was right, you know. You're probably just doing this out of spite. If you die, they'll swear I murdered you. Is that what you want, you stubborn, arrogant fool? Do you want me to hang because you were so foolhardy as to rush out in the storm after I tried to warn you it could kill you?" Her voice broke on a raw sob. She doubled over and buried her brow against their entwined hands, watering his flesh with her tears.

She was so distraught it took her several seconds to feel the hand gently skimming over her unbound hair. Trembling with disbelief, she slowly lifted her head.

Dravenwood was looking right at her, his eyes alight with a tender regard that stole the breath right out of her throat. "There you are, angel," he said, disuse deepening the husky note in his voice. A half smile curved one corner of his mouth. "I always knew you'd come back to me."

Chapter Twenty-nine

Anne gazed into Dravenwood's eyes, mesmerized by their crystalline clarity. It was as if he was seeing her—*truly* seeing her—for the first time. His regard was like the most rare and costly of gifts, giving her back something she had believed to be forever lost.

Herself.

He slid his hand through her hair, his fingers toying with the velvety locks, then curled his palm around her nape and gently drew her mouth down to his. His fever might have faded, but he was probably still under the sway of his illness. He couldn't possibly be thinking clearly, if at all. Anne knew she should pull away, should ease him back to the bed and urge him to rest, but she had neither the will nor the desire to resist him. As he tenderly molded her lips to his, she breathed in his breath as if it held her only chance of survival after being submerged beneath the water for a lifetime. His breath was no longer scented of sickness, but of peppermint and hope.

She felt her shawl skitter from her shoulders to the floor, but didn't care. She was too lost in the tantalizing flick of his tongue against hers as he

breached the seam of her lips and tenderly ravished her mouth.

When her tongue responded with a bold foray of its own, he wrapped both of his arms around her, groaning deep in his throat. This was no groan of pain but of a pleasure sharper and more dangerous than pain.

The two of them might never meet on a ballroom floor to share a waltz, but he swept her into his bed in a dizzying turn until she was lying beneath him. Even as his mouth continued to work its dark and delicious wonders, one of his hands slid down her side, lingering ever so briefly against the fullness of her breast before tracing the graceful dip of her waist, the flare of her hip, then slipping beneath her thigh to lift one leg so he could wedge himself in the cradle of her hips.

Anne gasped, her hips arching off the bed of their own accord to embrace the evidence of his desire. There was no cure for this delirium. The fever was contagious and had infected them both. She could feel its flames licking higher as his hand slid around and up the silken skin of her thigh, easing her nightdress up with it.

The cold, distant man she had once believed him to be had vanished, leaving a hot-blooded stranger in his place. There was no time for thought. No time for caution. No time for regrets. There was only the warmth of his tongue stroking the velvety recesses of her mouth in a rhythm

that was unmistakably and irresistibly carnal. The heat of his hand as he slid it to the side and pressed its heel against the tender mound between her thighs, urging her to ride him to some extraordinary place where pleasure was not only possible but inevitable.

A shuddering sigh trembled on her lips as his fingers followed the path his palm had forged. She buried her face against his shoulder to hide her burning cheeks as his long, elegantly tapered fingers slid through the softness of her nether curls and began to have their way with the silky flesh they found beneath—stroking, gliding, caressing until her sighs turned into breathless, little gasps. When the callused pad of his thumb brushed the throbbing little bud at the crux of those curls, her womb responded with a shiver of delight and a pulse of pure liquid pleasure that made her ache to clench her thighs together.

But his hand was still there, urging them apart, urging her to cede dominion of all that she was—all that she would ever be—to his desperate hunger. Even then, he was not content to simply seize the prize he had won. He continued to toy with her, each deft flick of his nimble fingertips threatening to incinerate her in a consuming fire.

"You came to me, angel," he whispered hoarsely, the scorching heat of his lips tracing the column of her throat until they settled against

the pulse beating wildly beneath her skin. "Now come for me."

He was her master. She had no choice but to obey his command.

The waves of pleasure broke over her in a blinding torrent. But instead of dragging her down as she had feared, they sent her shooting up out of the darkness and into the light.

Anne was still quaking with delectable little aftershocks when he covered her again. She clung to his shoulders, torn between drawing him closer and pushing him away. He suddenly seemed very large, very overpowering, very . . . male.

His mouth closed over hers once more, sampling the honeyed sweetness of her lips with a tender ferocity that soothed her panic, gave her the courage to open her thighs for him when he sought to nudge them apart with his knee. She felt the heavy weight of his arousal settle against the part of her still throbbing from his touch. He rubbed himself in the creamy pearls of nectar he'd coaxed from her melting core, then entered her with one long, smooth stroke, sheathing his rigid length deep within her.

Rent asunder by both the agony and the wonder of it all, Anne dug her fingernails into his back and sank her teeth into his shoulder to muffle a helpless wail. She had been foolish enough to believe she had known passion before, but that had been only a pale shadow compared to this, a

frivolous little ghost of pleasures to come. A guttural groan tore from Dravenwood's throat as he rocked hard against her, deepening both the pace and the intensity of his thrusts until her wordless pleas swelled into shuddering moans she could no longer contain.

Still he did not relent, making it clear he wouldn't be satisfied until those delicious shivers of ecstasy began to wrack her womb once again. The second they did, he stiffened and surged within her, an even deeper groan tearing from his throat as he was swept away by the same relentless tide of rapture he had sent spilling through her.

Anne's eyes fluttered open to find the misty light of dawn breaking through the French windows of Dravenwood's bedchamber. She sighed, her limbs weighted with a delicious languor that made her feel as if she had somehow melted during the night, then been reformed into something finer. Unlike Pippa, who whined and groaned and buried her head beneath the pillow when required to rise before ten o'clock, Anne had always been a cheerful riser. She would bound out of bed and dress quickly, eager to face the challenges of the day. But on this day, she would have been perfectly content to lie abed until noon, her every muscle a little sore, but still tingling with satisfaction.

She stretched with all of the languid grace of Sir Fluffytoes as she rolled over to seek the source of that satisfaction.

Dravenwood was lying on his back, one muscular forearm flung over his head. She sat up on one elbow to study his rugged chest and beautifully sculpted profile at her leisure. He looked so incredibly peaceful.

Her eyes widened in alarm. Dear Lord, what if his heart had been too weak to withstand their exertions? What if she had inadvertently finished him off?

She touched a hand to his chest. She could feel it rise and fall with each even breath, could count each steady beat of his heart beneath her palm.

She collapsed back on the pillow, grateful tears springing to her eyes.

Love is still the most powerful medicine of all.

As Nana's voice echoed through Anne's mind, a smile touched her lips. She had somehow accomplished what all of the poultices and medicinal teas had failed to do—she had saved him.

She was still feeling rather pleased with herself when he reached over without opening his eyes and drew her into his arms. She settled against him, her back pressed to his broad chest. When she felt his arousal nudging the softness of her rump, she couldn't resist giving her hips a taunting little wiggle. His immediate response

made her grin. Yes, he was most definitely showing signs of life.

He tugged her even closer, his possessive embrace making her feel warm and safe and cherished for the first time in a very long while.

"Maximillian," she murmured, savoring the taste of his name on her lips.

A husky groan escaped him. "Hmmm . . . my angel . . . my sweet . . . my Angelica . . ."

Chapter Thirty

Anne froze, glaring blindly at the French windows. One of Dravenwood's hands closed around the softness of her breast, gently squeezing. Anne hesitated a moment, then reached down and flung his hand off her. As she struggled out of his embrace, he grunted in protest, then rolled to his opposite side and began gently snoring.

Anne slid out of the bed and snatched her discarded nightdress from the floor, determined to make her escape before he could discover he had taken the wrong woman to bed.

When Anne came marching across the gallery a short while later, bathed, dressed, and starched to within an inch of her life, Angelica was lying in

wait for her on the landing. Anne was determined to ignore her, but as she started down the stairs to the entrance hall, she could feel the legendary beauty's taunting gaze boring into her back.

She swung around, pointing an accusing finger at the portrait. "If you don't stop smirking at me like that, you conceited cow, I'm going to draw a pair of mustaches, some bushy eyebrows, and a wart or two on your disgustingly perfect nose. And then we'll see just how fetching your precious Lord Dravenwood finds you!"

Angelica continued to gaze down her disgustingly perfect nose at Anne, her amusement at Anne's expense undaunted by the threat.

From the entrance hall below came the sound of someone clearing his or her throat. Anne jerked around to find Pippa standing at the bottom of the stairs.

The girl was eyeing Anne cautiously, the same way they all tended to eye Hodges whenever they caught him jousting with the chickens or scampering through the gardens at twilight trying to catch a gnome. "Just who were you talking to?"

"No one," Anne snapped, casting Angelica one last baleful look before descending the rest of the stairs at a brisk clip. "No one at all."

Max awoke to find himself alone for the first time in days. He struggled to sit up. His head spun and his stiff muscles throbbed in protest,

forcing him to flop back to the pillows with a groan. He lay gazing up at the canopy, waiting for his muzzy head to clear.

Despite his lingering weakness, he was flooded with an undeniable sense of well-being. For as long as he could remember, he had felt as if he were suffering from some ravening hunger that made him snarl and snap at everyone around him. But now he felt deliciously sated, like a giant jungle cat that had just devoured a nice juicy gazelle.

Closing his eyes, he lifted his balled fists above his head and stretched, his rusty muscles rippling with exhilaration. He'd never felt quite so happy just to be alive. Ironic considering his last visitor had been a ghost. His eyes flew open, his memory honing in on the source of his satisfaction.

Angelica.

She had come to him in a dream, just as she had before. Only this time when he had reached for her, she had melted into his arms instead of back into the night.

Max sat up, his confusion growing. Pale, early-afternoon sunlight streamed through the French windows, shining on the empty rocking chair that had been drawn up to the very edge of the bed.

He would almost swear the woman in his arms last night hadn't been a vapor of mist, but flesh and blood. She had been warm and responsive, her mouth a living flame beneath his. Surely no hallucination could be *that* vivid.

He raked a hand through his tousled hair, scouring the blurred edges of his memory. If he concentrated hard, he could almost hear a voice gently coaxing him to part his parched lips so the cool metal of a spoon could be slipped between them. Could feel the scrape of a straight razor wielded by steady fingers against the bristles of his beard. Could feel a cool hand on his brow, gently testing the temperature of his fevered flesh.

He could see a woman bending over him, her skin as fine and pale as alabaster, exhaustion shadowing her hazel eyes. Her hair had escaped its unraveling chignon to hang in limp strands around her worried face. A face that suddenly came into focus with brutal clarity.

It was the face of his housekeeper, Mrs. Spencer.

Not Angelica, but Anne.

A wave of horror washed over him. Dear God, what had he done? Had he dragged the woman into his bed and forced himself upon her in his delirium?

That scenario didn't fit the tantalizing glimpses stealing through his memory—the softness of her lips flowering beneath his to welcome his kiss; the trusting warmth of her hand twining through his hair to caress his nape; the enticing way her hips had arched off the bed in an invitation no man could resist; the throaty little cry she had tried to bury in his throat when his fingertips had coaxed her over the precipice of pleasure into ecstasy.

As the memories came flooding back one by one, Max could feel himself growing hard all over again. He swore beneath his breath.

There was only one way to prove the *memories* were nothing but the ravings of his feverish brain. He would seek out his housekeeper and no doubt find her calmly going about her duties, proving nothing untoward had transpired between them.

He had no intention of ever telling her about his lurid fantasies. If he did, she would probably either recoil in horror, slap him silly, or laugh in his face.

Max slid out of the bed, taking the comforter with him to wrap around his waist just in case anyone should come barging into the bedchamber before he could reach his dressing room. When the blanket's hem snagged on the edge of the bedpost, he turned around to give it a yank.

That was when he saw the rusty stains marring the silk sheets.

Max gazed down at them, his disbelief slowly hardening into certainty. He had been right all along. The woman who had spent the night in his arms and his bed had not been a vapor of mist. She had been flesh.

And blood.

When Max descended the stairs that afternoon, no tantalizing aroma of baking bread greeted him.

Lisbeth, however, was passing through the

entrance hall, feather duster in hand. "M'lord!" she exclaimed, a snaggletoothed smile lighting up her freckled face. "So glad to see you up and about. Mrs. Spencer told us your fever had finally broken."

"Oh, she did, did she?" He supposed the deceitful woman hadn't bothered to tell them it had been replaced by another sort of fever altogether.

"She said you'd had a *very* hard night and we were to let you sleep as late as you wanted." Lisbeth frowned at the heap of bedclothes in his arms. "There was no need for you to strip the bed, m'lord. All you had to do was ring. One of us Elizabeths would have run right up to fetch the sheets for the laundry."

"I don't want them laundered. I want them burned. We need to make sure no one else in the household falls ill."

"I don't believe what you had was catchin', m'lord. Why, none of us has had so much as a sniffle!"

"You can never be too careful about that sort of thing." He loomed over her. "Carelessness can cost lives. Just look at what happened to poor Mr. Spencer."

Clearly alarmed by his ominous leer, she backed up a step before reluctantly reaching for the sheets. "Very well, m'lord. I'll see that they're burned."

Max yanked them out of her reach. "I'd prefer to see to it myself. Unless, of course, Hodges is

available. I've heard he excels at that sort of thing." Without another word, Max went striding toward the kitchen, leaving Lisbeth gaping after him and no doubt wondering if the fever had boiled his brain.

Max's determination to confront his housekeeper right away was doomed to be thwarted. Everyone he questioned insisted she was in a different location.

Pippa and Dickon were convinced they'd seen her heading for the chicken coop to gather some fresh eggs, while Nana swore Anne was in the drawing room helping Bess swab the remaining soot from the ceiling. Bess claimed she had spotted the housekeeper from the drawing-room window just a short while ago "thtrolling toward the orchard with a bathket over her arm." When Max arrived at the orchard, his muscles screaming from the effort after so many days spent languishing in bed, he found Beth and Betsy halfway up an apple tree with their skirts tied up to their knees, but no Mrs. Spencer. Lizzie informed him Anne was last seen in the dining room helping Hodges polish the silver. Hodges insisted she was in London having tea with the king.

Max would have suspected them all of deliberately trying to confound him if their own bewilderment hadn't been so convincing.

As the afternoon melted away and his house-

keeper continued to stay one step ahead of him, Max's frustration deepened to anger. He was as angry with himself as he was with her. After Clarinda had left him, he had sworn he would never allow himself to feel this way again. Would never abandon reason for the madness that only love—or lust—could inflict.

Growing weary of the chase, he finally retreated to his study, leaving explicit instructions that Mrs. Spencer was to report to him the very *instant* she was spotted by one of the others. The infernal woman couldn't elude him forever.

He was rewarded for his persistence by a crisp rap on the door just after sunset.

"Enter," he commanded, caught off guard by the heavy thud of his heart. Perhaps he'd overtaxed himself with his exertions. Perhaps he was on the verge of a relapse. Or death.

The door slipped open and Mrs. Spencer came gliding into the room. Max wasn't sure what he had expected from her—an accusing glare or tearful recriminations perhaps? But she looked as calm and unruffled as she had on the night he'd arrived at Cadgwyck Manor.

Except for her snowy-white apron and that provocative bit of lace at her throat, she was garbed in black from throat to toe. Her hair was sleeked back from her face and confined to its usual net. Her lips were pursed as if they'd never softened beneath a man's kiss. Her

expression couldn't have been any more bland.

Max scowled, finding her cool aplomb some-how more infuriating than a foot-stomping tantrum might have been. She could have had the common decency to look more . . . well . . . *ravished*.

He wanted to see her with her cheeks flushed and her hair tumbled around her shoulders. He wanted her lips parted and trembling beneath his. He wanted to see some evidence of the pleasure she had found in his arms and the pleasure she had given him. Seeing her look so untouched—and untouchable—only made him want to see what he could do to rectify that situation.

She arched one eyebrow at him. "You sent for me, my lord?"

"Sit." He nodded toward the chair in front of the desk.

As she obeyed, he watched her face carefully for any sign of strain. Was it his imagination or did he detect a faint wince as she settled her pert little bottom in the chair?

"I'm glad to see you looking so well," she said after every fold in her skirt was arranged to her satisfaction. "Would you care to review the household accounts or discuss the repairs to the drawing room?"

Max's mouth fell open. Lisbeth had been wrong. His fever must have been contagious after all. The woman was obviously delirious.

"Oh, I don't know," he drawled. "I thought we might review what happened between the two of us in my bedchamber last night."

She was silent for a gratifying moment. "I was rather hoping you wouldn't remember that."

He didn't bother to hide his incredulity. "Did you truly believe I could forget something like that?"

"I must confess the thought did cross my mind." She leaned forward in the chair, studying him intently. "Just how much *do* you remember?"

Leaning back in his chair, he propped his ankle on the opposite knee and met her gaze squarely. *"Everything."*

Every kiss. Every caress. The sharp dig of her fingernails into his back as he had slid deep within her and made her his own.

Her slender throat bobbed as she swallowed. He had finally succeeded in ruffling her composure. "I hope you don't think I intend to blame you for what transpired between us. You'd been half out of your head with fever for days."

"Only half?" he said drily.

She blinked at him. "What are you implying, my lord? That a man would have to be completely out of his head to take me to his bed?"

"No, Mrs. Spencer, you know damn well that is *not* what I was implying!" He surged to his feet and paced over to the window. He gazed out into the deepening shadows of twilight, struggling to

gain control over his temper. "You'll have to forgive me. This is all new to me. I'm not in the habit of debauching the help."

"That's fortunate. Nana will be ever so relieved."

Max swung around to give her a reproachful glare. "Yes, do assure the Elizabeths it should still be safe to bend over to scoop the ashes from the hearth if I'm anywhere in the vicinity. I'll try to resist the temptation to toss their skirts up over their heads and have my way with them."

A becoming blush crept into her cheeks. "I fear you're making far too much of this. You're a man. I'm a woman. We've probably both suffered more than our share of loneliness in recent years." She shrugged, lowering her gaze to her lap. "Was it any wonder that we reached out to each other during a difficult time? You needn't trouble yourself any further, my lord. As far as I'm concerned, last night never happened."

While most men might have been relieved, Max was shocked to discover that was the one thing he would not allow. He leaned against the windowsill, folding his arms over his chest. "Perhaps you're right, Mrs. Spencer. After all, you are a widow. I'm sure you were accustomed to welcoming your husband's attentions with equal . . . enthusiasm." She yanked up her head to stare at him. "Why, one might even consider your Mr. Spencer a lucky man were it not for his being crushed to death in such an untimely manner

by . . . what was it again?" Max tapped his lips with his forefinger. "A runaway team of horses?"

"A wagon," she bit off, giving him a stony look. "He was crushed by a wagon."

"Every gentleman in London knows there's very little challenge involved in tumbling a widow into his bed. He doesn't have to squander his time or effort on all of that tiresome wooing —the compliments, the flowers, the endless round of balls and operas and rides through Hyde Park." He sighed, as if savoring some particularly salacious memory. "Widows are always so eager to please . . . and almost pathetically grateful for any scrap of male attention. Why, I remember hearing about the widow of a certain Lord Langley who could do the most extraordinary trick with her tongue—"

Anne surged to her feet, her blush replaced by a flush of anger. "I'll have you know I am neither eager to please nor pathetically grateful!"

"Nor are you a widow, Mrs. Spencer," he thundered. "Or should I say *Miss* Spencer."

She paled. "How did you know?"

"Let's just say you left behind certain . . . clues."

"Oh, God . . . the sheets," she whispered, realization dawning in her eyes. "I was in such a hurry to make my escape, I forgot all about the sheets. If one of the maids sees them . . . or Dickon!" She started for the door.

"There's no need," he said quietly. "I've already destroyed them."

She collapsed with her back against the door, eyeing him with grudging admiration. "A gentleman to the bitter end, aren't you?"

"One wouldn't know it from my behavior last night." He tilted his head to study her. "So why did you lie to me? Why have you been pretending to be a widow for all these years?"

"I don't expect a man of your rank and privilege to understand. It's difficult enough for a woman to find employment in a reputable household, but it becomes nearly impossible when everyone around her equates being unmarried with weakness and inexperience."

He leveled a mocking look at her. "Ah, yes, and you are a woman of *vast* experience."

"I learned very quickly that most ladies aren't willing to hire a young, unmarried woman to manage their households. They're too afraid their husbands might . . ." She trailed off, lowering her eyes.

"Do precisely what I did last night?" He took a few steps toward her, unable to help himself. "Did it not occur to you that had I known you'd never been . . . married, I might have at least shown you more consideration?"

"Married?" Her rueful little laugh mocked them both. "You didn't even know I was alive. You called me Angelica."

Max winced. Apparently, he hadn't remembered everything about last night after all.

"Don't be so hard on yourself, my lord. At least you didn't call me Clarinda."

Max was surprised by how little her gibe stung. Loving and losing Clarinda was no longer a searing wound in his heart, but a bittersweet ache that was already fading.

Retreating behind the desk, he sank back into his chair. He'd successfully negotiated treaties between countries that had been warring for centuries, yet this one hardheaded woman continued to confound him. "It was one thing to steal a kiss. Quite another to rob you of your innocence. If you don't wish to remain in my employ after my deplorable behavior toward you, I wouldn't blame you. If you choose to go, I'll make sure you receive the compensation you're due." He watched her face, holding his breath without realizing it.

"And what's the going rate for that sort of thing?"

He felt himself color. "That's not what I meant! I meant that you were deserving of a handsome severance sum. With my name and connections, I could secure a position for you in one of the most desirable households in all of England. You'd be free of this accursed place forever."

She lifted her chin. Max would almost have

sworn he saw a faint quiver in it. "Cadgwyck is my home."

Max nodded, feeling a curious kinship with her. The rattletrap, old manor had somehow become his home, too. "Then I suppose there's no help for it, is there?"

"For what?"

"If you won't let me atone for my sins by sending you away, then you'll simply have to stay and punish me for them."

"Punish you? How?"

"By agreeing to become my wife."

Chapter Thirty-one

"Your wife?" Anne croaked. If she hadn't had the door to support her, she might well have slid to the floor in a heap of skirts. "You'll have to forgive me, my lord. I was under the mistaken impression that you had recovered from your fever. I'll ring for Dickon at once so he can help you back to bed."

Dravenwood gave her a chiding look. "I don't mind if you make me grovel a bit just to placate your pride, but you should know I've no intention of squandering nine years of my life wooing you."

"You can't possibly marry me! Why would you even suggest such a ridiculous thing?"

350

"It's what a gentleman does when he compromises a lady," he patiently explained. "And as you just pointed out, I am a gentleman to the bitter end."

"But I'm no lady! I'm . . . well . . . I'm your inferior!"

Dravenwood rose to his feet, looking as dangerous as she had ever seen him. "You are inferior to no man. Or woman, for that matter."

"But . . . but you can't just take your housekeeper and make her your countess. Why, you'd be the laughingstock of all society!"

"It wouldn't be the first time, now would it? Do you honestly believe their scornful glances and cruel gibes have any power left to hurt me?"

"It's not just society who would scorn you. You have your family to consider as well."

Instead of looking alarmed, he looked rather delighted by the prospect. "When I offered for Clarinda, my father threw an enormous tantrum and my mother took to her bed for a fortnight. And all because Clarinda's father was a 'commoner' who had made his considerable fortune in trade. Can you imagine what they'll say when I write to tell them I'm marrying my housekeeper? Why, they might even go so far as to disinherit me and drag Ash back from his adventures to take my place!" His smile deepened into a bloodthirsty grin that made him look more like a pirate than an earl. "Perhaps we should travel to London and

give them the news in person. It would almost be worth it just to see the look on their faces."

Despite all of her noble intentions, Anne's heart had begun to lurch with reckless hope. But his words dashed that hope. She could never travel to London. She could never become his countess. She could never be his wife.

"I'm sorry, my lord," she said softly. "I appreciate your single-minded devotion to propriety, but I'm afraid I shall have to refuse your offer."

He scowled, pondering her words. "Then it's not an offer. It's an order."

She gaped at him in disbelief. "Why, of all the high-handed, arrogant, presumptuous . . ." She briefly sputtered into incoherence before blurting out, "You can't just order me to marry you!"

"And why not? You're still in my employ, aren't you? I can order you to serve fresh pheasant for supper or bring me a cup of tea. Why can't I order you to marry me?"

"Because I have no intention of continuing to work for a madman. I quit!"

"Marvelous. Now that you're no longer my housekeeper, we'll be free to marry."

Anne threw up her hands with a strangled little shriek of frustration.

He came around the desk, the coaxing look in his eye far more dangerous to her resolve than his bullying. "The two of us aren't so different, are we? We're both bound by duty and the

expectations of others. There's no need for you to spend the rest of your life attending to the needs of others until you're as stiff and dried-up as you're pretending to be." Her mouth fell open in outrage, but before she could speak, he continued, "As for me, I have no choice but to marry someday to provide an heir to carry on the family line. And I'd already made up my mind I'd never be foolish enough to do it for love."

Hoping to hide the fresh blow his words dealt her heart, Anne said crisply, "I'm so glad you decided to spare me the tiresome wooing."

"All I'm saying is that in my world men and women marry for convenience every day. There's no reason you and I can't do the same."

"It won't work. We don't suit."

"Are you so sure about that? From what I do recall about last night, we seemed to suit very well." The silky note in his voice deepened, sending a reckless little shiver through her womb. "If we marry, we can do that whenever we like, you know. It's not only legal and condoned by the church, but encouraged."

Anne had once heard that when a person was drowning, the person's entire past could flash before his or her eyes. But in that moment, as she felt herself bobbing beneath the waves of his persistence, it was her future that flashed before hers: waking in the warmth of his arms on a chill winter morning, her cheek laid against the crisp

fur of his chest; watching him heft their daughter in the air just as he had hefted little Charlotte, twirling her about until she collapsed in helpless giggles; seeing the silvery frost at his temples slowly melt through his sooty locks; spending the years softening all of his scowls into smiles until their children's children danced around them, making the halls of Cadgwyck ring once more with the music of love and laughter and hope.

But it was a future that could never be. She'd surrendered her future in the same moment she'd surrendered her past.

"You make a compelling case," she said. "But I'll need some time to consider your . . . proposition."

"I believe I can afford to grant you that much."

She straightened, smoothing her apron and donning Mrs. Spencer's bland mask. "Will that be all, my lord?"

He scowled. "No, Mrs. . . . *Miss* Spencer. I don't believe it will." She stood frozen in place as he came sauntering toward her, a predatory glint in his eye.

Her mask slipped as he framed her face in his hands and brought his mouth down on hers. This was a kiss no woman could resist. He crushed his mouth against hers, the harsh demand of his lips tempered by the sweeping mastery of his tongue. He raked his fingers through her hair, loosening the silky tendrils from their net until

354

they tumbled around her face in wild disarray. By the time he stepped away from her, she was limp and breathless and aching with want. Her cheeks were flushed with heat and her lips were parted and trembling in anticipation of another kiss.

He surveyed her, his satisfaction with what he saw evident. "*That* will be all. For now." His passion-darkened eyes and roguish grin promised her his kiss was only a taste of the delights to come should she be sensible enough to accept his suit.

Angelica Cadgwyck stood over Maximillian Burke's bed. It wasn't the first time she had slipped into his chamber just to watch him sleep. But it would be the last.

Moonlight drifted through the open French doors, bathing his handsome features in its silvery glow. His lips were slightly parted, the stern lines of his face relaxed in boyish repose. The sheet had slipped down to his hip bones, exposing the impressive expanse of his chest and the chiseled planes of his abdomen. She had always found it fascinating that despite his fondness for propriety, he didn't sleep in a nightshirt or nightcap like other men, but was content to wrap himself in nothing more substantial than a moonbeam.

He was a greater mystery to her than she would ever be to him. She was still searching for clues as to what manner of man he might have become

had he not been prone to such hopeless affairs of the heart.

If the two of them had met at a ball in some other lifetime, would he have asked her to dance? Would he have scrawled his name on her dance card and waltzed her out the nearest terrace door into the moonlight so he could steal a kiss? Would he have wooed her with pretty words and bouquets of roses and trips to the opera and rides in Hyde Park?

She had promised herself she wouldn't touch him this time. But the rebellious lock of hair that persisted in tumbling over his brow posed too great a temptation. She reached to gently brush it back, her fingertips grazing the satiny warmth of his skin.

He stirred. She froze. What would she do if he reached for her? Would she be able to resist him if he sought to tug her into his bed and into his arms? After a moment, he simply nestled deeper into the pillow, murmuring a name in his sleep— a plain name that sounded like a sigh on his lips. A name that sent a wistful lance of yearning through her heart.

Not *Angelica,* but *Anne.*

It seemed his destiny would always lie in loving the right woman at the wrong time.

She withdrew her hand, holding it up to the moonlight. She could already feel herself fading. For all these years she had been nothing but a

shadow, flitting through the corridors of life. But then he had come along and done everything in his considerable power to give her substance again.

She couldn't afford to let that happen. A ghost couldn't be hurt by the sharp edges of life. A ghost couldn't bleed from a broken heart or dream a dream that could never come true.

A ghost couldn't fall in love.

She pressed a tender kiss to his brow, then turned away from him and drifted across the room. She cast one last longing look over her shoulder at the bed before melting back into the wall and the past.

Max awoke enveloped in the sultry scent of jasmine. He sat up abruptly, his nostrils flaring. His heart was pounding wildly in his chest, but he couldn't remember what he had been dreaming. For some reason, that deeply disturbed him. He didn't want to go back to being the man he had been before he came to this place—a man who didn't dream at all.

Whatever he had been dreaming, it had left him with a nearly inconsolable sense of loss. This was different from what he had felt when Clarinda had tossed him over—deeper and more piercing to the heart. It was as if something had gone terribly awry that could never be put right again. He'd had the exact same feeling when he

had ruffled through the blank pages at the end of Angelica Cadgwyck's journal.

He glanced at the empty bed beside him, surprised by how fiercely he wanted to find Anne there, wrapped up in those rumpled sheets. He wanted to pull her into his arms just as he had last night and bury his doubts and fears in the lush sweetness of her warm and willing body.

The ethereal aroma of the jasmine hadn't dissipated along with his dream, but had only gotten sweeter and more overpowering. He slowly turned to find the French windows standing wide open, just as they had been on his first night at Cadgwyck. He was no more able to resist their invitation now than he had been then.

He tossed back the blankets and reached for his dressing gown in the same motion, compelled by a peculiar sense of destiny. It was almost as if his every choice since coming to Cadgwyck had somehow brought him to this moment.

Slipping into the dressing gown, he padded across the room and out onto the balcony. Lacy tatters of clouds drifted across a luminous opal of a moon. He closed his hands over the cool iron of the balustrade, his gaze instinctively seeking the tower on the far side of the manor.

At first glance the tower appeared to be shrouded in shadows, the blank eyes of its windows still jealously guarding its secrets. But when Max squinted against the darkness, he saw

something else—a faint glimmer that could have been a trick of the moonlight . . . or the flickering flame of a single candle, the exact sort of beacon a man might light to guide the girl he was seeking to seduce to a secret rendezvous.

Although it still made the tiny hairs on his nape prickle, Max wasn't even startled when the first tinkling notes from the music box came wafting across the courtyard to his ears.

Perhaps he had always known the night would come when Angelica Cadgwyck would be ready to dance with him again.

Chapter Thirty-two

Max could still remember the weight of the silver music box in his hands, the way its wistful notes had tugged at his heart like the echo of a waltz danced in the arms of a phantom lover. It could have been his imagination, but on this night the notes sounded even more off-key than usual, giving their song a sinister cast.

He already knew what would come next. But this time he wasn't going to allow himself to be seduced by that tantalizing ripple of feminine laughter. He wouldn't be lured into the darkness by a promise that could never be fulfilled. He'd had his fill of chasing ghosts. He was ready to

trust his heart to the hands of a warm, living woman—one strong and sensible enough to keep all of his ghosts at bay, even the ones he'd created himself.

He straightened, loosening his hands from the balustrade. "I'm sorry, sweetheart," he whispered. "I would have saved you if I could have."

The music abruptly stopped.

He was turning away from the balcony railing when a woman's scream, ripe with anguish, tore through the night, followed by the sharp report of a single gunshot.

Haunted by that heart-wrenching scream, Max raced across the second-floor gallery, dragging on his shirt as he ran. He rounded the landing and headed down the stairs without sparing Angelica's portrait a single glance.

Unwilling to waste precious minutes crashing his way through the darkened house, he wrenched open the front door and went pelting across the weed-choked flagstones of the courtyard. Except for the wispy clouds and a misty scattering of stars, the sky was clear. On this night there could be no mistaking a crack of thunder for the report of a pistol.

The tower loomed up out of the darkness. Max had to circle it twice before he finally located an outer door. At first he feared it was bolted, but when he set his shoulder to it and shoved with all

of his might, it gave way with a full-throated groan of protest. He found himself on the first floor. Shafts of moonlight pierced the arrow slits, illuminating the winding steps leading up to the top floor.

As he started up the stairs, he could hear Anne's brisk, no-nonsense voice warning him away from this place: *The stairs are crumbling and are quite dangerous to anyone not familiar with them.*

He hadn't taken the time to yank on his boots, but he was moving too fast to feel the bite of the crumbling stone beneath his bare feet. Centuries ago he might have had a sword in his hand as he made the dizzying charge up the stairs to storm the keep. Now he had nothing but his wits and the instinctive urge to help whoever had let out that terrible cry.

The iron-banded door at the top of the stairs was closed, a flickering ribbon of light visible beneath it. Max's steps slowed. What if he was running straight into some sort of ambush? What if his suspicions were founded after all and someone in this house wanted him dead? What if someone was waiting on the other side of that door with a pistol that had not yet been fired?

His mouth set in a grim line, he shoved open the door, sending it crashing against the opposite wall.

This time there was no egret to greet him. The tower was deserted. As he padded across the

room, the vacant eyes of Angelica's dolls watched him from their shelf.

A single candle was burning in a silver candlestick on the edge of the dressing table, its dancing flame casting a warm glow over the tower. In that forgiving light it was almost possible to imagine the chamber exactly as it had been on the night Timberlake had died.

The report Max had received from Andrew Murray had brought the events of that night into crisp focus. As Max turned in a slow circle, the room seemed to revolve around him, the present melting into the past. Instead of a brisk autumn wind, he could feel a warm spring breeze drifting through windows that weren't shattered, but propped open, their diamond-paned glass fracturing the candle's glow into a thousand tiny flames. The lace draped over the half-tester's canopy drifted in a snowy-white fall over the shiny brass bed. The keys of the harpsichord weren't cracked and yellow, but white and even. The trailing ivy painted on the freshly whitewashed walls was verdant and green.

Several silk and satin bolsters had been removed from the cream-colored coverlet adorning the bed and piled on the velvet cushions of the window seat. It was a stage set for seduction.

Angelica would have had to wait for the perfect moment to slip away from her own

birthday fete so she could meet Timberlake for their rendezvous. They would have already publicly celebrated the triumph of her portrait's unveiling together—Timberlake basking in the delighted gasps and applause of the guests, Angelica stunned to see herself through his adoring eyes for the first time.

Hearing the ghostly tap of a woman's slippers on the stairs, Max whirled around to face the door.

As she hurried up the winding stairs, Angelica could probably still hear the muted laughter, the clink of champagne glasses, and the music of the string orchestra drifting into the night through the open French windows of the ballroom. She would have appeared in the doorway, breathless from ascending the stairs so fast, the color high in her cheeks, her sherry-colored eyes sparkling with both nerves and anticipation.

Timberlake would have been standing just *there,* Max decided, where the candlelight would show him off to his best advantage. He would have given her that teasing smile she loved so well, his hair gleaming like spun gold. He would have looked so handsome, so dashing—like a young prince who had scaled the walls of her tower to steal a kiss. How could she resist him? How could any woman resist him?

Max closed his eyes, inhaling a phantom breath of jasmine as Angelica rushed right through him and into Timberlake's waiting arms. Had he

wooed her with a private waltz around the tower before claiming the softness of her trembling lips as his prize? How long had it taken for his embrace to become too tight, his kisses too forceful, his groping hands too free? How long before he'd shattered all of her hopes and dreams by shoving her down on the window seat and falling on top of her, his greedy hands tearing at the finery she had chosen just to please him?

Was that when she had screamed? Was that when her brother had come rushing up those stairs and burst into the tower, pistol in hand, and put an end to Timberlake and his wicked schemes forever?

Max opened his eyes. A darkened stain was on the timber floor next to the window seat over-looking the sea—a stain that hadn't been there the last time he had visited the tower.

He crossed the floor and crouched beside it, touching two fingertips to the dark blot to find it still warm and sticky. As he lifted his fingers to his nose and inhaled, there was no mistaking the coppery tang of fresh blood.

He slowly stood, wiping his fingertips on his trousers. A gust of wind soared through the tower, extinguishing both the candle and his glimpse into the past. Moonlight revealed the chamber for the ruin it was. A jagged crack divided the looking glass in two. Rotting lace drifted from the canopy of the half-tester like a shroud for a body that

would never be found. The window seat was a gaping mouth, its rotted wooden teeth lying in wait to devour anyone who ventured too near.

Without the candle to hold the darkness at bay, the night beyond the window came into sharper focus. Max sucked in a harsh breath as he spotted the woman standing on the very tip of the promontory.

He must not have forgotten how to dream after all. Hadn't he seen her just like this once before in his dreams? Standing on the edge of those cliffs with her buttercup-colored skirts billowing around her?

He wanted to shout her name, but he knew she would never hear him over the bullying voice of the wind and the roar of the waves crashing against the cliffs.

Max took off down the stairs at a dead run. He slipped on a crumbling step and almost fell, but didn't slow, not even when he reached the foot of the stairs. He burst out of the tower, emerging from its shadow to find the wind had scattered the clouds, but left the stars hanging like shards of ice against a field of black velvet.

He sprinted through the breezeway and went racing along the edge of the cliffs toward the promontory. He might be dreaming, but the sharp stones tearing at the soles of his feet felt painfully real.

As he drew closer to the promontory, he half-

expected to find it as deserted as the tower. But she was still there, a slender figure standing all alone on the fragile shelf of rock that jutted out over the water.

The White Lady of Cadgwyck.

Moonlight silvered the crests of the waves behind her and limned her in its loving light, making her look less than solid. Max stumbled to a halt, his chest heaving with ragged breaths. He was terrified that if he drew even one step closer to her, he would startle her right over the edge of the cliff. The wind buffeted him with the force of a fist, as if trying to keep them apart.

She slowly turned to look over her shoulder at him, her long, dark hair whipping across her face until all he could see was the wistful regret in her eyes. Then she turned back to the sea, spread her arms as if they were wings, and vanished over the edge of the cliff.

"No!"

The hoarse echo of Max's shout was still ringing in his ears when he lunged forward and went diving over the edge of the cliff after her.

Chapter Thirty-three

Max was sinking.

The darkness enveloped him in its seductive embrace as if it had always been waiting for him. He could hear its sibilant whisper through the roaring in his ears, promising him that all he had to do was close his eyes and open his mouth and he could sleep, never to be troubled by dreams again. He wondered if it was the same voice Angelica had heard all those years ago.

Fighting to resist both the voice and the pressure swelling in his lungs, he kicked frantically toward the undulating orb of the moon. He broke through the surface of the water just in time to catch a salty wave square in the mouth. He coughed and sputtered, then dragged in a desperate breath and dove again, ignoring the painful scrape of thigh against rock as another wave sought to hurl him to his death.

Trying to peer through the murk was futile. Closing his eyes, he raked his arm through the water, seeking any evidence that he was not alone.

That he was not too late.

His groping hands closed on emptiness again and again until he could feel both his breath and his strength begin to flag. It seemed his White

Lady was going to have the last laugh after all. He could almost see Anne rolling her eyes over his foolishness as she was marched before the constable to explain how their latest master had drowned after plunging over the edge of a cliff to rescue a ghost.

Then he felt it—the silky ribbons of a woman's hair drifting through his splayed fingers. He lunged forward, half-afraid his arms were going to close around the rotting bones of a corpse that had been trapped beneath the sea for a decade. But living flesh filled his arms, its squirming softness undeniably feminine.

Triumph coursed through his veins, fueling his determination. He was not going to be too late. Not this time.

Anchoring his arm around his prize, he used the last of his strength on a mighty kick, sending them both shooting toward the surface. They broke through the churning water, gasping for breath. The outgoing tide tried to suck them out to sea, but Max's powerful kicks drove them away from the deadly rocks and toward the gentle curve of the cove, where the surf murmured instead of roared and the sand shimmered like crushed diamonds in the moonlight.

The waves continued to batter them from behind until they washed up on the shore and collapsed in the wet sand, still sputtering and coughing.

Max was too exhausted to protest when his

companion struggled her way out of his arms. She crawled a few feet away from him, then staggered to her feet.

Still panting with exertion, she swung around to glare at him through the strings of sodden hair plastered to her face. "Damn you, Maximillian Burke! *Would you stop rescuing me?*"

Even with its crisp tones softened by fear, it was impossible not to recognize that no-nonsense voice. Max sat up, tossing his wet hair out of his eyes. If he hadn't looked like a beached herring before, he most certainly did now. Especially with his mouth hanging open in shock.

His housekeeper was standing before him, the yellow dress from the portrait clinging to her every luscious curve and revealing *exactly* what she'd been hiding beneath her staid gowns and aprons for all these weeks. Without the restricting net to confine it, her hair hung nearly to her waist. The weight of the water couldn't completely dampen its natural exuberance. It was already beginning to curl into charming little ringlets in the moist sea air.

"You *idiot!*" she shouted. "What in the bloody hell did you think you were doing?"

Rising slowly to his feet to face her, he said evenly, "Don't you think I should be the one asking you what in the bloody hell *you* were doing?"

"Oh, I was just in the mood for a little midnight

swim," she said, sarcasm ripening in her voice.

"Perhaps you should consider swimming in a place where you aren't in danger of being dashed to death on the rocks."

"I know exactly where all the rocks are! You don't! You could have landed on one and cracked your fool skull wide open. Of course as hard as your head is, it probably would have cracked the rock instead! And I wouldn't have been in any danger of being dashed to death on the rocks if I hadn't had to jump back in the water to try and save you."

"If you didn't want me to dive in after you, then just what did you want me to do?" he thundered, his temper mounting along with his confusion.

"I wanted you to go away, you silly, stubborn, dear man," she wailed, tears welling up in her eyes. "I wanted you to be just like all the rest of them and tuck your expensive tailcoat between your legs and go running back to London!"

Max pondered her words for a moment. "If you didn't want to marry me, you could have just said so. There was no need for you to throw yourself over a cliff."

A strangled sound between a sob and a shriek tore from her throat. Still swaying on her feet, she bent to scoop up a gout of wet sand and hurled it at his head.

He dodged it easily. "It was you all along, wasn't it?" he asked, the pieces of the puzzle

finally beginning to click into place. "The mysterious lights, the music box, the ghostly laughter. *You're* the White Lady of Cadgwyck Manor." He drifted across the sand toward her, no more able to resist her now than when she had been standing on the edge of the cliff. "But why, Anne? What would you stand to gain by perpetrating such a dangerous hoax?"

"It wasn't what I stood to gain! It's what I stood to lose!"

Before she could elaborate, Dickon and Pippa came spilling out of the shadows at the base of the cliffs, all five of the Elizabeths fast on their heels. Max stared as they came pelting across the sand toward them, Dickon in the lead. Even if a path had been carved into the rocks, they could not possibly have climbed down the steep face of the cliffs that quickly.

The sea caves, he thought. The ones Dickon had promised to show him before the fire. The coast had been rife with smugglers only a few decades ago. Why should it surprise him to learn the caves were hiding passages leading up to the house? Hell, why should anything he discovered on this night surprise him?

Dickon and the others stumbled to a halt. As Pippa bent over to rest her hands on her knees so she could catch her breath, Dickon jumped into the air, pumping his fist in Max's direction. "I can't believe you're still alive!" The boy flashed

Anne a delighted grin. "You should have seen the way he went flying off that cliff after you. He didn't hesitate for even a heartbeat. It was magnificent!"

"It was insane!" Anne shouted at him before rounding on Max once more. "I was a ghost! I was supposed to already be dead. What was your brilliant plan? To join me?"

"I didn't really have a plan." Max eyed the others through narrowed eyes. "Although obviously the rest of you did. What was your part in all this, lad?" he asked Dickon, hoping to take advantage of the boy's exhilaration to ferret the truth out of him.

Dickon cast Anne a questioning look. When she responded with a weary nod, his grin widened. "It was my job to light the candle and open the music box when Annie gave me the signal."

"And I was the one who provided the scream," Pippa added eagerly, plainly tired of hiding her light beneath a bushel. "Bloodcurdling, wasn't it? I do believe I might have an affinity for the stage. I'm thinking of going to London to tread the boards. I could very well be the next Sarah Siddons!"

Max shifted his darkening gaze to the wide-eyed huddle of Elizabeths. "And you?"

The maids briefly conferred among themselves before nudging Lisbeth forward. Eyeing him shyly, she bobbed an awkward curtsy. "We was

to clean up the tower before you returned, m'lord. You know . . . so you'd think you'd gone all squirrelly in the head and catch the next coach back to London like them others did."

"Why didn't you just throw a sheet over poor Nana's head and make her shuffle up and down the lawn, clanking chains?" Max asked.

"Nana strangled the chicken we used for the blood," Dickon cheerfully offered. "We're having stewed chicken for supper tomorrow, you know."

"Which one of you had the job of sneaking into my bedchamber in the dead of night?" Max suspected he already knew the answer to that question.

"That would be me." Anne folded her arms over her chest, looking decidedly unrepentant. "Your armoire has a false back that leads to a secret passage, one that was once used to hide Cadgwyck's priest when the soldiers of Henry VIII came looking for him. It was a simple enough feat to slip into your bedchamber, open your balcony doors, wave a bottle of perfume around."

Max glared at her, wondering if it had been her on every occasion he had felt Angelica's presence hovering near his bed. "I ought to have the lot of you hauled off to jail. But, unfortunately, I don't think impersonating a dead woman is a hanging offense." He started toward her, trying to figure out how a woman could look like a drowned rat and yet so beguiling all at the same time. "I may

just save the constable the trouble and strangle you myself."

She took a wary step backward, but before he could reach her, another shape came melting out of the cliff face. Max shook his head in disgust. "And I suppose it was *his* job to fire the pistol?"

They all turned to find Hodges crossing the sand in the moonlight, an ivory-plated dueling pistol gripped in his hand.

"No." Dickon's grin faded. "That was my job, too."

"Dickon," Anne said softly.

Heeding her unspoken command, the boy immediately wrapped his arms around Pippa and the maids, shepherding them out of harm's way.

Max rolled his eyes. "I don't know what you're so worried about. The pistol has already been fired."

"They're a matched pair of dueling pistols," Anne murmured calmly, as if a maniac with murder on his mind weren't marching across the sand toward them. "They were both loaded and I have no way of knowing which one he has."

Max lunged forward, determined to put himself between her and the weapon. Before he could succeed, Hodges raised the pistol, his hand surprisingly steady, and pointed it right at Max's chest. Max froze, afraid to make any sudden movements. He might accidentally goad the butler into firing, and if the man's aim was off, he could still easily hit Anne.

Hodges's voice rang with a confidence Max had never before heard. "Step away from her, you scoundrel! Or I'll blow you straight to hell!"

"Put down the pistol, Hodges," Max said gently, inching away from Anne instead of toward her. "Then we can discuss this man-to-man."

"You're no man! A man wouldn't try to force himself on an innocent girl! You're a monster!" Hodges raked back the hammer of the pistol.

"No!" Anne cried, stepping toward him with hand outstretched. "He's not the one who tried to hurt me. He's the one who tried to save me." She forced a tremulous smile, a coaxing note creeping into her voice. "Why, just look at him! He's all wet because he jumped into the water after me! Isn't he such a silly goose?"

Hodges cocked his head, still eyeing Max with open suspicion. "But I would have sworn I heard you scream."

"That was me," Pippa said desperately. "I . . . I saw a spider. A very *large,* very hairy spider."

Hodges's hand had began to waver.

"There now, darling," Anne said soothingly. "Why don't you hand over that nasty pistol and let Dickon take you up to bed? You must be ever so tired."

The butler shook his head. "It's all my fault. I'm the one who brought him here. I won't leave you alone with him. I should have never left you alone with him."

"Hodges!" Max snapped, imbuing his voice with all of the authority at his command. "I'm your master and I order you to give Dickon that pistol! Right now!"

It was almost painful to watch Hodges's shoulders slump, to see his features soften back into a mask of bewilderment. "Aye, my lord," he whispered. "As you wish."

His hand fell to his side, leaving the pistol dangling from his fingertips. As Dickon rushed forward to gently remove it from his grip, Anne closed her eyes, breathing a shuddering sigh of relief.

"You're right," the old man mumbled, reaching up to ruffle his hair. "I'm ever so tired. Not accustomed to staying up so late . . . the ball . . . so many guests to look after . . . such a dreadful fuss . . ."

"Come now, sir," Dickon said, taking him by the elbow. "I'll see you to your bed."

Before Dickon could steer him back toward the caves, Hodges turned to look at Anne. "I'm so glad you decided to wear that gown to the ball. You look absolutely stunning in it. It was your mother's, you know. That's why I wanted you painted in it. She would have been so proud of you."

Anne took a step toward him, her face constricted with some painful emotion. "Do you know who I am?"

"Of course I know who you are." Hodges

beamed at her, all the love in the world shining from his eyes. "You're my darling little girl—my angel . . . my Angelica."

"Dear God," Max breathed as he realized his butler was no butler at all, but mad old Lord Cadgwyck himself.

Anne went to him, then. Cupping his ruddy face in her hands, she touched her lips to his brow, then drew back and whispered, "Good night, Papa."

He gently smoothed her wet hair away from her face, gazing tenderly at her. "There now, don't cry, poppet. You know I can't bear it when you cry. You're my good girl, aren't you? You've always been my good girl. I'm so glad you came back. I've been waiting for ever so long."

He was still beaming at her over his shoulder as Dickon led him away. Avoiding Max's eyes, the others trailed after them, leaving Max and Anne all alone on the beach.

Still standing with her back to him, Anne wrapped her arms around herself, shivering in the cool night air.

Max shook his head, stunned by what he had just witnessed. "That poor devil. No wonder he's so confused. He actually believes you're his daughter. After all this time, who would have ever thought . . ." Max trailed off as she turned to look over her shoulder at him, the beseeching look in her eyes more devastating than a blow.

He should have seen it before. It had been

there, right before his eyes the entire time—in the proud tilt of her head, the sparkle of mischief in her eyes, the mocking smile that always seemed to be poised on her lips even when she wasn't smiling. She might never live up to the absurdly idealized vision of herself in the portrait, but she was beautiful in her own right—even more beautiful in Max's eyes because of the very flaws the artist had chosen to conceal.

He was haunted by his own smug words: *I've always believed every mystery is nothing more than a mathematical equation that can be solved if you find the right variables and apply them in the correct order.* How had he managed to find all of the wrong variables, then applied them in no particular order whatsoever?

As the girl from the portrait and the woman standing before him merged into one, Max sank down on the nearest rock, gazing up at her in speechless wonder.

Chapter Thirty-four

Surprised by how good it felt to finally have substance and form again, Angelica turned to face Max, tossing her wet hair out of her eyes. "You needn't berate yourself for not seeing the resemblance sooner. Laurie's gift was to flatter

his subjects until they were all but unrecognizable, even to themselves. And I am ten years older than when the portrait was painted. I lost my baby fat a long time ago. Of course, in my vainer moments I still like to think I bear some passing resemblance to that spectacular creature. But my hair was never quite that glossy, my nose so perfect, or my cheek so rosy. And Timberlake did insist on painting me with my mouth closed to hide that unsightly gap between my teeth."

"I adore the gap between your teeth," Max growled. "But why? Why on earth would you fake your own death?"

Unable to bear the weight of his searching gaze, Angelica turned toward the sea, watching the moonlight dance across the crests of the waves. "When I stepped off the cliff that night, I had every intention of ending my life. But it seems God, with his infinite wit and wisdom, had other ideas. I missed the rocks entirely, and when the current started to drag me beneath the water and out to sea, I discovered I was just as selfish and strong willed as I'd always been. It wasn't in me to just give up and sink into the sea and meet the tragic end I deserved. So I took a deep breath and struck out for the cove. I had always been a strong swimmer, you see." A faint smile touched her lips as she remembered warmer days, summer idylls with her laughing, freckle-faced brother by her side. "When we were little, Theo and I used

to sneak down through the caves and swim here whenever Papa was otherwise occupied. It took every ounce of strength I had, but I finally managed to haul myself up on this very beach." She turned to look at Max, meeting his fierce gaze with one of her own. "A girl went into the sea that night. A woman came out. A woman who would fight to survive and win back everything she'd lost."

"Anne Spencer," he said softly.

She nodded. "They would have never let Angelica Cadgwyck back into the manor. But with patience and planning, I knew Anne Spencer just might be able to sneak in through the servants' entrance. So I tossed my shawl back into the water, slipped back up to the house through the caves, packed a bag, and ran away."

Max rose to his feet, his face a study in frustration and rage. "I still can't understand why you were driven to such a desperate act. Was there no one to help you?"

"Theo was already on a ship bound for Australia in chains, and they'd come and taken Papa away to the asylum in Falmouth. It was to be my last night in the only home I'd ever known. Papa's solicitor had paid a call earlier in the day. He was kind enough to point out that there might be certain *opportunities* for a young woman of my looks and breeding who was considered to be 'soiled goods.' He even very generously offered

to take me to London himself and set me up in a small apartment he could visit whenever the fancy struck him."

"Give me the man's name," Max said flatly. "I'll see him ruined within the fortnight . . . if I don't kill him first. How in the name of God did you survive after you *died* that night?"

She shrugged away all the years of drudgery and loneliness. "I went into service. I became exactly who I was pretending to be. I learned all there was to know about managing a household so I could come back here someday and mismanage Cadgwyck." A rueful little smile played around her lips. "If Papa had his wits about him, I've often thought how it would have made him laugh to imagine his pampered little princess changing linens and scrubbing baseboards."

Max didn't look the least bit amused. "Why come back to this place at all? Why take such a risk? Is it because Cadgwyck was your home?"

She lifted her gaze to the top of the cliffs, where the uneven roofline and crumbling chimneys of the manor were just barely visible. "My home and my prison. There have been days when I think I'd like nothing more than to set a match to it myself and watch it burn." She drew closer to him, desperate to make him understand. "But from the time Theo and I were very small children, Papa told us tales of a mysterious and fantastic treasure that had been brought back from

381

Jerusalem by one of our ancestors after the last Crusade. Papa never worried about his creditors or his mounting debts because he told us that if things ever became too dire, we would simply sell the treasure and be so fabulously rich we'd never lack for anything." She sighed. "But he never would tell us what the treasure was, just that it was hidden somewhere within the walls of the manor."

Max's words would have been less painful if he hadn't taken such care to gentle his gruff tones. "What if this treasure never existed? What if it was just some fanciful tale concocted from legend and wishful thinking to amuse his children?"

"I couldn't afford to believe that. I knew if I could find it, I would be able to hire a solicitor to clear Theo's name and an investigator to locate him and bring him back from Australia. We could buy a new home somewhere far away from this place and be a family again."

"Your father looked very comfortable with that pistol in his hand. It wasn't Theo who pulled the trigger that night, was it?"

Angelica closed her eyes briefly, haunted by images she had spent the last ten years trying to forget. "They both heard me scream, but it was Papa who made it up the stairs first and found me with my dress half torn off and Timberlake on top of me, trying to . . ." She swallowed, surprised by how fresh the memory of that night still was. "I went there believing he was going to offer for

me, to ask Papa for my hand. Or perhaps even try to coax me into eloping with him. What a ridiculous little fool I was to fall for that charlatan's tricks! And my folly cost my family everything."

"You might have been young and innocent and naïve," Max said softly, "but you were no fool."

"Papa shot Timberlake, but the strain was too much for him. He collapsed to the floor, clutching his head. Theo and I both knew he would never survive prison, especially not in that condition. So we made a pact never to tell anyone what really happened. When the first guests came rushing over from the ballroom and up the stairs, it was to find Theo standing over Timberlake's body with the gun." She lifted her chin and met Max's gaze squarely, no longer forced to hide the bloodthirsty glint in her eye. "I wish it had been me who shot him."

Max slowly nodded. "And I wish it had been me. Just how long did it take you to make your way back here?"

"Six years. After five years, I managed to collect Papa from the asylum by pretending to be a long-lost cousin. He'd been there so long no one remembered he had once been a powerful lord. His *keepers* thought it was just another delusion. I found him living in squalor in a dirty cell that was little more than a stall." She lowered her eyes and bit her lip, reluctant to reveal such a private pain. "He didn't remember me. He talked about

Angelica all the time, but never seemed to realize that I was her."

"Until tonight," Max said softly, reminding her of the tender adoration in her father's eyes as he had smoothed her hair away from her face. "What about Pippa and Dickon? Where did you manage to collect them?"

She dragged the chain of her locket over her head and handed it to him. He snapped the locket open, a puzzled frown furrowing his brow as he studied the two miniatures nestled within. "I recognize you and the boy who must be Theo. But who are the two children on the other side?"

Angelica leaned over, pointing at the little girl with the riotous dark curls holding a scowling baby boy in a long, white gown in her chubby arms. "The girl is Pippa and the boy is Dickon. They're my half brother and sister."

Max looked nearly as stunned as he had when he'd discovered she was Angelica.

"Please don't judge Papa too harshly. To honor my mother's memory, he chose never to remarry. But he had been a widower for a *very* long time, which resulted in a certain *friendship* with a pretty, young seamstress in Falmouth. When she died during a cholera outbreak, he brought Pippa and Dickon into our household and passed them off as distant cousins. He was determined to provide for them in every way, both emotionally and financially."

"What happened to them after your father's collapse?"

Angelica felt her face harden again. "Papa's oh-so-helpful solicitor managed to find homes for them—at a workhouse in London. It took me almost five years to track them down. Pippa had been adopted by a wealthy tradesman and had grown accustomed to lolling about in the lap of luxury, and Dickon had run away from the workhouse and was living on the streets, picking pockets to earn his bread." She couldn't help laughing at the memory. "Although they both came with me of their own accord, you've never met two more surly brats. Pippa still fancies herself quite the little lady of the manor, but Dickon began to blossom after I brought him here and turned him loose to run on the moors."

Max arched an eyebrow at her. "And just who might the Elizabeths be? Long-lost cousins?"

"Just girls who had lost their way in this world. I found most of them on the streets of London, half-starved and abandoned by the men they had believed would take care of them."

"And Nana?"

"My former nurse. Since my mother died in childbirth, Nana all but raised me. She was staying with her son and his brood in a nearby village when I came back to Cornwall, but leapt at the chance to return to Cadgwyck and live out her final years. Everyone I brought to this place

had one thing in common: they understood the power of secrets and knew how to keep them."

"Aren't you forgetting the most important member of your cozy little household?"

"Who?"

"The White Lady."

Anne lifted her chin to a haughty angle. "Nobody around these parts had ever forgotten Angelica Cadgwyck and her tragic end. We started spreading fresh rumors about the ghost long before we arrived. As you've already discovered, the locals are a superstitious lot, only too willing to attribute a will-o'-the-wisp or a banging shutter to some restless spirit. Before long Cadgwyck's new owners couldn't find anyone brave enough to spend the night here, much less staff the manor."

"And that's when the ever-practical Anne Spencer stepped in to save the day," Max said, irony lacing his tone.

Anne Spencer's dutiful smile appeared on Angelica's lips. "Who could resist a reputable housekeeper with an entire staff of servants at her disposal? Once we were in residence, it became even easier to keep the legend of the White Lady alive. With each new master, the manor became a little less hospitable, a little more haunted."

"How did you keep the villagers from recognizing you all?"

"Dickon does bear a striking resemblance to

Theo, but he and Pippa were only small children when they were taken away. And we never let Hodges—I mean Papa—go into the village."

"What about you? You go into the village every week. How on earth could they fail to recognize you?"

"Even without the portrait to confuse them, I bear little resemblance to the pampered child they knew. People see what they expect to see. And most people don't see servants at all. They're nearly as invisible to the rest of the world as ghosts."

Max shook his head. "When I think of your poor father reduced to living as a servant in his own home . . ." He frowned. "Wait a minute. You told me it was a stipulation of his that Angelica's portrait never leave the house."

"There was no stipulation. *I* was the one who dragged the portrait down from the attic and hung it on the landing to keep the legend of the White Lady alive. And to remind myself of the girl I had once been . . . and who I never wanted to be again. Then you had to come along and ruin everything! To prove I was still the same romantic fool who would give my heart to a man for the price of a kiss."

Dangerous storm clouds had began to gather in his eyes. "*You're* a romantic fool? I just flung myself over a cliff for you."

She shook her head sadly. "Not for me. For *her.* For Angelica."

"You *are* Angelica," he growled. "My head wouldn't let me admit it, but somewhere deep in my heart, I think I always knew."

They stood there glaring at each other in the moonlight for a long moment before Angelica said quietly, "If you're not going to send for the constable and have me hauled off to jail, I suppose I should start looking for another position."

"Yes. I think that would be best. For the both of us." He drew himself up, every inch the cold, forbidding master who had come to Cadgwyck Manor all those weeks ago. "I'd be more than happy to write you a letter of recommendation."

"Considering the circumstances," she said stiffly, "that would be incredibly gracious of you."

"It will probably read something like this: 'Angelica Cadgwyck, also known as Anne Spencer and any other number of unknown aliases, is the very model of everything a gentleman would seek in a housekeeper—sharp-tongued, bossy, deceitful, proud, sneaky, conniving, unscrupulous, utterly ruthless when it comes to achieving her aims—' "

Although his words flayed her tender heart like a barbed whip, Angelica held her tongue, knowing she had earned every acerbic syllable of his rebuke.

" '—clever, courageous, honorable, sensible, determined, patient, generous, kind, devoted, an outstanding cook, marvelous with children, the

elderly, the mentally infirm, and small, annoying pets, loyal to a fault, and by far the finest kisser I have *ever* had the pleasure of taking to my bed. Any man would be blessed to welcome her to his household, not as a housekeeper, but as a wife. Which is why I pray she'll do me the honor of becoming mine.' "

Angelica turned her back on him, not wanting him to see the fresh tears welling up in her eyes. "I know what you're trying to do, Maximillian Burke, and I won't have it! I'm not some damsel in distress anymore, and I don't require rescuing by the likes of you!"

His hands closed over her upper arms, warming her chilled flesh with their irresistible heat. He touched his lips to her hair, the smoky rasp of his voice making her shiver with a need deeper than longing. "I'm the one who needs rescuing. Save me, Anne . . . Angelica . . . sweetheart. Save me from going back to being the man I was before I came here. Save me from all the years of loneliness I'll have to endure without you in my arms. Save me from spending the rest of my life longing for a woman I can never have."

Angelica turned in his arms. His dear, handsome face blurred before her eyes as she reached up to touch her fingertip to the furrow between his brows, smoothing out the scowl she loved so well. "Beneath that fearsome mask you wear,

you're nothing but a hopeless romantic. It's what I've always adored the most about you."

He gazed down at her, his gray eyes no longer cold, but smoldering with a fierce heat. "I don't want to be hopeless anymore. Will you give me hope?"

"I'll give you more than hope," she vowed, smiling up at him through a shimmering veil of tears. "I'll give you my heart, my body, and my love for as long as we both shall live."

He shook his head, his expression solemn. "That's not long enough. If you should die before I do, God forbid, you have to promise to come back and haunt me until we can be reunited again."

"Have no fear. I promise to wail and clank my chains so loudly you'll never get another decent night's rest. Especially if you're foolish enough to remarry and bring your new bride back to Cadgwyck."

Max's lips curled in a wicked grin. "If I have anything to say about it, you'll never get another decent night's rest after we're wed."

As a joyous peal of laughter burst from her lips, he swept her up into his arms and off her feet, swinging her in a wide circle. He had finally succeeded in catching his ghost, and there on the same beach where Angelica Cadgwyck's life had ended, it began again.

Epilogue

Maximillian Burke's coach rolled through the imposing wrought-iron gates and up the long, winding drive of crushed shells. He stuck his head out the window of the elegant vehicle, eager for his first glimpse of home. As the steep gables and soaring brick chimneys of the house came into view, his heart leapt with an undeniable mixture of satisfaction and pride.

Cadgwyck Manor was one of the shining gems of the Cornwall coast. No one could say it had seen better days because these were undoubtedly its best. A gleaming cherrywood door had been set in the mouth of the ancient gatehouse that served as both entrance hall and the heart of the house. Graceful Elizabethan wings flanked the gatehouse. The leering gargoyles that doubled as rainspouts had been replaced with chubby stone cherubs.

The manor looked not only well cared for, but well loved, as if its sturdy walls might well stand guardian on the edge of the cliffs for another five centuries.

A tower right out of a fairy tale crowned the far corner of the west wing, capped by a pretty little red-tiled turret. The autumn sunshine winked off its diamond-paned windows, and just enough ivy

had been left creeping up its stone walls to give it an enchanted air. Max felt a roguish smile curve his lips. The tower now served as the master bed-chamber of the house, and he had every intention of making some magic there on this very night.

As the coach rolled to a stop in the courtyard, its handsome team of matched grays still prancing restlessly, a footman in blue-and-gold livery came rushing forward to whisk open its lacquered door.

"Welcome home, m'lord," Derrick Hammett said, his ginger hair and good-natured grin a welcome sight indeed. The lad's cheeks were no longer sunken. His broad shoulders filled out his livery so nicely that the Elizabeths all blushed and stammered and had to fan themselves with their feather dusters whenever he sauntered by.

"Hammett." Max greeted the young man with a nod and a smile as he descended from the carriage. "I hope your mother and sisters are well."

"Indeed they are, m'lord! Indeed they are!"

Max had no reason to doubt Hammett's words, especially now that the young man's mother and sister were working in the Cadgwyck kitchens. There seemed to be no shortage of help at Cadgwyck these days. The generosity of its master and mistress toward their staff was becoming something of a legend around these parts. Just last December, they had hosted a Christmas ball for the servants featuring bowls of warm, spiced punch, individual flaming puddings, and a bonus

of two pounds apiece. Each servant had also received a colorful wool muffler knit by Nana herself to ease them through the cold winter months.

Max handed his hat and walking stick to Hammett and turned toward the house, breathing deeply of the scent of the sea, which had come to mean home to him.

The front door of the manor came flying open.

He had once imagined returning home from a long journey only to have a loving wife run out to greet him, trailed by a moppet or two, all eager to leap into his arms and smother his face with kisses.

That face split into a huge grin as Angelica came running down the steps of the portico and across the courtyard, her lovely face alight with joy and her arms already outstretched toward him.

Dickon was right behind her. At fourteen, he was finally on the verge of growing into his lanky legs and arms. Pippa strolled behind her brother, twirling the parasol she carried everywhere to protect her fair skin from the sun. She was far too dignified and elegant a young lady to be caught sprinting across a courtyard.

Max opened his arms and Angelica flew right into them, smothering his throat and jaw with eager kisses. He wrapped his arms around her, burying his face in hair that still smelled of freshly baked bread and cherishing the solid warmth of her in his arms. He supposed he would always

secretly fear he might reach for her only to have her vanish into a wisp of jasmine-scented vapor.

She tipped back her head and he claimed her smiling lips for a tender kiss. He could feel the firm swell of her growing belly pressing against his groin. Soon he would have a moppet of his very own to run out and greet him when he returned from a journey. Not that he intended to make many more journeys without Angelica by his side.

For now he would have to content himself with Piddles, who capered around their merry little group on his stout legs, barking in staccato bursts designed solely for the purpose of piercing the human eardrum.

"We missed you so much!" Angelica exclaimed. "I can't believe you let that nasty old Company drag you away from us again."

"I'm sorry, darling. I told them I wouldn't come back to the Court of Directors, but there was a very important matter that required my attention."

She gave him a haughty look. "*I* am a very important matter that requires your attention."

"And I can promise you now that I'm home, I have absolutely no intention of neglecting my duties." He gave her a wicked leer, then seized her mouth for another long, fierce kiss that made Dickon groan and Pippa duck behind her parasol, rolling her eyes.

"How was your voyage?" Dickon asked, always

eager to hear about adventure and exotic climes.

"Far too long," Max replied.

"Did you bring me a present?" Pippa inquired, peering hopefully toward the coach.

"I most certainly did, poppet. But I couldn't bring it with me. I'm afraid you'll have to be patient until it arrives." Max could hardly wait for her to meet the stout, balding, seventy-three-year-old artist who would be arriving within the fortnight to paint her portrait as a surprise for her eighteenth birthday.

Angelica patted the pocket of her apron. She still had a habit of wearing a plain white apron over the exquisite gowns Max had ordered from the finest modistes in London for her extensive wardrobe. "I received another letter from Clarinda while you were gone."

Since he and Angelica had wed, she and Clarinda had struck up quite a correspondence, a rather unnerving prospect for any man who had ever loved two women at different times in his life.

"She and Ash are coming home in November for a few months and she wants to know if they can bring Charlotte and spend Christmas here with us at Cadgwyck."

Max heaved a long-suffering sigh. "If I'm never going to be rid of that ne'er-do-well brother of mine, I suppose I might as well get used to having him around. Perhaps I can drag out the toy soldiers and best him in a mock battle."

"They'd also like to bring Farouk and Poppy and their brood. If you don't mind, of course."

"Why would I mind? Wait a minute," he added, warned by the mischievous sparkle dancing in her eyes. "Just how large is Farouk's brood?"

She blinked up at him, all innocence. "At last count, I believe they had twenty children."

"Twenty?"

"Well, they only have one son of their own so far, but Farouk did have a harem before he fell in love with Poppy."

Max shook his head in dazed disbelief. "Dear God, and to think I was willing to be content with an even dozen."

"Ha!" Angelica said, resting a hand on her belly. "You'll be content with two if I have anything to say about it. Or maybe three, if you don't scowl and growl at me too much."

Max leaned down to nuzzle her throat, murmuring, "I thought you liked it when I growled."

She giggled like a girl, then leaned away from him to peer into his face. "Was there any word this time?"

Max hesitated. Every time he'd been to London in the past two years to meet with his team of investigators—the finest money could hire, including Andrew Murray, the man who had ferreted out the truth about Laurence Timberlake—Max had returned to Angelica only to quench the hope in her beautiful hazel eyes.

"There was no word," he said softly, watching her face fall. "But I did bring you something that might be of interest."

Max crooked a finger toward the coach. A man slowly emerged from the shadows of the vehicle. If his tawny hair hadn't been bleached pale gold by the sun and his freckles buried beneath a deep-bronze tan, it would have been like seeing an image of Dickon as he might look twenty years from now.

The man stood beside the carriage, clutching his hat in his hands and hanging back as if uncertain of his welcome.

"Theo?" Angelica whispered, a mixture of wonder and disbelief dawning in her eyes.

"Annie?" The man's throat bobbed as he swallowed back a visible rush of emotion.

Max felt his own throat tighten as Angelica ran to her brother and flung her arms around his neck, a sob of pure joy spilling from her lips. When Pippa and Dickon would have joined her, Max held them back, wanting to give Angelica and Theo time to savor their reunion. After a few minutes of laughing and crying and murmuring among themselves, Angelica beckoned Pippa and Dickon over to greet their half brother.

Dickon immediately began to tug Theo toward the house. "I want to hear all about Australia! Are there really little bears that live in trees and eat leaves and jackrabbits as tall as a man who

can knock a bloke out with a single punch?"

Pippa followed, still twirling her parasol. "Are there lots of handsome convicts in Australia? Are very many of them looking for brides?"

Angelica linked her arm through Max's, resting her head against his shoulder as they followed the others to the house. "I can't believe you did this for me."

He patted the hand she'd wrapped around his arm. "I would do anything for you. Even fling myself off a cliff."

"If you'll meet me in the tower tonight after everyone else is abed, I'll show you everything I would do for you."

"Everything?" he echoed hopefully, cocking one eyebrow.

"Everything," she promised, smiling up at him.

They climbed the stairs of the portico and entered the house to find the others had already headed for the kitchen, no doubt following the irresistible aroma of the freshly baked bread Angelica had taken from the oven shortly before Max's coach arrived. At first they thought the entrance hall was deserted, but then they heard a peculiar melody of clanging and cursing.

The door to the longcase clock at the foot of the stairs was standing open. Angelica's papa had crawled half inside the thing. All that was visible of him was his black-clad rump.

"He spends most of his time dodging the nurses

you've hired to take care of him," Angelica whispered. "Since the clock will probably never work again anyway, we decided it wouldn't do any harm to let him poke around in the works. It keeps him out of trouble."

Her papa emerged from the clock, his snowy-white hair standing on end and his nose smudged with grease. "You there, lad," he said, pointing a wooden wrench at Max. "Fetch me a cup of tea right away."

As he disappeared back into the clock, Angelica explained apologetically, "He thinks he's master of the house and you're a footman."

"Then I'd best fetch him some tea so he doesn't sack me."

Max was drawing her toward the kitchen when the first majestic bong echoed through the entrance hall. The two of them exchanged a disbelieving look as the clock continued to chime, finding its voice for the first time since the night of Angelica's eighteenth birthday ball. The clock didn't fall silent until it had chimed exactly twelve times.

They turned as one to find Angelica's papa triumphantly holding up a glowing ruby the size of his fist. "I thought it would be the safest place to hide it with all those fools traipsing through the house for your ball. How was I to know the damn thing would get stuck in the works?"

Max and Angelica exchanged a wondering look,

then burst out laughing. Now that they no longer needed it, the Cadgwyck treasure had been found. They were wise enough now to know that the only true treasure lay in the love they had found in each other's arms.

As Max swept Angelica off her feet, still laughing with delight, the girl she had been gazed down at them from the portrait on the landing, her cheek finally dimpling in the smile she'd been holding back for all those years. Max winked at her over his wife's shoulder.

It seemed Maximillian Burke was a man who dreamed after all.

And she was the woman who had made all of his dreams come true.

Center Point Large Print
600 Brooks Road / PO Box 1
Thorndike ME 04986-0001 USA

(207) 568-3717

US & Canada:
1 800 929-9108
www.centerpointlargeprint.com

LARGE TYPE
Medeiros, Teresa, 1962-
The temptation of your touch